To Kirk,

Late Bet

In friendship

by

Douglas Stewart

Warm regards

[signature] *November 2007*

Bloomington, IN   authorHOUSE®   Milton Keynes, UK

AuthorHouse™
1663 Liberty Drive, Suite 200
Bloomington, IN 47403
www.authorhouse.com
Phone: 1-800-839-8640

AuthorHouse™ UK Ltd.
500 Avebury Boulevard
Central Milton Keynes, MK9 2BE
www.authorhouse.co.uk
Phone: 08001974150

This book is a work of fiction. People, places, events, and situations are the product of the author's imagination. Any resemblance to actual persons, living or dead, or historical events, is purely coincidental.

No part of this book may be reproduced, stored in a retrieval system, or transmitted by any means without the written permission of the author.

First published by AuthorHouse 3/23/2007

ISBN: 978-1-4259-8910-1 (sc)

Library of Congress Control Number: 2007902292

Printed in the United States of America
Bloomington, Indiana

This book is printed on acid-free paper.

Also by Douglas Stewart

Fiction

Case for Compensation
Villa Plot, Counterplot
The Scaffold
Cellar's Market
The Dallas Dilemma
Undercurrent

Non-Fiction

A Family at Law (with Gavin Campbell)
Piraten (In German)
The Brutal Seas
Roulette - Playing to Win

Acknowledgements and Comment

Considerable research over several years was essential for this book. Along the way, many people helped me and some have become good friends. I appreciated the interesting and helpful background information given by Andrew Tottenham, the London based international gaming expert.

Representatives of the Gaming Board of Great Britain were also very supportive when I visited them, even though they knew that in this novel, I depict one of their number as corruptible. I intend no slur on the hard-working dedicated people at the Board. They operate in a demanding environment and over many years have upheld the highest standards. In any profession or occupation, one can find an occasional rotten apple, giving opportunities for an author writing fiction. I know of none at the Gaming Board. I was however satisfied that in some casinos in poorly regulated countries, they can and do cheat. Thanks to the Gaming Authorities in the UK and Nevada, the integrity of casinos under their control is enviably high.

Several employees and senior management of casinos in the USA and United Kingdom helped but preferred not to be identified by name. A good friend also refused to be identified because she is a blackjack card-counter and concerned about repercussions if this were known.

Naturally, neither Dukes Casino nor Space City exists, nor are they inspired by any particular casino. The real names of some Formula One racing drivers are used but actions during Grand Prix races are fiction. Paul Lew and Freddie Spencer, through their connections in racing circles, overcame hurdles for my research at the Indianapolis Grand Prix. The characters in the book and their behavior are fiction and any resemblance to any person, living or dead is unintentional.

My friend Bruce Mastracchio helped with the editing, his own talent as a writer being invaluable. Martin Edwards, himself a prolific and successful crime writer, was also able to assist me in more than one way. Nick Barton of Clouds House boosted my background knowledge of treatment for addictions. He and his dedicated team have helped so many people to fight their demons. Peter Wagstaffe, valued friend and always a solid source of obscure facts, has yet again proved his worth – with more obscure facts! To you all, I hope that I have accurately interpreted your input. Any mistakes are mine, not yours.

Finally, by way of acknowledgement, my wife Bridget has been a tower of strength during this long project. There have been times too when my young daughter Lara, with her fascination for keyboards, has made the project seem even longer and more demanding. But a child's smile can make anything forgivable!

In the plot, I make much of the roulette *system* called *Reverse Labouchère*. Of all roulette *systems*, this is the one that, given the right conditions, can create millionaires – but on the bad days, can lead to ruin. Be warned.

Douglas Stewart

February 2007

24th June 2002 – London

Don't panic!

Dex did a quick calculation as he took in the slowly revolving roulette wheel. The ball rested on 31, the fourteenth black number running. There had been six already before he had even started betting. He counted his money again. In front of him were stacks of blue chips and multi-colored plaques worth £790,000, all that remained of his cash hoard from just minutes before. Just yesterday, like a thousand years back, he had changed over two million US dollars into sterling. Now it was half gone. Not one red number had hit!

Not one, he muttered to himself.

Just one Duke's Casino plaque could buy a swanky BMW. Four of them would leave change against a Ferrari. Never before had his strategy gone so horribly wrong. The choice was stark. Double up again? Shove out over £700,000? That would claw back today's monster losses and win two grand on top? Or cash out and lick the wounds till dawn?

This past year he had turned the five thousand legacy into a staggering cash hoard even after tossing money around on every luxury he wanted. Now after just eight bets backing red, he was one spin from ruin. He thought of the lifestyle to which he had grown accustomed – the burgundy Aston-Martin, the Knightsbridge mews cottage and jetting to Vegas or *anywhere* first class.

For months, pocketing twenty thousand a day from Dukes had been a doddle - and all from watching a small white ball land on his winning numbers. He wavered, debating whether *to go all in* like a poker pro. Surely tonight's piss-poor run would end? He looked at his chips and then at the wheel. Hell, after eight black taxis, a red bus was way overdue. Hit any of eighteen red numbers and he'd be rich again. Any black meant *oh fuck*. Andy, the dealer spun the ball.

It was now or never.

In a sudden impulsive move, Finlay Dexter pushed out his bet, all £790,000. As they'd say in Vegas, *he'd bet the farm*, nearly one and a half million dollars. Eyes following the ball as it sped rapidly under the rim of the wheel,

Dex gripped the edge of the green baize table, his face blanched and his jaw muscles taut.

"No more bets," said the dealer, a Geordie called Andy.

Without even knowing he had done so, Dex stood up to watch more closely, the vein on his forehead throbbing, his palms now moist. The ball was moving fast, tight beneath the wheel's rim. Dex could scarcely breathe, his heart pounding, his eyes unflinching. His rollercoaster past flashed through his mind – the tormented childhood, the bankruptcy, the inheritance, the winning roulette system and the cosseted lifestyle that his winnings had brought him. Was it all ending in disaster?

As the ball slowed, it was torture in slow motion. Like stepping into thin air tied to a bungee. Like free-fall parachuting before the chute opens. The die was cast. No turning back now. No time to say *sorry mister I've changed my mind*. Suddenly the bet seemed crazy, risking everything on a bouncy white ball. In agony, he watched it dance erratically as it hit the strikers.

Reality. The outside world. Everything disappeared. Nothing mattered but a white ball and a red number as it skittered around the wheel.

8 Black.

Bounce on.

30 Red.

Bounce on.

11 Black.

Still got legs.

36 Red.

Teasing me.

13 Black.

Faltering.

Barely moving now.

Stopped.

But no!

There was just enough energy.

The ball trickled over the metal fret.

I've won.

Shit! I've fucking won.

27 Red. After all those black cabs, that fucking red bus has arrived!

Yes, yes, yes!

Bliss, oh bliss!

Nearly eight hundred thousand smackeroos!

Nearly eighty thousand profit!

Distantly, he heard Jeb Miller's voice. From his stool behind the wheel, the inspector had spoken but nothing registered. Dex was still emerging from his trance. He felt exhausted, had been to hell and back. He was breathless, drained. Scarcely able to comprehend his return from the abyss, he stared almost hypnotized as the ball slowly circled on number 27.

Miller's tone was sharper now. What was he saying? Dex looked up. "Mr Dexter. Sorry but that was a late bet, a no-bet. You must get your bets on earlier. The ball had dropped."

Even as he heard the words, Dex saw that Andy had pushed his chips off the layout. "I bet long before the dealer said *no more bets*. What's the problem?"

"Not so, I'm afraid. I told Andy to remove the bet. You obviously didn't hear."

Dex squared up his considerable physique and took a step nearer the man on the stool. "Bullshit! My bet was in plenty of time." His glare was met with a glassy look and Dex suddenly felt impotent against the inspector's power. Somehow, he resisted the urge to smash a fist into the uneven teeth beneath the chaplinesque moustache. Instead, he thumped the table hard with both fists, the noise carrying across the near silence of the other gaming tables. "Fuck you! I'm right," he shouted.

From somewhere, Nigel Forster-Brown, the casino manager appeared with the Pit Boss and his Shift Manager. Miller edged his fat bottom from off the stool to carry on the conversation at closer quarters. Noisy scenes in an exclusive Mayfair casino like Dukes were an embarrassment. Like publicly shooting fallen racehorses, a row like this was unwelcome. It could unsettle their wealthy international players at the other tables. FB, as he was known to everyone, waved his arms soothingly. "Mr Dexter. Please keep your voice down."

Dex looked at the tall stooping figure with contempt. "Come off it, FB! This stinks! This short-assed runt called my bet *late*. In his dreams! I had £790,000 on red and it won. I saw the ball circle the wheel many times after my bet was on." Seeing again the dead fish look from Miller and a shrug from FB, he continued. "No way had Andy called *no more bets* when I put my chips out." In his classless accent, each vowel well articulated, Dex spat out each word so that players at other tables were now watching the confrontation.

FB spoke quietly, trying to defuse the position. "Please be quiet, Mr Dexter otherwise I shall have to ask you to leave and your membership will be terminated. If there was, er, shall we say some small, er, misunderstanding, our cameras will resolve it."

For a moment Dex' rapid eye movements suggested he was going to ignore the warning but something made him draw back. To be banned would be crass. He looked around for support but remembered that he had been the only player at the table. Scotty and Glenn had gone. Only Andy knew the truth and he was saying nothing - just avoiding eye contact.

But Dex knew, indeed was *abso-bloody-lutely positive* he was right. Miller moved in even closer, all soothing voice and aftershave. "Look Mr Dexter. My job is to make sure there are no late bets. The dealer had called *no more bets*. The ball had dropped. That's why I ordered Andy to push your chips off. You were so busy staring at the wheel you never heard me speak. Never even *saw* the chips being pushed off."

Dex looked down at the dumpy figure whose head was at shoulder level. "As I had time to watch the wheel, *Mr Miller*," he spoke the name with deliberation and contempt "I *must* have placed the bet in time." *There! Get out of that, short-arse!* Slowly and with an icy calm now, he emphasized each word again. "As I had time to watch the wheel, I *must* have placed the bet in time."

Miller ignored the logic. "As FB has said, the man-in-the-sky will have recorded this." The inspector made it sound like a favor rather than a stitch-up.

"I'll get the tapes played back," FB hastily agreed. "Remember when we had dinner that night? I explained we had cameras everywhere."

"Even able to spot if I'd clipped my nails since my previous visit." Dex quoted back FB's words. "Yes. I remember. Okay. Take a look. You'll see!"

FB moved away to a telephone out of Dex' earshot as Miller struggled back onto his stool, the seams of his dinner-jacket straining at every movement. "Do you want to carry on or wait?" He puffed. "Normally, we'd carry on but as you're the only person at the table, it's your choice."

"I'll wait." Dex snapped back as he returned to his seat. Gradually his own breathing became more controlled. He pressed his broad shoulders back against the thick upholstery. An uneasy silence prevailed. Andy's eyes were everywhere but on Dex. With not a single witness, Finlay Dexter felt uneasy. Could he trust these bastards? Pity Mick Glenn and that American Scotty Brannigan had just left the table. They'd have known the truth. With every passing second, his concern grew. The wheel had stopped now, the ball still tantalizingly on 27. Dex sorted and re-sorted his chips, his initial confidence starting to fade. The uncomfortable stand-off lasted just over three minutes but in the silence it seemed much, much longer.

Dex saw FB answer the phone, nod his head once or twice and then walk across, his eyes looking at some distant horizon. Dex knew that this meant nothing. FB had never met anyone's gaze in his life. He stood beside Miller. "I'm sorry Mr Dexter. I'm afraid the inspector was right. The cameras caught it all. After the other two players left and with nobody else playing, the dealer was spinning rather sooner than before. Perhaps it caught you unawares. You started to put out all your chips but then you hesitated. After Andy said *no more bets*, you finally pushed the whole lot on. But the ball had dropped. Not onto number 27, you understand. But it had reached that moment where no casino allows any more bets. You didn't lose but unfortunately you didn't win."

"This is what is known as a fucking stitch-up! Unbelievable! It's just a big unfunny joke. Who writes your gags? Bob Hope? I insist on watching the recordings."

By his standards, FB's tone was abrasive, his nose sniffily upturned. "Not permissible! Club Rules. We're not running the Odeon Cinema."

Dex thought for a moment. "I want to see Audley Shawcross. He'll sort this crap out." Even as he said it, Dex realized that the Chief Executive, his personal bête-noire, would simply shovel on more bullshit.

FB looked at the wheel as he replied. "He's having dinner. Mr Shawcross will talk to you later. But he can't go against the cameras any more than I can." He turned away and addressed Andy. "Carry on. Spin the wheel"

"Hold it," commanded Dex. "Nobody else is playing this table. I need to decide whether to bet again or not. I wouldn't want *another* late bet." His sarcasm was lost on Miller who was picking a morsel of food from between his teeth. Dex saw FB mouth a yes to the inspector.

"Take your time then," replied Miller as he smoothed down his receding hair and pushed his glasses higher up his nose. He then summoned a colleague to watch the table while he slipped away after FB. Dex watched him leave, convinced they would now be briefing Audley Shawcross - arranging the hymn-sheets; squaring the circle and getting those ducks in a row.

He felt strangely relaxed. *Deserving to win* counted for nothing. The fear of defeat tightened his balls yet the demon within told him to go on. In a determined move, he again pushed out every chip, all seven hundred and ninety thousand to back red.

This time, Dex felt none of the passion that had pumped him up earlier. He was almost dispassionate as the ball hopped and jumped over the frets. It flirted with black 2, red 25, black 17 and red 34. Would it make it across black 6 and land again in red 27? Yes ... still it tottered on, touching 6, then 27 before rolling next door into black 13.

"Sorry," said Andy. "Not your day."

Dex rose from the table. "That's enough punishment!" He wasn't going to admit he was cleaned-out - bust and buggered.

"Better luck!"

"Sure." His face lengthened, the blood draining from his cheeks. As he took in the plush regency style surroundings, he wondered when he would be back– the antique furnishings, the works of art and the crystal chandeliers. Fleetingly, he relived those godforsaken destitute nights in the Kilburn attic room. That had been home after the snooty bank manager had bankrupted *Louche*, his fashionable nightclub in Dover Street. But he had fought back from that. Now once again, he was destroyed.

Around him, as he crossed the room, it was again business as usual. Nobody even stared at him. Altercations were a rare but inevitable part of casino life. In Dukes, millions changed hands every evening. Those previously curious eyes never saw him leave. The scattering of players risking their millions were all locked in their own private battles. Nobody knew the truth; nobody cared that he had been mugged.

His shoulders slumped, his head lowered, hands deep in the pockets of his tailored slacks, Dex' every step was leaden. The cushioned carpet felt like a sea of treacle. For a second he saw himself in a gilt framed mirror. It was not something he wanted to see again. *Dickhead*, he muttered! *You're skulking out like a dog that's been caught crapping in the corner*! He pulled back his shoulders, changed his stride and from somewhere forced out a politician's smile as he headed for the bar.

"Mr Dexter, welcome back!" The Spanish bartender from Seville was always cheerful. "I'll fix your usual. CM on the rocks with a salted glass."

"Don't spare the tequila, José." Even as he chatted with the Spaniard about Real Madrid's new signings, Dex had convinced himself that he was not Miller's first sucker. Boosting profits like this without any witnesses was just too easy. The inspector's timing had been perfect. It was the biggest bet he had ever placed. *Bloody typical*! He could see it now. Dukes had been waiting to get him – waiting for months till he was alone with a big, big bet riding on the ball. Waited till Mick Glenn and Scotty Brannigan had cashed in. Not that Glenn would have noticed much. The international soccer star was too full of shit. But Scotty, the legendary racing driver from Las Vegas – hell, he was smart. He wouldn't have let them get away with any crap.

He was still reliving the confrontation with Miller when his Cadillac-Margarita appeared along with a plate of canapés and cheese cubes with biscuits. Meticulous as usual, José placed everything neatly on the low mahogany table in the half-light of the inviting bar. "Staying for breakfast Mr Dexter?"

"No. Just waiting to see Audley Shawcross, then it'll be home for the hot chocolate and Reader's Digest tonight." He was rewarded by José's laugh. From through the door, as if from another planet, he could hear the distant sound of the ball hissing round the wheel. He shuddered at the unwelcome reminder that at thirty-three, once again he was a busted flush.

From across the bar, Arthur Yarbury came across to join him. Lord Yarbury had been sitting alone with a Campari. The drink and the color of his complexion had much in common. The silver hair was neatly cut, very short and with a precise parting. His face was flattened as if somewhere among his ancestors, a pug had featured in the fertilization process. The eyes were rounded, the nose was retroussé, the ears slightly curled and he had trained the eyebrows to stand upwards like an out-of-control thicket hedge. The hands were small and podgy, barely reaching out from the sleeves of his regimental blazer.

Dex had known him all his life, though with the generation gap, they had never been close. As he grew up, the peer had been a near neighbor in the glorious village of Bladon in Oxfordshire. He had mainly dropped by for cocktails with his parents. Inwardly, Dex groaned. Right now he needed space, not Yarbury trotting out the same tired anecdotes. He eased off his chair to greet the family friend. On sitting down again, he drank deeply, savoring the salt that clung to the rim of the crystal glass.

"Finlay, dear boy! Long way from Bladon, eh?" The peer laughed. "A pleasure to see you! Winning as usual, I suppose?" At university, Dex had abandoned his given name of Finlay for Dex but Yarbury had never got into the change

"Caught a bit of a cold." Dex had no intention of pouring out his heart. He had no time for golfers who relived every slice or gamblers who sought pity for self-inflicted wounds.

Yarbury was wearing his cricket tie, maroon and gold, with the navy blazer and grey flannels. "Happens to chaps. I'm now sixty-eight. Played for nearly fifty years. Deuced if I can remember winning. Not the point, is it? Love gambling, simply love it dear boy. But winning? I mean like cricket - it's *playing the game* that counts." He grabbed a handful of pretzels before continuing. "Family okay?"

""Father, mother and Beth are flying back from New York tonight. Mother's relatives were celebrating something. I had no interest."

"Damnably fine Lord Chancellor, your father."

Normally Dex would have let it pass but tonight was no ordinary evening. "You think so? Forgive me Arthur but when I was growing up I always admired your opinion." It was an exaggeration.

Yarbury looked at him thoughtfully for a moment or two and then put down his drink. "Your mother's a saint of course."

"I love her dearly."

"And Beth – such a delightful sister for you. Tragedy to be born blind."

"She's done remarkably." His twin was into Hedge Fund management in the City and made the journey with her dog every day by public transport.

Yarbury leaned forward. "Your mother confided in me once."

This was new territory and not on the peer's usual list of hackneyed tales. Dex looked eager to hear more. "Unlike her. What did she say?"

"Local Hunt Ball. Must have been over twenty years ago. I stumbled across her crying her eyes out behind a marquee. We sat down on a bale of hay. We'd both drunk too much. Must have chatted for an hour or two. She told me more than she should. I caught her at a low point, I suppose."

"What did she say?"

"About your father's womanizing. But it was worse than that."

Dex nodded thoughtfully.

The peer leaned even closer. "Your father's an absolute sod. Can't stand the man. Not after what your mother said. Chasing skirt half his age is one thing but knocking her about and abusing you and Beth." He growled surprisingly deeply for a small man. "I mean it was damned disgraceful. That and calling you *Boy* all the time!"

Dex was shocked, not at what he was hearing but at the source. He had assumed nobody outside the family but dear old Reverend Hillyer knew anything about the tempestuous household – the drinking, the fights, the swearing - his mother often on the point of leaving. But every time she had relented to father's pleas for forgiveness. For a second, he relived the nights he and Beth had hidden in the closet on the landing, listening to the shouts and screams from downstairs. "There was no sexual abuse. Don't think that,"

"You put up with a great deal." He placed his hand on Dex' knee. "Finlay, from what your mother said, you were a very brave lad. Always stood up to him, even intervened once when he was smacking your mother around."

Dex hesitated and then acknowledged the truth. "Several times, actually. I was about nine or ten then." He laughed in a self-deprecating way. "Didn't do much good, pounding father's thighs with my fists."

"He's a big man. And so are you now, come to that. But back then, you always looked a bit puny, if you don't mind me saying so."

"I toughened up later. Boxing, wrestling, weights, cross-country." It was an understatement. He had been school champion in several athletic events. Dex ordered more drinks as if he were paying for them but like dinners, hospitality was always courtesy of Dukes. "José! Same again please. I scarcely noticed that one! And you, Arthur? Campari-soda?" He met the peer's look with his most intense stare, brown eyes thoughtful and penetrating. "You don't really think father's a good Lord Chancellor do you, Arthur?" It was barely a question. He saw the slight shake of the head and continued. "Personally, I prefer the view of the journalist who tore him to shreds."

Douglas Stewart

"Remind me."

"One of the Sundays said that calling him a *Champagne Socialist* was an insult to champagne, socialism *and* politics. I remember the precise words. The article said *there was no man alive who had stuffed more lobster, foie gras and pheasant into himself than Alexander Arbuthnot Dexter as he cunningly brown-nosed his way to be Lord Chancellor.*"

Arthur chuckled in a high-pitched way, almost like a naughty child. "I remember that now. He was livid. Too close to the truth of course. But he *is* a damned fine politician. He has all the qualities - devious, smarmy and plausible. Frankly, I've despised him ever since your mother confided in me."

Dex tapped his nose. "Ever noticed the old hooter's a bit off center? That was father when I was about twenty after I had been chucked out of university. He was boasting that he would be the next Chancellor with a change of Government. I told him he was a Tory *and* a hypocrite." Dex shook his head as he relived the flying fist that had left his nose streaming blood down his Black Sabbath T-shirt. "He was too quick for me despite the age difference. We've never spoken since then. That's thirteen years. But I still see my mother and Beth."

"Sister still at home?"

"Beth won't leave my mother. Mother won't leave father. Mother's too dignified for that. So they all live together. She and me - we're typical twins, very close but still fight with bare knuckles." He offered the listener some stilton. "Actually, I'm still shocked mother ever confided in you or *anyone* about what she suffered. Not her style at all. These days, she has her own sitting-room on the top floor. Father is banned."

"Poor dear." Arthur cocked his head as he spoke, his teeth too gleaming white to be his own. "And you? Not doing insurance broking any more?"

Dex' face was transformed as he let rip with a mocking laugh, his impudent look heightened by his quizzical eyebrows. "No way! I was just a pin-striped hod-carrier carting files round the Lloyd's Building for *scratching*. Talk about Cemetery Junction! It was like a morgue working there, a living death. I was lucky though! Just when I was looking for the escape hatch, I inherited a few thousand; picked up a book on roulette and proved I could win more at the tables in a few days than working for a year. That was a year ago. I told them to stuff the job."

"Don't blame you. Deuced boring - work, that is. I did it once. Not my scene. Prefer to toddle down to the Lords for lunch, snooze off the claret in the Chamber and then slip in here for dinner."

Dex recognized the understatement. Arthur liked to play the buffoon but his brain was quick. He knew too that Arthur had so much inherited wealth that he could afford to lose his thousands to Dukes. "I only tried broking to please mother when I was bankrupt. That was after *Louche* folded and I was nearly jailed. "

"Nasty business that. Memory is not what it was. Come to that, not much of me is!" He glanced down at his crotch with a rueful appraisal. "Didn't your partner ...?"

"Boris was a Polish Count and an old school *friend*. Least I thought he was. I hated school. Happiest days of your life? Crap. Propaganda put out by someone with the cunning of Goebbels. But we got on well. After I was thrown out of university – too much time watching slow nags at Hexham and York - I left home and moved in with Boris. He had private money. We opened *Louche* as the hottest nightclub in town. He put in the big cash. I gave a bank guarantee for the rest."

Man-about-Town? Jack-the-Lad? That's what I read about you."

Dex realized that Arthur Yarbury's memory was far better than he usually made out. "Arthur! Didn't realize you stooped to reading tabloid trash!" His mind drifted back to Durham University, recalling those wintry days in the north-east as his wilderness years. There had been just one redeeming feature: they had put down an indelible marker. For eighteen years, he had been *Boy* - molded by his father's determination to clone him as an opera loving lawyer, someone never happier than when headed for Covent Garden after the Law Courts.

Dex however, had secretly harbored other plans. *Not quite true*, he now realized. *Absolute balls actually*! Never had a plan, not ever. Not unless you counted being as different from father as possible. Then a wild idea had turned into an act of defiance. Instead of registering for the law faculty, he had turned to theology. If anything would get up his father's nose, he knew that was it. He had no interest in the course at all. As he had said to his friends, the only two courses that interested him were race–courses and intercourse.

In the second year, bedding dowdily dressed students before heading to York races once too often had led to him being *sent down*. It was only then that he told the truth to his father. Alexander Dexter's wrath had carried several doors away through the open window of Porcupine House, their elegant London mansion on Hillside Road in St John's Wood. It had been no surprise when his father had first thrown a hefty punch and then Dex' clothes, his music collection and Formula One memorabilia out of the bedroom window. From the street below, the blood still streaming from his nose, Dex had shouted back, "If you think I'd be proud to follow in your footsteps, dream on. It would be like treading in shit." They had never spoken again.

Dex realized that he had enjoyed the conversation with Arthur rather more than usual. It was certainly better than thinking of being penniless and wondering how to get used to bailiff dodging once again. "Another one, Arthur?" Dex signaled to José. "My trouble, arrogant shit that I was, lay in believing the hype about me in the papers. I mean I knew it wasn't the real me at all – but I played up to all that media *Man-about-Town* crap."

"Those gossip columnists certainly loved you. Always dating some popsy or another. Fast cars. Annabelle's, Tramp, Ascot, Henley, Wimbledon."

"Bloody fool that I was! I got to believing my own image." He wondered why he was telling Arthur all this. "But hell, I was early twenties and every tabloid was full of me. I was too cocky to understand that the hacks were fawning over me because *Louche* attracted the celebs and royals. I thought it was because they *liked me*." His healthy raw-boned face showed his regret but even in repose the craggy features were always tinged by insolence. "Joke! I was just the sucker helping them fill their columns. So when I was arrested, my journalist *friends* happily dragged me through the gutter."

"So what went wrong at *Louche*?"

"We'd had six great years, me and Boris. Then a tabloid journalist wrote a story that fashion models were snorting coke by the yard in the ladies' restroom. Fifty cops crashed in and we were busted. Me? I was clean. But what I didn't know was that Boris had been the peddler." Dex' face darkened and an angry scowl creased his forehead and he sucked in his close shaven cheeks. In an irritated gesture, he flicked his hand through his tousled golden brown hair. The unkempt look with generous strands flying in most directions was the work of skilled hands at a fashionable hair stylist not far away in Brook Street.

"It's coming back to me. Didn't that little shit Boris blame you?"

"Too right! He ran a defense that *I* was the peddler, so the cops charged me as well. Threw the book at us both. The media blood-fest ran and ran. The trial was pure theater of course - erstwhile friends fighting to the death. But I got off and he went down on a seven stretch. Bastard! Only seven! Too short by far." He caressed the lapel of his velvet jacket. "Then the bank called in the guarantee. I was bankrupt at twenty-eight. Thanks, Boris." He eyes flashed anger. "That's when I appeased mother by getting what she called *a proper job* in insurance." His face lit up. "But since then, courtesy of Dukes, I've paid off the last creditors."

Yarbury looked at his watch. "The witching hour. Time to go home to her ladyship. Delightful talking to you, young Finlay. See you at Silverstone. Audley's invited you?"

"I'll be there." It was Dex' turn to look conspiratorial as he inched towards the peer. "What do you make of Shawcross?" he realized that even as they had been chatting, his subconscious had been in overdrive.

"Shawcross? He's dining with that sheik from… forgive me dear boy. Somewhere full of sand and oil. *Sucking up to him* as we used to say when I was young. Audley's not my type, dear boy, not my type at all but he's damnably generous with the freebies, what?"

Dex laughed. "Your freebies, Arthur, have cost you enough to own Silverstone, not just going as his casino guest."

""Don't remind me. This place will be my ruination. And you? Like Audley, do you?"

"If they squeezed him, there'd be enough oil to interest Esso." Dex debated whether to confide in Yarbury but decided to say nothing. "I had my usual run-in with him before dinner. Sometimes I think he's sinister. Other times, I reckon he's one great phony."

Yarbury's laugh was mocking. "That accent!"

"Precisely!" They both stood up, Dex dwarfing the slight figure of Yarbury who laughed again. "Tell your mother I was asking about her. Beth too." Dex sensed a wistful sadness as Arthur mentioned his mother.

"I will." Alone with his near empty glass, reality quickly returned. Waking in the morning and facing total ruin was going to be bloody unpleasant. Soon, there would be court summonses and visits to the West London Court pleading for time to pay bills at a tenner a week. He looked at the remains of his Cadillac-Margarita as if the answer lay there and then accepted the barman's suggestion of another. By the time it arrived, his mood had changed.

Once again, he was bloody angry, his brow knitted. He started rehearsing some choice adjectives for Shawcross. But then he thought it through again.

13

There was no point in getting banned. Not if he wanted to come in again. And he might.

That is … if he wanted *revenge*.

You bastards have ruined me. Now I'm going to ruin you.

The citrus flavors swirled around his mouth as his thoughts gelled. Why just take revenge on Dukes in London? They own Space City, that glitzy palace - all three thousand rooms and two billion dollars of it. As he watched the door for a glimpse of the boss, increasingly crazy thoughts raced through his mind.

You destroy me. I destroy you.

His jaw muscles flexed and his neat teeth worked on his lower lip. This had been no honest mistake. Not when the cameras knew the truth. His knuckles whitened at the stark reality. Then, his features changed again as he debated how to tell Beth. She would go apeshit. Together, they had just registered a charity to help abused kids and each had committed to donate five hundred thousand by the year end. His contribution had just gone. Gambled away in a mad rush of blood. Well … cheated away! He needed it back. Couldn't let her down.

No! Fuck that, Dex. Win it back. Don't take this shit lying down!

Fessing up to Beth would be tough but he knew what she would say. *Get that money back, every last penny. That would be fair. The charity needs this money.* "No Beth! Fair? Fuck fairness. That's not bad enough for these bastards. That's what I'll say. I've been *fair* all my life. Did father get to be Lord bloody Chancellor by fairness? These bastards have destroyed me. Total revenge. That's what I want."

The vague concept of *revenge* percolated through a succession of exhilarating ideas, some of them absurd. For the next ten minutes, he could think of nothing else - just kickaround notions that ebbed and flowed without substance. They made him feel better.

An *obsession* had been born – a glorious obsession.

What had Beth said over dinner at Langan's last week? She'd heard that Dukes were under financial pressure due to delays on the new tower they were adding at Space City. He made a mental note to check that out just as Shawcross emerged from the dining-room. Still uncertain of what he would say, he left the bar to confront him.

Their paths crossed near the foot of the broad sweep of the marble staircase leading up to the front entrance onto Mount Street. "Mr Dexter! I'm so *very* sorry about the, er, *small* problem in there tonight." The lean figure, with the looks of a matinee idol, was just a tad shorter than Dex but his physique and haughty demeanor were ideal for the tango. He spoke in the hushed tones of an undertaker comforting a bereaved widow and Dex watched his hands wringing in mock despair. "These … er," Shawcross fought for the right word, "er … *misunderstandings* happen. Rarely of course. Thank goodness! The cameras. Marvelous technology. Captured the truth. It was a late bet."

It was like listening to FB all over again. Dex' face did not show what he thought of the lying bastard. He shrugged. "Shit happens." He paused to shake his head. "Disgraceful though that you won't let me watch the recordings myself."

"Club Rule 47(b)."

"Nothing in Club Rule 47(a) about justice being seen to be done, I don't suppose?" As Dex spoke, contempt in his face and voice, his brown eyes were fixed on the Chief Executive's frozen smile. Then he did something he had never before done. He touched Shawcross just above the wrist, lightly, ever so gently with no hint of a clamp. "But *you* know the truth, Mr Shawcross. What's more, so do *I*."

"No doubt we shall see you soon." The silky urbanity and the false cultured accent irritated Dexter. Shawcross would know from the cashiers that Dex had lost a year's winnings in a torrid twenty minutes.

"See me again?" The edge to Dex' voice did not escape Shawcross. "Oh yes! Count … on … that." He snapped out the words.

For a moment, a flicker of puzzlement showed on the listener's face. Shawcross' hand fingered the obvious scar on his cheek, an involuntary movement. A brilliantined Saudi prince had just come down the staircase. Noisily, Shawcross cracked his knuckles as he waited for them to be alone. Both men watched the Arab flounce across the squelch of the carpet in his oh-so-western Ravazzolo suit. He would probably lose between five and ten million at blackjack before dawn. Shawcross waited until he was out of earshot and then adopted his most patrician tone. "Would you like our limo perhaps? Knightsbridge isn't it?"

"I'd rather walk."

"As you wish. Good night then, Mr Dexter. And I am *so* sorry." He watched as Dex took the stairs, two at a time. Then he strolled through to the casino and quickly cornered Miller and Nigel Forster-Brown. "No trouble from Dexter at all."

"And he's cleaned out! Just as you predicted." Miller grinned like a fat kid with a toffee-apple.

"Prats like Dexter always lose, given half a chance." They were grouped behind an unused kidney-shaped baccarat table. Shawcross, eyes cold and hard now, adjusted the crispy white cuffs that peeped from below his normal working uniform of single-breasted tuxedo.

Jeb Miller nodded. "Doubling up after each losing bet. Crazy system! Bound to get you in the end."

Shawcross nodded, his eyes less menacing now. At forty-four, he still looked a hard bastard well able to hold his own in words or a brawl. When excited, his abrasive Essex accent broke through the usual tutored vowels. "I'll never forget when the creep told me that doubling-up was *his* system – I mean do me a favor … that he had invented it." The accompanying laugh was not funny.

The scar hinted at a rough edge and the ladies adored it. The angular latino looks had seduced most of the women on whom he had set his sights. Miller guffawed, too heartily for Shawcross' liking. The man's teeth were uneven and stained by years of pipe smoking – or as other staff suggested - from ass-licking the boss.

"You're joking," Miller scoffed. "The Martingale? Doubling up stakes after losing? Been around since King Canute burned the cakes. Mugs' game. Dexter just got lucky for too long."

The third man, Forster-Brown, smirked at Miller's memory of schoolboy history. So far FB had said nothing. Respectful as the parish priest delivering the last rites, his eyes had been lowered, hands clasped behind his tall stooped back. Now his head nodded like a toy dog in a car's rear-window. "You were right, Audley," he gushed. "*Be patient* you said. Then pounce. And Jeb here did just that! Perfect timing." Despite being number two to Shawcross, FB never said much, especially to his boss. He knew his place, took his orders, pampered the bastard's ego and dreamed of retirement in nine distant years.

Shawcross smiled at the flattery but the eyes crying *shark* were narrowed. His Class-A brain was at work. "Credit where due FB. Good idea of *yours* to raise the maximum bets to a million for even chances when Dexter's around. For Martingale players, it suckers them right in. Worth the risk."

Miller relished picking over the bones of the corpse, though it was FB with his stoop who looked more like a vulture. The inspector's face was alive, his piggy eyes alert. "But with tossers like Dexter, it worked a fucking dream. He went down to the wire … and…"

"….Then *Operation Cyclops* wiped him out!" Shawcross finished the sentence for him. A leer played around his lips as he continued. "It happens."

"Lot of *Cyclops* about recently," Miller showed his raddled teeth.

Shawcross chopped his right hand in a decisive movement. "Wipe the tapes, FB. Not that Dexter's trouble. No hint of that." For a second, he wondered if he was trying to persuade himself.

"Damned *technical problems*. Same as last week when we rolled over those Greeks." All three laughed.

"Martingale's for jerks," said Miller. "Run of fourteen blacks. Rare but nothing remarkable."

"I've seen twenty-six. I knew we'd get him. Cyclops made it easier." Shawcross punched a fist into his other palm with an impressive smack. "So we took Dexter for ….?"

"About a million and a half," Miller eagerly provided the figures. "Sucked him dry. Spat him out and sent him home to Mummy." It was a line he had used about the Greeks and the Peruvians before them. Miller knew Shawcross would slip him a tasty cash bonus.

"You did well, Jeb." The CEO's delight over *Cyclops* was tempered by impatience for the start of the big one – *Operation Snowball*. Shawcross rubbed his slender hands in anticipation before again fingering the old scar on his darkened cheek. Then he was gone, effortlessly working the room, shaking hands here, sharing a polite word there. Yet beneath his smooth banter, something was troubling him.

Not what Dexter had said. Just that insolent defiance on his face.

Dex ignored the rain as he strode angrily down Park Lane. He was reliving the evening. It had all started much as usual – dinner with a bottle of Richebourg and then onto the gaming floor. He had sauntered towards the roulette tables, his back ramrod straight, head high and hands in pockets. He had spotted Nigel Forster-Brown. The General Manager was watching a busy blackjack table where an Argentinean was being paid out just under a million for a split that had left him with two hands of twenty-one. "There goes your Christmas bonus, FB."

FB looked at the table, still watching the payout. "Bonus? Christmas? We're a casino, not a merchant bank. "

"Judging by the thickness of the carpet, I guess you're right, though I heard you're in a spot of bother over Space City."

FB looked away. He shrugged and watched the payout. "Nothing serious, that's for sure." He scuttled away with indecent haste.

"I wouldn't fancy being a shareholder, not after what I heard," Dex called to the departing back. He saw Scotty Brannigan and Mick Glenn playing roulette and joined them. He had admired the American for years. As a Formula One world champion three times over, he was the stuff of legend. Glenn played soccer for Arsenal and England - played well too but his brains were in his feet. Though he had seen them once before, Dex had never played at the same table. Down the far side of the room, on a dais beneath the oil by Reynolds, was the Baccarat Pit. From there came the occasional laugh and a triumphant murmur of "Pay the Bank" from a Chinese diplomat.

Already the numbers-board behind the wheel showed the last six numbers had been black. *Perfect!* "How're you doing?" It was the usual greeting on joining a table and rarely answered in detail. Brannigan smiled, shrugged as if to say *just about okay.* Glenn just mumbled about his *bleedin' luck* as he tossed chips around like confetti. Dex watched them as he started his own play, backing red numbers. Each was true to image – Brannigan cool and showing no reaction when he lost while Glenn scowled, his eyebrows knitted together. With his beaky features, the soccer star was hovering over the table like a bald-headed eagle, splashing chips around as if money meant nothing. Pocketing two hundred grand a week for kicking a ball, it probably didn't.

"Let's hit it, baby" Mick Glenn prompted the dealer. Wearing a turquoise kimono-style tunic with a generous split, Nancy leaned across and spun the ball. As it lost speed, it dropped down beside the diamond-shaped metal strikers.

"Last bets," Nancy warned as the footballer shot out his muscled arm to place a final chip as an after-thought. "No more bets." This time, her tone was sharp, her voice forceful. This was a command. *No more bets* meant just that. She waved her left arm above the layout to prevent anyone placing a late bet.

"Seventeen, Black. Odd"

As Dex lost yet again, Glenn was a big winner. "Scotty, me ol' pal. You gotta go with the wheel. Stop pissin' about with sweetie money on even chances. Think big, win big." The accent was London suburban, rough and uncompromising.

Brannigan grinned at Dexter for the first time. Gone was the austere severity of the man who never flinched when cornering at one-forty mph. The grey eyes told the story – *heh just ignore this fella*! "Listenin' to him, you'd think he never lost." He turned away to Glenn. "Tortoise and the hare. Call me a tortoise, Mick."

"Minardi against a Ferrari?" Dex chipped in. "Don't remember seeing Minardi drivers on the podium too often." Dex met the full force of the American's penetrating stare. He'd seen TV close-ups of Brannigan in the cockpit but that was nothing compared to this. The eyes were stripping him naked, searching to test his mettle. Something about them struck him. Something different. Unsure what, he mentally noted to look out his old race recordings.

Dex watched Scotty manipulate a chip between his fingers with deft movements, a sure sign of too many hours spent at the gaming tables. The cool stare bored into Dex. "More like my RGB and a Ferrari! It's shit this season."

"I've noticed."

The next two spins produced more black numbers, losers for Dex as he doubled and doubled again. "Petrol-head are you?" Scotty resumed the conversation.

Dex shook his head. "No interest in what's under the bonnet. I like the power struggles, the race for the first bend, the ambience, the macho images, the forked-tongues, the lies."

"Plenty of those aroun' the pits, that's for sure. That Machiavelli guy would have learned a bit!"

"Been a fan since Ayrton Senna won his first championship in 1988."

"You at Monaco last year?"

Dex said no and decided not to comment. He remembered the race well enough though. "I get to some of the circuits though."

"Maybe I'll see you again somewhere."

"Silverstone maybe? I'm going there – courtesy of Mr Shawcross. He's flying us up."

"You're goin', aren't you Mick? Amount you've lost, you've paid for everyone's trip anyway."

"Yeah. I'm goin' funny man." Glenn's polished bald head added to the fierceness of his appearance but he seemed ready to take ribbing from his friend.

"I'll see you both there then. Shawcross wants me to say hi to his guests at lunch." Scotty turned to face Dex again. "I'm Scotty Brannigan, though I guess you know that." He spoke modestly in a lazy Nevada drawl.

"Finlay Dexter. People call me Dex."

"People call me worse'n that, buddy!"

Dex was about to reply when Nancy set the wheel spinning. The table fell silent. Dex thought back to Monaco 2001. He remembered watching the race on a small TV in Kilburn. It would be interesting to see it tonight on his giant plasma screen. *Those eyes?* The mystery intrigued him.

"35. Black. Odd."

Fuck that!

A repeat!

Still ...no problem.

Bound to be a red bus soon.

"Nancy, love. Do that again and I'll effing marry you tomorrow." Mick Glenn pummeled one meaty fist into the other. "You up for it?"

Nancy continued stacking his winnings – just over three hundred thousand. "Tempting, Mr Glenn but I'm married." She had heard it all before. She pushed over the winnings.

"Come on Nancy. Scotty here's owns a jet. He'll fly us to Vegas. Divorce your old man one day. Marry me the next. I understand how to treat a lady, know what I mean." He growled like a randy mongrel sensing a bitch on heat.

"So why aren't you married Mick?" Scotty enjoyed the dig, knowing the answer well enough.

Glenn scratched his nose. "Come to think of it, why buy a bleedin' book when I can visit a library? So do yourself a favor Nancy. Just come on back to my pad tonight. What's another slice off a cut loaf, eh?" Dex noticed Mick's fists. They were like ship's piston heads, tightly clenched.

A shift change ended the banter. Nancy nodded goodbye to be replaced by Andy. Scotty Brannigan pushed back his chair. "I'm quittin' Dex. Lost enough. Mick'll be buyin' down at Brown's Club tonight. See you at Silverstone. An' man – better luck, eh! You're down a bunch of money."

"Thanks. Until Silverstone then. And get that RGB sorted," Dex replied exuding as much confidence as he could.

Dex was now alone at the table.

Earlier that day, Dukes' board had met upstairs for their monthly dogfight. "Get off my back," protested Audley Shawcross. "Space City will win through." The Essex boy from the end-of-terrace home with rusting bikes dumped in the unkempt garden thumped the boardroom table. The Waterford decanter trembled. He had been speaking fast, the words tumbling out. For a second, his finger ran down his right cheek, a mannerism he no longer noticed. "Ignore the delays. Forget the cost over-runs on the new tower." He looked at each board member in turn before fixing the chairman with a look reserved for his personal Judas. He always regretted speaking too quickly, knowing that his acquired vowels broke down.

Sir Cedric snorted, his pink face wrinkling in disapproval at the very thought of Space City – a vulgar place that he judged a tasteless behemoth. "The new tower is months behind schedule. Strikes. Contractual disputes. Listen here, *Audley*." Though he used the name, he might just as well have said *office boy*. "We planned to float the Dukes Group once we'd added these new rooms." Again the snort. "Some hope! Your master-plan of *hitting Vegas running* has totally buggered the cash-flow." His voice, thin and reedy anyway, became thinner when he was riled. "We're servicing going on two billion dollars. The wolves everywhere scent a kill."

"Our biggest players wanted us in Vegas. Last thing *we* want is our wealthy Arabs losing money in Bellagio that *we* could take off them. Until nine-eleven it was a no-brainer." The Chief Executive continued his circle of the table. His flared nostrils took in the mix of odors – Sir Cedric's clothes reeking of cigarettes, Vivienne Healey's delicate perfume, O'Keefe's curry lunch, Kyte's unctuous Old Spice. The strength of his own Padron Cigar followed him everywhere. He had chosen it from his humidor with loving care before the meeting, thinking even then that it would be his sole pleasure over the next ninety minutes.

21

"Unless we win more in London," the chairman harrumphed "we can't meet the bank interest. Fat chance! Since nine-eleven, too many of our Arab members have retreated to their tents instead of losing their oil wealth to us." He looked at his cronies for support. "Cut our losses. That's what I say. Sell Space City to one of the big players in Vegas - say MGM-Mirage, Harrahs, or Steve Wynn."

Shawcross shook his head very slowly. Then he sighed as if telling a snotty nosed kid something for the third time. His tone was exasperated. "The big boys won't rescue us. My guess? They are *enjoying* our discomfort. *Schadenfreud.* They'll wait until we're bust before pouncing. So we have to survive."

"Drunken rednecks on weekenders from Albuquerque won't balance the books." Sir Cedric drew heavily on his cigarette and exhaled with contempt.

"Carlo has no doubts we'll win through. By the way, he sent greetings and apologies. He's too busy in Vegas delivering the project instead of listening to you whining." Carlo Letizione was President of US Operations and the director charged with delivering the new wing on time. Shawcross treated the tough American with his strong Vegas pedigree as an ally. With his swarthy Italian features, he looked the part. What the board did not know was that they shared a secret common interest in *Snowball* and *Cyclops*. But beneath the arm-gripping and back-slapping, Shawcross despised the man, viewing him as a lousy man-manager who had created most of the financial problems that were swamping them.

The dislike and mistrust were mutual. Except that he had appointed him, Shawcross would have dumped Carlo two years back. But he was not going to give the board the pleasure of crowing about that. Not when he had secured Carlo's agreement to *Cyclops* and *Snowball*.

"This damned Space Shuttle launch every hour." Kieran O'Keefe opened with a gentle Irish lilt. His voice evoked rolling hills, splashing streams and misty rain. You could almost hear the infectious jiggety-jig of a three-piece band and the raucous laughter from a bar by a small quay. The softness of tone did not fool Shawcross. O'Keefe's face was mean and chiseled, the hair gelled completing his *smart Alec* appearance. "That mock Shuttle attraction cost thirty-two million. It's so popular, it's keeping the losers *away* from the slots and tables. Is that daft or just plum crazy?"

"Get real. What do you know? Stick to bean counting." Shawcross turned towards the empty fireplace. Leaning against the intricate plasterwork, he looked elegant in repose, hands hanging relaxed beside his hand-stitched suit. There was an easy transformation in the Jekyll & Hyde sides to his character.

He could slip from charismatic allure to fearsome predator with just a touch of overdrive. He wanted to tell them they were two-faced bastards. Each one had supported the Vegas investment. *Especially you Cedric. Yes ... perhaps you'd like your life rearranged? Like that guy in Panama.* He cut the train of thought. *Don't go there! Panama never happened. Never.* "Business downstairs *has* been slack. But it's just a blip."

"Some blip!" Sir Cedric Oakley waved his squat hand at the quarterly figures. "You've barely broken even." He spluttered out his assessment and then nodded in agreement with himself.

"I've asked around," continued Shawcross. "We've done better than most." It was a lie. "Carlo believes it won't be long before normal service in Vegas will be resumed." Another lie. "But the great American people are still scared to fly." He clenched his fists as he thought of Mohammed Atta and his hijackers. "Scarcely helpful so soon after opening."

"When we voted on the new tower, business was good," continued the Irish Finance Director. "What's your forecast now?" He looked for brownie points from the chairman who smiled paternally.

The lights from the twin chandeliers above the oval table barely reached the corners of the spacious room but each painting had its own spotlight picking out the reds and black of a London long before the days of Henry Ford. The deep blue carpet had the corporate logo running through it, matching the place mats and coasters. Shawcross sipped at his gin and tonic and sensed the hostility. And he didn't give a toss. From his position by the Adams fireplace, his eyes flashed warnings at the eight directors. His only ally was Reggie Kyte, the Director of Security, a man with a critical role in casino operations with millions in cash turning over daily.

Shawcross glanced at Vivienne Healey. She was a true floating voter and the one who could swing the chairman's vote ... or the chairman's *anything* come to that. Her glazed look showed that even she was losing patience with him. *Bloody amateurs! Know fuck-all about running a casino.*

He thought of his own career - dealing blackjack for the aristocracy in illegal London casinos. *Then working the cruise ships and that rough joint in Antigua. And then Panam.... Stop! Access denied! You've never been there! Fast-forward to Moscow. Ran that dump for those hoods, snub-nose always to hand. And now you lot!* His gaze looked at the great and good around the table. Reggie Kyte apart, they had barely visited the gaming floor. *So? Don't complain Audley! They're suckers!*

As he listened with one ear to O'Keefe droning on about adverse trading conditions and mock Space Shuttles, Shawcross wanted to boast that his *personal* surveillance system bugged the cloakrooms, the telephones, the corridors and was under every table in the bar and restaurant. Best of all, he had bugged the Irishman's office. He had listened to their plotting. But nobody knew of *his* personal hidey-hole full of tricks.

"City pundits reckon Space City to be a voyage too far," observed Vivienne Healey with an icy smile.

Shawcross nodded. "I saw the newspaper. *Mission Impossible* – wasn't it? Look Vivienne: do you trust them – journalists and city analysts still wet behind their ears? Or do you trust me?"

"Too many snakes and not a ladder in sight." Sir Cedric read aloud from the Financial News about the strikes on the Vegas building site. "My friends at the Athenaeum Club thought that very droll." His face reddened a shade deeper. "Ha-ha! Very funny! That wretched article probably put back flotation prospects indefinitely." He shook his head before tossing back his Glenlivet. "I never expected to find Dukes' profits being insufficient to buy a small round of drinks at Boodles."

Shawcross could take no more. "And I didn't expect to have my chairman leading dirty little cabals. For nearly forty years, you've grabbed every non-executive job your society friends at Boodles could offer. Your achievements, except always being first with your snout in the money-trough, wouldn't fill a postage-stamp."

He raised his hand to prevent Sir Cedric from interrupting. "Know what? Somebody told me your catchphrase down in the Square Mile." He paused for effect and mimicked the chairman's sibilant voice. "*Spare a moment old bean?*" Shawcross' laugh was captivating and he saw several of the listeners trying hard to keep a straight face. "Sounds like something from *Billy Bunter's Schooldays*. Well, *old bean*, do us *professionals* who run this place a favor. Let me and Carlo see this through. Without us working our balls off ... this company is doomed. Bankrupt. Think how that will read on your next job application – all of you."

Nobody wanted to break the silence. All eyes were on Sir Cedric. At last he spoke after stubbing out his cigarette. "What next then, Audley?"

Shawcross moved to the head of the table, standing behind the chairman, forcing him to twist awkwardly to stay involved. Talk of bankruptcy had rattled them. There were nervous sideways glances; papers were being shuffled.

Someone coughed. Keeping them waiting, he stooped to help himself to a smoked salmon sandwich. With deliberation, he sipped at the double Gordon's as if waiting for someone else to speak. In poker terms, he knew he had *the nuts* – and better still *they* too now understood it. Only *he* could save them.

At last, after chewing through a couple of mouthfuls, he spoke quietly, one hand in pocket, the other stabbing the air. "If you, Cedric, can't keep the city boys in the bank happy, then you don't deserve your monster salary. Frankly, you've fucked up from start to finish." The gloves were now off yet he had spoken so gently that his audience had been craning forward to catch what he said. He liked this useful ploy for ensuring attention. "In contrast, *I* can and will deliver."

"We need bigger profits. The omens are...well...ominous." O'Keefe looked like a contestant on *Millionaire* who had just answered a one hundred pound question without phoning a friend.

"Well, thanks Kieran for that incisive analysis. No wonder you graduated so well." *Patience, Audley, patience.* Still speaking softly, he continued. "Kieran. I don't have the advantage of a degree, like you – postal course, Third Class Honors, wasn't it? So I can't bring such useful platitudes to the board. But as a self-made success let me tell you: during the next quarter or so the drop will be transformed."

O'Keefe wriggled uncomfortably in his chair. He thought Shawcross had believed his top degree from Trinity College Dublin mentioned in his job application. Seeing the Irishman's discomfort, the chairman intervened. "Transformed, eh? Sounds like twaddle," he chirruped as he wiped his hands with a napkin. He looked at O'Keefe. "What'll keep the bankers happy?"

Shawcross placed his elegant card-sharper's hand across his mouth, concealing a smirk. He had recorded every word of their secret meeting a couple of hours earlier. "Two million sterling a month more," Kieran lobbed in the demanding figure, confident that it was impossible.

Shawcross said nothing.

Cedric snapped shut his briefcase. "Fine. In four weeks, I'll expect just that."

"No way!" Shawcross enjoyed the provocation.

"Huh?" The grunt was aggressive.

"You heard." The CEO continued to speak from above the tufted white hairs that flapped like ailerons either side of the chairman's head. He grabbed a calculator, aware that all eyes were on him, tapping in figures to imply spontaneity. Then he looked up. "I won't be judged on four weeks. Give me until next December. I'll deliver an extra *forty* million. Let me repeat: at least forty million more here in London."

He loved taking in the shocked faces. The Financial Director looked bemused. "But that's over six mill a month."

"Congratulations, Kieran. And you didn't even need your beads and counting frame either. Six point six million actually!"

Sir Cedric looked around and saw that the mood had changed.

"Worth waiting for," said Vivienne Healey. She looked at the chairman for endorsement but saw only bemusement. She was twenty years his junior. Business-like with Slavic features beneath jet-black hair, her model-girl height contrasted with the Winnie-the Pooh physique of her chairman. "Come on Cedric. If Audley delivers, that would be amazing in this dismal market. *And* we can keep the banks at bay."

Cedric's flabby cheeks wobbled into a forced smile. "Quite so, Vivienne, my dear, quite so." Sir Cedric nearly patted her hand but refrained. He turned to Audley. "Forty million then but at least an extra three by the next meeting. Just to prove you're not playing for time." He looked round at the nodding heads. "Meeting closed."

Shawcross leaned heavily on the chairman's shoulder. "I haven't finished!" he snapped. "I want a bonus of one million for delivering this." He waved a cheery hand. "Think about it! Must be better than er …. bankrupting the company, wouldn't you say?"

Sir Cedric looked round the table and saw the resigned looks on the faces. "Done. No mercy if you fail." He eased back his Chippendale chair and waddled towards the door, the rolling gait due to a touch of gout. Pausing only to adjust the flower in his buttonhole, he disappeared from sight, eager to discuss Newmarket down at Boodles.

"Dickhead," Shawcross called after the departing figure.

"You're an employee, Audley. You ought not to speak of Cedric like that." O'Keefe sounded petulant in a limp-wristed way.

"Oh piss off will you! Only one person can save you. And it is not Cedric."
The notion of saving this lot was singularly unappealing. Shawcross nodded
his own goodbyes and once back in his own office, summoned Pru. His PA
bustled in, all bum and hearty - dressed as if she had been judging a Sussex
gymkhana. Her voice was pure Roedean and Lausanne finishing school. Her
cheerful smile and voice filled the room. "How was the Crazy Gang?"

He grimaced.

"Another gin bad was it?" She saw his nod of appreciation and returned with
a generous slug.

"No interruptions now please, Pru." Alone in his paneled office, he dialed a
chum from his schooldays at the Essex comprehensive from where he had been
removed for cheating. To Arnie Fisher, this had earned his pal *more* respect.
Fisher and his brother ran a shady investigation bureau in Goodge Street and
had grown prosperous on the fees that Dukes paid them.

"Arnie? Can we meet? Two-thirty tomorrow? Excellent. And your report?
Finished? Good news is it? Thanks." There would be two items on the
agenda. Digging up dirt on Cedric would be one. But that was a sideshow,
an insurance against the bastard trying more tricks. The main item was the
surveillance that would underpin *Operation Snowball*. That chance sighting
on the Bayswater Road had been pure gold.

A shiver of anticipation went through him. He downed his drink and leaned
back in his swivel chair. A dangerous look creased his rippling features, the air
of a rogue enjoying a moment of quiet satisfaction. He knew the look well and
reckoned that a movie of his life would star Antonio Banderas. The actor could
play *sly* in such a disarming manner. He checked his watch. It was time to see
today's lemmings throwing themselves over the money-cliff downstairs.

He moved effortlessly into his dressing-room to change from his tailored
suit into dinner-jacket. As he fiddled with his bow tie, except for the first
developing wrinkles on his forehead, he liked what he saw in the mirror,
Without them, he reckoned he could pass as thirty-four instead of ten years
more. Maybe a Botox treatment? That and a replacement for Claire Weatherley.
He thought of her strapped to the bed, the leather thongs straining, sweat
glinting from her buttocks. Pity she detested the rough stuff. Hearing her
squeals had been *so* pleasurable. Still, she was l doing a great job downstairs
with the blackjack. It was just in the bed that he needed a replacement. His
eyes glinted in anticipation.

Downstairs on the gaming floor, he saw Finlay Dexter arriving and wondered when *Cyclops* would get him. An opportunity was overdue. He was still smiling at the prospect as he greeted the insufferably loquacious Indonesian couple who were always good for a big loss. No need to cheat them. "What a pleasure! And how was your flight?" Then he moved across to greet Dexter as he stood beside the seascape by Turner.

"Oi! Guv! Got any spare change?" The gruff voice from a doorway startled Dex. He was nearing his mews cottage, hurrying along Knightsbridge through the steady rain. He saw a man, bearded, unkempt and eyes deep-set beneath the wrinkled folds of skin. He was lying beneath some soaked cardboard close to the entrance to the Park Tower Casino. The image struck a painful chord. The vagrant could have been sixty or maybe thirty years less. It was hard to tell. Dex fumbled in his pocket for change and found thirty pence. He turned to his wallet. Next to his Amex card was a solitary fifty-pound note, his last cash and he handed it to him. "Better luck, eh."

The vagrant looked at it suspiciously. "Blimey You're a gent an' all! A red note! Ain't seen one of these before."

"And me? I won't be seeing one again! Goodnight, pal!" He regretted the comment. How could anyone have a *good night* sleeping rough on a London street? As he quickened his pace toward the lights of Harrods' windows, arms swinging briskly, the vagrant's whiskered face taunted him about the shallowness of his hedonistic lifestyle. Large raindrops splashed his Italian shoes as he crossed Sloane Street, dodging between an accelerating Porsche and a pair of cops on motor-bikes. The vibration of his cellphone against his hip puzzled him. "Yes?" The grip that clasped the Nokia glistened under the street lamp. His face lit up as he recognized the voice. "Beth! Hi!"

"I'm at JFK Airport. They've just called the flight. How are things, kiddo?"

"Mum's folks as boring as ever?"

"You didn't miss anything. No alcohol. Daddy hated it. And you? Stuffing Dukes as usual?"

"You know ring donuts?"

"Go on."

"All I've got is the hole in the middle. I'm flat broke again - just like after *Louche* went down."

"What! Lost the lot? *Everything*?"

"Not *lost*. I could take *losing*, Beths." The plural was a throwback to toddler days in Bladon.

"Meaning?"

"Those bastards cheated me."

"Highest truth?"

He smiled at Beth's childhood expression and replied in kind. "Cub's Honor."

"Can you prove it?"

"Like hell I can. No witnesses." He relived the moment and scowled. "Scotty Brannigan, y'know the American Grand Prix driver and his mate Micky Glenn the Arsenal player had just left the table."

"So?"

"I'm going to ..."

"Get a job?"

"No."

"Get even?"

He paused to gather his thoughts but then spoke with far more certainty than he felt. "No. That's not enough. I'm going to *destroy* them." He had made his point with icy clarity but his sister said nothing. "Beths. You do see what they've done to me? I'm stony broke. *Everything* will have to go. The car, the flat, everything I've lived for."

Beth's tone was less sympathetic than he had hoped. "You lost over a million, didn't you? Well, tough titty! Get a job. Most people have to work."

Dex ignored the jibe. He knew the long hours she put in. "Beth – I'm not kidding. Call me fucking stupid if you want. Guilty m'lud! But it took fraud to sink me." Was he getting anywhere? He was unsure. "And when I say destroy, I don't just mean Dukes. I'm going for Space City."

"Space City Casino? Taking on the mob? You been drinking again?"

"Eye for an eye."

"When did you ever read the bible?"

29

"I was robbed. Don't you understand? I'll need your help. Delving into their figures. Junk bonds and so on."

"Isn't there something else you want to say?" Beth snapped. She waited for his response but heard nothing, so she continued. "Like a huge *sorry* for screwing up the charity?" Dex was unsure whether to be defiant or play the whipped pup. He said nothing. "Sheer greed," she continued. "You *are* a bloody wastrel. Drifting around all day like a knotted condom in the Thames." He heard the sniff of derision. "Until you've got the half million back for the charity, you can take a hike."

He snorted at the knotted condom jibe. This had gone even worse than he had feared. "Right. If I'm on my own, so be it." He nearly told her to go fuck herself but somehow refrained. "Thanks for nothing Beth… and goodbye." The phone clicked and she had gone. One minute and a thousand regrets later he called her back. She was on voicemail. He left a message. "Beth! Sorry! Really am! You're absolutely right. But I'll get it back. And more. Promise. Safe flight. Love you."

Back home, dry and anxious to forget his plight, he sank a slug of rum and coke and crossed to the music centre. He riffled through a stack of CDs and DVDs – *Queen in Concert, Black Sabbath, Ozzie Osbourne, Shawshank Redemption, The Ryder Cup 1998, Last Tango in Paris, Casino, Playgirls Exposed* and *Four Weddings and a Funeral.* Then he found it, tucked beneath *Fawlty Towers* – the Formula One *Grand Prix Season 2001.*

The mews room was compact, snug in winter and decorated in warm positive colors. He adjusted the dimmer switch, closed the heavy drapes and slumped back into the leather recliner. He fast-forwarded to Monaco, 27th May 2001, the race that Scotty Brannigan had mentioned. He wanted to see the eyes. Seconds later, the familiar evocative whine of 16,000 RPM engines filled the room but the pictures were of bikini-clad beauties drinking on a yacht followed a view of all the rich men's toys that crammed the harbor. It set the glamorous tone.   Monaco was *the* race to be seen at.

Ever since his teens, he had absorbed Formula One stories. He loved reading of the testosterone-charged drivers. He envied the way they mocked death's kiss on the winding and unforgiving roads through the Principality. For the tanned beauties and skinny models the dream was to date legendary hunks - iron men like David Coulthard, Jensen Button, Eddie Irvine or the enigmatic Scotty Brannigan. For his part, Dex would have given anything just to sit behind the wheel or to discuss G-forces with a world champion. But Scotty these days seemed more interested in G-spots than G-Forces.

He waited impatiently for the shots he wanted, his mind drifting back to revenge. Scotty! Perhaps Scotty was just the man to help - Vegas background. Icy cool. Knows all about roulette. Knows Shawcross and Dukes. He must know the Vegas power-brokers, the way the place ticked. Maybe. Just maybe ... Dex flicked fast-forward to the start of the race and the close-ups.

The camera zoomed in on the red Ferrari of Michael Schumacher in pole position. The eyes were unblinking, the concentration total. *That man was just so impressive.* Dex flicked on and then fast froze on Brannigan who was second on the grid. In contrast to the total focus of Schumacher, there was something troubled about the American. Dex leaned forward to look more closely. True, you had little of the face to work on – barely more than the eyes were visible but they seemed to reflect an inner turmoil. He played the segment again at normal speed. The grey eyes were restless, always on the move. Then he flicked back to March and the Australian Grand Prix, the first race of the season, for comparison.

"Yes!" He thumped the arm of the chair in satisfaction. Brannigan's eyes earlier in the season had been unflinching, just like tonight. So what had been tormenting Scotty at Monaco last year, May 2001? Not fear surely? Was he thinking about Schumacher? The notorious bend at Sainte Devote? The instability of his RGB? Something else?

Monaco - 27th May 2001

Just before two pm the Mediterranean sun was beating down on the cars, a shimmering haze rising above the hot road surface. The Monaco Formula One Grand Prix was seconds from go. The rays bounced off the bodywork of the most sophisticated driving machines on earth. Brannigan had just completed the formation lap, not racing - just going round in a procession as the drivers warmed the tires.

He parked on his mark, waiting for the drivers behind him to get into their positions for the start. There was nothing else to do now but await the last arrivals at the back of the grid and then watch for the five red starting-lights ahead of him.

Until this season, Scotty had always loved Monaco. Not today. As he waited for the first red light, he tried to keep focused, kept telling himself to concentrate. But it wouldn't happen. In eight seasons, he had won here three times, afterwards partying until dawn, sometimes bedding a Hollywood star and once even waking up with a contented but shame-faced married member of the British Royal Family. He rarely drank much anymore – the odd beer perhaps. What turned him on was the buzz of the Monte Carlo Casino, the danger of the circuit and the supply of beautiful women. But not this year. The troubles had been piling up all morning.

For starters, the RGB was fucked, way off the pace. For a triple World Champion, it was no fun being the butt of the oldest pit-lane joke around.

Heh! Did you hear? Last time Scotty was back home in Vegas. He stopped to offer an old woman a lift. She was shuffling along, one leg in plaster. No thanks, she replied. I'm in a hurry!

Hoots of laughter from the mechanics down the Pit Lane.

Fuck you Nanda Datt.

Fuck you Roxy.

Get outta my head!

Should be thinking of beating Schumi into Sainte Devote.

Earlier, in the team motor home, he had been swilling down water and wearing his sponsor's cap, peak up. Roxy, his separated wife had called. He slumped to a chair, littered with his clothes. "Oh it's you. What now?" His irritation was obvious.

"I've been thinking." Roxy's accent was English, the words lazily slurred together, Tony Blair style. "About yesterday's offer. Twenty-two million dollars to settle? Forget it! I want thirty-five. Same timescale. Twenty-eight days to agree or see you in court."

"See you in hell, first."

Roxy Dawson wrote in-depth profiles of sporting personalities for an English tabloid. That's how they'd met. She paused for a menacing moment. "Your choice. Pay or I'll tell the judge about your hot cash in Gibraltar. He'll really go for your balls." Her chuckle was familiar to Scotty. It spelled warning in large letters. "You won't be bedding models two at a time after that, Scotty dahr...ling."

He imagined her flame red lips pouting. "You're just a greedy bitch. You conned me into that Little White Chapel in Vegas - sayin' you were pregnant. Lyin' little vixen." Brannigan had learned a fair line in abuse from his father who'd been a trucker in Reno. His mother had worked as a server in a diner and tolerated her man's ways, though too often he was in jail for thieving or fighting. "I'm losin' sponsors like crazy. Now, you and your leech-like lawyers are bleedin' me dry. As for Gib – hell, there ain't no crock of gold there. Go ask the apes."

"Cut the crap! The only ape around is you. Wait until my Queen's Counsel lays into you. He'll squeeze you till your balls pop out of your bum."

"Like I'm crappin' myself waitin'. Sure. I had cash there. Thirty-eight mill. Not now. Gone. Lost."

"Oh *puhlease*! Do me a favor! I'm reaching for the Kleenex. Roulette again, was it?" He imagined her heavily made-up face contorting as she crossed and re-crossed her shapely legs. "Don't lie to me. You've shifted it somewhere else."

"Twenty-two mill is the offer. Get this Roxy! I did a few calculations. That's one million a blow-job." He examined his well manicured nails and scowled as he recalled her pampered existence at his expense. "Seven months of hell we had." He looked at his notes. The writing was large, bold but neat. "That's 312,480 minutes. Twenty-two mill is seventy bucks forty cents *a minute* for our marriage." He heard her intake of breath at the figures he'd worked out. His grin reached wall to wall. "Roxy: I'll do time for tax evasion rather than pay you a dime over twenty-two mill."

"Go cry in that jet of yours. Life must be tough."

"It is, you thievin' bitch." He shouted at the mouthpiece. "An' the Lear ain't mine no more than those breasts are yours. So jus' get the fuck outta my life." He switched off the phone and stormed outside. He needed space, a rare commodity in Monte Carlo. He needed to walk by the Thames, go climb Mount Charleston or kick sand on a beach in Phuket.

Some chance on race day!

Instead, in the warm morning sunshine, he leaned against a tree that lined the crammed pit area. He tried to pretend that he was invisible behind his mirrored sunglasses with his cap now pulled low. His body language read *keep away*.

I need to unwind.

Damn Nanda Datt.

Damn Roxy.

Damn my contract.

He glared at the spanking red, black and gold car, littered with logos. Despite its beauty, Scotty knew it only peaked when parked up. "Don't waste your time – the car's a pig", he mouthed towards his head mechanic who had been working to improve its handling. All around were floral displays, striped bunting and colored awnings, just like Chelsea Flower Show. He could smell no flowers. The air was too heavy with other race day odors so familiar to him – somebody's distant barbeque, high-octane fuel, sun-oil, cigarette smoke, scorched rubber, hot oil and the cloying smell of cellulose.

He checked the time - nearly eleven and getting hotter by the minute. He wished the Parade Lap would start and he could clear his head. Mick Glenn rang asking whether to place a bet. "Back Schumi, not me. Sure, I start second today but that's only because of others' mistakes. The quick guys are behind me. Hell Mick, I don' know why I bother. Roxy was threatenin' again jus' now. Man, why the fuck should I keep her in fur-lined frillies? Bitch!" He paused. "Gee! Forget it! Shall we hit the tables an' play some roolly tonight? Good. See you then."

From his shady spot, he absorbed the noise of 80,000 spectators. He checked his watch. Three hours till the start. First though, he'd have to meet his Race Engineer and do the Parade Lap with the other drivers. He sighed. From the yachts, came canned music, the laughter of the beautiful people chomping, swigging and braying their way through champagne cocktails, crab salads, lobster and huge dishes of moules. In the bars and restaurants above the ninety-degree corner at Sainte Devote, Scotty could imagine more of them - Italians, French, Germans and English bantering and joking. At this bend, rich fans dined well, risking their livers not their lives. They'd paid to see the probability of a *big accident*, front row viewing like Madame DeFarge in Paris in 1789.

The night before he had partied till two with Mick Glenn at the Tip-Top bar. On the way, they'd passed Repossi, jewelers to the Grimaldis, Monaco's Royal Family. "That's where I bought Roxy's ring," Scotty confided. "Diamond cluster. Over a million bucks. She still has it. Dodi Fayed bought one there for Princess Di before they flew to Paris. Didn't bring either of us any luck."

"C'mon Scotty. Cheer up. Let's hit the totty." They headed for Casino Square, Scotty brushing away requests for autographs.

"Can't be too late, Mick. The other drivers are already tucked up and readin' their comics."

"Scotty!" A shout from a fan with an American flag ended his train of thought. He waved back more cheerfully than he felt and slid back further behind the tree. Once, Monaco had been the high spot. No more. The fun had gone. Beyond the barriers across the track, he watched the fans, the tifosi, mostly draped in Ferrari flags or wielding huge banners with pictures of macho man David Coulthard. Two Americans were carrying the Stars and Stripes coupled with Brannigan's picture. He waved across to them, made their day.

He shifted further into the shade and removed his peaked cap. With restless movements, he wiped the sweat from the nape of his neck and ran a small hand through his thick crinkly hair. Sandy in color, he always swept it back. The unfashionably wide sideburns were a trademark and featured on his website and PR photos. When he was a teenager, his mother had reassured him his looks would improve with age. "Capricorns always do," she had insisted. At thirty-six he hoped she'd be proved right before too long. He'd weighed himself that morning – 172 lbs of packed muscle with a weathered face, hollow cheeks and a wide mouth. But he had no illusions: it was the job, not his looks that the women loved.

He walked across to his V10 race car, capable of doing the ton and stopping dead again within six seconds. But it was still off the pace.

Heard the other one about Scotty? They're putting go-fasta stripes on his car so we think its moving!

"Fuck my contract." He muttered the words as his anger rose. He was contracted to RGB until November 2003, *tethered to a go-kart* as he had told Mick. Last season he had cleared over thirty-five million but sponsors don't like losers. With his poor results, making ten this year was more likely. Who'll sign me up then? Sympathy votes didn't feature in Formula One. Today the Slow Lane, tomorrow the Exit. So I need big bucks … and fast too. The IRS wanted twelve million like yesterday, to say nothing of that bitch Roxy.

He kicked angrily at the thirteen-inch Michelins and wished he hadn't when he saw the scowl from Jason, his mechanic who loved the car like his baby. He thought of telling Jason that he didn't have to drive the pig.

Now as the race was about to start, he gripped the small rectangular steering-wheel while he waited for the red lights. The soft tones of Nanda Datt's elegant English again filled his head as if they were the answer. Maybe the Malaysian's offer hadn't been such a heap of shit. He shook his head, fighting temptation. His eyes flickered, reflecting the turmoil. The dapper businessman had pulled no punches. "You're finished, Scotty. Great career but you're washed up." The approach had been in the bar of the Mandarin Oriental in Kuala Lumpur after the race at the Sepang Circuit. "So help us. You'll be well rewarded."

Scotty had told the diminutive figure in the silk shirt, lightweight suit and alligator shoes where to shove his crooked offer. But since then the season had been one glorious fuck-up. Shall I call him? Or forget it? He eased his tight butt in the seat as he glanced up at the five lights. Not a red in sight but in his rear-view mirror there was still some movement. Surely the last two cars on the grid must nearly be in position.

The first red light appeared. The professional in him at last took over. Nothing mattered now but those lights. Ahead of him was the Schumacher Ferrari. Behind – another twenty cars, five of them faster than the RGB and hoping to out-brake him at Sainte Devote.

Gotta get a good start.

Beat Schumi on the straight.

Shut the door on him in the first three hundred yards.

Six seconds to Turn One at Sainte Devote,

No time at all.

But long enough to win or lose the hundred minute race.

Long enough to destroy a career.

Two lights,

Three,

Four.

Five

Wait.

They're all lit!

The lights went out.

Go! Go! Go!

The tires fighting for traction, his RGB roared away at 16,000 rpm, his frame pinned against the low slung seat. At once, his head was swaying to the bounce of the wheels, his body held rigid in the seat belts that held him almost horizontal in the car, his head low to the ground. Behind him, the purple and gray smoke from the burnt tires and noisy exhausts filled the grid.

Fuckin' cool start.

I'm up ten yards on the Ferrari.

Go for it!

Edge left.

Foot down.

80 mph.

100 mph

120 mph

165 mph

The steel barriers raced by, a blur in the violent acceleration.

I can do it!

Nose in front now.

Ahead was empty road except for the right-hander coming up fast.

Too fast.

Shit!

Schumi's gainin' again.

Front wheel up by my rear.

Now he's level.

Fuck!

I can't make it.

Gotta back off.

His line.

Not mine.

Game over.

Gotta follow him through the bend.

Slam down to second.

Gotta drop to 55 mph.

The chassis shuddered, the suspension struggling. The engine screamed with the violent deceleration, the brakes white hot as the shriek of the 800 horsepower drowned the cheers of the crowd.

Fuckin' balance.

The G-forces seemed to be tearing him apart as he bounced around, the RGB fighting for grip on the hot tarmac.

Okay pal.

Round we go.

What the....?.

The back end's going.

Correct it.

A touch of the wheel.

Now the front's losin' it.

It's Sainte Devote baby.

Turn damn you. Turn.

Fuck!

I'm crabbin' it.

Bounce.

Brake.

Steer.

Gloved hands wrestling.

Barrier ahead.

Barrier!

Shit!

Wallop!

Wallop again.

I'm goin' up.

Up.

No. I'm not.

I'm fallin'.

Shit, oh shi…

The crowd just above the track saw just what they had paid to see – drama big time. The RGB sideswiped the barrier, jumped vertically nose first and then flipped, the nose flying off into the safety fencing. The fuel tank was full. Flames flickered and became an instant inferno, brilliant orange surrounding the upturned cockpit. Twenty following cars somehow slewed, spun and skidded to avoid the wreck, two others colliding and spinning to a stop. The crowd was silent now.

From the RGB there was no sign of life as marshals and safety crew ran to douse the flames. Professor Watkins, the medical specialist to the sport was now sprinting towards the inferno. As always for the start, he had been following the pack in a fast saloon car. The smell of burning drifted down the circuit as the surviving cars disappeared towards Casino Square. An announcement said that they were stopping the race.

The flames were quickly doused and the fire marshals lifted the twisted wreckage to get to the trapped driver. Suddenly a roar rose from the crowd as a gloved hand waved from the cockpit.

"I'm gettin' too old for back-flips." Scotty later welcomed Mick Glenn in the private ward. He was propped on a couple of pillows, a cage propped around his midriff to his feet. "No shit Mick - controllin' that fuckin' car. Like a dinosaur on ice. I'm done for this season. Maybe for good."

"Nah, mate. Not you! Spring chicken!"

"Broken femur. Maybe make the last race at Suzuka, if I'm lucky. That's what they say."

"Could've been worse. Your dick might have been burned."

"Saved by the fireproof briefs." He pulled Glenn towards him. "I've already picked the best-lookin' nurse. Nadine. Reckon she'll do a trick for me before I'm outta here."

"Just to keep you warm."

"Just to keep me warm. No funny business." The exchange was a running joke between them. He paused. "Look, you go on down to the casino. Put ten thousand bucks on black numbers for me. I'm feelin' lucky today!" They both laughed. Later though, when he was alone, there was precious little to laugh about. Locked to this contract, Scotty knew he was washed up. Next year it would be the same car, the same problems scrabbling around for points. It was no life for a champion.

But Nanda Datt could change all that. Maybe it would be worth phoning him. The devil on his shoulder had won.

London - 25th June 2002

Dex watched Brannigan's rescue on his recording. The operation was slick but as the gurney was loaded into the ambulance, the crowd guessed that the injury was significant despite Scotty's big wave. He felt pleased that he had been right. This *had* been the race when the driver had looked distracted. The question was why? And since his return this season, why had he been creating so much controversy.

He poured the last of the coke, swilled it down and went to bed. After a tormented night, he forced himself to go for his daily jog though his mind was more tired than his limbs. He entered Hyde Park through Alexandra Gate at just after eight-thirty. The rain had passed on and the sky was now cloudless, though the forecast was of rain later.

So do I go to the Job Centre? Become a minicab driver, a night watchman. Thanks Mr Audley bloody Shawcross. He quickened his pace. Beth would have ideas once they had talked things through. "Money changes things; money is power," she'd told him. "Lack of money causes crime."

Away to the south-west around Hammersmith, he saw a pall of smoke against the pale blue. At first it seemed like morning pollution before its intensity changed his mind. Black smoke seemed to be rising fast and then darkening the sky for miles around. Quite a big fire, he decided, as he switched direction towards Garforth Mews but probably never meriting a line in the evening paper.

Just when Dex in his training togs was crossing Knightsbridge by Brompton Oratory, a ringing phone disturbed Mick Glenn's sleep. He was at his North London home, about eight miles away.

"Mick! Hi! How y'doing, man!" Scotty sounded as if he were speaking with his head in a bucket.

"Christ! What sort of time is this to ring anyone?" Mick Glenn's voice was abrasive, his throat parched after their late-night session at Brown's. Sophia, an Italian hairdresser with good long thighs was sprawled across the circular water-bed. Still breathing heavily, the ringing had not disturbed her. He grabbed for a glass of juice, reaching past a giant stuffed panda dressed in red and white Arsenal colors. On the floor were a purple mini-dress and two pairs of G-string pants – his and hers. "Why so early Scotty." He looked at the football-shaped clock. "I'm not long asleep."

"My rule. If I'm awake, then *everybody's* awake!" He laughed. "I'm drivin' to team HQ near Oxford. Enjoyed last night. Glad you got lucky. Lips like a carp. Still there is she?"

"Sleepin' like a baby. What you want anyway?"

"Sympathy. That jivin' last night – jiggered up my old fracture."

"Gettin' old mate. Painful is it?"

"A cactus up the rectum would be better. Anyway, the team wants me to stay on in the UK. Guessed we might try some more roolly?"

"Sure. Last night was pretty fuckin' tasty." Mick admired the girl's generous cleavage and played with the black curls of hair that lay damp behind her ear. He checked to make sure the girl was asleep and spoke quietly, unusually for him. "I'm off to the bank to pay in Dukes' check. So tonight. Dinner first?"

"Nah! There'll be a long inquest into the handlin'. Damned car - still more jumpy'n a Mississippi bullfrog, more nervous'n a colt." Even as he spoke, Scotty knew this wasn't true. But he couldn't tell Glenn about Nanda Datt. Couldn't tell anyone about the devil on his shoulder and that he could've won in Austria and San Marino.

Over dinner at Dukes they'd been playing catch-up. Mick had recently returned from the Far East as one of England's World Cup team. "Should've stuffed Brazil," he said, the hurt still apparent in his face. "Gutted, we was." Scotty had noticed his eyes narrow as he'd continued. "But what about you? I've seen most races, read about them all. Heh! Scotty you've been like a kid havin' drivin' lessons. What's goin' on? A coupla collisions. Then, you brake-tested that Miguel Escona geezer that was carted off to hospital. Then took some heat for holdin' up Schumi on his flying lap. Coulthard – you dumped in the gravel during a risky overtakin' attempt. You certainly been spreadin' the shit since your crash last season an' no mistake. Any drivers still talk to you?"

Scotty took the comments as vintage Mick Glenn and not a criticism. "That's Formula One, son. Big boy's sport. You win, you lose or you're gurneyed away. Boo-hoo! Wipe your eyes, kid. You know the shit."

Glenn didn't but inferred that he did.

Scotty eased his foot from the pedal as he saw the queue ahead at the ring-road. "Tonight then. Say we meet at Dukes at around nine-thirty…" Glenn never finished the sentence as Brannigan cut in.

"Hold it! There's a news flash." There was silence on the line except for some background talking from Brannigan's car. "Holy shit! A big jet's crashed approaching Heathrow. Coming in from New York. Just fell from the sky."

"Where?"

"Near Hammersmith Bridge. Yeah, Barnes they just said." Brannigan paused. "Hope none of my fans were coming in for the next race. Haven't many left."

"See you at the bar. Say 1030."

"Sure."

Dex relaxed under a piping hot shower. He'd finished his jog in respectable time, not his best but, for a *nouveau pauvre*, he was feeling good.

I'll have to get a job. But not today. I'll go the library. Search the web. Read up on Dukes Group at Companies House. Pop into the Gamblers Bookshop. Plan where to live. "I hate you, Shawcross but just you watch it!" he shouted above the torrent of water. "I'm coming to get you."

On the shower radio, Chris Tarrant was chatting away during his Capital Radio spot. After some jokes about his TV Show, *Who Wants To Be a Millionaire*, the program unexpectedly cut to the Newsroom. "First reports are coming in that a passenger jet from New York to London has crashed in a field near Barnes, south west London. Emergency Services are going to the scene of what witnesses have described as a major disaster. A further update will follow on the hour."

At first, Dex only half absorbed the news, interesting but tragic. Then it hit him. New York to London. Beth! He threw open the shower door and toweled down hurriedly. Lots of flights from New York land now. He switched on Sky News as he rang Beth's mobile number. No response. That meant nothing he told himself.

He powered up his computer and checked Beth's email sent yesterday. Flight ZXB 278. Barely had he found the number than he heard the presenter confirm that flight ZXB 278 had crashed. He sat numbed at his computer. His mind was blank, incapable of coherent thought. His eyes were transfixed on the number ZXB 278. But they were seeing nothing. How long he sat motionless, he had no idea. The TV brought him back to reality. "First reports say there may be some survivors. The flight was carrying three hundred and twenty nine passengers and crew."

He wasted no time. After dressing in seconds, he headed for the scene and ran all the way to Knightsbridge Tube Station for the train to Hammersmith. He remembered little of the next twenty minutes, except wanting to shout *laughing's out of order* to some cheery passengers in his carriage. It had been a relief to get off and head for the river. Even before Hammersmith Bridge, he could see the smoke and smell the fuel - the same smoke he had seen when jogging. The stench stifled him - clinging to everything, invading his clothes, his throat, and his eyes. Lonsdale Road was chaotic - ambulances leaving, a BBC TV crew in a small van arriving, the female reporter talking into her phone.

Dex scowled at her, suddenly jealous that she had someone to talk to.

"Sorry, sir. No further." The young constable was guarding the barrier.

"My family was on the plane."

"Sorry, sir. No exceptions. Could get in the way of the rescuers and the crash investigation boys."

"Does it help that my father is a Government Minister – the Lord Chancellor?" Pulling rank was not Dex' style and he felt bad about even trying it on. The policeman chewed his moustache for a nervous second before confirming it made no difference. He saw the resignation on Dexter's gentle features. "Oh and sir, like - I'm sorry – for you personally. Hope they escaped." He didn't add that there was speculation that over three hundred had died.

Dex nodded his thanks. "Where can I find out if my family survived?"

The constable spoke into his two-way, listened, scribbled and then handed over the Emergency Number. "Good luck. You know, sir, you're better off not going too near anyway." He was about to add something about burst open bodies and shredded corpses but thought better of it.

While he had been listening, a woman Dex recognized now as a BBC-TV news reporter had been standing close by. She appeared to be watching the jammed traffic but as soon as he stood looking bemused by the cordon, she approached him. "Hi! I'm Tiffany Richmond, BBC-TV News. I couldn't help overhearing. Your father, the Lord Chancellor, was on the flight."

He took in her appearance – red blouse under a black jacket with a simple silver brooch in the lapel. She looked smaller than on the evening news, maybe five foot six and daintily built. Her hair, cut short and two-tone chestnut with highlights was lacquered enough to avoid being blown about at even the windiest locations. She had barely made up her pale skin at all. The gentle smile came more from the almond shaped eyes than her small mouth colored by a hint of pink lipstick. "Father, yes but my sister and mother too." Later, Dex wondered why he hadn't told the reporter to piss off. Perhaps, because he'd seen her so often on TV that she didn't seem to be a stranger.

"When I go on air, can I mention that? Do you mind?"

Dex answered like an automaton. "That's your call. I hope they missed the flight."

The journalist had been at home in Chiswick when the BBC had summoned her to the crash site. Tiffany Richmond was a 31-year-old veteran of several disasters and of droughts in Africa. Her positive jaw and steely blue eyes gave her an attractive but no-nonsense look, softened only by the elf-cut hairstyle. The fan letters came by the sack. "I'll be tactful." Dex shrugged and moved towards the police cordon again. Uncharacteristically, she moved quickly to stop him going closer. "You should get away from here. Please go. I *have* to be here. I've done it before but *you* can't achieve anything." She nodded towards the smoldering fuselage. "It's not pleasant. Better to be close to the hospitals." Dex hesitated. He thought of his last angry exchange with Beth. He was fighting an urge to hurdle the tape and rush towards the wreckage, shouting, searching, looking for Beth and his mother. Doing something. Doing anything. But the pleading look on the presenter's face and her gentle tug on his arm stopped him. "If I can help, these are my contact numbers." She slipped a BBC card from the hip pocket of her black trousers. Dex noticed that it felt pleasingly warm.

"Thanks. I'll try not to bother you." He spoke like a voice from the dead. "Where are the survivors being taken?" His voice was cracking.

"St Mary's, Charing Cross and Hammersmith. By the way, what's your name?" Her true professionalism returned.

"Finlay Dexter."

"How old are you, Finlay?"

He seemed barely to notice the question and answered without thinking. "Thirty-three. People call me Dex."

"Address? We won't be precise, don't worry."

"Here's *my* card." He produced it from an expensive calfskin wallet. "Call me if you hear anything, good or bad."

"I will. Oh … and Dex. I hope this works out for you." She turned away quickly. Tears were welling in her eyes. He looked so helpless despite his age and strong physical presence. The big brown calf's eyes were so gentle, yet there was dignity too – in his masculine stance and the determination in his jaw. She understood just what he was going through. She had been there herself.

London - 25th June 2002

Shawcross threw aside the Evening Standard. He had been interested in the Barnes crash only because of the story suggesting that Finlay Dexter's family had not yet been accounted for. *Maybe he'll inherit and play in Dukes again.* "No interruptions Pru. And thanks for the tea." To be certain, he locked his office door and then opened the box-file left by Arnie Fisher. He spread out the photos, the typescripts of phone calls and records of bugged meetings. Besides the tapes themselves, there was even what Arnie had described as an X-rated video, full of action. He owed everything to a chance sighting of Adrian Ryder and his Zara woman on the Bayswater Road, Watching her on the video would be a pleasure.

Ryder's job history was unremarkable. Wife, no children. Kent Constabulary, rising to Chief Inspector. Early retirement with a disability pension after a thug destroyed his neck with a brick. Joined the Gaming Board when aged thirty-five and was now aged forty. Shawcross studied the picture of the familiar figure. Looks good for his age, despite the iron grey hair. Zara Belfield knows how to keep him young.

He glanced at the picture of Molly. She'd been married to Ryder for years but in the photo, she was sitting on a swing chair, passionately kissing a younger woman – apparently a student from her Art College.

He turned to the transcript dated 19th June – just a week before.

Location: Champagne Bar Poirot, Adwater St W1.

Time: 1745 - 1805.

Ryder: "Unlike you to be late."

Zara: "Bloody taxi. Snarled at Oxford Circus."

Ryder: "Go by Tube. Quicker. Champagne?"

Zara: "Only time I'm going underground is when I'm dead. Cheers." **Pause.** "But I'm not staying long."

Ryder: "Oh?"

Zara: "Adrian, this is a P45 moment. Tell that dyke you're leaving. It's her or me." **Pause**. "Not what I want. But I can't take you pissing about any longer."

Adrian: "Heh, sweetie-pie! We've something special." **Pause**. "I'm thinking *so* much about how to create a life together. About nothing else really. But I'm not wealthy. Divide that by two for what the legal eagles say Molly'll get. What then?"

Zara: "Just do it! I've saved a bit. I can't wait to chuck this casino accountancy stuff. We just go. Disappear. Run a bar in Spain or Antigua. Go crewing on a yacht. Get into real estate. Make love all the time."

Adrian: "Sounds like bliss but you've expensive tastes. It's unrealistic. Taxis, designer things, cashmere jumpers, clothes from Escada. Champagne bars. Besides, we can't just disappear. Can't leave Molly with nothing."

Zara: "Why not? Quit acting like a plodding copper. Show me the man you were when we first talked. Get a life!"

Long Silence.

Adrian: "It's not so easy."

Zara: "Easy as me walking through that door."

Adrian: "Wait. Wait. Give me a month."

Zara: "Remember that afternoon in our little place? What you said. I believed you. You've got two weeks. Adrian: do it for me. Bye"

End

Shawcross didn't rush to the rest of the evidence. He looked lovingly at his selection of cigars – Cuban, Nicaraguan and a few from the Dominican Republic. He could barely contain his excitement at what he had read. The door to *Snowball* was open wide. The fun would be getting Adrian to walk through it. He picked up a Padron but decided this was a really special moment calling for one of his three classics – a 1980 Montecristo No 2. He looked at the label, rolled it in his hand, held it to his nose and admired both smell and deep chestnut color. With a sigh at the perfection, he looked out his cutter and then lit it with meticulous care using a match from Dukes' own box.

He was about to continue his reading when his cellphone rang and he looked at it with irritation. He waited until the caller had left a message. Few people had the number and mainly he gave it to women who passed through his life in London. He was in no mood to chat but was interested to know who had called. As the smoke from his cigar drifted lazily towards the ornate workings on the ceiling, he played back the message and recognized Leila's guttural Arabic voice at once. She was a lithe beauty from Morocco who had been visiting London. They had first met last year while staying separately at La Mamounia and he had rapidly checked on her wealth, hoping to lure her into Dukes but she had refused to gamble.

"I'm at Gatwick, about to fly to Massachusetts. Audley, we had great times. You've torn my emotions to shreds. You really know how to play *this* woman's emotions. Those roses at the hotel this morning, so thoughtful. I'm going to display them on the plane's boardroom table. They'll remind me of your gentleness and the exciting ways you touched me. As for the clock, you're too generous. It's a *timeless* reminder of your sweet ways. You don't talk of love, so neither shall I. But our time together gave me such happiness. I wish I could have said this to you in person. I long to see you. Goodbye, Audley, until I am in London again."

He rose absent-mindedly from his chair and strolled to the window. He looked at the sky, so black now above the London lights. He thought of Leila about to soar away in her private jet. The first night, they had dined in the romantic surroundings of *La Poule au Pot* on Ebury Street before going on to rock and smooch at *Tramp* on Jermyn Street. The next night he had taken her to a charity ball at the Grosvenor House Hotel and had bid four hundred thousand pounds for a carriage clock, originally engraved on instructions from Diana, Princess of Wales and gifted to an unnamed admirer who had died, leaving it to the charity.

He knew it was a crazy price for a clock you could buy in Harrods for around five thousand but the pedigree and the good cause made it worthwhile. The generosity had impressed Leila of course but he had really wanted the other guests to know that he was charitable, could afford it and that Dukes was not strapped for cash as they may have read in the paper. *Yes, a win-win all round.*

He looked down at the Lamborghini that was dropping off someone at Dukes' front entrance before returning to his desk and checking his diary. Ana-Maria from Portugal was arriving tomorrow with her banker husband. She had phoned earlier. "He'll be at city meetings both afternoons. Does that interest you?"

Yes.

Seducing married women was so much more fun.

His bachelor life suited him fine. He wanted no commitment and always promised nothing more than sex, preferably the rough stuff and chivalrous attention. If he were lucky, and he often was, then she would like the studded leatherwear and thumb-grips. But this time he needed somebody to trust beyond his private life, someone who would be involved too in *Snowball*.

He called Arnie. "I'm going through this material. You've done a great job. I want to know more about the woman."

"Zara? She's got him right *there*. He'd do anything to keep her. She's the real brains but he's solid enough. Honest too. She comes from Ealing. He lives in Ashford – the Kent one. No kids. She's close to partnership with these accountants but she's bored. I doubt she'll stick it."

"Nothing in her cupboard? Nothing that rattles?"

"Yes. Surprisingly. Get this: she was sacked from her first job for fiddling expenses."

Shawcross was taken aback but said nothing. "Yes," Arnie continued. "I didn't expect any skeletons either. But she airbrushed that job – one whole year - out of her life. Her resumé says she was on a gap-year in the USA. The present firm never knew she'd worked before."

"How'd you get this Poirot bar stuff?"

"Easy. Bugged his briefcase when he was visiting Dukes. I watched the entire episode from another table. And the pillow-talk, that was easy too. Once we had the briefcase chirruping, I knew where and when they would meet up. Not always, mind. You'd seen them slip into that seedy place off the Bayswater Road before. When I heard them arrange to take a room there, I arrived first. Slipped the lazy old Greek at the front desk a couple of ponies. He agreed to fix it so they had room 12. So I used it before and after them. Bugged under and behind the bed, installed the camera lens in a vase of plastic flowers. Result: some cracking shots of the Adrian and Zara Show."

"Anything worth listening to?"

"Bed springs mainly. But the video – yeah. Do yourself a favor - watch that. That tongue of hers"

"You mean nagging? Pressuring him even in bed?"

"Come off it Audley. Licking his dick like an Ice cream!"

Shawcross mentally noted to watch the recording as soon as possible. "But did she nag him afterwards?"

"Nothing more than you know. They're well-suited in an odd way. She's University. He's Police College. She's sexy, jutting hips, almost sleazy but she wields a vicious tongue. Great for a quick bunk-up, know what I mean. Likeable she is not. But he's so calm. Rides the punches, gets the pleasure. They talk mainly about pipedreams – meeting movie stars, Elton John, David Bowie. You know. Going to shows, riding off into the sunset when he wins the lottery. She's high maintenance all right. On his disability pension plus the Gaming Board job, she'll bleed him dry, no time at all."

"Yes." Shawcross spoke slowly as his own thoughts fell into place. "I can see his dilemma. And I'm grateful. Cash will suit you best?"

" 'Course."

"Drop by tomorrow evening then. I've some cash chips from the Golden Orb. Cash them in down there. Don't go losing them mind."

London - 26th June 2002

When you're weary, feeling small,

When tears are in your eyes,

I'll dry them all.

From the sound-system, the plaintive tones of Art Garfunkel broke the silence of Dex' living-room. Though the room was warm and the blue porcelain lamp with the deep orange shade threw a comforting light, the words made him shiver. It was well past two am and he was pleased to be alone. Two aunts had offered to join him but he didn't want banal and morbid chit-chat. Though he had planned that his next home would be ultra-modern, all chrome and Scandinavian furniture, antiques were more suited in the mews cottage. He gazed around at the furnishings, remembering the happy hours at Lots Road auction rooms, bidding for items to match the 18th century building. Then, the world had been full of excitement, of hope, a time of living for the moment. Now, everything would have to go, probably sold as a job-lot to buy food and pay for the basics.

The CD ended, even the silence now seeming intrusive after a day of emergency sirens. He unplugged the phone and switched off his mobile. The day had seemed endless - meeting helpful officials who could not help at all. On TV screens he watched Tiffany Richmond, the consummate professional reporting from the scene. But nobody seemed to know who had lived or died. Nobody seemed to know why the jet had thundered into the ground just a few miles short of Heathrow either. Experts were already making bricks without straw, speculating as to the cause. To Dex that mattered not a jot.

When he had returned home close to midnight, he stopped to look at the moon, the heavens and the starry night. Somewhere up there if you believed dear old Reverend Hillyer, were Mummy and Beth. *Whatever*, he sighed. Tonight, the moon was shining down on an empty world. To him, London's lights had gone out, leaving him in a sea of black. In the sitting-room, he looked at a picture of Beth, dressed for Royal Ascot last year, a wide-brimmed hat over her toothy grin. He thought of his mother, now at peace. *At peace.* Never had the words seemed so apposite after her tormented marriage.

About tea-time, his phone had rung. "Dex? Tiffany Richmond. I've just had the latest list. Not pleasant news but I promised to phone. I'm so sorry. Your mother and sister are among the confirmed dead but your father is alive and at the Charing Cross Hospital."

"Alive? Father? Just father? I'll get over there. "

"Dex. I'm so sorry. I know just what you're going through. I lost my brother Roger in the Paddington rail crash in 1999. We were very close. I was at the scene, reporting, not knowing he was a victim." She caught her breath. Her tone was gentle, far softer than her busily matter-of-fact style when on the TV News. "Call me if I can help. It must be pretty desperate."

Charing Cross Hospital was nowhere near Charing Cross but Dex found it – a gaunt mix of high and low rise ugliness on the Fulham Palace Road. He had spent all evening there sitting, standing, walking and enquiring. He had wanted to phone Reverend Hillyer to ask why God would take the wheat and leave the chaff. What mysterious ways of God explained why father had not received his red card from the Almighty.

A distinguished looking man had then appeared. "I believe you're Lord Dexter's son?"

"Correct."

"Sorry. You've had quite a wait. Simon Carson. I'm a neurosurgeon. Shall we go in here? We'll get a bit of privacy." His face brightened. "Tea and biscuits too, if we're lucky. It's been a long day – for us both." Carefully, with a surgeon's precision, Carson closed the door of the small meeting room. As Dex seated himself on the utility chair, he wondered how many times Carson had brought bad news to families in this windowless green-painted room. There was a no-smoking sign on the wall but there was an ashtray and the air was fusty.

"I'm whacked! Not an easy operation, so let's relax!" Carson removed his jacket and slung it carelessly over a spare chair. The man exuded compassion and competence. Most of the consultants he'd met had been *prima donnas* and arrogant as hell. Dex warmed to him at once, placing Carson at about fifty-four, as slim as his delicate fingers, graying at the temples and with small eyes. The face was bulbous, the beard neat and well trimmed. "Your father is alive but only just. He is in a deep coma following a severe head injury. There were three leg fractures and several cracked ribs but his spine miraculously is intact."

"Will he come out of it?"

"Too soon to say." He raised his hands defensively. "I'll tell you the possibilities." Carson stretched out his shapely hands and spread them on the table. "He may die tonight, tomorrow or soon. Prepare yourself. He may never come round at all and simply exist in a *Persistent Vegetative State*, alive but unaware. Then again, he may recover enough to live a reasonably normal life. I have to say, I don't regard *that* as too likely. Finally, he may emerge from the coma but never really find the plot again. He would be alive yet unable to do much. He would hear, see and perhaps understand but would play no meaningful role in life at all."

"That sounds worst of all for him. To be half there."

"Not even half – it's a penalty beyond belief. Not great for the family either." A nurse appeared with a tray of tea and some plain biscuits. "Thanks, Lucille. You're a star!"

"For you, Mr Carson. Just for you." She grinned hugely and spoke with a deep West Indian voice. "And there's a load of photographers outside the front entrance. For you. Your father? Famous I believe."

Not the word I'd have used, Dex thought as he nodded abstractedly.

Carson offered the biscuits and helped himself. "Anyway, don't expect miracles. Finish your tea, no hurry but I must get back to the coal-face. If you don't want to face the cameras, Lucille will take you to the back entrance."

"Did you know my sister and mother were both killed?" Dex spoke without emotion, as if he were passing on news about strangers.

"Oh no. I am sorry. I had no idea."

Beside him now, in the chilliness of the sitting-room, the 18th century grandmother clock chimed three and London was as quiet as it ever was. The pizza he had ordered lay untouched. A bottle of Jack Daniels and a coffee cup lay empty beside him as his eyes closed and he fell asleep rocked right back on the recliner. When he awoke, nothing had changed; nothing was any better. Beth and his mother were still very dead.

He scratched at the stubble round his chin, stretched and then riffled his fingers through the bird's nest of hair. He peered round the edge of the drape. Down below, the media circus had arrived. There were about a dozen photographers, journalists, vans with roofs plastered with aerials and at least three TV camera crews with mikes covered in fluffy material like giant grey dusters.

He showered away the booze and debated what to tell the media. Ever since they had hounded him after his prosecution, he had been both suspicious and resentful. He switched off the radio off. The news was too somber, the disc-jockeys too banal. He put on a red sweat-shirt, chinos and the black boots he had bought less than forty-eight hours before. Impulsively, he decided to call Tiffany.

A male answered the phone. "Sorry to ring so early. It's Finlay Dexter." His normally mellow voice was throaty. "I met her yesterday."

"Who?" The man sounded brusque, uninterested, as if he'd just been disturbed doing something very personal. Dex nearly put down the phone with an apology.

"Sorry. I wanted to speak to Tiffany Richmond. My name is Finlay Dexter. She gave me her home number." The listener did not respond and Dex wondered if he'd replaced the receiver. Then he heard the man shout. "Tiffany. Can you come? Someone you met yesterday. Dexter someone, I think." Then there was silence until he heard padding feet.

"Tiffany here. Who is it?"

"It's Dex. I'm sorry. I really shouldn't have rung you. Especially not so early."

"What's the news on your father?"

"Barely alive. But it's not that. I'm besieged! My street is crawling with journalists, cameras. What should I say? What should I do?"

"At this hour? Offer them coffee. You'll have friends for life. Then talk!" Her tone was calm, and reassuring. "They're not out to crucify you, just chasing a human interest story. They'll – want a good picture and a quote. With your father's ... er... position and your mother and sister, you're seen as a perfect victim to highlight."

"You're sure about that? I've had some right dirty bastards chasing me when I was in the news before."

"Not this morning. That may come. Editors will soon have everything known about you to add to what quotes you give now. They're not going to dredge up unpleasantness in this interview, believe me."

"So tell me what to say after Maxwell House all round." As he listened to her crash course on media relations, an invitation caught his eye. From Audley Shawcross, the gold-embossed invitation was to the Grand Prix at Silverstone on Sunday 7th July.

"You say that, you'll be just fine." she concluded.

"I'll tell you later how I got on."

"We should get together," she said, her voice softer now. "Talking to me might help you. I can guess what you're going through. I learned so much over Roger's death. Perhaps a Starbucks one morning?"

He looked at the invitation again and debated what to say. "Thanks. I'll be in touch about that."

"Talk to me any time. Counseling. Consoling, whatever." She seemed lost for words. "Look. I'm sorry I was so hard on you yesterday. Part of the job – meeting people in distress and nearly shoving a mike up their nose. Not a day goes by without me hurting about Roger. Or about the incompetence that took *his* life. Be strong."

London - 28th June 2002

"Carlo!" Shawcross knew 2pm in London was a good time to catch the American director. "6 am isn't it?"

"Hi Audley!"

"You getting up or going to bed?"

"Goin' to work. I'm in traffic on I-95. The rush hour here gets worse and earlier." Carlo Letizione had stumbled into a blue Space City T-Shirt, yellow shorts, red socks and a pair of Nikes – a man in need of a color co-coordinator or a wife who had not given up on him. Outside, the temperature was already 88 degrees but the air-conditioning in the aquamarine 8-Series BMW sorted that. He had positioned the seat fully forward so that his legs could reach the pedals. His stomach bulged towards the steering-wheel. "Played poker until four. An hour in the sack and now back to base. I've a meeting with the unions at eight. But I'm on top of it now. They're purrin' again."

"Good." Listening to him, Shawcross recalled how much the strikes had aged the American, his hair rapidly receding in the last fourteen months.

"Lost eighty fuckin' grand playin' Texas Hold 'Em. A bad beat to a little old guy who should have been in bed with his teeth in a jar. Life sucks."

"You can afford it!"

Dukes' US director had not finished yet. "Fuckin' three deuces with a five kicker. Got his last deuce on the river."

"Stop whining and listen! What this agent didn't find out about Ryder ain't worth shit, to speak in your uncouth New York style."

"Unbelievable. I had a pair of kings, for fuck's sake - and an ace kicker."

The tough New York accent grated on the Englishman. The man's brusque style had created any manner of problems during construction. "Listen damn you! Adrian Ryder is arriving in thirty minutes. I want to bounce my plan off you. You feature in it, big time."

"The Gaming Board guy? What do Inspectors do?"

"Ryder visits his little patch of casinos. We're just one. He checks us out for compliance. Mainly he deals with Reggie Kyte or FB but I chat him up occasionally."

"Spot checks, eh?"

"Rarely. More routine. He looks at our finances, the membership list, compliance issues mainly. He *could* take a roulette wheel away. Stop a game of baccarat or blackjack. Check the decks of cards. Mainly they don't but some, shall we say *insurance* is worthwhile. "

"The UK's gaming people have teeth then?"

Shawcross strolled to the window and watched with pleasure as a traffic warden stuck a ticket on somebody's Rolls-Royce. "Yes ... and no."

"Meaning?"

"The teeth are there but so too is complacency."

"Explain. No – wait one. I'm just joining I-15. Real black-spot." He switched lanes and then accelerated around a custom-built Dodge truck. "Okay. Shoot."

"Familiarity can breed coziness, something of an Achilles heel."

Letizione rummaged among the burger trash on the passenger's seat until he found a pack of Marlboros. "Meaning?"

"We always make Ryder welcome. But it goes much deeper. Gaming here was out of control until 1967. The cops grew concerned that the Vegas and Chicago mobsters were moving in. So Parliament passed the Gaming Act. This draconian law has everything running like a nanny-state."

"Your crazy membership rules. Forty-eight hour notice before being allowed to play."

"Twenty-four now. Changed recently. But anyway, for years, the Gaming Board seemed to be a soft touch. The rules were strict but some clubs increasingly ignored them. A war to woo big players broke out – casinos were offering all types of inducements. The balloon went up when Ladbrokes shopped the Playboy Casino to the Board."

"Okay. I get the drift. So?"

"The Board pounced really hard, banning directors, shutting down casinos. Licenses were lost. Brutal isn't a strong enough word. I just missed being caught up in it." He adjusted one of the photos that Pru had put out in readiness for the meeting. "That scared the shit out of the survivors. Everybody realized there was big money in owning casinos. Better to keep them legit. Why risk losing a license to print money? Better to obey the law."

"And?"

"And so for about twenty years the law's been obeyed. There's been the odd infringement but nothing like before the 1981 bloodbath." He paused. "Pretty tame I expect compared to the seventies in Vegas."

"I guess so," growled the American, reminded of the violent years. "With Tony *The Ant* Spilotro and his brother around, *respect* was essential. I kept my distance. Didn't do to cross the wrong guy. Pretty much, there was torture and whackin'. That controlled our minds, everythin'. Then the Feds started to make inroads, arresting *made guys*. Some ran for it or were whacked and dumped in the Mojave Desert. Didja know even Spilotro ran out of luck? He was buried *alive* in a cornfield." He coughed some phlegm from his throat and spat through the window. "Since then, things've changed but I learned one lesson – no whackin'. Sure, it works for a while, keeps the stench in the pot. But, you go whackin' folk, in the end it'll jus' bite you back."

"I agree," said Shawcross almost too hastily. "Anyway, over here it's always been different. Inspectors like Ryder don't *expect* to find infringements. Not serious ones, not any more. Complacency."

"Cool. So what's the plan? Heh! What a beautiful sight. Our new tower's really takin' shape now. Fillin' a big chunk of skyline. Sorry. The plan?" He stubbed the cigarette and took a bite from the cold burger bought two hours before.

"Pull this off and *Operation Snowball* is nearly go. The last element, I'm working on now. Hook Ryder and we've an ace in the hole. Let me explain."

Ten minutes later, Carlo had grunted approval. "Could work. Phone me later."

Shawcross replaced Arnie Fisher's report in a locked drawer of his leather-inlaid desk. He eased himself up. He sat down. He felt restless, eager to start the meeting. He'd even noticed a touch of damp under the arms of his pink Turnbull and Asser shirt. *Not nerves surely. Just pumped up. I can piss gaming knowledge all over him.*

He sipped coffee from a bone china cup, one of too many that day. Glancing across to the corner table now brimming with photos, he smiled, though not his womanizing look. This was the other Shawcross, dangerous and not pretty. Though the lips were parted, the cheeks were sucked in, his eyes as unflinching as a crow's. Yet the other Shawcross presented a smile that was wide, generous, giving access to the neat teeth. The cheeks then seemed less hollow and the eyes more inviting than sinister.

"Why do you want these out?" Pru had asked earlier as she dusted off the pictures and put them on display

"Call it *Memory Lane*. Old age. Nostalgia. I might keep them out for a few days. Might not."

Pru looked quizzically at him but his face was a mask. "Vegas?" She pointed at a group picture.

He nodded. "Dealing School. I learned to spot card-counters, cheats, how to deal all the games." He didn't say so but what had been really useful were the lessons learned from Abe Wattsen, a *banned* dealer. Between Rancho and Decatur, he ran a discreet school from his single-story timber-frame with the air conditioner on the roof. There in his family room, he gave private lessons in cheating. Shawcross had learned how to deal seconds; to shuffle the decks into the order he wanted or to deal from the bottom. He could steal chips, spin neighbor bets at roulette or switch a pair of regular dice for loaded ones. Within a few weeks of hard work, he was as quick-fingered as any illusionist. Though Abe was knocking on a bit now, he had not retired. In February, Dukes had sent six dealers over to Abe on the pretext that he was rewarding them as employees of the month. *Operation Cyclops* had begun.

Pru picked up another color print. "Looks like Antigua."

"Right. I worked there for a while."

Polished my card-sharping.

Dealing Single-Deck blackjack to drunken sailors and ignorant tourists.

Until the Jamaican stoker, nobody had queried how, too often, he could make big bettors go bust with a ten when they needed a six. Or how he could so often pull a blackjack for himself. The stoker had grabbed a stool and tried to hit him before security carried him away. "And this one?" She picked up a colored picture of an old church. On the buttresses and the bell-tower sat several hunched vultures. A young Shawcross was in front of it, dressed in shorts, garish shirt and flip-flops. Beside him was a beautiful Latino girl. There was a caption scrawled across one corner in thick blue ink: *Spot the Vulture*!

Shawcross tried to cover his confusion. He had thought he had removed it from the collection. "That one?" He tried not to sound shaken. "Mexico City."

"That's odd. Only last week, I saw that movie of the Le Carré book – *The Tailor of Panama*. I could have sworn this church was in the Old Town in Panama – where the young woman lived."

"No. Definitely Mexico." He shook his head vigorously. "I expect the architecture is similar. They're both Latin-American countries with a strong Catholic influence." It sounded smooth enough but he didn't think Pru had bitten on it. "I'll put it away." He laughed. "I don't want any reminders of that temptress. Took me years to forget her." Pru picked up the brown-framed photo and abstractedly handed it to him. "Get the kitchen to send up some fish soup and a mixed salad. Brown bread and iced water. I want it now please so I can be clear when my two-thirty arrives. Remind me. Who is it?" His giant bluff was needless.

"Adrian Ryder."

"Hmmmh! I wonder what he wants. Hope nobody downstairs has been breaking the rules."

"Not that I heard." She left the room, each step much slower than usual. Shawcross watched her ample posterior disappearing. Not for the first time, he thought her style would be better suited to working at the Guards Polo Club.

Then for a long minute, he gazed at the photo. He stroked the girl's face and remembered their animal passion in a swish hotel overlooking the Panama Canal at Colon. He could almost smell the sultry heat and see the toucans with their vivid beaks. He remembered her flinching when the tropical thunder had crashed overhead before the afternoon showers had lashed over their naked bodies on the terrace.

His memories drifted to the Gran Paradiso Casino where he had dealt blackjack. His fingers twitched and the familiar dry feeling grasped the back of his throat as visions of his Bowie knife, his *Master Bowie* danced in front of him. The feelings intensified and his fingers twitched as he relished its power – the life and death that it commanded. The love affair had started in San Antonio when he had visited the Alamo – James Bowie had been one of the heroes to die there in 1836, slaughtered by General Santa Ana's Mexican army. But not before he had invented this most savage of weapons, a grave shaped handle with razor edged steel blade curving to the point of death. He had stared at it longingly – 10.5 inches in length and two inches wide – God's earthly messenger of death.

He removed the photo from its frame. He raised it to his lips and kissed the girl's face before slowly feeding it into the shredder.

At two-thirty sharp, Pru ushered in Ryder. Shawcross had his loafers on the desk but he was quick to cross the room with strong, positive strides to meet his guest. "Adrian!" Shawcross pumped his hand as if they were old friends. Ryder had never been to Shawcross' office before. He looked uneasy, his hands now fidgeting and one foot scuffing the carpet. "Have a seat. Tea, coffee, scotch - whatever you like." The handshake was firm both ways, though Shawcross also gripped his guest on the shoulder in a gesture of reassurance.

"Oh. Let me see. Yes. Tea please." His voice and mannerisms were both unusually wooden in this formal environment. He seemed even more like a Kent policeman than usual.

"Indian or Chinese? We have both," said Pru.

"Regular. Dark brown"

"Just like you had it down the nick," laughed Shawcross, referring to the police-station. "Thanks, Pru. You're a star." Shawcross dismissed her with a friendly wave. He put on his *trust me, I'm a nice guy* smile - the one he'd used when dealing from the bottom of the deck.

Ryder looked round the office with admiration. Shawcross said nothing, content that his guest was feasting his eyes on the *ad hoc* image. Ryder noticed the mixed aromas. The spacious office with its high ceilings of decorated plaster smelled of leather, a touch of sandal-wood, of pot-pourri and moist earth from the evergreen plant by the window. Matched against them was the lingering smell of cigar smoke, trapped in the richness of the fabrics. "I like the room, very comfortable." As he spoke, Ryder was still taking in the burgundy drapes, the Chinese ornaments, the wood paneling, the memorabilia and the original watercolors that adorned the walls. In front of him was the width of the leather-topped desk, at least three times larger than his own metal-top.

Shawcross compared the man in front of him to the gyrating figure in Arnie's video. His guest was still a fine-looking man of commanding appearance. The moustache was too thin for his face to be entirely friendly, a remnant from his police days no doubt. The iron-grey hair added gravitas without ageing him. The cheek bones were prominent and high, his face close-shaved and slightly tanned. He looked like a weight watcher and keep-fit fanatic. Only the slightly stiff movements of his neck showed why the Chief Constable had discharged him from the force.

Shawcross was able to take in other details that he needed to know in making the pitch: the blue shirt was clean but old, the tie well chosen to match. The grey suit looked like Ryder had bought it *off the peg* in a low-end department store that morning. The watch was a cheap digital, the tie polyester. Shawcross was pleased - everything was consistent with Ryder's important job and unexciting salary. He thought of Zahra's expensive tastes, guzzling champagne while her lover wore shoes he should have discarded months before.

"Help yourself, Adrian," Shawcross suggested pointing to the tray now left by Pru. He fought to keep a smirk from his face. Snowball *was now much closer to reality. "I thought a quick chat would be useful but first let me show you round... it won't take long." Shawcross reckoned on a lengthy meeting but there was no point revealing that. He wanted Ryder to relax. "No problems downstairs?"*

"Nothing to worry about."

The two men, the spider and the fly, were standing by the photos on the corner table. "We've kept our license then! Fooled you again." The jocular tone broke the ice but Ryder still acted as if out of place. He stood, hands in front of him, shoulders hunched, shuffling both feet now.

Looks as if he's embarrassed about his shoes.

I would be.

Big, black, cheap, old and clumpy.

"Where was this?" Ryder was looking at a picture of Shawcross with Sophia Loren, Robert Redford, Mick Jagger and David Bowie.

"The Cipriani. Venice. Great days." He flourished his arm expansively. "Those ones were Las Vegas - where else!" He was pointing to a pair of photos - Shawcross with Sinatra and another of Tom Jones with an arm round his shoulder.

"And that one?" Ryder need barely have asked. The picture of Shawcross, bronzed and rippling with muscle, clutching two scantily clad young women told a story. His smile added the rest. His height of over six feet, his sleek black hair, neatly groomed and swept back were then his obvious assets. The near pointed jaw-line was more evident in the youthful man, an inheritance from his Brazilian mother.

Shawcross laughed suggestively. "Halcyon times on the QE2 as a dealer." He rolled his eyes. "Adrian, you just wouldn't believe the life aboard for a young man. I'm too old now," though the way he spoke showed he didn't mean it. "Gaming on ships was so different - Texans, Germans, Greeks, titled people all dripping with wealth. No idea how to play. The women! Gagging for it, especially the married ones. I had to quit. Needed some sleep!" he pointed to the next photo. "That's me at the St James's Club, Antigua – London Society in the sun. I worked the roulette tables there. Fun for a while but I became bored - switched to another place – a real dive." He fixed Ryder with a knowing look and touched his scar. "Roughest place I'll ever work."

He motioned Ryder towards a chair. Deliberately, he had ignored the biggest photo – one of himself with a white-suited Elvis but it had captivated Adrian. "Is that really you with the King?"

"Some guy, he was. Las Vegas International Hotel – now the Hilton. What a performer! Signed it to me personally." The best lies are the biggest. Elvis had left the building and been buried in Gracelands six years before Shawcross had ever visited Vegas

"Makes my life look a bit tame!" Adrian Ryder meant it. "Still it's important work I do," he finished lamely.

"Indeed it is, oh yes indeed." Shawcross crossed his legs and tried not to look too pleased at the precise entrée he wanted. "Adrian. I know you're busy. Sit down, relax,. Take your jacket off if you want. I'll come straight to the point." Ryder ignored the invitation but did his best to look relaxed by leaning back in his chair, unbuttoning his jacket and folding his arms - gestures that did not fool Shawcross.

"This is, oh, nothing to alarm you. Quite the reverse." He looked away and watched Concorde banking westwards like a giant bird of prey. "Beautiful plane. Love it every time she passes over. I simply have to watch. Anyway, as I was saying, I need to talk to you in confidence. It's about Space City. You know a bit about it, of course."

Must mention that at once, put him at ease.

Bet he thought I was going to compromise him over his job in London.

Ryder's face brightened. "Las Vegas casinos are, er, *just* beyond our reach." The pedestrian style of speech was consistent with twenty years nicking speeding motorists. The dry, sardonic humor was his typical understatement.

"We open the new tower on 30ᵗʰ December. Critical mass is the name of the game – as more people come to Vegas to gaze rather than gamble, so you need more rooms for more guests to fill the table games and slots. We expect our casino drop to surge with all these new rooms. But … here's the rub. With more players come more problems. Recruitment for key positions has started. We need bigger guys to fill the big boots. Carlo Letizione, he's our US director, says he wants a top guy to run security – y'know compliance, that stuff - a fresh face, someone not tainted by working in Vegas or Atlantic City." He stopped and selected a chocolate biscuit.

Ryder said nothing. He looked to be studying every detail of one of Shawcross' favorite pieces by Olivier – a French Mantel Clock *Au Nègre*. It had cost thirty-five thousand Swiss francs, a good investment and easy to sell if he ever tired of it. "Carlo asked me to suggest someone with good experience who really understood gaming." He gazed at the ceiling and then smiled warmly across the desk. "Adrian, I'll be blunt. I've recommended you." He paused to push the biscuits closer to his visitor. "Sorry! I should have asked before even mentioning your name." Then he fixed Ryder with an appraising look. "Interested?" His smile said *don't rush. Ten seconds ago, you were Adrian Ryder, Gaming Board Inspector, ex-Kent Constabulary. In deep shit with Zara and Molly. Now, a new life in Vegas is yours for the taking.*

Ryder shifted in his seat as he adjusted the crease of his trousers. Shawcross studied the body language as Ryder started to speak and then stopped. He rubbed his chin, re-crossed his legs, looked at the ceiling, opened his mouth and then as quickly closed it. The man would be useless at poker. *It's obvious you want to leap over the desk and sign. But there's a problem that's holding you back. And I know what it is. I'll get there, don't worry.*

Shawcross pretended to have misread the signs. He raised his hands, palms towards Ryder. "I quite understand Adrian. Moving five thousand miles, giving up a lifestyle here – well I know it's not for everyone. Kids at school maybe. But you might be able to point me to a colleague. It's one hell of a job for someone who wants glamour, sun, big money, the bright lights and the pressures of a seriously big role. Carlo has the last word but I bet him a magnum of champagne that he'd choose you, however many candidates he saw. But," he lied fluently, "I know nothing of your personal life. Are you married? Kids? Maybe your wife wouldn't want to leave the UK or it would disrupt education." He offered Ryder a cigarette from a silver box but the inspector declined. Then he waited and watched for a reaction.

The Inspector straightened himself in his chair, patted down both graying temples and then shifted again. "Look, I *am* interested. I've no children and I'm telling my wife that I'm divorcing her. But …"

Shawcross managed to look surprised and concerned as he cut in. "I'm not sure whether to say good or I'm very sorry."

"I'd like to hear more."

"Carlo wants the appointee to build a new team. Call it a revamp or a makeover. The appointee could even assist in choice of a deputy – someone who would understand casino accounting – a new broom. Someone who will keep us on the right side of the money-laundering laws. Tougher every day." He saw the Inspector's eyes register *Zara*, just the reaction he'd wanted. "I don't expect you'd have anyone in mind. No matter. We can look ourselves. It's you we're after."

Ryder spoke slowly as if he were answering a hostile barrister in cross-examination. "Funnily enough, I might. I mean I might just know someone. It would depend."

"On salary? Silly of me. I hadn't touched on that. But I doubt it's a deal-breaker. You'll find it attractive."

"Would I be on contract here in London?"

"Good question. No, definitely not. We envisage you'd contract with Space City using a tax efficient Bahamas corporation – call it Casino Research Consulting, if you will - CRC for short."

Ryder shrugged. "If it's legal and saves tax."

"Am I moving too fast?"

"No. What about income, start date, removal allowances and accommodation? Medical insurance. I gather that's hellish expensive over there." Shawcross could judge from the less strangulated tones that Ryder was now feeling increasingly comfortable. At last too, his arms were unfolded. "Y'know. Just the minor details," he joked.

Shawcross played up the joke by rocking back with laughter, like a Black Widow baring her deadly fangs. "Removal, medicals. Take for granted. All picked up by Space City. As for the basics, Carlo would start you on $200,000 a year. If you had a suitable deputy, then his salary would be $125,000. There'd be a car thrown in, say an open-top Chrysler and a two bedroom apartment for the first year. There'd be Health Club membership and a heated

66

pool and spa, of course. You'd have to rent or buy after a year settling in. On your salary, Carlo says you'd get a place out at Seven Hills of say 6,000 square feet – that's just the house plus a big garden, tennis court and private pool. Strip View. Houses of that caliber usually have what they call a home theatre. Like the Empire Cinema in Leicester Square – only bigger." They both laughed. Shawcross guessed that Adrian could now barely sit calmly and seconds later he was proved right. Ryder stood up looking dazed. He turned away from Shawcross and stared at the photos on the mantelpiece and corner table. There was a lengthy silence.

Ryder turned round, his face troubled. "There's one real issue. When would I, or maybe we, start?"

Shawcross knew he had to tiptoe through the minefield. "Full time - probably from 1st April. Nearly nine months. Ideally, we'd like you there now but that's unrealistic with immigration delays. But Carlo's prepared to wait for the right person." He made a note with his black Mont Blanc pen with the white crested top. Then he flicked through his papers. "Oh! Damnation! Sorry Adrian. I've missed something." He saw the concern on Ryder's face as if the sweet shop had slammed the door in his face. "Relax. It's nothing too bad. At least, I don't see it that way." Shawcross did not hurry to speak. He wanted to build the negatives; to get him more worried. The balance was vital – making him think his Vegas dreams were shattered but preventing him from handing in his notice.

If he did that, he'd be useless.

He eased himself forward, hands clasped behind his head, deliberately casual. "Carlo needs some consultancy work done. You'd prepare a report. He doesn't need to interview you – well, you've earned my endorsement – but there *are* other good candidates. If he likes the report, you get the job. Until April, he'll need occasional advice on gaming issues. See how you'd approach some of the problems that he's facing even now. Nothing demanding for a man of your experience – and, if I may say so, sound judgment. How much notice would you have to give?" Shawcross already knew the answer.

"Three months. I could do this report in October."

There was an uncomfortable silence as Shawcross' continued his charade. He shook his head before taking a deep intake of breath. Then he sighed and shook his head again. He sat back, slapped his hands in front of his face as if in despair and desperately seeking a solution.

"Sorry, Adrian." Every word was from the Shawcross Book of Porkies. "No can do. Carlo *urgently* needs to select the Head of Security. Sorry, didn't I say the job title before? Yes it's Head of Security. That's a non-Board position but with prospects. You're still young. In five years. Well ... I'd say you should be Vice-President of Security. You get the drift. But he needs to see how good you are." He looked quizzically at Ryder. "Not unreasonable?" He quickly continued before the listener could comment. "Carlo needs a report on the Atlantis Casino in Nassau within a month."

Ryder didn't say anything and Shawcross was pleased. He stretched before strolling to the window. There he perched on the ledge, swinging one leg casually. "Wish I could escape to a top job in Vegas." He pointed to the teeming rain. "A summer day in London. In Vegas, Carlo told me its blue skies almost every day from March until November." He gazed down towards the corner of Mount Street and shook his head in despair. "Adrian. I must say it. Time is a deal-breaker. If you can't do the Nassau report by the end of July, then we'll look at someone else. Shame because Space City would pick up the tab for the Nassau trip, y'know its in the Bahamas, then on to Vegas to meet Carlo."

Shawcross looked across at the broken man. Ryder shook his head in despair and then gnawed at the side of his thumb as he stared at the carpet. Shawcross turned from the window and walked slowly back to his guest. He patted him consolingly on the shoulder. He returned to his notepad and skimmed through the pages. "Ah! Here it is! Probably academic now but forgive me. Carlo would definitely pay for the report on Atlantis *and* for any occasional advice before you start." Shawcross shrugged his shoulders in a moment of shared sympathy. "But I can't see any way round your roadblock." He pointed to a draft brochure on his desk. "We're planning to celebrate the new tower in December with a big concert, perhaps Tom Jones. You'd have been there with all the stars - Leonardo DiCaprio, Michael Douglas and that gorgeous Zeta woman. George Clooney, Matt Damon - all Vegas regulars." He stood beside the bemused figure and again rested a hand on his shoulder. "I'm glad I tried anyway." He stretched over to his humidor but the listener declined the offer of a chunky Havana. With slow deliberation, he selected one for himself, cut off the end and set it alight. "I've done all the talking. Maybe you didn't really want the job anyway?"

"It's the three months notice."

Shawcross saw that he was absent-mindedly stirring his tea. No way could he tell her he had spurned the offer. He would have to say nothing to Zara.

You tell her and she'll say you're a fucking wooden-topped copper.

Shawcross sensed that his pitch had worked a dream. He snapped the notepad shut. Without saying as much, he was apparently closing the meeting. "I guess we'll look elsewhere now."

"Wait. How about this? How about I go to Nassau using some holiday while my notice is running?"

Shawcross compared the meeting to breaking in a young colt. It had needed strength and willpower. Shawcross recognized a desperate man. The spirit was breaking. He sucked in air and shook his head slowly. "I like your style – good lateral thinking but it won't fly. Don't give your notice, not yet. Too risky for you." Shawcross was firm. "Unlikely but suppose Carlo says your report is the biggest heap of goddamned shit he's ever seen. He's polite that way! I can't let you take that chance. You'd have ripped up a safe career with the Board." He gave Ryder an *I'm-on-your-side* smile of reassurance. "Secondly, I can't *fairly* let you give your notice until the USA Work Permit is certain. That'll take a while since 9-11. More scrutiny. More delay. My guess is you give notice on first January."

"There must be a way to get round this, surely." The pleading in the voice was not lost on the listener, who judged the inspector to be his poodle, ready to beg at the snap of his fingers.

Shawcross nodded and opened his arms in a welcoming gesture. "Let's think like winners. We want you to work for Space City. You want the job. No time to be defeatist. Your colleague, does he work at the Board?"

"Can we speak in confidence?" Ryder ran his finger around his collar. He colored slightly.

"Of course. This entire conversation is just between us." In the cupboard, the tape decks whirred relentlessly, picking up every word from the mike under the desk. The camera in the painting behind his head saw every twitch.

Ryder lowered his voice yet further. "The colleague doesn't work at the Board and it's a she actually." He wiped his hand on his trousers. "You've met her briefly. I was thinking of Zara Belfield."

"Zara? Zara?" He paused as if thinking. "I know. Isn't she the independent accountant your Board uses?" He waited for Ryder's embarrassed nod of agreement. "Quite a stunner as I now recall. Not like most accountants, pebbledash glasses and ten cheap pens in their top pocket. So you'd like to take her to work in Vegas. Well, who wouldn't?" He leaned across the table and shook Ryder's hand. "You sly old dog! Zara, eh! All I can say is - you lucky bastard!" He enjoyed watching the sickly grin on Ryder's face. "Zara Belfield, eh? Clever with it. Sounds ideal. We were looking for someone with accountancy training."

"No one but absolutely no one knows about this. I'm married. We won't be going public - not yet."

Shawcross nodded thoughtfully. "Maybe this would work: you *both* go to Nassau. You write the report. Go on to Vegas. Meet Carlo. If he's happy, his legal people will set up CRC. You then apply for your Work Permits. Okay so far?" The spider paused within biting distance of the fly. The *coup de grâce* was near.

"Go on."

"This is the clincher – at least I think so. Comes of us *both* thinking positive. Space City pays CRC, *your offshore company,* for the report and for occasional advice on staffing and compliance issues. Space City won't pay you personally. There's no contract between you and Space City! *You* are employed by CRC – not Space City – and CRC is ..." He paused to see if Ryder had followed.

"Me and Zara."

The spider's fangs had delivered the poison.

"Precisely. See. You're not breaking your contract with the Board. Nobody else is employing you. You and Zara will be employing yourselves! That way, you keep your job at the Board until the US Government grants your Work Permits. Not a boat burned. And it's worth saying – nothing you do for Space City interferes with your duties to the Gaming Board." He knew that by January, both *Cyclops* and *Snowball* would be history.

Ryder thought quickly, his face flooding with relief. "Brilliant! You've cracked it Mr Shawcross! My job with the Board wouldn't be prejudiced. I could travel next week with Zara. Take some holiday."

"Don't say this was me. This was *us* – *our* resolve to crack it, Adrian. And oh, it's Audley please when you're off official duty." He paused while he selected the next lie with care. "You give notice on 1ˢᵗ January. Start on 1ˢᵗ April. But to be clear - *we've* no need for confidentiality. Tell the Board about the job offers any time you want." This was a dangerous gamble and he tried to conceal his anxiety as he watched for any reaction. The smell of Montecristo hung heavily between them as he continued. "To us, your role is not a secret. We've nothing to hide. For you, well it might be different." Shawcross held his breath. If Ryder told the Board, they'd appoint a different Inspector to watch over Dukes – and that would be a right fuck-up. "Your call Adrian but if you tell them before January and your Work Permits are delayed or refused, you'll have a black spot against you. Could work against promotion."

"It *would* work against me. No question."

"And the accountants would know that Zahra's going too. Her prospects would vanish – and the Board wouldn't let you two ever work together again. Rightly so. Still, this is a decision only you two can make."

Rather quicker than Shawcross had expected, Ryder agreed. "You're right. We'd say nothing until we give notice. Nothing wrong in that. You're sure we wouldn't be signing a contract with either Dukes or Space City?"

"Positive. CRC would receive a monthly retainer of 10,000 dollars a month. You get zilch." The concept of Letizione needing advice from Adrian Ryder on anything was a joke but somehow, Shawcross' trust-me look oozed his sincerity. The dark eyes held steady, the lips slightly apart, his head pushed forward in emphasis. "Talk to Zara. Give me a call tomorrow to confirm." He gave him the full arm over both shoulders treatment as he ushered him to the door. "Congratulations. You won't regret this. I hope Zara likes the idea."

"She will. Believe me, Mr Shawcross, she will."

Alone again, he switched off the recording and the camcorder. Triumphant, he slumped into his rocker and grabbed the intercom. "Pru? A gin please. Large." From the drawer, he pulled out the box-file from the Enquiry Agent. Seventy-eight pages about Adrian George Ryder and Zara Amanda Belfield. Thirty thousand pounds worth but the key to multi-millions.

"Not skimping on the gin, are you Pru?"

She gave him a dismissive look.

"No calls now please. I'm switching to Vegas problems."

"And the Gaming Board?"

"No trouble. Just coming up to mid-year reporting. Due diligence and all that crap." He watched her leave, tinkled the ice round the glass and took a thoughtful sip. He heard the chime and saw it was four fifteen. *Breakfast time in Vegas.* He picked up the phone. "Carlo! I've hooked your new team, Adrian and Zara."

The American had a great view of the building works through the floor-to-ceiling window of his office. He swallowed a mouthful of waffles with maple syrup. On the side were hash browns and crispy strip bacon. "Good job."

Shawcross cringed at the accent – *good jaarb*.

"Zahra's somethin' else is she?" Carlo's chuckle was earthy.

He knew Letizione well enough – they'd partied with showgirls at Cheetahs and Crazy Horse Too. "She's class. Not into fat slobs like you. Lose forty pounds, grow six inches and change your after-shave – even then you still wouldn't have a chance. Take a look in the mirror."

"You smooth limey bastard. I get my moments." Even as he said it, he was thinking of his wife's contemptuous comment a couple of nights back about him having more chins than a Chinese phone-book. Until they'd partied and become really drunk together, it had been much worse. Friendly meetings had been rare during the first building operations. Most had involved shouting, swearing and arguing about everything. Shawcross instinctively despised the American and doubted that Letizione felt differently. But despite the myriad problems, Space City had opened on time with a typical Strip fanfare of fireworks. Tensions had eased for a few months only to flare up again with the bad attendance figures after 9-11. The winter strikes on the new tower had reopened the deep fissures until a couple of months back, a better rapport had been struck. In a VIP room at a local nightclub, they had been given *the treatment* by a couple of topless dancers with blonde hair and endless legs. Afterwards, they had relaxed with beer and pizza at the company's penthouse in Turnberry Tower. "Look, Carlo. We need to work together. If not, we're both out. Dukes can't win enough in London to pay the bank loans over here."

"So?"

"Those bastards on the board may fire us both and cut their losses."

Carlo had looked unimpressed. "Pointless them cutting their own throats. Keep talkin'. Ain't heard nothing yet to tell my Mom about."

"I've two ideas – call them *Operation Cyclops* and *Operation Snowball* for now. This is just theory. I've done nothing. But believe me - I can turn this fucker round. But I need you aboard."

"So?" The stubbing out of the Marlboro was contemptuous.

"I've no intention of setting up these operations only to find there are more cock-ups in Vegas. I can't fill the bath if you keep the plug out."

"*Cyclops* and *Snowflake*. Are they legal?"

Shawcross looked foxy and shrugged his no as if unable to admit anything in words. "Needs must. It's now first of May. I've already sent my four best dealers over here to a crooked dealing school. That's part of *Cyclops*. We'd start benefiting by early July."

"How much?"

"Two million a month. Can't squeeze any more out of that. Enough to get me through the mid-year board meeting. *Snowball*, not Snowflake as you called it, is the big one. More complex. We can raise fifty, maybe sixty mill by Christmas. Your bank here will love that."

Shawcross could tell that Letizione was impressed but reluctant to show it. "Any whackin' involved? There's more skeletons out in the desert than rattlers. I ain't into whackin'."

"No." Shawcross shook his head, short and sharp *perish-the-thought* movements. The effect was disarming though the Englishman still noticed Carlo's eyebrow rise. "White collar crime only. Low risk."

"So what do I get?"

"You keep your job for a start. Second, we feed the bankers. Third, the best bit, we'll cream off some of the money from *Snowball* to our own account. Caymans or Aruba. I'll set it up. Split 70-30. On first January 2003, we divide the money - perhaps fifteen to twenty million. You could get around six mill sterling but *you must deliver*. We must open on time. No more delays before the New Year. Understood."

Carlo nodded. "The delays weren't my fault. But I want fifty-fifty."

"Not on Carlo. It's my idea. I do the work. I'm the one taking the big risks. But I'm buying your loyalty. Seventy-thirty' and non-negotiable. If you say no, then the entire shooting-match goes belly up by 30th June. We won't survive the board meeting. Agreed?"

The scowl broke into a grin. "Deal. And the Board will know nothing?"

"No."

Even now, recollection of the late-night deal was still uppermost in Shawcross' mind as he continued the transatlantic call. "I'm sure as hell I've snared this

Adrian Ryder. His floozy Zara won't let him be dumb enough to say no. But she's smart. *She'll* see through this offer. Not at once … but before the game's over."

"But smart enough to play along."

"She wants the good life. If I'm right, she'll keep her legs open and her mouth shut. Not him! Unusually for a copper, Adrian has a boringly honest side to him."

"Heh! Send over that video of Zara humpin' him."

Scotland – 5th July 2002

Overnight, a hundred quid for the flight to Scotland seemed a fortune. Amex would soon be squealing but this time, the card had gone through.

As the 757 made its final approach, Dex looked down at the sprawl of Glasgow. His face which had been bronzed from visits to Dubai, Las Vegas and Barbados was now pale, adding to his look of youthful innocence. He saw the blue seating and towering brick-red stand of Ibrox stadium to the east. To the north-west lay Loch Lomond and the man he needed to meet.

I'm leaving on a jet-plane.

Don't know when I'll be back again.

The John Denver lyrics had haunted him for a week now. The poignant words seemed especially emotive. He had read about Denver's last solo flight over the Pacific from California never to return. Had he been singing those words even as he took off? The lyrics had even stuck with him as the organ had played during yesterday's family-only funeral at Bladon Church. There had been just seven mourners – six too many for Dex who had wanted to be alone.

After the aunts and uncles had gone on to the Bear at Woodstock for the family lunch, he had spent twenty minutes alone with Reverend Hillyer, before driving on through the drizzle to join them. Looking back, Dex appreciated what a marvelous father-surrogate the vicar had been, always providing friendship and love when Alexander Dexter QC had provided neither.

Though Dex had no time for religion, a throwback to force-feeding at school, Hillyer had always been someone to whom he could chatter. In his teens, Dex had spoken to him often about life at home, the violence, the drunken abuse, the shouting, the stony silences and the constant attrition of any self-esteem. The advice had usually been the same – counseling him to work harder at the relationship – advice he had always considered but never accepted.

Sheltering in the porch from the wet after the other mourners had gone on, Dex had quizzed Hillyer, who thought for a few seconds before responding. "I can't explain why your mother and Beth were taken. I could say that God moves in mysterious ways. I could say that God wanted them for his own.

But I *don't know*. Try to forgive your father – both for the past – and for surviving when you'd wish him dead. He needs you now. Hating him won't help." The tall kindly man spoke gently. "Today's not the time but in a few weeks, maybe more but not too long – we need to talk. There's something you need to know." What Hillyer had meant troubled him as he drove through the rain to Woodstock in the Fiat Uno with 48,000 on the clock. He cursed the squeaking wiper-blades and relived the smell of the leather in the Aston-Martin that he had handed back two days before.

The change in the plane's engine noise brought him back from Bladon churchyard to the final approach as the flaps slid out and curved down behind the trailing edges of the wings. With a slight bounce, the 757 was down, everything juddering as it braked along the runway. It was good to be doing something, escaping from London. The prospect of returning tonight to Porky House where he had moved in. He had never liked the place but now it was too full of painful memories. The prospect of clearing out clothes, make-up and personal knick-knacks was a real downer. There would be so many little things; so many big memories. The only positive was that father would not be there to crow over Boy's return.

But for now, it was time to concentrate on Walter McKay. Today's meeting was the start of the fight back against Dukes. But would he help? As a member of the team that apparently broke the bank at the casino in Nice, he seemed just the person. As the plane taxied to its gate, he let go of the arm-rest, aware now that he had been gripping it since take-off. At 35,000 feet, he'd suffered flashbacks, natural enough when the press were still buzzing about the crash. His own paper today had run the story under the benchmark picture of the cockpit in front of a cricket scoreboard. An enterprising photographer had made his fortune by displaying the numbers 307 and 22, matching the dead and survivors, a chilling reminder.

Throughout the flight, he had stared through the window at the distant horizon. Having to meet McKay in Scotland had been useful – forcing him to get into a plane. Not that he had any personal fear or superstitions at all. Not walking under ladders, being careful on Friday the Thirteenth or being aware of the Ides of March were all so much crap. Life and luck were no more complex than this: three hundred and seven people had run out of luck because a part of the plane had failed, because the pilots or someone had fouled up or because terrorists had willed it.

He filed off into the dour grey of a Scottish morning. It matched his mood as he took the M8 west in the hired Skoda and within moments was crossing the Clyde over the magnificent Erskine Bridge. His route took him beside Loch

Lomond but he was meeting McKay further on at the Loch Fyne Oyster Bar about forty miles away. He was early and so he dawdled, stopping at Cameron House Hotel. From a paneled room that must have heard many an angler's lie about big salmon, he could see Ben Lomond, shrouded in low cloud beyond the loch, the glory of the heather lost in the sunless morning. Even the loch looked black and foreboding, clasping the secrets of past dramas and violent deaths close to its soul.

"Thanks," he smiled to the fresh-faced young woman who placed coffee and biscuits in front of him. He started to scribble.

The owner of a gambling bookshop in Holborn had been a fund of information. "You ought to read this book." He returned from the crammed shelves clutching *Gambling Scams* by Darwin Ortiz. "Essential reading that one. Here's another - *Thirteen against the Bank* by Norman Leigh. He organized the coup against the casino in Nice. Norman's probably dead now for all I know but someone called Walter McKay came in a while back. He claimed he was one of the thirteen. Some people still speculate that the team never existed and that the book was fiction. McKay was convincing though. Just on the sane side of eccentric. He'd be about seventy now. Lives alone in Scotland. He's on our mailing list, a real gambling expert, used to play in Vegas."

"I don't like cold calling. Can you ring him? Introduce me."

"You're not a journalist are you? He won't talk to them. Told me he never gives interviews about his coup."

"I'm going to break a casino." Immediately, Dex wished he hadn't said it.

The owner looked at him as if he were insane. He blinked behind his large spectacles and his laugh bounced round the small confines of the crammed walls. "Good luck, mate. That's all I can say. Except for the special few professionals, if you want to end up a millionaire in a casino, start with two million." He laughed again like a parent kindly putting down a child's stupidity. "I'll phone. He's more often fishing than gambling these days."

As he watched a boat carve a creamy white wake across the blackness of the loch, Dex munched an Abbey Crunch. His thoughts were on the gripping story of Norman Leigh's outrageous plan to break the casino. Dex wasn't concerned that McKay's name had not appeared in the book. The team, using *noms de guerre*, had been put together by Leigh and disbanded after the French police had, so he wrote, busted them. An embittered Norman Leigh had claimed the casino had been infuriated at a group of gamblers winning so much and had brought in *les flics*.

Outside again, the stiff westerly had blown away the clouds and a bright sun was emerging to mellow the loch while accentuating the greens, purple and yellows on the hills and mountains. As he descended the steps to the silver car, the wind made him glad of his leather jacket and the knitted scarf bought in Milan. "The Oyster Bar? It's a bonnie spot. Ye'll like it fine. Forty minutes. Nae bother," the doorman told him as he said goodbye. "Try the Bradan Orach. As fine a flavor of smoked salmon as ye'll get anywhere in the wurrld." The Highland lilt was soothing. As he sped along the narrow and winding road past Tarbet his spirits had lifted with the cloud. The meeting promised so much.

He found himself speeding, foot too heavy on the pedal after the tiny Fiat. He soared up Rest and Be Thankful and then descended to the shallow waters at the head of Loch Fyne. The oyster beds lay scattered over the waters, piercing the placid surface. Beyond them he saw the long low white building, his lunch venue selected by McKay.

"I suppose you expected a Rob Roy figure. Name like mine and living up here," said McKay with a twinkle in his watery blue eyes. He was small, wiry, looking full of energy to keep his waist trim and his walk sprightly. "But I was brought up in Surrey, not far from London. Never had an accent - just felt Scottish. I've picked up the odd word of course." Dex took in the appearance – appealing unless you expected a dandy. Dex liked the easy comfort of a man who had no interest in his attire – the greeny - blue jacket was old, the brown woolen tie slung too low and off-centre. The shirt was grey flannel, matching the shapeless trousers that he wore over a pair of elderly brown brogues.

The eyes were small, the skin waxy and pallid. A nervous tick must have confused poker players trying to get a tell from looking at him. Every few seconds, McKay's head twitched and twisted. "I haven't hit the tables for two years. Quadruple bypass. Roulette, smoking, drinking, blackjack, all-night poker. Caught up with me. I keeled over at Heathrow. Still, its been a full life – lost three wives and two fortunes. Careless really. Shall we eat or talk first?"

"Let's eat and talk." Dex sensed this would be a long meeting. The sheer enthusiasm of the bouncy little man was overwhelming.

"Try the Bradan Orach. Best anywhere. All the fish is good, kippers especially, the cheese too but I'm not allowed that." They seated themselves in a light wood booth with pew-type seating either side of the table. McKay ordered the Muscadet to be served in an ice-bucket. "You want to break the bank, I hear."

Dex nodded with enthusiasm. "I want to bring down a casino – two in fact. London and Vegas."

"Why?"

"They cheated me out of every last penny. I'm flat broke. Now I'm going to destroy them."

The small man looked thoughtful. "Cheated, eh?" he weighed up the possibility like his first two cards in a game of Hold 'Em. "Possible. Revenge?" he shook his head. "Impossible. Even if you win big, you'll be as effective as a flea on an elephant's ass." For a man who stood less than five feet four, he had a rich resonant voice. He wiped a watering eye. "Look laddie, casinos are too experienced, too rich to be broken. They're run by mean *bastards*." McKay spat out the last word with surprising vehemence. "They're not good losers y'know. A smile from a casino boss is another man's lie." He looked across the narrow table and his eyes held a warning. "Here's what they do - if you're a big loser, casinos smarm and grease you until they've bled you dry. If you're a big winner, they red-carpet you to keep your business – to win back *their* money. Then, after they've bled you dry, they drop you. The smiles, the handshakes, the banter all disappear like snow from those mountains out there. Sometimes too, especially in America, they'll make your life hell." His eyes closed as he revisited some private corner of his memories. "Ruthless. That's the word." After a slight pause, he cocked his head and continued. "Which casinos?"

"I'd rather not say."

McKay scratched his silvered hair with a gnarled hand. Considering he lived in gloriously soporific surroundings with soft highland air, Dex reckoned that somewhere his body had taken excess punishment over the years. "Take care. You're just a young fella." His eyes narrowed. "London may not be Vegas. No teeth extracted or pulled fingernails in Mayfair but as private clubs they'll ban you. No need for a reason. If you started to hit them big, you'd be out on your ass long before you've scared their accountants." He paused to light his pipe, a slow ritual. "Are you really serious? I mean you're a big man but you're well – a gentleman, not a street-fighter.. I was expecting a Russian mobster type. Sorry, son. No offense!"

"None taken. Don't underestimate me. I'm like granite beneath the surface. Like my father."

"Your father? You speak as if I should know him."

"Alexander Dexter. Lord Dexter. Lord Chancellor and now slowly responding in hospital after the Barnes crash."

McKay looked as if he was about to say something typically blunt about Lord Dexter but then stopped. "Tragic. Thought I recognized you from somewhere. I remember now, right enough. I saw you on TV. You lost your mother and sister. You spoke well. Head held high. Proud, like a wounded stag – big eyes hurting yet showing admirable dignity. But don't you think, with your father and all, you've enough to worry about without this, well … crazy idea?"

Dex tried not to sound or look as exasperated as he felt. McKay seemed to have past his sell-by date." I'm going to do it. Don't underestimate me."

"*Nobody* can bring down a casino."

"But they do go bust?"

McKay gazed through the small window and watched some gulls land on the glassy water. "Bad management usually. Or perhaps a convenient liquidation, like a fire at a loss-making business. Never ever destroyed by a solitary punter with a grudge."

"But you did it, broke the bank." His tone was strident.

McKay shook his head and a smile flickered round the small mouth filled with false teeth. "Good headline. Back then I was about your age – cocky, ready to risk anything for easy money. But *breaking the bank* doesn't mean what you think. It means forcing the casino to close a table because of the losses. That goes back to Charles Wells in 1891. Y'know the song – *The Man who broke the Bank at Monte Carlo.* That was about him. Wells won a fortune but died broke so they say. But the casino wasn't bust. Not even close. When Charlie boy had won all the chips at his table, they simply placed a black cloth over it like a shroud. These days, they would keep the table open, topping up with more chips."

Dex' face showed disappointment. "So Wells never did make the Monte Carlo casino go belly-up?"

McKay laughed but not unkindly. "No, no! No more than did Norman and me. It sounded good on the news. We won a fortune but were no more effective at destroying the casino than a Pekinese yapping at a bus."

The brown bread and starters arrived. "This Bradan Orach. The way they smoke the salmon is fantastic. Delicious." Dex' boyish enthusiasm wasn't lost on McKay. "Tell me about your coup."

"First, we tested our system in London. It's called Reverse Labouchère. We won a great deal. Then we went to Nice where Norman wanted revenge for personal reasons. Look: if you go to the casino as we did, thirteen of us, working in shifts, filling every place at the roulette table betting against each other on even chances, it's scarcely subtle. We stood out like a boil on a stripper's bum. In London, yes, we made waves but we hadn't got too greedy."

"And in France?"

"Dear old Norman wanted to humiliate the casino. He had a vendetta over a family slur. It was an obsession." Dex liked the word. It fitted his own feelings. "We won enough to be, er … well, at least comfortable if not rich. I bought a wee place up here to go salmon fishing. Waste of time now. There's scarcely a fish in the water. All in Japanese trawlers or the nets I guess." He sighed. "Don't get me onto that!"

"So the system was infallible?"

"You could win a fortune but never bankrupt the bastards. I told you. They don't let you get near to ruining them."

"Could I do exactly what you did – but on my own?"

"Yes. If you started betting ten pounds on red and ten pounds on black at the same time, you'd eventually win a lot of money."

"But if you back red and black, you'll lose one bet each time. Plus ten, minus ten and if zero hits, both lose half stakes."

"Precisely. But using the *Reverse Labouchère* system, imagine you and me playing at a tenner each. I bet black. You bet red. One of us will win unless zero hits." He wiped his eye on a tartan hankie. "Suppose you win. You increase your stake. I keep mine at a tenner. Most of the time, the two will jog along - each winning about fifty percent. We both end up losing. But at some point, who knows when, red may race ahead, winning over seventy percent of the spins. Still with me?"

"So far." He watched the dumpy waitress place the Loch Fyne kippers in front of them along with a pot of strong tea – essential according to McKay, who'd added that the rich oiliness of the kippers would kill the wine.

"Suppose that red keeps on winning. Not every spin but far more often. Every time red wins, *you* increase *your* stake. This cranks up fast. Meantime I'm mainly losing only a tenner each spin. You're winning thousands while

I'm losing tenners. You could easily reach the table maximum. Between us, we're quids in. And what's the beauty of this?" McKay eyed his plump kippers with love before answering his own question. "Say that basic tenner has been increased and increased as red keeps on winning three times out of four. Your next stake is say five grand. That's all winnings – you're using the casino's money to bet big."

"Like it!" Dex sipped the tea again, its dark brown emphasized by the white of the cup. "Say I lose a spin with five grand, what happens?"

"By then, you'll still be tens of thousands ahead, so it's just a flesh wound. Your next bet isn't back to a tenner. You reduce it to your previous bet. About the same amount. If you win next spin, you increase your stake again. But of course, you can lose that fortune quickly if black suddenly dominates and red completely stops winning. You need to quit when the imbalance starts to self-correct. But so long as red's hot, you're cleaning up."

"So what happened in France?"

"We had six playing all the time in shifts covering High, Low, Odds and Evens, Red and Black. As one of us left, another took our seat. Stupid really. Over-egged." He shook his head and his small eyes closed so long in remembrance that Dex thought he had nodded off. "We played each imbalance up to the table limit. But the casino later turned nasty. So we divvied up. I took off back to London with my share. I was pissed off. I didn't share Norman's obsession to make the casino grovel. I just wanted to be rich."

"And you succeeded."

"Soon lost more than half at the poker tables." A twitch of his head accompanied the unflinching look. "High stakes no-limit poker's like that – rags to riches to rags. It's no answer to *your* pipe dreams either." He tapped his briar in emphasis.

"Would you help me? This Reverse Labouchère?" Dex wasn't convinced this was the answer.

McKay looked wistful for a moment. "Sorry, laddie. I'm too old. Anyway, you're like Norman. You want to go beyond winning. You want them to grovel, don't you?"

Dex looked down at his plate. Then, he grew determined as he relived those moments when Miller had robbed him. In a rare show of emotion, he found himself stabbing the air with his fork. "They destroyed me. Lying and cheating."

McKay gazed through the window at the road winding down the far side of the loch. The gentleness of the scene was so far removed from the noise of the Vegas Strip and the thronged gaming tables. But he never commented directly. "Play alone, backing the two opposites. That way you won't have to share the profits. The casino won't bother you until your stakes get seriously high. In London, they might ban you or close the table. In Vegas, it's different. If they don't like you, they'll *invite* you to leave with a pair of gorillas to encourage your departure. It's shit-yourself time, believe me."

"Happened to you?"

"My gorilla moments? In Vegas *and* Atlantic City. Seven years ago and then three years later. I'd been headhunted by a Harvard student. Brilliant kid, long hair and dirty finger-nails. Looking for older players to join a card-counting syndicate to win big at blackjack." He wiped his weeping eye. "Six of us rolled over five places in Atlantic City and fourteen in Vegas." He paused to decline dessert and started tamping down his pipe instead.

"But you won big time?"

"Over a million."

"Just blackjack?"

"Right. Edward Thorp in 1962 and then Stanford Wong turned blackjack on its head by card-counting. The high octane part is disguising that you're a counter." He relit the fruity Erinmore tobacco and sighed. "The stress started my heart troubles – angina. You live on your nerves. You're like a thief cracking a safe. Every moment you're expecting the alarm to go off or the cops to arrive."

"But I read that card-counting's not illegal."

"True. But the casinos don't approve. If you play good *basic strategy*, that's okay - the odds are still against you. The casinos accept that. Most people lose their entire wad anyway. But card-counting is different. You, the player gain an advantage over the casino of up to two percent – the reverse of their position. If they can make millions on two percent, so can you. But they don't accept that you're playing fair by counting cards."

"You actually count the cards?" Dex glanced at the menu and fancied the local cheeses.

"No. You're keeping a count of the number of high and low cards. If, by deep into the shoe, the cards have been mainly low, then that favors you. Better chance of getting twenties and blackjacks. Low cards remaining in the shoe favor the house. So if the shoe has delivered mainly low cards, it becomes *rich in tens and aces*. That's the phrase." Dex could see the pale blue eyes lost in recollections of when the count had justified socking it to the bastards. "You then raise your stakes dramatically. Instead of playing five bucks a hand, you might start betting one hundred. You're then winning so much more than you ever lost."

"Sounds fair. Skill."

"Tell that to the Mob boys who ran Vegas. Today is no different – except you won't end up dead. Look: this is the problem. If you suddenly turbo-charge your bets from one thousand pounds a hand up to fifty thousand, it's too obvious you're a counter. The bosses, the cameras, the dealers will spot this a mile off. They'll ban you."

"And *your* gorilla moments?"

Dex saw the small man look shaken, as if a bolt of lightning had passed through him. His eyes closed and the sallow face seemed to blanche even more. Dex watched the right eyelid develop a sag all of its own. "The second time finished me. I was working alone, no syndicate. Card-counting. I'd won about ninety thousand that morning around Downtown Vegas, the rougher, tougher gaming area. Suddenly, heavy meat, hoodlums with arms like tree trunks took me somewhere downstairs along an echoing concrete corridor. I was shitting myself I can tell you. Ever seen the movie *Casino*? Watch it. The scene with the guy's head in a vice? That really happened. And I knew what had happened to a guy called Kyle. Poor Kyle – I'll tell you about him in a moment."

Finlay's writing grew increasingly scrawled as he struggled to keep up with this bouncy dynamo. McKay could talk without pausing for breath, his agile mind jumping effortlessly from incident to incident. "So where was I? Oh yes! I was frogmarched along this darkened passage. Both guys would have enjoyed beating me to pulp. Biceps like bodybuilders. Faces like angry bulldogs. Voices like they had breakfasted on gravel." He looked across emphasizing sincerity. "So, I was dumped in a room - call it a cell, bare walls, no window and a naked bulb. No plush carpets or glitz down there. More like a Gestapo interrogation zone. They made me stand, back against a wall. They photographed me. Mug shots from every angle. A big guy in a tuxedo appeared, flexing his fingers, as if preparing for a strangling. Name was something like Ambrosiana. Anyway, I stood there pissing myself looking up at his huge chest." His smile was rueful and low key, as if he were recounting some fictional incident. "I thought I'd won a single ticket to the Mojave Desert. But after making me sweat while he barked and growled, he just said that "your play is too good for us. Don't come back. If you do, you will regret it. Understand." McKay smiled again as he relived his moment of release. "But I kept the winnings. Some counters don't but they could sue the casino. As you said, card-counting's not illegal. But look Dex, this is no way to destroy a casino."

"So you gave up?"

"They sent my name and photos to every casino in Vegas within seconds. Everywhere I went, I'd barely feel the air-conditioning before the security guys escorted me out. I was blacklisted everywhere. My crime was using my brains. To those bastards, it *is* a crime. Ken Uston, one of the greatest blackjack players ever, was so hounded and victimized, he turned to disguises." He shook his head. "But what you can never easily disguise is the way you play. To win you must bet high when the time's right. Dead giveaway. That's if you do this alone."

"But this team? The first incident."

"Oh yes. Sorry. The Kyle story. Tragic. We'd done Vegas and never been caught but we were edgy. So we flew to Atlantic City, NYC's Vegas on the East Coast." He saw the hovering waitress. "To hell with doctor's orders. I'm enjoying this. Two glasses of port." He leaned forward, elbows of his tweed jacket on the wooden table. "There were six of us. Remember I said the problem is disguising the huge change of stakes? So we worked round that. Imagine you are playing as a card-counter. Suddenly, the count favors a big increase. *You* ignore it, still playing low stakes like a typical tosspot. I'd be watching close by. You give me a sign, perhaps by scratching your ear. I join the table and *never* play low stakes at all. I'd *start* as a big player because you'd signaled me over. Between us, we disguised that you were a card counter. I win big and we share the profits."

"How did that end?" Dex was hoping for something positive to take away but he saw McKay's hands started to shake. "Forget it! I don't want to scare you." He looked pleased when the port arrived. "No. Second thoughts, I will tell you. You must understand the dangers. This is no game."

Dex watched McKay's hands shaking. "Go on. I'll be fine." He sounded more confident than he felt.

The old man swallowed a pill with his port, leaned forward and clasped his hands together to stop the trembling. "Kyle, he was our organizer. We'd been in AC for about a week. Cleaning up. He was just going to his car in the multi-story at the casino. We'd just won over one hundred thousand. Two gorillas he knew to be off-duty casino security in plain-clothes appeared from the shadows, beat him to pulp and told him to leave town."

"Not just a mugging by people who saw him winning?"

"No. He identified them to the cops. But they had alibis, all bogus. Cops did nothing to help him. The gorillas took the cash, a diamond tie-pin, everything. Made it look like a mugging. I heard from Kyle the other day. He's still deaf in one ear, lost his right eye and has metal pins in both thighs. Talks slower now. He tried litigation. Gave up. The casino said somebody had mugged him. The video recordings in the garage disappeared."

Dex gave the little man a wry grin. "My casino wouldn't let me see their videos that would have saved me."

"No surprise." He gave an unexpected double twitch, fooling Dex who had almost become able to anticipate the involuntary flicks of the head. "After a while, when I'd recovered from the sight of Kyle in a hospital bed, I played in Europe, Africa, Australia, using disguises. Eventually, I decided to try Vegas again. Big mistake. That's when they caught me for the last time. I was luckier than Kyle. No physical abuse. Just torment. But I retired on a high. I'd won over a million that tour." He looked wistful but whether from old memories or the empty glass Dex was unsure. "I was banned anyway, so I banked my money. Good thing. I'd have probably lost it playing no-limit Hold 'Em in Binion's." He refused to let Dex pay. "I went to London last week. Just to watch. At blackjack, the greedy bastards cut the deck so deep now, it dilutes card-counting. The table maximums are low. Automatic constant shufflers have made tracking the deck impossible. Some casinos don't let a newcomer join a table until the end of the shoe. Cuts out the Tom and Jerry team stuff we did."

"So Reverse Labouchère's my only chance."

"If you can survive long losing spells, you can win big but you won't destroy the casino."

Dex looked crestfallen. He stared at the table, the cost of the trip now outweighing achievements. "Is there *nothing* positive?"

"Make *this* a positive, son: I've stopped your pipe-dreams of destroying a casino by winning at the tables." He beckoned Dex to come closer, although nobody could hear them in their wooden pew. "Strike them where they are vulnerable." He leaned forward to whisper. "It's Dukes, isn't it?" His face suddenly looked young again, the grin broad.

"How did you know that?"

"You mentioned London and Vegas. It was a sixty-forty bet. Dukes opened in Vegas. The only other British involvement there is London Clubs with the Aladdin. True, the Aladdin project went sour but I rated the management at London Clubs among the best. Couldn't imagine you'd have had trouble at any of their London casinos. It's a major public company. But Shawcross at Dukes? Never liked him. It's a private company too. Means they have a better chance of financial manipulation."

"And Shawcross?"

"Women adore him. To me, he's so obviously a total shit. But there *was* one thing: he lied to me. Said he'd never been to Panama. But I knew someone who dealt blackjack there. When he quit, his replacement was Shawcross. They worked together for two days."

"Did you challenge him?"

McKay eased a bit of kipper from his tooth as he shook his head. "No. Just stored it up here." He tapped his head. "Why deny it? You might find a skeleton in Panama."

"Anything else?"

"I heard Space City is burning money. So they'll need to maximize the casino drop in London to meet bank guarantees in Nevada. Not easy. Since 9-11, the market's bombed out. The real whales aren't coming to London so often." He emptied his pipe with a grubby cleaner. "Hard times are when casinos cut corners, maybe break a few Gaming Board rules, like in the early eighties."

"Could that happen now?"

"With a Shawcross in charge and cash flow problems – possible. You prove they've broken some serious Gaming Board rules – and they're toast. That's one way to destroy a casino." He thumped a weathered hand on the table. "Bang goes their gaming license. No Dukes, no cash-flow to Vegas. No Space City. Job done. Destruction"

"You make it sound so easy."

"Uh–ho. No way! If they find out you're after them, watch your back. Be careful who knows what you're doing."

Dex realized how stupid he had been telling the owner of the bookshop. How needless to share his intentions with a stranger. McKay was different but there was a lesson. "Shawcross is a ..." McKay's voice trailed off. "No I can't prove that. But watch him. Ever wonder how he received that scar below his right eye?" He saw Dex nod his yes. "I can't prove anything but I've heard rumors. Be warned." He looked almost paternal as his eyes rolled out the danger sign. "Shall we go? Your secret's safe with me. But keep it close. Big money at stake. Spells trouble. So take care, laddie. And find those skeletons in Panama." He dabbed his eyes and then tapped the side of his head. "There *is* someone who might help you. I met him once in London – a good card-counter. I doubt he's what you need but his name was Mark."

"How do I find him? He's not a priority. But ..."

"He used to play at the Victoria Sporting Club, the Sportsman, the Palm Beach, Russell Square, the Golden Orb and some place in Bayswater. Even saw him once in the Ritz, though that was a bit posh for him. Generally, he worked the middle-market places."

Dex was desperate to take away something more positive "Surname?"

"Mark?" He sniffed the air as if it would give inspiration. "Edwards. Mark Edwards. No. That's not right. Evans. Aye! Mark Evans. As clever a counter as I've ever met outside of Vegas."

"Thanks." Dex made a note about finding needles called Evans in casinos. "Your friend – the one from Panama. Can I meet him?"

"Dead these past ten years."

"What was the casino?"

"The Gran Paradiso. It's a dive. Be careful. Life out there is cheap and the sharks aren't all in the ocean."

London - 7th July 2002

As he trekked across London to Battersea, Dex had agonized about what to say to Tiffany about his finances. How did you explain to a TV presenter that the Cash Point yesterday evening had gobbled up his card due to insufficient funds? The planned trip to Tesco for food and a fill-up for the car had been jettisoned. Asking her to join him at Silverstone had been an impulsive gesture when the planned Starbucks meeting in Shepherd's Bush had been cancelled by her. Her acceptance of the day out had been a surprise.

As he maintained a brisk stride, he rehearsed the planned meeting with the bank manager. Begging for an unsecured loan would be tough. "Twenty grand please."

"And repayable when, Mr Dexter?"

"When Man walks on Mars. When I win back my money from Dukes. Or later please. Perhaps for Mars read Saturn." *Fuck you Shawcross.*

The previous evening, after eating his last Loch Fyne kipper, he'd begun sorting out Porcupine House. He'd started with Beth's room. A white stick was propped in the corner beside Lucky's empty bowl. Everything was precision-placed, organized to a fault. In her small office beside her en-suite bedroom, he found a metal cabinet filled with bulky files. She had duplicated many of the documents in Braille. They needed to be looked at, especially her Will and an insurance policy.

He also found a copy of his mother's Will but his father's papers were a mess – a mix of Government circulars and utility bills stacked high, some of them needing urgent attention. For a clever man, his personal affairs were a mess as if he had been swamped by Government business or whatever it was that took up his weekends away from home. As Dex walked into the Battersea Heliport, Tiffany was just parking her blue Toyota Celica.

"You walked? That far? St John's Wood? That must be five or six miles." Her tone was incredulous.

"Left yesterday. Packed sandwiches for the journey."

"I'd have picked you up."

"Thanks but I like walking." He led her into the crowded and noisy terminal. Anybody who could afford a helicopter to Silverstone thought the money well spent to avoid the annual traffic chaos. "Coffee?"

"Love some. Thanks." He led her through the throng and begrudged three pound twenty for two cups.

Thank God she didn't want a fudge brownie too!

Dex had rushed an early breakfast of the last grains of Blue Mountain coffee, no juice and toast without butter or marmalade. Then he had started the unwanted hike across London. In the terminal, guffawing laughter surrounded them, many of the fans in caps, cord trousers, suede shoes and shirts with a Porsche or Ferrari logo. The only person he saw from Dukes was Nigel Forster-Brown, the General Manager. There was no sign of Audley Shawcross.

"Morning FB. This is Tiffany Richmond. She's my guest."

"And our privilege. I like your no-nonsense style on the News, Ms Richmond. Delighted you could join us." FB knew how to say the right things but any good impressions made were lost in his presentation. Glad-handing members did not come easily. Invariably, he never looked people in the eye and his handshake was soft and clammy.

"Duty or do you like motor racing?" Tiffany asked.

The tall man with the unsmiling face and rimless glasses forced a rueful smile. It wasn't pleasant as his teeth when bared were uneven and prominent like a camel's. He had lost most of his hair when in his twenties and today his pate was reddened. "Strictly duty!" He spoke while looking out of the window at nothing at all. The tone of voice showed that FB was not a happy man. "Audley Shawcross is traveling. He's *so* good on these days. Cricket, golf, rugby or Formula One. He's like a chameleon – knows all about it, able to chat on for hours. When its over, he never gives the sport another thought."

"And you?" Tiffany intervened. "Where would you rather be?"

FB's eyes studied the flooring and sounded defensive. "Me? I'm a computer nerd. Besides that I enjoy pottering round my veggie garden in South Norwood." He patted his sunburned head in emphasis. "Broccoli," he added absent-mindedly.

"Surfing? Chat-lines?" Dex followed through.

Head lowered, FB thought for a moment as if he were revealing the depths of his innermost secrets. "Beyond that. I *do* join chat-lines. I do surf too but only because I'm always learning. I did a course on computer science. I'm what's called a *tweaker*. I write programs for *tweaking* – a technical term for improving computer performance. But my first love is encryption – security." For FB, this was a long speech. When Dex had dined with him in the casino restaurant, he had been monosyllabic.

"Posh form of hacking?" Tiffany's voice showed she was joking. FB never noticed.

"I could hack. But I prefer to make things *more* secure. He wrinkled his strawberry nose in disdain. "This Formula One stuff - I'm told the cars are *very* noisy. Still." His face brightened. "The lunch and wines will be first-class."

Dex wanted to get closer to the subject of Shawcross. "I suppose the big boss is swanning about in luxury?"

"Schmoozing members it's called." FB didn't seem keen to elaborate and looked relieved as the flight was called. "Time to go!" Then his fingers twitched and he studied the floor again. "Look, I really am most dreadfully sorry about your family. Shocking, shocking business. I really didn't expect to see you here at all."

Dex gathered together his Sunday Times for the flight. "Why wrap myself in a black shroud? The funerals are over. There's nothing I can do for my father either." FB was now looking at a crack on the wall. "Anyway, I love Formula One." Dex did not add that today was a chance to talk to other members, an opportunity to find out if Dukes had ever cheated them.

And a day's free food was handy.

As the Augusta A109 with seven passengers sped northwards, small talk was difficult and so he divided the paper with Tiffany. Dex kept the Business Section, something he usually skimmed last after devouring the color supplement and the articles on lifestyle. A headline jumped at him. "Space City: Costs spiral. Gloom Deepens." He read on. The *Vegas project is hemorrhaging money with poor attendance and the costly new tower under construction. But Audley Shawcross says no problem. "We're still on course for a flotation. The new rooms and extra gaming area will be sensational. We're predicting a strong cash-flow. We're confident."*

He recalled McKay's advice - *desperate people, desperate actions.*

Silverstone, the top English Grand Prix circuit, came into view, the tarmac track winding and twisting like a giant black snake through the Northants countryside. As the helicopter joined a long line hovering to land, Dex looked down at the regimented lines of team motor-homes, all precision parked to avoid the displeasure of F1 supremo Bernie Ecclestone. He saw, the red, gold and black colors of the RGB team and hoped he would get a chance to talk to Scotty Brannigan. His help would be the cherry on top of the day.

Scotty Brannigan's mobile phone rang as he entered the motor home. The inside looked as if Hurricane Andrew had just passed through – clothes, papers and fan-mail lay everywhere. The TV played in the corner. A half drunk cup of coffee was on the table. The computer displayed the weather forecast for the Silverstone area. On a chair, the Sunday Scope lay open at a photo of a topless model. His racing helmet, plastered with logos was on the floor by his boots. "Yes." His voice showed his irritation. He hated interruptions when he was psyching himself up, especially today when God willing he had a chance to win. Would it be the Team Boss or Roxy? Or worst of all, that Malaysian bastard.

Nanda Datt's singsong voice sounded close and as precise as always. "Scotty - we are most unhappy with what you said yesterday, most unhappy indeed." The English diction was perfect despite the oriental accent. As he listened, Scotty could imagine the small head tilted to one side like a sparrow. "You say you need to win to restore your credibility. So we will go along with it. Reluctantly. But for this race only." The well-educated voice rose and fell with a precise rhythm. From where Nanda Datt was speaking, Brannigan had no idea, unsure even of the man's true name.

"The handlin' problems have been overcome. On the straight, we're fast. Startin' from third on the grid, I've a great chance."

"Win then. We're backing you to win! Big money."

"Then you're crazy! Do yourself a favor. Don't bet at all. I can't *fix* a win. This is fuckin' F1. Anythin' can happen. Screwin' up someone else's race ... well jus' maybe ... but sure as hell, I can't guarantee *a win*."

The Malay ignored the advice. "We are most displeased. We'll pay you nothing for today. Besides our bet riding on you, we'll bet two hundred thousand for you. At two to one, you'll get four hundred if you win. Nothing if you lose."

Yesterday, Datt had ordered him to lose and to play games with the championship contenders but he had refused. He knew his refusal would cost dearly - just when another million would have been handy with Roxy.

"Fuck you! If you think...." He realized he was talking to nobody. He threw the phone against the wall where it left a dent before landing on one of his red racing boots. For good measure, he hurled an apple against it too. Whatever happened today, next race he was going to stuff Nanda Datt and to hell with the consequences.

He grabbed the cold coffee and thought of his chat with Mick Glenn at the Oxo Tower restaurant last November. He'd been careful with his words. "Been readin' about Malaysian bettin' syndicates. Fixin' Premier League games. Even bettin' on that crazy cricket game too."

"Yeah! It happens." Mick was in training and had sipped at his juice. "They pay well. Least, so I've heard. But if you get hooked, their claws ain't lettin' go. One syndicate even sabotaged floodlights – to get the game abandoned at the perfect moment. The score at that time counts out in the Far East."

"You're not in on it then? Fixin'."

Glenn grinned sheepishly. "Naah, mate. Not me." He leaned forward. "Get involved in that shit, it's bandit country. Ever heard of Wolfgang Schimmelsohn. No? He played in the top German football league – the Bundesliga. He was murdered a couple of months back. The cops think he was bein' paid to fix matches but then tried to, y'know, get out of it."

Scotty nodded thoughtfully but said nothing.

"Then there was a cricketer, can't remember his name. Indian Test team. He was taking bribes to throw his wicket. Friend of mine reckoned in the end, he'd had enough - told this fixer where to shove it. Only ended up dumped in the bleedin' Bombay docks, didn't he?"

"Tell you what I don' like, pal." Scotty called for an iced tea for himself. "Somethin' the same but different. Take David Coulthard. A great driver, super-fit and incorruptible. Remember his private jet crashed back in May 2000? I assumed this was an accident. Everybody did. Then that champion jockey's plane crashed – Frankie someone in the next month."

"Yeah! Frankie Dettori. At Newmarket."

"Right! Another accident or so I thought until I read an English Sunday paper."

"Go on! I look at the pictures mainly. The rest's all fiction!"

"The journalist said the cops were investigating a connection with both crashes – suggesting a link to Malaysian betting syndicates."

"Nah! Coulthard and Frankie – they ain't corrupt." Glenn was emphatic.

"I agree. That wasn't the police theory at all." He played with a whiskery sideburn for a moment before continuing. "According to the theory, this syndicate had bet big money on who would be F1 champion that season and who would be champion jockey."

"Okay. And?"

"David Coulthard was driving too well for their liking. Getting in the way of their bet. Not the person they wanted to win the Championship at all. Same for this Dettori guy. Neither had done anything wrong. Just innocent professionals goin' about their job. Doin' it *too well* for some oriental bastards betting on *someone else's* success."

"So the two crashes were attempts to take them out? To help their bets?"

"You got it. That's if the story was credible. If it's true, fuckin' terrible, isn't it? Coulthard doesn't buy this theory but with millions at stake, well it makes you think. Amazin' that DC and his girlfriend survived."

He slurped some coffee and looked again at the weather forecast. Though he had never read Shakespeare or heard of Lady Macbeth, he went to the basin in the motor home and washed his hands as if the action would cleanse himself of the dirty deeds. He thought back over the season. He had been suckered right in. Eyes wide shut. "Oh yes, we only want background - tires, team gossip, likely weather conditions and refueling strategy," Nanda Datt had said. But after hooking him had come sinister orders. "Take out Coulthard. Get Schumi off pole."

He kicked his helmet with a bare foot and wished he hadn't. "I'll get you, Nanda," he said, his jaw clenched. He checked his Rolex, willing it to be race time but no such luck. He wanted to escape. From the team. From Nanda Datt. From himself.

To Dex, the chance to see the race from above Copse Corner, one of the best positions on the circuit was like a dream. To be with Tiffany was a giant bonus. Champagne in one hand and a smoked salmon canapé in the other, they looked along the track. "Down below us is Turn One, the big action point. That's because they start just over there." He pointed to his right. "I picked up some earplugs for you."

"It's that noisy?"

"No. Just thought you'd want to avoid listening to me banging on."

"Shall I put them in now then?" She was already slipping them into a pocket on the front of her pink denim tunic.

Her laughing smile was reassuring. "Fancy a stroll?" Dex wanted to be alone with her, to get to know her away from the noisy chatter of the hospitality zone.

"Sure. But haven't you done enough walking for one day?" They were still laughing as they clattered down the stairs, her boots with stacked heels ringing from the metalwork. She looked up at the scudding grey clouds. "Going to rain?"

"Every driver, every team are asking the same question. There's more seaweed in the Pit Lane than on Brighton Beach! Huge strategic advantage if you guess the weather correctly. You wait – if it rains during the race we'll see some real action. Michael Schumacher – they call him the *Rainmeister* – he's a genius in the wet. It'll be a real fight between the American Scotty Brannigan and Schumacher. Scotty's dropping by at lunch. Can't say I know him but we played roulette at the same table at Dukes. He was in with the footballer, Mick Glenn."

Tiffany's brow furrowed. "Glenn was upstairs."

"Right. The big guy."

"Not my sort. The Sports Editor gets to hear most rumors. We can't always broadcast them though. He'd heard stories … very vague, probably crap and nothing proved but they centered on match-fixing and drugs."

Dex thought back to the night in the casino. "He won a large fortune when I was watching. I don't see why he needs to get into match-fixing."

"Like most gamblers, he probably loses more than he wins. Anyway, footballers are chancers by instinct and most don't have too much brain. They're around clubs, bars, other celebrities, the agents, the hangers-on. It's easy to get involved with some sleaze." Dex nodded thoughtfully. Everything she said reinforced his feelings that Glenn was not the man to help him. She cast him a sideways glance, wondering why he hadn't responded and so continued. "Strange isn't it? Us being here. You don't know me. I certainly don't know you. But it just seems right."

"You'll have been told this before. I feel I *do* know you because you're so often on screen."

"True. People do think they have some type of right to talk to TV journalists – because we invade their homes and talk to *them*. It's a compliment – but it can be damnably irritating when all you want is to be left alone and anonymous. That's why I'm wearing this low-brimmed hat and sunglasses."

"A hat suits you. I thought you'd chosen it because you didn't want to be seen with me."

"You catch on quick." When she laughed, her head shook, something that seemed out of character to the briskly efficient television personality image. "So how's it been? Better since the funeral?"

"Bladon left me numb. The Vicar up there's an old friend. Told me to eat a huge breakfast and to suck strong mints during the service."

"Did that help?"

"Not that I noticed! Now the problem is father, there's no finality. He's the living dead."

She nodded her head in understanding. "I felt a release after Roger was cremated. Are you religious?"

"No. I prefer right and wrong as my creed."

"You're the judge of that?"

"Can't think of anyone better. Just to be true to myself."

"After Paddington, I dabbled in Buddhism, trying to make sense of life without Roger. That didn't help. Then I went to a psychic, trying to open communications with him again."

"What? You mean you tried one of those medium people who sit in a dark room speaking in a strangulated voice asking: *Is there anyone out there?* Too spooky for me."

"Something like that. I wasn't sure whether it was the woman who was mad or it was me for paying for the consultation. I never heard any voices, least of all Roger's. When he was alive, we shared extra-sensory perception but it didn't survive him. Do you believe in that?"

"ESP? Never thought about it really. But I'd love you to explain."

"Not now. We need to be sitting somewhere cozy, intimate. Red wine, candles. Somewhere like Julie's in Holland Park."

"That's a deal." The thought of picking up the tab for Burger King, let alone Julie's until the bank had come across made him change the subject. "What do you make of FB?"

"Why do you ask?"

"I sense you're a good judge of character."

"That's no answer." She poked him playfully in the ribs.

"I'm interested in everything about Dukes."

"Ever been told you're enigmatic?"

"Never met anyone who knew such long words."

"Dex, you're not answering my questions."

"Let's wait for Julie's, shall we?"

"Pity to wait so long."

"Oh?"

"I'm going to Los Angeles and Washington for three, maybe four weeks. Our American correspondent is unwell. I put in for a change from Home Affairs."

Dex found it hard to conceal his dismay. "But you're coming back?"

"That depends. On me and how I do – and on his health. I've done foreign before. Africa mainly."

"Why the change?"

"Don't take this wrong but I decided because of *you*." She chuckled as she watched his reactions. He touched her sleeve, just the slightest tap, almost biblical. She stopped instantly, the way Jesus had done, as if he had pole-axed her. They were under one of the big stands just away from the stream of fans going in all directions. He turned so that he could face her, looking slightly down at her upturned face. Without even thinking, he pulled away her sunglasses, tilted up the brim of her hat and met the full force of her eyes, green and naturally slightly narrowed. Now they were wide open, surprised at his actions, her facial muscles showing the underlying pleasure. Though her mouth was small, her lips were full and they now parted as if caught out by his intrusion. The twitch of her small nose also showed her pleasure and as he stood just inches from her, he was intensely aware of her sexuality and even more of her inner strength.

97

Despite the smell of fast-food not far away, he noticed the perfume, something light and delicate. He watched her pinkened lips open further as if she were gasping for air, their fullness now emphasized. He placed his hands on her bare shoulders and pulled her closer but though he could now feel her breasts brushing lightly against his safari jacket, he sensed no invitation to kiss her. There was something else on her mind. "You put in to work five thousand miles away because of me? I didn't know I had such a powerful effect on people. Like a skunk, am I?"

She patted the end of his nose with her index finger. "That day in Barnes. Well, maybe that evening too, I saw myself, my inner soul – stripped naked. I saw myself for the horrible person I'd become."

"I don't understand." Dex tried not to imagine what she would look like stripped bare.

"When you spoke to me, I was a right bitch – a hard-nosed professional."

"I never noticed."

"No excuse. I'd have been worse if I'd had a mike and the camera-crew had been available. I'd have put you in front of the camera. As soon as I overheard your tragedy I was imagining soundbites like: fears are mounting for ... or there is increasing concern about the Lord Chancellor, Lord Dexter, his wife and daughter. I was thinking: even better if the uncertainty of their survival could be carried forward. Son at the scene. Held back by police. Now that would be a real story, one with legs. That's what I was thinking." She shook her head slowly. "What a shit!"

"I see." He spoke slowly and then shrugged dismissively. "Those thoughts never showed."

"I'm glad. Paddington and my time in Africa hardened me to starvation, withered limbs, screaming pain, suffering, death. I became talked about as a journalist always close to malnutrition or suffering. The image took over. Others' suffering became seconded to feeding my ego, my screen image."

"Don't punish yourself. Forget it. I thought you were so very caring about me."

Beneath the chestnut highlights of her elfin cut, her eyes welled with tears. "I truly want to say this. Don't stop me." Her voice was all choked up, her labored breathing showing the deepness of her soul-searching. "In Barnes, after I finished speaking to you, I felt that my professional instincts had dragged me to new depths of inhumanity. I watched as you gazed at the wreckage, looking at what was probably your family's funeral pyre. I saw those Bambi eyes. You were so brave and fearless, desperate to race into the wreckage. Yet for all your manliness, I saw only this lost child, just like when I was at Paddington and had been told Roger was among the victims. I realized then how desperate, how on the edge you were as you watched in those jeans and sweat-stained shirt. And yet seconds before, my only instincts had been to get a microphone to shove up your nose. I felt sickened at what a hard bitch I had become."

"So you put in for a change from famine and disasters?"

"The USA or Paris. My other brother Simon is in real estate there." Dex felt her shoulders start to tremble. She struggled to get out the words. "*You* were the catalyst. As I watched you turn away to visit the hospitals, I started to cry. I nearly bit through my lip forcing myself to be as tough as my image. *Tiffany Richmond crying? Never. She's tough as old boots.*" She looked up at him. "But *you* know better." She slumped forward into his arms and for a few moments, just sobbed with her head buried in his chest. "I had sold my soul to the Great God News."

"Heh, heh! Just relax." He found himself squeezing her shoulders and then gradually stroking her back with one hand and a moistened cheek with the other. As he gently pulled away he wiped a tear from her cheek. "I admire your courage in telling me. But don't reproach yourself."

She smiled a watery smile. "Dex, those TV interviews you gave – amazing considering how much you had feared the media when we spoke. Despite that impudent look, you revealed such a rare resilience against pain. I don't know how life has treated you but on the screen, I recognized an inner strength. I could never have spoken like that about Roger." She pulled a tissue from her pocket and dabbed her cheeks, then fixed him with the force of her eyes. "Sorry - It was *you* who needed earplugs." They both laughed, faces close and she hugged him. "You said something a few moments ago - something that triggered this outpouring. Remember what you said back there? About being true to yourself. That's so right." She screwed up her face. "Well, I wasn't – not when dealing with tragedy. I had become true only to my image."

Dex was surprised at how brittle she was and recognized the lingering effects of her brother's violent death. He felt a shiver run through him as he wiped where her eye-shadow had started to smear. He clasped her hand and gave it a reassuring squeeze. "You'll need a cloakroom before lunch. But before that. There's something we need to get straight."

"Go on." He saw her head cock to an *I'm-all-ears* angle. She swept back a tinted strand of hair that was drifting too low over her forehead.

"We know nothing about each other, our private lives that is. And when I phoned early that morning a man answered the phone. He didn't sound exactly pleased to hear from me."

Tiffany leaned forward, her eyes so quizzical. "Oh, you might see him off." She laughed. "That was brother Simon, over from Paris. Not an incestuous relationship that I've noticed." She enjoyed watching as his right eyebrow rose, his face colored and a cheeky grin broke through.

"I'm glad."

"He'd had a heavy night with the boys, that's all. But don't get ahead of yourself. I've defense mechanisms that I learned were essential at the Beeb." She stroked his cheek. "Play a slow game. I like to know a man really well, not just the suave sexy side displayed in a rush for the bed." The cheeky look he gave her was appealing and she pulled him up close. "No point you trying that *come on, I'm not like that look* with me." She pecked him gently on the cheek. "You're a man!" She twisted him round towards the ten-deep crowds heading for their seats.

"Slow games are fine but now you're disappearing. There are things, deep and personal, that I want to share with you too. Things that I need you to understand."

"It won't be long. We'll share."

Back in Dukes' hospitality area, with TV monitors around the wall, the fourteen casino guests were starting to mellow. The Arabs weren't drinking but the English guests were making up for them, though Mick Glenn was sipping iced water. He was however voluble. Dex heard the odd words - *open goal, choked, unbelievable, losin' to Brazil, David Seaman.* He was obviously holding court on England's failed campaign to win the World Cup.

FB was talking to Lord Yarbury. He led Tiffany over to hover beside them, waiting for a chance to get into the conversation. FB was explaining why the game of craps had never really caught on in England. Dex knew that his father had always spoken disapprovingly of Yarbury as someone loaded with cash, none of it earned by him. Yet he had been a revelation the night they talked in Dukes. FB introduced Tiffany first and then turned to Dex. "Arthur - have you ever met Finlay Dexter? I'm sure you know his father, the Lord Chancellor."

"Know him well, FB. Finlay, dear boy! Haven't seen you since before the crash." The hand was soft as it gripped Finlay's. "Dreadful business! How is your father?"

"Not good."

"I wrote to you of course." Dex didn't believe him and expected soon to receive a back-dated letter.

"Are you a regular at Dukes?" Tiffany enquired.

Yarbury's laugh was infectious. "Blackjack mainly. When I've lost enough at that, I try baccarat. After losing my damned shirt there, I toddle over to the roulette. That's my main exercise for the day, walking between the tables." He chortled as he patted his generous stomach. "When I've lost everything, I go home. Happy as a pig in shit." He cast a glance at Tiffany. "Sorry my dear." Dex noticed something different about his teeth. "I'm one of life's losers. Just as well I was born rich or I'd have died poor. Can't do anything at all. Well, I vote occasionally on obscure Bills though what they are about is quite beyond me. Good grub down at the Lords though. Decent claret too. Can't work a video recorder or set an alarm-clock. The trip recorder on the car's a foreign lingo. My lady-wife does all the difficult jobs – ties my shoelaces, makes the toast, boils kettles and stirs my tea without spilling it. One day, she's promised to teach me how to open the microwave door."

"You're too modest, Lord Yarbury." FB's eyes were raking the floor. "You took a first at Cambridge. Distinguished military service against the Mau Mau and in Cyprus. I've read your *Who's Who* entry."

Dex saw Yarbury in a new light. "And no doubt you've had some spectacular wins too."

Yarbury patted down his slicked down silver hair, a needless gesture and then grabbed another champagne from the passing waiter. " And then you get to come to days like this. Good company, damned fine lunch. Drink yourself silly. Bray like donkeys at every joke. Can't beat it. Never watch the race though. Overgrown kids driving round in circles! Now, if you'll excuse me, I'm just popping down to put on some bets. A pleasure to see you again, young Finlay."

FB gazed at the tiny figure of the departing peer. "Quite a character! And beneath all that self-effacement, he's no fool. I'd say we should get seated. Sit where you like. Audley told me I *had* to sit next to Arthur Yarbury - even if half his lunch does end up on my left sleeve. Something to do with his new false teeth I understand."

"Send the boss the cleaning bills." Dex seated Tiffany next to him. Opposite was the footballer who immediately introduced himself. "Mick Glenn. You'll know me."

 "You'll know me too. " Dex enjoyed bouncing back the cockiness. "We've met – roulette a couple of weeks back. You had a big win. I'm Dex and this is Tiffany."

"You was there, was you?" He rolled his eyes. "Tasty. Lost it all since then mind you." He was wearing a black Armani suit, with a deep red shirt open at the collar. A red hankie peeped from the top pocket. The dark single color of the suit helped to disguise but could never conceal the strong physique with the arm muscles bulging against the finely woven expensive cloth.

Dex looked at the orange-juice. "Still in training even though the World Cup's over?"

Glenn's face turned sour. "Trainin' never stops. I'm pretty much rationed on booze. I've drunk so many gallons of orange-juice, I dream of it. The season's twelve months long now. I've built me own pool back home. Swim two hundred lengths every day, then I do the weights, spot o' running on the machine. Then there's the horizontal joggin'. That helps." He winked at Tiffany as if to say *and you could be next*. "But if there's no big games around, like now, then the boss doesn't mind me letting me hair down." He saw Dex laughing. "Well, so to speak." He patted his shaven head and joined in the joke. "Is this a Methodist Convention? F'Gawd's sake, someone pass the red wine," he continued. "I'm allowed one glass. Haven't been so parched since I flew on Saudi Airlines." He saw that two of his neighbors were Arabs with glasses of water in front of them. "No offense, mate. Each to his own, that's what I say." He sloshed the Santenay into his glass and toasted the guests. "Cheers dears, here's to queers. Cheers chums up yer bums – as we say among friends". He turned to Tiffany who was looking bemused. "What you do then, *ducks*?" The pugnacious face made the question sound like a police interrogation and Dex was unsure whether Glenn had forgotten her name or was pissing about.

She was about to answer when Scotty Brannigan appeared. For a second there was silence and then Mick Glenn led the clapping. "Scotty, you Yankee son-of-a-bitch," Glenn shouted. "Over 'ere. What's news?" He stood up and towered over the driver who was resplendent in his driving tunic, his sandy hair starting to crinkle again after a recent flattening in the shower. Brannigan smiled acknowledgements to people he knew and to people he didn't. Some of the faces were familiar from his evenings in Dukes. "Hi, FB! Hi, Mick! Not much time but I thought I'd just drop by."

Glenn put an arm like a python over his friend's shoulders. "Goin' to win?"

"Even losers win sometimes," he drawled. "Sure, today I fancy my chances. Schumi's favorite but what the heck. Two years ago, he crashed out big time at Stowe Corner. Broke his leg. Bad vibes for him. Or is that wishful thinkin'? If I'm in sniffin' distance, Stowe might be a good place to overtake him. Psychology, see?" He turned to face Mick Glenn. "Guess that's a bit profound for you as a footballer." He was rewarded with laughter. Dex saw Glenn's eyes flash with anger at being laughed at but then, realizing the joke was from a friend, he joined in.

Dex reckoned Glenn's face with his prominent nose was even more fearsome in profile than from the front. The combination of bald head, thick black eyebrows, beak, designer stubble and sharp chin were compelling. Dex was fascinated by the vein throbbing in his temple and the clenched hands. There was something of the coiled spring about the man. His fists seemed ready to judge every remark as an insult only to back off when his brain worked out it was harmless. Being close to him was like sitting by a grenade with the pin removed. The nervous energy was exhausting. The man was totally unsuited to help bring down Dukes.

"Mind me asking?" It was one of the other English guests. "How did you get into this, Scotty?"

"Well, my Pa, he was a long-distance trucker. We lived in Reno, Nevada but most times, he was away drivin' or in jail. His trouble, he liked a fight and a drink – the drink usually came first." Laughter greeted the comment . "We were pretty darned poor – me, my kid sister and my mom. Man! We was so poor when he was in jail, we used to eat our Kellogg's with a fork, so's we could use the milk again next day." The applause caused the driver's eyes to sparkle and the corners of his mouth twitched in pleasure. Then once again, his eyes were almost lost in the developing creases and wrinkles of his weathered face as he worked the room with an easy experience.

The questioner persisted. "So how did you get into F1?"

"Back in 1981, Pa, he got out our beat-up ol' pick-up and we drove to Las Vegas to watch the Grand Prix at Caesar's Palace. They do say now it was the worst race ever – drivin' roun' the car park. But for me, those cars, the colors, the noise, the spins and crashes - the money, the glamour, they kinda grabbed me by the throat. Ain't never let go. So I drove go-karts, NASCAR, Formula Three. The rest you know. Any more questions?"

"Been a disappointing season?" It was the same guest with a flat Birmingham accent.

"Sure. We had a bunch of problems with the car. It's been slower than molasses in January, more frisky than a fart in a glove." He touched his forehead in an exaggerated gesture as he saw Tiffany's smile broaden to a grin. "Excuse a country boy's language, ma'am."

As he caught the driver's eye, Dex waited until the laughter had died down. "The weather looks significant. What type of tires will you be using?"

"Heh buddy!" Scotty recognized Dex. "Good to see you again. Hope you're beatin' hell out of Dukes at roulette. They can afford it." There was more laughter, a few cheers and some table-thumping. "Good question anyway." Brannigan looked towards the window. "We'll be lucky to get through the race without rain. So I guess we'll all start prayin' the rain jus' keeps away. But English weather ain't like Vegas, that's for sure. So, if we have to, we'll all change into some heavy grooved stuff. You spectators like the rain. Means we get all out of shape, crab-like, slippin', slidin' an' beatin' hell out of each other's cars. To us though, it mainly means that Schumi, Michael Schumacher, will prove his greatness. They don't call him *Rainmeister* for nothing. I remember watchin' him at Interlagos, Brazil 1996. I spun out, second lap. Man, that rain was comin' down like a cow pissin' on a flat rock. He drove that car like he had glue on them tires. Same in Spain a year or two back. So me? I want it dry."

Mick produced a bulging wallet. His cufflinks briefly appeared from beneath his jacket – a mini roulette-wheel on each sleeve. "Worth ten grand backin' you?"

"Been listenin' have you, Mick? The bookies are usually right. Rain or dry, Schumacher's Ferrari is quicker'n shit through a short dog." He looked at his watch. "I've gotta get back. Can I sign any autographs?" Nearly everybody asked him to sign their programs and then he left, shadowed by Mick Glenn's hulk as he headed for the bookies.

Nobody said a word as the duo left. "Seems quiet without Mick," Dex whispered as he turned to Tiffany.

"But you can't help but like him. He's like a friendly bear with a thorn in its bum. But Scotty. He's one sharp cookie. Yet outside Mick's cocky bullshit, I'm told he's ..."

"Kind to dogs and he's bought a decent place for his old mum in Epping Forest?"

Tiffany grinned, ear to ear. "That and charitable too. He does appearances at Boys Clubs, fund-raising events. Visits Great Ormond Street Hospital every week to cheer up the sick kids. Gives big money but always insists on anonymity. Not the long word he uses I doubt. But it says a lot for him."

Dex pushed back his chair as if ready to move on. "Unlike those society toadies who grab the headlines with their generosity just to get a knighthood."

"Besides being big, bouncy, strong, rich – and famous, there's an animal intensity about him. - enough to find the feminine side of most women. But he's a turnip-head. Not my type."

"Which is?"

"Onions – people with one layer after another to unpeel."

Dex rose and held the back of her chair. "If you've finished dividing the male species into veggies, let's watch the start"

"Of course. Ear-plug time." She searched for her little foam lumps. "I must admit, I told a bit of a porkie - saying I liked Formula One. Bit of an exaggeration really. I've never been. But now, I'm excited. Meeting Scotty helps – makes it personal, doesn't it? Him down there, risking his neck just to entertain us."

"I can't understand why he hangs out with Mick Glenn."

"Roulette maybe? Both self-made from poor backgrounds. Besides that, they're both womanizers."

"Heard any other rumors about Scotty?" Dex was thinking back to the recording of the driver's eyes before Monaco.

"People say he's been driving badly this year. That's all."

He led Tiffany outside just in time to see the cars taking up position on the grid. They leaned against the railings and he found himself pressing against her as they craned forward to see the Start Line and the red lights. As he nestled against her slim body, he felt no resistance and so he pushed himself a little closer until it seemed natural to drape an arm around her waist. He saw a flicker of a smile but she made no comment. Or perhaps he heard nothing because of the roar of the engines and the effectiveness of the earplugs. Either way, he felt slightly too aware of her warm body pressing back against him.

The noise rose to a crescendo as the five lights went out and the race was on. The pack of cars screamed and weaved their way through the tight bend beneath them, engines backfiring, a glow of flames occasionally appearing to lighten the grey gloom of the afternoon. "Either Scotty hasn't the speed to overtake or he's biding his time," Dex shouted but it was lost in the deafening wall of noise. A couple of cars collided but somehow raced on with a damaged wing and a torn nose-cone.

Once the pack had spread out, Dex removed Tiffany's earplugs, a good enough reason to nuzzle up to talk her through the developing pattern of the race. The rain started and the cars began stopping on a dime in the pits for tire changes and refueling. Sheltering beneath an umbrella as the drizzle intensified into a downpour, they watched lap 34. Looking right and over Tiffany's head, the pit straight seemed endless but at over 200mph, it was quickly come and gone. "That's the McLarens finished," Dex explained. "Their strategy on tires was a gamble. It didn't come off. This worsening rain has put them right off the pace."

"So Michael Schumacher loves this," she shouted about the increasing roar. Just then his gloriously deep red Ferrari appeared sending up blinding spray for Scotty as he followed in the RGB.

"But it looks like Scotty's on song too. The RGB hasn't the zip to take Schumi this lap but the way he's driving, we may see some fireworks pretty soon."

She turned to look deep into his eyes. "Let's go in and watch the TV monitors. This rain is just getting too awful." Inside, they helped themselves to hot drinks. "Scotty has had a poor season," said Jock Argyle the TV commentator. "Controversial too. It's understandable, y'know: a former world champion under pressure in a car that hasn't performed. Doubts creep in. Am I as good as I was? Can I still do it? That's when accidents happen. You try to prove you've lost nothing. You try too hard. You make mistakes. There was muttering down in the pit lane about the brake test some drivers reckoned he made over in Montréal. Brannigan denies it. And Coulthard wasn't impressed at being dumped in the gravel in Brazil. Brannigan called it a racing incident. Debatable. He also ruined Schumacher's flying lap in qualifying a couple of races back. I guess it's the pressure to succeed. But if he can overtake Schumacher in the wet, then we'll really know he's back."

Dex watched the leaders take Copse Corner in the blinding spray at nearly 145 mph, before heading away towards Stowe, the highly-tuned engines threatening ear damage to the unwary. Mick Glenn was leaning against a wall, cigar in one hand and orange-juice in the other. Tiffany was on her feet now, arm punching the air. "Go on Scotty! Take him! Take him!" The RGB started to make its move on the race leader. Dex guessed the crowd at Vale would also be standing, sensing a great racing moment. For Scotty to overtake Schumacher in the wet would be unforgettable. Dex saw the American feint left and then right. He pointed to the screen. "Schumi's struggling to close the door. Yes ... he's offline now, you can do it Scotty, go, go! Just look at that acceleration." They watched the RGB wiggle as it strained for grip on the slippery surface. The two cars were side by side, the wheels inches part, two craftsmen striving for every inch of road. The RGB was now inside Schumi, as each driver tried to command the racing line for the corner. "He's done it!"

Tiffany whooped and jumped, still punching her arms in the air as Scotty forced the Ferrari to give way. From outside, the crowds braving the rain were all on their feet, shouting as the old maestro accelerated away from the *Rainmeister*.

"Hope you placed that bet," Dex shouted to Glenn. "Scotty's looking good for a win." The star gazed at him as if he had never met him before in his life. With studied concentration, he managed to get the unlit end of the cigar into his mouth. "Late night. Sufferin' now. But that's good, winnin' a bet. After the beatin' we took at Dukes last week. Lost a bundle."

"Playing roulette?"

Glenn waved dismissively. "None of your fuckin' business."

"Ignore him, Dex. Let's go outside and cheer Scotty on as he goes past." Tiffany's face was flushed as she grabbed his arm and they swept out of the glass doors onto the tiered steps. "Go! Go!" They shouted as the RGB took Copse as if it were a straight road on a dry day. "He's two hundred yards up but there's a long race ahead. If there's two things no driver wants, it's having Schumi either just ahead or just behind. He'll harass the life out of Scotty." Dex wiped some rain from Tiffany's forehead. It seemed so natural to touch her now after her release of emotions beneath the grandstand. "Let's grab some more tea."

Inside, Mick Glenn had slumped onto a chair near the TV monitor, his eyelids drooping. "Disaster!" Jock Argyle was shouting. "Looks like the RGB's engine has just died. I saw a puff of purple smoke from the back end. Brannigan's out. He's parking up just short of Woodcote. Could be gearbox problems. So

Michael Schumacher regains the lead and looks unstoppable. Montoya won't trouble Barrichello now, so we're looking at a Ferrari one-two and a Williams in third. But what a disaster for the American! His big chance. He'd done the hard bit. And now this. Oh! Look at the anguish on Brannigan's face!" Dex and Tiffany joined FB in looking at the screen.

"Get that!" Dex saw Scotty pounding the car with his fists. "Just like Basil Fawlty. Who can blame him?" The room fell silent. Nobody was going to catch the two Ferraris now. The driver removed his helmet, tucked it under his arm, straddled the barrier and started the long walk back to the pits. The limp was evident, the gait tired, the head bowed. But the fans were on their feet, cheering every labored step.

Dex offered Tiffany a chair. "Wonder what's he thinking?"

"*I* feel drained - so God knows how he's feeling."

Scotty felt the pain from last year's injuries as he raised his leg to get over the Armco barrier. The helmet seemed to weigh a ton, his legs were like lead. As the rain spattered his head, soaking into his sandy hair, he remembered the crowd. His heart was still pounding, his mind arcing. He knew he had to p[ay the hero, absorbing the cheers from the crowd but it was barely within him to do it. That shudder and the loss of power had sapped everything from him. The energy that had sped him past Schumi had long gone.

He pulled off his long gloves and acknowledged the standing ovation. He could almost feel the affection as row upon row of fans rose to watch the weary figure limping through the steady downpour. As he trudged slowly beside the Armco, he knew that Nanda Datt would be in a raging fury. "Tough shit, you bastard," he muttered as the main stands came into view. He managed another wave. The soaked crowd cheering his long walk only made him feel worse. For too long , he had cheated them.

As Dex watched Schumacher receive the checkered flag, he could hear Glenn mumbling abuse at the TV screen over his lost bet. He had discarded his cigar in a half-empty glass, his head now propped in his hands, eyes closed. For a second he wondered about drugs but dismissed it as unlikely. Dex had not abandoned hopes of talking to him about Glenn's loss but it seemed pointless now. He looked at Tiffany who was watching the three top drivers appear on the podium. He wandered across to Lord Yarbury who was standing alone, munching a generous slice of chocolate gateau. Dex arrived just too late to warn him that a blob of cream was about to fall on his tie.

"Do you always find it hard to win at Dukes then?"

The peer nodded cheerfully as he mopped away the cream. "Won here though. Know damn-all about this motor stuff. Just put a bet on the favorite as that Yankee said. Some German name. But down at Dukes? Me, dear boy? I'm their ideal member - a happy loser."

"Will they survive?"

"Probably, though with nine-eleven, Space City has been a huge mistake. Somebody might buy them out, I suppose. Any company with cash-flow problems is vulnerable. FB told me that Shawcross is away on a new membership drive. With this damned recession, deuced if I know where he'll find new players. Not big ones."

"You've played casinos for fifty years. Do casinos cheat? Use magnets under the roulette wheel? Anything like that?"

"In London? Not that I've ever heard. Opportunities may be there. People like me – I'd never notice! Some foreign dives – I'm sure there'll be crooked games. Johnny foreigners. Never trust them." He shook his head. "Dukes win because of people like me, more money than sense. Chocolate cake or a salmon whatsit, young fella?" Dex accepted a salmon sandwich. "Anyway, I'm off to pick up my winnings."

"See you again, sir."

"Pleasure dear boy, always a pleasure. Such a good man your father. Cheer-ho!"

London – 27th August 2002

"It's been too long," said Tiffany. "Can't believe we haven't been together since Silverstone. So much has happened – to you and to me." They were in a discreet alcove at Julie's. At the last minute, Dex had called her saying Dukes was not a good idea and she had volunteered to book her *favorite table* at Julie's. They were now seated in the darkened Gothic Room where their secluded table was surrounded by heavy drapes and high-backed chairs with monastic overtones. Her expertise about Julie's had troubled Dex slightly, even more so when he took in the intimacy of their table. It was just so perfect for the type of dreamy evening he had in mind but she seemed to have lost the glow while traveling in the USA.

Dex clasped her hand. "To me Silverstone was like a dream. We became so close that day. It was tough losing momentum. By the way, that hat is just sensational, so very Julie's." It was 1920s, small, purple, and perched daintily towards the back of her head with an eight inch feather rising like an antenna. And that black dress - it really suits you. I love the tassels."

"Thanks. It works in here, doesn't it?" She grabbed an olive. "At the Grand Prix, we barely scraped the surface to reveal ourselves. You're rather a *large* onion." She removed the matching pashmina to reveal the sheer lines of her simple sleeveless black dress. The earrings were dangly twisted steel, almost *objets d'art*. The black stockings and gold necklace with a large amethyst heart pendant completed the bohemian vamp image.

Dex laughed uncertainly. "Not true. You opened up, big time before lunch. It was me who was enigmatic, remember? If you start peeling the onion, perhaps what you'll find is pure turnip-head."

"I missed you."

"So, are you back now for good?"

"I'll explain later."

"That doesn't sound promising."

"We've so much else to catch up about. You said on the phone you wanted to take me to Dukes for dinner. I agreed, so here we are - eating in Julie's. Give." She waited expectantly while Dex fiddled with his red and blue tie.

His shirt was pale blue, the suit was well cut but formal in navy blue too. He had guessed that he should look casual for Julie's but the sudden change of plans had left him dressed for Dukes. "Okay Mr Enigma. I'll continue. I've never been to a casino. Too decadent for my convent girl upbringing but I was really looking forward to it. Seeing FB again, meeting this Shawcross person you mentioned. Seeing the wealth. I don't see the bright lights as often as you'd think. In my job, I live with my mobile, my passport, a bleeper and a packed suitcase. Whenever I was based here and had a spare moment, I'd usually bunk off to France or hide in a B & B in the New Forest. What went wrong?"

"Let's put Dukes on hold until after we've eaten. Let's order?" The formalities with the server over and two glasses of Kir Royale now standing between them, she asked about his father. Silently, he toasted the kindest bank manager he had ever met.

"Positive news," he replied without great enthusiasm. "Carson, the consultant, says I should decide the next moves. He reckons father would do well at the Kemsway, a specialist unit up near Northampton but otherwise I need to take on a nurse, maybe two, to keep him at home. It's a miracle. As I told you on the phone, he's really progressed."

"And he's what - better?"

Dex shook his head. "Never will be. Doesn't seem to recognize me. He's unable to walk, can barely talk – well he can't other than to grunt. He's incapable of doing anything – and the bugger is, none of this is likely to change too much. Carson says if he goes to this Kemsway Unit, he might improve slightly. But to change him from one type of vegetable to another – a cabbage to cauliflower seems barely worth it. Heh – all these veggies! It's like we're making minestrone. Anyway, Carson reckons father's never going to regain the plot."

"Typical consultant! Sounds a bit unkind to me." Her tone was less harsh than the words.

"I've hated my father all my life. Too complicated to explain our relationship. We'd be here for days." He looked at her over the rim of his glass and his brown eyes oozed sincerity and a cry for understanding before disappearing beneath his hooded look. "But yes, to be honest, with Mummy and Beth gone, I do resent that he's alive and they were taken."

Her face showed her interest but no sign that the bitterness of his feelings had offended her. "I admire honesty. But we're certainly stacking up no-go zones. We haven't cleared those about FB or ESP from Silverstone yet."

"I'm playing a slow game." He winked. "There'll be plenty of other days to tell you the nastiness of it all. For now, you've got my soundbite."

"But you'll do what's best for him?"

"Yes. Dumping father sixty miles away in Northampton would be the easy option. Having him at home would be tough. I don't want to see him as a wreck every day. I'd rather he was the bastard of old. If sending him to the Kemsway really would make him better, then it's a no-brainer. But it won't."

Tiffany looked uncertain and played with her tapenade. She raised the glass of Meursault and clinked glasses. "I'm *intrigued* by you. You look ready to run a marathon before breakfast. You're big, trim and strong and yet you look so, oh I don't know, naïve, innocent. But my guess is that like your father, you're a hard bastard too. Right?"

Dex' grin broadened. "Maybe I need a new hairstyle. Something more butch. En brosse? Shaven? A tattoo? A touch of the Mick Glenns?"

"See. Dodging the bullets! But I'm serious! Your Artful Dodger look is an asset. You'll find that people underestimate you. One day, somebody will rue their mistake. As for me, I want to keep digging, exploring." She leaned forward so that her words could be whispered across the narrow table. "Look, let's be straight. I'm trying to find out more. I know you're hiding something big, maybe more than one thing. So …I'm *intrigued* by you. Not love, nothing like that. We had this in common: we'd both lost vital people suddenly and violently. I wanted to help you, to counsel you … but at Silverstone, I found it was *me* who needed *you*." She tightened her grip on his hands. "I'm enjoying seeing your different layers revealed. But I feel there's so much more to come."

"You may not like what you learn."

She shrugged. "Maybe."

He felt more wine was needed before opening up on the Dukes fiasco. "I must warn you, pretty it ain't! I'm the onion who's lost his onions!" He poured more of the chilled white Burgundy. "I've some big troubles to unburden after we've eaten. Perhaps for the moment we just both need each other – maybe for different reasons." Her parting words when the Silverstone day ended - *we could be great chums,* had put a dampener on his testosterone.

She nodded thoughtfully and then cleared space for her field mushrooms in filo pastry. The waitress then served Dex with his wild boar sausages and olive oil mash. Tiffany lowered her slightly flared nostrils towards the plate. "Wow! These mushrooms smell just amazing. They remind me of childhood, red wellies and a wicker basket - walking through endless meadows near Cerne Abbas."

"Cerne Abbas! I saw the Giant there once." He was recalling the figure carved on the hillside, his naked body so clearly outlined in the chalk. "Mother told Beth and me to close our eyes. But of course I didn't. What a whopping erection!"

"Us convent girls used to climb up the hill to kiss the tip when we thought the Nuns weren't watching." They both laughed until they saw that the waitress was waiting to pour Dex' favorite wine. She lowered her eyes demurely, pretending not to have overheard but Dex recognized a laugh bursting to emerge when she returned to the kitchen. Dex studied the Chambertin 1999. He sniffed and approved. It was the first good bottle he'd bought in weeks.

"We've my bank manager to thank for this meal." He raised his glass in a toast and wondered where he would have taken her without the thirty thousand.

"Have you seen that solicitor I recommended? The one in Lincoln's Inn Fields? He was brilliant sorting out Roger and everything."

"Rufus Chandler? He's as good as you said - sensitive but tough as nails. Would you believe it? My mother left me nothing in her will. Not even a kind word. On the other hand, if Beth had survived my mother by twenty-eight days, she would have inherited the lot. Instead, so the lawyers say, it all goes to my father - as if he can spend it."

Tiffany was shocked. "Why did she cut you out?"

"Father's doing, that was." He shook his head, a sharp dismissive toss. "About three years ago. She had nothing. Then he put some of his assets in her name, so he dictated their destiny – to Beth or back to himself." He smiled, eyes lowered in sadness. "Mummy and me, we had a deep rapport. That was true love."

"You could challenge the will."

"I could ... but wait!" He smiled at first but then it turned into a chuckle as he started to explain. "I tell you, this is the funniest thing since Beth's dog peed down father's leg when he was asleep in front of the telly. "The legal eagle says I get the last laugh. He spoke to the old man's solicitor. Father hadn't left a will! Can you believe it! Only the Lord High and Mighty Chancellor. Apparently, he was due to visit his solicitor before he went to New York but had to put it off. He'd ripped up the previous one."

Tiffany caught on quickly. "So when he dies, everything comes to you."

"If he never recovers enough to make a new will, as he won't, then yes. I'm the only next-of-kin. But that's not what excites me. Not the money. *It's getting one over on him*. He'd rather have given everything to the dogs' home than see me get a dime - and he hated dogs, especially Beth's Lucky." Dex topped up her glass. "1999. A great year for red Burgundy. We should drive down there sometime. You love France. I love driving. Least, I do when I've a car that doesn't threaten to break down any second." She looked at him quizzically but made no comment. They sipped appreciatively and he sensed a wavering in her position as she stroked the back of his hand. He hoped that *chum* was disappearing to become close friend and then lover.

"Cheese? Pudding?"

"Just coffee. Decaff please."

"You'll know from the Paddington crash, there's large damages claims being made for father, mother and Beth. The lawyers are sitting in the middle taking fees from everyone. God knows who's to blame for the crash – and the lawyers don't care if everyone denies responsibility. They're just toasting delivery of their next Bentleys. I'm not in Beth's will either but she nominated me to benefit from her life insurance but her Will directs everything else to the RNIB. Quite rightly. At thirty-three, I shouldn't need charity."

"You mean you do need charity? Money problems?"

"Self-inflicted wounds."

"Not another *Louche* disaster."

Dex looked surprised. He had never mentioned his business career. "You know about all that stuff?"

"I've checked you out. The Beeb's archives are magnificent. So yes, I know your past pretty well – the appearance at Southwark Crown Court, the flash cars, the gossip-column stuff - the tempestuous affair with Miss October, her with the ring through her navel."

"She needed ring-fencing, not one through her navel."

"Let's get down to Ground Zero. Have you drunk enough now to tell me about Dukes? The sudden change of plans?"

He leaned forward and touched her hand. "That's the face you put on when questioning an evasive politician. All jaw and suspicious eyes." He saw a flicker of amusement but then the same intent look. It was time to answer. He suddenly wanted to pour it all out, to risk her scorn, to ride her derision. "We can still both go to the casino. If you want."

"Look. You're not the impulsive type. In fact I can see that you're calculating. So there's a reason you made the last minute change of plan. So give! Did you expect to charm me into bed by bringing me here? This cozy little hideaway?" She looked him straight in the eye and tried to keep a straight face as his impish look teased her.

Dex put up his hands in mock protest at her full frontal assault. His mouth was creasing into a suggestive smile. "No. No. Well. No but it's a great thought. I mean if you're … No? But it wasn't the reason." He tried to catch her eye but failed. "But put me down as a yes vote anyway."

"Friend of mine says she's had more orgasms after dinners here than anywhere in the world – and she's cabin crew on British Airways so she must have had plenty. I can't speak for the orgasms but Julie's is number one for soul-searching. So don't get ideas yourself. We're here to get to know each other. Seeing if the books are as good as the jackets."

"You'll find my pages are well-thumbed." His face changed from flirtatious to deadly serious. He sought to bore deep into her eyes. "Before I start, I want two promises from you. One – absolute secrecy. Two - no knee-jerk reactions. Hear me out to the very end. "

"You've got three bums and a penis implant? You used to live with a Slovenian waiter called Marko?"

"You heard that already?" He glanced downwards as if checking. "But I'm deadly serious. So …agreed?"

"Promise."

"This'll take time. You'll get no ten-second sound-bites for the News at Six."

"It sounds like you've some heavy baggage. Order me a calvados, please. I always drink that when I zap off to Normandy." Dex waited for the drinks and they sat silently, he planning what to say, she in eager anticipation. The fiery golden calvados arrived, large measures and forty years old.

"I'm going to Dukes tonight. Please come. But dinner there was impossible." He leaned forward, lowered his voice and clasped his hands beneath his chin as if in silent supplication for strength to get through the oncoming storm. He knew, just knew she was going to explode. She waited with suppressed impatience as he fought for words before giving him a nod of encouragement. When he started, Dex spoke with slow precision. It was if he were mining deep into cavities of hard rock, unveiling an inner self. "Before the accident, I was a regular at Dukes. Then on the night before Barnes, I lost. Everything. Home, car, lifestyle, savings – the lot. Bust with a capital B. Playing roulette. But ..." He faltered, seeming to lose his courage.

Tiffany tilted her face as she leaned closer to share his confidence. She clutched her glass in one hand and now his wrist in the other. "Go on."

Dex could smell a heavier perfume than before and a body lotion too, seductively heady as she leaned towards him. Avoiding the detritus of the meal, she now clasped both his hands. He saw at close quarters the highlights so easily picked out by the small light in the alcove. He took in the purple and black feathers in her hat, the colors shimmering as her head moved. "I was shafted."

"What?" Tiffany's firm gaze was incredulous. "Cheated?" She sounded disbelieving as she savored the aroma under her nose and breathed in. "How? Were you short-changed?"

"I was robbed, mugged, cheated and lied to. They flung off my winning bet. Late bet, they said. Wouldn't pay me." Tiffany watched as his face relived the moment, his cheeks going red and his knuckles now white as he clenched the glass. Gone were the soft brown eyes from which she had drunk deeply. Now they were dark and deep and impervious like manhole covers. The words came out staccato-style, dragged from a recess marked *horror*. "It wasn't true. They checked their camera tapes, *so they said*. Told me I was wrong. They lied. They robbed me. Believe me Tiffany."

"You lose your shirt gambling, then more fool you. As for cheating, dream on! Not here in London. Not at Dukes. Too *Establishment*. Sounds like a typical gambler's lament. Bollocks and sour grapes." Tiffany saw the flash of anger in his eyes but her own dander was up now and she did nothing to cool him.

Dex spread his arms out in a helpless gesture. "Hear me out, damn you! Remember your promise? I *know* they defrauded me. I was ruined, bloody ruined. They stuffed me rotten." Despite his vehemence, he could tell she was not buying.

Her eyes were like slits and even her lips had lost their fullness. "If you gamble, don't cry if you get whipped. But it still doesn't explain why no dinner at Dukes."

"There's more." He ran his hand into his tousled hair and played with it. "Look, Tiffany. They *wanted* to clean me out. Knew I'd staked everything."

"A few hundred?"

Dex shrugged and lowered his eyes as he moved both salt and pepper from left to right with snappy precision. "If only!"

"A thousand?"

"More." He fiddled with the stubby glass, picked it up and drained the last of his calvados. Then he looked her full in the face. This was it. "I lost about one point five million instead of winning it."

"What!" Tiffany's exclamation was loud enough to carry three alcoves and Dex shuddered. "Excuse me! Did you say *one point five million*? On a spinning wheel?"

He fixed his look on the table but acknowledged she was right with the slightest nod.

"Dex, I can't believe what I'm hearing." She stared in disbelief. "The word *pratt* doesn't do you justice. Asshole is closer. At Barnes and Silverstone, I had total respect for you. After Silverstone, I had growing affection too. I felt we had the basis of a real and deep friendship with so much going for us. No rush, just building a relationship as opposed to the usual *get your kit off and first one to orgasm wins*. But shit, I mean hell — underneath what I saw at Silverstone, you're just a selfish, greedy, brain-dead creep. Affection? Forget it. Just crawl into a deep hole. One point five million?" Her generously broad cheeks and curved mouth made no pretense at friendliness. Her head shook and she spoke through clenched teeth. "You could have saved thousands from starvation. Little kids have died because of your greed." In a brisk movement, she bent down and gathered her black suede shoulder bag. "This evening started well." She exited the alcove and stood in the middle of the small darkened room. She hesitated. "And finished …like a dog turd in the mouth," she shouted. Another shake of the feathered hat and she was gone.

117

It was five minutes before the waitress came to the table. "Another calvados? On the house? You look a bit distraught."

Dex nodded abstractedly. "My cunning plans weren't too successful." He swirled the dregs as he waited. "Well thanks, Tiffany! Never did hear me out."

Across London in the heart of theatreland, a white stretch-limo was parked close to the fashionable Ivy Restaurant. Moments later, Scotty Brannigan, Mick Glenn and two young women appeared. Amid hoots of laughter, they tumbled into the back. "Dukes Casino please," ordered Brannigan, the father-figure of the group. The bottle blondes were from the cast of the TV soap, *Essex Girls*.

"Coupla vodkas and Sharon's anybody's," Mick had told Scotty before the two women had arrived. "Been workin' on this a while. Started the old chat in the hospitality suite out at Sky Television Studios. Tonight's the night. Her bloke's out of town. Boxin' match in Atlantic City. And her best mate, Lynda something from the program, she's right tasty. Plays an Essex nympho, no actin' ability needed, know what I mean?" He had nudged Brannigan enough to hurt. "You'll make out there me ol' mucker. Even with a face like yours."

Now, as they cruised through Mayfair, Mick Glenn's voice was as loud as his shirt and tie. The two girls, with their bare stomachs, jeweled navels and dripping in glitter, filled the car with their clashing perfumes. "We're going to stuff Dukes, Sharon. Playin' the old roolly. You watch me."

"I'm watching you already, you naughty man," she giggled. "Get off, willya! Take your hand off me thong."

"I've a right, ain't I? Bought you two vodka and Red Bulls and a Benedictine, didn't I?" He twanged the material against her buttock. Her short red skirt rode up even higher as she wriggled in pleasure at the attention. Scotty, meanwhile, was quietly persuading Lynda that she needed to come back later to check out his silverware from his biggest victories.

Lynda agreed. "S'long as you've bought the new Robbie Williams CD, sort o' background stuff. Really turns me on, he does."

Scotty grinned. "Funny you should say that. Bought it this morning." He saw that she believed him and grinned even more. "Here we are." After piling out of the limo and signing in their guests, they headed for the tables. "Mr Brannigan, Mr Glenn, what a pleasure." Audley Shawcross oozed his normal charm as he eyed Sharon's obvious breast-enlargements. "Thanks so much for your appearance at Silverstone. Pity about the gearbox."

Scotty shrugged. "It happens."

Glenn draped his arm across Shawcross' shoulders. "I'm 'ere to squeeze a coupla hundred grand off you." The footballer breathed garlic into the Chief Executive's face as he fingered his new gold earring.

Shawcross flinched. "Dukes enjoys your company, win or lose. Now if you'll excuse me gentlemen, perhaps I'll join you in the bar later." As soon as Shawcross had turned his back, the smile turned to contempt. He slipped away, adjusting his bow tie. Despite the recent Botox treatment on his forehead, a frown puckered Shawcross' features as he saw Finlay Dexter descending the stairs, not someone he had expected to see. He forced a friendly wave but hurried towards the internal telephone. "FB? Get Jeb to Roulette Table Two with One-Eye dealing please. And if the South African arrives..."

"Mr Blomstein?"

"If he arrives and plays at his usual table, I want Andy dealing. All clear?"

Moments later, Jeb Miller raised himself into the chair behind the roulette wheel as Wong Chi started to spin for Brannigan, Glenn and the two women. Popularly known as One–Eye, the Hong Kong born dealer had trained in Macau. With his quicksilver fingers, the oriental could have made a great living as a magician.

After signing in, Dex looked round the so familiar basement surroundings. It seemed like he had never been away. Everything looked the same, the same hiss of the ball, the same Japanese businessmen playing baccarat. Tiffany was right – Dukes is *Establishment.* Everything was working at the usual calm measured pace with scarcely a sound from the players or staff.

Did I really sit here and get stitched up?

It seemed hard to believe.

He changed five thousand into chips but with no intention of playing. Seeing Miller's portly figure on the high stool, he wandered towards his table. Only then did he recognize the seated players. "Scotty! Mick! Good to see you." He smiled towards the two blondes who were too busy gossiping to notice. "Sorry about Silverstone. But they'll be talking of that overtaking maneuver for years."

Scotty pushed out some chips. "Thanks pal but only winnin' counts. S'been so long since I went to a podium, I'd need a map. But gearbox failure - that's Formula One. Not everyone likes Michael Schumacher but he came to see me afterwards – shook my hand, real gracious." He lowered his eyes. "Life goes on." He added more chips to back Red.

FB arrived at Dexter's shoulder. "What a pleasure Mr Dexter! Playing tonight?"

"Maybe. I took a bath last time. I'll see how it goes."

"Anyway, your guest has arrived. You'll have to sign her in."

"Guest?"

It could only be one person. With a calm appearance, he strolled through to the reception, where he saw Tiffany, still wearing the hat and outfit that had been so very Julie's. In the casino, the hat now looked out of place but her poise and well-known face carried it off. "I'll sign you in." He showed no great enthusiasm. "But watch out for dog turds. There's plenty more about."

"I could do with a drink. Not too late am I?" Her face showed no trace of remorse or anger – indeed Dex could read nothing into her attitude at all.

"Let's go to the bar." After they were seated in a quiet corner, he fixed her with a sinister look. "You've got a bloody cheek crashing in on me here." He spoke quietly but firmly. "After your pathetic little display in Julie's. I've seen kids of three behave better. And keep their promises too." He ordered Bellinis as they sat on a chaise-longue under a portrait by Sir Peter Lely. Somehow, Dukes had persuaded the planners to permit a reduced ceiling height in the bar. The walls were bottle-green hessian, the decorative features in gilt so that overall, what was a large room now appeared smaller, more intimate.

"I should have heard you out. I shouldn't have stormed off." She helped herself to a cocktail onion. "But I was right to call you a deadbeat for losing the money."

Dex guessed this would be the nearest to an apology. He looked around nervously, suspicious that somebody could eavesdrop their discussion. Nobody was close but he remained uneasy. "I'll tell you," he continued. "When I left Julie's, there was a deathly silence. Then some joker started barking like a terrier. I disappeared to a chorus of derisive laughs." She gave a half-smile, inferring he had deserved it. He leaned across as if to whisper sweet nothings. "Be *very* careful what you say in here. I'll explain later." She looked puzzled.

There was still no softening in her attitude. "You'll need to explain a great deal later. But for now, tell me about roulette. I'd like to watch."

"Play if you want. I'll take you through."

"Gambling on a ball landing on red or black? On what the Beeb pays me? Do me a favor!" Dex had barely started explaining about bets *on the layout* and even chance bets *on the outside* when Audley Shawcross appeared, his eyes exuding pleasure. "Welcome back, Mr Dexter. So *sorry* about your tragedy. You received my letter of course. And the floral tribute." Dex had received it and had personally dumped the wreath in the waste bin. Audley Shawcross almost licked the floor in his greeting as he took in the snappy Italian suit, blue shirt and club tie. "We've missed you."

"This is Tiffany Richmond."

"I'm a great fan. Loved your book. *Pain at the Sharp End*, wasn't it? Very moving. Read it when I flew to Sun City. The flight simply passed like a flash. Punchy stuff."

Dex kicked himself that he had never read her book and hadn't even known that she had written one. Typical of Shawcross to have done so – *or to say he had*. He noticed that the wrinkles above the boss' eyebrows had gone but the long scar on his right cheek remained. Keeping it must have been deliberate. It added an aura of hard centre and mystery to the image. As Shawcross small-talked Tiffany about some of her work, he was standing, hands at ease, utterly relaxed and leaning slightly forward, exuding *matinée idol playboy*. Dex sourly reckoned his sultry looks would have been well suited for tea-dancing. As if reading Dex' mind, Shawcross gently ran a finger down his cheek as he admired Tiffany's elegant legs when she crossed them demurely.

Dex couldn't wait to get away. "Come on Tiffany. Let's go to the roulette."

"Have a pleasant evening and I do so hope you will visit us again, Ms Richmond. Perhaps come in for dinner as my guest?"

"I'd like that. Thank you." Tiffany watched him as he slithered from table to table. "Sexy bastard isn't he? But too shallow. Is he married?"

Dex flushed, feeling more than a tad jealous at her readiness to accept dinner. "Don't know. My impression is he plays the field. He often dines with members' wives while their husbands gamble. Gallant to a fault."

"Where did he get the scar?"

"I'd heard he had a car accident."

They left the bar and wandered slowly into the gaming room, pausing to look at the artwork and the figurines. "Too grand for my liking," Tiffany volunteered. "I prefer art to be simpler like pen and ink or etchings. These frames are so ornate. But it works well down here."

"Reminds me of the Palace of Versailles – awesome but after a couple of nights there, I'd run screaming to find a cave."

The tables were comfortably busy and a soft chatter greeted them. Shawcross was trying not to look bored as he chatted to a Hong Kong banker. "The Beeb's littered with Shawcross clones. I'd love to question him, put him on the spot. Sincere he is not."

"He's an Essex boy," Dex prompted as if that explained everything. He wanted to ask what she thought of his accent but again he held back, avoiding saying anything controversial that the microphones might pick up. He felt uneasy, on edge and irritated with her. Her arrival without a proper briefing was a danger to his own agenda.

"You'll recognize the four at the roulette. There's two of the cast from that dreadful *Essex Girls* soap. Mick Glenn and Scotty Brannigan you've met. Mick's orange chips, he bought in at one hundred pounds each. As usual, he's plastering the numbers with them - over ten thousand quid out there. Five hundred on zero. So he's playing *on the layout*. Scotty Brannigan's playing the even chances – *the outside bets*. Like I do. Did." He was quick to correct himself and was rewarded with a flashing smile.

"Mick looks a bit quieter than at Silverstone."

"He's okay when he's winning. Wait until he loses." He then nodded towards the Chinese dealer. "Everyone calls him One-Eye because his Chinese name is a bit similar." Only Scotty and Mick were playing seriously. They'd tossed Sharon and Lynda a few cash chips so they could put out the occasional bet and *ooh, corr* and *aah* over the winning number. "No more bets." One-Eye spread his hands above the layout. "Miller – the fat guy on the stool watches that nobody adds to their chips or places bets after *no more bets* is called."

"18. Red. Even." One-Eye swept away the losing chips. Despite having covered almost every number, Mick had lost. Scotty, using blue color chips each worth a thousand, had backed black and lost three chips.

Glenn glared at the thin Chinese figure with the big black-framed glasses. "Give over mate!" One-Eye ignored the comment. "Only backed thirty-three bleedin' numbers, didn't I? Last spin was 22. Now 18. Next door. Only four numbers could lose. That's the second time you've done me over. That is out of order. Big time. Shake it up a bit. This place spooks me. Bleedin' magnets in the wheel. 'S all rigged."

One-Eye shrugged at the typical loser's rant. "The wheel has no memory, Mistah Glenn." Dealers usually trotted out this hackneyed response. It paid lip-service only to the full truth.

"And we don't use magnets," chortled Miller trying to add some frivolity.

Scotty laughed but Mick just scowled. "Don't shoot the messenger, buddy. I couldn't hit a *dead* fly with a banjo – let alone place a winning bet! It'll change, Mick."

Mick was not appeased. "Thirty-three numbers I'd covered." He shook his head angrily.

"Cool it, Mick." Scotty's voice was sharper this time. "The sun don't shine up one dog's ass all the time. I'm tellin' ya, your luck'll change."

Jeb Miller shuffled his bottom from the Dickensian stool at the head of the table and came across to Dex offering a handshake. "Glad to see you back, Mr Dexter. Haven't seen you since . . ." His voice trailed away. "Terrible business. So sorry."

"Yes! Since you called *late bet*! Terrible business – for me. Good business for you." Dex with calculated rudeness turned away, delighted to have shoved an Exocet right up Miller's fat ass. Tiffany glanced at Dex, one thin eyebrow raised in surprise but her smile at Miller's discomfort was supportive. Dex watched Scotty double up his stake and switch to Red – playing small beer compared to the thousands that Mick was putting out in a series of short-arm jabbing movements. The footballer had again covered thirty-three numbers but this time the stacks of orange were even higher. "Mick's betting over twenty grand. Looks like a Manhattan skyline, doesn't it?" he whispered, sensing some relaxing in her mood. "The four numbers he hasn't covered are all next to each other - again."

"No more bets." The ball slowed and dropped. It appeared to land on twenty-two Black before slowly edging next door. One-Eye spoke like a metronome. "Nine. Red. Odd." He swept away Glenn's towers.

"Shit! Bloody 9. 22, 18 and now 9 again. All neighbors. You bastard! You fixed this. That's three running I've lost. I'm down thirty-five grand." He scowled at Miller. "Get this dealer changed. Send him back to China for all I care. A slow boat." He didn't expect a reply. Miller fingered his moustache.

"Yeah, yeah" Glenn burbled on. "Don't say nothing. Your smug face says it anyway: Shit 'appens!"

Scotty scooped up his winnings and glared at his friend. He spoke quietly but firmly. "Shut the fuck up, Mick! Big boys don't gripe. What you've lost - just an hour's work for you anyway. A few throw-ins, two free kicks an' you're there. So quit the shit, big fella."

Mick was unreceptive. This wasn't quite what he had promised Sharon in the limo. "When I'm losin', I'll fuckin' gripe until my ass falls off. Hey! You! One-Eye! Don't spin yet. I ain't ready. Gotta get more cash."

When Mick returned from the cage he had another one hundred thousand pounds in plaques. These he changed into cash chips and more orange. Though Dex was standing close to Tiffany, he felt none of the Silverstone vibes. She was almost like a stranger, the magic elixir had vanished. She showed no flickering of warmth towards him but instead was totally engrossed in Glenn's behavior. Just as at Silverstone, Dex found himself intrigued by the pounding vein on the footballer's temple as he now gambled forty-thousand across the layout. "Spin 'me up an' watch me clean you out!" He glared at One-Eye and then winked at Sharon.

Scotty pushed out twenty thousand pounds in blue. "Hate to say it but anything Ferrari red'll do me." Dex saw that Tiffany was craning forward to watch the ball. The only sound now was the relentless hiss while it circled the wheel. The ball teased 22 again before skittering like a stone across the waves. "1. Red. Odd." It was not that far from the previous clutch of numbers.

"Done it! I've done it!" Mick's relief was obvious. There was sweat dripping down his neck, his eyes stood out and he snorted in excitement. He was as breathless as if he'd just played a ninety-minute game.

"How much will he win?" Tiffany looked at Dex.

"Thirty-five times his stake. With fifteen chips on that number, he wins, er, £52,500. But it won't see him right. He lost £38,500 that spin on the other numbers. So he's only won £14,000. Needs to win another two or three spins to get in the money after what he's lost." He silently watched the dealer pay out Scotty's win. One-Eye *sized into* the bet. Dex had seen this dozens of times when he had won but had never bothered to watch closely. His mind had always been on the next spin. Tonight was different. He was here to *watch* using his new knowledge from a growing stack of gaming books. He knew that *sizing into a bet* involved the dealer judging the height of the staked chips and then building a matching one to be pushed across the table as winnings.

With the two stacks side by side, the dealer then leveled them off. One-Eye should then run a finger across the two stacks to check the height. If too tall, he would keep any surplus leaving the player with an equal amount as winnings.

Dex watched One-Eye assemble the blue chips to pay Scotty. He then raised the stack slightly above the green baize and shifted it to beside Scotty's bet. The American was busily chatting with Mick who was getting back his noisy swagger now. The two stacks came together with a slight bump. Dex did a double take as he saw a small, sharp but definite movement. Coming in one chip high over the baize and then bumping had moved the bottom chip from Scotty's stake into the bottom of the winnings. In a flash, One-Eye's forefinger ran across the two stacks. They were now level - as they should be. Dex was shocked. For a moment he had to convince himself of what he had just seen. An action replay would have helped, so quick was the subtle movement.

Scotty was busily stroking Lynda's neck as Dex counted the two stacks. There were nineteen in each. There should have been twenty.

I was right.

Instead of paying out twenty chips, One-Eye had pinched a chip from Scotty's stake making the stacks equal. He'd *sized in* with only eighteen chips, bumped one across. Result nineteen in each pile. Dex moved round the table to tap Scotty on the shoulder but then faltered. Jeb Miller and One-Eye would lie. Say Scotty had staked only nineteen chips. You'll just blow your plans. He decided to watch some more.

Tiffany looked at him, a question in her face but Dex smiled back as he picked up a card from the table showing the wheel and the way to position bets. He handed it to her. "This'll help you understand."

"What's up?" Her mouth was deliciously close to his ear but the pleasure was lost on him. He did not need an intruder on his thoughts right now.

"Say nothing. Just watch!" His voice was a whisper but the tone was acid.

One-Eye was preparing to pay out Mick. Sitting on top of the fifteen orange chips was the glass dolly, the marker always placed on the winning number. Mick was watching half-heartedly but more interested in leering down Sharon's low cut top as he stood behind her. Dex had *seen* the payment routine a thousand times but had never really *watched*. His homework yesterday on gambling scams had prepped him on what to watch out for now. Paying out a bet on a single number involved *breaking down* the single tower of orange chips into groups of five. One-Eye broke the chips into three offset groups of five. Cameras all round could now verify the stake. He then rebuilt the tower. "Five Twenty Five orange."

"Yes." Miller nodded approval and gazed down as One-Eye prepared to pay out £52,500.

"What would you like, Mr Glenn?" enquired the dealer in his robotic style as if he were taking orders in a Chinese take-away. "Four purples, some golds, a few pinks and the rest in orange?" The suggestion was routine.

"No. Give me all cash chips. Three purples, twenty-two golds and five pinks. No orange." Mick turned to Sharon. "This is where I win big using the golds. They're one thousand each. The purples is ten thousand. The pinks is one hundred. Shove the pinks on your birthday. Even if you lose, remember that today's gonna be your lucky day, know what I mean."

Dex saw her grin and heard the dirty chuckle as she muttered *you beast but I like you.* "Aggressive strategy," Dex murmured to Tiffany. "He'll cover just twenty-two numbers plus his winning stake left on number one. That leaves him fifteen losing numbers." He watched One-Eye counting out the winning chips, again breaking them down so that the cameras could check he was not over-paying an accomplice. Dex checked the value of the piles put together. They were correct. Miller nodded consent. One-Eye then re-stacked the winnings, at once attracting Dex' interest. Contrary to all usual practice, he had positioned the golds on the purples, pinks at the bottom. The purples should be on top being the highest value. Dex overheard Mick whispering to Sharon what he was goin' to do to her later. He saw the friendly punch and heard her giggle as the dealer stretched out with the winnings. One-Eye pushed the stack towards Mick with his left hand and steadied with his right across the top. Then he let go, withdrawing his hands.

Christ!

I saw that flash of color.

Under One-Eye's right hand, he had glimpsed a gold chip — one thousand pounds that should have reached Mick had been held back. In a swift movement, One-Eye gathered a few other chips that were by his work-station and dropped them all down the hole. The gold chip went with them. The footballer had seen his winnings counted out but had never bothered to check what had actually *reached him*. Instead, he was already scattering the golds, while telling everyone his luck had changed.

No wonder One-Eye had put the golds on top.

Even Mick would have missed a purple worth ten grand.

Dex counted the new bets placed - only twenty-one gold chips on the layout – one short.

The wheel spun and the ball rolled to a halt on 14 Red – a losing number for Mick and Sharon. "Heh! Chinky! You're getting' on me tits! 'Ere. Change these for gold." He pushed the three purples across the table.

"Well I'm doin' jus' great now," Scotty volunteered not altogether helpfully. "These kind folk keep givin' me money." Dex reckoned that Scotty was winding Mick up but the big man was too busily muttering to himself to rise to the comment.

"Let's have a drink," Dex suggested to Tiffany as he resolved to do his own filming down here.

They passed Audley Shawcross, who had paused to watch them from a few paces away. In particular, he had been admiring Tiffany's black stockings and the tasseled dress, so different from her television image. Whenever Tiffany had moved to watch the wheel, standing tip-toed as the ball was spinning, she had provided him with a tantalizing profile. "Not risking your money tonight, Mr Dexter?" He fell into step with them as they left the room.

"We'll have a drink. Tiffany's too tired to learn tonight. I'm going to explain to her *what's going on*."

"You must learn how to play well Ms Richmond. I'm sure you're in *excellent* hands." He rubbed his palms together. "I'll set up membership for you. Sign up at reception when you leave." Shawcross adjusted his dress shirt, flashing his teeth and his cufflinks simultaneously. "Be our guests for some drinks, Mr Dexter. I'll show you to an excellent table." He walked them into the bar and settled them at a thick-cushioned sofa for two. "We're *so* pleased to see you back. Some champagne cocktails perhaps?" After he had organized the drinks, Shawcross excused himself and headed for his office.

"Want to stay a bit longer?" Dex draped an arm across the back of the sofa.

"Pure theatre but enough for tonight!"

"Mick Glenn'll lose the lot. Wild bets, no strategy."

"Look who's talking! Your strategy wasn't so great either. But losing three times when he'd covered so many numbers?"

"It happens. With a clever dealer."

Tiffany's face turned sharply towards him but she lowered her voice. "What was the matter in there?"

"I saw the dealer…" His voice trailed away. "It wasn't important." She caught the warning flick of his head and changed the subject. "Let's drink up. It's late."

Upstairs in his office, Shawcross had locked his door and gone to his box of tricks. Hidden behind a work by Reynolds, it contained his private eyes and ears. From an array of switches, he clicked one. At once, the conversation from the sofa was live, picked up from microphones in the armrests. The hidden lens, built into the wall fabric, missed nothing either. The dimmed wall-lights and comfy chairs encouraged intimate exchanges, not least from guests relaxing on the sofa. That's how he had trapped a Frenchman boasting to his girlfriend that he was the cleverest blackjack counter in the *Midi* and had never been caught. The player had never understood how they'd identified him so quickly. Moments later, his membership had been terminated and he was standing in the London rain.

Shawcross listened to the chatter. "What was the matter?" Then came Finlay's reply. "I saw the dealer. . ." Then there was a pause. "It wasn't important." He continued to listen to the inconsequential chit-chat. But the cameras had caught something in his facial behavior. It looked as if Dexter was shutting her up.

Wondering if he was becoming paranoid, Shawcross poured himself a Baron Otard brandy, larger than normal for this stage of the evening. He'd observed that One-Eye had been spinning neighbors to stuff Glenn. You had to give it to the little Chinaman – he could land that ball into the same section time and again. If it suited – and the way Glenn had been playing was just perfect for this. He selected a Padron cigar from his humidor. What's that she's saying about moving to Washington?

"So please don't get too close, Dex. Don't build your plans round me. Not after you … you know. My feelings are too confused."

"Me too! I wanted every day to be like Silverstone but tonight's shot that to buggery."

She patted his hand as an act of kindness but not love. "I fly in two days. Our correspondent's cancer has spread. I did enough to convince the Editor to send me over there indefinitely. It's a big career move." The mikes fell silent. Shawcross saw the sadness fill Dexter's face. Then there were sounds of movement.

"Let's go."

Shawcross switched off and stretched out on his easy chair. He tapped the cigar ash. Like everything he did, even this simple act was delicate so that the dollop fell with precision and unbroken. Careful planning was his creed. Leave nothing to chance.

"I don't really owe you an explanation, now." They were passing some car showrooms on Park Lane as Dex spoke. "Not after your puerile behavior in Julie's. Your promise wasn't worth much, was it?" He looked at her. His anger still evident. "Don't bother answering. It wasn't a question." Yet even as he spoke, he wanted to rekindle the curious bond that had grown at the Grand Prix.

"We could try again."

"Keep your promise this time?"

She nodded."

"I'll sign us into the Dorchester Club. Let's talk in there." He led her downstairs into the clubby atmosphere. Down below the hotel, the rooms were filling with that demi-monde who regularly rose late and partied until dawn. Tiffany spotted two large chairs in a corner away from the dancing beat of Leo Sayer. Then, over consecutive rounds of vodka-martinis and with smiles of encouragement from Tiffany, Dex decided to unburden himself. "Shoot!"

Her question came quickly. "Why Julie's?"

"Because of something I read just before I was about to meet you in Dukes." He signed for the drinks. "I'd bought a book on casino management. Do you know what? Besides the obvious cameras and the hidden mikes all over the *gaming room*, this book said there was no law that said that bars and restaurants can't also be monitored."

"Bugged? Go on." He saw that she was softening.

"I wanted to explain to you how I was cheated, what I've found out – but also what I'm doing about it." He ran a hand over his hair and nodded. "It would have been a total snafu if we'd been bugged over dinner." He nodded again as he saw she understood. "It would have blown everything. Then to cap it all, you turn up without me briefing you and start gabbing away. Hell, I was pretty pissed off."

There was no apology. "Dex. Precisely what *are* you doing about it?" Coming from her, this was now under-arm bowling, easily played back.

"They robbed me. Destroyed my way of life, self-indulgent though it was. My new charity I've had to shove on a back-burner. You have no idea of the hell I've been through by their fraud. That day we went to Silverstone? I *walked* to Battersea because I had no money to buy petrol. That's how ruined I was! You were right - I was a bloody idiot risking so much but don't forget that I actually won and secondly every penny lost was from my winnings.." He opened and closed his hands and then gestured with a strong flourish of his index finger. "Now it's *my* turn to sort that bastard Shawcross out." His voice was business-like, his tone matter of fact. "I'm going to put Dukes out of business. Crush them, the way they crushed me."

"Sorry?" Tiffany tried not to laugh, though her hand was already rising to cover her mouth. "A bit extreme perhaps, Dex?"

"You think so?" His tone was scornful and dismissive. Inwardly, he was seething too, reminded of his final haunting conversation with Beth. He said nothing, fearful of saying something he would regret. Instead, he selected a square of cheddar and chewed thoughtfully. An earnest look, the type she had seen from preachers on TV on Sunday mornings in America seemed to fill his face. An all-consuming zeal filled his features from the broad forehead to the clear lines of his chin, an image so effectively adopted by American evangelists. "You've never been broke. Never been down to bread without butter and reused teabags. Never walked to court every week to beg for time to pay debts." He saw her flinching and so continued. "You have no idea what humiliation means until you've been destitute. It happened after *Louche*. But for the bank manager now, It would be happening again."

"Anything else?"

"Yes. I thought it was arrogant beyond belief that you stormed off without understanding. You jumped to a conclusion that I had dreamed up the crime to cover for my own stupidity. Well, thanks. But I'll tell you something, no two things. Firstly, you would never have behaved like this at Silverstone and secondly, after what happened in Dukes tonight, I'm more determined than ever."

"What do you mean?"

"I caught One-Eye cheating both Scotty and Mick."

She looked confused. "I saw nothing." Her attitude was defensive now.

"Neither did they. People are trusting, off-guard. I was looking for something, anything. I had worked out – well, why just roll me over? And I was right. One-Eye performed two different tricks tonight." For the next few minutes, Dex explained what he had seen. Tiffany listening intently.

"Maybe you *were* cheated." She was uncomfortable at yielding even this bit of ground. "Do you know why I came back? I was just paying off the taxi when I realized something."

He shook his head. "You wanted to be with me?"

She smiled, briefly placed her dainty fingers on his hand but shook her head. "Because I realized that a casino just might cheat you out of a big sum. Unless they're desperate, small sums would be pointless. At first I thought it absurd. But for that type of money – it's possible."

"You wouldn't believe the value of their frauds."

"How much?"

"At a quick guess, what I saw tonight could easily save Dukes one hundred and fifty million a year."

"What?" Her voice and face showed her shock. "How?"

Dex knew he had got through. The bitterness in his voice disappeared and he used his hands to make his point. "Extrapolate like this: from just one spin, One-Eye stole two thousand from Scotty – that's peanuts. But in a typical evening, on just one table, there could be three hundred spins between eight pm and four am. If they can steal on just fifty of them, that's one hundred thousand. Multiply that by four roulette tables and you're looking at four hundred thousand a day or nearly three million a week."

"Equals one-fifty million," Tiffany's enthusiasm seemed to be growing. Her nostrils twitched as she thought it through. "That's beside calling late bets and getting the odd one point five million."

Dex was now into full flow, his enthusiasm now rampant. "Precisely. I've been reading the financial pages. Dukes *must* win big in London to repay borrowings to banks in America. They're stuck in a pincer between a post 9-11 drop in revenue and a fatal decision to expand with a new tower." As she visibly mellowed, they clinked glasses of Absolut Citron. "That type of funding takes a load of cash. I didn't learn much law from father but I do remember the basics for proving adultery – inclination plus opportunity. Seems relevant here."

Tiffany winked. "Different sort of shafting perhaps?" Dex grinned and encouraged her to continue. She thought for a moment. "Reminds me of algebra, my pet hate when I was fifteen: cash crisis plus inclination plus easy opportunity equals guilt. But you must prove inclination."

"Not plus. The cash flow crisis *is* the inclination. There's more. I saw another dealer tonight called Andy pull a different trick before you arrived. Much, much better for the casino. The player had twelve chips on number fifteen. Each was worth a grand. I counted. It won. The dealer *broke down* the bet but in doing so, the bastard palmed off the top chip."

"Stole it?"

Dex nodded yes. "I counted before and after. Hidden under the palm of his hand. This poor South African guy won thirty-five multiplied by eleven instead of twelve."

"Hang on? That means." Tiffany paused as she did her math. "Thirty-five thousand?"

"On just one spin. Try that trick a few times an evening and my one hundred and fifty million figure is left for dead."

"Just because players aren't watching out for cheating?"

He looked serious as he agreed. "I know most of the dealers, they know me. They know which players check their winnings. I never did. Neither did Scotty or Glenn. There are a few who know precisely what's due and make sure they get it. They're the rarities. I was typical - built big piles of chips and so long as I ended up with another equal stack as winnings, I was happy. Never thought they might have *bumped* me. The dealers and Miller, FB, Shawcross –know everything about the players. Some are always drunk, some are chatterers, some scatter chips so randomly they have no idea what they've bet. If the South African who won on the next table had bet just one chip, then no way could Andy have done anything. But with a stack of nine or twelve chips, then palming one off is easy – if you practice."

"How do you know all this?" Tiffany sounded impressed. She removed her hat and shook her hair like a wet dog. "That's better."

"Reading books. I know what to look for now." He stretched and then clasped his hands behind his neck. "There was one other thing going on – not illegal but clever. Tonight, Glenn was betting against the wheel – piling chips onto all the numbers that had not hit. But clever old One-Eye just kept landing the ball on the same small segment – his landing strip. It stuffed Mick rotten. If Mick had switched to back those numbers, One-Eye could change his spin so that the ball would keep landing somewhere different."

"I thought roulette was random?"

"The very best dealers can keep hitting the same part of the wheel. One Eye looks really slick. But even he can get it wrong. When he hit 1 Red, I'm sure he was aiming for the same numbers again. Only the slightest variation in the spin can send the ball bouncing very differently, especially if it hits the strikers. At illegal schools, dealers learn dirty tricks – card manipulation, palming chips, double-shuffling. I expect One-Eye was schooled in illegal gaming in Hong Kong – a tough baptism."

"Could this just be the dealers cheating? Nothing to do with Shawcross."

"No. One-Eye didn't palm the gold chip for himself. He dropped it down the hole for recycling." He shook his head. "This is organized fraud coming from the top."

Tiffany pulled her chair closer. "Dex – I feel really bad now. I over-reacted. I was in a foul mood because you'd switched to Julie's. I misinterpreted your intentions."

"If Shawcross knew what I've found out, I'd be in deep trouble. This is fraud, big time." Even the impish look was gone.

Impulsively, she grasped his hand, her eyes full of warning. "Beneath those smiles, there's evil. Take care." Her smile was encouraging and he ordered the same drinks again.

"I won't be deflected."

"I can see that. And there's more to tell?"

He looked down, his eyes now concealed beneath the heavy lids. "My last conversation with Beth ended up with a row." He swallowed hard. "I can never forgive myself for that. But my final pledge was to get the money to kick-start the charity." His words faltered.

"I've pushed you into places you don't want to go."

Dex shook his head. "I can't run from the truth. Beth was right. I never thought about the kids. Should never have risked losing money I had pledged. But I never expected to lose."

He saw that Tiffany looked unimpressed and he steeled himself for another wound. "So what next? The Gaming Board? The Police?"

"Filming. Once I've gathered all the evidence, then I'll decide how to use it."

"But this is a powerful company, Dex."

"I thought that once." He shook his head dismissively, his mind back in Scotland listening to the wisdom of Walter McKay. "They're pygmies."

"Go on." Though it had gone three, she was still alert, eager to listen.

Dex could see she was trying to fathom him out. "Weak because they have guilty secrets; weak because they *need* to cheat. A successful casino has no need to cheat."

"But you're cornering a rat. That's danger. Why risk it?"

"Because, oh ... it's hard to explain."

"Tell me." Her tone was sharper but full of encouragement now.

"Because I've never achieved anything really worthwhile. The charity would have changed everything. Father called me a *louche youth* once. That's how the nightclub got its name."

"*Louche?* Remind me what it means."

"Shady; disreputable; seedy; immoral; shifty, of questionable taste."

"Fathers are often right."

"Mine was never wrong. That's what he kept telling us."

"A seedy nightclub shut down for drug-running; a suspended prison sentence; a busted gambler. Hmmmh. I'd say your father got that one right. Scarcely the ideal employment history for a Baptist Minister."

"But I help old ladies across the street."

"Not enough to balance the scales. Even a few thousand Hail Marys wouldn't be enough."

"Beth was the achiever. Me? Every ladder has been a snake in disguise. This time, I'm going to succeed. But don't ask me for my plan. I haven't thought of one yet." He gave her a defiant look, head upright, eyes once again hard. "I'll tell you something else. I'd have explained everything in Julie's, the charity and so on, but for the..."

"The dog turd bit. Sorry. A bit extreme that. But I was *really* pissed off with you. I'd put you on a pedestal only to find you weren't even worth a plinth." She shifted slightly closer to him. "I like the charity stuff. Tell me more another time. That's a Dex I'd like to know better." Her face softened, her eyes fluttered and her mouth broke into a delicate smile. "That's a beautiful idea."

"Right now, *I* need your help. Ask someone at the Beeb's Sports Department to slip you the phone numbers and addresses for Glenn and Brannigan. I want to talk to Scotty especially. I'm also going to trace that South African they rolled over tonight. See if he'll help me. Mick Glenn will be a last resort."

She agreed. "Nearly four. Late for me. I must grab a cab back to Chiswick. I'll call you before I fly." The kiss on the lips was soft and warm but too perfunctory to carry real meaning. "Be strong. Be careful. Keep in touch."

"Friends again?"

"Better than that. We're real chums. *Illegitimi non carborundum.*"

London - 30th August 2002

"Hello! This is Mick." Dex listened to the recorded message. "I've either struck lucky and I'm with some little raver or I'm unlucky and trainin'. Leave your details. If you sound sexy, I just might ring you back. Keep scorin'!" The message ended with a coarse laugh.

Dex faltered but then plunged in. "Call me about Dukes." He added his number but deliberately gave no name. Immediately, he regretted his actions but the inaction had got to him. He tried to rationalize that he had no choice. According to FB, Karl Blomstein, the cheated South African had gone back to Durban. Scotty Brannigan hadn't returned any calls and was now at Spa for the Belgian Grand Prix. The loose cannon footballer was now the best possibility and the direct route to Scotty.

"Celebrities' cellphone numbers are hard to get. I did my best," Tiffany had said. "As it was, my pal at the Beeb was suggesting oral sex behind the studio couch. I told him to go and play with himself."

"Couldn't you have been a bit more adventurous?"

Tiffany had laughed. "Been there, done that. He's history. Keep in touch, Dex. Lots of emails. And I'll let you know when I'm back. Or if you happen to be in Washington, then let me know."

Dex felt as if he had been labeled *a keep in touch friend* but without the touching. Yet he was unsure of his feelings towards her anyway. Perhaps that reflected her ambivalence about him. With her flight now somewhere over the Atlantic, sultry London seemed unpleasant, hot, dusty and devoid of Londoners. He felt alone, acutely aware of the emptiness of his life. The rich were all on yachts in the Med or in villas in Tuscany, up mountains or hills, by private beaches or pools and far from the grime and the smell of diesel fumes. The rest were in Blackpool, Brighton, Spain, Las Vegas or Disneyworld.

For the past hour, he had been relaxing in a quieter part of Regent's Park, close to the canal. He'd wanted time to reconsider his decision about his father and to concentrate on Dukes. He eased himself from the deckchair and binned his ice-cream wrapper. His back felt clammy and his *Au Bar* T-shirt was stuck to him. His jeans seemed too tight and he wished he had worn shorts. He walked over the thin parched grass, hands deep in pockets looking out for a discarded can to kick.

He had decided to have father nursed at home once the old man's lawyers had guaranteed to pay for the care from trust funds that they managed for him. He paused by the zebra crossing and waited for a truck to stop. Then he walked in front of it, the metalwork on the grille radiating heat as he passed. Why the juggernaut should have made him think of Jude Tuson he wasn't sure. But it did and as he headed for Wellington Road, his mind was full of her. Perhaps both she and the juggernaut shared the same uncompromising power and the same blunt front. Her power certainly came without subtlety. Jude would be the live-in nurse, starting tomorrow.

Of all the applicants, she had impressed him most. Aged twenty-seven with deep copper hair, she had a bottle-brown skin and a rounded face with an arrogant cockiness never far beneath the surface. Though she had caused no problems during the interview, Dex had reckoned that subservient she was not. She'd interviewed well and saw no need for him to hire two nurses. She was pure Aussie from her Sydney accent and Doyle's sweatshirt right down to her Earl's Court address. The open-toed shoes revealed well-manicured toenails with green varnish. On her bare arms, gold bangles and bracelets adorned both wrists. She exuded confidence – in her ability, her looks and her appeal.

A deep voice that would make itself heard calling for lager across the throng in the *Rat & Parrot* accompanied her outdoor-athletic frame. Her hair was well groomed and slightly bouffant making her look taller. Even so, she stood a good five-eleven with hands well suited to strangling crocodiles in the Northern Territories. As he'd looked at them, he'd remembered Lord Yarbury's whispered comment at Silverstone. He's been admiring Tiffany's delicate hands and when she was out of earshot, he'd said. "Pretty young thing. Lucky you, old chap. Small hands. Remember, always date women with small hands. It makes your dick look bigger."

Not the case with Jude Tuson.

After she had gone, he'd looked at his notes: *tough, blunt, cynical, ambitious, sexy, grasping, "efficient, not loving"* – her own description. He had asked about her experience. "Yeah. Started in Sydney. Full nurses training including geriatrics. Worked at Westmead Hospital. Brain damaged victims. Then Saudi. Couldn't stand that. No drink allowed and randy Arabs wanting to sodomize you. Turned my back on that I can tell you." Her laugh revealed good teeth, well cared for. "Well, so to speak."

A watch that looked like a Piaget but which could have been a fake or a gift from a rich Saudi gleamed on her left arm. Jude's eyes were deep-set and darting and there was something of the adventurer in her face; the brazen recklessness of the streaker in her look. Perhaps it was the way she stood - chest thrust forward and shoulders back that emphasized her figure and epitomized her character. He'd seen her sort clutching pints of lager heading for Twickenham to support the Wallabies.

"I've nursed everything from koalas to kinkies, babies to baldies. Yeah! Put me down as experienced. Your old man? Piece of cake. He's an in-and-outer, right? Shove it in, clean it out." Her appraisal was typically robust. "Talking of which - who gave you all that stuff about needing two nurses? Is he a big fella?"

She saw him nod yes. "He was. Looks to have lost weight in hospital."

"No sweat. I could throw a Sumo wrestler over the Eiffel Tower."

"What about the law? Working hours, lifting weights?"

"Aw, c'mon! Politically correct bollocks. I want the money. I've one aim in life – to get rich quick – hence Saudi. Now I'm looking for the main chance in London. Don't expect me to be giving bed-baths in five years. I want to meet some rich layabout who'll keep me in Gucci and champagne. Meantime, save your money. Pay me more. Just hire in a relief nurse for my evening off." With her confident reassuring style, she had made it all seem so simple. After she'd left, her personality had lingered with a smell of Gitanes and Gaultier perfume that she had applied as she was leaving. But after she had gone, some doubts crept in and he had revisited them while slumped in the deckchair. Had he been too hasty, turned on by her eyelashes and by the thought of her living in?

His mobile rang as he crossed Hillside Road. "Mick Glenn here. You phoned. Who you? What you want?"

"I've met you now and then. Silverstone. Dukes last week." "Who you then?"

"Finlay Dexter. Dex. Sat opposite you at Silverstone."

"So what's it to you?"

" I need to speak to Scotty. You were both cheated."

"Shit. No kiddin'? I told Scotty . I said Dukes had spooked the wheel. Bloody magnets everywhere."

"Don't know about magnets. But I saw it. The three of us need to meet."

"Nah, mate. I'm too busy to piss about. Tell me all the shit now or just fuck off."

"Fine. I'll fuck off." Dex switched off the phone leaving Mick wondering what sort of asshole would hang up on him.

Dex was still worried about that call when he reached Porky House. Agents would have described it as elegant, three-story, double-fronted and late 18th century. The family home was set back a few yards from the road in a street filled with gentry – though Dex knew better than to expect sightings of them in August. He stopped to smell the climbing roses that festooned the stone wall of the house. They were in need of some loving attention.

A few miles north, Mick angrily threw Dexter's number in the bin and wiped the message. He slumped into an armchair, poured a can of Diet Coke and switched on a TV reality show. "Heh, Sharon?" His shout carried to the pool area. A few moments later, the blonde appeared from the sun bed, towel around her head.

"Yeah?"

"When's your bloke back from America?"

"Creole? He's back."

"What!" Glenn jumped from the chair. "I said no chances. I thought he was still in Atlantic City."

"Take it easy. He flew in this mornin'. I slipped away after he went out. Business. We've plenty of time for another one - a quickie. He thinks I'm seein' me sister in Enfield."

Glenn thought about Creole Henry and suddenly didn't feel interested in sex at all. "Nah! I think you'd better go love. Play it safe. Don't want Creole findin' out about us."

She sighed. "Pity. I was lyin' there getting' all turned on thinkin' about you, me and that porno movie you got. But play it your way. He'd be a right bastard if he found out. I'm gonna leave him soon anyway. Then we can have lots of time." She wrapped her arms round his neck and kissed him, long and lingering.

"Yeah," he said drawing back. "Get your kit on. The man's an evil bastard an' that's for sure" He patted her backside as she turned away. "Your sister? Won't split will she?"

"She'll cover. She hates Creole."

After Sharon had driven off in her customized Mini Cooper with its black stripe down the white bonnet, Glenn had been restless. He'd done some lengths of the pool to think about the conversation *with that stupid dickhead who rang off*. Instead, he found images of Creole Henry haunting him instead. Thinking about Dukes was less worrying and after one hundred laps, Mick made up his mind. He had a Vindaloo delivered by the nearest Indian take-away, toasted his manager ironically with a pint of pineapple juice and decided to confront Shawcross.

At eleven-fifteen, Dukes was starting to fill up when Mick parked further down Mount Street. Tom, the doorman, nodded cheerfully as Mick Glenn bounded up the steps. Being polite to some members didn't always come easily. Too many were examples of the pond-life that the management tolerated only because they were hefty losers. He had no time for prima donnas but he saw Glenn differently. Despite his obvious lack of breeding or brains, Glenn usually stopped for a quick word. But not tonight. "Going to beat Chelsea then?" Arsenal and Chelsea had a long-standing London rivalry.

"Yeah!" Then he was gone. Wearing a mustard color jacket, black shirt and tie, Glenn strode down the marbled sweep of stairs, leaving the doorman wondering what was bugging him. His jaw was set and his lips were already rehearsing what he wanted to say. Glenn signed in and at the entrance to the gaming room he paused, looking round for Audley Shawcross. No sign. He peered into the restaurant. Not there.

He spotted Ken, the cloakroom attendant. "Boss in tonight?"

"He's away, Mr Glenn."

"Who's in charge?" The tone was aggressive and the jaw pushed forward.

"Mr Forster-Brown."

" 'E'll do! Fetch 'im mate can you?"

"Sure!" Ken disappeared down the corridor. "FB. Mick Glenn is outside the cloakroom. Y'know, the England footballer." He lowered his voice. "Sounds angry. Wanted to see Mr Shawcross."

"I'll sort it out." FB was not as confident as he sounded – even less so when he saw all six foot four inches of packed muscle looking ready to explode. He swallowed hard and his small eyes blinked behind the thick lenses.

"Mr Glenn. Delighted to see you again. Mr Shawcross is traveling. He's back next Thursday. Can I help?" He tried to sound calming as his eyes avoided the listener.

"Fu-uckin' disgrace this place." Mick's voice was raised. "Full of shits in penguin-suits. Cultured voices, oh yes la-di-dah - but you're only out to bleedin' cheat us."

"Please keep your voice down. This is really most... unwelcome." FB's accent was far from posh but compared to the uncouth star, he spoke like the Queen's tutor. His own career experience in top-end casinos hadn't trained him for dealing with an uncouth giant, his eyes flashing like a copulating stallion and with his pants on fire.

"Now you listen to me rabbit-ears." Glenn moved closer so that his chin hovered close to FB's bald head. He rapped the acting boss on the shoulder. "Listenin' – little man?"

FB, despite his own height felt very small indeed. "I really think we should go into the office. Talk this out like civilized gentlemen."

"Ain't no gentlemen round here. You'd be unsold as a used pisspot at a car boot sale an' that's a fact. And we ain't goin' nowhere. Anyone mug enough to gamble at Dukes needs to hear this. You tell Shawcross I know this place is fuckin' crooked. Your dealers cheat us, that's what. Last time I was in, you shits rolled me over. So just watch it. You lot was seen. Caught in the bleedin' act."

"You must be mistaken."

"Listen you bald headed bunny. You tell that ponce Shawcross: I'm not leavin' without all me money back – all £480,000 of it or I'm goin' to Scotland bleedin' Yard. I know the fuckin' works on you lot. An' I'm goin' to tell every fuckin' member the way it is. Got it, you carrot cruncher? I'll be in next Thursday evening. 10-30."

Overhead, the security cameras captured the scene and the mikes picked up every word. "Please go now." Above Glenn's shoulder, Forster-Browne could see Lord Yarbury faltering as he descended the stairs. He had heard the commotion and was looking embarrassed. FB held his breath as Glenn spun around on his Cuban heels and then ran up the stairs. Halfway up, he glared back down. "The game's up, chum. You're all goin' to jail."

The peer stepped aside for Glenn and then waddled round the carpeted curve to the bottom.

"I'm so sorry, Lord Yarbury."

"What a bore! Methinks he needs some lessons in how chaps behave. I'll complain to Audley."

Las Vegas - 30th August 2002

Shawcross and Carlo Letizione exited the visitors' car park at Yucca Mountain, somewhere not usually on the tourists' agenda. President Bush had just approved dumping 75,000 tons of nuclear waste deep inside it. They had driven out from Vegas to see the volcanic mountain and had then journeyed far inside by train to assess the controversial project. The experts had convinced enough people that the plans were safe and most congressmen were happy to use Nevada as America's trashcan.

Shawcross was concerned about floating the company in a year or two if tourists were avoiding Vegas for fear of coming home with luminous hands. They had both been reassured. The BMW was now speeding back to Vegas across the brown and rust colors of the desert landscape. Carlo Letizione scratched his head. "I dunno but it seems kinda dumb and dangerous shippin' waste here by road and rail from all over the USA. An invite to terrorists."

Shawcross agreed. "That seems to be the main worry. I'm less concerned now about sending our high-rollers home glowing in the dark."

Letizione swore at the roar of a passing Harley Davidson. "The casinos here lobbied but no way were we ever goin' to win. So now we just say how safe it will be. Ten years until it happens anyway. We'll have floated on the stock market long before. Made our pile." Letizione scowled again as another scruff with a long beard roared past, hands on handlebars way above head-height. Shawcross was happy to keep the conversation trite, especially as he sensed that Letizione had been edgy all morning. There were far more immediate issues that both men were anxious about than Yucca Mountain.

"C'mon Aude. You've been duckin' talkin' 'bout *Operation Snowball* for too long. I'm havin' a real tough time not payin' contractors. I've started so many bogus law-suits to delay payment, our goddamned lawyers are workin' overtime. We're nearly fucked. Where have you been? Give."

"Gibraltar. Cyprus. Monaco. Liechtenstein. Geneva."

"Not Panama?"

He picked nervously at his fingers. "Panama? Never been there. No contacts."

Carlo grunted. "So who's gettin' this cocksucker rolling?" The bite in the nasal voice was clear. "You told me *piece of cake, old chap. Relax.*" He mocked the English accent. "I'm so relaxed now, I ain't got no more fingernails to relax with." He waved a hairy hand in emphasis. "So?"

"Cyclops has been a smooth operation. That's all in-house stuff. Conjuring tricks. Late bet calls, palming chips. That's done well - kept Sir Cedric's lot docile. Bought time with your banks." He paused as he thought how much cash he had creamed off and already sent to his personal account in Vanuatu. Only enough to satisfy Sir Cedric had gone through the books. Increasing the profits too much without more players would have got that shit O'Keefe asking questions.

"Meantime, your job is to *kick ass* with the contractors – get the bills reduced. Keep the creditors worried. We can play the poverty card pretty well. Even if soon we won't have to."

Letizione was not appeased. "Fat cigars all round. Anything gone offshore to our account in Aruba?"

"No. Not yet. Wait for *Snowball*."

"Yeah but *Snowball*? What's goin' on?" Letizione grabbed a Snicker bar and munched hungrily.

Shawcross watched the overweight man wolf into the chocolate. "Don't you ever stop pigging out?" Shawcross bought time to sort his lies. "Little bit in from Gibraltar. But I'm closing the big one at lunchtime."

"Who with?"

"Krieger from Liechtenstein."

"You said these guys you was talkin' with would *howl at the moon* when they heard your plan. Your words, not mine. I ain't heard nobody howlin' at nothin'. Heh and I thought you said Krieger was a done deal?"

So too had Shawcross but the little runt lawyer had been playing hard to get. "Krieger's in the bag. Just a small detail to resolve today and then *Snowball*'s going to roll. It'll deliver cash like you won't believe." Shawcross looked out at the vast nothingness of the Mojave desert, the barren rough ground and the mountains etched clear in the noonday sun. Outside the temperature was 108 degrees and likely to peak three degrees higher by mid-afternoon. The stunted shrubs looked beaten to death by the savage heat. "Bugsy Siegel had balls sticking up the Flamingo back then in the middle of this desert."

Letizione talked through the remains of his snack. "That motherfucker *Snowball* should have been rollin'. Now everything turns on a goddamned phone call. Like waitin' for a couple of aces on the flop. Believe it when it happens."

"Krieger will come across." He wished he was as confident as he'd sounded. Pinning all hopes on a tight-assed weasel like Krieger was dangerous. He recalled without pleasure the lunch in Geneva the previous week.

Letizione seemed to have been reading his mind. "Thought you said that meetin' in Geneva went well. Rollin' over like a spaniel to be tickled, you said. Again, your words, not mine." He turned his head but received no eye contact. "Look Aude, piss in your own pants if you want. Don't piss in mine."

"It'll be okay. I told you."

Shawcross closed his eyes to kill conversation. He wanted to get his head round the call from Krieger. He relived and rehearsed the spiel he'd peddled over lunch in Geneva. It should have been an easy sell. But it had been tough." Heinz," he had opened, "Osama bin Laden did *us* but not you a favor! Governments everywhere are trying to cut off his money supply. In Washington DC and Brussels Commission the cry is to close havens for dirty money – like Liechtenstein, Heinz! They are after professionals like you for laundering drug cartel money."

"Not true!" snapped the lawyer. "We don't!"

"Agreed. But the truth becomes what Governments say it is. They're ending your banking secrecy; making bank accounts transparent; killing off anonymous offshore corporations and secretive trusts run by faceless men like you. Banks and professionals must report suspicious transactions. *Know your customer; know your client* – that's the creed now as ordained by the great god *due diligence*. Casinos too, so they say, are hotbeds of money-laundering. Casino controls will be tough but there's nothing like knowing the law. I know how to beat it – and that is a window that will be closed in Britain but not yet. Your clients should be using Dukes to clean their money and bring it onshore so they can use it."

Krieger had seen the logic of that but had still declined to act.

Carlo Letizione had booked lunch at Cili, Las Vegas' favored power-lunch restaurant at the golf club near the Mandalay Bay. What he had assumed would be a celebration of *Snowball* started as if between strangers. They played with their appetizers in silence broken only by trite monosyllables until the maitre d' came across. "A phone call, Mr Shawcross." With a smile, the Englishman left the room to take the call.

"Heinz! Right on time."

"But not good news, Mr Shawcross. I have decided against."

Shawcross tried not to sound desperate. Krieger represented his last chance. "Did I not make myself clear? This is a fantastic deal."

Krieger's law firm specialized in secreting and managing other people's wealth through use of anonymous companies and a labyrinth of Caribbean trusts or local anstalts. But bin Laden had made life more difficult. Shifting money, hot money, had become increasingly complex. The lawyer was speaking from his steeply roofed office in the tiny Principality of Liechtenstein, a mountainous enclave between Austria and Switzerland. "Fantastic deal?" He threw back the words disparagingly. "For you, certainly. For me? Aggravation. Loss of management fees. Risk. And for what? To help you and your Dukes Casino." The negative message sounded even worse in the guttural Germanic accent.

"No, Heinz. *To help your clients.* To free their money. I made you a good offer."

"I disagree. It is nearly midnight here in Vaduz. I'm tired. So, I will say goodnight."

"Wait! Wait, Heinz. If I'm reading you correctly, the problem is money."

"Your idea of generosity and my idea of a fair offer are as different as Vegas and Vaduz. So, goodnight."

Shawcross could imagine the bird-like head nodding, the thin lips parted and the darting tongue licking them. No way would Heinz Krieger put sleep before profit. Shawcross hated this beady-eyed little worm getting one over him. For a second he remembered last week's lunch at the Hotel des Bergues in Geneva. The bastard was always first to order the most expensive wines but last to pick up the bill – over US$7,000 for two last week.

"This loophole I'm offering – a godsend for your clients. Heinz, this is your chance to change their unobtainable locked-away funds into daily wealth. We must act quickly - before the UK's casino loophole is closed. What terms did you have in mind?" He feared the worst.

"In Geneva you made your best offer. So you said." Krieger broke off to let the words sink in. "I believed you. Are you now saying that was not your best offer? That you lied to me?"

"Not at all," Shawcross retorted. "Others considered the offer generous ... and had accepted." The deception came easily. "But tell me your terms. I can only refuse."

Shawcross mouthed *tight-wad* as he waited. He knew that this millionaire lawyer was too mean even to pay for a haircut. Despite earning at least eight million Swiss francs a year, he used his wife's scissors for his graying hairs. And it looked like it too.

"You offered to split four percent of the funds. Insulting! I want four percent just for me. If you want two percent, your choice. I get my four whatever." Shawcross saw red and gripped the receiver as if he were throttling the little miser.

"Heinz, I really ..." he started.

"I'll take that as no. So goodnight."

Shawcross imagined Carlo Letizione awaiting his return. He knew he had no choice but to lie back and enjoy it. "Okay Heinz. It's a deal. You drive a hard bargain."

There was silence. Parsimonious in everything, Krieger rarely gave away words, taciturn as a gargoyle on a Viennese palace. "Good." There was silence. Then he started talking as if he had relaxed and wanted to release some of his worries. "You were correct about banks. All my life - no questions. Now since nine-eleven, they're running scared. Forms to fill; passports to produce; Compliance Officers. Phone calls asking questions. Beneficial owners. Know your client. The Bank of New York story has been damaging for financial centers. Now I hear a Nigerian scam using offshore centers is surfacing. Every day it is getting harder to maintain the confidentiality and to access funds that the clients want. Concealing big money is a problem. Moving money is becoming too difficult. I will retire soon." For Krieger, this was like a Gettysburg address. But he hadn't finished. "For big sums, the risk is greater. Four percent was for small sums. Say under one million American dollars. Above that, I want an over-rider of one hundred thousand in addition."

Krieger's avarice made the listener's eyes mist over with a red haze. He felt the lawyer was dragging him downhill by the nose. "But Heinz, why don't you deduct that sum at your end?"

"Because the clients will *blame me* for the high fees. I want them *thanking me for my help*. For *my* solution to *their* problems. Not hating my fees. So, you agree the deal?"

"Yes." Somehow, Shawcross uttered the word. "Agreed."

Back at the table, Shawcross ordered vintage Veuve Cliqueot. "Told you, Carlo. No problem. *Operation Snowball* is ready to roll." But the bottle had barely been opened when the maitre d' again appeared. "Your office phoned Mr Letizione. Can your guest please call London urgently?"

"Wonder what that's about," muttered Shawcross. "FB can panic sometimes." He returned to the phone booth and rang. When Shawcross returned to the now cold prime rib, Letizione knew there was a problem. The bounce in Shawcross' step had disappeared.

"An English soccer player came in. Big name, well-known. Started shouting that we'd cheated him. Wants near half a mill back on Thursday. Says he's going to tell all the members and go to the cops. Or else."

"What does he know?"

"*Know*? Of *Cyclops*? Nothing. *Suspect*? Who knows? Might have spotted something. Devil's job to prove it. Unless he has good witnesses."

"Pay him off," growled Letizione.

"No way, Carlo. He'd still shout off his big mouth. Crowing that we'd admitted cheating him. He's pig-ignorant. I'll think of something."

Letizione nodded as he chewed thoughtfully. Suddenly and unusually, he spoke like an old style Mafiosa. "Do that. Scare da fuck outta him but no whackin'."

"No need to kill him. I'll have a couple of heavies waiting next Thursday. They'll see him off the premises."

Letizione nodded as he looked through the picture window across the water to the golf course. "I brought your Inspector guy, Adrian Ryder and Zara here. Knew it would impress them. Robert de Niro was sittin' just over there. Least I said that's him!"

"How was their report on the Atlantis?"

"They got the jobs. Does it matter?" He pushed the orange-chocolate dessert round his plate and chuckled. "I put them in your company penthouse at Turnberry Place. Wired every room for sound. Cameras too. She's the smart one. He's blinded by her. We've got them right here." He pressed his thumb on the table.

"Good move. Does he realize yet we're holding him by the *cojones*?"

"Coffee, please. Decaff for two. We'll sit on the patio for that," Letizione ordered. They went outside. The misters cooled the air across the tables. "Sure. They had quite a debate while splashing around in the hot tub. She'd worked your game out in Nassau. He didn't agree. He didn't want to believe he'd been bought."

"But," Shawcross interrupted "life was so good, he no longer cared?"

"You got it." Carlo Letizione produced cigars. "One glimpse of her stockin'-top and he just whimpers like a pup. If you're doin' nothing later, we'll sink some tequila and watch what the cameras picked up. You won't be disappointed."

"Don't get carried away, Carlo."

"By the way. I always thought you'd worked in Panama."

"Never been nearer than Aruba." Shawcross could see that Letizione was enjoying himself.

Enjoy your little digs, you fat shit.

But you'll regret it.

Spa, Belgium - 31st August 2002

Scotty Brannigan was in a long de-brief with his Technical Director and team boss after the qualifying session. He would start in seventh position, six places ahead of his team-mate. The driver knew he had forced the best out of the troublesome car in qualifying and the boss had been pleased. "Get a good start and maybe tomorrow you can get into the points. Our sponsors are trigger happy. Otherwise." He pulled his index finger across his throat.

Scotty thought about the first bend at Spa before responding. The hairpin called *La Source* had been the scene of some spectacular pile-ups. "Twenty-one cars hitting La Source is a lottery. Specially if it's wet. If I get round in the pack without a shunt, then we may be on. Specially if the front four screw each other up. But the handling's still wrong. We need more down-force without compromising speed."

At last, the long sweaty meeting was over. As Scotty left the RGB team's technical centre with its array of computers that had monitored his performance, he switched his cellphone back on. Then he looked at the sky. The air was humid, heavy with rain just waiting to torrent from the dark clouds that scudded over the Ardennes. There were four messages but only one grabbed his attention: Nanda Datt had called and would be ringing again every 30 minutes. In his motor-home, he showered and changed. Though the helicopter was ready to whisk him to his hotel he waited for the call. Nanda Datt was punctilious to a fault. "Given the limitations of your car, a perfect position on the grid. Once the pit stops begin, throw some weight about. Clear? Just as we discussed and agreed in Oxford"

"Remind me." The driver was being deliberately obstructive. Scotty remembered every word of the face to face meeting in a suite at the Randolph Hotel the previous week. He could imagine Nanda Datt reclining in that easy chair, the bottle of Black Label and the small hands, forever moving. Though from Kuala Lumpur, or so he said, he sounded and looked so very English with the highly polished shoes, immaculate white shirt and oh-so-British club tie with crowns on it.

Scotty had no illusions – the man was a mega-crook and probably behind the match-fixing murders. He recalled gazing at the Ashmolean across Beaumont Street and thinking how permanent and civilized it looked compared to the nastiness of the sordid discussions in which he was involved. The slow precise oriental voice with the sing-song tones had made the threat plain. "The French Grand Prix", he said "was a disaster but the collision was not your fault. But in Germany and then Hungary, you disobeyed instructions. You did not delay Montoya – quite the reverse. Your explanations are unacceptable. Spa is your last chance Scotty."

Outside the pits, the rain was falling now, large splattering drops. "Scotty? Still there? Deliver or else."

Scotty paused long enough to irritate Datt. "Remind me of your orders."

Down the line from somewhere anonymous, Nanda Datt continued. "We're backing Michael Schumacher and Rubens Barrichello for first and second, either one to win - short odds but a good bet. We want Coulthard third. Get Coulthard into as many points as possible. Prevent both brother Ralf Schumacher and Montoya from scoring points."

"Is that all? That easy?"

"Don't fuck with me Scotty. Our big bet's on the Drivers' Championship. You know that! When they total the points for the season, we must have the following order: Michael Schumacher, Barrichello, Coulthard, Ralf Schumacher, Montoya and Raikkinen. Your failure to deliver in Hungary has dropped Coulthard behind Montoya and the younger Schumacher in the points. After tomorrow, there are only three more races to get this order correct. The syndicate can win over seventeen million if we forecast the correct order. Understood?" The words came out, staccato-style. "You will get your reward too."

"Yeah! Sounds kinda familiar."

"If you fuck with us tomorrow, keep looking over your shoulder. You'll never race again. Our good nature has limits." The line went dead.

1ˢᵗ September 2002 - Spa, Belgium

Dex had been to the Grand Prix at Spa several times but never before in the Paddock Club. He had taken the last minute decision to dig into his loan to go to Belgium. While watching Saturday's qualifying the commentator had mentioned that Brannigan would not return to London after the race. Instead, he would fly to Spain to test the suspension before going on to Monza for the Italian Grand Prix. That had been the clincher – plus the knowledge that Beth's life company had promised his check for four hundred thousand. Three hours later he was at Gatwick Airport and on the flight to Brussels where he picked up a car to drive down the autoroute to the circuit. The nearest empty hotel bed had been an hour from the track at Maastricht in Holland.

The months of what politicians called *a period of severe restraint* would soon be over. There would be no return to the free meals every evening at Dukes; no mornings spent choosing sunglasses or designer clothes; no freshly squeezed with fluffy scrambled eggs while looking across the gardens from the breakfast room at the Carlton Tower. The policy would however bank-roll his plans, even though the details were still unresolved. The expenses were stacking up - cameras, travel, maybe more private detectives, the people digging in Panama. But a bigger picture was emerging. Merely winning back his losses was for wimps! He wanted to get back more, much more on top and only then to put in the boot on the Dukes empire.

Dex knew how hard it was to get close to the drivers but the privileged few with Paddock Club tickets could do a Pit Lane Walk, right in with the cars on the morning of race day. Sometimes, the drivers mingled at lunchtime in the marquee with sponsors. Dex reached the circuit by seven, somewhat ahead of the rush. Fans cooking eggs and boiling coffee after camping out in the forest overnight filled the approaches. He breakfasted well in the Paddock Club and checked out his seating. Nobody seemed sure whether Scotty was likely to drop by at lunchtime.

He wandered down the footpath, thinking of Tiffany, wondering what she was doing at eleven at night in Los Angeles where she was doing some interview. Her last email had been three lines, telling him how busy she was having *a blast*. It was crazy trying to read plusses or minuses from a few lines but there was no sign that she was missing him. He had signed his last email *Your Pedigree Chum* but she hadn't even commented.

As he jostled through the fans lining the narrow footpath, his thoughts turned to Jude, so, zany, so upfront but sly for all that. Already, he had learned just how ambitious to get rich she really was. There was no future with her but as a passing fling? He thought of her in those figure-hugging jeans. Or maybe she's wearing that short skirt again today. She must have noticed my eyes popping out like headlamps on a frog-eyed Sprite yesterday afternoon but he had made no move - the nagging reminder that compromising his relationship would be dumb kept returning.

He studied the chicane and then killed time by crossing to the other side of the circuit, walking up beside *Eau Rouge,* the legendary left, right, left bends all on a fearsome gradient. By driver acclaim, this was the ultimate F1 test – taking the bend over the brow of the hill *on the flat* - 180 mph, full speed, foot fully down. Lesser drivers eased off and even the best were liable to misjudge the line and crash into the tire barrier beside the track. He wondered what it took to be a World Champion. *Anybody* can drive, do three-point turns. So was it brain speed? Eyesight. Or just being able to quash that shit-yourself feeling. I must ask Scotty. If I ever get the chance. Why in hell doesn't he return my calls?

The Practice Session started and he watched while leaning against a Shell hoarding. The drivers sped past him, engines coughing, occasional noisy spurts of flame flashing from their exhausts. He watched Scotty guide the RGB through Eau Rouge but was sure he was not *on the flat*, probably due to lack of trust in the car's handling. That - or he was getting past it, driving within himself. The session ended and the track fell silent, only the lingering smell of high octane fuel and the blackened road surface reminding Dex of the slide-rule risks taken by the drivers just moments before.

He crossed the footbridge over the track near La Source. With a flourish of his Paddock Club pass, Dex gained admission to the Pit Lane. He saw the gleaming red Ferraris of Schumacher and Barrichello, the red and white McLarens and the blue and white Williams. Immaculately dressed mechanics surrounded each car, feverishly working to fine-tune and check settings that can gain or lose one-hundredth of a second – the difference between success and defeat.

He kept on walking past each team garage until he reached the two RGB cars. The garage was as clean, calm and orderly as an operating theatre. He hovered, one of several fans looking admiringly at Scotty Brannigan's car, reminiscing about his great days. But of the drivers, there was no sign. He knew that when not in team meetings, they were like performing seals for the sponsors. During every spare second, they were expected to meet and greet and pose with their backers. Ground down from the non-stop crass questions, Dex guessed they had no more interest in meeting their public than most celebrities. Scotty was probably happier discussing strategy, telemetry and set-up.

There were two young mechanics working on Brannigan's car, one polishing, the other checking the giant Michelins. For a flickering second, Finlay's eyes met those of the mechanic nearest to him. "I'm a friend of Scotty's. Can you give him this note please?"

"Sure. I'll be seeing him in about twenty minutes. They're round the back in a meeting." The mechanic stuffed the envelope into the top pocket of his team color overalls.

"Will Scotty come out front?"

The mechanic started polishing the bodywork. "Scotty keeps to himself before the race. Afterwards, sometimes he's relaxed."

"If he's done well, you mean."

The mechanic grinned.

"Okay. Just see he gets the note."

Scotty Brannigan did not appear during lunch at the Paddock Club and, by Spa standards, the race itself was uneventful - no thirteen-car pile-up at La Source this year. With a sense of frustration and anticlimax at not talking to Brannigan, Dex boarded the coach back to Maastricht.

Usually, the squally showers that are a feature of the Ardennes weather make for exciting racing with the track dry at one end but greasy and treacherous at the other. But today, the overcast skies and a dry track had made the result too predictable. Dex had watched the two Ferraris romp home with Montoya third. Scotsman, David Coulthard had beaten Ralf Schumacher into fourth place. Brannigan had retired with gearbox trouble in the fiftieth lap. As the coach crawled along the jammed roads, he dozed fitfully, thought of Tiffany and wondered what she was thinking. He doubted it was of him. The only thing to look forward to was checking for a message from Brannigan at the hotel.

"No sir. I'm sorry. No messages." The receptionist's English was nearly perfect.

The London morning newspapers had arrived, so he picked up the Sunday Scope and the Sunday Times. After ordering room service, he yawned, weary from the early start and dispirited at his failed mission. He switched on the TV and glanced at the papers. Mick Glenn starred as front page news in the Sunday Scope.

ENGLAND STAR'S NIGHT OF LUST

Last night Mick Glenn, 29, was taking no calls at his luxury home in North London. The Arsenal and England star, whose form on the pitch has been poor so far this season, has even been off-target in his choice of girlfriends.

Yesterday, he missed three good chances to beat Chelsea in the derby game but the news we broke to him before the match might have upset his shooting boots. Glenn has been involved in a torrid relationship with fun-loving Sharon Reid, the busty star of Essex Girls. The star's problem is that Sharon lives with reputed Yardie boss Creole Henry who found out and most definitely is not amused.

"Yeah, it's true," confessed a tearful Sharon who was sporting a black eye. "Yeah, me and Mick we've been seeing a bit of each other. I've stayed at his place now and again while Creole was in America.

The Ivy

"Me and Lynda from the program, we had dinner at The Ivy with Mick and Scotty Brannigan." International celebrities like Joan Collins and Tom Cruise favor this top West End restaurant in the heart of theatreland. "We had a right old laugh I can tell you. So we all went on to Dukes Casino in Mount Street. Mick gave me a few chips to play with. He lost a bundle. He was throwin' chips everywhere. We left after an hour or two. In the white limo goin' back to his place, he told me he'd lost near five hundred thousand.

North London Palace

"Anyway, we dropped off Lynda and Scotty at his pad near the casino. Dead posh it looked. Then we was driven to Mick's, like a palace it was - big

security gates, a heated pool and a snooker room. Inside, I had a few vodka and Red Bulls and then, well ...you can guess the rest."

But last night as our reporter waited outside, Glenn was alone in his fortress-like home just off The Bishop's Avenue. Buying a home around Millionaires' Row won't leave much change out of four million pounds.

A Gentleman

"Mick was real nice, a gentleman. In the morning, he gave me a bowl of muesli and an Arsenal shirt and fixed me a limo straight to the TV studio. Creole thought I was staying at Lynda's but somehow he heard I wasn't. He went wild. He never hit me though. I tripped over a cable in the studios. But he's ape-shit with Mick."

Grievous Bodily Harm

Creole Henry, 36, arrived in Britain thirty years ago from Jamaica. He lives with Sharon in an £800,000 terraced house in Camden Town. He was not available for comment but in Yardie circles, he is well known for his violence. He's done time in Feltham Young Offenders Institute for using a bicycle chain. In 1994, the Jamaican received four years for grievous bodily harm after pushing a broken bottle into the face of Roland Dupree, a known drug dealer from Dalston. Increasingly in the last few years, gangland killings in North London have become commonplace as turf wars over drugs have been settled in cold-blooded executions.

Piss Off

When we phoned Mick Glenn to ask if he denied the story and to enquire how late night gaming and alcohol were affecting his performance on the pitch, he said. "Piss off. It ain't none of your business." When we asked if he knew Sharon was living with Creole Henry, he put down the phone.

Dex looked at the photo of the Jamaican. He was built like a bull with no neck and a face that shouted *beware*. The eyes were fierce, the whites wide and fixed but then mug-shots were rarely flattering. He thought of his truncated discussion with Glenn and wondered if he was wearing *shit-yourself* underwear now. As he looked at Creole's brutal face, he found himself feeling sorry for the footballer at the prospect of the black thug coming after him.

As the Spa crowds jammed every country road for miles around, Scotty Brannigan relived the race, knowing that Nanda Datt would not be opening any champagne this evening. He shrugged and told himself that it was done now, too late to repair the damage.

After the stormy debrief about the engine failure, he had sat alone, freshly showered and casually dressed in hipster slacks and an RGB sweat-shirt. On the desk by his laptop, lay the note his mechanic had given him. He read it again. *Urgent. What happened at Dukes. Very confidential. Please phone.*

He frowned as he recalled the evening at Dukes. His thoughts flew fast – losing money, Mick behaving like a jerk, the two women with scarcely an ounce of brain between them. The frown turned to a flickering smile as he relived what happened on his king-size after he'd shown Lynda all his trophies. That had been the best part of the evening but even that didn't make him want to see her again or be reminded of a pisspoor evening overall.

He looked at the note, a reminder that this Dexter guy had phoned a while back and he had never bothered to return the call. And now Dexter had been in the pit-lane to try to see him. *Persistent to a fault. something must be bugging him real bad.* He scowled angrily as he thought of the phone call this morning from Mick Glenn warning him their names were all over the Sunday Scope. He wondered if Lynda would now spill her story. Not that it mattered. Or maybe it did.

Magazines had always relished his playboy style anyway. But even so, sponsors would not appreciate specifics – like photos of her wearing very little, supporting lurid details of the love-making. He sighed, ran his fingers through the wiry hair and flicked open a can of iced water from the fridge. He looked again at the note, started to pocket it but then felt sorry for Dex and grabbed the phone instead.

He hadn't even dialed when his team-mate interrupted him. "Scotty?"

"Yeah? What is it Pierre?" He saw the balding head peering round the door.

"The pilot wants to leave at once. There's a severe storm around the Pyrenees. Landing at Barcelona may be a problem. We can beat it if we go now. Otherwise, he won't fly until tomorrow."

"I'm sure as hell not staying here. I'll be quick." He picked up the note. Saw the three numbers to try. Cellphone, hotel in Maastricht or London. *Ah! Good. He says the London number is always manned or there's voicemail.* He dialed, tapping his fingers impatiently.

No answer.

No voice mail.

"Fuckin' waste of time that was, you asshole." He stuffed the note into his pocket, packed his laptop and notepad into his black leather briefcase and bounded down the steps and under the darkening sky. He wanted to get away. There was something brooding about the Spa circuit – probably brought on by the blackness of the forest and the lowness of the clouds. At least in Barcelona there would be life, laughter and usually better weather. Except everyone interested knew he'd be there. Including Nanda Datt. The post-race conversation with him was imprinted like a scar on his memory.

"Game's over, Scotty. You didn't fuck up. You deliberately fucked us up. You let Montoya through. You slowed Coulthard down, weaving around. Total reverse of instructions. Don't practice your Italian." The phone had clicked dead.

2nd September 2002 - London

By Monday mid-afternoon Dex was back home in St John's Wood after an uneventful flight from Brussels. He checked the message-pad. Still nothing from Brannigan. "Hi Jude!" She was coming down the stairs in a red shirt, less well buttoned than it might have been and a tight black skirt. "How's father been?"

"No problems. No change."

"Let's take a look." He followed her back up the two flights of stairs, their footsteps silent on the expensive grey carpeting. With seven bedrooms, the Hillside Road home was not short of space. What had been his mother's *quiet room* had been easily adapted for his father. Her TV and his mother's old but comfortable chair were already there. Only the single bed was new. Jude's own room was next door, ideally situated for the regular attention his father needed. Dex had always found the *quiet room* a sad place. Now it smelled of disinfectant masking less pleasant odors. This was where his mother had spent too many hours alone – her sanctuary from the man she refused to divorce. Dex looked at the room, memories flooding back. He wondered if his father had any comprehension of the irony of being housed in this room.

"Hello, father," he said as cheerfully as possible. The pallid figure was flopped back in his chair. Dex sat down on the edge of the bed so he could be at eye-level. Lord Dexter, looking a shadow of the burly figure he had once been, was wearing a thick woolen dressing-gown and yellow pajamas that were now too large for him. A tartan traveling rug covered his legs. Dex expected no response and received none. His father's once proud head, typically held back so arrogantly, was now slumped, lolling against his neck. His plentiful hair that he had swept back in giant silver waves was still thin from the operations. Dex tried to see the eyes without being sure whether his father was awake or asleep. The hands were fidgeting, one bony finger pushing against another.

"No change?" he whispered to Jude, still unsure how to cope. "Is there no way you can stimulate him?" Dex surprised himself at how concerned he was for father's welfare, far more than he had ever been before the crash.

"Waste of time." Jude spoke with hardened experience. "Yesterday we looked at photos from his past. Your old home in Bladon, your mother, him in his socking great wig and black and yellow robes. Zero reaction. I played some of his CDs that you said he liked – Wagner. Miserable stuff that was. Not a flicker of recognition. I gave up. I even tried him on some of my Rolling Stones stuff, just to see if I could get him angry. Nothing. Not a flicker." She turned to face him and he felt uncomfortably aware of her stance – hands on hip, pelvic area thrust forward, shoulders pulled back. In her eyes, he thought he could read an invite but he let the moment pass. "Look Dex. Stimulate until you run out of breath but he's never going to improve."

Dex sounded unconvinced. "Carson said we'd see advances if we worked on it. You make some coffee. I'll sit here with him for a while, talking to him about the old days."

He sat on the floor so that he could see clearer into his father's eyes. They seemed fixated yet on nothing, showing no response when he raised and turned the head towards the television. Dex gently lowered the head to its lolling position and wiped some dribble from around the mouth.

What's the point in this, God?

Alive but locked in a life without meaning.

Only weeks before the jet had tumbled from the sky, Dex had stood a few feet from his father in the hallway. Neither had said a word. Lord Dexter had been engrossed in the Law Gazette and once the Government car arrived, he had left without a goodbye to wife or son. Dex' animosity had lingered long after the car had sped away.

Okay, he had been a right bastard, uncaring about who he scrambled over to meet his own ends. True, he had shouted, sworn, drunk too much and seduced far too many young barristers in his days as Queen's Counsel. Dex remembered stumbling across a cheerful young thing doing up her red bra in father's downstairs study when his mother had been in Cheltenham. Father had said nothing about keeping quiet, his face just showing resentment but no remorse. But at least he had been a person, a character. Now, he was, oh shit, say it – a waste of space.

After the crash, it had been like reading an obituary of someone who was still alive. Colleagues had described father's acid brain, his skill at cross-examination, his voracious appetite for good food and hard work. Yet nobody had said they liked him. *Effective, dedicated, demanding* – these words had dominated the papers.

"Father, this can't go on." He spoke with pedantic diction and addressed the eyes in the hope that he was getting through. "As you would have said with your love of Latin maxims: the *status quo* is not an option. There are two choices. I ask a doctor to risk his career to ease your passing - morphine or contrived pneumonia. That's one way. The alternative is to try hard, bloody hard to make life more meaningful for you. You'd go to the Kemsway. It won't help much – but then it might. Simon Carson believes you *can* hear and understand but can't give out messages yet. I want you to work on that. We'll go for one blink for yes and two for no." He looked in vain for some sign of a blink. "Well, think about it. We'll try again another time."

He looked at the skin sagging under father's chin, saw the hair damp and without life or style. *This man had given him life and then wanted to dictate it.* He blinked back tears he could not believe had welled up as he wondered about his parents. Had he been conceived from love? Over thirty-four years ago, had there been real affection? Or had there just been fleeting moments of mechanical passion, a wife meekly submitting to the male's domination? "I'll never know, father but whatever else …you gave me life. And for that I'm grateful." He leaned forward and kissed the cold and moist forehead. "One thing I know: being you now isn't fun, you poor old bastard. You're going to the Kemsway. I'm going to give you the best possible chance." The decision now made reminded him that Jude would not take well to being out of a job. He sighed as he went to the en-suite bathroom to wipe down his face, asking himself how often his mother had dried away *her* tears while sitting up here.

He heard Jude singing an old *Men at Work* number as she entered the room. He took the coffee from Jude and said he was going to shower and then make plans.

"Did an American call while I was in Spa?"

"No. Just the dry-cleaners wondering if you'd forgotten about a suit you left there two months ago. Oh and a travel company wanting to know if you needed a tour package to Monza for the Grand Prix. That's all."

Dubai – 3rd September 2002

Nanda Datt stretched back on his *chaise-longue* in his spacious suite at the Jumeirah Beach Hotel in the United Arab Emirates. He dropped a grape into his mouth and turned down CNN News. He was psyching himself for the difficult meeting with the syndicate. He sighed. They had all grown too greedy, assuming success was their *right* rather than the result of his hard work. Rich people didn't like losing money. To them, explanations were excuses. They did not care that the English Premier League had been a tough call despite the failed prosecutions against Bruce Grobbelaar, Hans Seger and John Fashanu. Formula One was chancy, even with unquestioned loyalty and Scotty had behaved like a shyster. One–Day International cricket was still doing well though trickier with Condon's anti-corruption shadow still lingering.

Far below, he saw the fine sandy beach and the endless blue of the Gulf. A white Bayliner left an impressive swell as it sped seawards. He selected a large brown date with care and pushed aside the remains of his lunch tray. The telephone interrupted his line of thought. "Yes?" The single word revealed the shadowy existence of his life. There was suspicion, caution and hesitation in the word. He listened for a moment and his unlined face relaxed. "You're ready? Excellent. So when will ...? A week? So long? Yes, yes. I know you don't want to be caught. No! Stop! I don't want details. Just results. Don't call me again until everything is finished."

He replaced the receiver and poured himself a large malt in celebration. Today was his 31st birthday.

London – 3rd September 2002

"It's all balls, of course." Jude took the stairs of Lord Dexter's home two at a time. "These experts calling the slightest improvement an advance. A vegetable's still a vegetable. Believe me, there's only been one recent breakthrough."

"Being?"

"Too many patients demonstrating lack of response were condemned as hopeless cases." She bustled through the hall, past the portrait of Lord Dexter in his legal gown and wig. "In fact they were blind, not brain-dead. It should have been an international scandal but it never was. The emphasis was on the positive – that medical science had caught up with best practice – and lessons had been learned."

Dex raised his voice excitedly. "So my father?"

Jude came up close to him and looked him deep in the eyes. "Sorry, Dex. Carson would have checked out the eyesight, no sweat. Any improvement now is going to be of no help to him – or you."

Dex was reluctant to agree. He had still not told Jude of his decision. "But Carson's team said to keep stimulating him." He took a chair by the kitchen table, its black, grey and pink surface matching the granite wall above the large red Aga that his mother had loved so much. Meanwhile Jude percolated some coffee.

"He might *get* better but he won't *be* better. See what I mean? He'll still be in a wheelchair, head flopping and face contorted, making unpleasant noises from different parts of his body. Confused muttering."

"But he seems to recognize me." Dex was now convinced of it. "I've spent hours with him since yesterday." Knowing she would scoff, he refrained from telling her he was trying the one blink, two blink approach he'd read about.. "He seems to understand when I talk about the past. He grunts and his head moves slightly – as I see it, at the right times. Maybe he would be better in the Kemsway, getting more stimulation."

Jude's bouffant hair stayed flawless as she shook her head vigorously. "Dream on, boss." She handed him a cup of Kenyan and sat down close to him, helping herself to a lump of stilton. "Stimulate him 24 -7 and he still won't be

Brain of Britain. But the nursing unit will be richer." Her look was dismissive of medical psycho-babble as she turned to face him, crossing her legs with deliberation as she did so. Her yellow kilted skirt was so short that Dex received an eyeful of flesh and a flash of black. He knew she was seducing him for the third time in twenty-four hours. Last evening, he felt sure she had been hovering outside his bedroom drooling for an invite.

Jude placed her elbow on the counter, leaning towards him, her black V-neck suddenly seeming low cut and obvious. "Remember, it's my night off? Liz is my relief. Ask her. Get a second opinion."

"I'm surprised you're taking a night off so soon – you being so ambitious. Thought you'd rather be working. Getting money for your piggy-bank."

"Naah!" She laughed and patted his knee as she rocked forward. "If I don't go out, how am I going to meet this rich Romeo who's going to pamper me on his yacht or ravage me in Trump Tower overlooking Central Park?"

"How come you're so obsessed with being rich and pampered?"

"Because it sure as hell will beat being poor – that's all bedpans, burgers and Kentucky Fried."

"So your family. Tell me about them."

"My dad, he was a stevedore – red-hot trade unionist and a great supporter of Bob Hawke when he was PM in the eighties. But he grew disillusioned with him when there was a hardening of finance policy. Reckoned Hawke had turned his back on his true supporters. Dad ranted and shouted at the TV all the time – always wanting to march or strike."

"You were brought up in all that?"

"As long as I can remember. Trades Union talk was a steady diet - every meal."

"So what was your attitude?"

"Don't get me wrong. I loved my mum and dad. When I was nine or ten, he was my hero. I watched him being interviewed on TV, being filmed outside Parliament after meeting the PM. But by fifteen, I saw it so differently – realized that his ideals were just so much crap. *Strikes and rights*, his favorite words were no way to get rich. You only had to look around our home and all the cheap furniture on credit to prove that. Dad was clever, always buying books on Lenin or Marx. He spent hours reading about Scargill, Scanlon and Jones, the Miners' Strike and union power in England. He called that era the

Golden Days of the Glorious Struggle." She raised one eyebrow in disbelief. "Dear old Dad - he could have made us rich with that brain. He died of cancer two years back, a sad and disillusioned man." She sighed. "Passive smoking during too many hours arguing about rights instead of achieving great things. Catch me following that route?" She revealed her orderly teeth as she laughed at the very thought. "Poor bastard! Mum's still in the rented place in Woolloomoolloo, worrying how to pay off the carpets. She doesn't earn much as a train cleaner."

Dex warmed to her, sensing a more human side. "But why become a nurse if you want to get rich? Wrong job surely."

She leaned forward again as if sharing a confidence. He noticed a faint aroma of her strong French cigarettes that clung to her clothes. Her eyelashes were curled and mascara-prominent. Again, he felt the hand rest on his knee, staying fractionally longer this time. "No. My qualifications are portable. I knew I could get jobs anywhere, opening up a new world far from dock strikes. Coolest night in Sydney was Saturday – *all-fall-down-night*. Out with the mates drinking stubbies of Tooheys until we dropped. Then Sunday morning, head throbbing and a strange man snoring in the bed. I mean – get real. Can you believe that was the highlight? Pissed as rats and a shag you can't remember." She looked at the ceiling and shook her head. "No more of that shit. My qualifications are taking me up-market. Travel equals opportunity," she pouted and he saw that as she'd been talking, the skirt had shifted again.

Dex nodded thoughtfully, trying to ignore the increasing amount of thigh. "Makes sense. But don't look at me. No chance of Gucci shoes or yachts from this employer."

"You don't do so badly." Her eyes flashed round the room, taking in the Smallbone kitchen units, the Aga with its two spanking red lids, the American-style fridge-freezer with built-in ice dispenser.

"Not mine. None of it. I'm unemployed. I squat here. Unemployable probably. I'm looking for a rich woman to sweep *me* off my feet. Sex on demand, a fast car, a house near St Tropez and a private jet to go to every Grand Prix." He scratched his cheek and smiled, eyes quickly looking away.

"No good looking at me then," she laughed. "Well, except for the sex."

There was a moment when the only sound was the mellow chime of the wall-clock in the corner. Dex' voice was suddenly throaty as he blustered on, trying to pretend she had made no invitation. In the past, he would have needed no better invite but now, his mind was confused by the way she was manipulating him already. "Oh, I don't know. On what I'm paying you, you're getting richer by the second – being paid to sit here and chat to me. When's Liz arriving?"

"Couple of hours. Plenty of time." She winked at him before swivelling her buttocks on her chair and placing a hand on each knee of his Levi's.

He paused and looked at her intently. This was getting out of hand, attractively so - but against his promise to himself. He remembered the old line from schooldays.

An erect penis has neither conscience nor commonsense.

He tried to ignore his mounting excitement. "You're right. I'll ask Liz about the Kemsway." The words came from an autocue as his mind was fast-forwarding to what was happening all around him, his eyes eager to take in the curves of her body. The intensity of her presence and the availability of her lust suddenly clouded everything.

"Sure, you ask her." She shifted clumsily on the chair flashing more pink flesh and jet-black stocking-tops. Her well-groomed hand moved further up his leg as he studied her three different rings, all expensive looking stones and he wondered what stories lay behind them.

Trying to pretend nothing unusual was happening was becoming impossible but he battled on. "So your night off looking for rich men. What are you doing? Hitting the town?" Her hands were now stroking both thighs, her fingers delivering sensuous messages. Her arms were outstretched, her body leaning even closer to him so that her copper hair was nearly brushing against his cheek.

"Any ideas?" The cocked head and tone of voice were not even subtle.

Dex took an age to reply, wondering whether to do so jokingly. "Madame Tussauds or the Tower of London?" He looked up and smiled, face beaming. "Or if you prefer maybe dinner at my casino? Do you like gambling?"

She seemed ready to leap onto his lap in her eagerness to accept. "You kidding! Me? An Aussie! Bet on anything – even the color of the next car to round the corner. So, you're on. The Tower and Tussauds can wait. I'll wear something slinky." As he watched her mouth, his inner battle continued, though he knew there would be only one result. He was aware of her breath, hot and coming in short bursts, her anticipation becoming overwhelming. He felt the driving force of his own needs taking control. The brief fling with Beth's married friend Amanda had fizzled weeks before Barnes. He smiled fleetingly as her description of their affair had flashed through his mind. *The Grateful Dead* from a corpse of a marriage she had called herself, praising Dex as her erection and resurrection. There had been no pretense of a relationship, just an energetic process involving a human dildo. Shortly before the crash, she had phoned saying it was over, leaving Dex wondering if she had returned to battery-powered satisfaction.

For no obvious reason, Dex stood up looking tall and lean in profile. She too eased off her chair and for a second, they were holding hands before he drew her close as she tipped up her head to receive his lips in a lingering kiss that locked them while their bodies rubbed against each other. The kiss started gently and searchingly but then a shared force gripped them both and he found himself heavily aroused, pushing his pelvis towards her in anticipation of what lay beneath the kilted skirt.

He knew now there was no going back.

Jude moved her exhausted arms to flop back on the table, legs dangling either side of him. He bent forward, head against her cheek, aware of the rapid cooling of the sweat. She twisted her head to put her mouth by his ear. "Dex, I've been dreaming of that ever since I first saw you." She spoke gently. "But that beat the hell out of any dream."

"Takes two!" Even getting those words out was a problem. But he was happy about that. No pillow talk, no intimate confessions, no hints of his plans for Dukes – and heaven forbid no suggestion that he was considering ending her contract. They went upstairs and showered in the bathroom of the master-suite. As they soaped away the pleasures, Dex' thoughts were troubled but he smiled and chatted about casinos and the games she played.

He knew he had compromised himself, leaving her the victor in her undeclared war with him. Now, as he listened to her singing rather badly as she dried her hair, he laid out a favorite suit on the bed, regretting what had happened yet in awe at the frenzy they had shared. But he was still resolved to talk to Liz.

London - 4th September 2002

FB hopped from foot to foot and then pushed his glasses back up his nose. "Dining alone?"

Dex said no. "Jude Tuson enjoyed last night so much, she's joining me again."

"I'll get your table laid up for two. Perhaps a flower?"

"On my guest's plate, yes, thank you."

"And you'll be playing later?"

"Some roulette. I'm due some luck." Dex felt no choice but to play to justify being present. It was inviting curiosity if he just stood around watching. He checked that Jude wasn't in earshot. "I read that stuff about Mick Glenn. Half a million! Has he been back?"

FB's mouth opened and shut before at last an answer emerged. "Dropped by once but didn't play. Personally, I'd be more worried about that thug Creole than half a million." The eyes studied a distant mark on the carpet. "Ms Tuson I presume! Welcome back. Sorry not to have seen you last evening. I hear you enjoy roulette." FB was characteristically eager to change the subject as he acknowledged Jude, dressed to kill - white leather suit, cut tight with a black chiffon blouse and slingbacks with high-heels. The colors emphasized the copper hair, even more commanding than usual. Dex saw her imperious look. It was disconcerting. *She* was now boss – and then some.

"Jude. This is Mr Forster-Brown. He was off duty when you cleaned up last night. Everybody calls him FB." He turned to the manager. "FB – this is Jude Tuson."

"I'm so excited," she trilled. "Until yesterday, I hadn't hit the tables since Sydney. I'm going to take you apart again tonight."

"Bit different here than that emporium in Sydney." FB's tone was sniffy. "But good luck. Enjoy your dinner." Forster-Brown tapped his watch. "Excuse me. I'm nearly late for a meeting." He headed for the stairs to get an update from Shawcross who'd flown in earlier from Vegas.

Jude wanted Dom Perignon. "Y'know. The fizzy one that costs an arm and a leg. And some caviar canapés. Beluga preferably." She dismissed the barman with a nod.

Dex looked her up and down as she pushed her shoulders back to maximize the prominence of her breasts. "You look stunning. That outfit."

"Got lucky. An old wrinkly I was looking after croaked. He left me a few thousand in his will. Mind, after some of the things he'd made me do with his dong, I deserved it." She laughed coarsely at the recollection and demonstrated the size of his organ with her finger and thumb. "Magnifying-glass job. So I treated Jude to a few goodies. Like this little number from a boutique in Paris. Glad you like it. After winning so much last night, I'm in the mood to do it again. Not drinking?" Her face showed her disdain at his orange juice.

"I'll have wine with dinner. I need a clear head."

"You think so? I've had my biggest wins when I was running on neat vodka. I feel a big win coming on."

He grasped her hand and felt her sexual energy remind him how good she was in bed – where they had spent most of the day. "Hope you're right. Gamblers Anonymous is full of bankrupts whose lucky underpants let them down."

She wiped some crumbs from her mouth. "No room at roulette for sweaty palms." She beckoned the Spanish waiter. "Some menus please. I'm starved. I could decimate a rhino's ass." The caviar canapés had all gone, along with the nuts and crisps.

She's a locust, devouring anything in her path.

Me included.

Upstairs in his office, Audley Shawcross beckoned FB to sit down. In front of him was a large gin and a smoked salmon salad but he offered nothing to FB. The relationship was less headmaster and deputy than headmaster and new boy. "When Glenn arrives tomorrow night, I want no scenes, no outburst like last time. Have him brought straight in here, two security people with him at all times. Any nonsense and have him bounced onto the street. Do I make myself clear? I've seen the recordings of last time. Bloody disgraceful behavior. But for a *bald-headed bunny*, you did fine." Shawcross laughed at FB's discomfort at the reminder of Glenn's insults. He always enjoyed watching FB squirm.

FB wanted to justify his performance to the boss. "So unexpected. No security around. Big fellow. Boorish. Most unpleasant." His face relived the incident.

Shawcross ignored the comments. He was reaching for the Signing-In Book. "Don't go, FB."

"So you reckon he'll show?"

"Maybe, maybe not. He lost nearly half a mill. Mind you, he has bigger problems now with Creole Henry." He watched FB hovering uncertainly. "But he's not getting his money back."

He studied attendees for the 27th August. There had been forty-six members and guests in that day. He listened again to the tape of the exchange. "You lot was seen. Caught in the bleedin' act." He knew all the members and some of the guests. If Glenn had seen anything himself, he'd have turned a few tables over there and then, no mistake. Anyway, he didn't say he'd seen it. Just *you lot was seen*. Brannigan would have said something too. Unless he knew Glenn would trash the place. The two soap stars? Just froth. Forget them. Wouldn't have seen or understood anything. There was the baccarat crowd, the blackjack players, those two Triads who played roulette but always on the other table. It had to be someone who played roulette, someone who knew the game well. Someone who had taken the trouble to contact the soccer star. Someone convincing.

In the end, he had just six names. He tried to remember the evening. In most ways it had been like any other. One person made it stand out: TV journalist Tiffany Richmond. Her first visit. And with that tosser Dexter.

He phoned the cage. "How much did Scotty Brannigan win on 27th August?"

"He changed fifty thousand into chips and cashed out fifty-six thou, two hundred."

"Finlay Dexter?"

"Didn't play at all. Bought in for five thousand. Changed it back."

"I remember. He just watched."

"Cheeky bastard!"

"Tiffany Richmond. Did she play?"

"No trace."

"Asif Wasaz? Mushtaq Sehwag? Shohib Khan?"

"Changed six hundred grand each. None cashed in. All three, cleaned out." The cashier laughed before adding "as usual."

Shawcross thoughtfully put down the phone. The evening was flooding back. He thumped his fist into his other palm. That was the night I cut into their chat on the sofa.

He summoned Jeb Miller and Shift Manager Mark Ferrera to his room. "Mark: make sure the other Shift Managers are told. Keep Jimmy, One-Eye, Juan-Carlos and Andy away from Finlay Dexter. While he's at the table, make sure it's played straight. Otherwise, go for it as usual. Understood?"

"No problem but ..."

"You want to know if Dexter has spotted something. The answer is no. But I'm taking no chances."

FB intervened. "He's down there now. Tasty bit of crumpet with him."

"Tits like a roll-top desk." Miller added, rolling his eyes. "She's winning too. Roulette."

"Not that Tiffany Richmond woman?"

"No. Some Aussie bit called Jude Tuson."

"I'll be down later."

"You're playing like a wet fart." Jude glanced across at the small pile of chips in front of Dex. He was betting small, dabbling really. The owner of the gambling bookshop had suggested a modest staking system and though he was now winning it had been a grind. He felt like a tortoise in a casino full of hares. As she leaned forward to place her next bets, her breasts knocked the top chips from her own seven stacks of yellow chips – all winnings.

"Let's see who laughs last." Dex replied with a squeeze on her arm. "I've seen big stacks disappear. Why not cash in? You're over thirteen thousand up."

"Dream on Dex. Me? I'm going to make them wish they were still being breast-fed." She was expertly covering sections of the wheel. The ball seemed to follow her hunches. "Spin away, dealer. Get ready for a big payout."

"Nine, red, odd." Lee, a Singaporean dealer with a gentle manner, saw he had hit another winning number for her. "This is your night, okay."

"See, Dex. That's another five grand. Like I said earlier. Think like a winner. Play like a winner. Be a winner."

"Have you *ever* lost?"

"Same as my virginity. Just once, long ago and best forgotten. Nah! Losing's for wankers." Dex laughed as he watched the payout. Not once all evening had there been a sign of conjuring tricks by the dealers. But one thing had been odd. He had never got to play at a table with One-Eye or Andy. They were always quickly taken off.

He glanced round the room. Miller was supervising One-Eye two tables away. "I'll leave you here. I fancy a change of table. No point you moving."

"I'm stopping at a million," she called after him, ignoring the protocol of hushed tones and discretion.

Dex took a vacant chair at One-Eye's table. "Treat me kindly. Couldn't get going over there."

The Chinaman grinned. "You should know better, Mr Dexter. I'm only the messenger. The wheel has a mind of its own."

"You don't expect me to believe that? Coming from you, it sounds like Chinese junk."

One-Eye laughed but did not respond. A German stranger sitting next to Dex spoke up, his breath heavy with whisky. "So! If the wheel has its own mind, it must hate me!" He leaned towards Dex as if revealing his safe-deposit box number. "Listen to me. Don't play at this table. He's killing me. Go to any other table. Watch TV. So, for sure, I'm having the worst night of my life."

Dex grinned cheerfully. "Stop then."

The German wagged his finger, laughingly "*Nein, nein!* The next spin may be better." His small teeth emerged from a compact and rounded mouth, giving him a goldfish appearance. "I've been playing here for hours these last few days. I say each time, Gerhard: tonight will be better. It never is." He laughed in self-mockery and then shook his head slowly, drawing Dex' attention to his trimmed and thinning black hair that was plastered meticulously across his head like a member of the Adolf Hitler fan club. "My name is Gerhard Hoge - optimist."

"Got to be in this place, Gerhard. I'm Finlay Dexter. Dex. I'll keep you company."

The Englishman placed his bet on red, his single pink chip, his mind drifting to Scotty Brannigan. The American hadn't seemed a total shit. So why ignore an urgent message? It made no sense. He turned to study the German who was around fifty, corpulent and breathing heavily. The man's face was heavily lined with fleshy cheeks and tanned in a weathered way. Hoge would have looked good in a Tyrolean hat and *lederhosen* yodeling *The Lonely Goatherd*. He was betting tens of thousands and taking an age to place his chips. In front of him, he had a complex betting attack neatly typed out.

"More pages than Einstein's Theory of Relativity," suggested Dex. "Good system?" Dex tried to keep a straight face. "I mean occasionally you get ahead?"

"It's called *Infallible Techniques*. I bought it from a website. Five hundred euros to download." Dex had anticipated some sardonic German humor and was not disappointed. "It is infallible. I put out the chips and the dealer then takes them away. It never fails and better still, it has a pleasant symmetry." Again, there was a hearty laugh.

Dex joined in. "I admire your philosophy … and your English."

"I had a Jaguar dealership. I was often in Coventry for meetings. I retired seven years ago. Then I did some wheeling (he pronounced it *veeling*) and dealing to keep my brain working. I'm new to roulette, to all this. Now I'm hooked. I lose thousands. It is painful," he shrugged "but I'm happy."

"Gerhard," Dex saw that his own bet had won and retrieved his two pink chips, "if you like pain, I can give you a phone number. Blonde, a whip, handcuffs and thigh boots. Cheaper than losing to these bastards."

"Maybe later." The German grinned, his eyes disappearing behind the wrinkles, his jowls wobbling. Dex looked across at Jude where she was holding court. She loved being at the centre of things. He caught her eye and she waved, pointing to her mountains of chips. She half-stood, leaning across the baize to spread her chips. As he admired the leather tightly stretched across her buttocks, he realized he was not the only person taking in the pert *derrière*. Audley Shawcross had appeared and was standing, one hand in pocket, the other with a finger resting on the side of his face. His thoughts were plain to see as he switched positions to get a profile. After a pause, he went around the table to watch her full face.

Gerhard was holding his *Infallible Techniques* calculations close to his eyes to read while One-Eye yawned and looked at his fingernails. The yawn was infectious and Dex yawned too as he hummed a U2 number from their Joshua

Tree album. Suddenly, his humming stopped. Eureka! That's the answer! Gerhard's infallible system! It meant lots of scribbling. Ideal cover for using a pen incorporating a hidden camera

"Gerhard, I'd like to talk about your system. Maybe give it a try."

"You're crazier than you look. But for sure. We can talk at the bar. Let me finish losing first!" He returned to his notes and then placed more chips with Teutonic precision. Dex looked around the other tables. There were so many new faces, like Gerhard, none English. Good for business if they all lost like him. But who were they? All three blackjack tables were full. Both baccarat tables were open – unusual for mid-week, as were all the roulette wheels. The new players generally looked loaded too – expensive suits, tinted designer glasses, well-groomed hair and hand-stitched shoes. He took in several gold tie-pins and the invariably designer watches. It was nothing unusual for members to be wealthy but finding a rash of new players in a recession was remarkable. How had Shawcross attracted them?

He could hear Jude's raucous laugh and saw that Audley Shawcross had moved again and was now talking to her. She was giving him the treatment, talking, laughing, her head thrown back as Shawcross fed her a witticism. Maybe he then mentioned Dex. Whatever the reason, Jude seemed to sense he was watching her and she laughed as she looked across at him.

"You leaving, One-Eye?" Hoge sounded disappointed. The voice brought Dex back to the table.

"Change-over time," replied the dealer as he prepared to make way for his replacement. He spread his fingers wide open and turned his hands palms down and palms up – a requirement to prove to the cameras that he had not concealed any chips between his fingers. "Didn't think you'd miss me - not after what I've done to you."

"So, I wanted to win despite you."

"Fiona will look after you. See you later." The Glaswegian dealer was early thirties, tall, strong in features and with the bosom of an opera singer. Her low cut evening-dress was compensation enough for the loss of One-Eye and Hoge's narrow eyes responded behind his wrinkles with obvious pleasure. Seconds later Jeb Miller was replaced by an inspector that Dex had never before seen at the roulette. Usually, he was on blackjack. Was this all coincidence or are they being kept from me?

Fiona leaned over the wheel and with a strong flick sent the ball spinning. From behind him came the whoops as Jude noisily scooped up more winnings. He felt irritated that Shawcross was still chatting to her. "Thirty-six. Red. Even," said Fiona.

"So. Very agreeable. Thank you my dear. Do it again please." After his stiffly formal order, Hoge produced cigarettes from a deep yellow pack and offered one to Finlay, who declined.

"Optimism rewarded. Well done!"

Dex had also won and the dealer paid him out. He then watched Fiona count the staked chips that had almost hidden the number from view. She turned to the Inspector, a New Zealander with a bullet head and a gold tooth. "Seventy-three thousand?"

He looked at the confusion of splits, street and straight-up bets and shook his head. "No." There was no smile or softness in the inspector's response and no offer of help.

After a moment's fluster as her cheeks colored, Fiona smiled across the table. "Seventy-seven thousand. Sorry about that sir."

"Not at all, my dear. A repeat please. Then I will be nearly even. A triumph." Dex wondered how much One-Eye had stolen while Hoge had been alone at the table.

By four am, when Jude cashed in her win of just over twenty-seven thousand, not once despite his efforts, had Dex played with One-Eye, Andy or Jimmy for longer than one spin. But he'd had an interesting twenty minutes in the bar. Gerhard had won nearly two hundred thousand while Fiona was dealing and was bubbling at his first ever win. The *Infallible Techniques* system Hoge had bought was called *Labouchère*, a formula involving placing bigger and bigger bets to win back losses. Dex politely took down the details and promised to try it though he knew that too often it was ruinous, so different from the less fashionable *Reverse Labouchère* explained by Walter McKay while tucking into his Bradan Orach. There were things to do: chase up Panama *and* study *Reverse Labouchère*. Dex accepted FB's offer of a limo as Jude chortled about her win. "How much are you ahead?" Jude asked.

"Three hundred and seventy five pounds."

"Pathetic. You gotta go for it. Like me. You're like a pensioner playing dominoes."

175

"I know." For a second, he nearly told her he'd won and lost over a million. He was glad he resisted.

"That Audley guy is a real sweetie. Makes me laugh. Turns me on too. "

"I noticed."

London – 5th September 2002

At his mock-Georgian home in a cul-de-sac just off The Bishops Avenue in north London, Mick Glenn answered the phone and turned down the volume on the sound system. Bob Marley's *One Love* had been booming in every room, upstairs and down. Heralded as Millionaire's Row, this undulating district was known for flash money, entrepreneurs, Greek shipping magnates, Indian accountants and company directors from the rag trade. Every home was gated. High walls and wrought-iron fences lined the boundaries. The large gardens, some of them running to three or more acres, gave privacy from neighbors and the public. In the garages might be six or more cars, a power-boat and a large Harley-Davidson or two. Costing him just under four million, complete with clock tower over the stables, Mick reckoned he had a bargain. *Get an 'orse one day*, he'd told himself several times. A black BMW cruised slowly past the gates and turned round.

"Not doing' so good then Scotty?"

"Too right! Testin' in Barcelona was jus' the usual shit. Good to be back in Monaco, look at the sea, visit the casino." Scotty spoke without enthusiasm.

Glenn thought how distracted his friend sounded - his voice seemed listless, full of weary resignation. "Then Monza?"

"Sure, I'll drive there. But heh – this Creole guy. You gonna be okay? He looks meaner than a cross-eyed coyote. How's it been, bud?"

"Yeah. Been a rough ol' time an' all. Me Mum in tears, me old man getting' the piss extracted at work. The photographers have gone now. Fair got on me tits, they did, waitin' outside me gates. I ain't heard from this Creole Henry geezer though. Sharon said he was still spittin' mad and to watch out." He patted his gleaming head. "She's leavin' him. That's got right up his nose an' no mistake."

"I guess he'll forget real soon. Plenty more Sharons around for a Yardie boss." Scotty sounded less convincing than the words. "I read you crapped out against Chelsea too. Missed three open goals."

"Nah, mate. They was not *that* easy. Get the bleedin' press on you and they make a drama, linkin' it with Sharon and the roolly. It's ass-kicking season on Mick. But it'll pass. If I do well this Saturday up at Newcastle, I'll be the hero again."

"Gotta go, Mick. See and take care. Watch out for that fella with the dreadlocks. Life's cheap. Believe me. I know." It sounded as if Scotty was going to add something but then he just closed. "Be lucky."

He turned up the volume and stripped off, his chest a mass of black hair, his muscles mean and hard from his keep-fit routines. His body was tanned all over from his sun-lamps. He looked what he was, an athlete in peak condition. Just time for fifty laps before going to see that bastard Shawcross he told himself as, surrounded by Grecian statues, he dived into the pool, Bob Marley still thudding all around.

Let's get together and feel all right.

Let them all pass all their dirty remarks, One Love.

It was early evening as Dex joined Gerhard Hoge and his friend Jacques Crabant in the bar. Jude had gone to play blackjack before dinner. For the third night, Jude had taken time off. Once more Liz was standing in and welcoming the money. Only a few minutes later though, the Australian had reappeared with Audley Shawcross and they sat on the bar stools, deep in conversation. She saw Dex and waved but made no attempt to join him. For the next twenty minutes, he chatted and listened to Crabant, a Breton who had taken early retirement from the European Commission in Brussels. In the lively way he told it, he had grown bored and wanted to have fun traveling and spending a recent inheritance. Casinos were a novelty.

"See you again," Dex said as he saw them leave for dinner at Le Caprice. As they climbed the stairs, both puffing with exertion, his phone vibrated. It had been a bad line but the American's familiar voice was instantly recognizable. Dex raced up to the street where he could not be overheard and reception was better. For about five minutes, he did more listening and less talking than he had expected. "Thanks. See you soon." He turned abruptly away from Dukes and with angry strides, set off for Berkeley Square. He was still seething, his knuckles clenched when he had finished a circuit and was heading back to Mount Street. *Bitch!*

Back in the bar, he could see Jude was still playing Shawcross like a trout, gripping his arm, laughing in an exaggerated fashion at his every remark.

"Audley says I can join Dukes," said Jude as soon as he approached.

"*Mr* Shawcross talked you into it?" He glanced at the boss who was the picture of unhurried calm, one slender leg swinging, the other foot tipped up against the bar. Jude had been shopping in Davies Street and looked seductive in her heavily patterned silk chiffon tank top with simple skirt. Her large gold earrings hung heavily beneath the striking hair, the muted lights barely doing them justice.

"Nah, mate. I talked *him* into it." She grinned across at Shawcross who preened his slicked back hair, sucked in his cheeks and smiled like a schoolboy with a trophy.

"We like her play," he said as if Dex deserved an explanation.

Shawcross' pointed stare did not impress Dex, who judged foreplay was more on his mind. "Real risk-taker isn't she," Dex observed. "Unlike me. So, *darling*, shall we eat? It's nearly ten." He liked the way he had emphasized *darling*, though *bitch* was the word still uppermost.

"Eat like starving dingoes. Slosh back some vintage red stuff and then bankrupt the place." She grinned at Shawcross whose eyes froze at the word *bankrupt* before urbanity returned. "Enjoy your dinner both of you. And good luck at the tables."

Dex had thought freebie meals at Dukes were history but with his guest playing like a whale, the generosity continued. He offered a hand to ease Jude off her stool and ushered her to the wood-paneled dining-room, all white table linen and candelabras with blue candles to match the carpet. On the way, they passed FB talking to two thugs in dinner-jackets who were unsuccessfully trying to look like gentlemen. He wondered what they were doing.

When they reached their table, he felt an icy calm, his inner fury controlled, his action plan coming together. He politely held her chair as she sat down and let her take the lead in choosing the wine, a great burgundy. Culminating in the call from Scotty, everything had come together in just two hours. By comparison, her flirting with Shawcross was only an irritation.

As darkness fell over north London, the last of the starlings' chatter died. The trees swayed gently in the evening breeze. Just before ten with all quiet, Mick Glenn locked the front door. He was wearing a black shirt with a black jacket and red and white striped tie. Eager to get to the confrontation with Shawcross, he almost bounded across the gravel to his car. That he had little idea who had seen any cheating or the details did not trouble him at all.

He settled into the bucket seat of his Arsenal red Porsche 911 Carrara and fired the engine. He saw the reminder on the passenger seat that in the morning he had to visit a kid with leukaemia. Elton John's *Crocodile Rock* resonated from six speakers. Sixty yards away out of sight down the curved bush-lined drive were the large security gates and he pressed the zapper to have them open by the time he reached them. He hoped for a quick and easy confrontation with Shawcross as he had to be

With a scuffing of gravel, he moved off and rounded the bend in the sweeping drive. As the gates appeared, he realized they were blocked by a car without lights that was driving in. Then suddenly, the other car's headlights split the night, blinding him. He slammed on the brakes, gravel flying in all directions. He opened the door and climbed out, right arm gesticulating towards the other vehicle. "What the fuck you doin' comin' in 'ere?" Glenn's rasping voice rose above the purr from the two motionless cars. "Clear off, you snooping bastards. Bloody journalists." He had almost reached the other car when from the black shadows of the trees and bushes to his right, he heard movement. A knee slammed into his back and an arm gripped him around his throat. He felt himself being pulled backwards until his left leg was pressed against the car. He tried to shout but only a strangulated grunt emerged as he felt something cold and hard pressed against the right side of his head, behind the ear. A single shot from the 9mm Beretta was enough. Glenn slumped to the ground near the headlights. The intruder glanced into the car for a second occupant and then with a gloved hand switched off the lights and engine. A second later he ran to the gate. With inches in it, the car and the pedestrian beat the clang as the wrought-iron gates clamped shut. Within ninety seconds their stolen BMW was cruising in the traffic heading north on the busy Finchley Road.

Eyes still wild with anger, Jude pushed back from the remains of her dinner,. She stood up, pulled in her buttocks and rolled out the full majesty of her breasts. "And Dex - I suggest you go boil your prick."

Dex was not surprised or concerned that she wasn't coming back tonight. "Pick up your things sometime or I'll send them to Oxfam."

"Too bloody right I will." Then she was gone. He watched her swivelling hips as she stormed from the restaurant, head held high, steps short and brisk. The earlier anger had been replaced by pleasure and he poured himself a glass of the Chateau Cheval Blanc. The showdown and noisy parting had been inevitable and unlike the fracas in Julie's, it had been just the outcome he wanted. Dex silently toasted Shawcross for the magnificent wine as he ordered cheese while he mulled over the evening. "I've decided to send father to the Kemsway," was how he had opened the discussion.

"Oh? Why?" Jude frowned and instantly stopped eating her veal cutlet. She laid down her cutlery and looked at him with venom from across the table.

"Because I think he'll do better there."

She snapped back. "You're wrong, ask anyone."

"I didn't ask just anyone, I asked Liz – just as you said."

"You didn't tell me."

"No reason, not until now. I phoned her while you were lapping up attention from your good friend Audley."

"Jealous are you? You should be. And Liz?" She picked up her crystal glass in a fierce movement and held it near the rim. Clenched in her large hand, it reminded Dex of how a baboon would clutch a banana.

"Liz is getting some response from father. I've been trying a one blink, two blink routine. I wasn't sure whether I was dreaming a response. Liz is positive."

Jude chopped her hand across the table dismissively. "Nah! Dream on! Wishful thinking."

"No. You don't work hard enough with him to make progress."

She leaned across the table, her voice low and defiant. Her nostrils were flared, her teeth bared. "I spend hours sitting with him, reading, talking, trying to stimulate him – that's unless I'm in bed with my boss. What do you mean not work hard enough?"

"Well," Dex tried to keep his excitement from showing, "how about last weekend, while I was over in Spa? Saturday evening and Sunday?"

Her eyes narrowed. "Saturday? Sunday? What do you mean? Typical days. In one end and out the other. TV on, reading to him, you know – the full works. Even tried him on the Rolling Stones, like I said. You said he hated rock music. Trying to get a response. Result – not a flicker, not a sign of recognition."

"All day Sunday?"

"Too right, mate – all day."

"So how do you explain this?" Dex fumbled in his jacket pocket and produced a crumpled receipt from the Outback Retreat on Earl's Court Road. "See. Sunday 1ˢᵗ September. You paid for a meal for two at 2230"

"What the ...? How did you get that? Snooping in my room?"

"I'm asking the questions. Who was looking after father?"

Jude looked evasive.

"You left him alone didn't you?"

"I fixed for Liz to come in. I needed a break."

Dex' eyebrows rose. "Liz? That's a poor lie."

"Liz was there. I swear."

"You left him alone."

"Ask Liz."

"I did. She was at the Royal Free Hospital."

"That's it then, if you don't trust me."

"Why should I trust you? You cheated me, lied to me, abandoned father for hours."

"Nah, Dex. Not hours. Just a quick meal out. He was fine anyway. Never missed me, nor will he ever miss anyone."

"So what time did you go out?"

"About nine until eleven. He was asleep when I left."

"So why didn't you answer the phone at just gone seven?"

"I didn't hear it."

"Cut the crap, Jude. You're lying again. If you didn't hear, then the voice-mail would have kicked in. It didn't." Dex looked her straight in the eye and saw again into the soul of the woman with whom he'd shared his most intense ever orgasm. Now it counted for nothing. "You switched it off while you went out, thought *that* a lesser risk than leaving it on." He saw that she was cornered and was not prepared to listen to much more. "When I got back, I was puzzled that the phone-clock was over five hours slow." Dex paused, anxious to pick his words carefully. *Mustn't mention Brannigan's name in here, not with the tables bugged.* "A friend of mine phoned at around seven pm. Said there was no answer, no voice-mail." He swirled the deep red claret and sniffed appreciatively. "Jude - our relationship, business and personal is over. I'm firing you now without notice but you can spend the night back at Porky if you want."

"I'll sue. I'm not taking this shit from you. I'll consult a solicitor in the morning."

"See you in court." He saw her wipe her mouth and could see what was about to happen. "Jude, just calm down. Accept you're a cheat and a liar and find another job."

"And Dex - I suggest you go boil your prick."

Dex spread some ripe camembert onto his Bath Oliver and thought about her parting words. *Boiling his prick* did not seem like a sensible option. He looked at the receipt that he had found this evening, screwed up on her bedroom floor. He had been shocked but it had prompted him belatedly to speak to Liz, something he knew he had stupidly postponed. She had been most helpful but the call from Scotty had been the clincher. The American had sounded apologetic for not getting in touch, explaining he'd been busier'n a bee in a field of clover, before adding that he had tried the London number on Sunday evening.

Dex wiped his mouth and looked forward to the morning flight to Nice and the meeting now fixed with Scotty in Monaco. He poured a coffee and wondered whether Jude was already fawning around Shawcross. No matter. He thought of Tiffany and was unsure how guilty he felt. The flowers he had sent two days before? Had that been guilt or an attempt to build a bridge? Whatever, her emailed response about wanting to talk had been an improvement on her cool hands-off attitude. He debated whether she was softening or perhaps jealous at the news that Jude had been living in.

The cheese had gone, every Bath Oliver finished. The cherry brandy chocolates lay untouched. He put Scotty's Monaco address into his pocket and pushed back his chair.

Upstairs, Shawcross had been busy with paperwork. In the background, a CD of the light jazzy tones of Diana Krall was soothing. The speaker on the desk had been delivering every word from Dexter's table. His most wolfish look had lingered after Jude had stormed out, telling him to *boil his prick*. Every word had been music to him. Jude was now unemployed. She was as hot as hell and best of all, a thoroughly devious and dishonest little vixen. Just what he had been looking for to supplement Claire now that *Snowball* was coming on-stream. There might even be a bonus of learning what Dex had said to her during pillow talk. The phone rang.

"Yes, FB?" He listened to the report. "Glenn's a no-show? It's no real surprise. All talk! Yes, you can stand them down." He decided it was time to chat to Jude.

Dex thanked the maitre'd and walked purposively into the crowded gaming room. He wanted to find FB. At the roulette table, he saw Jude rolling a green chip between her fingers but FB was not there, nor in the bar. Dex walked through the flower-filled reception area to the men's room. The two bruisers that he had noticed earlier at the foot of the stairs had gone. He opened the door to the men's room and heard earthy London voices, so he hovered unseen.

"Easy money then. A no-show. FB said don't hang about. Mick was due by midnight latest, he said. What you say we go down Soho. Taste a bit of action."

"Yeah! Pity though. I was hoping to land one on him."

There was a laugh. "Typical Spurs supporter. Anything to get at Arsenal."

Dex had heard enough. He banged the door as if he had just arrived and breezed in. The two security men were about to leave the urinals. "Evening." With a nod, the men acknowledged him and were gone. As he washed his hands, he knew now that Mick had been expected. But had he named Dex already? Was that why he could never get near One-Eye, Andy or Miller's tables? Pensively, he returned to the gaming-room and watched some Japanese playing baccarat before deliberately sitting at a roulette table where One-Eye was the dealer. One spin later, the dealer was gone. "My break," he murmured as he handed over to Gordon, a Mancunian with a broad accent.

FB appeared and started chatting to Gerhard Hoge, so Dex went to join them.

"Gerhard. How's it going?"

"So I am losing. But I am happy Dex. For sure, it's fun here."

"Think how much happier you'd be if you won more often."

Gerhard looked perplexed as if winning was still an alien concept.

"We like to keep our members happy," prompted Forster-Brown.

"That reminds me." Dex improvised. "I expected to get match tickets from Mick Glenn tonight. Has he been in?"

FB looked away and spoke as if each word was a wisdom tooth being extracted. "Sorry but I can't help. Did he say what time he'd see you?"

"No. I assumed before midnight."

FB shrugged as if he had no information to volunteer. "Need a limo tonight?"

"Thanks. A ride home would be helpful." Dex tried to catch FB's eyes without success. "Amazing how busy you've become recently. Considering 9-11, the economy, and the recession everywhere."

"I'm surprised myself," FB volunteered. "But Mr Shawcross says when times are tough, people drink more, play harder. With the favorable British gaming laws and our gourmet restaurant, there's nowhere better than here. Don't you agree Mr Hoge?"

"For sure. This is a great place. So friendly. So international. I've made many new friends. Dex, we must eat one evening – perhaps with Jacques Crabant. He didn't bother to come back after dinner."

Dex studied the dumpy figure of the German. "Does he enjoy losing too?" He checked the time. "I'm having a swift drink. Care to join me?"

"Thanks but I want to play. I'm feeling lucky." Hoge's body rocked with laughter and even FB smiled politely but Dex' mind was already elsewhere as he had seen Jude strut into the bar. After watching One-Eye pay out after several spins with no sign of cheating, he headed into the bar. She was sitting on a sofa in the back corner beside Shawcross who was handing something to her. It was like looking at a stranger and seemed unbelievable they had shared so many hours in bed.

As he approached, Jude saw him and hurriedly slipped something, Shawcross' address and private phone details no doubt, into her handbag. Shawcross rapidly removed his hand from her knee. "FB's fixing me a limo, Jude. Want a lift back to St John's Wood? Or can I get you dropped off somewhere?" He was rewarded with a piss-off look but it had been fun asking. He turned to her companion. "How was Las Vegas? Space City?"

Shawcross stroked his cheek and laughed, an unfunny and nervous sound. *Yes- definitely giving her an address or phone number.* "Vegas? Hot. Building work's going well. Can't wait for December. I was just saying to Ju..., er Miss Tuson, we may be able to invite you over to the grand opening. Space City will invite about forty of our members from here."

Dex didn't believe a word. "Let me know. So your cash flow's okay then? I was reading the FT this morning. Pretty bearish article about London casinos."

Shawcross' eyes disappeared before reappearing with a ring of confidence smile. "Don't believe journalists. Look around. Business is fine."

Dex braced himself and plunged in. "Did you see Mick Glenn tonight? He promised to give me some tickets for the Manchester United game."

Shawcross pulled a cigar from his pocket. "No. Mr Glenn hasn't been around for some while – not since the night you were here with, er, another guest. Keeping a low profile after that muck in the papers, I expect." Dex noted that Shawcross could recall the very night he and Glenn had been in together and the failure to acknowledge that he had been expected tonight.

 "I was saying to FB. Those two thugs in bow ties you had on earlier. Made me uncomfortable just to look at them. What was that all about?"

"Sorry?" Shawcross fumbled for words and for a match.

"Those guys like night-club bouncers."

Shawcross recovered his poise. "Oh! Them? You must have seen them before, surely. We often hire in extra security - when money is being delivered or when someone very special is visiting. We had the Sultan in earlier."

Dex saw the eyes telling a different truth. "Ah! FB's signaling. Sure I can't drop you off anywhere, *darling?*"

"I'm staying," Jude snapped, eyes glaring at him.

He had taken a few steps when on impulse he turned back and leaned down to Shawcross who looked confused. "A word of warning." Dex drew even closer to whisper. "She farts in bed." Then before Shawcross had time to react, Dex had swiftly moved away. Moments later, he settled into the dark brown leather of the Bentley Turbo, registration Dukes 1. "Hillside Road. Up in St John's Wood, please." As he reclined in the comfort, he was exhilarated that the past few hours had seen so much fall into place. But he still only had more questions than answers.

"I'm hungry. Barely ate any dinner tonight. Due to that tosser." Jude nodded towards the door. Audley Shawcross summoned the barman and ordered Bollinger champagne and prawn sandwiches. With Dexter gone, he could continue on his mission uninterrupted. He moved closer to her, slightly uneasy about the drift of Dex' comments.

She brushed her hair against his cheeks, too embarrassingly close for discretion, even though the bar was deserted. "Like my perfume? Vera Wang."

His smile was delivered beneath eyes that had softened. "Tantalizing, Jude. It suits you. You look wonderful too. So, to continue from before the interruption, I guess you're not working for Dexter tomorrow."

"I'm out of work. No home. I gave notice on my room in Earl's Court. A friend from Melbourne's storing my stuff in her place. The rest - I'll have to collect from St John's Wood sometime."

"I just might have an ideal job for you. We can't discuss it here. I've already spent too long with you. I don't want gossip flying. Finish the sandwiches and enjoy the champagne. I must glad-hand a few of the new members. Maybe half an hour or so. Fancy a drink back at my place? You can sleep over if you want. Sounds as if you've nowhere else."

"Gee thanks, Aude. Thought you'd never ask!"

"You have the address." He gave her the keys, a surreptitious movement under the table that took overlong as their hands touched. "We can't leave together, you understand. Take a cab, not one of our limos. Don't give my address in front of the doorman. Fraternizing with the members is not allowed."

"Fraternizing? That's a long word for a fuck isn't it?"

Back in Porcupine House, Dex booked a flight to Nice on the web and then prowled round, unable to settle. Liz had agreed to stay for a couple of days while he sorted out the Kemsway. He looked in on his father who appeared neither awake nor asleep. "You poor old sod," he muttered as he crouched close to wipe away some dripping mucus that was staining the pillow. "But you're going to a far better place as a priest would say. And don't think I'm just dumping you. I want only the best. And I'll visit you – often. Believe me. Let's get that one-blink, two-blinks system really working, eh?" He turned to leave. "Sorry about Jude. My fault. Too captivated by her charisma rather than her credentials. But you'd understand that, wouldn't you, you randy old goat?" He cast a last look at the frail left-overs of the former Lothario figure. It was pitiful and hard to take. Back in the kitchen, he sipped a coffee and flicked through the TV channels until he found MTV. A young black singer in orange hot-pants was gyrating herself into a state of ecstasy, so he watched in a semi-detached way, the sound kept low.

He was convinced there was something odd about Mick Glenn and the no-show. He checked the footballer's address and grabbed for his A to Z map. He turned to page 28. Mick's home was no distance. Impulsively, he decided to go there even though it was nearly two. So what? He felt alert, all pumped up by the rush of action. Anyway, as his mother had always said *knowledge is power.*

With the roads nearly empty, he reached The Bishop's Avenue in just over ten minutes, passing through the leafy open spaces of Hampstead with its charming grand houses looking out over the Heath. The wide tree-lined Avenue was deserted, the houses, some unseen beyond large gardens had floodlit drives. He found the cul-de-sac where Glenn lived and turned in and quickly reached the turnaround at the end. On the right, he had seen Score House, or at least the house name beside a pair of high and heavy gates. He pulled up.

Outside the car, he stretched, relishing the night air. The fragrance of damp firs, pine and newly cut lawns filled his nostrils. Though still very much London, the night air told a different story, the firs reminding him of the fragrance of Kielder Forest in Northumberland. Somewhere, an owl screeched but otherwise everything was quiet. He paused for a moment, wondering what in hell he was doing here in the middle of the night. If a patrolling police car chanced to pass, it would take some explaining. He walked along the unmade path beside the road until he reached the gates. When manufactured, they had been wrought-iron, painted black and designed around an equestrian motif. But someone, Mick Glenn perhaps, had then added two large steel plates on the inner side so that gawpers could not see inside.

Dex moved closer. He grabbed the gates and pressed his eye to the one-inch crack between the two halves. Inside, there was no security lighting. As his eyes grew accustomed to the shapes beyond the gate, he saw the silhouette of a car parked just a few yards away, its outline obscured by the towering trees and the dense mass of rhododendron bushes. There was no noise from the house, no evidence of a wild party. He was barely there ninety seconds before he was back in car, wondering what power his new knowledge had given him.

French Riviera - 6th September 2002

At shortly after seven a tall figure waited in cap and navy overalls by the car park entrance to *Aristide Bleu*, Scotty Brannigan's apartment block. The narrow residential streets of Monaco were still quiet. The day had barely started for most of the residents. He had circled the building, vetoed the front entrance deciding that the best access was through the underground car park. The security camera was geared to checking arriving vehicles, not pedestrians. He stood behind a concrete pillar, just outside the metal grille, as he waited for his chance.

Within less than two minutes, he heard grating and grinding. An emerging motorist had activated the chain-link barrier which rose to the ceiling. A silver Lexus coupé appeared and with a touch of the accelerator was gone. In a trice, he had edged sideways, back pressed against the white stucco and ducked under the closing grille. Earlier, over a croissant down beside the port, he had studied his sheaf of papers. He would recognize the driver anywhere - those distinctively large sideburns, the lack of height and mop of sandy hair. Now as he stood in the gloomy light of the basement, he started to remember other details. At a glance there were around thirty vehicles, each in a reserved spot. Brannigan owned the penthouse on the 18th floor.

He looked at the black Renault Clio with custom alterations parked in Brannigan's spot. Precisely as he had read in F1 magazine. "I love my motorbike and my Clio," Scotty had been quoted. The intruder debated whether to take him out upstairs or beside the car. Eighteen floors up was less appealing and so he looked around, wondering how to plan the attack.

There was a lift with a camera watching the door. There was also a door-less emergency exit leading to bare concrete stairs. Then he saw a grimy black door built into the wall. It housed the fire hose, spooled on a large drum and an extinguisher clamped to the wall. Other than a squashed beer can, there was nothing else in the small space. He stepped inside, pulled the door closed leaving a crack just big enough to see the driver's side door of the Renault. When Brannigan entered, he would have his back to him.

He settled, hoping it would not be a long wait. From his pocket, he produced his Ruger Mk II pistol, ideal for an internal job like this. With an integrated silencer, it was compact, accurate and its .22 bullets deadly at close range.

Once Brannigan's back was towards him, a couple of steps in his rubber-soled shoes and it would be nearly point-blank. He laid the gun on top of the hose, close to his right hand and ready for immediate use.

From another pocket, he produced a pack of brie and salami sandwiches that he had picked up at a pull-in on the A8. Carefully, he opened the perspex pack and munched steadily before returning the waste to his front pocket. He leaned against the wall, occasionally grabbing the Ruger whenever someone appeared from the lift. Every arrival was a false alarm and he stayed concealed but alert and watchful. By eleven–thirty, he was aching from standing still for so long. He stretched as far as he was able and did some exercises, rocking from toe to heel to keep his circulation moving. Another pack of sandwiches would be welcome, along with some black and piping hot French coffee.

The lift door opened.

He saw Brannigan, unmistakable even in the light from the dusty bulbs fixed to the ceiling. He picked up the gun in his gloved hand.

"I'm off to lunch up in the hills."

The gunman looked again and realized that Brannigan was not alone. An older man, probably over fifty, had emerged from the lift behind him. "Enjoy yourself Scotty but what about an early evening snifter. The casino bar?"

"Great idea, Gerry but I'm meeting a friend back here at six. I guess we might eat out somewhere later and hit the tables afterwards. Could catch up with you then."

The older man stood beside Brannigan as he clambered intro the Renault. "Sounds good. I'll be at the baccarat pit. Enjoy your lunch. Someone interesting I expect."

The gunman heard Brannigan's laugh as he closed the car door and the engine was fired into life and with a sharp turn was gone.

The gunman swore silently as he watched Gerry follow in his Citroen. He debated what to do. Stay put or come back after lunch? Brannigan would be gone for hours. Do I wait on the eighteenth floor? Leaving the block and trying to sneak in again was pretty damned risky. Unacceptable. Staying put was grim but had the advantage that Brannigan would return here. But sod's law dictated that Brannigan again might not be alone. Reluctantly, he decided to look upstairs and climbed the emergency stairwell. He checked the ground floor and then the second and third levels. It was unpromising. Except at front-entrance level, entering the residential areas from the wrong side of the emergency doors was impossible. Only someone on the other side could open them. He returned to the basement. There, he studied the camera by the lift. Fixed to the wall just above head height, it looked well-angled but was on a swivel. Carefully, he pushed from beneath. A slight but valuable shift was the reward. The bottom three feet of the door were now out of shot. He crouched down as he entered the lift and quickly pressed the button marked PH.

After a swift ride, he emerged into a light airy foyer, from which there were only two doors – one into Brannigan's two-level home, the other the emergency stairwell. As the lift descended, he assessed the area. The tiles were red and black. There was a simple ebony side table. On it stood a bronze ornament of a naked lady on a plinth. There was nowhere to hide except behind the door to the emergency stairs. He pressed the pewter handle on the door and it opened giving onto the barren grey stonework of a feature designed never to be used. He jammed the door open with his hankie, knowing that once closed, there was no way back inside. He had a fair view of Brannigan's light oak door with its spyglass at eye-level but better still, he could get a shot in perfectly as the driver exited the lift - easy with his Ruger at around fifteen feet. The escape routes were okay – the lift if essential or the stairs to the basement. He sat down on the cold hard floor and turned up his nose at the smell of something dead rising from below him. His stomach growled and he wished he had stocked up better. It would be a long wait. Perhaps a lost waiter would drop by with a rare steak and French fries.

The French Riviera – 6th September 2002

As the Airbus carrying Dex circled low and easterly over the azure of the Mediterranean on its final approach to Nice, Scotty Brannigan was gunning his high-performance car towards a rendezvous with Estelle, a fashion consultant from Cannes that he had met the previous evening. The black Renault Clio made light of the steep climb from Monaco. Scotty Brannigan enjoyed driving something small, zippy, anonymous and suited to the crowded narrow streets of Monte Carlo. He fingered the wheel impatiently, anxious to make the lunch meeting on the shady terrace at *La Tuile Rouge*. His favorite restaurant was up in the hills behind the coast. He had also booked his preferred suite for a siesta *à deux*, plenty of time to be back for his meeting at six.

This first date had followed a meeting of eyes in the casino. Estelle was taller than him but not much, a blonde with a sharp nose, strong chin, pencil slim and had been expensively dressed in a lemon cord trouser-suit. He had seen her watching him at the table and she had accepted his offer of a seat and a drink.

"You should have a rear-view mirror," she had suggested later when yet again, he had glanced around the gaming room as if looking for someone.

"Cool idea, honey. What shall I fix it to?" His wink had suggested the answer and created a flirty atmosphere even before they had crossed the road to the Hotel de Paris for a quieter location. He was captivated by her delicate skin, tanned and without make-up. He loved her style – expensive bracelets on her wrists and a magnificent gold necklace with a teardrop charm on her creamy neckline. It swayed when she talked. Hanging just above her small breasts, he found it hypnotic.

She noticed that in the new bar, he made a point of sitting in a corner, back to the walls. "No need to use the mirror here," she joked. "There's no Michael Schumacher about to overtake."

"As if he could." Still laughing, he ordered Pimms. Since a swapping party organized by a Tory grandee at a Cotswolds manor earlier in the year, he'd taken to the taste, though until then he had been alcohol-free for seven years, sinking enough Diet Cokes to dream of them. He knew he had to resist the urge to drink. It was so pleasurable, that hazy alcoholic escapism. If some wine with Estelle over lunch kept visions of Nanda Datt at bay, it would be worth it.

He flicked down a gear and accelerated past a Mercedes as if it were not there. Now, as he deftly crossed lanes onto the A8 and swept towards the Viaduc de la Nuec, his face glowed with excitement. He always felt this way when embarking on a new seduction. He wondered what she would wear – something simple but absurdly expensive from a boutique on the Croisette no doubt.

Perhaps a bare midriff, bronzed and flat as a pond.

And not much underneath either.

Mmmh!

The speedometer showed one hundred and fifty kilometers as he switched on his CD player and a Bryan Adams concert thumped and thundered all around. The Nanda Datt fatwa hanging over him added to the poignancy of the new relationship and his fingers drummed to the beat. Perhaps Datt's threat added to the urgency too. He anticipated the planned seduction with confidence. The place never failed him. *La Tuile Rouge* held fond memories, especially the chosen suite. The views beyond the terrace were of rolling hills littered with olive trees, lavender – lilac, blues and reds and the deep green of the distant firs. Yet no thoughts however erotic or pleasing could remove today's shadow of Nanda Datt. He would have to have a glass of red with the rare beef.

As he sped west, through the tunnels and over the soaring bridges at 90 mph, his eyes were constantly flicking between the three mirrors, suspicious of every car in the fast lane. He'd driven about fourteen miles when he saw the time. Twelve noon. He silenced the CD and flicked on Europe One for the news. Though his French made no attempt at the accent, his understanding was perfect. Scotty listened to the reports of rising tension in the Middle East and talk of a dock strike in Calais. Then he heard it, translating verbatim to himself. "The Arsenal and England footballer Mick Glenn was found dead this morning outside his home in North London. A police spokesman said he had been murdered some time yesterday evening. His car was close by. The police are looking for a motorcyclist who was seen parked in the area mid-evening.

"Mick Glenn had been named recently as involved with the girlfriend of reputed Yardie gangster Creole Henry. The police spokesman refused to speculate on motive. This death follows the murder in Germany of Wolfgang Schimmelsohn the Bundesliga player. That murder remains unresolved but police there have been working on a theory of match-fixing. Of that, there is no positive evidence."

Creole got him then.

Holy cow!

Though maybe not Creole.

Surely not Nanda Datt?

Had Mick been match-fixing like the German?

Those three goals?

He found he'd covered several miles debating who had killed his friend. He drove like an automaton, remembering nothing of the journey– just like the San Marino Grand Prix 1994. Then he'd been in fourth place approaching the sweep of the Tamburello Curve on the fifth lap. Beside the track was the wreck of a Williams-Rothmans, barely recognizable. No sign of life. Still grieving for Roland Ratzenberger killed in qualifying the day before, the unthinkable seemed to have happened again. Scotty recalled forcing himself to drive beyond the edge, defying the suddenness of death.

Next time round, there was still no sign of Ayrton Senna – just the ambulance crew struggling by the cockpit. Still trapped and not moving was his friend and the greatest driver of all time. The rest of the fifty-six laps were a battle between wanting to cry out for his Mom; to park up and then run for the hills or to show an iron-balled determination saying *fuck'em all, I'm going to go faster than ever.*

That's what he had done. Like the other drivers. Balls out for glory. Ayrton, the King, is dead. Long live Grand Prix racing.

As the Renault hugged the twisting road into the hills, Scotty recalled his last warning to Mick .

The prospect of Estelle in bed suddenly seemed unappealing. "Hell, after this, I couldn't get an erection with a truckload of Viagra," he told himself. But if this were Nanda's doing, then I'm in deep shit. Hey! You can't hide for ever, buddy. Only bin Laden can't be found. There'll be the funeral, the sponsors' events at Imola. You can't become a hermit because of that Malaysian bastard.

London – 6th September 2002

Audley Shawcross was enjoying his usual late breakfast.

Same place, same food, different woman.

Just the way I like it.

In an alcove by the casement window of his maisonette looking across to Holland Park, he and Jude sat almost side by side. The leaves had started to fall and winter's premature grip was in the air. Black clouds scudded above the trees. Rain was imminent and likely to last. In the background, Kilroy was burbling on the TV. Shawcross was still in a white toweling dressing-gown with a Beverly Hills motif. Unusually, his sleek black hair was tousled and he had not yet shaved, making him appear swarthier than usual, his Latin blood showing through.

Jude, looking more than her age without any make-up and too little sleep, had made herself comfortable in his home which was a cross between an art gallery and a museum. As he read the Financial Times, she had quickly put together his request of grapefruit juice, scrambled eggs, brown toast, chunky marmalade and coffee. The marmalade was from Fortnums, the coffee from Costa Rica.

"Interested in antiques?" he enquired.

"Besides you, nah, not my style."

He laughed but then looked disappointed. "I bought this cutlery last week. Do you like it?"

She picked up the heavy spoon and knife. "Yeah, it's fine. But then to me a spoon is a spoon."

He picked up the knife to show to her. "This is nearly two hundred years old. King's Pattern Flatware. Made by William Traies probably around 1828. Solid silver – well as solid as any silverware – around ninety-two percent. If it were one hundred percent, it would simply bend without Yuri Geller going near it. I found it at the Chancery Lane Silver Vaults. That's the largest collection of dealers in fine silver in the world."

"I didn't know that. Bet it cost you."

"It did but the pleasure of using it outweighs any expense. Maybe we could go down there. I saw a beautiful Mantel Clock. Over one hundred years old. Made by the Goldsmiths and Silversmiths Company. I would have bought it on the spot but, well," he paused with perfect stage management "last week, there was nobody special in my life. I have a passion for clocks and couldn't really justify it for myself. Look around. I have so many." He reached across to kiss her lightly on the lips. I hope I'm not being too pushy or reading more into last night than I should but I sense, a certain magic, a *frisson* as the French would say."

She gave a dirty chuckle. "If you mean did the earth move, then it certainly did." She moved closer and kissed him back, full on the mouth and wiped a speck of marmalade away from his cheek. "And though we Aussies spell culture with a capital K and know even less about it, yes, I'd love to see this clock. But I don't deserve such generosity."

"Think nothing of it. We may have a spare hour this morning."

She ran her pink varnished nail down his cheek. "Tell me about your scar," she demanded with all the directness of her upbringing in Woolloomooloo.

 "A drunk hit me with a chair in Antigua. A bad loser." He returned to the point he wanted to make. "I'm sorry Jude, I rather foisted my idea of a clock on you. My tastes aren't everybody's. Maybe we could stop off at say Caroline Charles' boutique and pick up a little something for you to wear too."

"Heh, Aude! You're even sweeter than you look. But the boutique I really fancy is just near here –The Cross in Portland Road. Mind, I've never been in."

"Easy. We'll do that – and the clock too. I really enjoy giving. To the right people of course."

"Of course." Her smile was coquettish and he could tell that she was getting horny again. But there was work to do before pleasure.

 "So how long did you work for," he paused "er Mr Dexter?"

"Days. Like I said last night, he made me redundant. Decided to put his father in a home."

"Bit sudden wasn't it? Just days after starting? No other reason?"

"Nah. He felt the old man needed more stimulation. Felt I couldn't do what a special unit would manage. That's it."

Shawcross compared her explanation to what he had overheard. "Hmmmh. Well, make sure he pays you some notice."

For the next twenty minutes, Shawcross chatted on, regularly bringing the conversation back to Dex, nothing cutting edge but still going beyond mere casual interest.

Jude shifted herself closer to him. "I don't know why we keep talking about Dex. He's history. A jerk. I don't want even to think about him. Tell me more about yourself, your ambitions. That's what interests me. I mean you've been so successful. Antiques, fast car, shares in Dukes. You've been a real success."

"Thanks. But Jude, I'm not really comfortable talking about myself. Part of the job really. My role at Dukes is to get the members talking - to show I'm interested in them. I remember their likes, dislikes. That's what pleases them. To show I care. They don't want to know about me. Most of them want to talk about themselves." He laughed, his smile sincere. "Most gamblers are egomaniacs. I mean listen to the way *you* talk down there. Going to bankrupt us, you know. Full of braggadocio."

"Is that a posh word for bullshit?"

"Let's stick to braggadocio, shall we." He played with a ring on her right hand, wondering where such a big rock had come from. As she helped herself to more coffee, her sleeves rode up and he saw the marks on her wrists from the handcuffs. "Liked the rough stuff, didn't you." The look was intent, the eyes a touch too penetrating and she looked away. "Plenty more where that came from."

"Mmmh. Domination's a turn-on. I hoped you'd noticed." She blew into his ear.

"I've ideas for after breakfast. We can still go shopping. But first, I said I had an idea for you – a job."

"Is it a better offer? I still have to earn a crust."

"Here's the deal. Live here. All the flagellation and bondage you'd ever dreamed off plus fifty grand until the end of the year. Cash."

"For fifty grand, don't bother about the sex." Her smile was teasing. "Cash will do nicely." She was wearing one of his shirts and a pair of purple panties. She ran her hands through his hair as he gazed into the distance, his mind somewhere else.

"I was hoping you'd put it the other way round."

"What do I have to do for fifty gee? And don't tell me it's nursing *your* father!"

"For fifty grand, I'd want you to nurse the entire British Legion." He twisted in his chair to fix her face to face. "I've another job in mind. Helping me at the club. Trust me. Perfectly legit. But not going through the books."

"Explain." He nuzzled close to her ear and ran a hand across her nipples. Then, just as he was about to do so, a change in the droning background noise attracted their attention. They both turned to the huge screen in the walnut cabinet. The BBC was breaking into *Kilroy* to go to the Newsroom. "The Arsenal and England footballer, Mick Glenn, has been found shot dead outside his home in north London. His housekeeper found his body when she arrived this morning. A Police Press Conference will be held at noon. More news of that in our regular bulletin."

"Bloody hell!" Shawcross had jumped from his seat and approached the big screen. "Mick Glenn dead! He's a member. So that's why he didn't visit the club last night. Dexter told me he was due to see him - expecting match tickets."

"Will you tell the police?" She watched his dressing-gown flop open as he turned to her. "About him coming – well not coming to Dukes, I mean."

Shawcross thought for a moment, his deep-set eyes disappearing. "I doubt that's of interest. People's plans change. But yes I may phone."

"I've never met him."

"He was a regular. Big player. Brains of an ant-eater but he told some good stories about the Premier League."

"Who'd want to kill him? Creole Henry?"

"That makes sense. Bedding that soap star wasn't clever. Or a drug connection. Or match-fixing. These top footballers – all so flash."

"Talking of flash," she pointed to his open dressing-gown before leaning forward to kiss his trim stomach, savoring the warmth of his skin and the smell of his manhood.

"My ace in the hole," he winked at her. "In the big built-in there's a PVC kit … plenty of studs and a black mask. Help yourself. Game on?"

"Can't wait." She returned to the bedroom and opened the sliding door. There was a human sized crucifix, the leather restraints for ankles and wrists obviously much used. There were leather outfits, a cap with a swastika, leather in several colors and at the end, the PVC outfit, shiny black and beside it an assortment of whips and leather. Something else caught her eye – down in the corner, flat on the floor under some brown wrapping paper lay a knife, a large one in a leather sheath. She stooped down and picked it up. At once, she recognized it as a Master Bowie from a hunting trip years ago in the Outback. She suddenly felt nervous as she pulled the black handle and over sixteen ounces of knife emerged. Puzzled about why he owned such a fearsome weapon, she fingered the nine and a half inch pointed blade, guiltily looking over her shoulder as she did so. Disturbed by the finding, she quickly pushed it back into the sheath and concealed it once again. As she pulled on the PVC jacket, studded hot-pants and tried on some boots for size, she struggled to force the stainless steel image from her mind

Monaco – 6th September 2002

By the time, he had driven for nearly an hour from the airport and wound down the long descent to Monaco, Dex was too late for lunch but he sat on a terrace beneath the Hermitage Hotel and ate a snack of *crêpe au fromage* with some Provencal wine, impossibly robust without strong goat's cheese. As the sun gradually disappeared behind the swish apartment blocks, he passed the time by creating a file about Dukes on his laptop. Almost at once, he felt chilly out of the sun, the sea breeze feeling cool on his bare arms. He was eager to get moving but it wasn't even five-thirty.

He called the new file *Obsession*. In it, he started to list all the facts that he could remember, every conversation, every oddity. He re-read them, marking inconsistencies with an asterisk. Nothing made sense yet everything stank like mackerel rotting on a Cornish quay. Looking across the small port, life felt better now – the sunshine, the blue skies, the life policy money apparently in the mail. Best of all was trying to make an ally of Scotty. That would be real progress on the Vegas side.

He created a *to-do* list - chase Panama agents for their report; meet Mark Evans for breakfast tomorrow; try again to find a pen-camera with a long transmitting range; interview Brannigan; talk to Lord Yarbury; pump Hoge and Crabant about how they came to Dukes; check their background on the web.

Success in finding card-counting Mark Evans had come suddenly – the owner of the bookshop had heard that he had been frequenting the Golden Orb recently, mostly early evening. Meeting Evans had not been a pleasure. The contrast between the bouncy McKay and Evans could not have been greater. He seemed a brittle character, unprepossessing in appearance and with a defensive wall around him. Only reluctantly had Evans agreed to meet for breakfast on Saturday morning. He doubted that much would be achieved.

He ordered an American coffee, checked the time and calculated it was morning on America's east coast. He dialed Tiffany's number. Instantly her well articulated voice was on the line. "Hi! How's London?"

"Al Qaeda permitting, still there. I'm in Monaco. Meeting Scotty."

"At last. He contacted you?"

Rapidly he explained an edited version about firing Jude, the missed message and the showdown the night before. "Scotty sounded interested, well intrigued anyway. Not like that dimwit Mick."

"Watch it, Dex. Don't speak ill of the dead."

Dex said nothing for a moment, trying to see the joke. "Sorry. You mean he's brain-dead?"

"Haven't you heard? Dead. Murdered last night. At his home."

"That's impossible. I was there."

There was an overlong silence. "You? There? What the hell were you doing there?"

"Snooping."

"When was that?"

Dex thought for a moment. "Around two a.m."

"What? Why?"

"Hard to explain. But things at Dukes seemed odd." He stared down the street, cursing a noisy motor-scooter that whined past up the hill. "Seems I was right."

Tiffany sounded less sure-footed now, her hesitancy obvious. "The news broke this morning London time. What, well, I mean – when you went there, did you expect to find a corpse?"

"I don't know what I expected. No, not a corpse anyway. What time did he die?"

"The cops haven't confirmed. So why, I mean what made you go there? Something must have triggered it. Sounds to me as if you need a good lawyer."

Dex laughed dismissively. "Nobody knew I was there. Nobody saw me – but anyway, I never entered his property – there are huge electric gates."

"So what did you see?"

"Not a lot. Trees. No sign of the house, no noise. His car, sorry – a car, was inside near the gate."

"That was his Porsche. His body was right beside it."

"No shit!" He thought back to the scene. "Hell! Mick was lying just feet away all the time."

"Single gunshot wound. We're running a story that the killer used a 9mm Beretta, typical of a contract killing. Highly professional."

"Counts me out!"

"Where were you before midnight?"

"In Dukes."

"You could have hired someone and then gone out later to check what had happened." She paused again. "Could look very bad if anyone knows you went there."

"Nobody but you. There were no cameras at the gate either."

"You'll need to handle Scotty carefully. He may not know."

Dex agreed, speaking slowly, assimilating so much new data. "He'll be choked. Couldn't be a worse time to talk about Dukes cheating. Compared to murder, it's just so trivial."

Tiffany fell silent, the seconds ticking away. "Unless its not trivial at all."

"Meaning?"

"Maybe Mick's murder is linked to your phone call to him. Wasn't he due in Dukes last night? To raise hell, you thought."

"God! You think that ...?"

"No. I think nothing – except that you should be *bloody* careful. God knows what Mick said when he went to Dukes the first time. Maybe nothing. Until the cops arrest Creole Henry or someone else, you can't rule out Shawcross or anything."

"Shawcross was expecting him. At least there was a *charade* of expectation. They had two bouncers hired specially. So that doesn't point to someone silencing him before he arrived. But then again, it just might. I must go. I'm due to see Scotty soon."

"Mmmh." The journalist in her sounded unconvinced. "Take care. And Dex, listen – suddenly, I'm rather missing you. *Special* chums. Remember that."

Dex visibly cheered but wondered why she had said it. This was a new mellowness. "Don't worry. I bet Shawcross is as puzzled about this as me."

"Relieved too. If he was expecting trouble."

He hesitated but then remembering the life policy continued. "Shall we meet? I can afford a cheap flight to Washington."

"I don't know what I'm doing one day to the next but I've put in for time off around the 25th."

"Done. I'll be there."

"Sounds good. Bye, Dex. Stay cool."

After the line went dead, he sat looking at nothing, excited by her change of attitude but puzzling over who had killed Mick. It was a given that Mick engaged brain later than most but nobody deserved a cold-blooded execution. So was it Creole or Shawcross ... or neither of them?

According to the waiter, Scotty's place was immediately behind him but a few hundred feet higher. He decided to walk, returning the computer to a bag he could sling over his shoulder. The climb was steep and when he reached the *Aristide Bleu* tower, he was glad of the work-out as he admired the clean futuristic style of the building. Each floor looked to be one large apartment and there were flower-decked balconies at every level on three sides. From the lower floors, the view was just of the building opposite but for those high up, like Scotty, the apartments overlooked the port and far out to sea. He approached the main entrance and pressed the buzzer for the penthouse, expecting the familiar voice to say hi and to open the door. Nothing. He rang again and after three attempts gave up. He rang Scotty's cellphone and left an angry message.

Just then, the door of the block opened. A couple of teenagers emerged arm-in-arm, engrossed in each other. With a smile, he walked past them and into the building. He doubted they even saw him. So much for security. There was nobody at the concierge's desk. The new all-mirrored lift whisked him eighteen stories to the top floor. When the lift arrived, he took in the smallish foyer, saw Scotty's front-door but went first to the picture window, marveling at the sweeping views. Then he tried the bell-push and he heard it sound somewhere inside. No answer.

Fuck you Scotty!

He crouched down and fumbled through his bag to leave a note. As he searched for his pen and notepad, he felt uneasy, as if he were not alone, as if he were being watched. *What had triggered this?* The hairs on the nape of his neck started to bristle.

Douglas Stewart

Yes. There it was again.

A creaking noise somewhere behind me.

Forget it.

I'm alone.

He continued scribbling saying he would wait in the bar opposite for an hour but would then be returning to London. As he finished pushing the note below the door, the creaking behind him was unmistakable. He swiveled round and noticed that the door to the fire exit was ajar. No question, the sound had come from that direction. Standing up, he walked the few paces and pulled open the green-painted door. He saw nothing as he peered cautiously into the small area. It was concreted and drab with the stairs down starting to his left. Then he saw a blue handkerchief lying just inside the door. He guessed someone had used it as a wedge. He took a step through, careful to keep a hand on the door to stop it closing on him. Almost at once, from his blind-side, a gloved hand appeared with a gun. He saw it raised towards him as a man of similar size in a navy overalls appeared, face concealed in a black balaclava.

Dex' stomach entered churned in shock.

"Kneel. Kneel. Right there. Facin' the wall." The speaker was unquestionably English.

Dex knew how professional killers operated.

Kneel and then a single precision shot.

Like that German pilot of the hijacked plane.

Like Mick Glenn.

La Tuile Rouge - 7th September 2002

Scotty stirred, emerging slowly from a deep sleep. Then he awoke, hair tousled, his naked body out of synch with his brain. Uncertain where he was, he tried to see familiar shapes. Gradually he recognized the suite - the paintings, the porcelain statuettes, the flowers on the small table. His mouth was dry and the bed was a mess.

La Tuile Rouge.

A cool breeze was blowing through the window. Outside everything looked black.

He fumbled to his right but there was nobody there. Estelle had gone, just the indented pillow as a reminder. He checked his watch. *Shit! Twenty after one!* Gradually, his life took focus. Shit! Mick is dead. A solemn lunch with lots of wine and some golden Armagnac. Estelle asking if that was why he had kept looking over his shoulder. "Coming upstairs?" she had suggested, oblivious to the decencies of mourning.

"Just keep me company." But lying on the large bed with her lips everywhere, his erection like a broom-handle had dictated events. He recalled the ecstasy and then the remorse as he had slumped into a deep sleep apologizing to Mick for the irreverence.

He found his phone. There were messages including one from Estelle as she drove back to Cannes, promising to be in touch. The next was from a rather angry Finlay Dexter phoning as he stood outside the front door of *Aristide Bleu*, saying he would wait an hour down the Columbus Hotel. He swore as he realized what had happened. Too much booze and too long licking those slender thighs. "Sorry about that Mick," he mumbled to his bleary face in the mirror." No respect at all but I'll come to the funeral and fuck Nanda Datt's threat. Sorry Dex. Should've set an alarm or fixed a wake-up call."

He clicked on to the next message - Dexter again. Timed at just after eight. He played it once and then repeated it. "I don't know what in hell's going on but there was a masked gunman by your flat. He pistol-whipped me round the back of the head. By the time I came round, he'd gone. I'm okay except for a sore head but I don't much care for the company you keep. I didn't tell the police as I must be in London in the morning. You tell them if you want.

Anyway - where the fuck were you? Don't tell me you had another engine failure?"

Scotty chuckled at the British humor in adversity but then his face became serious. He realized that Estelle had saved his life.

So when would Nanda Datt make his next move?

London - 7th September 2003

His head still aching as his souvenir of Monaco, Dex cowered beneath his umbrella. Sudden movement was not an option though this was impossible anyway in the driving rain and fierce wind that swirled through Bruton Street. The pen-camera just purchased, was the sole comfort. The prospects excited him as he looked in vain for a taxi. Fitted with a transmitter, a receiver down the street would pick up the images from the gaming room to a range of three hundred feet. He checked the time. The Press Conference at Mick's would be at noon.

He thought of Emily, Mark Evans' little daughter he had met at breakfast. They had breakfasted at Simpson's-in-the-Strand. Emily was a china doll. Meeting a stranger in a smart London restaurant seemed to come easily to her open and engaging personality. Dex had wanted to hug her and perhaps take up her offer to go with them to the zoo but the way breakfast had ended had killed that idea stone dead. Mark had arrived late, full of apologies. "As its Saturday, I'm taking Emily to the zoo. Hope you didn't mind her being here."

Dex had taken in Emily's pale pink and delicate features as she pulled off a tartan poncho and sat in the corner of the booth in a pair of red dungarees over a white jumper. She had the face of an angel, round and smiling with large eyes that beamed at the stranger across the table. Her hair was like flax and tied in a ponytail at the back. "Hello, Emily. I'm Dex. Did you bring something to read or play with?"

She nodded and produced a battered bear and a small book from a Barbie box. "These are my favorites," she said proudly. "Benjie goes everywhere with me."

"You're a big girl, aren't you? Tell me how old you are."

"I'm five. I'll be six in January."

"Well, Emily, us grown-ups are going to be talking about *very* boring things. But when we've finished. Perhaps we can play I Spy or Connections."

"Teach me Connections, Mr Dex. I don't like I-Spy."

"I will. Now let's all order." He turned to Emily's father, hoping his concern at Evans' appearance wasn't apparent. "If I'm like a bear with a sore head this morning, forgive me. I *do* have a sore head. Bumped it last night and it's pounding like crazy! I hardly ate yesterday, so I'm going for the Simpson's special - the *Ten Deadly Sins*. What about you?" As he was speaking, he took in Mark's strange appearance. The man could do with a square meal or maybe many. The way his jacket hung, it looked as if he had lost a hundred pounds overnight on the Atkins diet. The eyes were sunken with purple rings beneath them. For his age, his skin was too pallid and scrawny. His age? Twenty-five? Forty-two? It was impossible to know as he looked such a wreck.

Mark's accent and somewhat flat vowels suggested an upbringing in the Midlands. "Sorry I was late. Didn't leave the casino until four. Not much sleep. Usually lie in on a Saturday but I had to pick up Emily." His eyes were furtive, such a contrast to the openness of his daughter. "I'll share the Deadly Sins with Emily. Coffee for me, hot chocolate for her."

Dex poured orange juice from a large pitcher as he took in the image. The prospect of getting help from Mark wasn't appealing. He wondered what McKay would now make of the man he had rated the best blackjack player alive. "No problem Mark. Do you work locally?"

"Computer Programor in Eastcheap. It passes the time until I get back to the tables." He wiped his hand under his nose and then did it again. He glanced at Emily who was reading the menu to Benjie. "Let me tell you at once - I'm an addict."

Dex raised an eyebrow, not wishing to blunder in with the wrong assumption.

"The white stuff. That's the problem. Cost me my marriage. Kath and I - we're separated, not divorced. Rarely see Emily. Today's my day with her. Once a fortnight. Kath won't let me see her more because of the, y'know, problem. Can't blame her." He was not trying to get sympathy. This was factual, explained with the calm logic of someone who worked with computers rather than people. "My life's a mess. I exist just for Emily. My only other friends are coke dealers and casino bartenders."

Dex noticed that the man's hands were unsteady. He had chewed the fingernails almost to nothing. The eyes were dull, dead even and lurked between prominent cheek bones. His hair was cropped to a shadowy black, exaggerating a rather pointed skull. In one ear was a stud and the wide blue tie hung a full inch below the collar of a shirt fit only for a jumble sale. The eyebrows needed a trim, the nose was a mess but the teeth, above a chiseled jaw, were regular.

"I can tell you're looking at me and thinking - *My God, he's a bloody wreck.* You're right. At university in Sussex, I was a big guy - broad shouldered, barrel-chested and standing over six feet. When I was married, people said we made a handsome couple." He looked down, making his appearance even more forlorn. "Counting cards brings you to this." Mark Evans shook his head in self-disgust. "Can't live without it, coke that is. I don't eat properly. Can't afford to. My money goes up my nose, not into my mouth."

"But I'm told by a friend in Scotland that you're one of the most successful card-counters he'd ever come across."

"Wally McKay? I thought I was pretty smart until I met him. He taught me a lot. Me? The best? Who knows but I've no choice but to be pretty bloody good - just to pay for the stuff." He glanced at Emily who was looking at her book. "Vicious circle you see." The food arrived and he tore at a Cumberland sausage with obvious relish. "Mainly, I play the grind joints like the Golden Orb. At weekends without Emily, I go to Southend, Margate, Birmingham, and Bournemouth, tackling the provinces. I spread it about, never going to the same casino too often. That way I hope to avoid heat from the bosses."

"But blackjack's not *that* stressful, least I don't think so." Yet even as he said it, Dex regretted the comment, remembering Walter McKay's gorilla moments.

Mark looked angry, his hands restless and his lips pursed. He spoke quietly, his face contorted by anger. "You know bugger all about fuck all." He sipped his coffee. "It's the counting."

Dex looked shocked at the language in front of Emily and his eyes sent a message – *not in front of her* though he guessed that at home, she'd heard plenty enough until the couple split. Dex leaned back and put up both hands in surrender. "Sorry! Sorry! You're the expert. I'll keep my stupid mouth shut."

Mark cut up some bacon for Emily. "This is a real treat, isn't it Emily. I told you we'd have a fun day out."

"Thank you daddy. Thank you Mr Dex." The little girl wriggled along the bench seat to be closer to the father she so obviously loved.

"You have no idea what it's like – card-counting I mean." He twiddled his fork. "You're right. Playing blackjack *badly* isn't difficult. Just like Happy

Families or Snap. You may win but you'll probably lose, go home and play just as badly another day. But card-counting's different."

"Explain!" Dex wanted to test McKay's comments and advice.

"Tallying the High-Low count is a no-brainer. I could do that while playing with myself." His face looked even longer as he exhaled a deep sigh. "They're introducing technology here, real Big Brother stuff using image-recognition software to trap counters who try disguises. They've even built devices into the shoe from which the cards are dealt to permit player-tracking. For card-counters, once that hits all casinos everywhere, it's the end. Kaput. Stone dead gone. That and automatic continuous shufflers will kill off anyone using real skill."

"But what you do isn't illegal."

He laid down his cutlery and chewed thoughtfully, patting Emily on the head at the same time. "No but if I'm caught once, I'll be blacklisted everywhere. That's the problem – concealing that I'm a counter." He stabbed into the fried bread with an angry movement. "You live on your nerves, become paranoid. If you increase your stake too much, the bastards are onto you. So you have to look amateur, sometimes ignoring a favorable card count just to throw the bloodhounds off the scent." He raised his yellowed eyes, their look crying out for relief from injustice. "You're living on your nerves, just expecting to get caught. That's what's stressful. That's why I need the white stuff. And if I'm caught, what then? No way José can I afford to feed the habit on what I earn. Not after paying maintenance."

They fell silent, each weighing up the implications and putting away bits of kidney and fried bread. Dex felt more reassured by the bitter eloquence of the man and decided to advance the conversation. "I need help. I'm gathering evidence against a casino. I'll fund you to play plus a profit for your time. I want you to test the count over two or three weeks. But no bet changes based on the count. I don't want you caught."

"Explain." Mark looked puzzled and lit a cigarette, even though he was still eating.

"I want to know if the shoe has the correct number of cards in it. One member was griping that he rarely wins. Reckons that in this joint, there aren't enough tens and aces in the shoe."

"In London?" He stopped his fork in mid-air. "I've never noticed anything. Central Europe and the Caribbean? Maybe. I've heard unproven gossip."

"No matter."

"I could prove it. By counting through enough shoes, I'd spot whether they were spooking a deck."

"Mark: get me the evidence and maybe I could pay for your treatment at a top rehab place. Break the vicious circle. After all, card counting isn't making you rich – or happy. Stop the drugs *and* the counting. You might even get to see Emily more often."

Dex thought his approach generous and constructive but Mark simply glowered, his eyes sullen, his lower lip quivering. He ran his finger under his misshapen nostrils. Dex could tell he had no respect for do-gooders. "We've known each other less than forty minutes and already you're waving a wand and holy water everywhere. I've had your type right up to here – full of glib *tick-the-box* answers to a lifetime of problems." He waved an arm with a flapping sleeve above his head. "Well just go stuff yourself." He eased himself out of the booth. "Come on Emily, we're leaving."

"But daddy, I want my eggie. And Mr Dex is going to teach me Connections."

"Another time." He grabbed her arm, her poncho and toys and without a goodbye, turned to go.

Emily looked up at Dex with sad eyes. "Goodbye Mr Dex."

"I'll tell you about Connections another day Emily. Daddy's taking you to the zoo. Have a lovely day." He blew her a kiss as Evans led her off and out through the door. All that remained was a smell of stale sweat as he poured some English Breakfast tea and stared at the ceiling. He knew at once that he had blown it but then did he really need a Mark Evans aboard after the cock-up with Glenn?

Now as he stood on the Mayfair street corner, there was still not a cab in sight. He pulled the umbrella lower, a futile gesture as the rain lashed around him. His soaked chinos gripped his knees and his shoes were letting in water. "Taxi!" he yelled as the cheerful amber light of an empty cab appeared through the gloom. "You lot on wet days. Rare as rocking horse shit." Dex wiped the drips from his face as he settled in. "Mick Glenn's house. Just off The Bishop's Avenue."

"Fan are you?"

"Friend."

"Ask me, that Creole fitted him up. Catch me shafting his bird? No way mate. Evil bastard he is. Had him in the back of me cab once. Never paid neither."

Dex was about to respond when his phone rang. "Yes?"

Dexter slid the partition shut to get privacy. "Hi Dex! Jude here. I need to collect my things sometime. No hassle, no hurry," she'd said. "I've some keys. I can drop them off too."

"No problem. I'd like them back."

"Father okay?"

"Going to the Kemsway on Monday."

"Huh! Good luck but you're wasting your money." There was a silence, quite a long one. "And Dex, sorry about leaving your old man alone. But trust me, he never missed me. I'll see you at Dukes some time. Have a drink. Talk about old times."

"Sure." Dex sounded hesitant. "No hard feelings."

"You don't do *hard* very well, do you? I'd have told me to piss off. Take care."

"Hard enough to fuck you and fire you all in five hours. Think about it." He had scarcely cut the connection when there was another call. "Finlay Dexter? It's Scotty Brannigan." Immediately, his heart was racing.

"I'm glad you called."

"What's goin' on, man? What happened last night? You okay buddy? This guy hit you, right."

"Funny, it doesn't seem such a big deal today. Still sporting a lump the size of an egg. But yes, I thought he was going to kill me. Made me kneel down. Just when I expected the long black tunnel to nowhere, he must have just pistol-whipped me. I was out cold. Don't know how long but when I came round, my head was thumping and I was alone."

"I saw the blood. Gee, I'm sorry."

"So why was a gunman waiting outside your place?"

"I can't figure that. Nor what happened to Mick. Hey! I assumed that King Creole had fixed him – but not now. Not when someone seems to have been waitin' for me as well."

"Anyway, where the hell were *you*?"

"I had a long lunch up in the hills – drowned my sorrows with a friend and hit the sack. Didn't wake until gone midnight. That boozy lunch saved my life."

"But cost me a wasted ticket and a confrontation I'd rather never repeat."

"Dex. I owe you. You need to talk to me. I'll be at the funeral. How about I'll fly you to Monza afterwards, best seats for the race, pit-lane access, stay in my hotel. I'll fix all that. We can talk on the flight. I want to know about Dukes. I want you to tell me all the shit about Creole Henry, everythin'."

"You told the local cops?"

"About you? Thought about it but nope. Sure ain't nothin' they can do if some nut wants to kill me. But you can report it, if you want."

Dex said nothing but was puzzled. *Why wasn't Scotty more concerned about someone waiting to kill him?* "So where shall we meet?"

"After the funeral, be at Stansted Airport at six pm. The VIP lounge. I'll fix your admission. S'long!"

The taxi dropped Dex about eighty yards away from Mick's place. The familiar cul-de-sac this time was a hive of activity. From leaden skies, the rain had eased to a steady drizzle and the journalists and curious onlookers in their trench coats or anoraks had water dripping down their faces. With television cameras everywhere, memories of the morning after the crash flooded back. For a second, he wondered what Tiffany was doing – maybe breakfast or out for a morning jog by the Potomac.

The police had erected a small rostrum just outside the open gates to Glenn's house and a bulky figure appeared on it to address the gathering. "Good morning everyone. Sorry about the weather. My name is Detective Chief Superintendent Rod Blyth. I'm leading this investigation. With me here, I have Detective-Sergeant Jones." The lights set up by the TV companies shone on his face, the rain sliding slowly down over his forehead from his silver hair. "In the past twenty-four hours, we have continued our enquiries into the events surrounding the murder of Mick Glenn. We are now able to put out a formal request for help. We wish to eliminate a man seen loitering on a motorbike outside Hammerson House just south of here down Bishops Avenue."

Someone shouted *any description* and Blyth nodded. "Dark skin. Aged mid – twenties. Not English. Possibly Asian. Wearing a white crash-helmet." He checked his notes. "The bike may have had the letters LGP in the registration. We would like that person to come forward to be eliminated from our enquiries."

"Domino's Pizza Delivery?" some wag shouted from the back.

Blyth allowed as much of a smile as a murder enquiry permitted. "He was in the area between 2130 and 2215. Any questions?"

"Would that tally with the time of death?"

"Possibly."

"When was Mick killed?"

"Before midnight."

"How was Mick killed?"

"A single shot behind the ear. 9mm Beretta."

"Professional job?"

"A ruthlessly efficient murder."

"A contract killing?"

"Ruthlessly efficient."

"So no particular motives?"

"We are pursuing a number of lines of enquiry. No further comment on that." Blyth was not yet ready to announce either the profile of the killer or the motive. In his mind was the usual ragbag assortment of facts, suppositions and blind alleys that always cluttered the first days of a murder enquiry. Back in the nick, he knew an entire room was already taking calls, following up sightings and trying to build a picture of Mick's life and final movements. What he was not saying was that after the news broke, a phoned tip-off to Scotland Yard had said Mick had been match-fixing - indeed had taken big money paid from a Hong Kong bank. But the caller had been in a public phone box and had given no name. Until corroborated by real evidence, it was just filed along with all the other theories from cranks and nutters.

Blyth knew all about attempts by rich Oriental betting syndicates trying to fix sport in England. As a star player, Mick was an obvious target. And he *had* missed three easy goals against Chelsea. Blyth, a West Ham supporter, was looking forward to watching videos of Arsenal's last few matches while

Detective Sgt Jones was checking bookies for any sign of big winners or losers at the result.

Dex didn't buy theories in the papers about match-fixing. You'd pay a striker like Mick to miss – just what he had done. No reason to kill him there then. One paper had said Mick had been a randy bastard. Besides Creole's Sharon, he had been knocking off the wife of one of the Arsenal directors. To Dex, the Jamaican gangster still seemed more likely.

"Let me add just one thing," Blyth turned his head in a slow semicircle to ensure he had the attention of everybody. "I've seen the headlines this morning. I'm not responsible for what you write – or for the conclusions you draw but I must warn you that finger-pointing at Mr. Creole Henry is without any suggestion from us. We have an open mind on who killed Mr Glenn and why."

"Anything else the public can do?"

"Any member of the public who was in The Bishop's Avenue area Thursday evening and saw the motorcyclist or anything suspicious or unusual should get in touch. The man on the bike should make contact so we can eliminate him from our enquiries. If anyone has any other information that may be of help, then they should call us in confidence."

"Where was Mick going when he was murdered?" A woman shouted the question that Dex had wanted to ask.

Blyth flicked a glance at his colleague before answering. "We don't know. We understand he often went out later in the evening. Our enquiries are continuing. If anybody was expecting to see him on Thursday night, please come forward in absolute confidence. Here's our number. Thank you for coming."

Dex waited for a few moments while the journalists packed away cameras, microphones and chatted about the briefing. He was able to pick his way through the sixty or so people, many busy on their phones. He walked beside the rostrum and tried to peer through the open gates, intrigued to see the scene in daylight. A blue and white tape prevented him getting too close but he was able to see the bushes, trees and grass verge. Except for some markings on the gravel, it seemed so very mundane. Blyth was chatting to his sergeant and Dex picked up a snippet as he tried to appear as if he were not eavesdropping. "I reckon we'll never know where young Mick was going."

Sergeant Jones glared at Dex as if to tell him to clear off as he nodded to his boss. "You mean a secret meeting for nookie with a married woman?" The words were enough to reveal a Welsh accent.

"That's my guess. Someone who can never admit it."

"Reckon you...". The words faded as the two speakers moved out of earshot.

As Dex trudged off towards central London, he was glad he had been there. He now knew that the police had no idea that Mick was due at Dukes. He debated whether to tell them but then decided that it was better to see what Shawcross, FB or the two thugs did about that.

London – 11ᵗʰ September 2002

The tall Londoner pored over the funeral route just published on the Arsenal FC website. After the screw-up in Monaco, the pressure to deliver was on. Attempting such a public execution was a big risk but he had to deliver before Monza. Killing Brannigan at the funeral was the easy part - escape was the problem. *At my age, life means life,* he told himself as he checked a map. The website had explained that once the coffin was in the hearse, the Arsenal Team, the family and selected friends including Brannigan would walk behind it through the streets of Highbury. After a minute's silence, outside the main entrance to the stadium, they would go on to the crematorium.

In front of him were the A to Z and several newspapers. At only five-eight Brannigan's height would be a problem if bigger men obstructed the line of fire. Also, he was unsure how the mourners would play out a football tragedy. Would the crowds clap politely or have heads bowed in silence as the coffin passed? He would have preferred lots of movement and noise rather than tearful mourners but had to plan on working with an eerie silence.

He ran his finger down the plan of the route from the church in Finsbury Park. The hearse would go south down Blackstock Road, entering Gillespie Road before turning into Avenell Road. There it would pass alongside the East Stand of Highbury Stadium. He decided to walk the route. He slipped out of the small hotel behind Ealing Tube Station, ignoring the scruff with rings piercing his eyebrows. He kicked some Big Mac remains out of his path and walked to the Tube.

London – 12ᵗʰ September 2002

Dex had parked nearly a mile away from the church, leaving his overnight bag in the car ready for a quick dash to the airport after the funeral procession. The rain had stopped as he listened through his earpiece to the build-up on Capital Radio. As Dex hurried through the quiet streets, the commentator described at least five thousand around the church and a packed route. The biggest crowd was outside Highbury Stadium with a reported two hundred thousand people in the area.

By the church, the pavements were thronged several deep with shabbily dressed people. They were typical north Londoners, many of them living their lives only through the performances of Arsenal, their local team. The mourners could listen to the service outside on the tannoys. As Dex listened to the tributes to the slain idol, he felt uncomfortably aware that he may have played a role in Glenn's death even though Creole was the media's favorite suspect. He also now appreciated what Glenn's death meant to the community. Mothers consoled children, grandparents sobbed uncontrollably; skinheads with tattoos hugged each other in shared grief. To them all, Mick was part of their family, one of their own. The Arsenal captain spoke of Mick as a very human man, a footballer of rare talents, so generous with his money and with time helping disadvantaged children. He watched grown men unashamedly crying like children and shared the emotions, fleetingly imagining the beaky face swooping over the roulette table as he piled up the chips.

From just outside the church gates and amid hundreds of camera flashes, Dex watched Scotty Brannigan and the other pallbearers emerge. He had a good position and a height advantage to watch the pallbearers struggle with the heavy coffin. With obvious difficulty, they edged it into the rear of a black Austin Princess. Brannigan looked small, almost frail besides so many larger Premier League stars. The giant of so many racing triumphs was only larger than Rick Haley, the champion jockey who was also a chief mourner.

As the limousine slowly moved away, preceded by four police motorcycles, their blue lights flashing, it seemed unreal that he would soon be chatting to Scotty in an executive jet at 35,000 feet. As others from the crowd fell in behind the chief mourners, Dex did the same so that he was only about twenty yards behind Brannigan as the procession head south.

The menacing black clouds looked ready to prove the forecasters wrong with their predictions of a dry afternoon. He trudged in silent unity over the greasy tarmac. A rhythm soon developed and he found the sight of bobbing heads hypnotic, the throng advancing in unison between the shabbiness of the houses lining the route.

The silence was chilling. Dex found it hard to believe that so many people could make so little noise. As the cortège passed them, he saw onlookers look down to hide tears or just stare at the hearse with dead eyes, their minds filled with memories of the man's past glories for club and country, his hat-trick against Spain receiving endless replays on the TV. The violent purple clouds above the grimy poverty of the area added to the solemnity, as did the blacks, grays and dark blues of the wintry coats or anoraks worn by most. Only the red and white scarves of the Arsenal fans stood out alongside the few wearing the white shirts of England. Seeing the cortège had whisked him back to Bladon churchyard – the solemnity of the simple country church, the matching coffins and the wistful strains of Amazing Grace played by a piper outside the porch.

It could have been me in a maple coffin.

It could have been Scotty.

His somber thoughts kept being interrupted by puzzling about Jude. Her recent behavior made no sense. Each time he had gone into Dukes, she had been there, each time with a different man with huge money to throw around. Was she picking up rich men at the Dorchester Hotel or the Connaught and playing with their money? He'd watched her last evening, trying to understand what she was doing with an elderly West Indian. The day before, it had been a stern looking Russian who had to have been pushing eighty. "Into sugar-daddies are you? " he had joked hoping for an explanation. She'd simply shrugged and with a throaty chuckle in her voice, told him to stick to knitting.

Ahead, he saw the blues of the flashing lights reflecting off the dullness of the small homes and cheap guest-houses. A television camera was on a scorpion-like arm twisting around, rising and falling above its truck as it preceded the hearse. No doubt the camera was intruding on the grief of the chief mourners, the big names, just behind the jet black car. As he wiped away the first drops of thundery rain from his cheeks, Dex silently cursed at the disaster with his pen-camera. He had filmed Jude and the West Indian, Hoge and a few others, hoping to catch One-Eye or Andy cheating them. And he had.

As he had chatted from behind Hoge who was playing roulette badly, the pen in the top pocket of his jacket had caught One-Eye palming away the top two chips from a winning stack of a wealthy looking Greek woman who's husband was playing baccarat. With that slick movement, he had stolen seventy thousand pounds yet nobody had noticed. The camera lens was in the clip and the images were being transmitted only two-hundred feet along Mount Street. Kenny Jennings, an agent he had hired, had the receiver in his car but when Dex got home, all he saw were fuzzy black lines. The elation at capturing the proof he needed evaporated at once. The receiver had captured nothing.

This morning, he had angrily phoned the shop demanding his money back. "Must be the depth of the basement and the thickness of the walls. Perfectly good camera. It's the way you choose to use it that's impossible. Read the small print."

Dex had slammed down the phone. If the pen-camera was out, then the only option was using a concealed camcorder and that was not appealing. As he had breakfasted, chewing thoughtfully at a slightly blackened sausage, he concluded that the dwindling bank loan would have to fund Kenny filming with a digital camera. Getting him accepted as a member might be tricky but despite his ex- Met Police credentials, at least he looked the part - no cauliflower ears or stinted style of speech.

Ahead now, Dex saw the faded sign - *Blackstock Road*. Though Scotty was only twenty yards away, he was lost among the taller footballers and boxers as they walked behind the family and close to the Minister for Sport. Beyond them all, the lights of Highbury Stadium rose to illuminate the turbulence of the sky. The rain was heavier now and a distant rumble of thunder growled a warning of worse to come.

In Ardley View Guesthouse on Blackstock Road, the gunman checked his personal miniature TV. He saw the cortège and followers, most helpful in positioning Scotty, a small rather dejected figure limping slightly behind the Arsenal players. *Enjoy the exercise, mate,* he muttered as he checked the trigger and line of fire again. There was no need. His sniper's position was ideal and the rifle in perfect condition.

Though his escape plan envisaged nobody even seeing him, he had taken no chances. A pom-pom hat, false wispy beard, moustache, glasses and built-up shoes transformed his normal trim figure. He had added twenty six pounds to bulk up his physique. The final additions had been the boldly grey eyebrows and the wadding in his cheeks, puffing them out like a goldfish.

Unrecognizable, he had checked in to the rooming-house late the previous evening. A naked bulb hung from a wire on the ceiling. His room had a single bed and a hook on the door for clothes. Otherwise, the room was empty. Where a small chest of drawers had once stood was now only discolored lino marking its outline. No doubt a guest had carted it away. The floor was bare brown lino with a hole near the door. Countless visitors had worn a trail to the stinking lavatory across the passage. The Lebanese owner lived two doors down and the only other guest had gone out, probably to watch the funeral. The Londoner knew that he alone was tolerating the smell of damp linen and fresh mouse turds.

Ardley View was a mid-terrace property, probably one hundred years old and lacking in charm but perfectly positioned. His front room at the top of the stairs had an unobstructed view both ways along Blackstock Road. Opposite was the playground of a school, hidden behind a high red brick wall. At the rear, a garden had been paved to incorporate a rear exit into Finsbury Park Road, a quiet residential street. Within seconds, he reckoned he could be into the Ford Fiesta, stolen yesterday in Kensal Rise. Now it stood parked in readiness, just yards away. He had left the bonnet ajar so that he could quickly short-circuit the starting-motor for a quick getaway.

Before anyone would react, he'd be driving along busy Green Lanes heading for Arnos Grove tube. He listened to the hushed tones of the BBC TV commentator. "And there beside the tall subdued figure of Tony Henshaw, the Manchester United and England defender, is Scotty Brannigan, former Formula One World Champion. Brannigan and Mick had been friends for several years. He's flown in from Monza and will return today to get ready for the Grand Prix on Sunday. In front of him I see the distraught faces of Mick's Arsenal team-mates Lee Dixon and David Seaman..."

As the camera zoomed in, he studied the faces on the small screen. Brannigan looked older than he had expected, easily recognizable in his black suit, black tie and white shirt.

Brannigan was towards the far side, dwarfed by Tony Henshaw. The angle was not going to be ideal but he was sure he would get a clean sighting though for less time than he had hoped. To his right, there would be ten seconds, to his left about half that. For the first time, he heard the distant rumble of the approaching motor-cycles. *Fuck me, what a fuckin' bonus mate.* It was just what he needed to obscure the crack of the high-velocity bullet

He stood on the ledge by the sash-window. The top part was open just a few inches and the light in his room was off. He peered through the gap between the wall and the once–white lace curtains that hung limp across the dirty glass. Below his window, the pavement was jammed tight but across the street, there were less than twenty people, none looking his way. Even so, he wanted to keep any movement minimal as the procession drew near.

Needlessly, he again checked his beloved M24 sniper rifle, its high-velocity 7.62mm cartridge delivering death at 700 meters per second. Used by the Israelis against Hamas rebels, it would pass through Brannigan's brain rather than exploding inside. He looked through the laser pointer, caressing the butt for a brief second with the barrel just protruding beyond the window. The dark clouds and rain had dragged the horizon down to the road but despite the poor light, his sighting of Scotty would be perfect.

"And the police motor-bikes are now well down Blackstock Road," confirmed the commentator. "This normally thronged highway is stilled as the hearse carrying the football star draws closer to the line of shops before turning right to the stadium. Who killed Mick Glenn and why remains a mystery but now is not the time for speculation. Today, a nation's thoughts are only on the tragedy of the violent loss of such a talented young life, a life so full of fun. It took his death for us to know how he had worked tirelessly for poor kids and disabled children."

The sniper switched off the portable, pushing it into his packed bag. He edged forward and his heart rate quickened as he saw the motor-cyclists. Their headlamps were dipped, reflecting brightly from the greasy sheen of the tarmac. Behind the police came the TV crew, camera zooming low over the faces of the mourners. Next into sight was the chrome radiator of the Austin, its windscreen wipers working. Then he saw the first mourners, heads bowed, rain dripping from the black hats of the ladies and spattering on the pink baldness of Mick's Dad's head. The Arsenal team appeared followed closely by Scotty. Unmistakable: the familiar figure, the familiar face, even the walk was just as he had seen on the video - small steps with just a hint of a limp. He eased Scotty's head into his sights. His grip on the rifle was steady, his brain in deep-chill. The perfectionist was ready.

The red dot of the laser was just between and above Brannigan's eyes. *Easy pickings.* Missing at forty yards was unthinkable. But he wanted to wait. Better to let the motor-cycles pass, let their 750cc engines fill the air. By then, the bystanders would be staring at the coffin with Mick's Arsenal and England shirts draped across it.

Don't want them seeing the barrel protruding.

The noise from the motor-bikes reverberated everywhere, trapped between the buildings and the low clouds.

Bleedin' marvelous!

Never thought the fuckin' cops would be my friends.

He steadied himself by pressing his all black clothing against the wall. Just ten paces to go. A single shot and the cash would be his. He pulled the butt of the rifle closer to his right cheek. Five paces. Looking good. The laser pointer made it so easy. He started to squeeze the trigger.

Shit!

What the hell?

Suddenly there was nothing. His view had gone. A white mist had fogged the scene. *Nothing.*

Nothing but fuckin' white.

Like a fuckin' blizzard!

He lowered the rifle and glanced out. The operator had just reared up the TV camera on the scorpion arm to change the angle.

Shit!

He shuffled along the ledge, twisted his back against the other corner of the casement and pointed the rifle in the other direction.

Henshaw's black head was now blinding his shot as the mourners passed beneath him. He leaned back harder against the casement, anxious to get a clear view in the brief opportunity about to arrive. Now, the man behind Brannigan was obstructing the angle, a head shot still impossible. He paused, waiting for a few more paces. A shot through the back and exploding through his heart was now a runner.

Beautiful.

Easy.

He gripped the trigger as Brannigan's shoulders to midriff reappeared in a sliver of space between the two obstructing men. The gap was about three feet wide and twenty yards away.

Okay.

Now!

He tightened on the trigger and the rifle recoiled into his shoulder. He knew he'd hit him. Brannigan lurched, spinning slightly and then tumbled forward. There was no time to admire the handiwork. The killer was leaping down the stairs, pausing only to slam across the bolt on the front door with a gloved hand. Nobody could now just walk into the guesthouse. As he bounded out of the rear exit into a deserted Finsbury Park Road, he could hear shouting.

He threw the rifle onto the floor of the car before firing the engine from under the bonnet. Then he was away. No one was there, nobody saw him leave. They were either glued to their TVs or lining the route. In minutes, he had stripped away his disguise and was three miles away, ready to switch to his own car at Arnos Grove.

As Dex was gazing at the yellow glow of the stadium lights, he heard shouting and the steady rhythmic steps ahead faltered and then stopped. Screams broke out somewhere ahead. Everybody was yelling *stop* to those behind as the huge advancing army of fans threatened to crush those at the front. The relentless force of thousands of mourners trudging slowly forward into those who had stopped began to generate a sense of panic. Everyone around Dex seemed to be shouting as the crush from behind intensified. He was lucky being on the edge of the procession and as the pressure mounted, he slipped sideways to hurdle the tubular steel railings and join the fans outside Ardley View.

Someone said. "He's been shot."

All around people were screaming for an ambulance and police. From ahead, he saw the navy blue uniformed coppers arriving and could hear the occasional walkie-talkie. Dex was sure who the victim would be as he pushed his way towards the hearse. A sickening dullness grabbed his stomach. He looked around, wondering from where a shot might have come. Had the assassin been in the throng? On the pavement? He looked at the drab terraced houses and saw the slightly open upstairs window at Ardley View Guesthouse. "I heard the shot," a teenager in an Arsenal scarf said to an overweight policeman. "It came from up there." He pointed to the same window.

"Thanks." The officer spoke into his mouthpiece to direct the detectives and other officers. Dex watched as the police rang the bell and on getting no response, barged through the door, the bolt ripping chunks of aged wood from the frame. Dex peered over the heads to see where a circle of people had linked arms clearing a small area, around eight yards in diameter. In centre circle, someone was lying face down. A big black man was removing his jacket and crouching down to cover the crumpled figure. As the attendant moved, Dex saw the familiar bushy sideburns and knew at once that he had been right. The hearse had now stopped about ninety yards away, the motor-cyclists just beyond that. A woman claiming to be a nurse scrambled through the pack to kneel down on the filthy and blooded road surface.

Dex watched the cloudburst dancing off the slick tarmac and saw bloody water trickling downhill away from him. "He's alive," the woman said after checking the pulse and doing things that Dex could not see. The crowd seemed to echo the words. In the distance, Dex heard sirens as emergency services came from the Highbury direction. It seemed an age before the wails drew closer. The hearse pulled across onto the pavement to make room as the white Daimler ambulance made its noisy appearance.

As the crew rolled the stretcher into the circle, the crowd close to the body was silent, desperate to hear what was happening. The big black man stood up and Dex recognized the angular face of Tony Henshaw, his face numb, his eyes showing gleaming white. He moved back to give the crew more room and as he stood, scratching his face, a policeman spoke to him. "What happened?"

Dex craned forward to listen in to the Brumbies accent.

"Well, we was goin' along nicely. Not sayin' nothin', know what I mean? I was next to Scotty. He was to my right." He paused and then looked around. "Yeah. Look." He was pointing behind him at a pothole in the road surface, just on the edge of the ring. "I saw this hole, right ahead of Scotty. You can see, perfect for twistin' an ankle. So I says to him. "Watch out, 'cos I could see he was in a daze like, lookin' ahead.""

Dex could just see the nasty hole, about six inches across and a couple of inches deep, its edges, a mix of crumbling tarmac.

"And?"

"His right foot went into the hole, didn't it? He twisted but at that second, I heard this crack. I didn't know it was a gun. Didn't know what it was, truth to tell. He fell away from me. Didn't say nothin'. There was blood coming from near his head, left side back."

The policeman looked up and saw that this dovetailed with the upstairs window. "Thanks. It's Tony Henshaw isn't it? We'll need a statement later Tony."

As the police parted the circle that they had now themselves ringed, the crew picked up the body "Move away now please, move along. This is a crime scene." A policeman with a loud-hailer was just about audible against the wail of the sirens. Dex looked at the large pool of blood that was still spreading and flowing away with the rain. So my hunch and Tiffany's instinct that it was Shawcross behind Glenn's murder was a back-marker now. He felt better for the thought. Wait one. Not so fast! What if Glenn had named Brannigan. If he had done that, well maybe it *was* Shawcross and if it was … who was next? The uncomfortable truth hit him fast. Surely not me? If Mick had named me, I'd have been first to go, not third. He trudged back to his car. There he gazed distractedly at his packed bags, thinking how excited he had been to be jetting off to Italy. For the first time, he tasted fear, something he had never expected.

Shawcross was in his office enjoying a late lunch of over-stuffed ham sandwiches. The television was on in the background as he pored over figures from downstairs and more importantly his private records about *Cyclops* and *Snowball*. He sighed contentedly as he saw the millions that were passing through London.

True, he had to tolerate the Board Meeting at six but even the Irish slimeball O'Keefe had expressed satisfaction with business trends. Sir Cedric's views were still unknown but the bugs would pick up his usual pre-meeting chat with O'Keefe. He was about to pour a second glass of idyllic Montrachet from a cooler when the intercom buzzed.

"Yes FB." His tone was irritated.

"Sorry to bother you. Adrian Ryder is here with that accountant woman, Zara Belfield. The Gaming Board wanted a random check – as they do from time to time."

"So?" Shawcross tried not to sound alarmed. The Board only rarely sent in an outside accountant. This would be the second visit in two years.

"And?"

"He wants to see you."

"Can't you sort it, FB? I'm busy."

"He says he needs to see you. Won't say why."

"Better show them up, then. Give me five minutes." With fast aggressive movements, Shawcross shoved the bank statements and fund transfer documents into a manila file and then placed it in the safe. He brushed the crumbs onto his lunch tray and returned the wine to a fridge built into a Georgian mahogany fronted chest. He was about to switch off the television when he saw that the funeral procession was breaking up in disarray. It all looked chaotic but FB's knock on the door forced him to switch off.

Shawcross donned the jacket of his light grey suit and straightened his pink Garrick Club tie. In front of him was the open Gaming Board file.

FB hovered respectfully, uncertain whether to go or stay. "Thanks, FB. I'll let you get on downstairs." He waited until the door was closed. "Adrian! Good to see you." He pumped the hand warmly and then looked at Zara Belfield, recalling the shots of her clinging to a towel-rail while Ryder rode her from the back. She looked harder, meaner in the flesh but damnably challenging. "And this must be, Ms Belfield - Zara, if I may. Please sit down. I hope you're both looking forward to your new life in Vegas." He saw the nods, more enthusiastic from her than him as he went back behind his desk and swiveled his chair. "I'm delighted to see you. A random check I gather."

"Yes. The Board had noticed that Dukes' were beating the opposition in London – business growing when others are finding it tough."

"That's good news, then - beating the opposition! God! I've worked day and night for this place since nine-eleven, struggling to get our members to sign up new friends. I've been to every time-zone wooing the whales, trying to persuade them that London is safe." He patted down his hair with both hands. "And these last few months, well, I've seen what some Chancellor of the Excheckr once called the first green shoots of a recovery. But dammit! You say we're *beating* the opposition. That's great."

Ryder looked at the carpet.

"So the Board think we're doing too well – and needed to have you check us out?"

Ryder shifted uneasily. "Something like that."

Shawcross stood up and stifled a yawn. "And we get a clean bill from you I assume? As usual."

Adrian looked uncertainly at Zara as if taking instructions from a superior, which she was not. "We...ell, I wouldn't ..."

Zahra's face revealed the side of her recorded on the Poirot bar tape. She looked hard, the eyes now mean, the mouth tight, any warmth of personality subverted by a granite look. She gave him no chance to answer, waving him quiet in a sharp decisive fashion. "Not quite clean," she said breezily. "The usual odd queries. Nothing that we can't resolve with Reggie Kyte and FB. Nothing important at all."

Shawcross laughed. "Looking at Adrian's face just now, I was starting to wonder." He rested a hand on Ryder's shoulder. "Look Adrian, if you find anything, just *anything* down there that I should know about, you tell me. I trust FB of course but big money passes through here. Reggie Kyte runs a pretty tight ship on security but, well, you can't ever be too careful."

Zara handed over a small box which Shawcross quickly opened. "We brought you this. I hope you like it." Inside was a gold cigar cutter.

"You're too kind. I did nothing for you at all – just recommended your names to Carlo. The rest, well – you sold yourselves to him." He opened the humidor. "I shall christen it at once. A Padron, no less, is called for."

Adrian shifted again on his chair, still looking as uncomfortable as if seated on spiked fencing. Shawcross deliberately ignored this. "I'm delighted everything's fine. So go ahead - sort out the, er … trivia with FB downstairs and keep me posted about progress for your move to Vegas. I can tell you, Carlo was more than impressed with your report."

"Is Space City still going well?" This was Zara the coquettish again, perky and cheerful, her head tilted to one side, a pen playing around her lips. "As the Yanks would say – it is truly *awesome* – even without the new tower."

"Back on schedule. You'll get invites for the opening. There'll be so many stars, the biggest names from showbiz, we'll bring the Strip to a standstill." He was ushering them to the door. Ryder still looked as if he wanted to say something deeply profound but Zara had taken control and was almost hustling him out.

"Invites would be great, wouldn't they Adrian?" She opened the door and nearly pushed him through it. "So goodbye – and a pleasure to meet you Mr Shawcross."

"Oh, Audley please." His raised hands waved a protest and an invitation in a swift movement.

Ryder still had his back turned as she smiled at Shawcross, smile now dazzling him. Then she did something that Shawcross was unsure about, something he would replay in his mind for hours. She gave him a wink, quick but subtle and unmistakable. At the same time, she nodded her head backwards as if referring to Adrian. He thought he understood and hoped he was correct.

"Goodbye, Adrian." Shawcross waited for the inspector to turn and then shook his hand firmly but noticed that Ryder's hand was wet beyond clammy. "Drop by again if there's anything you need from me. Goodbye, Zara. A pleasure."

He watched them descend the spiral to the next floor and waved after them cheerfully. Back in his office, he flicked on the TV, poured the last of the wine and stood by the window. The glow on the tip of his cigar burned brightly as he listened to the crash of thunder almost directly overhead. Carlo had been right. Zara was onside. Adrian was the danger. The wink was the message that whatever worries Ryder had, she was in charge and everything was tickety-boo. He wondered if she would fancy a couple of nights at Chewton Glen or Hartwell House. But giving Jude the slip would not be easy. She was too street-smart to be fobbed off. That left the excitement of anticipation only.

He grabbed the phone. "Guess who dropped by, Carlo! Only our movie stars. They on *our* team, no question. Zahra's seeing to that. She's even flirting with me." They both chuckled. He glanced at the funeral procession. "And Mick Glenn is being buried today. "Convenient him being taken out by Creole Henry."

"Very convenient," muttered the American, still suspicious that Shawcross was implicated in the murder somehow. "Board meeting going to be okay?"

"With these figures I told you about? No problem. Better still, I've just transferred a couple of million to Aruba plus what you creamed off the other day via New York. Did you file that false invoice to cover it?" He heard Carlo say yes. "Good. Our little pension fund's stashed with cash – and plenty more to come." He was watching the screen as he spoke. "Hold it. Hey! Scotty Brannigan – the F1 driver from Vegas has been shot at the funeral."

"Isn't that guy a member too?"

"Two members shot in one week."

"Hmmmh." Carlo sounded unsure how to react. "Well, I guess them two, they jus' had somethin' goin' on we don' understand. Don' make no sense to me. Killin' them both, not unless Brannigan was layin' the pipe to Creole's woman as well. Anyway, don't you go losin' no more members. Kinda careless. We need more not less. I must go. My coffee's percolated now," Shawcross sat quietly mulling over the call. By the time he stood up to prepare for the Board, he was thoroughly riled. "The shitbag just coat-tails *my* brain, *my* work. Ungrateful bastard," he murmured. But then as he looked ahead, his anger eased. Carlo would get his come-uppance later. Once he was no longer essential.

Dex had listened on his car radio for news as he drove westwards through Swiss Cottage and down the Wellington Road. There was plenty of talk but no hard facts. Back home, he made himself some strong brown Yorkshire tea and helped himself to a biscuit. He yearned for a slab of Fortnum's rich fruit cake, a luxury now gone. His fear had now passed to be replaced by curiosity and determination. There was something he was missing - something obvious, a link between the shootings. He flicked on the News at Six and saw the scene on Blackstock Road and then the reporter standing outside the hospital. "A hospital spokesman has confirmed that Scotty Brannigan is in intensive care and in a critical condition but his injuries are not life-threatening. The bullet passed through the top of his shoulder just below his neck. A further statement will be issued at nine this evening."

The ebony black face of Tony Henshaw had then appeared. "Well, Scotty, when he was on the ground, I saw the blood pourin' from near his neck and shoulder. I thought – what the hell's that all about? He's only twisted an ankle. If he hadn't been kind of lurchin', reckon the bullet would have hit his back and maybe the heart and he'd have been gone."

"Any idea why he was shot?"

"No mate. Something between him and Mick, I s'pose but what they'd done to upset someone, I dunno."

Dex needed to think. With father now settled at the Kemsway Unit, the big house felt empty and too full of past memories, most of them unhappy. It creaked as the central heating warmed the autumnal air. He shivered, not from the cold but from the sense of isolation and the haunting memories of Beth tapping her stick along the wall behind him. He spread some blueberry jelly on wheat toast and debated whether to approach the police. *But what do I tell them? About the security guys at Dukes? About me being attacked in Monaco?*

He quickly decided that suggesting to the cops that Shawcross just might be involved was a non-starter. There was no evidence and if they so much as approached Shawcross and hinted at their source, it might not be pretty.

I could be tomorrow's corned-beef

He selected some mood music last played on the night of the crash and decided it was time to visit his father. His diary for tomorrow was once again empty. Then he picked up the phone and dialed the USA.

"I'm so excited," Tiffany said. "Tomorrow, I've been granted a one-to-one with President Bush at the White House."

"How long have you been given?"

"Fifteen minutes."

"Oval Office?"

"I don't know. So that's tomorrow written off. I won't be able to do anything else all day."

"Nervous?"

"Not yet. But I will be. I'm preparing some tough questions. My editor doesn't want a cozy chat. The Enron scandal, Al Qaeda, Iraq – but especially Enron where he's in danger of taking a serious hit."

"I expect he'll start a war. Politicians always do when there's trouble at home. Remember Dustin Hoffman in *Wag the Dog*?"

"Heh, Dex! Great idea! I'll ask Bush if *he* saw that movie and has plans to start a war in Iraq to deflect attention from Enron."

"Wear a tin helmet, then!"

"How's London? I know about Scotty."

"Pretty bloody."

"I keep saying take care. But afterwards, something else happens and the words have even more meaning. I'm , well … concerned for you."

"I could come over."

"No, bad timing. I'm going to be flying coast to coast for a few days on the Enron story and its implications for London. Keep with the original plan for later this month."

His tone was now serious. "I'm buying a new cellphone, a confidential hot-line that nobody will know to bug. Please do the same. Call me paranoid but I'm taking no chances after today. Tomorrow I'm seeing father. When I've done that, maybe we can speak again."

"Phone me any time. I get lonely here too. If I wasn't so busy, I'd notice it more."

"Good luck with the Prez. Maybe I'll see you on the box?"

"You will. Take care Dex."

London - 13th September 2002

"Please leave a message after the tone." Tiffany was irritated at her inability to get Dex on his mobile or at home. She knew he would be up around Northampton but he had not answered his old or new mobile. In desperation she left messages at his home "Hi, Dex. Tiffany here. One–thirty lunchtime in London. Eight-thirty, breakfast here. Call me anytime after four pm London." She tried not to sound concerned but the urgency in her voice came across. Having heard nothing by ten pm, London, she rang again. She was sitting with a glass of zinfandel in the roof-terrace bar of the Washington Hotel. Still no answer. "Tiffany again. Don't ring me in the next hour or so but catch up when you can. We need to talk."

Dex had been running behind schedule. A couple of accidents near Luton had caused huge lines on the journey north. Stimulating his father had been hard work too and so he had decided to dine at Dukes. He had tried calling Tiffany without success, keen to know about her trip to the White House. Unusually, after signing in, FB had joined him in the bar and suggested they ate together, something that had not happened since the heady days when he had played like a whale. If there were an ulterior motive, and he was sure there was, it never became apparent.

Dex picked every word carefully whenever the topics of Scotty or Mick Glenn were raised, indeed they both tiptoed around the subject. Afterwards, he had drifted round the tables, chatting briefly to Lord Yarbury and Gerhard Hoge about the shootings before playing some small stakes roulette.

Satisfied that Dex was going to be eating at Dukes' expense for the next couple of hours at least, Shawcross had slipped out of the emergency exit and hurried through the darkened Mayfair street until he reached the traffic racing far too fast down Park Lane. There he grabbed a cab northwards to St John's Wood. On the journey, he thought about the previous day's Board Meeting. It had been short and almost friendly. Neither Sir Cedric nor Kevin O'Keefe had caused any trouble. O'Keefe had confirmed the turnaround. "We're well able to service the bank loans," he'd advised with all the needless gravitas that only an accountant can muster when stating the obvious.

But nobody had thanked me.

He was still thinking of this when the taxi dropped him off near the zebra crossing immortalized by the Beatles outside Abbey Road Recording Studios. Despite the lateness, a Japanese tourist was scrawling graffiti on the wall as Shawcross walked by. With his raincoat collar turned up, his black bow tie and dinner jacket were obscured well enough as he turned into the shadowy confines of Hillside Road. A few upstairs lights were still on in the classy homes behind their high walls but the street itself was deserted. He saw the Dexter home just down on the right, its frontage part covered in ivy. He ambled past, taking in the details. He saw the name Porcupine House, deciding it appropriate with pricks like Dexter and his father around. There were a couple of lights on, one up, one down and a side passage to the right. The small garden was filled mainly with shrubs and a large horse-chestnut tree. Best of all, even on his second look there was no sign of any security cameras. That morning, he'd noticed a big bunch of keys on the dressing-table. "Keys to Lord Dexter's," Jude had explained. "I keep forgetting to return them."

"Oh. I'll take them to work. Probably send a car round to his place. The lazy bastards who drive our limos do bugger-all most afternoons anyway. I don't suppose you want to go back there. Is his father still there? And a nurse?"

"I can cope with Dex, no sweat. He doesn't give me the yips. And no, his father's now gone to a place costing over three thousand a week." She rolled her eyes to show her opinion. She had wrapped herself in a towel after her shower. He saw her drop it, hoping to interest him but he was in no mood. Since yesterday, he had become increasingly anxious to get to the truth about Dexter. The keys had opened up an opportunity that he had already been considering.

He grabbed the keys and put them into his pocket before she could change her mind. "No problem. Leave it to me. And what about an early lunch and then a little relaxation? San Lorenzo – 12 sharp?"

Aware from subtle probing over lunch that Dex hadn't renewed the alarm service since the accident. Confident that nobody was home, he walked briskly through the white gate into the garden. Somewhere, a dog was yapping and the empty street seemed full of movement as the stiff north-easterly battered the branches overhead. He scuttled down the side of the weathered building to the kitchen door, knocked and rang before slipping in and locking it behind him. No alarms, no flashing lights. For a moment as he stood in the silence with the red Aga at his side, he wondered if he was taking a risk too far. But the thought was quickly gone. He had to know more about Dexter.

He passed through the hall, where a ceramic table lamp was illuminated. He climbed the stairs and looked in disgust at the portrait of Lord Dexter. The air smelled of dust, lavender polish and a lingering staleness of cigarettes. On the landing, he flicked on the light and went from room to room, quickly dismissing the spare bedrooms as of no interest. A top floor room was set up for Jude and he saw her overnight bag, a few toiletries, some undies, a shirt and a single bed. He went to the main bedroom, facing the front. It had a king size with en-suite bathroom. A glance at the clothes in the built-ins convinced him this was now Dexter's room. A damp towel and a motor-racing magazine was further confirmation. He looked at the bed and fleetingly wondered what games Jude had played there. A red bra and pants lay on a chair and beneath lay a pair of her trainers flung casually on the floor. He glanced at the odds and ends on Dexter's dressing table, went through the drawers but found nothing.

Dexter must have an office somewhere.

Downstairs, he peered into the sitting and dining rooms – both neglected since the crash. With the doors to the rooms kept shut, they smelled musty. A picture on the wall showed the family plus dog sitting on a terrace marked Tuscany 1989. Dex looked even more cherubic than now.

Give the little shit a pair of wings and he'd look good on a cathedral.

He unlocked and opened another door in the square hall and put on the light. He found himself looking down a flight of flagstone stairs leading to the cellar. It too smelled of damp earth. A quick glance around showed it was a dumping-ground for a lifetime's junk and for a few cases of Bordeaux. The last door off the paneled hall was partly open and he glanced in. This was the study, lined from floor to ceiling with law books.

The curtains, heavy and lined were closed. A small brass light with a green shade sat on a leather-topped desk along with a Dell laptop in stand-by mode. He switched on the light and the computer. As he was poised to activate it, he saw the voice-mail light flashing on the telephone. There were three messages. He clicked play. "Hi. Tiffany here. One–thirty your time. Call me. Anytime after four pm London. Keep well." He clicked again and heard the second message timed just over an hour ago. "Tiffany again. Don't ring in the next hour or so but catch up when you can. We need to talk." He played the final message timed just twenty minutes ago. "Phone any time now. Urgent. I've had visitors from London." The mounting concern in her tone was unmistakable.

He carefully went through the stack of papers on the desk but they were all to do with accident claims after Barnes and lawyers' Conditional Fee Agreements. He pressed the Enter key on the Dell and the screen displayed an orderly desktop. He scanned the icons. There were shortcuts headed Barnes, Solicitors, Accountants, Life Insurers, Obsession, Media, Contacts and, intriguingly, Dukes Casino. He clicked open the casino file and saw a list of sub-headings: *Accounts. Wins and Losses. Card-Counting. Martingale. Contacts. Notes. Strategy.*

He clicked on Contacts and a list of names and addresses appeared. The computer was attached to a printer and he was about to run off the list when he realized that a car was stopping. He moved to the edge of the window and peered round the burnt orange drape. He could see nothing beyond the high hedge but the greenery was intermittently blue.

He moved back towards the hall, wondering if he had time to slip out of the side door. Before he had reached it, a loud knocking right beside him startled him and he spun round to look at the heavy wooden front door. He saw the three securely bolts. The police couldn't get in there. He entered the kitchen, keeping to the shadows but heard voices outside even before the bell there rang.

Shit!

He headed for the top floor to make out he was collecting Jude's things.

Bluff my way out.

He grabbed her overnight bag, threw in the few things and with light steps ran down to the floor below. He tossed in the trainers and underwear. Job done. He waited for the sound of the police forcing the door but all seemed quiet. It was strange. There was no shouting, no ringing of the bell or breaking glass.

He peered down from Dex' bedroom to the front garden and saw a uniformed policeman and two plain-clothes detectives exit the white gates. He heard the doors slam. The flashing blue stopped. Gone. But for how long? It was most odd. Hastily, he went upstairs emptying the bag, recreating the original scene. Then, he hesitated at the foot of the stairs debating whether to stay or go. The laptop held the answers. Dexter would still be on his main course. He hurried over to the Dell and pressed the Print button. He was rewarded as the first page of contacts emerged from the Hewlett Packard. Then it stopped, flashing for more paper. He looked around the desk but could see none.

He cancelled the print instruction and switched the printer on and off to delete the memory but the *no-paper* warning remained. He flicked through the contacts on screen but saw neither Glenn nor Brannigan's name. Looked like old school friends with nicknames like Buns, Bigun, Spock and Flatters.

He clicked open *Notes* and then *Strategy*. There he read of schoolboy dreams of how to win at roulette, baccarat and blackjack. The only positive was that he had found nothing to justify his suspicions. But the doubts still remained.

As Dex drove home after dinner through the quiet streets beyond Lord's, he was reflecting on the latest excellent bulletin on Brannigan. He was now out of intensive care though experts were speculating that his career was over. The nurse could only promise he would be allowed visitors *soon*. Overall, this morning had been good too – he admired the Kemsway's techniques for helping father. The first eight weeks involved an assessment and afterwards, they hoped he would be suitable for intensive rehab and cognitive behavior therapy.

At the Unit, he had tried asking his father to raise and lower his head for yes and no but without success. He had watched the therapists testing his responses and had seen some of the other patients who had improved under their care. The neuro-trained nurse and the neuropsychiatric consultant had both inspired him to keep hopeful. "We've seen improvements in worse patients than your father. We would like to see him advance to using a letter board and perhaps even a computer. There's a special program called *EZ Keys for Windows*. It's still early days." The euphoria had lasted a few miles but after that, the prospect of his father ever using a computer seemed utterly remote.

Back at Porky House, he parked up and entered the kitchen. He saw the granite topped table and for a second or two relived the erotic encounter that now seemed a world and a lifetime away. He wondered what Jude was now doing. Of any friendship with Shawcross, there had been no sign since that first evening.

From the fridge, he grabbed a Guinness and picked up the mail from the mat in the hall. He saw the usual sheaf of utility bills, a reminder from the alarm company and an invite to a Lord's Taverners dinner honoring the ITV Formula One commentary team. The last thing was a bunch of keys wrapped in a note, signed by Will Bates who he knew as a limo driver at Dukes. "1415. Your Keys." He tossed them all onto the Welsh dresser in the kitchen and sat down on the same chair where Jude had seduced him.

He drained the Guinness and decided to have a whisky chaser in the best Scottish tradition. Scottish ancestry, however tenuous, was useful at moments like this. He poured a large slug of Glenmorangie from a Waterford decanter, gifted by the Prime Minister to his father after the last Divorce Reform Bill had become law. Thinking of politicians suddenly reminded him that he had still not spoken to Tiffany about her trip to the White House. He topped up the glass and entered the study to check the messages. Instantly, something seemed not quite right. He saw two flashing lights on his father's antique desk. One troubled him more than the other. He was positive he had not left the printer light flashing.

He opened the paper tray. It was empty. He clicked on the *Word* icon and then on *File* and saw the list of recently opened documents. Dukes, Contacts, Strategy, Notes, Wins and Losses.

He reached for the whisky. "Bloody hell! Dukes' file!" The shock clamped him to his seat. He shook his head in disbelief and then shivered. Hell! Someone had been through the place today. Jude? Surely not. Unless her clothes had gone. Were there duplicate keys now? A creaking sound somewhere upstairs broke into his thoughts. For the first time, he felt a shiver of fear. Could somebody still be in the house? Was he a target like Scotty and Glenn? Would Shawcross be after him? No, Dex, he told himself. Wrong question. Had Shawcross been here while I was quaffing Chambolle Musigny with FB? He liked the logic but a rivulet of cold sweat still trickled down to the base of his spine. He sat motionless, uneasy having his back to the study door. His rather small ears were working overtime to make out the slightest sounds from upstairs. But once again, the place was as silent as a hundred year old house can ever be in steady breeze. Creaks, sighs and groans seemed to be everywhere.

Hesitant, he eased out of the chair to make a search. As he stood in the hallway and looked up the shadowy flight of stairs, he had a flashback to the brief image of the masked figure in Monaco, the eyes so eerie behind the hooded face. He shivered again. He returned to the desk, grabbed his father's paper-knife and silently climbed the walnut staircase, ready to bound back down at the slightest provocation. His breathing was labored as he reached the top floor landing. Mother's old quiet room was empty. A quick look in Jude's little room revealed nothing. Everywhere was orderly. Her few belongings were still uncollected. Nothing seemed to have been disturbed. He went down to his first-floor bedroom and put on the bedside lamp. The usual clutter appeared - credit card slips, keys, a ballpoint, old hankies, loose change, dirty clothes and yet more clothes waiting to be washed or hung up. His still damp towel lay across the end of the bed. Situation normal. Relieved, he turned to go down for his voicemail and another slug from the decanter but after a couple of steps he spun round. Despite all the clutter, something stood out. Jude's black satin panties were lying on the floor by the trouser-press. Yesterday, they had been upstairs in her room. He stared at them, trying to fathom out who would have moved them. He returned to the kitchen, tossed back the rest of the whisky and headed for the breakfast bar to get a refill. With no forced entry, Jude could still be eliminated as she had not taken her clothes. And only a man would have been interested in her black panties. So it was a sniffer, like that creepy Malone guy at school – but a sniffer who wanted to read about Dukes too. So why in hell would Shawcross pursue a knicker fetish when he was probably secretly dating her?

He sat down again at his father's well-upholstered chair and looked at his laptop. He tapped again at the recent files list. Thank God! The intruder had not opened *Obsession*. Everything he'd thought, everybody he'd spoken to and every move to fight Dukes was in that file. But the intruder hadn't found it. And luckily the Ortiz book and his current written notes he had taken to Northampton for reading over a pub lunch by the canal. He laughed, loudly, stupidly, a manic insanity of relief flooding him. That file would have revealed enough to fire up Shawcross into whatever nastiness he was capable of. He refilled the printer and ran off the entire contents of *Obsession*.

Then he double-clicked to delete the file and emptied the Recycle Bin. Finally, he ran the Defrag. *Obsession* had gone, though an expert could probably retrieve it. FB had once told him that computers had memories like elephants. Short of crushing the memory to dust and scattering it in the Thames, an expert could still retrieve all the deleted files. For now, this would have to do, until he smashed a hammer through all the drives.

He gathered up the copies, grabbed his computer and went to the dining-room. Father had built a safe inside the wide unused chimney. Scrawled beneath the Regency table was the code for the lock. Armed with a torch, he peered up, smelling the soot from log and coal fires, dating back to the days of London smog. With his head and shoulders right inside, he played with the combination and the door swung open. The heavy metal container was empty except for some of his mother's pearls, rings and a single document in a sealed envelope. In his father's bold hand-writing, it was marked "To be Opened after my Death." He was about to open it when he decided there was no point. Intriguing though it was, father was not yet dead. He locked his own items away, replaced the dried flower arrangement in the fireplace and returned to the study to listen to his voice messages.

Had the intruder listened to them? He sat in silence making notes as he replayed them. What he heard got him nervous, the intensity in Tiffany's voice in the third message echoing round the room in a metallic manner.

Using his new mobile, he dialed her number. "Dex! Thank God you've called. I need to talk to you."

"You sounded worried. Upset the Prez did you?"

She laughed. "I'll tell you about that later. Dex you're in deep shit. Two Met Police detectives flew over specially to interview me. They think you were involved with the shootings of Glenn and Brannigan." The transatlantic line went quiet for so long that Tiffany wondered what had happened. "You still there?"

"Yes, er ... yes I am. Did they say why?"

"Not precisely. At first, I thought they were reopening the Jill Dando murder but it soon became clear that they were interested in me and casinos. Asking about how often I played, where, who with. Only after about ten minutes did they make their point."

"Being?"

"After Brannigan was shot, they had received a call from my Sports Department pal saying that I had recently wanted details about Glenn and Brannigan for reasons I would not give." She snorted in anger at her colleague's behavior. "Naturally, they were on the next flight out. Asked if I was dating them, that kind of crap. Then when that door was slammed, they asked why I needed the names."

"You told them, of course? Said I wanted contact points?"

"Why not? But I didn't tell them why. Said I didn't know. Said I assumed you wanted to invite them to a party or to go gambling together. As for my pal, I'll sort him out later."

"Can't really blame him. It must have looked odd to him. Get their names?"

"Yes. There was Detective-Sergeant Fincham, a miserable asshole with a Midlands accent. Real Mr Excitement, he was." She imitated his heavy flat accent. "The other was Detective Constable Sealey. His eyes bulged out like a defecating bulldog, watering all the time. Between them, their brains would have disgraced a rather dim rhino. Can you believe it! The Brummie git spelled your name *Finnloigh*, just like he pronounced it." They both laughed before the seriousness of the position returned. "Only joking! Lucky for you they know Glenn was killed before midnight. They did not know you had been there that night. Least," she thought for a moment "they never mentioned it. Oh yes – and, no joke this time, Dexter in his notepad was Dexta. I didn't correct the spelling for them. They'll struggle to find you."

Dex heard noises at the front. "Don't be so sure. There's a blue flashing light outside."

London –14th September 2002

Shawcross took a last walk round the tables, joshing with the high rollers, though his mind was on Jude and what tricks she might have in store for him tonight. She'd been doing really well – in bed and in the casino. *Ideal woman for a short lease rather than in perpetuity.* The new members had taken to her and she had done everything asked of her. At home, she was insatiable and inventive, qualities that he admired. But at the moment, sex was no longer uppermost on his mind. As the silver Mercedes cruised slowly along the Bayswater Road, Ella Fitzgerald was scat-singing in a recording from Carnegie Hall. In his pocket were the keys to Porcupine House, duplicated during the morning. At the red lights at Queensway, he was irritated. He soon realized why. It was because the search had proved neither innocence nor guilt. Convinced that Dex was Mick Glenn's source, it was irritating that he had not found the proof. As the lights changed, a single word flashed through his mind. *Obsession.* He recalled the file on the computer. It was an odd name for a file and he regretted that he had not checked it out. He cursed the cop patrol for interrupting him. By the time he reached home, he had decided to try again.

The first thing Dex really noticed after being driven away in the back of the police car was the smell in the Interview Room. The short journey had just been a blur of confusion. Seated in the back between two detectives, he had said nothing, remembering advice from his father years before. "The police have to prove your guilt. You need say nothing, indeed the less you say the better. Best of all, say nothing at all. Resist the temptation to explain away your position, whether guilty or innocent. Oh and of course, Never trust a policeman."

Now, as he sat in the compact Interview Room, he looked around at the plain ochre painted brick walls. A single light with a low voltage bulb and a flying-saucer shade hung from the ceiling. The room had a small high window with parallel bars and by the door stood a constable with an ambitious look about him. His sneering curl of the lip *was an invite to try something so I can really thump you.* The metal chair was uncomfortable with its material sagging and the edges frayed. In front of him sat Det. Sgt Jones, the unprepossessing

Welshman that he had seen at the Press Conference with an accent that was pure Merthyr Tydfil. He had none of the grace of Detective Chief Superintendent Blyth.

Dex put him at around thirty-four, his hair cropped short, his mouth twisted upwards suggesting permanent disbelief at anything said to him. Indeed, his eyes were lifeless adding to that image. The air was stale, the body odors scarcely masked by the quick bursts of air freshener left by the Nigerian cleaner nearly 24 hours before. Jones, who smelled of pungent aftershave and a Tandoori take-away, had a habit of leaning across the plain wooden desk to put his face unpleasantly close. Already, Dex had felt like a boxer, ducking, weaving and pulling back to keep his distance.

"Let's try again, smart-arse." Jones showed his contempt with a sniff. "Where were you on the night of the fifth September?"

"No comment." Dex had used this format for nearly an hour but the detective was still not getting the message.

"If you've nothing to hide, why not answer?"

"Which of these two words don't you understand? *No* or *comment*? Or is the combination of them both together just too difficult? Anyway, no comment."

The detective tried wheedling, a change from the aggression of the first hour. The man had seemed to think that a successful interrogation involved barking the same questions increasingly loudly. "Look." At last he spoke quietly. "I only want to clear you. But let me tell you, sonny boy, this is a murder investigation and you're not helping yourself. I think you know far more about the death of Mick Glenn than you're saying. You wanted him dead, right? Gaming debts."

"No comment."

Jones leaned forward. "I will find the truth, oh yes. Believe me, I will, boyo. Just because you're the son of the former fucking Lord Chancellor, doesn't mean you can piss on a boy from the valleys."

"And just because you don't even know who your father was doesn't mean you can treat me as a murderer without evidence."

Jones jumped from his chair at the insult and grasped the far edge of the table. His face was close, too close. For a moment, Dex flinched, anticipating a blow as he saw Jones raise but then lower his fist. "You'd better take care

Dexter. I'm going to get you." He barked the words before slumping back. "Scotty Brannigan. The cameras picked you up on the Blackstock Road. Right by him just after the shooting. You set it up, right? You wanted to be sure he was dead."

"No comment."

"You're not a journalist but you were at the Glenn Press Conference. I saw you, snooping around us, eavesdropping to hear what we had on you."

"No comment."

"Why did you get both men's telephone numbers? Their addresses?"

"No comment."

"Did you contact them?"

"No comment."

"We know you contacted them," the detective tried to bluff.

"So why did you just ask me? Otherwise, no comment." Dex laughed and Jones angrily pushed back his chair. It banged noisily against the wall.

"That's a nasty bang you've had on the back of your skull. What happened?"

"Nothing as serious as seems to have happened sometime to your face. No comment."

"You're in trouble, cherub chops."

"Not half as much as you. You can't keep me here to shout at. Charge me! I know my rights. Shit or get off the pot. You've farted about long enough." Dex wondered if he had left fingerprints on the gate to Glenn's drive. He suspected he had, no reason back then to be careful. But they can't fingerprint me unless they can charge me. And they can't charge me without evidence. "Are you saying I'm here voluntarily or am I under arrest?"

"Under arrest. But not charged. Yet."

Jones stretched to his full height, the bulky shoulders from his mining tradition nearly blocking the door. "I suggest you stew for a while. Think about cooperation."

"I've thunk," he slanged back. "I suggest you consider what a complete dickhead you've been. Jumping to absurd conclusions and treating an innocent person as a confessed murderer. You're like an impressionist painter. Not interested in the detail, just the overall effect." The grin was huge now. "Why not try painting by numbers. See how far you can get."

The door slammed. Dex was alone with an empty cup and a lingering smell of curry. On his face was a smile.

Thanks, father.

Oxfordshire, England 16ᵗʰ September 2002

Dex had spent the morning in the pleasing grounds of the Kemsway Unit. At last the temperamental English weather had settled down and a sunny day had been forecast. Dex felt exhilarated at his father's progress. Even being in a Unit where so many people were living only through wrecked bodies and damaged brains, Dex found the visits therapeutic. Problems like being banged up and harangued by Jones overnight seemed trivial compared to the battles being fought in the Kemsway.

He left the grounds and headed west towards Oxford and Bladon, confident that father was responding. There were increasing signs of worldly awareness. His eyes now followed movements like an infant. He had told his father that the police had released him for lack of evidence and was convinced the old boy had responded with a smile. The pleasing thought helped take his mind off the tedium of driving round England in a noisy little car that was unlikely to pass its next test for roadworthiness. Even with his foot hard down, the battered yellow Fiat coughed and spluttered to reach forty-five and handled as if the road were a skating-rink. There was no radio, just the bare wires and an empty hole where the original had once been. He cursed the lack of music. The journeys seemed endless without Van Halen or the Jesus & Mary Chain to thump out from at least four speakers.

From the Kemsway, he had driven to the small churchyard at Bladon munching a tasteless burger from an unpleasant takeaway while reflecting on events at the hospital. It had been curious. The staff must have seen him on their televisions or on front pages. They must have gossiped about him, knowing he was coming in, fresh from a police cell. Yet nobody had said a word. He was news of the day, even though he was innocent and Jones had permitted his release. In their uniquely begrudging way, the police had released him without apology after twenty-four hours. "You're fucking lucky boyo," Det. Sgt Jones had commented. "We know you're in this, right in it. But Habeas Corpus and all that crap let's you walk free. But we'll get you."

"You lot make me sick. Just because the media are howling for arrests, you cover yourselves by arresting *anybody* to convince the world you're progressing. You're like blind ferrets trying to get out of a sack."

At the daily media briefing, a disgruntled Blyth had said just enough about Dexter to infer guilt without saying anything of the kind. The tabloids had lurid headlines about him, describing him as the *Victim of Barnes*, the *Man of Mystery* and a known associate of both men. Worse still, some dragged up the old stories of *Louche* as if dead companies gave rise to murderous instincts.

By the time he reached Bladon, it was late afternoon. The clock on the tower of St Martin's Church showed it would soon be six. The autumnal sun was weak now, peeking through the evergreens and hawthorns. Unusually there were no other visitors. Dex was glad of that. The headstones for the two graves stood out, so new, so white surrounded by other weathered ones going back centuries. Above him, swallows swooped and soared, scooping up the flies. The gales of the past few days had gone and the leer on Det. Sergeant Jones' face was a distant memory. The scent of honeysuckle and the clusters of roses that draped the stone walls purged the stink of the police station.

He enjoyed visiting graveyards, though religion had never meant anything. Among the graves, Dex felt at peace. As he sat beside the remains of Beth and his mother, it was like an extension of being at the Kemsway. The permanence of death added a useful perspective to life's aggravations. Each crumbling headstone was a reminder of the shortness of life's span. Each one was an invitation to appreciate the bigger picture, pigeonholing problems rather than being suffocated beneath them.

This was his first return to Bladon since the funerals and he found that rather than being grief-stricken as he had feared, he felt uplifted, almost exhilarated as he looked at the inscriptions on the headstones. He thought too of Mick Glenn heading down his driveway to demand his half million from Audley Shawcross. One minute, he was planning for the hour ahead, a day, a life. Next moment he was dead on a graveled drive. It was the same with his mother and sister, expecting to be on the ground at Heathrow in a few minutes. Then had come freefall from 2,000 feet.

Memories of their funerals came flooding back. That July day had been drab, misty rain drifting across the meadows, soaking the grass. The laments played by the piper had been poignant, capturing the somber mood. The clouds had been low, scarcely above the church tower, making heaven seem that much closer, making the parting seem somehow less distant. After the few other family members had gone, he had remained alone, ignoring the damp penetrating his trousers as he had sat on the wet wall questioning the meaning of eternal life.

Now, he reclined on the warmth of the newly mown grass and fought to imagine his mother's laughter when father was away but somehow her soft features and sad eyes eluded him. All he could see was black smoke and twisted metal rising from a cricket ground. But he could *remember* his feelings, the happier times, when she'd snuggled him on her shoulder and read him stories in his pale blue dressing-gown. He turned towards Beth, eyes sweeping the length of the grave that he knew held no more than a memory in a maple coffin.

So near, so far.

He stretched forward to touch each of the graves in turn, seeking that extraordinary strength that had made Beth his rock.

"I'm at peace with father. Can you believe that? I don't know why, Beth. But I'm glad." He looked at the two plots, side by side, the small caskets of flowers still in bloom from the funeral. "I promised you I'd sort Dukes and get the money for the charity. Remember? But look what it's done. Glenn dead. Brannigan fresh from intensive care. Me in a police cell overnight. Our home turned over and savaged by the police looking for evidence. Evans is a useless cokehead. It's all gone so horribly wrong, Beth."

He had never been closer to seeking spiritual guidance. Religion had been a no-go zone ever since the force-fed days at school. He looked down again as the purple and yellow pansies on the graves fluttered in the breeze. He turned to the sky for guidance as if expecting to see Beth's face emerge. Instead, an image of her plane tumbling from the sky, its wings ripping themselves free was his reward. The sky held no beauty for him today.

"It helps, doesn't it? The talking." Dex jumped in shock at the interruption. His old friend Reverend Hillyer was standing beside him. "People do, you know. Come here to talk." Hillyer slowly eased himself down beside him. His silver hair was thick and swept back. His face was bearded, grey and neatly trimmed. His nose was bulbous, his cheeks too flushed to suggest perfect health. But he oozed love and care. His words at the service had plucked tears from the few people present. He pushed his spectacles further up his nose. "I don't want to disturb you but I know you're troubled." He didn't admit he'd overheard every word of the plea for guidance. He had also heard the BBC News that Finlay Dexter had been arrested but released without charge.

"I feel out of my depth. I got into something thinking I was strong enough to cope. But too much has gone wrong. I'm getting crushed by the burden. Others are getting hurt. Together, Beth and I were so strong. You'll remember that. We still talk. And today of all days, I needed an answer."

Hillyer leaned across to put a hand on Dex' black T-shirt. "Perhaps *I* am the answer. Her way of answering. Was it just chance I was so close by? That I was here, ready to help? Perhaps not."

Dex smiled. This was like those days eighteen years before when he had chatted at the Vicarage in Woodstock about father's bullying. "Go on."

"How is your father? As bad as the papers say?"

Dex felt the question was curiously loaded and gave the vicar a second glance before he answered. "We've grown closer. He's never going to achieve much now. I'm fighting to get him the best medical result possible."

"I'm glad."

"Dex, I read the papers today, listened to the news. You're into something you can't control. Right?"

"Like a juggernaut without brakes. It's rolling away, unstoppable. I've done nothing wrong, just been the victim of an injustice. Not the arrest. I'm talking of long before that. I swore to Beth I'd get even. You'd say that was unchristian. Y'know, turn the other cheek."

"I don't agree." He offered Dex a mint and sat with his knees bent, wrapping his arms tightly round the black cassock that covered his legs. "Sometimes truth and right cannot triumph without a struggle, perhaps even a battle without great grief and suffering. Hitler's Nazi Germany was an example. Sometimes you must stand up and fight."

"But though I'm right, though my battle is just, though perhaps not truly Christian, everything has gone wrong. The gods are against me."

"Here in St Martin's of all places we have reason to remember 1939 to 1945. Britain, indeed the entire civilized world, nearly lost to Hitler. We faced disaster. The German war-machine was so mighty – yet courage and determination triumphed. Only a great leader, buried in this very churchyard, saved us all." Hillyer pointed across to the simplicity of the grave of Sir Winston Churchill. "Without his single-minded determination, his self-belief in the face of overwhelming odds, the jackboots would even now be trampling through the gardens of England."

He leaned across and squeezed a fatherly arm round Dex's shoulder. "Life must seem very empty. Your family destroyed. Your sense that God has failed you. Perhaps even that you have failed God." He smiled, a gentle and diffident look. "Truth and right will triumph. But it takes the iron will of a Beth or a

251

Churchill." He twisted awkwardly to make eye contact. "Dex, the *spirit* that is their legacy is something to which we must turn in moments of despair. God knows poor Beth had to struggle all her life. But she triumphed. Her very weakness became her greatest strength."

"So I should fight on for truth? Despite the adversity? Despite the unjust suffering that I've brought about? Perhaps being the innocent cause of people being shot and even killed?"

"Not *despite* it. *Because* of it. I don't pretend to understand what promise you made to Beth or why. None of my business. But if it was right to seek an eye for an eye, don't give up." He paused to caress a pansy. "Indeed, a journey unfinished is one better not started. You've embarked on seeking fair retribution. *Finish the journey.*"

Dex looked away and gazed at the austere simple grave of one of the world's greatest ever men. "I'm listening."

"It's a hackneyed cliché but the darkest hour comes just before dawn. When you've finished speaking to Beth, talk to our Winston. Look at the photos of him in the church – oozing defiance. Then imagine the drifting cigar smoke, that growling voice that gave us strength while striking terror into the Nazis as he relentlessly closed in on them." He shifted his ageing body with considerable difficulty to a standing position. "You consider your own efforts feeble but they may seem *very different* to your enemies who have things to conceal. Think how *they* perceive you. Perhaps you're doing better than you think. I talk to Winston often. He never fails me when I'm faced with burdens too great for a mere vicar in a small village church."

Each man fell into the other's arms, just as Dex had done as a confused schoolboy. "Thanks. I'll do that."

Unusually for Hillyer, he suddenly looked uncomfortable, his hands and feet all restless. "Dex, remember after the funeral, we spoke in the porch?" He nodded towards the entrance. "I said I would talk to you later about something."

"So you did. I'd forgotten."

"That wasn't the right time. Now, I feel I must breach a confidence. I think your father would want that." Dex thought back to the document he had found in the safe but not opened. "Follow me." They walked between the graves, Dex increasingly keyed up at what was about to be revealed. Towards the back of the graveyard, they reached a headstone, the marble scarcely weathered. In contrast, the flowers in the small urn on the grave were dead. "Read it."

Dex saw that the grave was that of Nathalie Rosemary Boxter who had died 14th January 1997 aged thirty-one. He turned to Hillyer who offered him another mint, which he accepted.

"Rosie – she never used the name Nathalie – lived in the village here. She worked in the tearooms in Woodstock." He paused. "Let's sit down again, shall we? Maybe on the wall there." Dex' mind was racing ahead, imagining already that Rosie had been yet another of his father's pretty young things. "Rosie had little money. In June 1995, she gave birth to a son, Bobby." He saw the look on the listener's face and shook his head. "No. It's not what you think. The father was in the SAS. It was a case of macho man plus alcohol equaled desire for what I'm told is now called a *quick bunk-up*. But the soldier never acknowledged the child as his and he was then killed on a mission in Central Africa. The child was born healthy and later christened right here by me. Rosie loved that child but, as a single mother, was struggling for money. Her own father was dead. He had worked on the Blenheim estate and had died poor. Rosie lived in a tiny cottage with her mum who is now about seventy-three." He fell silent, lost in his own memories as Dex waited, eyes looking across the fields to the distant woodlands. "After midnight one evening in early January, she was driving her car on a country road between Charlbury and Wootton, not far from here."

"I remember the road well."

"Bobby was in the baby-seat. A truck skidded on black ice and swiped her car like it was a toy. It was crushed beyond recognition and finished in a pond beside the road. The other driver was killed instantly. On a snowy winter's night, the road was quiet. The only car to come along was..."

"My father?"

"He'd been enjoying, shall we say, a pleasurable evening at the home of a young woman barrister who lived nearby. She was married but her husband, also a barrister, was away at a trial somewhere."

"Father was never one to spurn a chance."

"The safest thing for him to have done was to phone from a call-box – and disappear. The Lord Chancellor playing away from home with the wife of a fellow barrister was an unedifying story if the media had started asking what he was doing in rural Oxfordshire at that time of night. He did phone the emergency services from a box not far from the scene but gave a false name. He then raced back to the wreck, forced open a door and crawled into the mess. He found Rosie totally immersed under water. It was pitch black but he knew there was nothing he could do for her. But he battled with the seat belt and somehow pulled her out. He covered her up, tried to pump water from her but realized it was probably hopeless.

Then he heard a baby's cry and he crawled back into the wreck even as the car was sinking deeper. He then found the baby in the back, still cocooned in its seat. With the roof crushed in, he had to squirm and wiggle to find the buckle to release the belt. He twisted and shoved with the car settling deeper into the muddy bottom all the time. The rear seat area had been that bit higher and the baby's head was only just above the water line. Once he had undone the buckle, he tried to get out. Unfortunately, his efforts made the car move and he was trapped too but your father never panicked. Somehow, he lifted the baby upwards towards a broken window on the upper side just as the ambulance appeared. He shouted to attract attention and was able to hand the shivering little bundle straight to one of the crew. He himself was too bulky to get through the window but the fire team cut away the door and pulled him free."

"Did he ever give his real name?"

"No. He told the fire people that he was a rescuer and had not been in the car. He left a false name and address and after a quick chat with the police, got into his own car and drove off.

"Quite a hero." He ran a finger along the moss on top of the wall. "And he confided in you?"

"Yes. About two weeks later and before the inquest, he came to see me by appointment. We talked for a couple of hours. He felt deeply emotional about the baby. I became the link between your father and Rosie's distraught mum. Your father set up a significant trust fund to look after them both, though it was all cleverly done by London solicitors. His name as the benefactor was untraceable. From memory, he put a couple of hundred thousand into it."

"Does Bobby know my father?"

"Called him Uncle Angus." Hillyer lowered his eyes. "Bobby has been asking recently when his uncle's coming to see him. Your father was here most weekends. I think he combined illicit meetings in the Bear at Woodstock with taking young Bobby out to tea, to the swings or round Blenheim."

"My mother told me that he often just disappeared without explanation. She knew him well enough to assume he was with another woman but she never would have guessed he had an almost adoptive son."

"Who he treated with all the love that he had denied you. It was as if he knew he'd got it all wrong with you and wanted to try again. He told me only last April that he wished he could rewrite your upbringing."

Dex looked pensive and was silent for quite a while before replying. "My turn to be glad. But poor Bobby! He needs a father."

"Well, a father figure."

"I'm not really suitable am I? Not if you believe the tabloids."

"I'll talk to dear old mum. She doesn't know who your father was and I told her he was dead rather than brain-dead. It seemed tidier. I'll think about what's best. Leave it with me." He was unsure whether Dex was yet ready to take on developing a relationship with a small child already burdened with so much baggage. If half of what the media wrote were true, then Dex was scarcely the ideal role model. Yet he knew a different Dex, a caring loving person who had used his teenage years to cultivate the image of rebel the more his father reacted against him. "I'll let you know. The money of course still comes through. What the child needs is love from worthwhile relationships."

Hillyer looked at the clock on the tower. "I'm judging a Women's Institute competition tonight. I must go. But I want you to take your time, talk to Beth; talk to Winston. And do what your heart then tells you." He gave Dex a bear hug. "Winston used to come here often to see the graves of his parents." He fumbled in his pockets and found a history of the church. "Back in 1895 not long after his father died, he wrote to his mother." He adjusted his glasses. *"I went this morning to Bladon to look at Papa's grave ... I was so struck by the sense of quietness and peace, as well as by the old-world air of the place that my sadness was not unmixed with solace..."*. He smiled in a way that turned the clock back twenty years. "You see, it worked for him. It can work for you." He waved his arm in a thoughtful gesture and, showing his age, walked slowly towards the timbered archway of the lychgate.

Dex stayed a while longer, standing quietly beside the graves. From somewhere across the fields a cow, deprived of her calf, was blaring in agony. The world seemed full of anguish. Yet a feeling of peace descended on him and lingered as he fired the engine to head back to London. The solace that Winston had found in a country graveyard could still work its magic.

London – 16th September 2002

The journey into London down the M40 and M4 was about as hellish as usual, stop-go all the way from Heathrow. Dex lost count of the number of times he checked his watch but at least as he sat fuming in the long tailbacks, a new idea, *a big idea*, had struck him, good enough to help him get through the walking pace crawl from Chiswick through to the West End.

Being late was not his style. Being forty minutes late was an embarrassment and he looked sheepish as he apologized to Lord Yarbury. As it was, he had to save time by asking the hotel to valet park the little rust-bucket, something the doorman organized with barely concealed disdain. "My other car's even older," he told him as he slipped the man fifty pence.

The peer had downed a few pink gins already in the Rivoli bar at the Ritz Hotel and was keen to move on to the restaurant. "I'm dining with friends and you are *rather* late. Will we be long, old thing?" Dex said no and accepted a glass of Pouilly Fumé. Remembering the advice from FB, he sat well clear of the peer and let him waffle on about life at Westminster until he could take no more. "I know you're in a hurry Arthur, so I want to talk to you in confidence."

"My dear old thing! Lips are sealed. Mum's the word. What is it? This stuff in the papers? Problems over father, what? Women trouble maybe?"

"Dukes and Mick Glenn."

"Hrrmh"! The derisive grunt showed that death had not mellowed Yarbury's views of the man. "Disgraceful behavior at Silverstone. Then all that stuff about him and Kid Creole's popsy."

"Creole Henry," the laughed correction was gentle. "Did you ever come across him after Silverstone?"

"Socially, thank heavens no! Saw him at Dukes, once or twice. That was too often."

"When did you last see him?"

"Memory's not what it was. Does it matter? Well I suppose as you are asking, it must! Why are you asking?"

"Don't ask me yet please."

"Well, no matter." He violently swiveled a finger in his left ear. "The last time? By jove, yes. Remember that well. He was causing trouble again. As I arrived at Dukes, he was shouting off his mouth to FB. Embarrassing for a chap, so I pretended not to have heard. But of course, I heard every word. Ignorant man!"

"When was this?"

Yarbury rummaged in an inside pocket and pulled out a red leather diary. "Don't record these things but it must have been the day before I went to my cottage in Cromer. I'd planned to ask Shawcross to ban him but he was murdered before I returned. Chap was an embarrassment."

"The date?"

He flicked the pages, some of them food-stained and mostly dog-eared. "Went to Cromer on 31st August. So, night before."

"So what was he up to? Losing again and shouting about it?"

"Tom on the door let me in. Soon as I started to go down the stairs, I heard shouting. I recognized the voice. Straight off a dust-cart."

"What was he saying?"

"Called FB a bald-headed bunny. Good line that coming from an ignoramus but deuced impertinent, what? Then he was on about Dukes being crooked. Saying the dealers were bent. Said he had evidence from the last time in. Reckoned he'd been cheated of four hundred thousand. More maybe. I don't recall the detail. Something about they'd been caught in the act. He knew the whole works. He said he'd be in to see Shawcross on the next Thursday - the fifth that would be."

"The day he was murdered. Was he menacing?"

"Hell, yes! When he passed me on the stairs, his eyes were like someone about to be admitted to Rampton and never released." He downed the last of his gin. "Ignored me of course. Then he turned round and shouted at FB. Said they were all going to jail."

"And FB?"

"Apologized to me. Reckoned Glenn had been drinking."

"Was my name mentioned?"

Yarbury looked around as if the answer were written on a wall. "No. No, I'm sure it was not."

"Have *you* ever felt cheated at Dukes?"

"My dear chap! Never. Impossible. Only damned fools expect to win."

Dex looked uncertain but was not intending to challenge the peer just yet. "You enjoy a flutter. You always claim to lose. Suppose you loaned me one hundred thousand pounds and I promised you two hundred thousand back by third January, you'd think it a good deal. Tax free."

Yarbury's eyes rolled even more than Dex had expected. "You offering that?" The frown was excited but suspicious.

"Yes. I have a roulette system that will deliver all this and more. You have my word that you'll double your money." Dex raised an eyebrow and looked his most impudent. Beneath the table his fingers were crossed for more than one reason.

"Can't do it now. Meet me here tomorrow at noon. I'll bring the cash. You're a smart young fella. If you lose it, hell it's only what I'd lose myself. If you win, then damn me, it would be good to get something back from Dukes!'" He looked wistfully towards the beauty of the dining-room. "Now, if you'll excuse me, dinner calls."

"Of course. Thanks."

"Drat! Should have remembered before, young Finlay. There was one thing," he turned again. "There've been damnably few blackjacks and twenties recently. Some Johnny foreigner mentioned it. Sour grapes, I told him. Pull yourself together. Bad form for a chap to complain."

"His name?"

"No idea. Never seen him again. Small chap. But there have been damnably few blackjacks. Mind you, I'd lose anyway. See you tomorrow."

"Thanks."

"Good to see you dear boy. How's your father?" But he was out of earshot before Dex had replied.

London 17th September 2002

"Just a week and you'll be over," said Tiffany sounding enthused. She was phoning from Los Angeles. "I'm covering the build-up to the gubernatorial elections. Governor Gray Davis is up against it but clinging on."

Dex had little interest in any politics, let alone elections for State Governors in the USA. "Sounds ghastly. Try to stay awake! I went to the Comedy Store tonight. If *new* gags only had been the rule, it would have been a short evening."

"Tell me them next week. I'll be in Washington by the weekend. We must start planning what you want to see, to do."

"The usual tourist traps. I'll leave you to finesse the details. I'll book flights and a hotel."

"No hotel, Dex. Save the money. You'll stay with me at Foggy Bottom." Dex weighed the implications when she continued. "There's a spare room."

"Thanks, great." Dex mustered up more enthusiasm than he felt at the prospect..

"No more news from the cops?"

"Not a peep. They're still getting stick for lack of progress. I'm just a footnote in the stories now. I get the odd door-stepper but I can cope. Coffee comes cheap when its just for one." Though they were now both using new cellphones, Dex had insisted they occasionally used their normal lines as well, to avoid suspicion. He wanted to tell her the big news – about Panama, about one hundred grand from Yarbury and that he would visit Scotty in hospital the following evening. It would have to keep. "In the morning, I'm seeing the solicitor about the plane crash. Still no explanation of the cause."

"The black box and the cockpit voice recorder haven't proved anything. Too many vested interests. Difficult to get near the truth."

"I don't care to dwell on it. Not yet anyway. It's nearly midnight here. Doesn't do to start thinking about what went wrong. I'd never sleep at all. Enjoy LA."

Tiffany laughed. "Hard not to! Endless blue skies and a warm breeze. Tonight I'm dining under the stars at Santa Monica, looking out over the ocean."

"With someone interesting?" Dex' tone showed his anxiety.

"Famous and handsome too." She laughed at her teasing. "But don't worry. He'd no more try to seduce me than would Elton John. Not his scene."

Over the speakers came Sophie Ellis-Bextor belting out *Murder on the Dancefloor* as Dex padded round the house in his bare feet, cursing the cops for the mess they had left after their search. Nothing in the house seemed to be in the right place and someone had finished an entire packet of his chocolate chip cookies. But at least the bastards hadn't found the safe in the chimney and now with Yarbury's cash coming on tap, he had bought a new computer with no incriminating memory. Precisely how he was going to double Yarbury's payback, he was not sure. The big idea had yet to take shape.

The phone rang. "You are a night-bird I think." Hoge's accent was unmistakable. "So, I wanted to tell you. When I read you were in jail, I told the police you were in Dukes until after midnight. So you couldn't have killed that footballer."

"I might have hired someone!" Dex heard the German's sharp intake of breath at the implications. "Only kidding. I didn't and I'm really grateful for the alibi. Good of you. No doubt that helped them decide to release me." He hadn't the heart to tell his friend that the cops hadn't suggested he had fired the shots at Glenn or Brannigan – rather that he had hired an executioner. "See you soon. Hope you're winning with that system!"

"Winning? We Germans lose everything. Big football matches, 5–1 you beat us last September, the World Cup final 1966, two World Wars and probably at synchronized swimming too. So with my roulette, I am only maintaining the finest traditions of the fatherland. Goodnight my friend."

Dex loved the German's self-deprecating humor and laughed as he sat at the desk for a few moments lost now in thought about Panama. The report had been explosive. As he stared at the sheaves of paper, his mother's advice *knowledge is power* rang true. Yet again he had cause to thank Walter McKay. He now knew Audley Shawcross' most precious secret. Damning enough for the Gaming Board to remove him from the *fit and proper* list for running a casino in the UK or the USA. But not enough to destroy Dukes, let alone Space City.

For the third time, he picked up the report from Fernando y Fernando, the Panamanian agents turning to the Conclusions. "Based on our investigations, we are sure that Audley Shawcross was a blackjack dealer at the Gran Paradiso Casino, Panama City. Two other dealers, now in positions of senior management in other casinos both remembered him – though only reluctantly admitted it. The management appreciated him because he dealt crooked blackjack - producing suitable cards for the house to win or for players to lose. He could deal seconds whenever he wanted.

"On the night in question, the casino had been quiet. A young Mexican who had lost several hands caught Shawcross cheating. There was a scuffle. Shawcross pulled a large knife from inside his jacket and stabbed the youngster. The Mexican, in self-defense smashed a glass ashtray and then struck Shawcross with it, down his right cheek. Other staff tried to pull Shawcross off but they failed. He was crazed. Witnesses remembered several blows with the knife. Shawcross went from calm dealer to a berserk killer in seconds. One witness described him as a psychopath – a man who plainly enjoyed killing and showed no remorse.

"Management wanted to protect the license. Friendly people in the police were fixed. Witnesses who had not even been present told the police that the Mexican had attacked the dealer with the broken ashtray after being caught cheating. Then he had produced the knife but the dealer had wrestled the knife off the Mexican and stabbed him once. This was wholly untrue. We are satisfied that he always carried a Bowie Knife. Both our witnesses had been shown it, Shawcross saying he carried it in case of trouble.

"In the official police report, the dealer's name was recorded as Ben van Zandt, a South African, who had left the country. Our two witnesses who saw what happened each received a large sum in cash for their silence. Shawcross was smuggled into Costa Rica, perhaps even that night, and disappeared. He left behind a beautiful young woman with whom he had been living."

Dex grabbed a rich tea biscuit, the boring ones the cops hadn't eaten. It seemed reassuring to be munching normally, doing something mundane when surrounded by such disturbing evidence. The thought that a murderer, a psychopath to boot had been sitting at this desk searching for a link to Glenn's outburst made him shiver. Suddenly, his excitement turned to fear.

Dex locked the report in the safe along with the dossier from the fingerprint expert he had hired who had checked the printer buttons and the computer key-pad and had taken some prints from them. He had also retained some DNA and wanted Dex to get hold off a glass, cigar butt or cup used by

Shawcross for comparison. Then the case of burglary would be complete too.

For a moment with the safe open, he had again fingered the sealed envelope, tempted to open it. His father had dated it June 1st 2002 beside his signature across the flap only shortly before the crash. He was sure it was not a Will because his father had been planning to fix that with his solicitor. Perhaps it was a confession about young Bobby

He flicked on MTV to fill the house with noise and tried to concentrate on his Grand Prix magazine but his thoughts kept returning to the evil sounding Bowie Knife and the psychopath who had wielded it. He put it down and reflected how since visiting Bladon, he had started to climb from the black pit. Suddenly, so many things were falling into place. But even filmed evidence if Kenny, the agent he had hired, could get it would not destroy both casinos. He needed that extra something. But what that something was eluded him during a broken night's sleep, thinking too often of the Bowie Knife.

As dawn broke, he went downstairs and boiled a kettle for some instant. As he was spooning in the coffee he knew his next move – checking on Hoge and Crabant. Why had these big players and countless more joined Dukes? Was it something more than coincidence? And why was Jude so involved with some of them? She always seemed to be with a rich stranger.

He listened to the ticking of the kitchen-clock. Each movement seemed like Big Ben in the still hush. Since reading the Panama report, he hated silence. With a swift, nervous movement, he put on the early news to bring the house to life, hoping to quash the image of Shawcross creeping through the darkened rooms, perhaps armed with his Bowie. A thought shot across his mind, sufficient to make him put down the cup for fear of dropping it. The cops had said they had called round before to arrest him. Had Shawcross been there? Perhaps been disturbed and left the job only part done? It seemed plausible. So if he had been interrupted, then perhaps he would come back.

As the coffee went cold, a plan started to emerge, both audacious and dangerous.

Yeah, great plan Dex.

Made your own Will?

He decided to think it through again.

London – 18th September 2002

Dex was just backing the car out of the drive when Mark Evans rang, sounding in obvious distress. "I need to see you, man. I'm in real trouble. Today. Now. Like I'm sorry I walked out on you at breakfast."

"Busted? Card-counting?"

"Last night. By now, I'll be blacklisted everywhere. How'll I afford my next fix? Like man, you've got to help."

The man's attitude angered Dex. "I haven't *got* to do anything. I owe you nothing. Scarcely know you. Why would I want to rely on a cokehead? You're no use to me if you're banned everywhere."

Evans' voice was breaking. "If I don't pay the maintenance, Kath will stop me seeing little Emily. Then I might as well be dead."

Mention of Emily brought back warm but poignant memories of the child with the porcelain features who surely wanted no more than a father and mother together to love her. "I've a meeting at Coutts Bank in the Strand this afternoon. Then I'm free. Meet me in the Sherlock Holmes pub. Northumberland Street. It's just behind Charing Cross Station. 6 p.m."

"Thanks mate."

"Be on time. I've another meeting at seven-thirty."

The two big plans that had at first seemed so cunning now seemed absurd. Or was it just that the Bowie Knife was getting to him? As he drove past an empty Lord's cricket ground, not a flashy blazer in sight, his brain was asking why he was now tempted to turn to a cokehead after the disaster with Mick Glenn. Because, he told himself, I'm a soft touch where kids are concerned. Because I had no happy childhood and Emily deserves a better one than the mess she's now in. That's why. He swerved late to avoid a taxi in Baker Street but continued his thoughts even though he was not concentrating on his driving. Lord Yarbury could introduce Evans as a new member, unaware of the truth. They would never be suspicious enough to run the computer facial recognition software over him if Arthur Yarbury signed him in as a guest using a false name. "Dex – you're getting all those ducks in a row. Pity they're all lame though."

After the smokiness of the Sherlock Holmes pub, Dex appreciated the clinical surroundings of the private hospital behind Harley Street. Mark Evans had arrived on time but had cut a pitiful figure. Dex had felt uncomfortable even sitting with someone that looked to have slept rough with the winos on a park bench. Yet on reflection, the authenticity of the famous pub had proved ideal for the tempo of the meeting. Memorabilia of Holmes and Watson were everywhere. Plaster-casts of the hound's footprints and Holmes' pipe in a glass case had set the tone. Before arriving, Dex had virtually decided to sign him up. Yarbury's money and the life policy had opened new horizons.

On seeing the dishevelled figure, Dex had been torn, sound sense nearly being outweighed by need. The first few minutes of chat had made Dex increasingly uneasy. But then he had glanced up at the life-sized head of the Hound of the Baskervilles fixed to the wall. Its huge eyes flashed insanity just like the figure sitting opposite. To the left was a portrait of the great detective. The contrast was remarkable. The shrewd beakiness of Sherlock Holmes' face was so calm, so unhurried. The watchful eyes looked into the distance with a measured disdain. He seemed to be reproving of Dex' headlong rush - warning him to curb his Watson-like sentimentality. Elementary, dear Dex. Compassion, yes. But involvement no. Be patient.

"Sorry, Mark. You're no use to me like this. Your hands are shaking. The Gaderene swine have just crapped in both your eyeballs. They wouldn't let you into a dog-track, let alone accept you for membership at Dukes, disguised or not."

Evans started to get up to leave, wiping his nose with his hand. "So its goodbye to Emily. Not your fault, not your problem."

Dex waved him back to the bench-seat and his whisky-sour. He looked up at Sherlock, hoping for approval. "Relax! I hadn't finished. I *do* need your help. Here's what I propose." For the next hour, he had argued, cajoled and taunted Evans until at last the man had agreed. The meeting ended with a handshake and an unwelcome hug from the figure that was little more than a rattle of bones.

Now as Dex sat in the smoke-free waiting-room to see Scotty, Dex was unsure whether he would ever see or hear from Mark again. It had been a gamble, one where Evans could make him look very foolish – or an outright 35 to 1 winner. Evans had agreed to be treated in Clouds House at East Knoyle in Wiltshire. The cost would be an advance for his work in the casino. Dex reckoned it a big gamble, yet as he flicked through *Country Life*, he felt confident that the cost could be a great investment. It would help Evans, help Emily and hopefully rip the lid off blackjack at Dukes.

A young Chinese nurse appeared and led Dex along the corridor and into a light, airy and spotlessly clean private room. A pornographic video was on screen with two women and a man grunting and groaning theatrically. Scotty grinned and turned down the volume. "I'm still only up to watchin'. But it won't be long now, will it Kim?" He was wearing RGB colored pajamas. "How do you like my Chinese miracle? This is Kim. Saucier'n a bottle of soy!"

She shook a reproving fist at him. "He's terrible this man." Dex heard from her voice that she loved the attention. "He needs rest. Thirty minutes. No more."

"I'm jus' great. Never better." Scotty winced as he changed position. Dex pulled up a chair, feeling as if he knew the man and yet the reality was that they had barely spoken. Filtering from dozens of articles on the web, he had distilled the American into a tight-fisted womanizer; a man of great courage and a risk-taker with a sharp brain. There were stories of his sharp wit, a tendency years before to drink too much now cured and examples of violent outbursts from a short-fused temper *off-track*. The abiding impression was of a ruthless selfishness that rarely, if ever, wavered. If he had any loyalty, which one journalist doubted, it began and ended with himself.

"You're looking pretty good." Dex exaggerated, thinking the driver rather pallid and his face now more drawn than his PR image. "I was there, at the shooting. I thought you'd never survive."

"I've seen the photos. Looked worse than it was. But my left shoulder joint is pretty much crapped out." He shook his head ruefully. "But what's been almost worse - your goddamned limey coppers have never stopped fussin' my brain – roun' here always askin' the same dumb questions. Specially the guy with eyes like someone jus' poked a stick up his ass."

"That's Sealey. My girlfriend Tiffany reckoned he looked like a defecating bulldog." Dex liked that. *My girlfriend*. It sounded good.

Scotty laughed but quickly stopped as the pain racked his frame. "Constipated too, I'd say. No wonder they ain't got no clue who shot me or murdered Mick. Man! Have they gone on 'bout you, despite what I told them! They think I owed you money! Cops – all the world over, all the same. Jus' woodentops. How's your head? Looks good from here."

"Nothing now, really. You know I was arrested?"

"Sure. Bullshit, I told them. Said they were plum crazy an' even dumber'n they looked. That Sealey guy! He can talk longer'n the Mississippi river. Wanted to know how well I knew you. How much I owed you. Askin' why you needed my phone number. Mick's too. I told them. I said I was flying you to Monza for the Grand Prix. Told them we all had an interest in roulette and you wanted the three of us to play together. Right?" Scotty gave a generous wink and sipped a glass of water.

"Spot on. Perhaps that's why they released me. What you said, I mean." Dex leaned forward and could smell iodine and urine. And there was something else. What was it? Then he knew the smell from years back. His father! Late in the evening – Irish whiskey. *So Brannigan's back on the booze.* "I need your help, Scotty. More than ever."

The patient handed Dex a can of Coors Lite and seemed to ignore the implicit question. Either that or he had a strange way of responding. "I won't ever race again. That's what they say. I overcame the leg injury from Monaco. Well - jus' about. But this motherfucker's destroyed my shoulder. It'll take two years, maybe more." His cool stare was incisive, testing Dex for a reaction. Dex saw caution in the grey eyes. He recognized a man who gave away nothing easily - money, an inch of track or his true feelings. What you saw was not always what you got. "I need a purpose," Scotty waved his good arm at a pinboard covered with cards and messages from fans and friends. "Sympathy's fine for an hour. Give me a purpose."

"I could give you more than one," Dex almost cut in with enthusiasm. "I'm building evidence against Dukes – and Space City too. I want to clinch the last bits of evidence to sink them before the new tower in Vegas opens in December." He fiddled with his wristwatch before steeling his courage. "I'm going to wipe them both out. Raze them." He could see a mix of disbelief and curiosity fill the creased face. It was no time to be coy. It was a unique chance, the only chance. Now was a time for painting in violent colors before plastering on the bullshit afterwards. "Implode them. When I've finished, both casinos might just as well be dust." He leaned forward, looked around and then spoke in slow hushed tones, every word enunciated. "Space City's having a tough time. The building works are being bankrolled through Dukes by money stolen or cheated from members. You and Mick were rolled over that night I saw you. Before that, they'd mugged me for over one million. Ever since, I've been gathering evidence. I'm getting there." Dex looked round again. "I need help."

Scotty looked suspiciously at Dex. "You reckon Dooks is crooked?"

"I do." Dex looked and sounded sincere as he nodded his head in emphasis. "Together, we can destroy them."

"Sorry, pal. Your hobby-horse doesn't exactly do it for me," Scotty replied. "I've lived in Vegas too long. You go to casinos. You lose. Don't cry, son. Tough places. No boo-hoo." He adjusted the sling around his arm. "But if you know they're crooked, you go right on ahead and prove it but that sure ain't helpin' me."

"Suppose," Dex said after a long pause as he glanced at the cards pinned to the wall "just suppose I can also prove who murdered Mick and who shot you." He watched Scotty carefully. His hope for an immediate and positive reaction was disappointed.

"You gonna prove that the same guys shot us both?" Neither face nor voice showed anything but deep skepticism.

"Yes." Dex went for it, though he had no evidence at all.

Scotty tried to lean forward but the effort was too much. "I'll tell you somethin' straight. I sure as hell ain't been porking Creole Henry's broad."

"I don't think Creole Henry is involved. Nor do I think Mick was match-fixing."

Scotty shifted uneasily, his look furtive. It puzzled Dex as he watched the patient nervously twirl his sideburn between finger and thumb. Suddenly his eyes did not want to meet Finlay's. "I'm listenin', bud. No." He twisted awkwardly on the bed. "More'n that. I'm ahead of you. You think the shootings were linked with Dooks?"

Dex nodded as if afraid to say the yes-word - which he was. "Shawcross is a dangerous man." It wasn't comforting to stare that fact in the face when you were out to get him.

"Shawcross?"

"Listen. After I spoke to Mick – told him he'd been shafted, he went hell-raising. Threatened to bust Dukes. I've got a witness. The night he was killed, he was due to have a showdown with Shawcross. He was silenced before he could cause more trouble." He watched for a reaction but Scotty was inscrutable. "He wanted half a million. But from Dukes' position, they were damned if they paid, damned if they didn't."

"Why?"

"Because he was such a wild card he'd have shouted his mouth off either way."

"That was Mick. All the subtlety of a sex-starved jack-rabbit." Scotty's face was troubled. "You guessin' or do you know all this shit?"

Never had Dex met such a stare. He felt naked. "Deduction."

"So jus' guesswork." Scotty looked irritated. "Don't win no Grand Prix by guessin'. It's detail. Millimeters in set-up. Plannin'. Fuel loads. Pit strategy. Knowin' every bump. Know when you're goin' to find dirty air. That's what brings wins. Facts. Experience. That and commitment. Sure as hell, it ain't guesswork." He rolled his eyes dismissively.

Dex was in no mood to surrender and shook his head. "Judgment. That's what counts. Judgment based on *experience* is often inspired guesswork based on incomplete facts." He leaned across and fixed Scotty with his most direct look, the eyes not playful, the mouth hardened. "Give me credit, Scotty. I'm not guessing *the big picture*. I've joined the dots. What's inside them, well that's only the detail." Dex fought to sound less defensive than he felt. "Anyway, in your job, *you* guess too. Like not being sure what refueling strategy other teams are using. Like not knowing if it will rain on the third lap or the thirtieth. Don't tell me you don't guess – but you act on the best information." He finished his beer with a noisy gulp. "That's what I've done." He threw the can into a plastic bin. "Look Scotty. I need a team player. You're ideal."

"Huh! You think so? Me? Who the fuck told you I was a team player?"

"I'm looking for someone with a cool head who knows Vegas, knows the right people there, someone with a quick brain, someone who plays in Dukes." He stood up and jabbed his finger repeatedly. "Above all, I need a man with the balls to take on a psychopath."

"Psychopath?" The suspicious eyes and respectful tone revealed a watershed moment. Scotty pushed himself more upright on the bed. "Shawcross? A psychopath?"

"He's killed before."

"You're kiddin' me." He looked directly at Dex for the first time in a while.

"I can prove it."

"More than just killing – Shawcross enjoyed it. Bowie-knifed a Mexican."

"So how long was he locked up?"

"Never even charged. A big fix. Let me ..."

"Wait one." Scotty stopped Dex in mid-flow. "If Shawcross silenced Mick and Mick was tipped off by you ..."

"I'm in deep shit. Right. Unless Glenn didn't name me. And I don't think he did."

Scotty picked up an orange and threw it at the wall, baseball pitcher style with his good arm. He watched it squelch and tumble to the floor. "Well, damn me for a fairy-godmother! You're not quite what you look, son. Anythin' else?"

Dex ignored the dig as he plunged back in. "Shawcross burgled me - searched my place. Didn't find what he wanted."

"Shawcross – Mr Urbane. A killer *and* a house invader? That asshole sure must be worried about somethin'. An' I don't mean no small stuff like rollin' over Mick and me. There's gotta be somethin' bigger'n a pregnant elephant goin' on." He offered Dex an apple from the hamper by his bed. "Sure," Scotty's face was alight. "You've shown me an edge, somethin' I like, somethin' I *need* – danger, risk, livin' on the edge. But it still ain't enough." He went to pummel one fist into his other palm but found it impossible. "Life and death. Racin' for the first bend. Preferably life but at that second death doesn't matter, only the winning. That's what I need now I'm washed up. Ain't no future for me jus' toastin' my tootsies by a fire in an Aspen log cabin. Can *you* give me that rush?"

Dex sat down again and nodded agreement. "Closer I get to crushing Shawcross, the more dangerous it'll get. Shawcross is sitting on a powder-keg and I want you there when the fuse is lit. When will you be out of here?"

"Maybe ten days. But if Kim comes across with a few blowjobs I might stay longer. Oriental pussy. Keeps your mind off the pain." The ashen features creased from forehead to chin, laughter lines appearing but as quickly disappearing. As Scotty peed noisily into a bottle, Dex debated what he had to say to clinch a deal. There had to be something more than danger.

"Ten days isn't a problem. I've plans for you. Here and in Vegas. You have contacts there, of course"

"Sure. But like, aren't you forgettin' somethin'?" Scotty's face showed no friendship now.

"Remind me?"

"Money!"

Dex swallowed hard and told himself he shouldn't have been shocked. More than one internet chat-line had hinted at his lust for money. But Dex had never considered that his personal *jihad* wouldn't attract disciples like Scotty just for the beauty of truth.

Dex felt wounded as his hopes deflated. "How much?"

"Half a million upfront. Cash only. Agreed?"

"Shit!" Dex was dumbfounded. "Look Scotty. I'm not recruiting for the Chief Executive of Microsoft."

"An' I ain't wastin' my time for zilch. I could do with some big bucks, real good, real soon."

Dex played for time, stretching for a pear, wondering what to say about this greedy request. Then he thought again about his big idea, the one that had first hit him as he drove back from Bladon. What with the honey-trap plan for Shawcross and worrying about Mark Evans, the idea had gone on the back-burner. But Scotty's demand had forced him to make up his mind. Mentally, Dex crossed his fingers. "You chip in with half a million first. You'll get one point five back."

"What guarantee do I have?"

"None. Only my word."

"Dex, get real! I'm in Formula One. Your word ain't worth shit!" He snapped his fingers. His laugh was too mocking to be pleasant. "My word is my bond and all that crap disappeared when they stopped havin' a man with a red flag walkin' in front of cars. Cash counts."

Dex fell silent as he tried to weigh up the right psychology for this man. One thing was certain. Scotty would not respect weakness. Maybe he needed cash now, maybe not.

"Your choice Scotty. Hard to turn down a million profit, no tax, however rich you are. It's now or not at all. Want that million or not? If you do, then you play my rules. I don't need your half mill now, just commitment, total commitment and some help now but when things get tough, dangerous or even violent, you must be there. Your choice Scotty. I can find someone else but I hoped you'd *want* to be involved." He rose from his chair and turned towards the door.

"Dollars?"

Dex had been thinking in sterling worth around one point five million dollars. This was a bonus. "I wasn't thinking of roubles. Yes – a million dollars profit."

"Sit down. Have another beer." Scotty's eyes softened and disappeared inside a crinkly grin. "What do I have to do?"

"I'll come to that once we have a deal."

"Where in hell will you get a million bucks? Rob a bank?"

"Dukes."

"Dooks? A million greenbacks from them? How can you be sure? Bazookas or a Sherman tank?"

Dex tapped the side of his head. "With your half mill, I have a plan. That's *my* problem – for now." Scotty hurled another orange at the wall where it exploded and slithered to the floor in pieces. "We go on talking like this," laughed Dex "we'll be making marmalade."

Scotty appeared not to notice the remark, his eyes somewhere distant again. Then he spoke in an exaggerated English accent as he shook hands "Okay. Count me in, Dex – there's a good chap! My word is my bond too."

Dex replied in kind. "Spiffing, old bean. Now tell me about your Vegas connections."

"Vegas? André Agassi. Jus' the guy if you want to improve your backhand. The Mayor ... Oscar Goodman. He's powerful. Used to be the mob's lawyer. Knows how the city works better'n anyone alive. 'Part from them, I know Tony Curtis, a few attorneys and some classy pole dancers at Cheetahs Nightclub. Take your pick."

"I need an attorney who knows both gaming and criminal law. Someone with big balls. Someone prepared to fight dirty. Bringing down a two billion casino isn't a stroll in the park."

"Yeah. I know jus' the guy."

"Good. We need an agent in Vegas too."

"A private dick?"

Dex nodded. "And able to start working now. Someone who knows the dark and dirty side of casinos. Someone used to working with bent casino bosses."

"Bent casino bosses? Not too many of them in today's Vegas. But my attorney's pretty smart. He'll know jus' the guy you need. What's he gotta do?"

"I want the whole nine yards on Carlo Letizione. He's the CEO of Space City and a director of Dukes. Everything he's done; his connections past and present; anything shady whether rumored or proven. I want copies of all documents filed by Space City when they got their license to operate in Nevada. I want everything they've filed about the financing for the new tower." Dex had cleared the easy stuff first. "This is the best bit. I want copies of all Space City's bank statements between the first January to date and continuing to the end of this year. And Letizione's too."

"Oh sure. Nothing difficult then. Nothing illegal." Scotty laughed, clearly enjoying himself now. He hurled a third orange against the wall. "Vegas is a *juice town*. You need the bank stuff, someone'll fix that. But it'll cost more'n a few bucks."

Dex was ready to leave. "I want to speak to the agent within forty-eight hours."

"When do you tell me how you'll win big in Dooks?"

Dex thought for a moment. "You'll be at Indianapolis for the Grand Prix?"

"I was gonna fly there, sure."

"I'll meet you there. Maybe we can talk after the race."

"Sure. It's on Sunday September 29th."

Dex rose to leave. "By the way. Who do *you* think wanted you dead?"

"Fucked if I know."

"Dukes?"

"If you say so – as you did, then I'll believe you."

"*You* don't think that do you?"

"I'm paid to drive, not be a detective."

Dex shook hands and left. He was sure Scotty was lying. Scotty knew precisely why someone had shot him. "And my guess is, he doesn't think it was Dukes," he muttered to himself as he flung open the flimsy car door. "And if that's right, who in hell killed Mick Glenn?"

London - 23rd September 2002

Dex had spent the morning with his father in Northampton, watching the laborious task of getting food into him. Then, it was back to the *Yellow Peril* as he had nicknamed the baby Fiat with the lousy brakes and more rattles than a baby. The prospect of the drive cross-country to Wiltshire in the Fiat was not appealing but he needed to visit Clouds House. He stopped to pick up Kentucky Fried and ate as he drove. The car responded badly despite his skilled handling, the engine complaining as he dropped through the gears time and again round the back roads of Berkshire and Hampshire.

After the positive news on Mark Evans' progress, he then set off for the hundred miles back to London, passing the time by trying to add up how many days he'd recently spent in hospitals and clinics. No matter, in two days, he would be in Washington and then on to Indianapolis with Tiffany. And there, Tiffany could not play the spare room game. That's if she hadn't already granted him upgraded room arrangements at her Foggy Bottom home.

The prospect kept him smiling as he rattled along the slow lane of the M3 being overtaken by almost everything. His thoughts turned to Shawcross and the honey-trap, an idea that regularly surfaced only to be shelved yet again. Impulsively, he pulled into a service area and from a call box phoned Tiffany on her confidential line. "Just a quickie. When I get to London, I'm going to call you from home. Don't be surprised by what I say. Play along but don't believe it. The plan is still Washington until the 28th and then the Indy Grand Prix."

"You get more devious every time I speak to you." Tiffany's comment sounded like a compliment and it spurred him on through the early evening traffic as he mulled over his chat with the private detective. Gabe Fazziolli had an office on West Sahara, just off the Vegas Strip. He had called four am London, eight pm the previous evening in Vegas. "Gabe Fazziolli?"

"Sure."

"Finlay Dexter."

"Otto Schneider called me. Your Vegas attorney, right?"

"Right."

"I can do what you want, even the bank stuff. It'll cost *me*, so it'll cost *you*."

"'How much?'"

"Ten for me plus five to fix someone workin' for Space City or their bank. That's just for the bank records, okay?"

Dex gulped at the figures. "I'll wire it tomorrow Gabe. Fifteen thousand dollars. You can order that new Rolls-Royce."

The listener ignore the quip. "You needed some advice too?"

"Yes - on something I was reading. I need your opinion – and I need some contacts." Dex explained what he had in mind. Gabe was a good listener and when Dex had finished, he replied at once. "Sure. Here's what you do." For ten minutes, he explained every detail, concluding. "And this is the guy to do it - Max Chieseman. He's the best in the business and based in London. Call him up. Use my name."

"No Gabe. You call him first – soften him up for me."

"Sure. I'll call right now."

"Hold it, Gabe. It's four in the morning here."

"I'll phone later. Count on it."

From Northampton that morning, he had spoken to Max Chieseman who had heard from Gabe.

"Good, Max. I'll drop by tomorrow. Give you all the details. Can you do it? One month?"

"Nah. We're busy mate. Up to our bleedin' necks in work. Next March do?"

"I'll see you tomorrow. We'll sort something." Dex put down the phone judging that Chieseman would use thumbscrews to justify an extortionate demand for a quick job. The man operated from Penarth Street. It was neither precisely in Peckham or Bermondsey. It was a run-down no-man's land area that Dex was told was about twenty-five minutes from Big Ben. Not the type of area you'd walk round after dark but safe enough in daylight – if you looked as shabby as everyone else.

He guessed cash would talk down there, for those brave enough to carry it. He sensed he was going to be fleeced and recapped on his costly budget. *Fazziolli, Clouds House, Scotty, Yarbury, Gabe, The Panama people, Kenny Jennings. Now*

Chieseman – the key to everything. Near the Thame junction on the way back from Bladon, he had relived McKay's twitch and watery eyes and recalled the advice about *Reverse Labouchère.* Stopping in a lay-by, he had thought it through. Having mixed in his knowledge from the Ortiz book on gambling frauds he filtered back into the heavy traffic, a cheesy grin on his face. Now he was into implementation mode – that's if Chieseman would shift his ass.

Back in Porcupine House, it was honey-trap time. Dex phoned Tiffany using his insecure line. "Hi! I've been to Northampton today. Father's doing so-so given the issues. Are you still okay for me coming to Washington?"

"Looking forward to it."

"I can't wait to see you. But due to father, no way can I stay for the week. I'll fly to Washington as planned on Wednesday the 25th, the day after tomorrow. Plane lands at around lunchtime. But the bad news is, I must be back here on the 27th. The consultants are having what they call a *big tent* meeting about father's progress – all the medical disciplines are attending. I have to be there. Big tent, big *pow-wow.* I'm going dressed as a squaw!"

"You nutcase! But Dex, that's a real bummer. Is it worth you coming for such a short time?"

"You'd better make it worthwhile." Dex chuckled wickedly and Tiffany after a brief hesitation almost joined in. Dex had enjoyed that moment. Then after changing into his Cerruti suit that emphasized the width of shoulder and narrowness of hips, he had driven to Dukes. Part of his bed-time reading had been British casino laws – a real struggle as he hated anything about the law. Even the word gave him unpleasant flashbacks to his father talking about *aforesaids* and *fee simples.* But he knew it was essential.

McKay had been correct. The way to destroy Dukes lay in exposing their failures to comply with the law. That and being able to prove it. Last night, when most people his age would have been settling in for a night of lust, he had pored over the Gaming Act 1968. He now understood that all members and guests had to sign the register every visit. He knew the rules on casino staff socializing with gamblers. He knew the penalties for non-compliance.

As he stood under the subtle and subdued lighting in front of Dukes reception desk about to sign in, he heard someone descending the stairs and recognized the Aussie tones of Jude and heard her raucous laugh. She was carrying a ridiculously large black shoulder bag that seemed to weigh heavily, causing her to lean to her left. He appraised the wizened figure behind her. He held a silver-topped stick and wore tinted glasses. He must have been seventy or more, his face waxy and looking like old blotting-paper. The suit he was wearing was brown and it hung shapelessly on his small frame. He hovered by the passage to the cloakrooms while Jude signed him in.

"Mind you don't kill the poor old boy off with your antics," Dex muttered to her. "Or are you after his life insurance?"

She grinned. "Erection like a stick of rhubarb, no sweat. Your father okay?" She turned away without awaiting his reply, her attention now focused on the receptionist. Jude's bare midriff and shimmering blue skirt contrasted with the sophistication of the receptionist, immaculate in her red trouser-suit and cream blouse. Dex noticed Jude had added a tattoo above the cleft of her buttocks. He waited until he was sure she was listening. "Would you believe it? I was off to Washington on Wednesday for a week. Now, the Kemsway people want me back here on Friday. Something about a big tent."

"Medical baloney. A big tent!" Her look was scathing. "More like a circus. All clowns! Waste of time. I'd stay in Washington."

"They sounded insistent. I'll rush back." He nodded towards the old man. "Your toyboy appears to be flagging. Go ahead. Sign him in before me. I'm in no rush."

"Gee, thanks." She signed for herself and started to fill in the details for her guest. Dex pretended to glance at a magazine on the reception desktop while reading the guest's name: Alejandro Robledo c/o Claridges Hotel, Mayfair, perhaps the most distinguished hotel in London. Jude beckoned her guest to sign, which he did after a long pause and in a feeble scratchy style. He didn't seem to speak much English but looked happy enough as she led him slowly away to the cage to change some money.

He puzzled over why Jude would date someone with hands like a sparrow's foot. It made no sense. Convinced that the stick of rhubarb story was bollocks, he tried to reason out what was happening. Just this morning, Kenny Jennings had reported that she and Shawcross were an item. So no way was she fondling the old Spaniard's anything.

Dex signed in but told the receptionist he wanted to get some fresh air. The Dolce and Gabbana knitted scarf was welcome as he walked briskly to the corner of Park Lane and then on to the Hilton where the concierge gave him the number for Claridges. He found a payphone at the back of the lobby. "Can you put me through to Mr Robledo please? Yes. Robledo. Alejandro Robledo from Madrid. Thanks."

"I'm sorry sir. There is no guest of that name staying here."

"Did he check out earlier? I'm sure he said he was staying with you last night and tonight."

"No, sir. Neither night."

"Perhaps he checked in with his friend. Try under her name. Ms Jude Tuson."

"No luck sir. I'm sorry, sir."

"Thanks anyway."

As he walked back, he remembered more details from his book on British gaming law. Applicants to join a casino had to produce suitable ID – a passport, driving-license or similar. The casino would take a mug-shot and twenty-fours later, they would usually be granted membership. But guests could be signed in by members, no ID needed. So who are you Alejandro Robledo?

Back in the casino, he quickly spotted the unlikely couple. Dex took a seat at a low stakes game of blackjack giving him a perfect view of Jude and Robledo at the baccarat table. The Spaniard had at least six hundred thousand in chips in front of him. She was betting for him, switching from Bank to Player and loving the action. Robledo seemed bemused by the entire experience and kept nodding off. He awoke twice with a start when Jude called *pay the bank*. He could see she was staking large amounts, winning and losing heavily. After about fifty minutes, by which time, the Spaniard's fleshless skull was resting on her shoulder, she nudged him awake and together they went to the cage.

"I've lost enough. You seem to be getting all the cards I need," Dex said to the woman sitting next to him as he pushed back his chair. In the card-shoe, there had been six decks and he had no clue whether any cards were missing, though he had read that he should get a blackjack about every twenty-two hands. He had certainly not done that – but as he told himself, that's only an average.

Jude didn't notice him standing just behind her. She was too busy speaking to Robledo and the chief cashier. "Mr Robledo would like a check please in his favor."

So what was that all about?

He wished he could ask the cashier but didn't want to appear interested. "Enjoyed your evening Mr Dexter?" Dex was startled by FB's voice by his side.

"Very much. Can't get lucky with blackjack though. Never seem to get enough good cards."

FB stared at the wall somewhere behind his listener. "Goes like that sometimes. Then suddenly you'll be drowning in winning hands."

"Remind me to bring a lifejacket!"

FB coughed politely. "That police business. So sorry. Have the police given you the all-clear?"

Dex gave FB a look of disbelief at the question and laughed derisively. "No way! And they won't, not until they get someone else. Father told me years back that's how they work. So, I'm free to travel. Matter of fact, I'm off to Washington on Wednesday morning. Flying visit – I'll be back on Friday. Wanted to go for longer but the medics want me at the hospital about father." Dex nodded towards Robledo who was seated in a brocaded chair. "You're certainly getting some big players in."

"News travels we look after our high-rollers."

"But that old boy. I mean he wasn't even playing."

FB shrugged. "Not unusual. The seriously rich often humor their women like that. After all, at his age, he's never going to be able to spend it all."

"Who is he?"

FB looked across the room. "I think he's Spanish but excuse me. I'm needed over at the blackjack table. Another time."

"Of course."

Dex was about to move through to the bar when he saw Hoge at the roulette. "Gerhard! Winning I hope."

"I'm down." He laughed his usual guffaw. "But not out!"

"Fancy a drink?"

"For sure, I'll join you in a minute."

Dex ordered a bottle of Krug. As he watched the bubbles rising in the glass, he could also see that Jude and Robledo were drinking champagne that stood in a freezing ice bucket beside her long legs. There was no conversation between them and she seemed more interested in everybody but him. The stick of rhubarb relationship was plainly nonsense, so she had to be working to orders from Shawcross.

Gerhard Hoge appeared, rubbing his hands cheerfully. His face spoke of untold triumph at roulette. "Down two hundred thousand. But such pleasure! All those wasted years when I never went to a casino."

"You're certainly making up for it. Lucky for Dukes profits you joined here. Enjoy the champagne. To your happy losses!" Both men laughed and chinked glasses. "Before anything else, can you do lunch tomorrow on the terrace at *Le Colombier* in Chelsea. Dovehouse Street. I'd enjoy talking about roulette. I've tried your Labouchère system. Just as well I was wearing incontinence pants."

Like most Germans, Hoge enjoyed jokes about bodily functions. His guffaw bounced round the bar, causing everybody to look across. "Labouchère? History. Yesterday I downloaded another system. It cost a thousand bucks. Called the Fibonacci."

"Didn't cover the cost today then."

"It will, my friend." Hoge's laugh came from deep in his belly. "One-o-clock?"

"Perfect."

Time to play to the gallery.

"Glad you can do tomorrow. I'm off to Washington next day – quick visit. Just away the one night." Hopefully, somebody of all the people he had told would tell Shawcross. If he wasn't already listening.

Shawcross was indeed watching and listening, something he had done increasingly whenever Dex was in the building. The camera zoomed in as he chatted with the German but there was no sign of any conspiracy. He listened to the rest of the conversation. Banal stuff about some crazy system called *Infallible Techniques*. And Fibonacci. He didn't like Hoge's developing friendship or the planned lunch date but Dexter wasn't quizzing the German. Not yet anyway.

He judged Hoge as no fool, reckoned he would say nothing stupid. His eyes narrowed as he thought of that other loose-tongued tosser, the Frenchman,

Jacques Crabant. He smiled as he thought of the trip to Cornwall, one-way only for the Frenchman. For a moment, he felt the familiar dry sensation at the back of his throat as he recalled the Frenchman's surprised gasp as the blade had slit his throat before his corpse had fallen sixteen hundred feet down the disused tin-mine. His fingers still moving restlessly, his thoughts turned to Dexter again and his trip to Washington. It seemed the perfect opportunity, just the chance he had needed.

Back at Porcupine House Dex checked the telltales he had positioned around drawers and his desk. Nothing had been touched.

He clicked on Outlook to check his mail.

Good.

Message from Tiffany.

He opened the email and read in disbelief about the hurricane in Florida. Tiffany had to cancel his visit as she was required to be down there. "Shit! Bugger and damnation!" He sat in disbelief, staring at the screen. He rose to grab some instant, wandering around the kitchen in a daze. He put on a U2 CD and drowned his frustration in the remorseless booming rhythm. Then, just as he was raking through his Grand Prix recordings to look again at Scotty's eyes *this* season, a thought struck him like a meteor. It hit him so hard, he stopped what he was doing and slumped into the chair in the study.

If I'm not in Washington, then I'll be here.

And I've baited the trap for a psychopath's visit.

That tingling feeling at the nape of his neck returned.

London – 24ᵗʰ September 2002

Having cancelled his Washington flights and cadged a ride from Scotty straight to Indianapolis, he left the meeting with spivvy little Max Chieseman in Peckham barely convinced the man could deliver on time. He knew Chieseman had screwed him on price. For cash upfront, Chieseman had agreed to accelerate delivery to the first December. At least the short-assed shit had not lied when he'd said he had too much work. Invoices and orders swamped the ex MoD desk. Finished items, boxed and ready for delivery crammed the dispatch area from floor to ceiling. On the workshop floor, about sixteen staff were too busy even to lift their heads as he wandered round on his guided tour. Chieseman was not an enlightened employer and it showed in the sullen faces of the staff.

The contrast between Penarth Street with its small factories, taxi repair workshops and lock up garages to the fashionable chic of Dovehouse Street could scarcely have been more marked. The thirty minute drive took him into a fashionable part of Chelsea where he was surrounded by the wealthy locals who could stroll to Le *Colombier* from their multi-million homes. Dex raised his glass as they sat on the small wrought-iron terrace. "So why Dukes rather than say the Ritz, Gerhard?" Dex opened the more serious part of the discussions. After a couple of Kirs, a bottle of 1970 Hermitage and some banal gossip, the question was overdue. Dex watched for the reaction.

Gerhard knew his way around business. In the motor trade, he had learned how to avoid the truth but had never learned how to conceal his lies. At poker, he'd have been everyone's favorite sucker. His face smiled confidently enough but under challenge, his eyes wanted to dive even deeper behind the black frames of his spectacles. "I read about it in a magazine. Gambling that is. I've tried everything from horse-racing to lotto. So I decided to try roulette. With millions in the bank and no job, I needed excitement."

"But why Dukes?" Dex leaned across to pick up a petit-four. "I mean at Baden-Baden, you have one of the most beautiful casinos anywhere."

A shrug of the shoulders accompanied the growling voice. "I avoid Germany since I retired. Tax exile."

Dex looked so elegant against the mix and match look of the German's ill-fitting attire. "Yes, pretty understandable. So why not Monte Carlo, Las Vegas? Sorry. I sound like a police officer. I don't mean to. It's just so interesting as to how casinos pick up new members, especially high rollers, or should I say, good losers, like you."

"It's no secret," Hoge said but from watching the eyes search for refuge, Dex didn't believe what he was going to hear. "For sure, for top-end players like me, London is the gaming capital of the world. You know they are honest, strictly controlled – and so tasteful. London has the finest clubs, the most discreet ambience. Les Ambassadeurs, the Clermont or Dukes – that was the choice. I could have chosen any of them. I don't regret Dukes. I'm well looked after. In London, I've a rented place in Cheyne Walk. River view, penthouse. Delightful." He watched a daschund peeing against a tree. "Monte Carlo. No class any more. Just American and Japanese tourists watching old ladies playing roulette." His jowls shook in disgust. "I've been to Vegas. So, to me it is a crap place - hot, dusty, noisy and full of *dummkopfer* – idiots, you'd say. I never wish to see the place again. Everywhere, mechanics, fitters, grease-monkeys, all shouting *wooh* after every deal!" He laughed but Dex judged this as practiced patter - true so far as it went but not the real reason.

"And your friend – the one you wanted me to dine with? Crabet wasn't it?" The mistake was deliberate.

"Crabant? Jacques I haven't seen recently. Never even said goodbye or told me he planned moving on. A sudden urge to go to Tangiers I expect. He likes the gay scene there." Though the tone was convincing, Dex knew he was not getting beneath the surface. "And in case you're wondering, no I'm not. I have a wife who shops by day and does the theatres at night. I lose less than she spends." He rocked back with his infectious laugh, slapping his meaty hands on his meatier thighs as if an oompah-pah of a tuba were in the background.

"We were going to get together, the three of us."

Gerhard shrugged as if it were of no importance. "I expect Jacques got the urge for all those young brown-skinned boys. Paradise for a forty year old gay like him."

"What was his background? Someone said he played stud poker as if he had a death-wish."

"And blackjack too!" His eyebrows locked. "He worked in the Directorate-General for Agriculture. That's how we met."

Dex tried not to look startled at this curious fact. Gerhard had been a Jaguar dealer. He decided to let it pass but reminded himself that Agriculture was arguably the most corrupt department of the stinking cesspit of the European Commission.

"Have you met Jude Tuson? She was sitting opposite us last night. The Australian – she was wearing a skirt that damned near showed her pussy."

Hoge shook his head. "If only! Before angina and twenty years ago, I'd have tried. Those long legs! She makes my heart race. Plays big money too."

"You're younger than her last date."

"For sure but she has different men each night. Sometimes more than one. She must exhaust them." He looked up and shook his head ruefully. "I wonder how much she charges. But it's not for me though. My wife's jaws are like a rotweiler's. Her grip and my heart condition – these terrible twins keep me virtuous." Gerhard leaned across conspiratorially. "Anyway, the barman says she seems rather, how do you say, familiar with Audley Shawcross."

"Really! She's unstoppable."

He debated whether to volunteer anything. "I dated her a few times. Don't get me wrong! I didn't pay her! But she was high maintenance for all that. Judging by her present tastes, I was too young. Fifty years too young." He called for more coffee. "How do get along with Audley Shawcross? I'm too small a player for him to be interested in me."

"Chats about football. Politics. Never mentions the war!" Again he slapped his thighs as he laughed. "That's all. FB eats with me sometimes."

"Me too. He's as exciting as a dead dingbat. What did he talk about? Computer programs, modems, gardening and carp fishing?"

Gerhard's broad grin revealed his much-repaired teeth. "Pruning roses, ground-baiting and cracking Microsoft codes last time. Hard to keep awake."

Dex tried another tack. He wanted a reaction and was not disappointed. "I'm going to play in Les A or perhaps the Ritz casino tonight. Come for dinner. I can sign you in. Give Dukes a break," he continued. "Such elegant clubs. Your luck might change too."

Hoge thought for a moment, sipped his coffee but then declined. "You know Dex what they say about old shoes and comfort? That's how I feel at Dukes. I don't want to try a new shoe."

Dex resisted the urge to shout bullshit, bollocks and tosh. "Familiarity does help, doesn't it?" Finlay's look was impish. "At least you know who you're losing to." He nearly added something but then stopped himself. "What about match-fixing in Germany? It spills over into the story of Mick Glenn here."

"Footballers." He waved a dismissive arm. "I have no interest in them. I like the game, not the players. So yes, I'd say they are *corruptible*. Are they *corrupt*? I don't know. I'm not often enough in Germany now. But you? The police questioned you."

"They thought I was the plus sign linking Glenn and Scotty Brannigan because I'd been in touch with them about a motor racing and roulette trip. But I had no motive. Nobody seems to know if Glenn was taking bribes."

Excited by the lunch, Dex quickened his pace towards his old stamping-ground of Brompton Road. The four corners of the jigsaw suddenly seemed to be in place. Hoge, despite the lies, had let slip more than he knew or Dex had expected. Shawcross' game was becoming clearer. Odd though about Crabant not saying goodbye. It really was getting to be important to check him out on the web. He called Tiffany from a public box opposite Harrods. "I'm still getting over the bad news."

"Me too! My holiday's been blown away by the hurricane. They've whisked me from California. This is one big story. It's a Cat 5, winds over 150 mph. Hopefully it'll drop to a Cat 4. They're predicting thirty inches of rain and a load of deaths. The editor says I'll look vulnerable, meaning half-drowned, standing in driving rain, hair blowing everywhere. He says I'll ooze defiance. Bulldog breed stuff."

"Take care, sounds lethal. So I'll see you in Indy? Scotty's flying me over."

"I'll try. God knows why but I can't wait to see you. Life's been a real bummer."

"Absence, as they say. Aim for Indy."

In Knightsbridge, he bought some domestic surveillance equipment – nothing too sophisticated but still impressive. Once home, he worked on the finishing touches to the sting. In the background, he heard Detective Chief Superintendent Blyth on the radio reissuing his appeal for anyone who had seen the man on the motor-bike in The Bishop's Avenue. He sounded frustrated. He set up his old Dell laptop and destroyed every email in the Outlook program. Then he recreated the file called *Obsession* before writing copious notes, all trivia and left them around the desk. Then, for the next hour, he set to work creating a new file, one he hoped any intruder would find. He finished at nine, took a cab to Baker Street and seated himself at an Internet Cafe.

For ninety minutes, he surfed the web visiting sites he could not risk now at home. Looking around the packed room, full of young people of Middle Eastern appearance, he thought how hard it must be for the security forces to prevent another nine-eleven. Typing in *"Gerhard Hoge"* produced nothing from Google of any possible relevance, so he typed in *"Directorate-General for Agriculture" corruption "Jacques Crabant"*. There were over forty entries for Crabant, linking him to the Agriculture Department in Brussels and to his suspicious retirement.

Fingers flying excitedly over the battered keyboard with the letters *e* and *w* both defunct, the trail led to the European Community's Court of Auditors and then to OLAF, the Commission's anti-fraud agency. Captivated, he surfed from site to site, his eyes opening wider at the enormity of the corruption. There was page after page about sleaze, about sleaze-busters like Neil Kinnock, backhanders, nepotism, bribes and offshore accounts. Then he found what he wanted. Just ten days ago, a fearless editor of a gossipy newsletter had written about Crabant. He had connected him to dirty deals involving sales of surplus EC wine by tender to the third world, especially Brazil and the Caribbean. There followed some cheap laughs at the attempts of the Commissioners to root out endemic corruption. He scribbled notes in untidy writing:

EC fraud costing six billion a year.
Antonio Quantraro had "fallen" from a sixth floor window at the Agriculture building.
Tobacco scams alleged.
Masonic influence?
P2?
Mafia, Naples and Marseille.
Pedophile ring including a Commissioner.
Two murders in Belgium.
Nepotism in awarding EC contracts.
Fictitious deals.
Offshore companies in the Caymans.
Secret dealings hidden behind Liechtenstein secrecy.
Concern about tenders on sales of surplus wine – the wine lake.
Crabant involved in tendering process.
Sudden premature retirement.
Yet no apparent wealth.

Modest home in Leuven.
Old Renault car.
Nest egg somewhere?
Denial.
Absurd.
Wine sold for conversion to gasoline.
Used in Brazil, El Salvador, Antigua.
Denaturing process.
Conversion from wine by dehydration into ETBE.
Ethyl-Tertio-Buryl-Ether.
375,000 hectoliters a contract
Twelve million Euros per deal.
Who wins the tenders?
Ask "votre ami" Jacques Crabant.
Buggins' turn, Okay?
Rumors.
A good lunch for Frère Jacques.
Pay him his percentage.
Get your turn.
Nothing proven.
Official denials from the Directorate.
Scrupulous supervision.
Crabant another Quantraro?
Retire because of OLAF?
Or fear.
Or rich?
"Who wants to be another Quantraro? Freefall from six storys with no points given for style", said an official from the Court of Auditors who declined to be named.
Had Crabant protection in high places?
Perhaps yet another bent Commissioner?
Cars cruising beside Ipanema Beach using surplus Italian Chianti.

Dex could have surfed for hours but he had more than enough. As he re-read his notes, he now knew precisely what was going on and how Jude would fit in - Crabant, Hoge, those Russians, the West Indian, the Italians, the Spaniard Robledo too. He took a taxi to Hyde Park Corner where he was going to assess business at Les Ambassadeurs. Outside, a cold breeze was rain-flecked and he cursed the weather-man who had been wrong again.

As he dined alone in Les A, he barely noticed the fine food, so engrossed was he in working out why a middle-tier bureaucrat like Crabant aged early forties, would retire suddenly with no apparent wealth. With the new facts from Brussels, the inheritance explanation had already been filed on a shelf marked *fiction*. As he drained the last of his coffee, he had decided on the next move but it would have to be subtle. As the taxi cut through Hill Street, something else became clear. Crabant, the pauper, had been losing money like a drunken sailor in London but while using his own name. The realization that the Crabant scandal had only just broken seemed likely to be linked to his disappearance. So if he had hot money, who had paid him backhanders? People wanting to win tenders to turn Eurowine into gasoline. People like a former Jaguar dealer from Stuttgart? Hoge had been so casual about his friend's disappearance. Was that genuine? Or did Hoge know about the article? Had Hoge killed him?

"Enjoy Les A?" Hoge leaned away from the roulette table and his typed instructions on the Fibonacci numbers.

"So grand down there. Beautiful. Busy enough too but nothing like in here. This place really buzzes. Must be the charisma of Audley Shawcross."

Hoge looked uninterested and picked the skin on the side of his thumb. Dex sensed a coolness that had never been there before.

"Winning tonight, then?" Dex asked as he watched Jude lead another new face to the blackjack table.

"Not yet. These Fibonacci numbers – so they will make me a winner!"

"Maybe a drink later then? To celebrate."

The German licked his lips and patted down the hairs on the back of his head. "If I'm not too tired." Gerhard Hoge was such a hopeless liar. Dex knew that there would be no drink – not unless the German had no choice.

"See you later then. I'm going to play some baccarat." Dex bought in for two thousand, with the intent of playing the occasional hand only. He positioned himself for a perfect view of Jude. Her shrewd looking woman friend was buying in for five hundred thousand. This guest's diminutive body contrasted with Jude's well-built physique, yet she had the aura of power about her. Her clothes were expensive and in perfect taste for a woman in her late fifties. She looked South American with dark hair, graying but expensively tinted. At some point, her face had seen the surgeon's knife leaving it free of wrinkles.

The downside was that her features were now set in a permanent look of surprise as if someone had just goosed her with a rude shaped parsnip. Dex placed her as a senior executive of a big corporation or perhaps a politician. He heard her accented English and she reminded him of his trip to the Algarve, so she was probably Portuguese or Brazilian.

The dealer shuffled the cards for a new shoe as Dex watched Shawcross shaking hands with Jude's guest. He saw the slim hands differently now - hands that had wielded the knife; saw the eyes that must have burned with blood-lust; saw the figure that had almost certainly snooped through his house – and missed the Crown Jewels. He thought about the honey-trap and debated saying that the trip was off but that would be the chicken-out route. Despite a mounting sense of fear at what lay ahead, he steeled himself to go ahead with the plan.

"I'm cashing in," Dex said about an hour later as Hoge left the roulette. He watched impatiently as the dealer counted out his chips. He was ahead by two-fifty pounds. Guessing that Hoge must have gone to the cloakroom, he asked the barman to open a bottle of Chianti. "You want Italian wine, Mr Dexter? Unlike you. Are you sure?"

"It's been specially recommended."

He went down the corridor and trapped Hoge as he emerged from the cloakroom. "Gerhard! The wine's waiting. A Chianti – one of your favorites and a great vintage." He watched the reaction change from irritation to confusion to forced pleasure in split seconds.

"A quick glass then." With short busy movements, Hoge followed him to the bar and dropped heavily into a chair.

"Tell me you won!"

"It would not be true," he shook his head. "I must be playing Fibonacci all wrong."

Dex laughed with him. "Time to start looking for another system."

"Good wine." Hoge sniffed and swirled, admiring the heavy tears of Christ gliding down the glass. He helped himself to a slice of gherkin. "I didn't think you drank Italian wines."

"This was an exception – a great year and specially recommended." Dex hoped he sounded convincing. "Did you spot that attractive woman with Jude Tuson tonight?"

"The right word. Attractive in a strict way. Why? Do you want an introduction? If so, I don't know her."

"No. I don't go for *Mrs Robinsons* anymore, though it used to be fun." He asked the barman for more sun-dried tomatoes. "But I *was* trying to place her accent. Is she Hungarian?"

"No." The denial was assertive, almost mocking. "I heard her in the bar earlier. She's from Sao Paulo, Brazil. I recognized the accent but anyway she was talking about Jardim Paulista. I know that part of the city – the garden area. It's the best, though it has little competition." He shook his head. "A dangerous city."

Dex saw the opening – as wide as the Atlantic. "Selling Jaguars down there too?"

Hoge froze, gave Dex a quizzical look and then lied. "Vacation."

Dex decided not to interrogate him on why anybody with even half a brain would go to Sao Paulo for a vacation. "I went there for the Grand Prix once. I felt lucky to leave with my money, my faculties and all four limbs. The crime there! Everybody warned me of kids roaming the streets with guns and knives." He saw Hoge nodding in agreement. "I'll bet you a fifty note you didn't know this. When a pal told me, I thought he was joking. Amazing! He said the Brazilians run their cars on sugar cane or, would you believe, gasoline made from the European wine lake." He laughed. "That's all some Italian wine's fit for. But not this one."

Hoge looked away to study his Fibonacci records. "Sorry. I missed what you said. I was checking my addition. Oh, yes – the gasoline in Brazil. I heard about that when I went there. They de-nature the wine to make it suitable. Got that fifty?"

Dex tried not to show his satisfaction as he handed over the red note. Hoge couldn't lie to save his ass.

London 25th September 2002

Dex was restless. The moment had come. Maybe he was scared but he was not going to admit that. As darkness fell over Porcupine House, he could sense his mother's presence, almost hearing her sobs, the chinking bottles and his father's booming commands from the top of the stairs. Even these unpleasant thoughts were preferable to imagining Shawcross arriving, sheathed Master Bowie round his waist. From top to toe now, Dex was dressed in black, awaiting something that might never even happen. One moment, he felt exhilarated, the next wondering if he had lost his marbles sitting in wait for a psychopath.

Now, as he knelt uncomfortably in the darkened study, his face and hands blackened, he could feel the reassurance of the baseball bat bought that morning, lethal in a fight and suitable to keep him from the range of a lunged knife, however long the blade. He was behind the study door, where a large plant provided additional cover too. He swigged from a bottle of water and nibbled on a tuna sandwich, shivering as he swapped positions. The house felt chill and he noticed the smell of damp rising from the cellar. Around him, every light was off, every curtain drawn. He passed the time by planning his visit to see father, assuming I'm alive he kept reminding himself. He checked his watch again, stood up, yawned and stretched to avoid his legs going numb. It was gone eleven now and except for a rustle from the trees, there was silence. He was alone surrounded only by the ghost of old memories. He hated that, wishing he could set the speakers to full blast to kill the silence and drown the creaks, groans and sighs as the house settled for the night.

This morning, he had visited Scotty. The driver hadn't spent *all* his time removing Kim's suspenders, though he was quick to confide that she had come across *pretty darned good* during the long night-shift. Between glances at a recording of the Monza GP and occasional outbursts of *sonovabitch*, Scotty had expanded on the Vegas attorney now retained. "Otto Schneider. Meanest bastard in town – and that's sayin' somethin'," he'd explained. "Vegas is no ordinary city. Developers and casinos dominate the decision-making. Who controls them, well that's another story but if you wanna get rich or succeed, you need *juice*, you need *contacts*. You need dirt on those you want to fix. You need to have done a few favors to the power-brokers that one day you can call in. Elsewhere, you would call it corruption. In Vegas, it's jus' the normal way of doin' business."

"And Otto?"

"Plays this city like he owns it. He doesn't think he operates outside the law. Why? Because he sees himself as *bein' the law*. To him, the law is what he can fix, what he can get away with. Did his guy Gabe Fazzolli deliver?"

"He rang. Impressive."

"What Gabe don' know about casino scams ain't worth shit."

"Seems we have a good team," Dex was anxious to keep the subject away from Gabe Fazzolli's advice. "So it's Indianapolis Grand Prix here we come. You'll be fit to travel?"

"Ain't nobody gonna stop me."

For the first time since night fell, Dex smiled in the darkness as he remembered saucy Kim coming in, her night shift over and leaving for home. Dex could see she was exhausted, her hair was a mess, her lips swollen and there was a ladder down her left stocking. If Scotty could leave her looking as if she'd done ten rounds in a boxing-ring, then he was surely well enough to travel.

And that means I'll be with Tiffany.

He opened and closed his hands and wriggled his toes, did a few stretches.

Another hour disappeared. Still there was silence but at least it had passed quickly with madcap plans based on Max Chieseman. So much turned on him, especially paying off Scotty and Lord Yarbury from Dukes' money. He had just convinced himself that Shawcross had not taken the bait when he heard a scratching sound.

Nah! Just branches rubbing on a gutter.

Or one of London's rats scraping at the kitchen window.

Nothing to worry about.

A click.

Fuck me!

No question.

A key had unlocked the kitchen door.

A duplicate.

He heard the sound of night air moving. There was a creak, followed by another. Dex recognized the familiar noise of the navy blue kitchen door moving uneasily on its hinges.

What a dumb-fuck game this is!

What in hell's name got into me?

Poking sticks at psychopaths.

But he's expecting an empty house.

You're in the USA, remember?

So he thinks.

You have surprise.

That and a baseball bat.

Against a stainless steel blade.

Sharpened point too.

The giant horse-chestnut's waving branches sounded closer now as the door opened wide. The intruder closed the kitchen door and was now within thirty feet. Dex felt his stomach gripe and his bowels inch closer to free-fall. His heart was pounding, his mouth now dry, his breathing short and strangulated. His limbs has turned to water. He felt weak, helpless against the terror that the arrival had created.

Fight that panic.

Ignore it.

He dug his nails into his palms and by a slight contortion, twisted enough to peer through the crack above the lower hinge of the study door.

Nothing.

Just blackness.

Then breathing.

Then nothing again.

The intruder seemed to hesitate, unsure of his bearings.

He must be by the door from the kitchen into the hall.

Shawcross would know how to find the study.

But he wouldn't be sure in the dark.

His last visit, the lights had been on.

This time, the darkness was absolute.

Then on came a flashlight, its beam searching around the hall, its holder still unseen. Eye close to the crack, Dex scarcely dared breathe as the beam steadied and then advanced. Suddenly from the blackness, a face appeared but only in a shadowy way, half lit by the beam as it bounced off the wall. Dex' sphincter control was at failure point. Again, he dug his nails into his palms and tried not to cry out at the pain. Ten feet apart now, he wondered if the sounds and smell of his own fear were a giveaway. Disembodied, the face was fearful - green painted luminous stripes bobbing as the unseen figure below the face advanced with a confident step now.

Nightmarish.

Sub-human.

For a second he was back in the Sherlock Holmes pub, the ferocious Hound's head just above him.

Relax, Dex.

Be rational.

Like Sherlock.

It's just a man.

Nothing more.

A man with a kid's Halloween mask painted Zulu style.

Just Shawcross.

A psychopath ready to knife you to shreds.

The footsteps moved unseen now, just the thickness of the door away. Then the figure was in the study, the torch beam shining on the grey carpet and then rising towards the desk.

"Ah!" The man exclaimed as he saw the desk and the laptop. Then the torch picked out the closed curtains and the desk-lamp, which he clicked on. Dex peered from behind the deep green fronds of the King Sago. The man wore thin gloves, trainers, jeans and a black rollneck. He switched off the torch, put down his bag and seated himself at the desk. Then he eased up the mask so it perched across the top of his black beret.

In seconds, he had unpacked his own laptop, connected the two and had opened a link. With the intruder's back to the door, Dex could not see the man's face.

When he left, would he switch off the light first or would he look around and perhaps see Dex cowering behind the plant.

Or would the plant be enough to conceal him?

Play safe.

Don't wait to find out.

Hit him first.

Easy.

No.

Wait.

Remember the plan.

Wait until he's downloaded what he's after.

Find out if the plan works.

If not, let him put out the light.

Then hit him.

He saw the familiarity with which the man had booted up Dex' laptop, though he had deliberately not set any password protection. Windows' familiar jingle broke the silence and to Dex its friendly and mundane intrusion was so welcome. The intruder flicked from screen to screen, searching the programs and then exploring the contents. Dex saw Word opening and guessed he was after *Obsession* but he hoped the man would look further. The next file he had called *Onisac*. Both appeared at the top of the drop-down list of recently used files.

From his position, Dex had a partial view of the screen, obscured only slightly by the man's right shoulder. As he looked at the figure, hunched forward excitedly over the desk, Dex tried to see the profile. The look was familiar but the beret and angle made it difficult to be sure it was Shawcross.

"Obsession." The man almost grunted out the word and studied the screen. The shoulders seemed to sag in disappointment as he skim-read the pages. Then with a click, he copied and sent the folder to his own laptop.

He went to the next folder. "Onisac? Onisac? What the hell's that?" Dex heard the muttered question. The user clicked on the mouse and the page appeared. "Yes! Yes! Yes!" The intruder saw ONISAC typed large across the page. There was a scoffing laugh. "Onisac. Casino."

Dex knew now.

The voice.

The physique.

The tone of voice.

It was not the psychopath.

There was no Master Bowie.

It was the computer nerd.

The errand boy.

The Shawcross poodle.

FB.

Dex felt his chest muscles relax. His heart that had been pumping on turbocharge, started to slow. His confidence returned in spades as the specter of Shawcross disappeared. He felt released, wanted to leap up and cheer.

No Master Bowie.

Just FB.

And him thinking he's alone.

He thought rapidly, reassessing how to get best advantage from the new situation. He watched and waited, more confident in his planning now. It depended on one mouse-click and FB as an expert was never going to miss it. He studied FB's back as he read the introduction to ONISAC. Dex could have recited the words like The Lord's Prayer. Every one had been carefully chosen.

"This folder and the sub-folder are strictly confidential and relate to the crimes that I have uncovered at Dukes Casino. In the event of my sudden death, my solicitor holds one copy of everything and will draw the obvious conclusion. The sub-folder is listed under SEKUD."

The wait as FB read the introduction seemed endless but in truth lasted only seconds before he was ready to move on.

This is the moment.

Click. FB opened the sub-folder, mumbling *anagram of Dukes* as he did so.

A new page appeared. Dex again knew every word and found it hard not to snigger as he saw FB start to skim-read, then pause and then re-read. Every word had been selected to add to an impact. He saw FB scratch his ear, then look again at the screen before shifting uncomfortably in his seat. As if being manipulated by a puppet-master he then turned to glance uneasily over his left shoulder towards the far corner of the room. Slowly, he swiveled to look just above and in front of him. Dex was sure he was now hooked as the bewildered FB silently cursed Shawcross as he re-read the pages.

"I hope you enjoy my joke at your expense. I have caught everything on camera, a bit like you do to members. I have you filmed entering my home. Look over your left shoulder. Now look up. There! See that camera! Perfect mug shot, like the one as you crossed the hall. Look up in front of you, above the desk. See another camera? Get the picture? I have anyway, if you don't mind my second little joke. The microphones under the desk have captured anything said. As the cameras are linked to a silent alarm, **my** *armed response team are now surrounding the building. They will be taking you away.* **My people** *remember — not the police. Not yet. The heavies are briefed to talk to you — well they'll start by making you talk, Audley Shawcross. But you are dispensable. Know what I mean? If you don't cooperate. they will have some fun with your body parts. But I doubt you'll see the fun side at all. Nudge, nudge, wink, wink. Know what I mean? All doors have now been secured from the outside since your arrival. You are trapped with no escape route.*

The charges, if you survive the interrogation will include murder, conspiracy to murder, accessory to murder, keeping fraudulent records, conspiring to defraud members by rigging casino games and of course theft from me and burglary. There will also be charges for breach of the Gaming Act 1968. Your section 19 gaming license will be revoked. None of you at Dukes can be regarded as fit and proper persons to operate casinos under the Act any longer. Sentences will be savage. You will die in jail. But that assumes that we even bother with the police.

In conclusion, you may decide to surrender. In that case, you will turn out all lights in the room, use no torch and walk empty-handed to the French windows. You will find them to your left, about nineteen paces. You will stand beside them and tap on the glass three times. You will then face the window with your arms high up, legs apart, palms against the glass until someone opens the door in front of you. Sorry I can't be with you to see this."

Dex wondered how Shawcross would have reacted.

Impossible to predict.

Did that man ever panic?

The plan to hold and capture Shawcross until recompense had been made had to be shelved. A new plan had to fit FB's position instead. Dex saw him sitting as if frozen, lifeless. He was staring at the screen, hands now gripping each side of the computer. Perhaps sitting there seemed safer than giving the signal for armed thugs to take him away.

"Fuck you Shawcross! Fuck you." The sudden exclamation was a shock, shouted loud, spat out and full of venom. Then FB fumbled above his beret.

You stupid bastard FB!

What are you doing?

Replacing the mask.

Think that's going to scare a bunch of East End heavies?

Slowly, FB rose from the chair and stood looking again at the screen. Then he removed the mask and dumped it on the desk. He extinguished the light and counting aloud walked hesitantly to the distant corner of the room. There, now out of vision, Dex heard three sharp raps on the glass as he eased himself from his niche and peered down the room. FB was standing with his hands above his head, palms on the glass, legs apart. Unlike FB who had moved as if on autopilot, Dex was seeing and thinking in technicolor, everything now vivid. Of all the options, one stood out now with this particular intruder. It was the biggest break yet.

He tightened his grip on the baseball bat and started to cross the room with soft and silent steps. All the while he watched for the slightest sign that FB had heard anything, his baseball bat poised ready to strike a fearsome blow if needed. But FB, hands firmly on the window was expecting action from in front of him, his eyes staring through the glass. Dex crept to within three paces before he roared – roared louder than he had ever roared. It came from deep down within him and bounced off the walls, the windows and resonated through the house. In the darkened room it scared the hell out of the terrified FB, who screamed and turned to run, to escape, to go anywhere. In the shadowy light from outside Dex saw that the roar had been even more effective than he had dared to hope. FB had lost the plot. His face was gaunt, his eyes wide with fear and the dying seconds of his scream were still emerging from his open mouth. Dex could see the petrified man wanted to crawl back into his mother's womb. If the Baskerville Hound had been bounding towards him, he could not have been more distraught. But his path was blocked.

"One move FB and I'll club out your brains. You won't wake until morning and you won't like where you find yourself." Dex backed away to switch on the light. "Turn round. Back against the glass. Put your hands out in front of you." He stepped forward and in a swift movement had handcuffed the obedient figure. Then he roped FB's legs at knees and ankles and pushed him roughly to the floor, back against the wall. Dex turned to the window and rapped on it four times – in two bursts of two.

"You due back in Dukes?"

Silence.

"I said are you due back in Dukes? Answer me." He rapped out the command and acted on his father's advice about commanding attention. Speak slowly and to the point. "Don't piss me about or my boys will beat you to pulp. You won't *survive* the experience. But you *will* talk first. To them. They'll see to that. But I'm giving you a chance. I must confess I was hoping for Shawcross to drop by again but you'll do. So – it's your choice. Co-operate now or I send you to Braintree for the fingernail treatment – and that's just for starters." He saw FB shudder at the thought. "Then it will be electrodes attached to your scrotum. I'm told it hurts. Dreadfully. Or should I say shockingly?" He alone laughed at his joke. "Then I think they use dentistry - before bullets in your feet, your knees and ever upwards." Dex waited for the terrified man to look towards him. "FB – the time for pissing about has gone."

FB glowered silently, still trying to draw breath from the shock of the roar. Dex crouched down so that his face was inches from FB's. "You see FB, you and Shawcross have crapped on me for too long but you can't fuck with me any longer. Pity Shawcross sent the errand boy. I was looking forward to seeing him have the, er ... the treatment."

Dex grinned pushing even closer so that FB flinched away. "Your bad luck was to be here - but that's not my problem. So. Where was I? Oh yes. After the kneecaps, the boys go freelance. Your body, or what's left of it, will never be recovered." He smelled the remains of FB's Chicken Balti and drew back still speaking quietly to add to the impact. "Shawcross of course will distance himself – be of no help to you at all. You will be listed as a missing person." He moved in again to smirk. "Sad thing is FB - you're so beautifully *dispensable*." Dex enjoyed the contempt he had injected into the word. Dex went to the window and signaled, five raps and then another five. "There, FB. You have ten seconds to decide. Help me or go play with the Essex boys."

Without hesitation, FB spoke but his words croaked out like a dying man's death rattle. "Call off the bastards. I'll talk. But *you* know more than me. Murder? Who? When?"

"Don't piss about. Full co-operation. From now, you take orders from me." He gimlet-eyed FB again. "Yes or no?" He barked the words for effect. Dex waited for a few long seconds and then went to the window. "Last chance."

FB's eyes drooped towards his mouth like a weary bloodhound. "Stop them. I'll talk. But Shawcross," he faltered. "That bastard scares me just as much. Understand?"

Dex did but said nothing. He gave four bangs, two and two on the pane. "Is Shawcross expecting you back?"

"Yes."

"Time?"

"Soon."

"Then this is an offer you can't refuse. You'd better talk fast into this recorder. Then, after I explain what I want you to do, I'll let you go. You help me, I'll try to help you. But if you double-cross me, Shawcross will get the tape and know who squealed on him." He smiled in a disturbing way that made the listener shudder. "Me? I'd rather jump under a train than let him near me with his Master Bowie knife. You knew about Panama of course?" Dex was sure FB knew nothing of the kind. "Well, let me read you this from agents in Panama." He switched on the lamp and from a drawer, he took out the report and with painstaking emphasis read the account of the murderous attack. "This is your boss Shawcross. Know the expression caught between a rock and a hard place? Sure you do. That's you. My thugs or Shawcross. Or me – the one man who can save you. Meantime, regard Shawcross as on life-support. His days are numbered. Help me and you have a good friend. Anything stupid and he gets the tape."

"What do you want?" The voice was weak and pleading. "Shawcross doesn't give me an inch of slack. Doesn't tell me much. He's a right bastard."

"I know. But I'm losing patience. You know the scams going on, the cheating and money-laundering. Start talking now. Everything. All your tricks, which dealers are bent, what Jude Tuson's doing. How much Reggie Kyte knows. The people in the cage. Where all these new members come from. Why are they happy losing? How Shawcross hooked them. Then when I'm sure you've given me the lot, I'll tell you the deal."

"And Shawcross?"

"You help me – he will know nothing– until too late."

"And what do I tell the bastard?"

Dex needed time to think that through. "Relax. I've thought of that. I'll brief you after you've finished dictating."

As his watch nudged towards four, Shawcross was standing close to the cage, chatting to his security director. He tried to appear interested in Reggie Kyte's views on illegal immigrants flooding the country and killing the British culture. As he nodded politely, murmuring the odd *of course* and *couldn't agree more*, his thoughts were only on what had kept FB. He had expected him back by three.

There were only about a dozen members and guests still at the tables. He could see Jude at the roulette with another stranger, probably Belgian judging by the vulgar checked cloth of his suit. Then from the management relaxation room, FB appeared in his working gear of black tie and dinner-jacket. "Ah, FB! Good of you to come back. Barely worth it. How is your brother?"

"Still in intensive care. The worry is whether the stroke will leave him paralyzed down one side."

"Remind me tomorrow to send him fruit and a card. No better still, come on up to my office and I'll note it now. I wanted to show you some figures anyway. Goodnight Reggie."

"Goodnight AS. Goodnight FB."

The charade for the gallery over, the two men took their seats in the office which smelled of Mediterranean flower-spray struggling against stale cigar smoke. "No problems?"

FB looked at the corner of the desk, his eyes no more evasive than usual. Then he shook his head. "No."

"Leave any clues while you were there?"

"Gloves on all the time. When I left, I double-checked. Everything looked undisturbed."

"Good. And?"

"You'll be disappointed." FB's eyes looked at the carpet and then gazed towards the painting on the far wall. "I thought because you were so long, you'd struck oil."

FB shook his head and played nervously with his fingers. "The reverse. Knowing you were so convinced that the shit was onto something, I didn't want to give up. I took my time - searched every drawer, shelf, bookcase, cupboard from the top rooms to the bottom. That was after I'd checked the computer. I even broke his password to get into a secret section but this contained no more than rantings about his father." He paused. "Oh yes. That reminds me – I checked his father's computer. It hasn't been turned on since the crash." FB yawned into the back of his hand. "Sorry. I'm feeling pretty bushed now. You'll know. It takes it out of you being in someone else's house like that. Creeping round in the dark with a torch."

"I found it exhilarating," Shawcross was swift to riposte. "Adrenaline really pumping. But yes, I can see *you're* exhausted."

"On Dexter's laptop I even undid the defrag to see if he'd hidden any old material. Zilch. The Recycling Bin had nothing in it of interest. I also went through his emails. He's still corresponding with that Tiffany woman. That's where he's staying now – with her. Mostly, his letters and emails are all about the crash – y'know lawyers' letters, winding up the estates of his mother and sister."

Shawcross struck a match for another cigar. "The *Obsession* file?"

FB laughed. "Oh that! Big disappointment after your hopes. He's started a novel about crime in the city. I copied it in case you want to read it."

The snort of derision was response enough. "I can live without that prick's Le Carré efforts."

"Nothing concealed behind other passwords?"

FB rose to leave. By his standards he gave what was a withering glare of *do-me-a-favor*. "First thing I checked – looking for secret areas. That's what I was hoping for, something meaty. A bit of cryptology."

"I'm not sure whether I'm surprised or disappointed."

"Isn't it better that he's not onto us?"

"You're right. Of course it is. But I had a hunch. I don't like being wrong, that's all."

Indianapolis 29th September 2002

Scotty's personal chartered Bombardier Global 5000 had landed at 0710 Local Time in Indianapolis. Aboard were his pilot and co-pilot, a flight attendant, Scotty, his nurse Kim and Dex. At Indianapolis International, a limo bigger than a pop diva's ego was awaiting them. Despite the traffic, the slick organization meant they quickly reached the giant Speedway just west of the city. "Boring circuit this," said Scotty as the giant amphitheatre came into view. "Too flat except where there's banking on the oval. The Indy 500 boys go round this loop for five hundred miles. For Formula One, they built a detour with some windin' track."

"In the middle, isn't it?"

"S'right. But its flat. Too many circuits are too flat. Best bits for top skills are in Brazil – the Senna S or Eau Rouge at Spa. Get some rain there on those hills and boy, you earn your bucks. But this" – he waved his hand contemptuously at the towering stands – "magnificent but F1 racin' here unless it rains ain't the greatest."

The limo took them through a tunnel under one end of the circuit. As the car emerged into the light, the noise of the gathering fans and canned music surrounded them. "Dex – you and Tiffany will be up there." He pointed to the tall pale green VIP stand on his right. "You'll get a good view of a couple of hairpins and the in-field – Turns 9, 10, 11 and 12. There's lunch and tea. I'm told it's pretty darned good. Sorry but I just couldn't sweet-talk you both into the holy of holies over there." He was looking now to his left where Dex saw the marquees and striped awnings. Beyond them were the main grandstands looking across to the pit-lane. "That's jus' for me and my nurse. But I thought anyway, you and Tiffany would appreciate some catchin' up time."

Dex wondered for a moment if this was Scotty's legendary meanness in action. "Fine by me," Dex said though secretly he was disappointed. The white limo pulled up by a barrier with Fort Knox-type security. "This is the parting. Can't get you into here - Bernie Ecclestone's rules. Man ! They *are* somethin' else!"

"So where do we meet up? We need to talk before Tiffany leaves."

"I'll get us a table in the Paddock Club. Nobody'll care after the race. Say five?"

"Perfect. Enjoy the race." The limo entered the reserved area as Dex rather wistfully waved goodbye. The air was humid, the skies were patchy blue and Dex enjoyed soaking up the warmth and the atmosphere. A distant whine and then the roar of an engine by the main straight meant the first driver was ready for the final Practice Session. At the sound, the hairs on the back of his neck rose. They always did as the power reminded Dex of the finesse needed to prevent a young life from becoming a spectacular death. He took a deep breath and realized he was feeling better now than earlier. When the jet had been on its final approach, he had felt shattered. It had been a disturbed night but the sound now of more and more drivers revving up and the screaming protests from the brakes as the cars approached the hairpins were like a shot of black coffee, rejuvenating him.

And above and beyond all this would be Tiffany.

On the journey, Dex had scarcely slept. His mind had been racing at the coup over FB. He wondered how his plot would have played out with Shawcross. As the jet raced over Greenland, he felt sure that Shawcross would never have surrendered by the window. The outcome would have been a crapshoot, surprise his only asset.

In retrospect, even FB had caused less trouble than he might have done. Dex was confident that the tape would keep FB supportive until the end now. Fear and hatred of Shawcross were the best guarantee that FB would now do what he was told. The tape had been dynamite and a duplicate was in a safe in Lincoln's Inn Fields. His solicitor, Rufus Chandler had told him that while mind-blowing, it was no substitute for hard evidence. "Kenny Jennings should film as much as he can and try to get a statement from that Adrian Ryder fellow from the Gaming Board."

"But FB didn't finger him."

"No but FB doesn't know everything. What he did say is he didn't think Shawcross could carry on this big scam – *Snowball* – without having fixed Ryder."

"You're right – and didn't FB mention that when Ryder last came in he seemed very uneasy. Asked to see Shawcross."

"Here's the transcript, hot from my secretary." Rufus picked up a thick bundle of orderly pages. "This is what he said: *Ryder had random-checked the blackjack.*

He then went over to the woman Zara who had been asked by the Board to do a spot-check on why Dukes was performing so well. They had a stormy discussion which he could not hear but she was wagging her finger at him and her face was in his words bloody evil. Like a nagging wife was his description. Ryder though was shaking his head in disagreement."

"I'll question him."

"Don't do it when Zara is around. She seems to have quite some hold over him." The solicitor leaned back and clasped his hands behind his head. "I've already retained a top criminal QC called Charles Bart-Pemberton. He's going to check the evidence and advise when we have sufficient material to go to the Serious Fraud Office. He has a special rapport with the big cheese there. I'm fine on gathering evidence but I'm no criminal lawyer. You need him. Equally, I wouldn't let CBP near the damages claims from the Barnes crash. Horses for courses."

Dex had next phoned Chieseman. The uneducated voice had sounded even rougher on the phone but the man had still promised first December delivery. Moments later, a motor-bike courier headed for Penarth Street with the fifteen thousand that Chieseman wanted upfront.

The smell of cooking from lines of fast-food outlets reminded Dex that he was starving. He followed the powerful mix of aromas across the in-field until he found a stall selling giant turkey-legs where he bought two and a jumbo sized decaff coffee without cream.

The thought of Tiffany now so near excited him. So much had happened since their last parting. He'd called her from Gatwick and she had confirmed she would arrive for lunch but that with the story still unfolding with hundreds missing around West Palm Beach, she would have to return.

During the flight, Dex had been shocked at how much Scotty was still suffering from the gunshot. Despite pain-killers and a sleeping pill, Dex had observed him groaning and grasping his strapped shoulder while Kim mopped his brow with an icy flannel. As they approached the Newfoundland coastline, she insisted on giving him a hefty sedative so that Scotty quickly nodded off.

With a dismissive throw, Dex jettisoned the remains of the turkey into a waste drum and looked at the tiers of seating, now rapidly filling. The fans were arriving in hordes, waving banners, shouting, queuing for fast-food or walking round the in-field. Upbeat music blasted from thousands of tannoys and the smell of grilling burgers and onions seemed to waft from every direction.

Occasionally, the commentators spoke over the public-address system, chatting about the race prospects to help the one hundred and twenty thousand pass the time. Then from all sides, there was cheering, a roar rising to a crescendo. Dex looked up and saw that Scotty's face had appeared on all the giant TV screens. Dex could see the man beaming at such a spontaneous demonstration of affection. In front of him was a giant hoarding *America Salutes You, Scotty. God Bless You!* Everyone knew that his career was now over. He waved his good arm, owing them everything but with nothing to offer.

Nobody watching, Dex included, could have guessed his tormented mind as he stood surrounded by the media waiting for an interview. To a man, the crowd in the Grandstands stood to acknowledge their hero, the guy who the surgeons had rebuilt after one crash only now to be struck down again by a gunman's bullet. Even Dex felt moved by the huge show of affection, though he had grown surer that the man was not nearly as likeable as his adoring public believed. He admired the way that Scotty could absorb the beloved sugary American schmaltz, razzmatazz and sentimentality, all delivered in jumbo portions. In return, Scotty's Irish blood enabled him to play the harp to their emotions.

The cameras followed him as he limped down the pit-lane. Drivers and team bosses broke off from team talks and debates with mechanics to come forward to bear-hug him and to welcome him back as their friend. Bernie Ecclestone came from somewhere to shake his hand. Scotty ducked questions about whether he would race again. Asked who had wanted to shoot him and why, he was jocular. "Heh! The list's just too long! Angry husbands, disappointed lovers, other drivers, casino owners I've taken for millions, Maybe Roxy my ex-wife wanted the life insurance or it was some bad losers at poker. P'rhaps it was even Osama bin Laden. Could have been any of them guys." Then came the famous grin, eyes half-closed. "But it wasn't." The familiar tipping of the peak of his cap was the signal that a quip was coming. "Matter of fact, *I hired* this guy to shoot me. Reckoned the way I been drivin', I was worth more dead'n alive, so I left everything in my will to the best person I knew. Myself." He looked around grinning and relishing the laughs. "But man that gunman, he done gone an' screwed up. I didn' get no legacy, jus' a shoulder good enough for a critter with one arm. Reckon I'm gonna get me the best damned attorney and sue him for not shootin' straight." The crowd roared appreciation. Frippery and Scotty's public image went hand in hand. This was the nonsense they expected and he hadn't disappointed.

Dex joined in the cheers though he alone in the crowd knew just how cleverly Scotty had deflected the real questions, ones that Dex felt sure he could answer. With the interview ended, Dex headed for the tunnel to make his way round to the VIP Stand. He thought of what Scotty had confided to him as they had eaten steaks while the jet was climbing to its cruising height just south-west of Glasgow. "You ever been married?"

Dex had said no. "Don't go rushin' in like I did. Me, I've an ex called Roxy. She sniffs money from a country mile. My broker reckons this shootin' triggered a clause in my accident insurance. Like man, I'm better off with the cash than driving that RGB shit around in circles."

"So far, sounds great. But Roxy?"

"She remembered this policy. Memory like a computer. Her phone bill callin' me for her share is jus' somethin' else. I told her – I said I'll see you in hell first." Scotty had shaken his head. "But she's like one of them weebils. Harder you knock her, the quicker that bitch bounces back."

"Will she sue?"

"Maybe. But she's done pretty darned good. My lawyers reckon I can play the sympathy card now. Make it look as if she's takin' money from a fairground freak."

Dex had thought the conversation finished but then curiously Scotty had continued, his face turned towards the small window. The tone was bitter. "That bitch – she's to blame for all of this." Scotty had pointed to his strapped shoulder and his injured leg. For a moment, it seemed that Scotty was going to unburden himself but then his face hardened. Dex assumed he regretted volunteering as much as he had. Instead, Scotty started explaining about the history of Indianapolis, the *Brickyard Circuit*, and the central role of the Hulman family. Dex was left disappointed and as Scotty slept fitfully, high above the icy wastes of Canada, he was still fretting over what dark secrets Scotty was concealing.

Dex walked beneath the giant curve at the southern end of the circuit. All around was the blare of horns, the chanting of Montoya's Colombian supporters and the swathes of red-coated Ferrari fans. Normally, he would have relished the fevered activity - the mobile outlets selling overpriced memorabilia and merchandise and the smell of hot-dogs and burgers from the fast-food joints. Not now though. As the time for Tiffany's arrival neared, the slow moving people irritated him as he zigzagged between them.

As quickly as he saw a pay-phone, he made the decision that he had ducked for days. He stepped away from the unruly human tide, checked his watch yet again and hurried off to make a call. Afterwards, still looking like a schoolboy buying his first condoms, he had struggled through to the VIP Stand. On the top tier, there was a bar, comfy chairs and a few small tables set out for lunch. He secured an excellent table by the window above the steep rows of seating.

Tiffany was due at noon but Dex was twenty minutes early. In the men's room, he fixed his hair, shaved, dabbed on some John Varvatos and finally reached for his Serengeti Vedi sunglasses. Then he returned to the table to study the hype for the race. By twelve, he could have sung the grid positions backwards.

A tap on the shoulder was the first he knew of her arrival. He swiveled and took in her firm jaw, her laughing eyes that somehow still managed to be penetrating. She radiated fitness indicating hours in the gym. The Washington summer had tanned her face and arms. Even her hair seemed a shade blonder than when he had watched her interviews from the White House and while reporting from Singer Island with the wind shrieking into her microphone. She had lost some weight too or perhaps it was just the cut of her white flared trousers and deep red shirt.

"Hi! Remember me?"

"Haven't I seen you on the telly?" he asked as he stood up. Ignoring the other VIPs, he buried his head in her neck and hugged her. It lingered, two bodies locked with a warmth that he had not until now dared to assume. Her arms clung around his neck while his squeezed her back. Gently, she pulled away so that their faces were just apart, her familiar elfin haircut brushing against his cheek. She kissed him on the lips without passion but in a way that Dex hoped hinted at a deeper yearning.

"You look tired," Tiffany whispered. "Exhausted actually. The flight?" They stepped apart and agreed on lunch at once.

"A few disturbed nights." She recognized a typical understatement. "Life's been tough," he continued "but nothing compared to what you've been through. Yet you look … just amazing. I watched you standing near the ocean on Singer Island. I've never seen horizontal rain or waves like that."

Her smile was appreciative of the compliment. She wrinkled her nose and nodded her head. "God! I just needed to escape from the wind-blown heroine look. Now, I'm plain famished. Not a scrap to eat coming here. Internal flights in the US remind me of famine in Africa. The sound of my stomach rumbling drowned the engines!" She looked him up and down. "Looks as if you've been in training too. And I like the shirt." She was admiring the sweatshirt, black across the shoulders, white-fronted but with a red streak of a tire tread running across it.

"Appropriate for a Grand Prix, I thought."

"Goes well with those jeans. Jeans only look good if you've got the right bum. You have." Still with hands joined, they sat down, Dex bowled over by her approach. The Mumm champagne arrived and they toasted each other. "To us and to the spirit of Silverstone," he concluded. They chinked glasses "What's your abiding impression of your first hurricane?"

Without even stopping to think, she replied. "The noise and the coconuts. They were setting up my microphone near the waterfront. The roar of the sea and the wind was nearly deafening. I could hardly stand, let alone deliver any commentary. Suddenly this coconut hurtled towards us like a cannon-ball. I saw it too late. It hit the guy holding the mike at over a hundred. Broke his leg. He's still in hospital. He's lucky – on the head would have killed him. After that, we saw them flying everywhere, so we moved further from the palms. They were bent over just like bows."

"Scary."

"Unbelievable. The sheer power of nature in the raw. "I've *had* hurricanes up to here. I don't want to go back." Tiffany ordered Parma ham and melon followed by beef. "But I must! So what's your news?" she asked "You've been so cryptic even on our secret numbers."

"I've done things," he spoke slowly, not quite faltering "that you'd have said were crazy. If I'd told you, you'd have been worried. Well …terrified for me. But the risk against reward ratio was worth it."

"You're close to bringing Shawcross down?"

"Not close enough. My plan's nearly ready. The charity for abused kids is a big step closer. But if I can pull this thing off," he shook his head slowly, "well, there'll be winners all round at Shawcross' expense. *And* I'll clear some debts"

Her voice sounded edgy and she raised her penciled eyebrows. "Debts?"

"Mainly Scotty who lends me half a mill soon and I repay one point five in January. He's been useful. He's a mean bastard though, hard as they come. I sensed it was take it or leave it but he'll be centre-stage when the show moves to Vegas."

"For that money, he'd better be. What other debts?"

"One hundred grand to Lord Yarbury borrowed but double that due back to him. Oh … and a bank loan. But I need very penny to fund the plan."

"No Ferrari or Mercedes then?"

"Not exactly." She listened and laughed to his description of just a mile in the Yellow Peril. "So how much are you going to extract from Shawcross?"

"Ten million in sterling, say fifteen million US. After paying off everything, there's plenty enough for charity."

"You talk as if its in the bag. Are you going to blackmail Shawcross?"

Dex shook his head and grinned from ear to ear. "That might have happened a couple off days back but now, nothing so blunt. I'll explain – perhaps after the race. We're meeting Scotty."

"Can't you tell me now?" She stretched both hands across the table to hold his. Dex felt her energy pulsing through him as he looked deep into her eyes.

He winked at her. "No, not yet."

"Talk about a clam!" She shook her head in disbelief. "Play it your way you man of mystery. I can't believe how calm you are after Glenn's death and then being there when Scotty was gunned down."

Dex nearly told her about the strength he'd gained from Bladon churchyard but decided now was not the right time. "It's hard to know where to start. Can I, sort of, build up to the full story?"

She wagged her finger at him in mock anger. "Remember when you last kept avoiding the subject?"

"It's the onion in me! But I promise. I've no secrets from you." They clinked glasses again. But he knew he was never going to reveal about Max Chieseman.

"Sorry I landed you in it with those coppers. How was a police cell? When they ambushed me, I decided truth was the best option."

Dex shrugged as if it were nothing. "Quite an experience. Lower on the Richter Scale than being clubbed by a masked gunman. Lower than being burgled twice, once by Shawcross and once when I caught the intruder."

Her jaw dropped. "This all happened to you?"

He nodded as if the admission was the most natural thing. "I've hired an agent called Kenny and his woman Jackie to work undercover in Dukes, filming, observing. I'm also paying for a card-counting expert to be treated for addiction in Wiltshire. He'll be a while yet but he'll prove a case on blackjack fraud. He'll be fine if they can stop him shoving powder up his nose. I have a top QC who's weighed the evidence so far. He wants more flesh on the bones." Dex gave a gentle laugh. "Not something the QC needs personally! My God! What a stomach!" His face turned serious again. "Did I tell you about the report from Panama?"

"You know you didn't. Give."

"Shawcross is a psychopathic killer." Quickly, he explained everything he knew.

"My God! And you're not backing off? Dex isn't it time you just let the cops carry on now?"

"I promised myself I'd see it through. Anyway, the cops would only screw up. Pea-brains, especially the Welsh one. Trying to fit me up. I hate them."

"A legacy from the prosecutions at *Louche?*"

"Exactly. They played every low trick they could to get me to confess to drug-dealing." His face brightened. "I hate them. Let them solve these crimes without me." His eyebrow bobbed and his eyes twinkled to show the likelihood of that. He looked across at her, unsure now whether the highlights were darker or the rest of her hair blonder. The sun, streaming through the picture window caught the different shades to perfection. The new look suited her face, her smooth complexion so golden brown and fresh looking. He leaned across and stroked her cheek. "I want your support – I need you. I've done a great deal alone but I need you and Scotty – as part of my team."

Tiffany looked disappointed but said nothing. Instead, she downed her champagne and looked round the room, her eyes suddenly distant. Dex sensed something was wrong. "Is that why you asked me here today? Just to involve me in your plans." She shifted her cutlery and then looked down sadly at the table. She spoke gently and without rancor. "It's not why *I* came all this way."

He leaned across and pulled her hand towards him. "Me neither. That's the trouble talking in shorthand. Let's toast *us* again. That's why I'm here too. I so wanted to see you, to hold you, to laugh with you." Dex thought again that he saw some yearning in her face as he raised his glass. "To my best chum."

She laughed at his little joke and clinked glasses again, her face gradually softening. "To yesterday's chum and to ... today's Colossus. I mean it. You've changed, not just those new bags under your eyes. In London, when we were physically close, we were far apart. We had a big bridge to build. With the Atlantic between us, being so far apart, I've grown closer than ever. We don't need a bridge now. Time and the new you have changed all that."

Dex looked surprised at her outburst of sentimentality. "That's the most beautiful thing you've ever said." Again, he stroked the side of her face and her eyes closed dreamily. "That phone call. We agreed about absence. Remember?"

She breathed her answer. "Every word." Her voice had gone deep and husky.

He unwittingly imagined Jude and her glistening body arched and aching for him to enter. Despite the animal lust, they had remained strangers, yet somehow when Tiffany was like this the pair of them made music like a string quartet. He looked away to cover his discomfort at the untimely recollection. "In Julie's, we went to hell and back, all in one evening."

She paused while the server produced Beef Wellington in thick slices. The *sommelier* poured Volnay into deep, wide burgundy glasses. "We'll go there again. It'll be different this time."

"The Chinese have a saying – well they always do, don't they? May you live in interesting times. It's a curse and I've thought of it often. Hell, these past few months have been interesting all right. But like a cork, you have to keep surfacing. If I tell you everything in detail, I'll only gabble and babble but here's the agenda for the right moment." For two minutes, he rattled off the quickening pace of incidents that he had been through."

"All these new names. EC corruption? Zulu masks? With that agenda, I'll miss my plane."

"Good. Why not?"

"Duty and the editor call." She looked wistful, her eyes flashing a signal. There was something coquettish about her smile and her eyes darted back and forth as if in surprise at what she was about to say. "Dex my sweet - you seem so much, Mmmh ... older, more mature. But there's no rush to explain what else you've been up to." Birdlike, she tipped her head to one side. "Jude's left hasn't she?"

"Long gone!" His cheeks reddened at the insinuation and he wondered just what she suspected about Jude. Had her suspicions been a trigger to her new warmth? It seemed likely. "Are you peeling away another layer of the onion?" He chewed the tender beef thoughtfully and was delighted when he saw her enthusiastic acknowledgement. He wanted to say so much, so quickly. "Y'know," he said, "The big change. I'm out of father's cold shadow. And partly that's because in a strange sort of way, I've grown to love the helpless old bastard."

"Hatred is *so* futile, though I can see why Shawcross might be an exception to my rule. Journalism is dominated by hatred. Take any news program – everything's about war, terrorism, vendettas, revenge, crime, suffering and enemies." She pushed aside her plate and then changed her tone. "I hope you haven't been gambling?"

"Nothing serious. But I'm going to."

"Roulette?" Her tone was somewhere between a question and a command.

"Just once. Big money. It's a cornerstone of my plan."

"Even if you had the money, no more crazy bets." This *was* a command. He looked away. "Don't you ever learn?"

"I've learned, Tiffany. Trust me. I'll explain later." But he knew she would get only the sanitized version.

"Will you get a job?"

He played with the last morsel of pastry. "After Shawcross is history, I'll run the charity. For now, I'm fully engaged – destroying Dukes." His look and the way he spoke made the proposition sound eminently sensible. Dex waited for a grunt of disapproval or an angry shrug of the shoulders but it never came. Instead he saw respect, even an indication of support from the inflection of her mouth. He could sense the Silverstone magic, confident that he was drawing her closer. "My plans are different now."

"Go on. I'm not being a good listener." She swirled the burgundy. "This wine's amazing."

"Great bouquet."

"Different plan? But you just said ..."

"No." He pushed aside his plate. "Going for a triple whammy."

"So what's different?"

He grinned again, his eyes toying with her. His tired features came to life and his cheeks filled out, the impish charm fully restored. "As ever: Sink Dukes. Wham! Destroy Space City. Wham! Wham! But now," he paused to savor the moment "before that, I'm going gambling again. Big time. With Scotty. He doesn't know the details yet. We're going to win back every stolen pound plus interest and damages. Wham, wham, wham!"

"How much?"

"The ten million. Mind, I haven't told Scotty that figure, otherwise he'd want more from me."

"You're crazy." But he knew she didn't mean it. The words came from respect, not contempt. "But they destroyed you last time. What's different?"

Dex prodded the American Cheddar suspiciously. "What's different? I'll tell you. Me." His grin hinted that he was bursting to tell her something sensational. But he just returned to studying the cheeseboard. Tiffany waited for an explanation but it dawned on her after a few seconds that he had nothing to add.

She continued. "Not playing the Martingale then?"

His laugh was not even nervous. "Doubling-up? No way." His smile killed the obvious fatigue as he stroked her wrist and played with the charms on her bracelet. "We'll hit Dukes so hard, like a boxer's left and right that it'll be all over in one day, maybe just one hour. Just like they did to me."

"How can you be so sure?"

"Trust me."

She shrugged and then smiled. "I can't believe I'm saying this but, yes – with the new you, I guess I do." She put down her cutlery. "You know who shot Glenn and Brannigan?"

"I *thought* I did – but the short answer is no. I'll explain later. No secrets as I said. Coffee?"

She declined. "Trouble with living in the USA - you get bombarded with lifestyle gurus pontificating about health. So this week I'm off coffee. Ask me again another week!"

"There is," he smiled *"something else* I've wanted to ask you." He looked earnest. He whispered the words so that they edged closer across the maroon cloth on the table.

315

"Go on."

"You're not obsessed with Formula One, are you? So I mean – would you mind *awfully* if we missed the race?"

She caught the drift at once. "That depends."

"I'm well-tuned. I accelerate or slow down on demand, am good on clutches, any hills and curves and am incredibly easy to handle." The words tumbled out unrehearsed.

She wagged a finger at him before tapping him on the nose. "A naughty knee-trembler under the grandstand?"

"Better. There was a cancellation this morning." He nodded through the window. "At the Brickyard Crossing Inn."

"Just make sure we both reach the Checkered Flag at the same time. I don't like coming second."

"Better than being a non-finisher. Or a non-starter come to that."

She pushed back her chair with an alacrity that surprised him. "We can always watch the highlights later, can't we?"

"Kim, give us an hour, eh?" Scotty kissed her dismissively as he waved Dex and Tiffany into the Paddock Club. Inside, the atmosphere was *after the Lord Mayor's Show*. The blue and white table-cloths covered empty tables and staff were clearing away the remains of the huge party that had surrounded lunch and tea. Discarded race programs lay on chairs. A young woman was sweeping up champagne corks and scraps of food from the floor. Nearly everyone had left but the barman was quick to recognize a sporting icon and a bottle of champagne had appeared. Scotty autographed some programs for fans but then politely shooed away the last persistent pair who'd wanted to talk.

Dex went outside, keen to savor the view of the mighty stands lining the straight. Scotty followed. As he turned to Dex, he shook his head in disbelief. "What a race! The way that David Coulthard stole it. Overtaking from third in the final lap. Sensational."

Tiffany looked to Dex to reply. He clasped his hands in front of him and then behind, before patting his still damp hair. "Fantastic. Must have been one of the best races in years. Biggest upset since Mansell and the blown tire in Melbourne."

"Watch it all, did you?"

Dex looked to Tiffany who gazed at her program.

Scotty was enjoying himself. "You mean? No – you don't mean you guys missed the race? All of it? So much to talk about, had you?"

"So much to talk about," Dex's face colored and the hooded eyes provide a shield.

Scotty's face crinkled like his hair. He fiddled with his sideburn and then burst out laughing. "I was testing you about Coulthard. He was third. Barrichello led Schumi home. In case anyone asks you." He waved to some fans who were chanting his name and then they went back inside to their champagne now standing in a bucket of ice. "I phoned you. Oh twenty minutes before the start. I'd wangled you a couple of Pit Lane Passes. I called again about lap 15 and then gave up."

"Thanks. Next time." Dex kissed Tiffany on the cheek. "Let's sit down and talk things through." He waited for Scotty to wriggle into a comfortable position on his chair before continuing. "We're going to beat Dukes at roulette and no Sherman tanks needed."

"Roulette? Are you still sayin' I only get my bucks if you win at that crazy game? Sounds kinda dumb to me."

"By *us* winning. Playing Reverse Labouchère." With broad brush strokes he explained the basics of the system.

Tiffany looked puzzled. "But you won a fortune playing the Martingale, didn't you? You only lost because Dukes cheated you. Why change?"

"You're right but it's too risky and would take months. I want to blitzkrieg them!"

Scotty scratched his head and then spoke. Every word suggested he was angry. "The theory's fine. The reality sucks! One day, in the big blue yonder, maybe we'd clean up real good."

Dex looked away but rapidly composed himself to answer breezily. "We can *win* millions." Dex did not intend to divulge his math. He knew big reserves were essential, something he did not have and he judged now was not a good time to ask Scotty to pony-up with his cash.

Scotty waved his good arm dismissively. "Back home when I was a kid, we had an expression for guys like you. Seems jus' right now. You're plain full of shit. You sure as hell ain't gonna win - not in the first hour, not the first day even. Man, tryin' to better Dooks – hell next you're tellin' me you can kiss a cobra's lips." The tone was getting more noisily aggressive with the champagne on top of whatever had gone before. "An' I don' like that."

Tiffany looked on but said nothing as Dex started to say that Scotty could bail out if he wanted when the American's phone rang. "Yes," he said. When Scotty recognized the sing-song voice of Nanda Datt, he pushed back his chair and limped to a far corner of the marquee, where he stood head bowed, listening for a moment or two. "So you can fuck off, you cocksucker." Scotty's words still carried easily to Dex. When the driver returned, Dex noticed his hands were trembling. "Roxy, my ex-wife."

Dex was not convinced. Ex-wives wouldn't make a guy like Scotty look like a startled rabbit. He decided to attack. "Quit now Scotty if you want. You'll say bye-bye to a million profit."

Scotty grabbed for the bottle and refilled his glass. "An' you'll pay for your goddamned flight over."

Dex rocked his head back in exaggerated laughter. "Sounds like a good deal for me. I'll pay my fare but keep the profits. You're on." He nearly added *you mean bastard*. Scotty glowered across the food-stained cloth and flicked away some crumbs. Then he looked up and his eyes said *you're right, that's a bum deal for me*. Dex placed both hands on the table, fingers spread apart, eyes fixing first Tiffany and then Scotty where his eyes lingered long enough to make him look away. "You'll get your money back plus the million. Trust me!"

Scotty's grunt was hostile. His eyes were hidden as he looked down, his facial muscles working overtime as he wrestled with the renewed threat from Nanda Datt.

"*I'll* do it." Tiffany's surprise intervention seemed almost stage-managed. "If Scotty wants out I'll put up some cash."

Scotty was still aggrieved. "Trust me! Trust me! You're always sayin' that. Jus' like my boss at RGB."

Dex intervened at once. " I've tested Reverse Labouchère using my software program over thousands of spins." Dex mentally crossed his fingers. While true, the results so far had been dreadful. "I don't need any more crap from you, Scotty. Remember our deal in the hospital? I get the half-mill, you get it back plus one million profit. For that, you promised *commitment*. It's about time you started delivering."

Scotty tilted his glass to the bridge of his nose and drained the last drops. Dex stood up and beckoned to Tiffany. "It's your choice Scotty. Think about it. We'll take a stroll down to the pits."

Outside, Tiffany broke an overlong silence. "He's not as likeable as his image, is he?" Tiffany was not asking a question.

"He's desperate for money. His career's falling apart. That phone call came at a bad time. Fired him up. I don't know who was calling but I'd bet it wasn't Roxy. Thanks for that intervention! We may end up doing Dukes together but for the Vegas end I really do need him, awkward bastard though he is."

"You don't need him. You need *someone*."

"Were you seriously offering to replace him?"

"Me? I'm not sure. I wanted to gee him up. " Her shrug was non-committal.

"Scotty's nearly ideal – or was. Now, though I'm worried."

"Why?"

"First, he was quite a drinker back in the early nineties. Ever since, he's been dry – until recently. He reeked of Irish whiskey in the hospital. He sank three-quarters of a bottle on the flight - to kill the pain he said. But did you notice? His speech just now was slurred. He's been hitting the juice hard today. Understandable when he's all washed up."

"What's the other thing?"

"This battle against Shawcross will climax in Vegas. There could be trouble. If there were a chase, I'd need the fastest driver around. When I chose Scotty, he was. Now with that shoulder buggered, I'm hesitant."

"A drunken cripple you don't need."

They were watching the Jordan team, resplendent in their yellow overalls, packing to leave, loading tires into a huge truck. Dex kissed her. "You say the cleverest things." He pulled her closer. "God! I adore you! Especially after this afternoon." The kiss was long, deep and full of emotion. "So if he says yes?"

"If he says yes, then you've hired the wrong guy." She looked up at him eyes steadfast. "But the alternative is worse. If *you* backed off now and rejected him, I'd say he could turn nasty."

"How?"

"He knows too much. Suppose he turned malevolent. Phoned Shawcross after a drunken binge. That would blow you out of the water. Say he tipped Dukes off that you're planning a Reverse Labouchère coup. Shawcross would ban you from membership. You've told the man too much to be discountable. As the saying goes, Dex, you're better off with Scotty in the tent pissing out than outside pissing in."

Dex looked thoughtful but said nothing as he steered her along the littered walkway back to the hospitality suite. "But I think he'll say yes. It's a great deal for him. He needs the money. That's if you believe his tales of poverty. I don't! There's a great deal about Scotty we don't understand."

She tiptoed up to kiss his lips again. "If he says yes - is there a role for me? You wanted me here for a reason."

He stopped dead and turned to her. "I wanted you here because you're the most captivating, sexy, interesting, exciting, capricious, lovable person I've ever met. Could there be a better reason?" Standing on the bright green artificial grass, they kissed again.

"Sounds good to me. Well – except for the capricious bit. But seriously ... I do want to help."

"You will. If the plan develops, I'll want a decoy in Vegas and I'll need media coverage."

"Decoy? Explain."

"Another time. Let's see what he's decided." Back inside, Dex noticed that the champagne bottle was now empty. He approached the table with big confident strides, rubbing his hands and stretched to his full height. "So?"

"I'm your man, Dex."

Dex tried to sound pleased as he shook Scotty by the hand.

London – 3ʳᵈ October 2002

Kenny Jennings breezed into Porcupine House. "Some good news for you."

Dex needed action. "Nailing Adrian Ryder? The legal beagles are insisting on that." A phony war had set in, with too little to do until Clouds House had sorted out Mark Evans and Chieseman had delivered. "Tea? Coffee?"

"English tea, Dex. And if you've any of them cookies, y'know the Bourbons – well ..."

Dex gave a wry smile. He had grown to like and respect the agent. There was a calm authority about him that could almost pass as diffidence. "Take the packet when you go." As he waited for the water to boil, he looked at Kenny, seeing a slim anonymous Londoner aged late forties, average height, clipped wispy moustache, thinning brown hair and glasses. You could sit opposite him on a tube, watch him for a dozen stops but still forget him seconds after he left the train - ideal for his business.

"So what's the news?"

"I've traced Ryder. He's married, home near Ashford in Kent. Ex-copper. Invalided out after an attack. I got a woman at the Gaming Board talking. She thought I was a security guy for Maximus Casino in Marylebone. Ryder covers a few of the casinos in the West End but does a lot of his paperwork from home, like other Inspectors. She gave me his cell number for home / office. The rest was easy." He helped himself to a second biscuit.

"Don't know how you keep so slim."

"It's the hard work. That and pining for Jackie."

"Pining?" Dex sensed Kenny wanted to talk. "Explain – if you want."

"Me and Jackie, we're an item but we don't live together."

"How come?"

"She joined me at my little Ravenscourt Park office nearly twenty years ago. Well, you know how it is. One thing led to another. We were going to marry but then her father died. Her mother moved in with her and she's an embittered old shrew. Never liked me. I'm just a private detective, not a brain surgeon. Not good enough. So I won't live under the same roof as that old witch. Jackie and I get the odd evening together over at my place – but otherwise I'm left, well … pining."

"Tough story! Here's the tea. Dark brown."

"Luvver-ley," he over-emphasized his pleasure. "So do you want me to doorstep Ryder or will you?"

Dex wanted to do this one. "I'd rather you and Jackie covered the casino. That's your real value. Filming, watching, listening."

"Fine by me. I doubt Ryder could be dangerous. Might be a tough nut to crack though, what with his copper background. You know what they teach cops, don't you?"

"Tell me."

Kenny rustled the biscuit packet until his fourth biscuit tumbled out. "Never stand when you can sit. Never sit when you can lie. Never lie unless you can get away with it." Dex appreciated the joke.

"My father took me and my sister to Bow Street Magistrates once. In the gents was a machine dispensing combs and toothpaste. Even though decimal currency had been in for years, someone had scrawled on the metal casing – *Never put Bow Street Coppers in here. They're all bent!*"

It was Kenny's turn to laugh. "Believe me, I've suffered from the police too. They hate private detectives, so you going to see Adrian Ryder might work better." Yet even as he listened, Dex sensed some reserve. Perhaps Kenny had wanted the away-day and more chargeable hours. Or maybe he just thinks I'm too green.

"How's the filming?"

"Doing okay. Taking it slowly. Jackie and me, we arrive separately. We became members at different times and used different addresses."

"Reckon you can fool them?"

"We're careful. I'm not ready to film yet, though I've been getting them used to me being there. We've been practicing down in the Golden Orb. They've never seemed suspicious."

"That's twenty times busier. In Dukes you'll stand out."

Kenny nodded. "Operating a concealed camcorder isn't easy. My first attempts showed only knees. Jackie's film was like a roller-coaster zooming from floor to ceiling. But we're improving."

"Seen anything in Dukes?"

"Yes. Don't ask me to explain yet but I think I'm onto something you'll like. But I can't prove it in a day. It'll take a while to be sure."

"Plenty of big bills to deliver then."

"Brought one with me," Kenny laughed. "Just over a grand."

"Do I get a discount for every knee shot?" He slapped Kenny on the back. "No. Seriously, how much of my money have you and Jackie lost at the tables?"

"In the Orb, we play sweetie money. We're actually slightly ahead. I tried blackjack at Dukes. Winning is as hard as finding polar bears in the Congo. You gave me a float of twenty grand. I changed that the first time, so they knew I was a substantial player. Jackie – she's going to play baccarat. Maybe that's a tougher game for them to fix. She'll change about fifteen when she first plays. Or what's left of it."

"FB didn't mention fixing baccarat. This other guy you have scouting around. What's he achieving?"

"Leo? Good lad, Leo. Couldn't unleash him in Dukes or anywhere smart. He'd scare them shitless. He's a rough looking bastard but good for snooping, following like you asked. No progress yet."

"I'll drive down to Ashford this afternoon."

Kenny looked perplexed. He seemed unsure whether to speak or not. Then he did. "Are you sure door-stepping Ryder's a good move?"

"The legal beagles want a statement from him. I can see why."

"Sure I can see they *need* one – but is it *wise*?" Kenny pushed his thick mug forward for a refill. "You think Ryder may be bent. Why? Because FB suspects something. You assume Shawcross may have bribed him. I agree so far. But you barge in on him at home and try to scare the shit out of him. What's he going to do? You think an ex-copper is simply going to say: *Heh, Mr Dexter, you're right. I am a corrupt bastard and I've taken bribes. I know Shawcross' dirty tricks but he pays me to ignore them. So, thanks for dropping by Mr Dexter, it's a fair cop. Where do I sign my full confession?*" Kenny's moustache drooped in disdain.

The splash as Dex poured the tea was the only sound to break the silence. He frowned and pursed his lips. "Put like that, hell no. He's going to kick like a mule. Deny, deny, deny. And when I'm gone, worse still, he's going to tell Shawcross I'm onto them both."

"Can you take that risk?"

Dex slowly shook his head. "Put like that? No. It's impossible." He pushed across the tea and then walked around the table to stand behind Kenny. He dropped a hand on the agent's shoulder. "Thanks, Kenny. You've probably saved my life."

"But if anything changes, something that makes us convinced we can squeeze the truth from him, then let's reconsider."

"One thing. FB speculated that Ryder might have the hots for an accountant who helps check casino accounts. Zoe somebody." He flicked through the transcript. "Sorry, Zara Belfield of Crouch, Muir and Styles of Lovat Lane in the City."

"You should have told me that before. Leo can do some digging. We might find a pressure point yet."

Wiltshire, England 14th November 2002

Dex turned out of Clouds House into the country road. He was surrounded by waterlogged fields and trees, their bare branches swaying in the cold north-easterly. Looking remarkably different after his treatment, Mark Evans sat beside him. The paranoid wreck had gone. Indeed, when he had appeared with a neat haircut and no aggressive baldness, Dex needed a double-take to recognize him. He had gained some weight too. The gaunt haggard look had gone. He looked fit enough to leave the cloistered surroundings where he had fought his demons. In a time-worn brown leather jacket, jeans and a checked-shirt, he seemed transformed.

The Yellow Peril was filthy from the drive through the muddy lanes. "Sorry about the car."

"I did rather expect something rather bigger."

"I'm putting up with this old wreck until January. Then I'm getting a TVR." They splashed through the endless puddles of a gloomy morning, making heavy work of the winding roads leading to the A303. At last, they hit the London road and were heading slowly but noisily east. "Hungry?"

"I could sink a pint."

"Is that okay?"

"I'll be fine."

"There's a great pub called The Mayfly. It's right by the River Test - better in summer but always beautiful."

Until they reached the country pub nearly an hour later, conversation was desultory, trivia mainly - each with so much on his mind and neither mind meeting the other. "In the summer, the river is gin clear. You see huge trout, greedily sucking down a hatch of flies." Dex pointed at the fast flowing river which today was a muddy brown after the torrential rain of the last two days.

"I wouldn't mind dropping a worm in there."

"On the Test! Dry fly only. Fished upstream. If you used a worm here, the water bailiffs would have you. You'd never see another blackjack table for a long time. Or if you did, you'd never play sitting down."

Evans laughed, an all-time first. They went inside the low-ceilinged pub and each ordered pie, two veg and pints. "I never drank whilst I was in there. Didn't miss it. Booze has never been a problem. Kicking the coke, that was hell. But those people there, they know what they're doing."

"Think you're cured?" Dex eased himself into a chair close to the fire.

"They don't talk of cures. Sounds too much like Lourdes. I'm *in remission*." He played with a large ashtray. "The doctors, nurses, and my counselor – they all worked for me. Encouraged me to help others with their problems and to share mine. It's powerful therapy but, shit, easy it is not. I slept endlessly at first. Then I was in hell – cravings, then just so depressed ... like you'd want to scream. Maybe I did."

"How does it work then?"

"I had my personal counselor but we weren't encouraged to rely too much on him. Besides the doctors and nurses, peer support is the first help-point, but I found talking to the counselor useful. I think I'm going to be okay. Why? Because unlike many of the others, I was pressurized only by the card-counting. Well, the fear of being busted really. The marriage breakdown came from the gambling and coke." He paused to take a hefty swill of beer. "They were such great listeners, really wanted to understand. They worked on that angle. I'm never going to card-count again – well except for you. But that's going to be different."

Mark gripped the ashtray with obvious intensity. "I'm not going back there. Never." He shook his head. It didn't seem so pointed now with a growth of hair. The ear-stud had gone too. "It would be letting them down. Great people. I owe it to them. Respect for them, respect for me. And for you too." He nodded assertively. "Yes. That's it! I can respect *myself* again. Now, I have to get my life in order, pay Kath some money and see Emily. Get a life! "

"How's Emily been with you not seeing her?"

"Upset but I sent her letters and she sent me pictures she'd drawn."

"She'll love the new you. Maybe Kath will too." Dex saw the deep emotions surface as Mark tried to force back tears. He quickly moved on. "Am I expecting too much, y'know, asking you to play blackjack?"

"It's not the counting." He raised his head slightly sideways. "It's the edge. The nearly always being caught. But you don't want me to do that, do you?" He peered suspiciously over the rim of his glass.

Dex realized Mark had a good recollection of their breakfast discussion at Simpson's. "Quite the reverse. Or maybe not quite. I want you to count cards but not, absolutely not, to use the count to increase your stakes." Dex spread his hands gesturing simplicity. "All I want is the count after each shoe and your judgment on whether some tens and aces have been removed."

"Piece of cake. But I won't win, will I?"

"So what? It'll be my money. But playing Basic Strategy, you might win – well occasionally."

Mark chased a boiled potato around his plate and then chewed thoughtfully. "Will this take long?"

"Until you tell me that you are 100% positive that the bastards have taken out a wad of tens and aces. Or not."

Evans suddenly looked up and grinned. "If you're right, only a fool would increase bets with a favorable count."

"Precisely. If I'm right, you'll get a high count that says: *must be lots of tens and aces to come.* But there won't be, so the count will get increasingly higher until," he paused to thump the table - "bingo, the shoe's over. Now if that happens repeatedly, then it must be fixed."

"Agreed. But surely Dukes follow the official procedure - whenever there are new decks of cards, they semi-circle them on the table, face up so that the players can check that all the cards are there."

"Agreed. I've seen that, sometimes." Dex pointed to the blackboard. "Pud?" He saw Evans decline before continuing. "It's not just conjurors who do tricks. Plenty of dealers use sleight-of-hand." Dex wiped the gravy with a piece of bread. "I've learned this since we met:. Never play cards with an off-duty dealer. Granted, in London casinos, dirty tricks are unlikely." He ordered coffee. "But not impossible. That's precisely why it's so easy for a bent casino to get away with so much. The Gaming Board doesn't expect to find short decks, gaffed roulette wheels or crooked dealers. In Nevada, it's different. The Gaming Control Board people sometimes swoop and cart off a wheel for checking."

"How do you know this?"

"I traced a former casino director. The Gaming Board banned him for life from working in casinos during the great purge twenty odd years ago. The turf war between Playboy Club and Ladbrokes had gone way beyond the Gaming Act rules. Well, he'd come across slugged decks and missing cards too – though not, *if I believed him*, in the UK. He told me that on routine visits, the Board don't check the cards for missing tens or aces. They could but they don't." Evans was about to comment but then nodded Dex to continue. "How many times have you sat down at a blackjack table and played without seeing the semi-circle of cards?"

Evans was emphatic, head shaking positively. "Nearly every time. Hundreds, thousands of times. In fact, I avoid all that shit. Takes time. I go to another table."

Dex' face beamed pleasure. "Precisely. So you have no idea what happened to the new cards when you and nobody else was there. You've no idea what has happened to the cards in the shoe when you start to play."

"Go on."

Dex felt strange explaining scams to an acknowledged blackjack expert. "Ever heard of the *High Card Slug*? Perfect for beating card-counters and increasing the house advantage against everybody. Less 20s, blackjacks, double-downs." Evans looked puzzled. "This director guy told me. There are two mega-ways for the casino to cheat at blackjack. For management, the easiest but risky way of winning is to take some tens and aces from each pack. In a six deck shoe, there could be perhaps twenty-four cards missing – the precise ones you want to give you the edge over the house. As a counter you'd be expecting them to appear once the count is high and the shoe well advanced. But, and this is the point, you can't be sure because..."

"The casino doesn't deal out every card." The helpful interruption was immediate.

Dex gave Mark a high-five. "The shoe always ends with say twenty percent of the cards not dealt. It varies. Your expected tens and aces just might be there. I want you to prove it's impossible for shoes always to end with very high counts."

"And the less risky way? The High Card Slug?"

"More subtle. If the Gaming Board pounced, they would find all the cards were being used. But you, the player can be beaten by it time and again."

"Go on."

"A skilled dealer over a few shoes can manipulate the shuffle to create a slug of high cards all together. It's even easier for him with new decks of course. The cards are bunched anyway. When he shuffles up, he keeps this slug together towards the top part of the deck."

"Sounds unlikely." Mark Evans looked unconvinced. "Too difficult."

"Not so. *Commonplace* for a skilled dealer. Ask any magician or illusionist. *I have*. I also met a former dealer. He'd worked in Moscow until he had seen a gun too many. He challenged me to catch him cheating. Using six packs, he created a slugged deck when I was watching. He completely fooled me! I saw only a fair shuffle but somehow he'd maneuvered the aces and tens into a small part of the deck!"

Evans thought for a moment, his face puckered. When he spoke, he was almost triumphant as if revealing a Royal Flush. "But after the shuffle, a player cuts the cards."

"True." Dex was on song now. "Mainly, players cut near the middle. That's fine by the casino. You'll have seen this: if the player starts to cut too near one end, the casino won't accept that?"

"Yes."

"The dealer, after the cut must then divide the two batches of cards. The top part becomes the bottom. The slug, previously in the top end, sinks to the bottom."

Evans's face changed from disbelieving to respect. He'd understood precisely. "My God! I've seen untypical cuts rejected so often. Okay! So once the slug is at the bottom, the dealer inserts his own plastic card into the deck, judging this by where the slug is after the cut. Nothing beneath his plastic card gets dealt."

"Including the slug."

"And he can repeat that?"

"Keep that slug together when he next shuffles? Easy for a card-sharp. Those cards might not appear all day. Shuffling looks, er ... so ... comprehensive but it isn't." Dex was nearly finished. "Of course, it could work the other way - a bent dealer working with you could load the deck so that lots of small cards were undealt. You'd clean up."

"So long as I knew, yes. All these years I've been playing. Never thought of that." Evans was impressed. "I've had plenty of strange shoes in parts of Europe, even in London. But I assumed I'd been unlucky."

"Now we're going to find out."

"Can't wait." Evans frowned as a new point struck him. "Do they have continuous shufflers in Dukes?" He was referring to Shuffle Masters, an automatic shuffling-machine that removes the human element.

"They don't." Dex fumbled in his jeans pocket and pulled out a print-out run off from the Shuffle Master website. "Listen to this. If anyone knows about bent decks, these guys do. "*Before shufflers, games with large bonus payouts were a security risk due to concerns about the integrity of the shuffle. Shufflers eased those concerns and helped create a new genre of specialty card games in the process. And for the large blackjack market, the Company believes that its new continuous shuffler will provide improved game productivity and security.*"

"I'm going to enjoy this. But remember I'm banned everywhere."

"*I* can't sign you in. You can't join in your name as you're blackballed. You'll play at first as a guest of Lord Yarbury, using a disguise and a false name. He's played blackjack there for years. Never ever won. So he was delighted to assist. After a few days, you'll apply to join."

"Blimey! Me and a Peer of the Realm. And a disguise? Do I paint my face black? Have fuzzy hair?"

Dex brushed the crumbs from his thick polo-neck, laughed and nodded yes. "Sounds good but I was thinking of a wig to change hair color, a moustache, tinted glasses and some expensive clothes. A Lord Lucan look perhaps. Mustn't disgrace Arthur Yarbury."

"I'm going to enjoy this even more. What will I be called?"

"Something discreet." Dex grinned at Mark as he ushered him towards the door. "William Shakespeare from Stratford perhaps? We'll work on it."

"Stu Ungar?"

"Why?"

"Just about the greatest card-counter of all time." He grinned. "And a coke habit that killed him young."

They were still laughing as they reached the car. Dex felt pleased. The ten grand seemed to have been well spent.

London - 15th November 2002

"Hi Dex! I'm in New York." Tiffany sounded closer and excited. "Whatever you read or hear, believe only this. Blair and Bush are going to war with Saddam. I've been doing interviews around the United Nations building. All these resolutions are so much window-dressing. Saddam *must* reveal his WMD or he's toast."

"Reminds me of your Wag the Dog question to the President!"

"But remember, he dealt with it well - just grinned and said there were no comparisons between that movie and his position involving Enron. I enjoyed asking anyway. How's it going?"

"Keep talking! I just love hearing you. It's been a tough time without you. Sitting around waiting for everybody else. I hate this inactivity."

"Be patient. Far better to wait until every detail is fixed. Not that you're telling me them anyway. I sense that."

Dex wanted to move on. "Yesterday I picked up Mark Evans. That plus Kenny and Jackie – that's about all the action at the moment. Scotty's somewhere in the Far East with Kim." He trampled a fast-food wrapper on the floor of the phone-box. "I'm not panicking yet but Scotty has slipped beneath the radar. That doesn't help. Haven't heard from him since he dropped me off at Luton. He flew to the last Grand Prix at Suzuka and was having talks with RGB about his future."

"Short, I guess." Tiffany did not sound sorry. "Wasn't he supposed to be getting documents for you?"

"His local dick in Vegas, Gabe Fazzolli, was supposed to send everything to him rather than me. Security reasons. Made sense at the time. If they've reached Scotty, he hasn't told me."

"He's probably relaxing by a pool somewhere with Kim. It's not time critical is it?"

"Not yet - but I need to train him in Reverse Labouchère. And I want the documents. We were due some Nevadan legal advice too."

"Beyond gun law you mean?" What about Ryder?"

"Kenny thinks he may have a breakthrough. I'm expecting to hear today."

"When can we get together?"

"I can't really commit this month."

"Cooling off are you?"

"Right down to boiling point. Can you get over to London?"

"Unlikely. I've saved up my holiday entitlement to be freelance in December. Then perhaps we can get some real quality time."

"Can't wait! Especially looking at these call-girl postcards all over this kiosk. There's some right kinky bastards around aren't there."

"Time for your cold shower. Talk to you tomorrow." She blew kisses down the line, each one like music to his ears.

"Big hugs. Stay safe."

London 18th November 2002

"Lord Yarbury! Good to see you." Dex paused by the table. "I didn't realize you lunched here. Thought the Lords' dining-room was more your scene?"

"Damned fine watering-hole down at Westminster, granted. But here? Free lunch. Best value in town." He waved an arm. "May I introduce a splendid chap? I met Jeremy at Boodles. Turns out he enjoys blackjack so I've signed him in. Jeremy Legrange."

All three managed to keep a straight face as the charade continued. Evans looked the part – the tailored suit, red pocket hankie, silver buckles on hand-stitched shoes. His hair, thick and black was parted down the middle like an old-fashioned parson. The black moustache was generous but flecked with a touch of grey. The glasses had designer frames but no magnifying power at all. "Your first visit, er Jeremy?"

"Second. I came yesterday."

"Win?"

"Up a bit. Stopped at the right time. Didn't we Arthur?"

Yarbury smiled as if he had found a long lost son. "Bless him! Funny feeling this winning lark. Drat it, I've been playing since Britain ruled the waves and had never once heard of Basic Strategy until yesterday. Jeremy played my hands for me. I've always refused another card from twelve and up. Too scared of busting. Never split eights or doubled down in my life. Too damned complicated - like digital cameras and mobile phones."

Jeremy laughed. "Arthur was playing just like he learned Pontoon at Eton – incredibly badly."

Yarbury chortled. Legrange could do no wrong in his eyes. "Can't wait for today. Repeating it would be just spiffing." He suddenly looked puzzled. "But why are you in so early my dear old thing? Don't normally see you at the tables until the evening after I've sunk several pink ones and a decent bottle of claret."

Dex was ready for this. "I was telling FB. I wonder if I wouldn't play better if I gambled first and drank after. So I'll play in the afternoons sometimes."

Yarbury looked puzzled at the concept of not enjoying a drink at *whatever time* at all. He pointed at his dessert. "Enjoy your lunch. The treacle sponge, wonderful after the steak and kidney pie. Try the *Mouton* with that, something with body. Damned fine claret. The Stilton's always mature too. Take my tip. Needs a drop of Taylor's port. Don't let them fob you off with anything less than the best vintage."

A couple of hours later after a fun session playing roulette, Dex was ready to leave, slightly ahead. Hoge had been in. Again, he had been noticeably keen to keep his distance, though he had chortled about a new system called the East Coast Progression. *And no, Jacques Crabant hadn't yet sent a card from Tangiers.* While playing, Dex had seen a different crowd of people, not that a dozen strangers exactly constituted a crowd. Jude appeared with an Italian who FB told him was a Count somebody. Dex watched Kenny and Jackie cruising the room. If they were filming, Dex couldn't spot it. He hoped they had arrived separately as agreed.

At four-fifteen, Dex called Kenny as planned. "You're out of there now?"

"Jackie stayed on. I'm in a tea-bar at Marble Arch. I've some news."

"From Dukes?"

"No. I told the Shift Manager I'd be back this evening. I'm pretty sure that Dukes try the roulette fiddles much later - when there are more drunks around and the tables are busier. But no, the news is about Ryder. He's now shacked up with this Zara woman – lives with her in Islington. I bet the Gaming Board don't know that."

"So are you saying I should go there? Confront him?"

Kenny scoffed at the idea. "No. Go to his home in Kent. Talk to his wife but not as Finlay Dexter. Dream up something."

"Remind me of the address. I'll drive down."

Kenny read out the address, a small village just outside Ashford. "Box clever then."

"I'll think of something."

Just under three hours later, Dex drove into the small community of Bethersden finding it on the A28 from Ashford. It seemed as if everyone was watching television or at least not outside. The narrow lane was dark and silent as Dex drew up outside the semi-detached house. A solitary street-light stood unlit. On the edge of the village, Ryder's place looked like a former tied cottage. The grass was screaming for a cut. A silver Honda Civic parked on the short concreted drive needed its rust sorted and a new rear tire.

In the service station near Swanley, Dex had grabbed a scotch egg and a slab of cake, printed out a batch of bogus business cards and had then phoned the Ryder house. An unfriendly sounding woman's voice greeted him on the voice-mail. He left a message, promising to arrive in about an hour or two with good news.

The bell did not seem to work. However, a woman of about thirty-eight with a masculine look about her and a yapping Pekinese in her arms responded to his rap on the glass-paneled door. Her dark green trouser-suit was cut in a severe fashion and her hair was short, cropped almost *en brosse*. There was no smile. From inside came a dribbling doggy smell that Dex found repulsive. "Who is it, Molly?" Another woman's voice called from an unseen room.

"Yes?"

"Mrs Ryder?"

"It'll do."

"I'm Billy Naughton. I phoned earlier with the good news. Is Mr Ryder in? Adrian isn't it?"

"No."

"Will he be back soon?"

"No."

Dex heard a voice from somewhere yell that the Biryani was on the table. "That's a shame because he's won you both a cruise to Hawaii. Fly first-class to Los Angeles. Then the ship takes you in the penthouse cabin all the way to the islands – twenty-eight days of luxury." He fumbled in his pocket. "Here's my card."

She looked at it without interest. "When did all this happen?"

Dex beamed enthusiastically. "I love bringing good news! Can I come in? It's worth twenty thousand pounds. I'll explain the details." He enjoyed the gushing breathlessness. "We'll sort out your meal preferences, that type of thing. When Adrian gets back, you'll give him the surprise of his life."

"He's not coming back," she snapped. "He's shacked up with some bitch in London." Her face softened and a sly look broke through the unmade-up features. "When was the competition?" The crow's feet were very apparent and Dex judged that married life to Adrian had not been a happy experience.

"Can I come in?" he repeated.

"No."

He pulled his collar up. "Suit yourself but that wind seems to have come from Siberia."

She ignored him, her brain still working on something else. "When was the competition?"

"Last Valentines Day. In aid of police and fire charities. He bought a ticket for a fiver."

"We was still together then. That mean I'm entitled to half?"

"That depends on Adrian."

"Is there a cash alternative?"

"Could be. But the best value is the cruise." Dex leaned against the creaking porch and tapped the side of his nose. "Mrs Ryder, I can see where you're coming from. You want him to choose cash and then divide it."

"Seems fair to me. I was working too. I really paid for half the ticket, didn't I?"

"I might be able to help. Where do I find Adrian?"

"You'd try to talk him into it?"

"As you say, seems fair. I mean if I were you, I'd be pretty miffed knowing he was taking his new, er, lady-friend on a first-class cruise."

"He won't go."

"Oh, come now. He'd love cruising. Very romantic. But as I said, give me his home address and I'll drop by, see if he won't split the cash with you."

"No way's he getting away for a month. He's starting in Vegas – a new job. Some big casino, he said. Forget the name. Space Ship I think. Him and his bitch Zara."

Dex swallowed hard and tried not to punch the air. "Vegas, eh? Exciting but it's still not the same as cruising." He tilted his head up as if racking his brains.

"I remember! Space City. We're doing a competition offering prizes there next year. Huge place. Sounds fantastic."

The woman grunted dismissively. "Yeah, that's the one. Space City. So, my guess – the snivelling turd'll want cash, always did. Never spent it on me, nor the house. Spent it all on *Agent Provocateur* knickers for his bit of stuff. You'll let me know what he says?"

"Of course. Well, I hope he strikes it rich over there. Then you could get yourself a new place on the maintenance." He would like to have joked that the house was ideal raw material for a TV makeover program but decided she wasn't the type. "So if you give me his address, I'll let you enjoy your Biryani." He sniffed the air and noticed again the waft of Indian food and a stronger smell of dirty dog. "Delicious." He waited while she returned with a scrap of paper.

"Here. I've written it down. Shepherdess Walk, N1. You know, Mr er, er - Adrian ought to give me all the prize. Me and Cookie, we would really appreciate it. Adrian's told my solicitor, he's striking it rich next year. He don't need cruises."

"Life can be pretty unfair can't it? Good night, then." He felt uncomfortable about misleading her and decided he would buy them a holiday if Dukes paid up. In the car, he turned the heater up but noticed no difference. At least the excitement of the new information kept him buzzing all the way back up the M20.

London – 19th November 2002

Having laughingly received a job offer as an investigator from Kenny Jennings, Dex felt equipped to tackle Adrian Ryder. "Kenny, knowing as much as we do now, I think we can risk it. If he tells Shawcross, *a big if*, then it's time to run! But I hold too many aces now not to try."

Dex could see Kenny was unconvinced. "Maybe. But don't risk us. We're still hoping to get some really good stuff for you. So far, it's only snippets."

"There's so much Ryder can tell us. Risk against reward. I'm going ahead. When he finds out what I know, he'll crap himself all the way home to Zara. It's risky but so is you two filming. You being caught would kybosh everything too."

"I vote no. Never trust a copper like Ryder, even an ex-one."

Dex waved his arm soothingly. "I'll take care." Twice when he had phoned there had only been a voicemail and he left no message. A voice answered on the third time. "Mr Ryder? You won't know me. I'm from Department ML23 at the Financial Services Authority – International Division. My name is Graeme Brook and I need to speak to you on a sensitive matter. No. No. *You're* not in trouble but I do need to speak to you in absolute confidence – and urgently. How's your diary? This afternoon would be good. You can do that? Excellent. I work from Crawley, near Gatwick Airport so I won't burden you to come there. What about the St Ermin's Hotel? Caxton Street? You know it? Splendid. They do a good afternoon tea if that's your bag. Say quarter past three in the lobby. There are plenty of quiet corners. And again, I do stress the absolute need for confidentiality. Once we have met, you'll understand."

The ornate balconied lobby of the hotel had a delightfully tranquil atmosphere with a mix of formal seating at desks and other more welcoming arrangements. Dex chose a table with matching curved-back chairs away from the remainder of guests where confidentiality was assured. From here, he could watch both the revolving entrance doors. Besides that, he enjoyed a perfect view of the chandelier and baroque staircase that epitomized the style and elegance of the lobby area. From Boots, he had bought a pair of half-glasses with the lowest strength and he wore them perched way down his nose to add gravitas. In his best charcoal suit, a navy and red tie and with a leather briefcase beside him, he waited for Ryder who arrived punctually but looking as if he might have hurried not to be late. "Mr Ryder? Good of you to make time. Let's order tea. You want the full works – scones, cream, cake - or just biscuits?"

Ryder patted his waist. "Just one biscuit thanks."

"Me too. Here's my card. Do you have one so I can have all your contact points?" He watched the thin fingers delve into a surprisingly expensive wallet from inside a well-cut three piece suit. In light grey, Dex was impressed at the quality - hand-stitched and representing a considerable investment for a Gaming Board inspector. The pale pink shirt was a perfect fit too and someone had chosen the tie with care. *All the signs of a new woman's loving attention here.* As he chatted breezily about house prices, the traffic and the golf from America, Dex was delighted. Ryder had no suspicions.

"One thing, Mr Brook," Ryder chipped in at last. "I was *intrigued* about the meeting and so I checked the web but could find no Department," he checked the card "ML23 - International."

Good for you Ryder.

But I'm ahead of you.

"No you wouldn't – we work with the Serious Fraud Office, Interpol and the FBI on money-laundering. ML23 was only formed last spring to counteract money-laundering by organized crime and terrorists. We have secure, and boy, do I mean secure, premises away from the FSA headquarters. In part, ML23 was a response to nine-eleven but mainly we created it to meet Britain's obligations under the new European Union directive. We don't broadcast where we are or who we are – that's why I emphasized the confidentiality on the phone. One false word from you – and well not only would months of hard work be buggered but my life might be in grave danger."

"I see." Ryder nodded thoughtfully and Dex wondered if he had a riposte ready. But no. "I was in the police force– the Kent County Constabulary to be precise until I was retired on medical grounds. I understand secrecy – and the dangers of knowing too much."

Dex was struck by the formality and pedestrian style of speech and guessed he must loosen up off duty to have any chance of easing *Agent Provocateur* frillies off Zara Belfield. He ordered tea and biscuits and then continued but not before looking around to add effect. "Can't be too careful that nobody can overhear. Look: I know you work for the Gaming Board – and cover Dukes as one of your casinos." Ryder looked as if Dex had punched him in the crotch at the mention of Dukes but then drew breath and nodded yes. "Ever notice anything strange going on there?"

Ryder shook his head but Dex was unconvinced. "The casino is doing very well at the moment – very much against the London trend. Agreed?"

Ryder gazed at the balustrades above his head. Dex felt sure he was seeking the best evasive answer.

"Well to be frank, yes it *has* been busy when I've dropped by – but nothing, I mean, nothing off the graph. Shawcross, the CEO is a dynamic man and he told me himself he's worked day and night to restore profitability."

Dex held his chin, leaned forward, looked doubtful and muttered an over long "Ye...es," rather in a Jeremy Paxman imitation.

"Are you suspicious about Dukes? Money-laundering or something? I'd be shocked."

Dex shook his head. "No, no Mr Ryder. We're not *suspicious* of Dukes at all. We *know* they're laundering money. We just hoped that *you* had come across something that had made *you* suspicious. Your evidence would have been helpful."

Ryder shook his head too vigorously in denial. "Clean as a whistle, I'd say."

"You're wrong. A word to the wise, you might say. You'll have to be more watchful. Otherwise your bosses are going to be down on you for not spotting this when the shit hits the proverbial. You're going to have to get up to speed on Dukes or my guess, your ass is on the line down at the Gaming Board." Dex saw the waiter approaching and motioned Ryder to be silent.

Dex thought back to Molly on the windy doorstep. Considering that old cottage had been home until moving in with this Zara woman, Ryder had come far. The man now in front of him would not have tolerated the worn tire, the rotting wood over the porch and the lack of paint. The village home had yelled of neglect due to money and marriage problems, something not now apparent. The shoes looked new and were of Italian design, cut acutely with the softest leather and in keeping with the rest of his clothes. Besides the gold cufflinks, the watch looked like a Baume & Mercier.

"Help yourself. Well paid job, yours?"

Ryder weighed up the question as if handling gelignite. "The Board? Not great but I get by. Plus my disability pension from the police." He looked at Dex differently now, aware that for the first time, a sinister and more personal tone had come into the conversation. "So tell me. What should I be looking for?"

"The Signing-In Register. Phony names and addresses of guests signed in – especially by two ladies, Jude Tuson and Claire Weatherley. Names mean anything to you?" He saw Ryder look away and was unconvinced he had not noticed the stream of foreign guests they had signed in. "New members, some of them not exactly kosher. Ever heard of Jacques Crabant? No. Check him out on the web. Devious little Frenchman from Morlaix in Brittany. A shortass but worth millions. Made it big in Brussels. He's at the centre of corruption investigations being finalized by OLAF – the European Anti-Fraud Office. They approached us and suggested he was laundering millions through Dukes – money received as bribes from his work in the Commission's Department of Agriculture." Dex paused. "Is this all news to you?"

Ryder shifted uneasily and drained his tea. "I'm sorry to say it is."

Dex believed him. "In that case you'd better start building a dossier. Here's another name - Alejandro Robledo. He's a Spaniard. Former Mayor of Marbella. Reckoned to have enriched himself on the Costa del Sol with hooky planning applications. We believe he's also laundering his money through Dukes."

"But you're not suggesting Shawcross knows of this?"

"Aren't I?" Dex laughed. "Shawcross has been desperate to raise cash. Space City in Vegas was pushing Dukes to ruin. So he sucked in every person he could with hot money to launder. There's a cesspit swirling all around. My chief hoped you'd be on to this. Our view is they're guaranteed not to lose more than a certain percent."

"Boosting Dukes' turnover – and profits."

"Right. A hidden fee for laundering hot money. My Department can't uncover that information without alerting Shawcross." Dex clasped his hands together in a prayer-like gesture. "But if the Gaming Board combed through everything, that would not alert him. If we tried, he'd be on the first flight to *anywhere*." Dex joined his hands behind his head. "We're rather hoping that you could do this and report to us."

"Me?"

"Why not? It's just routine." Dex knew precisely why his guest was so uncomfortable. Ryder was now impaled on a barbed hook. Wriggling would make it worse. "I bet there's a pattern. When you next look at the books, check if Dukes are filing the correct Suspicious Activity Reports - the SARs to the NCIS. They should be. They're receiving huge cash sums in but drawing checks to pay members and guests cashing out."

"I can answer that. Zara Belfield who does the financial investigations told me that they had filed SARs. She'd seen the copies on file."

Dex tried to conceal his disappointment. He had felt sure that Shawcross would be ignoring the National Criminal Intelligence Service. "So Zara Belfield hasn't spotted anything either."

"Not that she's mentioned to me."

"So do you two agree on most things?"

Ryder appeared unsure of the intent of the question. "We discuss what we find at the casinos. I report to my superiors."

"Is Ms Belfield your superior?"

Ryder looked around for an answer. "Well no, not exactly. I do the routine stuff. She comes in occasionally as an independent accountant. I don't report to her, no. The Board are her clients."

"Do you recall a visit when you had a confrontation with Ms Belfield?"

Ryder's jaw dropped and he scuffed a shoe on the carpet. "Not as I recall." He looked around as if the answer lay somewhere else in the lobby. "We occasionally have an in-depth debate."

"What about?"

"I can't recall anything particular."

"When you were there on 12ᵗʰ September, don't you remember a bit of a bust up?" Dex saw conflicting emotions pass across Ryder's face. "If it helps, this was the day a second Dukes member was shot. Mick Glenn first. Then Scotty Brannigan at the funeral."

Ryder's lean face was starting to look ashen. "You're not suggesting?"

"We're working on it. So that day. Do you recall why you had *a lively debate* with Ms Belfield?" Dex could see that Ryder recalled every detail of the finger-wagging session.

"Put like that, no. I'd say we worked as a team - always. Of course, most visits, she's not with me."

"Why did you get stick from her that day? We had undercover people in Dukes and you were observed."

Ryder scratched his ear, then his moustache and sucked in his cheeks as he tried to find a coherent answer avoiding the truth. "Must be some mistake."

"No finger-wagging by her?"

"No."

"Not after you'd been checking out the blackjack?"

Ryder's face flushed horribly.

"I can see that you do recall something. So why did Ms Belfield give you, her client's employee, such a tongue lashing?"

"Did she?"

Dex wondered what his father would have made of the cross-examination so far. "My information is you found something wrong with the blackjack shoe. You told Ms Belfield and she was having none of it." This was into guesswork territory based on the FB tape but none the worse for that. "Why did you have to listen to what she thought? The blackjack was your baby, not hers."

"This is all way over my head."

"Did you report what you'd found wrong with the blackjack to your bosses back in Holborn?"

Ryder tried to hide behind his cup. "I didn't find anything wrong."

"You'd better smarten up your act, then. We have. Dukes is rotten from top to bottom. Every game is crooked. I can't believe you spotted nothing." Dex saw that Ryder was not going to respond and decided to throw him an apparent lifeline but one loaded with a lump of lead. "I'm sorry to have to ask you a delicate question but I must. As you yourself had no inkling of any wrongdoing at Dukes, do you think Shawcross has corrupted Ms Belfield? We know he's a real ladies man. Our boys think he seduced her and has snared her into a cover-up. So when you found something wrong at the blackjack, she didn't want you to report it."

"Zara? Corrupted? Ludicrous." Ryder raised his voice indignantly and Dex motioned him to keep his voice down.

"How can you be so sure?"

Ryder looked sheepish and reached for more tea. "I'm surprised you didn't know this – you seem to think you know so much. Me and Zara are an item."

Dex sensed it was time to hit him below the waterline. "We knew that, of course we did. Been going on for months and living together for the last three." He enjoyed seeing the nervous lick of the lips and the hands twitch as the inspector tried to compose himself. "Not that you two being an item would prevent Shawcross from seducing and corrupting anyone that he needed." Dex flipped open a notebook. "Moved in with Zara in about July, I believe. Might she have been involved with Shawcross before then?"

"You're on the wrong track, Mr Brook."

"But if Zara Belfield isn't corrupt, then it must be you. Or you're protecting her as well and you're both in this together."

"Mr Brook, you overestimate what an inspector can achieve. If Dukes were fixing roulette, or blackjack, I'm well known. Do you think they'd try anything with me there?"

"September 12th was a random check - unannounced. A spooked blackjack deck might have been prepared not anticipating your visit."

"Well rest assured, me and Zara aren't corrupt."

Dex adjusted the glasses. He was enjoying wearing them and he recalled how his father had used his spectacles for theatrical effect in court. He leaned forward and pointed with a single finger. "Look Mr Ryder, pussyfooting time is over. You haven't volunteered this, so I'll tell you something else we know. You've both lined up jobs in Space City." He stopped deliberately to take in the effect and was glad he had. Ryder's face looked like a death mask. "Big league for a Gaming Board inspector and a young accountant. Congratulations. Well sort of. Space City won't exist next year. Like the Monty Python parrot, it will be a defunct and very dead casino. Imploded … but by corruption. You might get a job as a demolition worker."

Ryder sat stunned for a moment or two. He looked like a carp out of water, struggling for air. It was as if he were wondering if there was *nothing* that Dexter did not know. "I came here to help your Department. I've had enough of this." He rose to leave.

"Sit down." Dex pointed a finger straight at him and barked the order. "I may yet be able to save your career." He watched Ryder hover uncertainly. "And your life. Nobody else can." The Inspector hovered caught in two minds. Then slowly, he sat down.

"You haven't told the Board you're leaving have you?" Dex paused long enough to see agreement. "Don't. You need to play the good boy now, reporting to me."

"I don't understand. If I report to my bosses, that's enough."

"We suspect that Shawcross has fixed somebody at the Gaming Board HQ - perhaps in Operations & Intelligence. If my Department is correct, then any report from you fingering Dukes means Shawcross will know as quick as a phone call. That would put you and Zara in grave danger. By that I mean *mortal* danger."

"So if I report to you?"

"We are filing our complete evidence next month direct with the Serious Fraud Office – and your Board will be notified when it is too late for Shawcross to receive any warning. In case you think I'm bullshitting you about the grave dangers, read this." Dex produced a copy of the Panama report now apparently addressed to Graeme Brook, Department ML23. He watched as Ryder read the document, his mouth falling open as he neared the end.

"Unbelievable. I'm staggered."

"I believe you – almost for the first time since we met. I've taken a real risk sharing this with you."

"I suppose you have."

"But you will not divulge the extent of what we know to anyone, not even Zara. Her loyalty to you is in question. If you ever have to mention this meeting to her, say only that you've been approached by a Government department on a top confidentiality basis to watch out for criminal behavior at a London casino. No more. Only if Zara asks, order her on no account to tell Shawcross or to discuss any of this with the Board. She's far more sympathetic to him than may be comfortable for you to accept." Dex saw the agonized look on his face. Dex changed his tone from forceful interrogator to family friend. "If I'm correct, and I haven't been wrong so far, Zara may tip off Shawcross and you'll be on the wrong end of over nine inches of Master Bowie."

"Look, I was never corrupt. Shawcross trapped us." Dex heard the admission and thought back to Kenny's confidence that Ryder would lie his way out of it.

345

"We thought that was possible. Spare me the dirty details now. Tomorrow, you must give our legal people a signed statement. Your best chance is to describe how Shawcross suckered you into accepting jobs at Space City. You will then explain you found out that something was going on but didn't report it because you suspected a superior at the Board had been fixed. Your intention was to get irrefutable evidence to take to the police direct. Then along came ML23 and saved you from your dilemma."

"Why can't you go ahead now?"

"We want the Feds to tie up the American end. They need three, maybe four weeks to nail wire-fraud, racketeering and money-laundering conspiracies on Carlo Letizione."

"And our jobs?" The Inspector's voice had gone thin and reedy.

Dex thought it pathetic that Ryder should be clinging to his shattered dreams of Vegas.

"Come January Space City will be an empty shell. Letizione will have *left the building* to use the jargon. Shawcross and the entire board too. But your statement will confirm that you had no criminal intent to be corrupted – that you agreed to work over there only after giving notice. You'll fill in the details of how much Shawcross and Letizione paid you both – and what they had promised."

"We never did work for them. A Bahamas company hired us."

Dex gambled with his reply. "We knew that. It sounds like a tax dodge. Knowing Shawcross, Dukes paid you nothing. Just used an offshore company to enrich you – new shoes, suit and so on." Dex nearly patted Ryder's arm but refrained. "Look, Adrian - I can see how he suckered you in. You weren't the first." He laughed heartily now. "But you'll be the last."

"Suppose I tell you go jump in the lake? That you can shove your ideas up your smug ass."

"Your choice." Dex produced a small recorder. "The tape and transcript would go straight to the SFO. But I will personally ensure that Shawcross is anonymously tipped off that you and Zara have shopped him – have discovered his Panama past. We'll give him time to find you both before moving in on him." Dex stood up, ready to leave. "Personally, I've always been scared of knives, especially a Master Bowie." He then rapidly explained precisely what the inspector now had to do.

After Adrian Ryder had gone, Dex went for a haircut at The Refinery – a complete restyling as Tiffany had suggested. He emerged with a new look that added to his maturity. With a more disciplined flat-top style, his face seemed less impish though the cheekiness returned when he grinned at the barber. During the restyling, the man had chatted about the usual inanities that left Dex cold but all the while Dex could only think of one thing - the nagging fear that Ryder would tell Zara. *That* would be like a spark in a fireworks factory.

London - 30th November 2002

With mounting irritation, Dex banged even louder. It had just turned nine a.m. The bell had gone unanswered but the brass knocker on Scotty's high-gloss yellow door was an invitation to vent frustration. Just as he was about to turn away, he sensed movement. Then he heard bolts being pulled back and a key was turned.

"Scotty?" The word was somewhere between an exclamation and a question. Dex was shocked. Any resemblance between public persona and the man now standing in front of him was hard to discern. The usually neat hair was dirty and matted and he had obviously crashed out in his shirt. The faded jeans were unpleasantly stained and his eyes were almost lost beneath swollen lids. It looked unlikely that he had shaved in days. Distinctly un-designer black stubble mixed with the sandy sideburns.

"Oh! It's you!" There was no invitation to enter but Dex edged forward to make clear that he had no intention of leaving. He saw Scotty's bloodshot eyes staring at the polished wood flooring in the hallway as he shuffled slowly backwards. Then, limping markedly and clutching at his left arm, the former icon made his way along the broad corridor leading into a kitchen-come-sitting-room.

It looked as if Hurricane Andrew had just passed through. Everywhere were dirty dishes, empty bottles and discarded clutter. Yet through it all, Dex could see that not long before, this had been a classy pad. Around the walls were framed pictures of Scotty at different circuits. In pride of place was one at Monaco with Prince Rainier. A framed letter on White House notepaper was from President Bill Clinton congratulating him on his World Championship. In a cabinet in the corner, were several large trophies, draped with ribbons and engraved in commemoration of some great drives.

Yet the biggest impact on Dex was not the trophies or the filthy clutter. He slid open a couple of windows to release the stink of booze mixed with vomit that seemed to have infiltrated the carpet and the thick turquoise curtains. To the left of the blank giant TV screen, a broken bottle of Jameson lay on the floor where it had been hurled as well as the squashed remains of several oranges. The pale blue wall just above was discolored and splattered where the alcohol had trickled down to stain the light beige carpet. Dex recalled the

348

thrown oranges in the hospital. Back then, it had seemed zany, exciting even. But what type of demons had invaded Scotty these last few days?

"You cure one, another one falls off the wagon," he murmured in anger to himself. "Where the fuck have you been? You're weeks late back with no attempt to get in touch." Any respect for the celebrated figure had gone. "Remember? I wanted commitment!" Dex' raised voice caused a shocked look from the driver. "Just look at yourself – you're a drunken wreck."

"Travellin'." Scotty turned away as if the single word explained everything. With studied concentration, he grasped the breakfast bar and poured a slug of Brennans, neat without water or ice.

"Put that down! I'll make coffee."

"Fuck you!" Scotty carried on pouring. "Anyway, there ain't no coffee."

"Fuck you too!" In a rapid single movement, Dex grabbed the full tumbler and threw it at the wall. It shattered adding to the stains a few feet away. The intervention seemed to shake Scotty who at first stood unspeaking as Dex poured the remains of the bottle down the sink.

"Motherfucker! Sonovabitch!" Scotty's tongue struggled to get round the words. For a second Dex thought that the driver was going to lay one on him. But Scotty was beyond that. After a faltering pirouette, he collapsed onto a chair. There he sat, head in hands, his bare feet trembling. Dex rummaged around the kitchen and, despite Scotty's denial, quickly found coffee and set the percolator working.

Dex opened a window to let some wintry air sweep through the place. "Don't look to me for sympathy, Scotty. We had a deal." He washed a couple of dirty mugs, sniffed the carton of milk and judged it beyond recall. Scotty meantime pulled up his feet so that he was almost in the fetal position on the leather rocker. There was no response. "Where are the bank statements and the agent's report on Carlo Letizione? The advice from our lawyer?" The scent of freshly brewed started to sweeten the stench. "I've been a sucker these last weeks. You've achieved bugger all."

"Keep your hair on". Scotty pointed at the new macho style. He tried to laugh but failed. "Too late for that, I see." He wrapped his arms around his head, hiding his face.

"No time for joking. I'll take that as a *yes, I've achieved nothing.*" He looked again at the huddled figure – a champion who had jumped and whooped on podiums everywhere from Magny Cours to Malaysia. *What had happened?*

Unnoticed by Scotty, Dex left the room. He found the bathroom and saw vomit on the floor, the towels and around the basin. In the bedroom, spacious and with a canopied four-poster that looked as if someone had slept on it in dirty boots, there was no evidence of Kim. Stacked on the dressing table, on the floor - almost everywhere there were odd papers, invites and crumpled receipts. He rummaged through the papers heaped untidily. It was rubbish mainly with nothing to explain his behavior

I still can't find what I'm looking for. He mouthed Bono's apposite lyrics.

Someone had converted the second bedroom into an office. There was a phone and computer, a copier and a fax machine all neatly positioned on a maple desk. To one side was an empty Out-Tray. The In-Tray was laden. On the desk was a large sheet of paper with the words **Nanda Datt** written in large black letters. Beneath it, Scotty had scribbled in red: *Sonovabitch*

Nanda? A woman? Could a woman be called sonovabitch? A man then?

He riffled through the In-Tray. The theme was constant. Money - lack of it mainly. Unpaid bills from everywhere. One letter was from his bank on Park Lane. "Due to insufficient funds, the bank had been unable to honor your check for one million dollars payable to Roxy Brannigan". There were faxed letters from lawyers in New York threatening lawsuits if Roxy's money did not arrive. The Internal Revenue Service wanted to discuss his non-payment of taxes and in default due process would follow. Alternatively, he could send a check for three million dollars by 14th December. He now had just two weeks to find the money. There was a letter from RGB terminating his services. But about Nanda Datt, there was nothing. Nor was there anything from Gabe Fazzolli or the Vegas lawyer, Otto Schneider. The only other item that caught his eye was a scribbled note with the words *Viperhead - 16.8m sterling July 02.*

He saw that the message light on the phone was flashing and decided to listen. He heard his own increasingly angry calls. There was another from the banker and another from his PR company. But in the middle was one message from someone with a precise foreign accent who left no name. "Scotty. You can run but you can't hide. I warned you. I will not leave the job half-done."

Slowly, he retraced his steps. His anger had changed to worry. It had to be the voice of Nanda Datt, someone to whom Scotty owed money or a favor. Half-done could only mean wounded not dead. The need for the Brennans was rather more understandable. In the sitting-room, Scotty had not moved. The coffee was ready but first he decided to get Scotty cleaned up. He tipped him from the chair and pulled the slight figure, half walking, part stumbling into the bathroom. He ran the shower, ordered him to strip and pushed him under the stream of water.

"Get yourself sorted." Satisfied that Scotty was responding, he left to make toast. He scraped some mould from the bread and popped it into the toaster. Twenty minutes later, Scotty appeared in an RGB black roll-neck jumper with red and gold hoops. His slacks were neatly cut, the creases sharp and also in black. He had shaved, smelled better and though his face looked as drawn as a milkman's horse, he looked closer to his website image.

Scotty looked sheepish. "It's been tough."

"Getting drunk is no answer." He nearly added *friends are.*

"I came back here. Letter from RGB. My two main sponsors, they jus' cancelled. Kiss your ass and a few million goodbye. Kim walked out." He avoided eye-contact. "My fault. I blacked her eye. Fists doin' the talkin' but she'd been stealin' from me – over eleven thousand." The laugh was self-deprecating. "Shouldn't have hit her though. Dumb."

"Drink the coffee. Eat the toast. Keep quiet for a minute. I need to think."

Scotty was in no mood to be silent and rattled on. "Remember Indy? I told you 'bout the accident policy makin' me rich. Them insurers have declined. They reckon because I had an *accident* policy, they don' owe me. Said shootin' ain't no *accident.*"

"Shit! Who've you been upsetting for so much to go wrong?"

"I've been as dumb as an Idaho chicken. Don' normally drink much. Pimms or a beer maybe but addicted I ain't. Not these many years. But oh, gee! That fucker Roxy's bleedin' me to death. She's gonna sell up my Vegas home, this place and Monte Carlo if she ain't paid. Deal was I paid her twenty-eight million bucks. But now I'm washed up and there's another million instalment overdue. No way I can pay her. Or the damned tax leeches."

"Just shut up and let me think, will you?" Dex was unconvinced that a driver like Scotty could be so flat broke. More likely, he was living the charade to shake off his liabilities.

The rant continued unabated. "That bitch Roxy. Just bleedin' me. Like a leech."

"But why pay her anything? You're out of work. Renegotiate the deal."

"Skeletons."

"Meaning?"

"She knows too much. Fuckin' snooped into everythin'. Always pryin'. My hot money, offshore accounts. She knew the lot."

"Pay her off from that."

"It's gone. Every goddamned last cent. Lost through bad advice. She don' believe that none. But one word from her an' I'm gonna get my balls whipped by the IRS. They'll tax me on money I ain't even got. Jail me as well, more'n likely."

"Nanda Datt still threatening you?"

Scotty stopped munching and looked resentfully at Dex as if the Englishman had just stabbed him. The shock started from his eyes, radiated through his mouth to his drooping jaw before spreading to every limb. "Nanda Datt? He's no problem. Ain't worth lick spit."

Dex watched the furtive eye movements and believed nothing. "You're lying Scotty. He had you shot because you defaulted. Right?" Dex picked a neutral word, concealing how little he knew. "Scotty, you're a total shit. You never play the regular guy with me. You still want to be part of my team?"

"Sure. Hell, yes." He drained the coffee and poured a third. "Need that million."

"Four conditions: tell me about Nanda Datt. No more drunken binges. Immediate help in Vegas and I need the promised half million from you to use for the Reverse Labouchère."

Scotty looked pole axed. "You know my financial position."

"Sounds like bullshit to me. You've cash, tucked away. I don't buy the line that your cash hoard had been lost on bad investments. You're far too mean to have taken that type of risk." He glared at the American who looked away. "You're a squirrel, hiding money away everywhere. Like in Viperhead." Dex saw the facial muscles twitch at the word and he knew he was right. "You're playing poor to fool Roxy or the IRS. But don't fuck about with me! Give me your half mill in *sterling* in two days and I'll pay you one million sterling in January. That's a great deal." Scotty scowled. "Every sonovabitch wants money I ain't got." He was growling like a wounded bear. "Datt's nothin' to you. He's the cross I'll carry until I'm crucified at my personal Golgotha."

"Our deal's off. No way but no way," Dex' voice rose again and he banged his fist on the dining-table, "can I risk playing Reverse Labouchère with you. I can't take on Dukes with a drunk. And I'm not cutting you in without your cash." Dex walked in a drunken, staggering crouch while Scotty watched bemused. "Remember Lee Marvin playing Kid Shellen, the drunken gunslinger in the movie *Cat Ballou*? I'd as soon team up with that old soak than a has-been like you." He walked round to tower over the seated figure. "Think of this like poker. The buy-in has now got greater. No money from you, no play at all and lose any chance of your million profit. Look under your bed and find me the money. Your choice."

Scotty did not reply but rose and started to wander around the room as if searching for an elusive flea. He bobbed down, looked under chairs, shifted cushions, moved papers until with a triumphant *yes* of satisfaction, he found a thick package buried beneath the Daily Mail of 28th November. "Knew I'd put it somewhere safe."

"Money?"

"No way."

The brown package couriered in from Nevada had arrived two days ago and had three sections. Dex opened it. The main bundle was twelve months bank statements for Space City. Dex flicked through them. Payments to bankers in New York. Three million dollars had gone to a bank on the Caribbean island of Aruba.

A pattern quickly emerged – large sums arriving from London – over twenty-three million dollars in fourteen weeks. Almost nothing before that. There were regular sums of 10,000 dollars since July going out to people called Casino Research Consulting in Nassau. That had to be Ryder. Dex made a mental note to get enquiries made there and in Aruba, guessing it would be impossible to break the secrecy. "Gabe's done well on the banking. Let me read the rest," he snapped irritably.

He skimmed through the report on Carlo Letizione. "Gabe didn't get much on him then." Dex was disappointed. Letizione was reportedly a hard-working experienced casino executive, a high stakes poker player with nothing violent known against him. Always distanced himself from organized crime. Reckoned to be law-abiding and an excellent choice for CEO of Space City *except* he was skimming money to Aruba, probably with false invoices for consultancy fees.

Dex flicked on through the final bundle, the advice from the attorneys - reams of detail on Nevada gaming laws, licensing procedures, the powers of the different authorities. He searched for the bottom line. "Heh, Scotty. This attorney Otto Schneider is shit hot – reckons funding Space City with hot or stolen money would splat their license. It's the money-laundering operation that's the killer-punch. The FBI would press criminal charges – RICO, wire fraud, money-laundering – if we give them the evidence. By his count, they're already guilty of thirty possible offenses. This Racketeering Influenced and Corrupt Organizations Statute is amazing."

Scotty replied as if his mind was elsewhere. "Sure. Yes …RICO."

"Background checks for licenses in Nevada are relentless," Dex continued reading and enthusing. "Failure by Shawcross to reveal his time working in Panama would not quash the existing license but he'd be banned. Proof of murder by Shawcross would not prevent Space City from holding a license but that would depend on other proper management being in place. A corrupt London end funding Nevada with stolen or laundered money would lead to loss of the license while Space City found new management and new owners.

"In the present economic cycle and with Space City unable to service its loans except by laundered money, it would need to file for protection from creditors – Chapter 11 or worse. In practical terms it will be doomed."

Dex wiped a drop of marmalade from the wrapping paper. "Those bank statements are dynamite. Being stolen evidence, Otto says we can't rely on them but we don't need to. We know the smoking gun exists of financial support from London using hot money. The Feds will quickly find what they want. As for us, you're off the team until you hand over the cash."

Scotty flicked a glance at Dex, his face sly. "If I found some cash, when do we play for real?"

Dex did not intend to reveal his plans. "When we're ready." He grinned hugely at the virtual admission that talk of poverty had been crap.

Paris – 7ᵗʰ December 2002

"Seeing you out of the blue. It's unreal," murmured Dex as he gazed from the window of their Ritz suite looking over the Place Vêndome. Tiffany tucked her warmth in front of Dex so that he got lean across her shoulder, arms tight around her stomach. After an afternoon catching up with each other in a bedroom, rich in all the deep colors of French classical style, Dex was dressed for an evening out. He was wearing an open-neck navy shirt under a fine cloth sports jacket in autumnal colors. A yellow hankie with navy spots in the top pocket added a dash of color.

"I wanted it to be a huge surprise. Telling you at the last moment. We'll drink a toast to my brother tonight."

"Unbelievable," Dex added. "It's a bummer he had to miss your birthday after you'd flown over specially. Where is he?"

"Some real estate deal in Frankfurt. God! What a dreary place to go." Tiffany looked in the mirror to check her make-up. "Normally after jetting the Atlantic, I feel whacked. Today I feel enervated. Must be down to you."

"I guess we'll both crash out after dinner."

"Where are we going?"

"*My* surprise." He turned away from the Christmas scene outside.

"I love surprises. Like that bouquet you sent, just because you felt like it. So am I dressed right for this place?"

He moved to stand in front of her and savored the perfume, the delicate eye-shadow and the slight highlighting of her cheek bones. Her hair shone and her eyes sparkled with excitement. "Looking like that you could dine with Chirac at the Elysée Palace. Stunning. That trouser-suit, so chic – so very Parisienne." Colored dark blue, beneath it she was wearing a red blouse with a ruff collar

"Its an American pant-suit! As French as a boutique in the Shopping Mall at Georgetown!"

"No matter. Let's head for the bar before grabbing a taxi."

"And remember. Not a word today about Dukes. Nothing until tomorrow. Today's *my* day."

"*Is* there anything else to talk about? It's going to be a quiet evening. Like a couple after thirty years of marriage when the battery has gone flat." The smile round his lips told her he was joking.

"It'll be my best birthday ever."

The following morning, they had breakfast served in the room before dressing in warm winter clothes. "I'm taking you somewhere you won't have been."

"If it's half as good as dinner by the Seine, then you're on. Those beamed ceilings, those huge burgundy glasses, the chintzy table-cloths, the candles. You do surprises well. That soufflé! I'll dream of that for ever."

"This'll be very different. Wrap up well and wear good walking shoes. There's a damned cold wind and snow flurries are forecast. We'll talk and walk. I've always wanted to go to this place." Forty minutes later, they emerged from the warmth of the Metro into the icy blast of the December morning.

Tiffany looked at the drab surroundings of an anonymous Paris backstreet. "Where are we? It feels like the back of beyond."

"We're out in the suburbs, the twentieth arrondissement. That Metro name mean nothing to you?"

She snuggled up closer and said no. "Should it? *Père Lachaise*? Nothing at all."

"I'm glad. It would have spoiled everything if you'd said *been here, done that. School trip 1988.*"

She looked up and saw the street name. "Rue du Repos. Sounds relaxing."

"Pretty relaxed, I'd say. Laid back even." He grinned as he led her towards the entrance at number six. "It's a cemetery – *La Cimitière Père Lachaise.*"

"Romantic place to bring me!" She brushed a snowflake from her cheek. "You have a thing about graveyards don't you? Your cathartic trip to Bladon. Now here."

"This cemetery is the resting-place for more famous names including the one at Westwood in Los Angeles where Marylyn Monroe and Natalie Wood are interred. There's more talent buried in this graveyard than anywhere in the world – politicians, actors, painters and writers by the bus-load. And you're right. I love graveyards - the feeling of being small, just a blip in the vast passage of time. Nothing beats them for putting daily angst into perspective. You can be so close to triumph, like Churchill, or tragedy like one of the first monuments we shall see. I thought you'd be intrigued. So much history here." They picked up a map of the sprawling area. "We'll start with tragedy but this tour can only have one ending."

"Someone I've heard of? Not some obscure French poet from the Loire?"

"We've talked about this person before." He guided her down a crunchy path, the gravel almost frozen solid and the trees overhead bare of leaves, their branches sharply etched against the background. "There!" He pointed to the monument to Abélard and Héloïse. Their story goes back about a thousand years. He was a poet."

"A tragedy, as I recall."

"No happy endings to that love affair – lives lived apart. Lives lived by letter."

"Today it would be email. Like us."

He pulled her close. "It's almost crunch time for Dukes. Happy ending time, God willing. Our lives will never be the same again. Nor those of so many others."

"So long as we're together, alive and safe, that's enough for me. That Panama report really spooked me."

"Me too. But I feel like a giant octopus. Every tentacle is playing a part, moving, stretching restlessly – relentlessly towards a prey. I can't stop them now. Soon they'll work in unison to throttle the stinking corruption of Dukes into oblivion. I feel like a conductor approaching the orchestra's grand finale, the crescendo, bringing all the different sections together."

"That was quite poetic. Must be all the artistic remains here. A conductor with eight arms perhaps?"

He tapped her nose affectionately. "See who's buried just there? Frédéric Chopin." They held hands as they took in the grave, quiet and peaceful. "There are plenty of other composers – Georges Bizet, Bellini, Pleyel."

Tiffany stopped walking and blocked his path. She looked up at him and clasped him close to her. "You aren't scared of death are you? You like being on the edge. But me? I don't want you to die. Dukes isn't worth that." There was a tear in her eye as she eased away from him.

He showed her his hand. "See my lifeline. It's long. I have no intention of dying just yet." Dex didn't say that he regarded palm-reading as a cunning device to extract money from the gullible.

"Remember Silverstone?" Her face was upturned to him, her cheeks reddened from the cold.

"I'll never forget."

"How I said I liked my men to be like onions – layers to be peeled off. That Silverstone feeling is back, drawing us tighter. I just wish you'd go to the police. You're too important to me now." She looked around at the waving branches and the somber black clouds that scudded so close to the ground. "Me? I'm always the same – just me being me. What you see is what you get. But you amaze me. Bringing me here. You're just a huge Breton onion with layer after complex layer."

"And you, Tiffany my sweet – just stay the way you are, don't change perfection." He kissed her slowly and with a deep longing. "I love you caring but please never prevent me from going on."

"Dex – I'm so scared."

"I'm not. I'm exhilarated. Now that Scotty has *found* his cash. My plan to take ten mill of Shawcross is coming along. There's now five hundred thousand in my Dukes account. My fear is that it's all going too well and it can't last." The biggest setback was Max Chieseman, who should have delivered six days ago but was full of crap excuses. "Ryder? Zara? Mark Evans? Scotty? Any of them, even dear old Yarbury. They're all weak links. The only one I really trust is Kenny. He's going fine with the filming, really careful." He squeezed her gloved hand as they moved on, no dawdling now, stepping out briskly as the threat of snow intensified under the near purple skies. They paid brief homage to Oscar Wilde, Édith Piaf and Balzac.

As they passed through the hundreds of less celebrated graves, he lightened the mood by talking of the burgeoning friendship between Yarbury and Jeremy Legrange. "Spoke to Mark two days back. He was like a cat with cream all over his chops. So happy. He's feeling well; he's lost the urge to gamble. And he and old Yarbury, they're like soul-mates! There's even a chance Mark and his wife Kath'll get together again. That would be great for little Emily – she's a poppet. Mark's played over four hundred blackjack shoes, enough he says to be convincing but he's going on to five hundred."

"Is it fixed?"

"He's positive. Different tables. Different shoes, same result. The card count predicts a shoe full of tens and aces to come – but they never do."

"So how in hell do Dukes fiddle that?"

"Ask me next week. Kenny and Jackie think they've spotted something subtle. They're still filming."

"What's your biggest worry?"

"God! That's not easy."

He knew it was Max Chieseman. "Worries? Problems? In one way, it's all downhill now. In another, this is a tower-block built of matchsticks. One mistake and the whole bloody thing collapses." He picked up a stick and scrawled a heart and arrow in the thin dusting of snow by the path. "We've gathered nearly all the evidence for the lawyers in both countries. When I give the word, they'll contact the SFO and the Feds." He paused to point out the grave of Camille Pissaro. "I just love that simple street scene of his."

"La Route de Louveciennes?"

"Right in one. So simple, so French. Maybe we could go to the Musée d'Orsay tomorrow morning and check out the Impressionists. Anyway, the lawyers don't get the nod until Scotty and I are clear of Dukes with the winnings."

"You're that confident?"

"Gambling is gambling. But if my plan works, then Reverse Labouchère is going to make Dukes wish they'd never cheated me." A robin flew across them and sat on the joint tomb of Yves Montand and Simone Signoret. "I've no single concern. I guess I'm worried about people on my side more than I am about Shawcross."

"What do you mean?"

The snow was settling fast now. "Scotty might throw another wobbly. He's brittle. There's someone called Nanda Datt who he won't talk about. I think Datt had him shot. If I'm right, he's going to try again. That or he's just leaving menacing messages to bugger up Scotty's life." He saw the shocked look on Tiffany's face. "So? The real worry is ..."

Dex thought swiftly. "Zara. Since I put Adrian Ryder through the spin-dry, he's been a trouble-free zone. Reports to me constantly. His statement to the lawyers confessed but put him in a better light. He's been snooping and digging but so low-key that Shawcross won't bite through his cigar."

"She has him pretty well under control though?"

"Poor bastard! I feel sorry for him. It's a doomed relationship. She's still daydreaming of Vegas and he can't tell her it's never going to happen. Their future at Space City was the glue. Now there's none. He's not too bright but he's under no illusions about *her*. On what he earns, the fabric of their relationship is damaged goods."

"But why feel sorry for him. He's been supporting Shawcross."

"He was conned. Zara was too hooked to care. After that, greed and lust prevailed over judgment." He used a gloveless hand to wipe some snow from her eyebrow. "He's terrified of telling her. That's the best insurance I have. If she knew the truth, she might confront Shawcross – looking for revenge or for a pay-off for silence." He rubbed his chin thoughtfully. "She's a chucker with a short fuse. Plates, forks – anything to hand." Dex scooped up a snowball and hurled it against the trunk of a chestnut tree.

"You must be frozen without gloves. At least I'm wearing woolly mitts. How much further? I'm sort of imagining a fondue and wine followed by the king-size."

"Fondue and fondle. Sounds good."

She rewarded him with a playful dig in the ribs as he continued. "There's just one more grave I want to see." He checked the map for plot 30. They headed up the wooded slopes, rounded a corner and both saw the tombstone together. It stood out because unlike others, fans had heavily smeared graffiti over the headstone beside the face of Jim Morrison. "Nearly two million visitors come each year, just for this. We're lucky to be here alone. Better that way." On the grave were several jars of flowers, struggling to survive the weather, their heads just above the snow. "He died just over thirty years ago, 1971."

"I was a toddler in a Minnie Mouse T-shirt."

"You and me both. The Doors were popular rock classics. That was a golden era. I'm sorry I was too young." He turned away with a sigh. "Only twenty-seven and he had achieved so much. But Morrison never saw it that way. He escaped to Paris from the fame of being *the pretty face* of The Doors."

"Wasn't he a talented poet too?"

"Never taken seriously though. He hoped Paris would help his career as a poet. Instead, drugs and alcohol overtook him."

"We shouldn't get too maudlin. His music lives on."

Dex wanted to stand longer, paying respects, his mind filled with memories of him listening to The Doors with Beth. He nodded and turned to join her. "Time for that fondue in the Rue Castiglione and then, *come on baby light my fire*. Together, they walked and hummed The Doors' big hit in reasonable harmony.

Much later, as the moon tried to break through the clouds over their hotel, Dex awoke from a deep sleep. In his arms was Tiffany, soft, warm and so innocent. He looked at the bedside clock. Nearly seven pm. He saw the message light flashing. Immediately he was concerned. Only Kenny had his number for any crisis. Dex had briefed everyone to contact Kenny *in an emergency*. He showered and dressed quickly, cursing that anything should be so urgent as to shatter the magic spell that only Paris could create so easily. He crept out and went to Reception. "Ah yes, Mr Dexter. About an hour ago. You had a message. Please ring Kenny urgently. It's about Zara." Dexter's face must have shown his concern for the young woman added. "Not bad news, I hope."

"Doesn't look good, does it?" But Dex' mind was not on what he was saying but on what the problem just had to be. Ryder must have blown the whole shooting-match.

Shit!

London - 11th December 2002

Dex walked along Southampton Row, deep in thought and oblivious to the swirling wind. At the Russell Hotel, he climbed the steps and sat down in the bar to wait for Kenny and Jackie. Since returning from Paris, each day had seemed too short, time running out until he had to start repaying his debts. Every morning he had shouted down the phone at Max Chieseman. Each time, he had felt better for it but had achieved nothing. If Plan A, the Chieseman version, was doomed, then Dex knew he had to create a Plan B. With that in mind, he had enriched the Gamblers' Bookshop by buying another book on gaming crime. He skim read it over a glass of house red and laid it down in disappointment. It contained nothing that could lead to Plan B.

It's Reverse Labby or a twelve-bore shotgun.

Through the window, he saw Kenny and Jackie scamper across the pavement from their taxi. He could tell something was wrong. Kenny's face was flushed and Jackie's pony-tail flailed out behind her as she scurried towards the steps. When he had seen her filming, she had been the epitome of cool – dressed simply but in good taste as she drifted from table to table.

"Tea?" Dex suggested calmly as they sat down beside him. "Or something stronger?" He hadn't quite forgiven Kenny for phoning him in Paris and taking the edge off the rest of the stay.

"No time for that," said Kenny, still standing.

"I'll decide that. Sit down, Kenny," said Dex. "Tell me the news. Tea for three please," he ordered. "You were caught filming?"

"How did you guess?"

"Didn't need a rocket-scientist. Who by?"

"Guy called Reggie Kyte. Weasel of a man. We've seen him around but he's never bothered us, nor we him. Until today. From when we arrived he seemed suspicious."

Jackie fingered her straw colored pony-tail and chipped in. "We hadn't even started filming, I was that spooked by him. He was always sort of near me, hanging around, leering, peering, know what I mean?"

"Sounds as if you were spotted yesterday, something that made the man-in-the-sky twitchy. Kyte's their Security Director."

"Our worry is someone may have tipped him off."

"Why?"

Kenny cleared his throat. "This is where it gets bad. Kyte stopped Mark just as he was approaching the gaming room. Lord Yarbury was already in, sitting beside me at the blackjack. These two big guys then escorted Mark towards the office behind reception. Jackie was on her way back from the powder-room. She saw him make a dash for it. Up the stairs like a whippet and he was gone."

"Did they follow him?"

"No." Jackie's creased face, though still attractive, spoke of too many late nights watching illicit behavior from her car in council estates. She knew how to apply her make-up. Her experienced touch smoothed the wrinkles that surrounded her eyes and which were starting to age her cheeks. From one side, her face showed a hint of past beauty but now overall she looked weary, though her smile was pleasing. Dex could see that Kenny doted on her and certainly today, dressed to kill for her time in Dukes, she looked the part of a rich bitch divorcee of a Brentford tycoon.

"Did you overhear anything said?"

Jackie's pony-tail bounced as she shook her head. "No. Not that I didn't try. But seconds later Kyte approached us with the same two security goons. They took the films from the cameras. There was nothing on them by then, of course." He laughed at outsmarting Kyte. "This little weasel wanted to *know our game*. "Roulette," I replied but he didn't laugh. "Got nothing from us. He told us he was terminating our membership. Then the heavies escorted us to the stairs."

Now Dex was looking concerned. "So we don't know if Mark said anything. Them nabbing him is much more serious. Maybe they recognized him." Even Dex was unconvinced by his own point. "And Lord Yarbury?"

"Playing blackjack when we were removed. I doubt he noticed. He never saw Mark today." Kenny's tone was now assertive. "Dex, we can't waste time here. Someone has blown it. We were busted due to a tip-off."

"Zara?"

Kenny nodded. "Who else? Since I called you in Paris, you've been so confident that she would behave herself… so, well I haven't really worried as much as I should have."

"Ryder was confident he had everything under control – said she'd been apeshit when she found out but was still one hundred percent onside. He'd warned her she'd go to jail if she didn't cooperate with Department ML23."

"Ryder didn't let me down. He hadn't told her anything. She stumbled on his notes about his secret visits to Dukes, doing the checks I wanted. She also found my false name - Graeme Brook but no number. When he came in, she went *berserk*, Ryder's word to me. He took a few blows, a nasty scratch on his neck but when he had calmed her down, she seemed to accept that the only person to blame was Shawcross."

"Maybe she changed her mind - decided to confront Shawcross. Sort him out."

Dex had to concede she was an unguided missile. "Or side with him." He stood up. "Enjoy your tea. I'll make a few calls." When he returned his face was grim. "It's worse than we thought." He looked at Jackie first. "Your lives, all our lives, *are* in real danger. Shawcross does not think rationally. He now knows I'm the spider spinning the web." He grabbed his cup and slurped quickly as his mind raced through an action plan. "Get back to your office. Strip it like locusts. Remove *everything* about Dukes. Take away the computers, files, the lot. Deliver everything to my solicitor's home in Wandsworth. His name is Rufus Chandler. I'm doing the same."

"We going to blow the whistle on Dukes now? We've everything we needed, One-Eye and Andy – both guilty as sin. Mark has completed around four-eighty shoes of blackjack – short of a round number but still plenty enough. We watched our films last night – all of them, one after the other. We now know their blackjack trick."

"Explain later. I'm not ready to blow the whistle." He could not explain why.

Kenny looked puzzled and cast a despairing sideways glance at Jackie. Dex saw the dumb insolence but ignored it. On what *they* knew, now was the time. But they didn't know everything. Dex looked at each of them in turn. "We meet tomorrow morning at Gatwick. Scotty Brannigan's jet will take us to the Caribbean. I'll fix the destination. You'll be there at my expense until after the New Year. By then, we'll have blasted the caboodle out of the water. You'll be paid for an eight hour day except Christmas holidays."

Jackie shook her head. "I wish ... but impossible. Can't leave my mother."

"Bring her."

Jackie shook her head. "No passport." Kenny looked relieved as he realized he was spared that.

"I can't tell you how dangerous things now are. If Shawcross got hold of either of you, it would not be pretty. This guy enjoys killing. He doesn't even need a good excuse, okay? We have to disappear until every final detail is in place. Jackie - you and your mother must go first thing tomorrow. Make sure nobody follows you. Leave no trace of where you're going. It can be anywhere - guest-house, small hotel, Devon, Scotland. Somewhere that a psychopath on the rampage will not find you. There's no room for any cock-ups. Kenny, I'll see you at the Gatwick Moat House at 0630." Impulsively, he hugged and kissed Jackie goodbye. "Be lucky. Be careful. I'm going to round up Mark, Ryder, and Zara. I'm meeting Scotty tonight." His voice showed his anger as he mentioned Scotty's name.

"Yarbury?" Kenny queried.

"Doesn't know enough. He'll be convincing this was someone he met at his club. If he tells Shawcross I put him up to the Jeremy charade, so what? Shawcross now knows I'm the orchestrator."

"You said Zara?"

"She's not the problem. I'll explain how you were all caught later. Kenny, make sure you're not followed to Rufus' home tonight or in the morning. Take care."

"I wish you'd just blow the bastard out of the water now."

"I wish I could too – but there's more to be done." He ran a weary hand across his flat-top. Then he whispered a final special instruction to Kenny, whose face beamed. "Good idea. I won't forget."

Dex cursed Chieseman all the way to Islington. But for his delays, they could have had everything buttoned a week or more back. Progress in the late afternoon traffic was slow but he enjoyed the lane-switching, cutting up the more patient drivers, remembering the back-doubles and quieter residential streets to speed the journey. When he entered their love-nest on Shepherdess Walk, it was evident that Ryder had been at home and Zara had just returned from the City. She was still in her office outfit of black suit, black stockings and white blouse. He was dressed in old jeans, a bottle-green shirt and a pair of socks. Ryder introduced him to Zara. "This is Graeme Brook from ML23." Dex saw at once that she was unimpressed

"Sorry to barge in but Shawcross has found out about the investigations. There's been a leak. You, both of you, are in great danger. It is highly likely that he will have you captured, taken somewhere for interrogation under duress and then who knows after that. The man is, after all, a psychopath. I suggest you both sign off as sick. Or take a sudden holiday. I'm offering two weeks or so away at my expense."

"Why?" Zara was defiant and resentful but her pout made her look even sexier as a result. Dex could see at once why Ryder was besotted with her - though not half as besotted as she was with herself. Her face had an arrogance that came mainly from the eyes. Their angle, the set of her chin and mouth showed she knew how to bring out the worst in men and was ready to use it. Dex took an instant dislike to her.

"Why?" Dex was scornful of such a naïve question. "Because if you stay here, you're both dead meat. Shawcross now knows I've nobbled you. He knows I've orchestrated everything against him."

Ryder looked puzzled. "Can't Department ML23 protect us?"

Before Dex had the chance to reply, Zara cut in with contempt. She snorted her contempt. "Of course not. It doesn't exist. I checked with the FSA this morning." She glared at Ryder as if he was a creep for ever believing the ML23 story. She stood, hands on hips, her breasts jutting forcefully under her suit jacket. Her anger turned to Dex. "Who the fuck are you anyway? Graeme Brook from near Gatwick you are not. Interfering with our lives, pretending to be an official. Why should we believe anything you say? Are you some kind of conman?"

"'Fraid not. Everything I said was true – except my status. I'm Finlay Dexter. Dex. I'm working to expose Dukes for massive crimes." He saw Ryder's jaw drop and shrugged as if to say sorry.

"Why?" Her voice was hostile and Dex looked around nervously to see what she might throw at him. A steam iron looked too close for comfort. He casually edged further away from her and close enough to the iron to grab it first.

"Because I found out that Dukes was a crooked con, a laundry."

"Well, I'm not going," Zara said crossing her arms defiantly with the look of an irate fishwife. "Not with a shit like you. Or him, come to that."

Ryder now gave a resigned shrug.

Dex jabbed with his right arm as he spoke. "Then you're both very stupid. Do you think I'd fly you off if this wasn't serious? I'm concerned for you - even though I neither like you nor have *reason* to care a damn about whether you live or die. But I don't want Shawcross to have the pleasure of carving you up. You know too much. I'd feel I'd made life too easy for him – letting him eliminate or terrify potential prosecution witnesses." Dex stood by the ironing board in the small and overheated room and watched the reaction. No wonder they had dreamed of Las Vegas.

Ryder didn't seem to know where to look, nor what to do with his hands and he looked gangly, his arms swinging loosely. He glanced at Zara and saw her eyes burning into him. He gave the slightest shoulder movement to suggest he was sorry. "Look darling. I didn't tell you this. I didn't want to scare you. Shawcross is a psychopathic murderer. We should do as he says."

"Scare me? Scare me? You useless twerp. What scares me is that I was nearly shackled to a berk like you. I'm not scared of Shawcross."

Dex decided pussyfooting was over. "You should be. I'm leaving. You do what you like. There are around two billion dollars at stake. *Nothing* will stand in his way to silence me and anyone who could give evidence." Dex edged nearer the door. "He may be coming here even now. So, if you change your mind, stay in the Holiday Inn Gatwick. I'll take now *everything* you have about Dukes, computers the lot. Don't tell anyone where you're going. I'll phone at five am tomorrow. If you're there, you'll get directions for the flight. If not, take care and check your life insurance."

"I'll be there," said Ryder. "I'll sort the papers for you."

"And if you're there," Zara snapped "I won't be. You and I are dead, like the dodo."

"Your call, Zara but if you don't help, then you're going to jail for a long time for corruption." Dex could see that she was unimpressed.

At just after ten pm, Dex picked up Mark Evans from his rented place in the cheerless surroundings of Elspeth Road in Clapham. "Passport?"

Evans smiled and joked. "In the name of Jeremy Legrange. Of course." He settled back in the Fiat and secured his seatbelt. "All very James Bond this – your cryptic messages."

"I'll explain tomorrow."

"Going away again! That's the real bitch. I told Emily and she was crying and shouting down the phone. Kath called me a bastard for letting her down."

Dex hated hearing this. "It's for the best after what happened this afternoon. But I'm sorry. Just when you were hoping to patch things up with Kath." He thought back to Emily and mentally noted to make things up to them all. "So this afternoon? What happened?" Dex checked for the second time that there was no tail as he settled down for the slow journey to the M23.

"It was nothing I'd done. No counting and changing stakes, not once."

"I believe you. I know *how* they busted you. They discovered your real name. They then used their computer software to check you out. What interests me is what they said and what you said."

"How did they find out who I was?"

"Later. So what was said?" Dex took a left and a right and they were onto the main road leading to the still distant motorway. The Fiat's noisy engine made conversation difficult as they crawled through the high streets of South London.

"This little fellow came up to me - within seconds of me arriving. Just as I reached the gaming room, this little shit held my arm. "*Mr Evans? Mr Mark Evans?* I was well shocked, I can tell you. I'd almost come to believe I was Jeremy. So this runt says: *Your attendance here in a false name is unacceptable.* Then two big guys appeared and I knew it was another gorilla moment – to use Wally McKay's terms. The small bloke who seemed important ..."

"That's Reggie Kyte, Security Director."

"Kyte. Yes – he said *come and answer a few questions.* So I walked in front of the three of them. They were herding me towards a back office behind Reception. Sorry, Dex but I panicked. I should have let them question me but when I reached the bottom of the stairs and saw daylight up there, I just bolted."

"Excellent. So no questions, no answers."

"Right. The two guards, near thirty stone between them, started to chase me. They couldn't get up the stairs like me. I heard Kyte shout *don't bother* but I still didn't stop until I was through Berkeley Square. I hid in a pub in Bruton Street. Then you phoned me. That's it."

"'You did well. Thanks. They might have tried to beat some information out of you."

"And Arthur Yarbury?"

"I've spoken to him. He's not concerned. They challenged him this afternoon. Told them he had been conned. They believed him."

"So where are we going?"

"It's a secret." The big blue M23 signs for Gatwick appeared, reminding Dex of his mythical ML23 office. "The motorway at last. Regard this as my private witness protection program. We'll need you to finalize your statement."

"Can I phone Emily while I'm away?"

Dex wanted to say yes. "You can write but phone calls are out. Shawcross – the big boss, who you probably haven't encountered, is desperate to get at us. He now knows the link from you to me. He'll be desperate to find out what you were doing. He'll bug your rented place and the family home in Thames Ditton. We've got to lie low until," Dex picked his words with care – "until we're ready to pounce." He saw the concern on Mark's face, his hands forever restless. "I hoped Emily could come too, so you could have Christmas together."

"No way would Kath let her leave the country. Can't blame her. I wouldn't … well I couldn't even tell her where I was going or why. Kath called me a heartless bastard and told me to take a hike."

They lapsed into a sad silence until he pulled off the motorway and moments later parked up in the Hilton. "You enjoy a steak and a couple of drinks. I can't join you. I've some urgent business. And thanks for what you've done. I'm sorry it ended like this."

"Forget it! I owe you. Clouds House changed my life – saved me from myself. I'll do what it takes."

Dex nearly gave him a hug but instead just shared his steadfast look. "Thanks. I value that so much." He left Mark to check in. "Be packed and ready in the lobby at 0545. Goodnight."

London Gatwick – 12th December 2002

Dex drove to the nearby Travelodge where Scotty was holed up. The post-midnight traffic was light as he drove through the murky night.

Oh yes, I'm the Great Pretender.

Pretendin' that I'm doin' fine.

The lyrics still plagued him after checking in before setting off for Scotty's room. This was not going to be pleasant.

I'm lonely but no one can tell

Pretendin' that I'm doin' well.

He banged on the door to Scotty's room and the American let him in. The bedroom reeked of beer. The American had downed a few but did not sound or look drunk. The bedside light was on and the bedclothes were rumpled but Scotty was still wearing a pair of blue trousers and a striped blue and white shirt. There was a truculent look on his face. Dex inwardly groaned at the prospects ahead. "Plane and pilots ready for the morning?" He was in no mood for niceties.

"Keep your hair on, what's left of it."

"The pilots, the plane?"

"Pilots need to know the destination. Gotta file a flight plan."

"We'll do it at the last moment. How long do Air Traffic Control need?"

"Minimum one hour – safer two."

"Do it at 0630 for 0800 departure. Destination Las Vegas. We'll drop off a set of the documents with Otto Schneider and then drive to Phoenix. Then we fly to our final destination. We won't use your jet for that bit but I want it to follow us later to use in emergency."

Dex grabbed a beer from a six-pack. He could see that Scotty was debating whether to be unhelpful as he flopped onto the bed and laid back, arms behind his head. "I'll tell 'em. Meantime, you'd better explain what in hell is going on. All this fuckin' urgency." As he listened, Dex recalled a couple of quotes about Scotty from an F1 website – *That man? Pig ignorant. Doesn't know how to say sorry* was one. The other - *He'll never defend his world championship title. He doesn't understand defense. With Brannigan it's always attack.*

Dex felt the blood racing to his head. He'd had a tough day, one of too many. He was tired, *beyond* tired and desperate to grab a few hours sleep. The last thing he needed was aggravation from Scotty. "Don't piss me about. You *know* what the problem is." He stopped to glare at Scotty who looked away and then swigged from a can of beer. "You broke all the rules. I warned you to put nothing in writing. I said you were a security risk. But did you listen? No." Dex stood at the end of the bed and pointed his finger in accusation. "You've blown everything. Shawcross' people must have pissed themselves laughing going through your apartment. A burglary was so predictable! But you knew best, so you thought, you bonehead! Hell, you're a former World Champion. Where's that quick brain, those well-tuned survival instincts?"

Scotty did not look apologetic and said nothing. He closed his eyes and eased his position, so Dex continued. "You're an obvious link between me and Mick Glenn. I *may* have distracted the bastard from me by my home revealing nothing - but that put you onto the front line."

"Fuck you! They didn't take nothin'."

Dex' anger boiled over and he had to resist the urge to land a fist right in the middle of the American's defiant features. "You liar. Notes. You made notes. *You* know they stole them." His voice rose to a crescendo as he thumped the bedside table so that the beer-can fell to the carpet. "*I* know they have them."

Dex rounded the bed and leaned over the reclining figure to shout the words eyeball to eyeball. "Nothing in writing, I said. Shawcross must have thought Santa Claus had come early. We had three people working undercover. Security busted them today. Your stupidity has ruined everything. Your disobedience to my order revealed my link to them, to you and to Ryder and his woman Zara." He banged his fist again on the bedside table. "Call that smart?"

Dex grabbed the sandwich that he'd picked up in Clapham. Lack of food and sleep was making his head spin now. He was feeling light-headed from trying to marshal his facts and re-jig his plans. "What did the notes say?"

"Nothin' much." He asked Dex to pass his laptop, opened Word and then a file called Dex. Without comment, he handed over the computer. Dex looked at the screen. The words **Dukes – Agenda** angered him. He read on, mouthing the words. Occasionally, he glanced up at Scotty whose curled lip showed pure aggression. "I can't believe you did this. You've given Shawcross a home run. You ran off a typed copy of this? I despair." He looked at the reclining figure, so unrepentant. Smug self-satisfaction was evident in the defiant set of the chin and the flashing eyes. Dex could not take the man any longer. Something snapped. With surprising force, he slapped Scotty across the face with the back of his hand.

Stunned at the ferocity and unexpectedness of the blow, the American cowered, hands now in front of his face in self-defense. "If I don't get your help from now, I'll do a fucking rain-dance on your bad shoulder. Finish it off once and for all. As it is, you don't get your money back or any reward."

"You want to fly to Vegas or not?" Scotty wiped blood from his nose.

"Oh we're flying to Vegas okay. You're not walking away from our deal. You've some ground to make up." Dex pointed at the screen, ignoring the blood streaming down Scotty's face. "***Item 1: Mark Evans / Jeremy Legrange. Item 2: Kenny Jennings and Jackie Morton aka Jim Shaw and Miranda Bell***. Shawcross had them all bounced. I expect Shawcross is already having their places ransacked. Mark? He had to run for his life to escape a hammering." His hand was shaking with rage as he read on. "***Item 3: Dex report from Ryder. Item 4: Co-ordinate SFO and Feds. Item 5: Panama. Item 6: R/L***. Talk about giving away the Crown Jewels. At least you shortened Reverse Labouchère. If we're lucky, they won't twig that." He glared at the American. "But he can guess I've found out about Panama." He let out a lengthy sigh of despair. A thought of just quitting everything suddenly seemed tempting but he knew it was too late to turn back now.

He took a large bite from the second sandwich and sipped his beer as Scotty struggled up from the bed, using his right shoulder to take the strain of his weight. Blood from his nose was streaming onto the pillow and sheets. He went to the bathroom and Dex heard the taps running. When he reappeared, a towel was staunching the flow of blood. He slumped onto the bed, head tilted right back. "Never thought they'd turn my place over," Scotty said from behind the reddening towel. "We can't go on with Reverse Labby now. We gotta quit. Get the fuck outta here. Get the Feds in." Scotty's voice was hardening. In Formula One, for years he had been the Lion King. Everyone listened when he roared. For a moment, his past aura returned. "I don' understan' why we ain't played Reverse Labby yet.." He lowered his voice though his resentment remained. "Sooner we get Shawcross locked up, the better. Why risk everythin'? Just for your crazy obsession with revenge."

Dex felt stronger now that Scotty had changed his attitude. "No. We go on. I just need more time."

Scotty dabbed away at his nose. "You don' get to be World Champion without being tough. Tough as shit. Ain't no more connivin' bunch of guys anywhere than in F1. You can be smart, you can hang tough but sometimes, it's smarter and tougher to back off." Dex' yawn was genuine but timely. "You and your dreams of bringin' down Space City when the tower's due to open – bullshit. Kid's stuff. Comic crap. This ain't no game."

"I'm still going for Reverse Labby."

"Now you jus' listen kid and listen real good." Scotty tried to get some beer to his mouth but spilled it over the towel. "You can't always be right. Now Shawcross knows, my fault maybe, delayin' is wrong, plain wrong. You're playin' games with this guy. Count me out. Don't fuck us all by livin' out your dream. Blow those cocksuckers away now."

"I'll do it on my own if you haven't the balls." A glowering look from Scotty was the response. "Just need Shawcross and Kyte to be off the premises."

Scotty was not persuaded. "Like I said, sometimes it's smarter to back off."

"I'll see you at five."

Dex phoned Tiffany on her secret number and heard similar advice. "Back off. We'll get that charity going somehow. *Your life* means more to me right now." Worse still, despite pressuring her to join him, she had refused. "I'd love to. It's sensible too. But telling the Beeb I'm off without warning just isn't on. But I doubt Shawcross would try anything on me."

"With a life sentence and two billion dollars at stake? Don't underestimate him."

"Dex – winning the money's not important. You have the evidence, enough to sink Dukes, Space City, and Shawcross – the lot. I don't know why you and Scotty haven't done your Reverse Labby thing already – but risking it now is crass."

"Once Shawcross and Kyte go to Vegas for the opening, I can take them for millions. All my life, I'll regret it if I don't."

"But now that Scotty's blown the game?"

373

"He's blown the *personnel*. For the next two weeks, Shawcross has to maintain business as usual for the celebrations in Vegas."

"He'll stop all the frauds."

"Too late now." His voice turned pleading. "Tiffany, I'm so worried he'll use you to get at me. You should join us. It would be safer."

"Not until Christmas. I'll be fine until then."

"Empty words. He's bound to assume you know something."

"If you're so worried, press the button now. Don't delay. Get Shawcross taken out."

"You know I can't do that." The conversation had ended on a cool note. The evidence for Otto Schneider lay beside him as he tried to sleep, all certified true copies made by Rufus Chandler and now neatly collated in seven black ring-binders. Just Kenny and Mark's final notes remained to be added. Dex barely slept after the call and when he did, it seemed to be only for seconds before the harsh fingers of reality tormented him again.

As the digital clock showed two-seventeen, he was wondering if someone had yet stripped Kenny's office. And where was Zara? Far from Islington if she had any sense. Then he'd relived the calls he'd made from the Russell Hotel. Using his code name of Alec Lucas, he had called FB about repairing his computer, their agreed format. FB had then returned the call from a phone box down Mount Street. "Reggie Kyte told me that Shawcross had found out who was causing trouble. According to Reggie, he was firing on twelve cylinders. His agent had turned over Brannigan's place and found some typed notes. He's hired some heavy boys to find you, hunt you down. Kyte told me they were going to bust some members after lunch if they appeared. Fooled me, those two filming. I'd never noticed."

"Jeremy Legrange?"

"Once we had his real name, we found he was a counter. Our computer imaging device nailed him in seconds. I tried to warn you but was scared to leave a message."

Dex had thanked him and then phoned Scotty. "Any news?"

"My place in Mayfair was done over last night. All my papers flung everywhere."

Dex thought of the trouble he'd had finding anything. "Where were you?"

"Birmingham overnight. Speaking engagement."

"They take anything to do with Dukes?"

"Nothin'." Dex blanched and he clenched and unclenched his fist at the lie.

"Your computer?"

"With me in Birmingham."

Dex decided a confrontation on the phone was pointless. Still seething, he ordered the American to bring his computer to Gatwick and to set up his plane for a hasty disappearance. "All our lives are in danger. Make sure you're not followed." Reliving Brannigan's lies, Tiffany's warnings and Zahra's defiance ruined any chance of sleep. He watched the red digital figures on the clock pass through three and then four. With sleep impossible, he showered and felt better able to face the challenges.

At the airport, despite feeling like a zombie, Dex tried to convey a confident image. Inwardly, the negatives were piled up like unsold books in a dump-bin. His head was pounding, his eyes showed the lack of sleep. He called Kenny across as they gathered to board Scotty's jet. Besides Kenny, Adrian Ryder, Mark and Scotty were also in the small waiting area. Dex' words were slurring from lack of sleep. "So you did what I asked?"

Kenny nodded and winked reassuringly. "Of course. We stripped the office of everything. He'll find nothing incriminating there." He looked around. "Where's this Zara woman? In the loo?"

Dex glanced across to where Adrian Ryder was reading the Daily Express. "Could be but not at Gatwick. She's refused to come."

"Silly cow! Does she want to be done over?"

"I tried to tell her but she's so pissed off with me and Adrian that she doesn't really care. She's dreamed the Vegas dream. It's been destroyed."

"Think she'll go to Shawcross and have a showdown?"

"It's a risk. Adrian tried to make her see sense. Zara told him she'd sooner sleep with a rabid dog than go to bed with him again. He told her that a rabid dog was all a bitch like her deserved. One-All I suppose but the end of that relationship! He reckons she's a survivor and wouldn't risk facing Shawcross. That's our best hope." He glanced through the smeared grime of the window at the murky half-light of dawn. "And your own report?"

"The final two pages will be shit-hot. I'll type them on the plane. You ..." he broke off as Brannigan appeared. "What the devil happened to Scotty?" He was looking at the black eye. "Tripped did he like Creole's Sharon?"

"Walked into a door I believe," Dex replied with a straight face.

"You look as if you could do with some good news," Kenny continued "so I'll give you some."

Dex nodded. "A good fix would be welcome."

"We cracked the blackjack fraud." He raised his hand for high-five and Dex managed to join in.

"I don't know how we missed it for so long."

"Go on." Dex grabbed his coffee and looked earnestly over the brim.

"Remember I told you about a woman that was always there at two pm sharp - Claire Weatherley – the one that looked like Charlotte Rampling. Like Jude, it became clear she had been signing in foreigners. When watching all the films *en bloc* it became obvious. She always went straight to the blackjack and briefly played *every table*. When the gaming started at 2pm the casino is quiet, the tables mainly empty. The few early arrivals are still having lunch and only the occasional person is eager to bet. The films showed she was invariably in first."

"She was the tall, elegant woman, a bit haughty and severe, you pointed out after one of your early visits?"

Kenny said yes. "Besides seeing her later on with a stream of wealthy foreigners, we never saw her do anything wrong. But we were missing the point. We started wondering why she was so keen always to be first in." He nodded across at Mark who was sitting alone looking rather sad and clutching an Ian Rankin novel. "He'll love this. Two pm sharp. Claire sits down at the blackjack. The dealer then spread out the new cards in the semi-circle, face-up but from packets *already open*. No cellophane wrapping. She never checked the cards at all. She played a couple of hands and then moved round, opening each blackjack table in turn. Mark told me that the correct procedure is to see them remove the cellophane. So you see how easy it was to go through a charade of spreading out the cards for inspection. Claire knew not to check."

"That bloody simple! So when genuine players arrived, all the shoes were ready. Decks with some tens and aces removed had already been set up. Players arriving had to assume that whoever had played first had seen new decks opened, semi-circled and checked."

"Easy wasn't it? Some days, another player might get to a table before her. They would get the cellophane treatment but most days, she opened each one. The rest of her time down there, she was tied up with the money-laundering."

"Bet you a tenner Claire Weatherley wasn't there when you were busted yesterday."

"No takers! No, she wasn't in. But every other day, by twenty past two she'd have opened every table, long before most members had reached the Stilton."

"Great job. Link that to Mark's evidence."

"Being?"

"The odds of the decks being straight were millions to one against."

Kenny tapped the side of the nose. "But it gets better. The day before yesterday, we outwitted Dukes. I told Mark and Yarbury to open a different table next to Weatherley. The Pit Boss had no choice. He produced *unopened* cellophane wrapped decks. And guess what?"

"The count was normal."

"Exactly. Averaged over sixteen shoes at that table, Mark noted typical honest counts with cards to match."

"Yo' the man!" This time, Dex gave Kenny an exuberant high-five. "Set up the gallows!"

Las Vegas – 14th December 2002

Audley Shawcross was not in the best of moods. The US Air flight from Washington to Las Vegas had meant a six am start after a long evening at a nightclub on K Street. It had turned noon when he checked in at the Bellagio. The size and power of the jets in the shower-room soothed away the worst of last night's booze and as he sipped a beer while looking down at the half-moon of water below and the fountains, he wondered whether Space City would ever compete at the top of the market. The Shuttle launch at Space City attracted a different crowd, eager for excitement, but not with such deep pockets.

Under the unusual grey skies of a dreary winter's day, the other familiar sights of the Strip looked tawdry. Only after dark would the neon create its enduring magic. In his suite, he admired the soft colors of the furnishings and the displays of yellow tulips and hoped that the executive suites in the new tower would create a similar sense of well-being among the high-rollers. He knew that luring them back with comps and pampering was essential.

There was plenty of time before he was due to meet Carlo. From the directory, he booked a showgirl for some relaxation. He checked his watch, calculated that it was now 9 pm in London and decided to phone FB. "Don't even ask me about the Internet Gaming Conference in Washington. The law's a bloody mess" he opened the conversation. "Any real news FB?"

"Not since you received those notes and Reggie busted that trio. No sign of anyone else – or anything else. Do you want Dexter banned too?"

"No. He's deposited that large wad. He'll be back. That's when we'll nab him. When he signs in, get security to give him the treatment for cheating until Arnie Fisher's boys take over. Then I'll be back personally."

He called the agent. "Heh Arnie! What's going on?"

"We got to Zahra's place in Islington by nine. Empty. Signs of a hurried departure. Suitcases gone. No passports. Nothing exciting except her twelve inch black dildo. Thought she'd have taken that with her."

Shawcross grunted, in no mood to fantasize over Zara.

"Then we did over Mark Evans' dump in Elspeth Road. He obviously left hurriedly too. There was a frozen chicken dinner for one lying on the kitchen table. Nothing helpful about where he's gone. Plenty of stuff about his marriage. Wife, young daughter. Solicitors' letters, the usual stuff about money, custody and access."

"Dexter and Brannigan?"

"No sign."

"You going to give me *any* good news?"

"Listen to this. Those two Dexter hired for filming – with the office over in Ravenscourt Park. They've done a runner too. Place is locked up. The voicemail says the business is closed for annual holidays. We got in of course but found nothing there about Dukes – or Dexter come to that."

"So they took any films, records or whatever."

"No question."

Shawcross knew better than to ask if they had done a thorough job. "So no good news there then. Nothing else?"

He heard a chuckle down the line as Arnie replied. "Interested in knowing where you can find them?"

"Tell me."

"We'd done over all the files, everything. Everywhere. Nothing. Fuck knows why but I checked the bin beside his desk. He must have taken a phone call from Dexter. There was a crumpled page torn from the message pad on his desk."

"And?" Shawcross sounded impatient.

"They had to meet D – that's all it said. Just a letter D. Meet at Heathrow. Passports. Return 8th January. The next bit was odd. Understand this? Big Bang Las Vegas - 4th Jan."

Shawcross scribbled a note, his face set in studied concentration. The writing was thick and heavily pressed.

4th Jan.

The Big Bang.

Arnie said nothing as he waited for a reaction. Shawcross could guess what a Big Bang might be. Call it D-Day. But why January 4th? After the opening?

It could only mean that Dexter was not yet ready. " Doesn't make much sense to me. Anything else?"

"Oh yes." Arnie was bursting to add more. "Oh yes, yes indeed. We know where they've gone!" Shawcross heard the triumphant tone of voice. "My money says we'll find them all together – a co-coordinated scarper"

"Where?"

"Boca Raton CC. That's all the note said. I've checked on the web. There's a Boca Raton Country Club. Five star place in Florida."

"Get it checked out."

"Florida in December sounded tempting. I was hoping to go over myself."

"No. I want you in London."

"Bugged everything yet?"

"Last one being fitted as we speak."

Shawcross felt in better spirits as he went down to meet Carlo Letizione at the Petrossian Bar. Donna, a long-limbed blonde with silicon implants, had entertained him with great energy for a couple of hours. As she waved goodbye, she was licking a sugary doughnut. As he closed the door on her, he puzzled how she kept her hour-glass figure though not why she was so talented with her tongue.

He flopped into a well-upholstered chair in the bar just beside the gaming-floor and didn't have to wait long before he saw Space City's CEO wiping a bead of sweat from his forehead as he emerged from the lobby. Carlo was dressed in a green checked suit, pink shirt and a wide yellow tie. The style made the Englishman reach for his Chivas on the rocks as he wondered who advised Letizione on taste in clothes.

Over Beluga caviar, they assessed progress. "Sir Cedric and the rest of the Board have arrived for tomorrow's board meeting." From the Englishman's tone of voice, Letizione could tell that relations in England remained frosty.

"Won't be no problems with them," Letizione observed assertively, his brow still gleaming with sweat, despite the chill of the air-conditioning. "They'll love my report. Occupancy prospects are just great. The whole place – tower and all is full for the openin'. We're runnin' at over ninety-seven percent for the whole of January. Full again for Superbowl." Letizione was bubbling with satisfaction as he greedily spread the caviar on the toast. The American watched the reaction and was disappointed. Though Shawcross mumbled pleasing noises, he seemed distracted. "All well in London, Aude?"

Shawcross hated being called that. He thought for a second or two before the words flowed confidently. "Well enough to wind down *Snowball* and *Cyclops*. We've met our banking commitments." He smiled with a downward glance. "If you send money along a tube, something always sticks to the sides. Know the expression? Aruba's now brimming with cash. All the invoices look good?" He saw Carlos's nod and continued. "Then you and me get the pension we deserve."

Letizione was still unconvinced. "You holdin' back about somethin'? Problems?"

Shawcross shook his head and looked Carlo Letizione in the eye. "Like what, Carlo? No, of course not!"

"I'm pleased. Come on then. Drink up. Let's take a walk round Space City. You'll be impressed." Letizione flicked some crumbs from his baggy suit. "Cedric and Kieran O'Keefe. Kyte? They staying here?"

"No. They're all staying in the corporate apartments at the Turnberry. Rooms bugged?" He saw Letizione's eyes narrow as he gave a derisive snort. Shawcross raised his hand. "Okay, okay! Sorry, Carlo! Silly question. Just make sure I get the transcripts of their chats before the meeting."

Las Vegas –15th December 2002

A bright sun filled the morning sky over Southern Nevada. There was endless blue from the Spring Mountains in the west to Sunrise Mountains in the east. Even so, with the stiff breeze, it felt barely above freezing. Dex and his team had the heating on full blast in the black Lincoln stretch-limo as they pulled away from the Venetian Hotel.

The previous evening, Dex had met Scotty's lawyer, the diminutive and ageing Otto Schneider. The little man had an ego the size of his giant desk in a room to match. He sat on a raised dais, holding court to the supplicants below who paid for his growled words of advice. No question, Dex had decided. The man was ideal, oozing aggression from every wrinkle. Schneider's hands never stopped. He might be polishing or brandishing his black-rimmed spectacles but mainly he was pointing, waving or chopping his hands repeatedly in rhythm to the staccato words he spat out, every one punctuated by an obscenity.

Dex had taken him through the stack of notes, films and reports. As he chewed on a constant supply of cookies, the attorney had enthused about raising hell with the Feds and at the Nevada Gaming Control Board. "We can fuckin' decimate every goddamned fuckin' one of these cocksuckers. Just tell me go get 'me," had been his parting words.

"Great, Otto … but I'm not ready yet."

The limo turned towards the sun, passing the lake in front of Bellagio as they started out on the long drive to Phoenix. Ahead on the Strip were the New York, New York and MGM Grand hotels. Of the roller-coaster that wrapped itself around the skyscrapers of New York, New York there was no sign. The chauffeur was about to turn left onto Tropicana by the huge lion outside the MGM when Dex ordered him to keep on the Strip. "I want to see how Space City is coming on."

"Quite sump'n ain't it" said the driver as he parked on the right just short of the Luxor's pyramid. Across the Strip to their left was the vast Space City complex, the main building gleaming white in the golden rays of the sun. The new tower to its south looked finished. Dex didn't reply. The size and sheer majesty of the vast building filled him with awe. When he had seen it before, he had just been a tourist. Now he was on a mission to destroy. The soaring height of the crescent building looked so permanent, his plans seemed absurd. The faux Space Shuttle, its huge cigar tube shape clinging beside the front entrance silenced each of the watchers.

Dex took in the details and for a second remembered that June night when he had vowed to destroy Space City. Now he could see the reality. Yet Otto Schneider's words provided comfort. *We can fuckin' decimate every goddamned fuckin' one of these cocksuckers.* He looked at the giant hoarding announcing the Grand Tower Opening on the 30th December.

The huge marquee sign, ninety feet high promised that Space City would continue to deliver *a new era of futuristic fun and gaming.* It already guaranteed *the loosest slots in town*, a boast he had read at least a dozen times along the Strip. Inside the limo nobody but the driver spoke. "Yeah, this city reinvents itself, blowin' up the old hotspots, introducin' new themes like this crazy Space Shuttle launch. Man, that's gotta be jus' *the* hottest ticket. The new tower's gonna be all high-tech stuff. Rooms are sold out for a year ahead."

To a casual eye, everything was complete. "See," the driver continued. "Jus' look at all them rooms." He was pointing to the fifty-three storys of towering half-moon. Dex hung on every word though he knew every fact and figure from the website. "Four thousand rooms. An' you get into this crazy place by those metal catwalks – jus' as if you were an astronaut." Everybody climbed out to take a look.

The giant replica of a NASA Shuttle was built to life-size and was called Galaxy. It stood on a launch-pad, towering nearly two hundred feet high and seventy eight feet wide. "Four hundred gamblers get selected every hour for a flight. Great marketing, see. You gotta be playin' for two hours before they'll offer you the *ride of your life.* I got lucky – knew someone with juice an' did it. Man! It blew my mind, flames underneath me, the rocket shakin', lights flashin' and then we were away into the Florida sky at nearly a mile per second. Ya gotta do it."

Dex swallowed hard and gripped the door handle as if it were his only way to keep his feet on the ground. Dex twisted his neck skywards to look up at the façade, so sharply defined against the blue background. "It's magnificent," Ryder commented. "Pity I'm not coming here to work." Dex noticed that not everyone laughed.

"There's a high roller suite in the new building," continued the driver tipping his cap backwards. "I seen round it. 12,000 square feet. That's eight times bigger'n my place out in Henderson. It's yours for twenty thousand bucks a night. You get your own private movie theatre, a bed the size of Texas, a bowlin' alley, indoor and outdoor pools, guest-rooms, a telescope for star-gazin', a spa and a night-club zone for the Britney Spears or the Matt Damons to give their parties." The driver fell silent as if imagining himself boogying on down with Britney.

"Let's go" said Dex. "Next stop Phoenix."

"That guy's right," said Scotty once they were all back in the car and Kenny had poured some strong black coffee from the flasks nestling in the door. "I been in the penthouses at the MGM, Caesar's and Palms. Man! They know how to make a celebrity feel like a *super-star*." He drew out the word, long and hard. Dex was pleased Scotty was even speaking. He had been surly, lower lip turned down, for twenty-four hours and his black eye now included a sickly yellow.

"You paid twenty thousand?" asked Adrian Ryder.

Scotty laughed, another first for a long time. "You kiddin'! Ain't *no* celebs pay. Least I never did. All the columnists, like Norm from the Las Vegas Review Journal, have their spies out hopin' for tabloid trash stories." The conversation gradually died away as the limo picked up speed and left behind the sprawling golf-courses and the endless suburbia. Dex had studied Scotty a great deal since leaving London, all the time trying to judge his mood. On the flight across, he had been visibly hostile but today he had seemed merely sullen. The laugh was the first plus. Mark Evans had not shared the excitement at Space City. He was locked in some private world of his own and from his rear corner seat, he was staring out at the vast rusty brown of the scrubby desert. Dex would have bet he was seeing nothing.

"Lonely?" Dex moved into the seat beside him. Evans looked down and nodded his head. "It's Emily. She's suffered too much."

"She's a real darling. She'll bounce back when you get home." He kept a one-sided conversation running but Mark's face remained frozen, his eyes never wavering from the distant horizon.

"Can I phone her when we get to Phoenix?"

"Sounds like a Glenn Campbell song," but this was lost on Mark so Dex hurried on. "Believe me. I understand. Kids are resilient – and forgiving too. Send her another postcard. If you phone home and Shawcross can trace the call, we're in deep trouble." Dex ran his finger across his throat but Mark never noticed, his shoulders hunched, his mind closed to reason.

"But if he traced us to Phoenix, by then we won't be there."

"True but it'll give him a trail to follow. Kenny pointed him to Boca Raton. Right now, I hope he's chasing shadows round Florida. If he traced us … well. Enough said." Dex maneuvered a reassuring arm round Mark's shoulder. "You know Dukes well. You've seen Space City. Shawcross isn't going to let you or me stand in his way. I wouldn't be spending my dead sister's life policy and dragging you across the world without good reason. But it'll soon be over."

True but not soon enough. Dex fell silent, reflecting on Scotty's anger and Tiffany's concern at the delays. *Act now they'd both warned. Don't mess with Shawcross. Leave it to the cops.* For a fleeting second, the lyrics of *The Great Pretender* flashed through his mind. He looked across at Evans and saw the sad profile and haunted look.

My message isn't getting through to him.

I have to help him somehow.

"Are you going to tell us where we're headed yet?" Kenny asked the question on everyone's minds.

Dex looked at Mark, debated whether to tell them and then responded. "Not yet. But you won't be disappointed. Let's just call it Paradise."

Scotty turned to face Dex, his demeanor still confrontational. "We just left Paradise."

"Different sort of Paradise, Scotty."

Audley Shawcross had plenty of time to get to Space City for the meetings and so decided to walk along the Strip. The wintry wind blowing from snow-capped Mount Charleston cut right through him as he realized after only a few yards. He walked increasingly briskly, briefcase in hand, grateful for his lined Burberry. He pulled up the collar and stuffed his free hand deeper into a pocket. Traffic was typically light at nine-thirty and he noticed how few pedestrians were about. Most visitors were still in bed or standing in long lines for breakfast. Mornings come late in Sin City.

Shawcross reviewed the junction with Tropicana before deciding to use the footbridge to cross to the Excalibur. Beside him, the first roller-coaster of the day had yet to thunder down beside the mock-up of the New York skyline. On the footbridge, he gazed towards Space City beyond the Tropicana Casino.

He saw a black stretch limo parked while a bunch of tourists gawped at his creation. It gave him a buzz just to watch them sharing his dream.

The pleasing emotions didn't last. His cellphone vibrated and he listened in quiet irritation as Arnie reported that his people in Boca Raton had come up with nothing. So where the hell were Dexter and his team? What were they doing? He looked again at Space City, its entrance closely protected by black-uniformed security guards. *That shit can't sink all this!* He saw the distant group climb back into their limo and speed away from him. A new idea, something he had termed *the nuclear option*, resurfaced. Perhaps it was time to use it.

He walked right round the perimeter of Space City, admiring it from all angles, his step bouncy again as he relished telling the Board he had delivered everything and more. *Snowball* could be mothballed. *Cyclops* was over. Dexter was the only irritation and he could be silenced, the safest and most pleasurable option. As he watched a coach from San Diego empty another fifty hopefuls into the lobby, he thought how amazing the past three months had been. But for the Dexter kid, it had all been so easy – fooling Sir Cedric's lot, sidelining the Gaming Board and seeing off the bean-counters. The auditors had been curious about the staggering growth in turnover but a few soothing words and blunt reminders of where their obligations lay had allayed their concerns.

Sir Cedric and the rest would soon be reading the accountants' report giving Dukes a glowing testimonial. Neither in Nevada nor their London office had they challenged the invoices from the Manhattan Island Bank of Commerce, a pompous name for their personal bank registered in Grand Cayman and the conduit for funds to be channeled to Aruba. Even Kieran O'Keefe had been satisfied that Carlo had fixed a secondary loan from that bank during the cash crisis during the strikes earlier in the year.

I've come so far.

No way is that little shit going to drag me down.

It's time for that WMD, the nuclear warhead.

He dialed Arnie's number and after that, spoke to Jude. When he'd finished, his face looked younger; his cheeks were flushed with excitement. He had pressed the nuclear button, a dangerous option but no question, one that would deliver game, set and match. Suddenly, he felt hungry, fancying a cup of coffee and a Danish. He doubted Letizione would have anything of the kind. In his office, any snacks would be food fit for carnivores, even at this time.

At the main entrance, the security guard nodded an indifferent greeting as he headed for the new tower first. Once there, he was greeted by the whine of electric drills, the sound of jack-hammers and the hum of polishers and other appliances as the finishing touches were made.

Shawcross walked round a pile of carpeting and took the emergency stairs up to Carlo's office. He felt a need to soothe Carlo. Yesterday's meeting at the Bellagio had been awkward and Shawcross knew he had performed badly, adding to the American's anxiety. Yet everything Carlo *knew about* had gone well. Like forty million well. Except maybe he was suspicious about Panama but as to the Dexter problems, he knew nothing.

Carlo's office was on the mezzanine floor and a secretary with big hair showed him in. The American had planned the decor of the spacious room himself as he immediately and proudly told Shawcross for the third time at least. The furnishings were pure Vegas and Shawcross cringed as he took in the clashing colors and patterns. The walls were red, purple and orange and festooned with blown up pictures of celebrities. The carpets were yellow with a red diamond pattern and a zebra skin lay across the floor by the picture window. The chairs were in mock leopard-skin while the bar-stools were carved like voluptuous nudes with over-rampant nipples.

"I like the style, Carlo. So restful after a long day, no doubt."

"Glad you like it." The sarcasm in the Englishman's voice had been lost on Letizione. He turned from the computer screen. "Help yourself to some wine. That's a real fine Mondavi." On the low table away from his desk, a tray of rare beef and a salad selection for two awaited.

"Bit early for that?" Even this throwaway line was enough to anger Carlo Letizione.

"What you suggestin'? That I'm some kinda soak? Dean Martin without the voice? To me, it's lunchtime. I work crazy hours here."

Shawcross never flinched. "Bit early *for me* then." The room was stale with cigarettes though the smell of replacement carpet and from a re-paint were both strong. "Subtle colors you chose – very restful." Letizione took this as praise and grunted happily. The noise of the construction work was gone. The only sound was the hiss of the air-conditioning and some canned *musak*, playing softly. "All the celebs in place for the 30th?"

"Sure. A-list guys from Hollywood. Plus all the top shakers from here. We've attracted the best." Letizione sat down on a wicker chair by the food. He didn't seem to be as excited about the opening as Shawcross had expected. They helped themselves to the Montana beef, cooked rare. Shawcross was in no hurry to talk. He leaned forward and poured himself some Opus One. "That's better Aude. Be in Vegas, behave like a local." Then as if he knew the answer, Letizione spoke confidently from behind his fork of avocado salad. "You gonna tell me what the fuck's goin' on in London? Yesterday you was so full of shit sayin' there ain't no problem. But it's straight-talk time now."

"Nothing we can't handle."

"Meanin'?"

"Just that."

"Stop pissin' on my carpet. Explain."

"Nothing serious. We caught a couple filming."

"And?"

"That's it. Well, besides evicting a card-counter with a disguise and a false ID."

"Filmin'? Bit fuckin' late knowin' that now. How long they been at it? Why? Who paid them? What could they have seen?" Letizione had put down his food and his face suggested his blood-pressure was running at 180 /125.

"Take it easy, Carlo." Shawcross stretched out his slender hand and waved it in a calming motion. He was as unruffled as the American was intense. "They'd only just joined the club. I doubt they saw anything."

Letizione looked across at the Englishman with barely disguised hostility. "Who set them up?"

Shawcross shrugged. "Maybe nobody."

"And the card-counter? Sounds trivial unless he was checkin' on the decks."

"Real name Mark Evans. He's disappeared. He has a wife and daughter we traced to Thames Ditton but he lived alone in a small place round Battersea Rise. His neighbor told my agent he left with a suitcase."

"So?"

"Trouble is the other couple disappeared about the same time."

"Your guy been out lookin' for them?"

"Too right. Arnie personally traced them to West London. A pair of dicks who had joined us under false names. He ransacked their place."

"Find anything?"

"Looks like they bunked off too. Justa piece of screwed up paper pointing to Boca Raton."

"They left the same day as Evans?"

"Their paper delivery was stopped the same day as Evans was seen with a suitcase." Letizione's left eye appeared to have developed a twitch, the eyelid fluttering. "Is there more?"

Shawcross decided not to get into Dexter, Brannigan or Ryder. He looked hurt. "Like what?"

Letizione stood up abruptly. "Fuck you. Quit treatin' me like a dumb-fuck kid." He pulled up his trousers over the bulge of his midriff and then wiped some sweat from his brow. "You wanted the rooms at the Turnberry bugged. You wanted the fuckin' transcripts. Okay you motherfucker. Take a read of this, then." He hurled over thirty pages of notes at Shawcross. "Why not start with your phone call from Reggie Kyte?"

Shawcross said nothing, a shocked look on his face as he recalled his earlier conversation with his Security Director. *Talk about hoisted.* His cheeks revealed a moment of inner turmoil. Completely forgetting that the phones were all bugged, Shawcross had spoken freely to his only ally on the Board. He stood up so that they were facing each other beside the window. "I didn't want to worry you. There's a problem with a member called Finlay Dexter, he's just a kid and nothing we can't handle. I'm pretty sure he's coordinating everything – making waves."

"Why?"

"Maybe a grudge. Either Dexter's got some evidence – in which case I'm working on that or he's not a problem."

"So Dexter an' all are holed up in Boca Raton?"

"We think so." Shawcross lied as he turned away to stroll around the office, taking in the paintings by Christian Riese Lassen and the Italian glass dolphins on an alabaster pedestal. "We interpret the note found by Arnie as jottings of a phone call with Dexter." He spoke over his shoulder. "Putting together the jottings produced this interpretation: Strip the office. Get to Heathrow at once. Destination Boca Raton Country Club."

Carlo closed his eyes as he assimilated the details. "And you and Reggie spoke of a Big Bang. Explain." The tone was sharp.

"So we did. Whatever Dexter's up to is planned for 4th January."

"Like what?"

Shawcross tried to recall what he had said on the bugged line. Had he mentioned the note found in Brannigan's flat? He decided he had not. "Our guess, a calculated one, is that Dexter doesn't yet have enough evidence. Otherwise he'd have gone to the cops in London - them or the Gaming Board. But we can't rely on that. We're working on the basis that he *does* have the evidence. We reckon he's cabooshed everybody to prevent me finding them."

"Scared you're gonna whack them, is he?" Letizione lowered himself into the chair, his spreading gut squashed against his desk. "Don' answer that! I won't believe you anyway. So what you doin' 'bout this shit?"

"Finding Dexter. Neutralizing him. When we've bled him white of facts," he paused "maybe we have to silence him."

Letizione thumped his desk. "No fuckin' murders! Fraud yes, whackin' no. Why you so goddamned keen to kill folk? You enjoy it or sump'n?"

Shawcross' lips hardened to paper thin. "Because it is ... effective. Because if Dexter can prove anything and maybe he can, then we're not going to enjoy our pension fund."

Letizione had heard enough. He left the shelter of his desk and stood uncomfortably close to the Englishman who tried to look unflustered. "Now listen you asshole. The game was to turn enough quick bucks to cure the liquidity issue. Low risk, you said. Skim off a slice for our trouble. Fine. Then once again become good citizens, everythin' legit." He let his angry features linger over-close a moment longer. "So now, you're ready to whack anyone in your path." He grasped Shawcross by his lapels and ripped him from his seat. Their faces were inches apart. "Goddammit! Ain't nothin' is worth killin' for."

"Let .. go .. of me." He waited until his jacket was freed. "Any better ideas? If I thought it would save us – and all this," he stretched out an arm to indicate the splendor of Space City, "yes, I would kill him."

"Okay, Aude. I heard what you said to Kyte. The time for messin's over. You're as worried as shit. The kid's got more'n enough to dump on us. He's outfoxed you real good. There's a lifetime in jail if we hang out here. I say we finish the meeting then head for Aruba. Strip the account. Then flip to Venezuela and then Brazil. See the guy in Recife for the face jobs. Then disappear. New life. No sweat. Leave Cedric and Kieran to sweep up the shit."

Shawcross moved to the desk and patted Carlo on the shoulder in a patronizing fashion. "Me worried? Look at the facts. It's December 15th. We've fifteen days until the ceremony, twenty days until 4th Jan to fix Dexter's lot. Why panic? We collect our performance bonuses on 1st January. If by then, they're still able to bust us, we empty the account and make a smart exit before Big Bang."

"Anythin' else you want to tell me?"

Shawcross frowned as he sat down again by the food and helped himself to some tomato and onion salad. "That was enough, wasn't it?"

"No." Carlo barked, fingers jabbing in accusation. "Like you and Panama. You held out on me. That guy you hacked to death down there."

Shawcross scowled but said nothing.

"Now besides not tellin' me – me who needed to know who I'm climbin' into bed with, you sure as hell said nothing on your application to the Gamin' Control Board here. No mention you'd ever worked in Panama. If they find out you been givin' them shit, these guys can be real mean. Not jus' with *your* license but all of us."

"I was young. A long time back. Self-defense."

"Not what I heard. So I'm tellin' you straight, man: any killin' between now and 4th January and I'm goin' right on down to the Grant Sawyer Building on East Washington. I'm gonna tell the Gamin' Board the truth. That I knew nothin' of Panama, wanted no part in whackin' nobody." Letizione's puffy face now showed he was angry beyond reason. All the festering grievances had erupted. "I'll tell them. I'm goin' to have you sent back to Panama. I bet their jails stink."

"If I go down, you go too. Believe me. I'll implicate you from your fat ass to your thick head."

"You go talkin' about whackin', then I'm past carin'." He looked from the window and saw the Shuttle glinting beneath the morning sun. "Space City was my dream. Sure, I was schooled here in Vegas with some of the hardest men alive but I learned from their mistakes. Keep scams simple, like skimmin' cash. *Snowball* was fine. Clever. But whackin'? Uh, oh. No! Y'know the lesson from those wise guy days? Once they started whackin' to silence rather than for revenge or discipline, they got busted." He sighed as if the anger had given way to resignation. "When Dukes appointed me President here, I thought I had a good partner. I trusted you. But with your la-di-dah limey accents, you and your Board stink like a steer's asshole." His face was now again disquietingly close to Shawcross. "Your trouble? You're too fuckin' arrogant. Won't listen."

"Cedric's lot will be here in ten minutes. You'd better go and clean up - wipe your sweaty face, change your stinking shirt, calm down a bit. Do something useful too - hire a local agent to see if Dexter's team are here. It's unlikely but get working on it anyway. I'm thinking maybe we can buy Dexter off."

Letizione was uncertain whether to believe this new idea but could see the logic. "Sure! Pay him off if need be."

Shawcross reached the door. "I'm going to the meeting room. See you in there – when you've relaxed a little. Well, rather a lot actually."

Alone now, Letizione stood in thought for a few moments before returning to his desk. He switched off the recording.

Mustique – 16th December 2002

Dex looked out of the cabin window on a perfect Caribbean morning. They were flying at six thousand feet now, starting their approach to the runway on the small Caribbean island of Mustique. They had left Barbados one hundred miles back and in the distance, the blip on the horizon was taking shape – the volcanic land rising from the deep blue of the ocean. "Must be one of the remotest spots on earth."

Scotty stared across in front of the young Englishman towards land. They were sitting next to each other in the Islander, the first sign of a thaw in the chilly relationship. "I guess maybe this *is* Paradise. But we could do with a few blondes to liven things up. Shawcross sure as hell ain't gonna find us here. Jackie doesn't know we're here does she? Nor Zara?"

Dex shook his head as the words of *Island in the Sun* played on his lips. "*Nobody* knows. Your pilot will follow to Barbados. He stays there until contacted, not knowing where we are. That's how it stays."

"I'm glad you'll be payin' me back for all this globe-trotting," Scotty observed in an attempt at humor. After landing in Barbados, the first signs of a thaw in his attitude had emerged.

Dex failed to see the joke. "Never forget it – *you* created this crisis. Those damned-fool notes you made. But I don't want to labor all that again. Paying for this trip is the least you can do." With another day gone and still no news from Chieseman, he sounded more confident than he felt.

He watched Adrian Ryder in the co-pilot's seat, his eyes studying the altimeter. Behind him were Kenny and Mark, each staring down at the Caribbean. He smiled reassuringly at them as the plane bobbled and bounced, wondering if they were both thinking of those left behind. He had lied about nobody knowing. Tiffany knew. But she wouldn't be saying anything. "Scotty, did you know that in it's heyday, Mustique was the number one party-place for the ultimate trendsetters. The Princess Margaret crowd were always flying in. She had a house here called *Les Jolies Eaux*. There were late night parties with her admirers and jet-set crowd. Though she's just died, some of the cachet had gone anyway. But you can't knock the place for privacy. Big movie stars and English titled classes still value Mustique for that. Lord Yarbury knows it well."

Kenny looked interested but Scotty's intervention prevented any comment. "What in hell's happening about our hit on Dukes? Why the fuck don't we jus' get on with it. That or forget it."

"I'll tell you when I'm ready." He pointed through the small window. "Look at that." Dex was admiring a multi-masted schooner that was making swift progress across the turquoise waters just offshore from a small cluster of buildings with red roofs.

Scotty peered down and took in the narrow strip of white sand with the foaming surf breaking onto it. He spoke softly. "You worried for Jackie?"

"Shawcross won't find her. She's staying with her mother in a rented cottage at Seahouses, a tiny village on the Northumberland coast. Cash paid upfront. Booked under a different name." The American weighed this up and appeared satisfied. He pulled his seatbelt a touch tighter as the plane dropped to under two hundred feet, for the final approach. It just cleared a low hill before dropping like a stone onto the tarmac just beyond.

Twenty minutes later, they had left the small yellow plane and were unpacking in a villa just across the narrow island. Mick Jagger's retreat was one way and Tommy Hilfiger's the other. According to their driver, *the rich guys* from London and New York would be arriving for Christmas *pretty damn soon, man.*

"It's beautiful," said Mark as he accepted a beer and stood beside the free-form pool. He was still wearing a long sleeved shirt and jeans, the only one not to have changed into tropical gear. The others had taken a stroll to the Cotton House Hotel just around the promontory.

"But you don't care about that, do you."

Mark's eyes wandered evasively, reminding Dex of FB. "Seven weeks away in Wiltshire and now another three." He shook his head. "Christmas here will be hell." He walked slowly towards the gazebo. "Sorry, Dex. Sometimes, I hate you. Sometimes I think you're my savior. Today, I'm pretty down about Emily."

"I understand."

"Me and Kath, we've been separated for ten months. When I left Clouds House, I told her I was in remission. She sounded sort of. Oh ..."

"More friendly?"

"Well, at least less hostile." He sat under the shade of the timbered gazebo and looked across the bay to a terracotta villa with a giant veranda facing a distant island. "I took it as a good start." The sound of the waves breaking gently a few feet away was soothing but Mark was beyond noticing. "I reckoned once I'd started a proper job rather than being Jeremy Legrange, Kath might have given me another chance. But disappearing, all mysterious, well she thinks I'm with some bit of rich stuff. I said a man was taking me but couldn't explain. 'Course, she thought that was worse!" His laugh was empty.

"If you can just hold out a bit longer, you'll be home. But remember what I said. No postcards mailed from here, no phone calls to home." Yet even as he said it, Dex felt a right shit. Once again, he was putting his personal dreams before all else. He made a mental note to chase those dilatory shysters in Peckham. "Cheer up. We'll go down to Basil's Bar later on, get a bit of party spirit going."

"Is Tiffany coming in?"

Dex felt embarrassed that she would arrive while the others remained celibate. This variation on *droit du seigneur* did not fit comfortably on him. "Yes. I hope she's coming."

"Scotty – he'll soon find some hot date here no problem, even with that eye of his. The rest of us? Adrian's a free agent but Kenny and me – hell we'll be the gooseberries."

Mark's viewpoint hit home. "I just don't know how I can help - short of renting some dusky maiden for you."

"I want Kath *and* Emily here."

Dex stood up, walked to the corner of the gazebo and watched a lizard scuttle into the undergrowth. A brightly hued butterfly flitted among the profusion of flowers and shrubs. Everything seemed so perfect – the depth of the colors, the fragrance of the oleanders, the sickly sweet frangipani, the pinks, the yellows, the whites and reds surrounded by the lush green density of the tropical foliage. And yet now their beauty was lost on him too.

He offered Mark a bowl of cheese biscuits as if it were enough to repair the damage. "She on email? Kath, I mean?"

Mark laughed his no. "But she has a phone."

"Let's walk down to Basil's Bar and phone a friend of mine in London from the village. It's a risk. He can then phone Kath - asking them to join us in Barbados. Mustique won't be mentioned. Do you have a pet name for her – so she'll know it's a genuine call?" He awaited a reaction but there was none. He looked across and saw Mark blinking back tears. "Think she'll come? I'll fix the tickets with a couple of calls."

Mark plucked a red flower and sniffed it for what seemed an age. "This must be the best place in the world to fall in love again." He rose and bear-hugged Dex. "It's worth a try. I call her T.T. She calls me S.B. Never ask me why!"

London 17th December 2002

Even in his own office, Shawcross had never before whooped. With his buttoned-up personality, he judged emotions as superfluous, even a problem. Apart from lust, blood-lust and greed, other feelings had never been a strong point. He had never cried at a funeral and had never paraded his heart on a sleeve. He recalled how thirty years ago Arnie Fisher had called him a cold fish. He'd been correct and had changed. Since then, he had learned how to squeeze out charm like toothpaste, dispensing banter to mask the powerful forces that ruled him. But now with nobody around, he jumped from his desk and strode round the room like a boxer who had just won by a first round knock-out. Arms punching the air in triumph, he shouted *yes, yes, yes* repeatedly as he circled his desk. Any lingering doubts had gone.

Mark is with Dex.

Mark is in Barbados.

He selected a chunky Bolivar and reclined in his chair. He kicked off his shoes and wiggled his toes, more at ease than for days. In front of him by his Mont Blanc pen were the notes of his conversation with Arnie Fisher. Originally, it had seemed like a long-shot, a needless expense bugging the phone at the Evans family home. But Arnie thought it essential and so he had approved the operation. Sometimes outsiders romp home at sixty-six to one. Just like this. The call had come in an hour ago London time. He re-read his neat writing. Someone called Declan had phoned from somewhere, speaking for Mark. After a few difficult exchanges, he'd asked Kath to bring Emily to Barbados all expenses paid. Mark would meet her at the airport. After some doubts and a few tears, Kath had agreed to take the Virgin flight on the 18th. With a sucked intake of breath, Shawcross' face hardened. The eyes grew cold, merciless. Now he had the luxury of two options – and twenty-four hours to decide which to choose.

He rang Space City. "Carlo. How's it going?"

"Good. All quiet."

"Don't bother looking for Dexter in Vegas. He's in the Caribbean. We'll get him in a couple of days, latest."

"Okay. What you doin' next?"

"Relaxing. Waiting for Dexter to entrap himself." The sly look on Shawcross' face was invisible to Letizione. "After that, I haven't decided." The lies slipped out easily.

Mustique –18th December 2002

Dex had been awake long before everyone else and so rather than cook in the villa, he had walked to the Cotton House for breakfast in the breezy openness of the Great Room. The large vaulted area was open on all sides to capture the breezes but it still needed ceiling fans whirring gently to fight against the sub-tropical humidity. Dex enjoyed the relaxed colonial feel but even more relished the luxury of being alone. There was no need to be funny, sympathetic, strong or ready to deflect any barbs from Scotty.

Stretched out in a wide and deep chair, it was easy to feel at peace with the world. In front of him were orange juice, exotic fruits and a basket of fresh bread and rolls with very strong Parisian coffee. Last night he and Kenny had put in place a plan to give any followers the slip once they left the airport with Kath and Emily. "That's the worry," he had explained to Kenny. "We must assume that Kath's phone was bugged. Therefore, someone will have either caught the same flight or will be at the airport to trail them to me."

"I know Bridgetown quite well. I've stayed there a couple of times to watch Test Matches. I know the perfect hotel on the West Coast. You can go in one entrance and out another. I'll fix a speedboat to whisk us to another hotel and a different car. No way, will they track us all to Mustique. But you will not go to Barbados. Like the Queen Bee, you must be protected."

Dex had not argued. He browsed a magazine about the island's history and when he had finished the last hot croissant, he went to the phone to catch up with Tiffany on her secret line.

"Hi, my darling. So how's New England? Everything just great?" Dex asked breezily.

She spoke slowly. "I'm so glad you rang. An hour ago, everything was just great. Now the bloody world has fallen apart."

Dex sensed so many emotions in her words. "Shawcross onto you? Al Qaeda? Something I've done?"

"Not exactly." Her voice sounded strained. He imagined her in a smart pant-suit and blouse, made up to perfection for the camera. "You obviously don't get the news out there."

"I can through the web but I haven't since yesterday."

"There's no easy way to tell you. Are you ready?"

"Go on."

"I was checking out the news from London. Usual stuff. Then they said that a five year old girl, Emily Evans had been snatched by a man in a car while she was playing near her home in Thames Ditton last evening." She paused. "Didn't you say she was flying over to join you?"

Dex stared at the wall, then at the receiver. He wanted to say something but no words would form. In his mind was the recollection of Mark yesterday. Dressed in a new red polo shirt and white shorts, he had excitedly bought clothes for Kath and Emily at the boutique in the tiny village of Lovells. "God! This is just too awful, Tiffany. I'll call you later."

He hooked up the hotel computer to the web and with restless fingers fumbled with the keyboard to find the page for Sky News. There was no mistake. Emily's cheeky grin filled the screen, together with more detail. She had been playing on her bike with an eight year old friend at a nearby hockey ground. Afterwards, while pushing her bike along the narrow track from the club-house to the main road a small blue family car had pulled up. A man in a cap had grabbed her and dumped her in the back seat. The other girl had described a tall man who was *old*. The police confirmed there had been no ransom demand. They had an open mind about the motive.

He thought back to that breakfast at Simpson's and the promise to play Connections. He remembered her big smile and sadness when Mark had whisked her away. "Goodbye Mr Dex," she had said. "Fuck you Shawcross. But I'm coming to get you." He inhaled deeply to ward off the panic that had gripped him at the prospect of telling Mark. Then after a last look at the little face, he logged off, hating himself for his mistake. The warnings from Tiffany and Scotty descended heavily onto his shoulders and he cursed the way that Chieseman had pissed him about.

He stood up slowly, his head spinning with anger. He felt as if his blood had drained to his feet leaving everything else running on empty. As he walked mindlessly along the track from the hotel to the villa, he never noticed the beautiful symmetry of the conical sugar-mill. Head down, he never acknowledged the gardener's cheery good morning as he exited under the hotel's pillared entrance. Every step brought him closer to facing Mark. His face, slightly tanned from yesterday's boat trip, was now ashen. He slowed even more, trying to rehearse what he would say, each step leaden as he drew closer to breaking the news. He knew it would be ugly.

"Hi!" exclaimed Mark cheerily as Dex appeared by the pool. He had donned a sunhat and was carrying a small doll for Emily. "The mule's all ready. Fed it ten minutes ago." Normally, they would all have laughed at the joke. Guests on the island used only electric golf buggies. The Royal jet set had started the tradition of calling them mules.

"Mark. We need to talk." He beckoned Scotty, Adrian and Kenny from their loungers. Grumbling that Dex was dragging them from the poolside, they followed. Nobody sat down. From the bleak look on his face, they soon appreciated Dex had something important to say. Remembering how his own legs had felt on hearing the news, he suggested Mark sit on a kitchen chair. "There's no easy way to say this, Mark. I've just read the news from London. Emily's been kidnapped."

Who said what, who did what was a blur when Dex later tried to recreate those torrid few minutes. Except for Mark who sat head in hands, everyone was shouting. So vile were Scotty's jibes as Dex tried to comfort Mark that he could not be sure precisely how he had responded. Mark clung to Dex. Dex gripped Mark. Adrian kept saying that *shouting won't help* as Scotty let rip with a torrent of abuse and *I-told-you-so's*. Eventually Kenny took charge. He alone seemed calm. "That's enough, Scotty. Mark – you have to be at home with Kath. She'll be distraught. She needs you."

Adrian nodded agreement. "She'll assume it's a sex maniac. At least we know it's not that." Dex did not care to add that it was rather worse.

"You can't fly back alone. I'll go with you," said Kenny.

"No. I must go back," said Dex. "I'm to blame. Should've realized that Emily was our weakest point."

"Master stroke by Shawcross," agreed Kenny. "But I want to be with Mark and get him home."

Dex took advantage of Scotty's silence to assert some authority again. "It's bloody obvious what Shawcross' game is. He's cornered, knows we have the evidence. He's blackmailing me to forget everything. If I act against him, Emily's not going to survive. So he knows I'll not move. He has nothing to lose. His one chance, crazy though it may seem, is to ransom her. I have to deal with him. Only I have the evidence. Apart from my bollocks on a plate, that's what he wants – all the evidence."

Scotty waited for the end of the exchange, his Dodgers cap worn back to front. "Right on! You sort this out. Give the bastard his evidence. Whatever. You've played God too fuckin' long, jus' lovin' pullin' our strings. Makin' us fuckin' salute you as if you were royalty. Well, I for one have had enough."

Kenny interrupted the rant. "Shut the fuck up Scotty, to stoop to your usual so-charming style of speech. That attitude won't help. Dex is still trying to deliver to help you; to help everyone." He pointed a stubby finger at Scotty and then continued in his slightly nasal tone. "Don't glare at me. You know it's true." Fingers pointed, he stared at Scotty as if defying him to disagree. The American was breathing heavily, his blue shirt heavily stained by sweat from the steamy heat. He screwed up his mouth, pushed back his cap but said nothing, so Kenny continued. "Same goes for Mark. Dex paid to save Mark from his addiction. Until just now, he was fighting to save Mark's marriage." He moved closer to Scotty who looked increasingly uncomfortable, fiddling with his hands, his eyes restless. Kenny again wagged his finger in admonishment. "Dex is obsessive, single-minded. Without that, he would have achieved nothing." Scotty pretended to be looking at yesterday's paper as it lay on the table. "But you? What have you done to help? Nothing. We're in hiding," he raised his voice "due to you. So this is your fault for disobeying orders and selling our Crown Jewels. Meantime, you sulk like Eeyore in a corner of the forest. It's time you gave up feeling sorry for yourself. That journalist last week was right. *You are just a washed-up driver - a slow-coach on the fast-track to oblivion.* Good description!" Kenny waved his hand with dismissive contempt. "So get back onside. We're in this together. *We* have a problem. *We* need to work together to solve it." He pounded his hand on the table as the American was about to reply. "Don't interrupt. I haven't finished." He paused to gather breath. "*You* used to be called ruthless, a power maniac. A selfish single-minded driver. As World Champion, you saw those criticisms as *qualities*. You said so yourself. Wouldn't be World Champ without them, you said. I saw you interviewed. So, you hypocrite, don't mess with Dex when he most needs help."

"Thanks," said Dex breaking an embarrassed silence after Kenny had finished. Scotty stood up, his eyebrows knitted and turned away to lean against the open door to the terrace. "You think you've covered every angle but someone else sees the gaps. I should've anticipated Emily as a weakness. I'm sorry. I've screwed up. Kenny: you go back to London with Mark and stay with him in Thames Ditton. Get a new mobile number and we can keep in touch."

"And all the evidence?"

"Surrender. Emily is all that matters. So I'm going to return the evidence to Shawcross. The man has nothing to lose now. He's a murderer and thanks to Scotty's leak, he knows I can prove it. Kenny: tip off the media from Barbados that Mark's coming home. Be his spokesman. Explain you're just a friend and were house-guests near Bridgetown of someone called Finlay Dexter. Say I've gone to Las Vegas on business. No more, no less."

"You going to Vegas?"

"London actually. I'll fly to Paris and then slip in on the Eurostar train. If Shawcross were to find me. " He shrugged the unsaid message. "I've got to retrieve all the evidence , then I'll do the deal with Shawcross, hopefully in Vegas."

"Why there?"

"Because it would be hard for Shawcross to smuggle Emily to the USA. So if I can get him there, there's less chance he'll harm her. Sort of divide and rule.

"And me?" Scotty was fiddling with an ashtray as if it were a child's comforter. "Do I go home to Vegas or stay here?"

"I'll need you in Vegas. To help with the hand-over of the papers. Can you get back there with Adrian – low profile?"

"Fly my plane into Phoenix and drive?" Scotty agreed without enthusiasm.

"Don't go home."

"Hell, yes. I'm goin' home. I'll know if they're watchin'. See I live in a guard-gated community. Ain't nobody gets into it without permission."

Dex was reluctant but decided to avoid a confrontation. He knew it was a mistake *and* weak leadership but he was still reeling from the shock. "Okay. We'll let it seem as if I'm there with you. Pick up a new cellphone somewhere. Phone me only on my private mobile. Don't use your land-line. Don't use my original cellphone number. Assume it's bugged."

"The hand-over in Vegas. What's your game?" Scotty looked interested at last.

"No games. No tricks. Once that bastard has proved Emily's unharmed, I want to hand over the evidence somewhere *very* public. Say in the middle of a hotel lobby. I don't trust Shawcross. He wants the evidence and then me dead."

"Will you contact him?"

"If need be. But my guess is that he'll email me. Maybe has already. Dukes have the details of every member." His confidence was returning and he was at once both animated and resolute. As he spoke, the usual rich tones returned and his voice was sharp and commanding. His words had been emphasized by the flailing arms of a tic-tac man. He'd ridden the body blows while Mark had been sitting quietly. Suddenly, Mark stood up, grasped Dex and broke down, sobbing uncontrollably. "Please ... with Emily ... no risks." The words were audible though spoken from deep into Dex' shoulder against which he was leaning.

"Mark, I'll do nothing to endanger Emily. And I doubt he will either. But I need to protect myself too."

Mark drew away. "Can I phone Kath?"

Dex shook his head. "From here? No. Both Shawcross *and* the cops will have your home phone bugged. I expect they'll have found the taps used by Shawcross when planting their own."

Adrian Ryder nodded. "If they found a wiretap, they'll assume this was no ordinary sexual predator. They'll keep that quiet while they try to find out who bugged the line and why."

"Good sense, Adrian. Shawcross certainly won't contact your home, Mark." Dex went to the fridge and poured himself an iced water. "We leave in thirty minutes. And Kenny don't contact Jackie. She's as vulnerable as Emily. As for Zara, I guess you won't want to contact her will you Adrian?"

Adrian shook his head. "No. "

Scotty scratched his muscular and hairy arm as he crossed the room towards Dex who was standing shoulder to shoulder with Mark. "You created this mess because you are one lousy listener. But getting the kid back – sure count me in." He looked at the tiled floor and spoke slowly. "See, I got a kid too. Her Mom won't let me see her. Brook'll be five in February."

Nobody said a word. The revelation was too full of implications. Dex eventually spoke. "Sounds tough. Tell me about it later. Right now, we need to get to Barbados." He gazed out at the richness of the colors in the garden with the blue of the ocean glinting from beneath the trees. "We'll come back. It's not Paradise Lost. It's Paradise Postponed." As the others went to their rooms to pack, Dex hooked up his laptop to the phone line and clicked onto Outlook. Among the usual smattering of incoming emails about losing weight and Viagra substitutes from Hong Kong, there it was: marked with a red exclamation mark for urgency – an email from an unusual address and signed Trent Harrison.

When you receive this, you may be unaware that unknown persons have seized Emily Evans, Mark Evans' daughter. As Mark is your guest at present, I am sure you will inform him. If you want proof, get a paper or watch British news.

I know someone who can get her freed. You will know what that person wants – the evidence - all of it with assurances that nothing further will come of your investigations and wild allegations. The police are involved now but if you do something as stupid as naming any suspect to them, that would be a death penalty for Emily.

Of course, if you went to the police anywhere about any of the other matters you've been trying to rake up, you would never find Emily alive. Total cooperation is essential. You may think this email is foolish. Think again. Emily's death will forever haunt you. Your suspect will never be caught.

After handing over the "evidence", you and your associates must never again raise any allegations or cause any trouble. Total silence is essential. To anyone tempted to ignore this factor, I can only say that some people are most unforgiving and have long memories.

I suggest we meet in Las Vegas on 23rd December - the safety of Emily until then can be assured if you agree to cooperate precisely.

Please reply urgently.

Trent Harrison

Two hours later as they waited for the London flight in the airport at Bridgetown, Dex had gained some kudos for predicting that Shawcross would be in touch. He had shown them all the email. "No surprises there then," suggested Kenny. "It has to be from him."

"Why would Shawcross choose Vegas to meet? Something stinks."

"Perhaps he wants the meeting in Vegas because *he's* there already," suggested Ryder. Everyone laughed supportively at the obvious commonsense. "I doubt Shawcross grabbed Emily himself."

Still amused by a remark that had broken the long tense period, Dex nodded agreement. "I'll find out." He put up a hand instinctively to ruffle his hair the way he used to but remembered it had gone.

"I won't be threatened by Shawcross about *my* life." Scotty Brannigan was all jutted jaw and defiance as he poured Diet Coke for himself and Mark. "Get the kid. Then we get him. To hell with his long memory. The sooner he's jailed the better."

"Double-cross him?" Unusually Dex was cautious. "I was planning on a quiet life, not having to look over my shoulder."

"Surrender?" Scotty's voice showed the contempt he felt. "I want two things: rescue the kid and then see Shawcross jailed. Or dead."

"Game's changed, Scotty. There's no hiding place now." Kenny provided more straight talking. Dex appreciated anything the agent now said. For a Londoner from a poor home with no advantages of a good education, he had learned the hard way and had a knack of pitching his views so well.

"You're both right." Dex jotted some ideas on a notepad. "I don't like Shawcross dictating our future either. Let's get Emily freed first whatever it takes and then review how we fix him. If we can." Dex pushed aside the crust of his pizza, stood up and stretched.

Adrian Ryder looked at each in turn. "Maybe an anonymous tip-off?"

"I expect Shawcross will have covered his tracks by then."

"Some tracks are hard to conceal – if you know where to look." Adrian had put on his most serious police officer tone. "Point is, nobody's been looking at Dukes the right way. Financial records that appeared kosher may not stand scrutiny. All those NCIS forms they have to fill for large or suspicious transactions. There's something odd there. I checked them. Zara checked them before me. They were all in order. But that of course is impossible."

"You mean because of all that cash they were taking in?"

"Right. It's all to do with prevention of money-laundering. They were receiving millions in cash and paying most of it out again by casino checks. That's reportable, big time. But I'm puzzled the NCIS never contacted our Board about it."

"The NCIS?"

"Sorry. The National Criminal Investigation Service. Casinos have to file reports with them. And Dukes did. I checked the forms."

Dex sipped a pineapple drink." So perhaps you saw the copies but the originals never actually reached the NCIS?"

Ryder looked at Dex as if he were the Messiah. "Heh! You could be right. So maybe we tip off the NCIS."

"But Shawcross would blame us – and be in pursuit."

Dex was hesitant. "Once Emily's safe, then it could work. Whether Shawcross would take revenge is impossible to guess. Not an attractive gamble."

Kenny had been bursting to add something. "But if the Gaming Board or the NCIS, for example, were to stumble on this themselves, a paranoid bastard like Shawcross would still assume we had tipped them off and would seek revenge." He waited to ensure they had the implication. "So we might just as well ensure they *do* find out."

"You're right, Kenny. That's just what the bastard would think."

London - 19th December 2002

Dex mounted the stairs to the Chambers of Mr Charles Bart-Pemberton QC. Called to Gray's Inn during 1966 and now also a Bencher, he had no wish to be a judge and was at the peak of the profession. With him was his solicitor, Rufus Chandler who had dashed over from his offices in Lincoln's Inn Fields at short notice. The grandfather clock by the Clerk's Room struck a melodious four. From floor to ceiling were All England Law Reports, Atkins Court Forms, European Community Reports and reams of legal magazines, many turning brown with age.

Dex felt stifled by the stale air in the windowless waiting-room. The small area smelled of dusty paper. He imagined the hundreds of previous clients nervously awaiting a *consultation* with one of Her Majesty's Counsel and worrying too about the legal fees running up by the second.

They were ushered into the presence of the *great man*, veteran of many a skirmish representing crooked company directors and other white collar criminals. Because he normally defended white collar crooks seeking to escape the rap, Chandler had chosen him as the best to test the weight of the evidence *against* Shawcross. The instructions he had delivered had asked the questions: *Could you get Shawcross off? If so how?*

After exchanged pleasantries, Bart-Pemberton's booming voice turned to the matters in hand. He articulated every word, speaking slowly as if addressing judge and jury. "I assume," he said after a noisy slurp of tea from a bone china cup "that you want me to set up a meeting with the SFO or somebody in the Fraud Squad. Indeed, I have just been debating whether to make a personal approach to Charmaine Waites, the Director of the Serious Fraud Office, something rather unusual. The SFO doesn't routinely take referrals from the public. But then this is a very unusual case. I expect you know her Rufus?"

"Not my scene."

"I knew her as a contemporary. I think she'll take it. The work you've done, Mr Dexter is, if I may say so, remarkable. Truly so. We don't need the Fraud Squad to investigate, though when they do I'm sure they'll find more. The groundwork is here, though Charmaine will obviously want to raid Dukes for more evidence. Probably use her powers under section 2 of the Criminal Justice Act 1987."

He grabbed a piece of fruit cake and paused to munch but gave no indication that he expected any comment yet. "We grew up in the law together. She often prosecuted where I defended. We have a plausible, no that's too strong a word ... a potential murder case against Shawcross for killing Mick Glenn. That evidence is likely to improve." He riffled through the ring-binders. "The disappearance of Jacques Crabant is interesting but just speculation. The Panama police may want to reopen their case on the fella that Shawcross hacked to death - but that's not our concern.

"The FBI," he continued "also has enough material here to throw several books at Dukes' Board. There's abundant evidence - the films, the extraordinary bank statements. I don't know what use can be made of them." He looked imperiously over his spectacles, impressed yet disapproving at the way they had been obtained. "But knowing they exist will encourage the Feds to get them anyway. So, we have in-house fraud, fixed card decks, cheating the players at roulette, two burglaries, a witness Forster-Browne who will turn Queen's Evidence, international money-laundering, fraud in Brussels and using hot or stolen money to pay off the American banks. Lot of international cross-border issues. Very serious indeed. Yes. I think Charmaine would like to put her team on that."

The Queen's Counsel tucked his thumbs into his bulging waistcoat pockets and rocked back in his chair, his small eyes afire with burning anticipation. "What do you think, Rufus?"

"I agree. The gaps in the evidence will soon be filled once Dukes' staff start squealing to the cops."

"Sorry to interrupt but might I say something, sir?" Dex' face and voice showed his hesitation. He was tired anyway after the overnight flight and the dash to catch the Eurostar at the Gare du Nord. The dry air in the room was heavy with stale pipe smoke and his voice sounded unusually thin.

"Please do," Bart-Pemberton flourished a meaty fist across the green and gold leather of the desk.

"I want the evidence back. I don't want you to go to anyone."

"Waste of bloody time my little speech was!" The QC bounced his hands off his pin-striped trousers and roared with laughter. Then there was a shocked silence broken only by Bart-Pemberton blowing his nose like a trumpet into an extravagantly sized red hankie with white spots. "You don't have to answer but I'd be interested to know why."

"I think," said Chandler sounding like a church mouse in comparison to the stentorian tones of the barrister "well, I mean, Dex, my take is that we'd like to know we've not let you down. That you don't want other advice."

Dex shifted uncomfortably. The staring eyes of the two lawyers bored into him – Bart-Pemberton's beady black eyes fixing him from over half-rimmed titanium frames and Chandler unblinking, somewhat owl-like behind a pair of Harry Potters. The QC's luxurious hair was pepper and salt, turning silver and swept back in a raffish manner. The barrister was stroking his silvered sideburn. "No. Don't think that. I'm very happy. It's just that, er, well. Ah, you see I don't want to go to the police *at the moment.*" He had given up hope of the QC offering him any of the fruit cake and so helped himself, believing reasonably enough he was paying for it at one thousand per hour for the two experts. "I haven't abandoned. I may want to continue later."

Bart-Pemberton shifted his bulk with much groaning and sighing and then leaned forward, elbows on his desk, face in his hands. "Old Shawcross pay you off?" The tone was gruff and direct.

Dex' laugh was strained, matching his voice. "No, no. I can't be bribed."

"Well, if you won't tell us why, that's your privilege. It's a pity. I think the Director of the SFO would have romped this home. And rightly so." He paused to gather the photos, film and sheaves of statements. He found his backing-sheet from Chandler and methodically stacked everything together until it stood some fifteen inches high. Then with a practiced flourish, he bound up the entire bundle in pink ribbon and scribbled a note on the backsheet. "So its goodbye Mr Dexter, at least for now."

"At least for now."

They crossed the sandy-colored Wilton carpet with a starburst motif. Behind the door stood a table covered with similar large bundles all neatly bound in pink ribbon. "Don't go losing this lot," joked Chandler as Dex struggled to adjust to their weight.

"I won't do that. But there's a duplicate set in Las Vegas anyway."

"Collecting that too?" The suggestion from the wily QC was delicately weighted.

Dex grinned without comment.

"Well, I found this a fascinating exercise anyway," said Bart-Pemberton heartily. "Thanks Rufus for instructing me. Most interesting case." He grasped Dex' hand in a huge grip. "By the way. Your change of heart," he pointed to the bundle "has nothing to do with that story in the newspapers. The little girl Emily Evans who was abducted."

Dex said nothing.

"That witness of yours," Bart-Pemberton continued. "Mark Evans. I was only just reading his preliminary statement after lunch. He had a daughter called Emily who lived in Thames Ditton. Funny coincidence."

Dex said nothing.

"But then life's full of coincidences. The evening paper say Evans was in the Caribbean when this happened. Dreadful business." He lowered his head to ensure full eye-contact at close range. "That's a nice tan, you've picked up."

Dex met the barrister's piercing stare without flinching. "Thank you."

"Well, take care. You're very young. You've achieved miracles in exposing all this. But don't play God. Especially with someone like Shawcross involved, otherwise you might be meeting Him rather sooner than you would prefer. Goodbye Mr Dexter. Merry Christmas." The darting black eyes hardened for a moment but then as quickly softened as the QC relished the discomfort he had caused.

Outside, the evening traffic was beeping and crawling through Fleet Street and westward into the Strand. The fumes of diesel hung heavily under the cloudy sky and the sound of boozy bonhomie drifted out from The George. After saying thanks to Chandler, Dex wheeled his heavy bag into Daly's wine bar. He dumped it under the deal table and eased onto the bench seat with a large Guinness.

He drank deeply into the smooth blackness and then gazed at nothing as he finalized the next moves. Staying at Porky House was too risky, a no-brainer. Even going there was chancy. But his new credit card starting from tomorrow would be there and his check book – both forgotten in the hasty departure. He phoned the Waldorf just across the street and booked a room and then called FB. Using his code name of Alec Lucas, he asked to be connected. After a few meaningless words with him about modems, he rang off and waited for a call back. It was a long five minutes. "FB. Thanks. Besides you, who would Shawcross use to do his dirty work?"

"It's Reggie Kyte inside. Outside he uses an agent. I'm pretty sure he's called Arnie Fisher. His office is in Goodge Street." There was a pause. "Heh! Was that a London number I just dialed. You back here?"

Dex thought quickly and replied without hesitation. "No. Vegas. That cell number is patched through to me anywhere. Some system called Global Roaming! Where's Shawcross?"

FB seemed satisfied. "In Vegas too and we're not expecting him back until nearer Christmas."

"Jude Tuson?"

"She was playing last night."

"Still signing strangers in?"

"No. She was alone."

"Thanks. FB. Is Shawcross at Space City?"

"Bellagio."

"Huh! That's odd. Bye."

Dex was disappointed about Jude. He had convinced himself that Shawcross would use Jude to look after Emily. She was an obvious person. That now seemed unlikely. He dialed Max Chieseman. As the number rang, he imagined the seedy figure seated at his cluttered desk, cigarette stuck to his bottom lip. "Is it ready?"

"Good news and bad news me old son. Yes, it's ready. The bad news is we're shut from today until 2nd January. Christmas y'know. Can't deliver."

Dex gripped the phone as if it were Chieseman's throat. "We've barely eaten our Easter Eggs and you're closing for Christmas! Look Max, get this clear! I don't care if you dress up as fucking Santa Claus and deliver on the back of a sleigh. You *are* going to deliver by noon on Monday 23rd December latest. That is an order! Understood?"

"It's a work of art, mate. Bleedin' van Gogh wasn't pressurized like this."

"Van Gogh cut off his own ear. In your case, I shall personally visit you in Peckham and it won't be your ears I cut off. Get this straight. The time for fucking me about is over."

Chieseman's whiny tone was pleading. "Be reasonable mate! That'll mean overtime for the lads."

"Merry Christmas, Scrooge. Deliver on Monday! If not, expect to be singing carols in falsetto. The pissing about is over. Got it?"

"You're a hard man Mr Cornelius. I'll fix it."

Dex was still smiling at the use of his false name as he rang Tiffany.

"Any news?" Her voice showed her anxiety.

"Not that you want. I'm expecting another email from Shawcross. Emily's still missing."

"Police getting nowhere?"

"I'm talking to Kenny in the morning. He'll know. There's nothing in tonight's Standard to suggest any progress. Where are you?"

"Middle of nowhere. Bowling Green, Kentucky. Shawcross will never find me here. *Nobody* could find this place. Nor would they want to in winter. Then tonight it's back to Washington and fly to Vegas in the afternoon. So what's your next move?"

"I'm trying to work out who Shawcross is using to look after Emily. And don't say Jude – it isn't her." He stopped, wondering if Tiffany would suggest something, but she said nothing. "I'm flying to Vegas tomorrow, collecting the documents from Otto. I'll meet you there. I've told Shawcross by email we'll hand over everything in return for Emily at the godforsaken hour of one am on the 23rd. All that's left to agree with Shawcross are the small details."

"Won't he double-cross you?"

"You mean kill Emily? I doubt it. He'll release her once he has my evidence. Will he try to out-think me? Yes. I'm sure he will. If he can get the penny and the bun, so much the better."

"Meaning?"

"Kill me. Grab the documents and release Emily."

"You sound relaxed about it."

"No choice," he laughed unconvincingly. "But I'm not going to carry the documents to the meeting."

"You'll double-cross him? That'll be a death sentence for Emily."

"No. No. Not that. No double-crossing. He'll get the documents, well one set anyway. He can't know if there's a duplicate. The clever bit is *I'm* not going to take them to the rendezvous in the Barbary Coast."

"Who is?"

"You!" He laughed as he heard her gasp. "You'll do it won't you?"

"I don't understand."

"You'll have the documents in the hotel room at the Barbary Coast, just opposite Caesar's Palace. Scotty will drive me to the meeting but without any documents. He should be able to shake off any pursuers, even with that shoulder. But if we're taken out, then Shawcross gets nothing in the car. But at precisely one am you'll hand them over, if Shawcross shows up. Which I doubt if he's tried to kill us first."

"Of course I'll do it. Anything to get Emily released. If this comes off, it'll be a great story."

"Except Shawcross insists on permanent total silence."

From the way she spoke, all clipped and terse, Dex could imagine her face, cheeks sucked in and narrowed eyes. "You won't be scared off by his threats will you?"

"I could be. I'd rather look forward to a peaceful life with you."

"No, Dex. You'll get no peace from me *or* yourself unless you crush that bastard. You'll have your duplicate documents. Once Emily is safe, use them. This man must be destroyed." She spoke with a determination that surprised him.

He muttered that of course she was right but in his mind he knew he could only decide on this once Emily was free. "When do you get to Vegas?"

"Around 8pm, Vegas time."

Timing was going to be tight. His mind fought to work out how he could be at the one am Monday morning rendezvous in Vegas and then in Dukes to play roulette that day. "We may even get Christmas together then. Somewhere."

"That's postponed. Dex, We can't celebrate Christmas while Emily is still a prisoner."

"If the plan works, she'll be free. You take a suite at the Barbary Coast from tomorrow. I'll come down the chimney when I arrive from the airport."

Tiffany laughed but then her voice hardened. "Dex. How about this? I check in under another name - say Alice Maltby."

Dex interrupted. "Sounds rather middle-age spread with a bun and a hair-net. Probably sucking a peppermint."

"Don't get carried away! Here's my idea. You *stay with me*, hair-net or not, until one am on Monday. You never do drive to the hotel. Shawcross *can't* get you. He won't know how you are getting there. You suddenly emerge from an elevator with the documents."

"Brilliant!" His exclamation was loud enough for a smooching couple in the next booth to break their clinch and look across at him. "And how about this? We somehow lead Shawcross to *expect* me to arrive by car. That'll expose whether he tries anything en route."

"That's a hard sell to Scotty. Setting him up as the chauffeur."

Dex had to agree. "You're right. I'll talk to him and then duck the torrent of abuse. But it's important Shawcross never imagines I'm in the hotel."

"We hide under the blankets from tomorrow until Monday."

"Reminds me of the old fruits of life joke."

"Yeah, yeah, yeah! I've heard it too."

"I'm off to Porky House now. Pick up some essentials. I'll be at the Waldorf tonight. With the papers."

"Take care. Call me later."

"Will do, *Alice*. Don't worry. Shawcross is nearer you than me. And thanks. That was a great idea." He blew a couple of kisses down the line and saw the young couple were still watching him as he picked up the evidence. An idea had struck him, something he could organize later from the hotel

London – 19th December 2002

Earlier that afternoon, Shawcross had studied the email from Dex. Its arrival had eased a great worry – that perhaps Dex wouldn't open his computer. Dressed in sweat shirt, parka, golfing trousers and suede loafers, Shawcross was far from Vegas, sitting anonymously in an Internet Café in London's Notting Hill Gate, not far from his home. He pushed aside the remains of someone's burger and considered his response. From somewhere close to him came the smell of garlic, making it hard to concentrate and harder still to touch the filthy keyboard. He read the email again.

• *I'll come alone. Meet me at the bar in the Barbary Coast Casino at one am on the 23rd.*

• *We toss a coin for choice of hotel from those adjacent - Caesar's, the Flamingo, Bally's and Bellagio.*

• *We get a security guard from the Barbary Coast to carry the suitcase with the evidence to the winning hotel.*

• *Hotel staff take us to a suite with special security provided by them. Without that, we do not leave the lobby.*

• *Hotel security will be on guard the entire time outside the suite door.*

• *A webcam video link from London to Vegas will be set up via personal computers.*

• *Emily must be seen seated in a van, moving and talking on camera with that day's Times held in her hands.*

• *I will produce all the evidence for inspection.*

• *Emily must then be dropped off by the seats outside the Queen's Head pub in Brook Green W6. Someone will be there to meet her between 9am and 12 noon London time.*

• *The van can be driven off.*

• *Your driver can confirm on the video link that he has not been followed.*

- *I have no problem if false number plates are used.*

- *Once my contact phones to say Emily is safe and the van has gone, I will leave accompanied by security.*

- *You will remain in the suite for thirty minutes.*

- *No double-cross is planned - not by me anyway.*

- *I just want Emily freed.*

Shawcross muttered in irritation as he read the terms. No way would he agree to be a rat in a trap. He went to the counter and ordered a biodegradable cup of something they sold as coffee. Quickly, he typed out a response.

"Your complex procedure in Vegas borders on the paranoid but my friend has agreed to the London end of the arrangements.

In Vegas, we shall meet at the Barbary Coast bar at one am on the 23rd.

*I will **not** be the last to leave the chosen hotel.*

*I will leave **first** with the evidence*

***You** will stay there for thirty minutes before checking out – and will pay off the hotel and security staff!*

Confirm this deal soonest.

Trent Harrison.

He pressed the Send button and sat for a moment, imagining Dexter perhaps even now reading it at Brannigan's luxury villa in Vegas. But he might not be there. Just because Sky News had mentioned he was traveling there from the Caribbean did not mean he had to believe it. He had not been at Boca Raton – an expensive red herring that had been. No matter. Dexter and the evidence would be at the rendezvous at one am.

He decided that it was time to hire some old Vegas friends. He rose from the battered chair and left behind the fetid atmosphere of the crammed internet room. Outside, he ignored a group of carol singers and their money bucket shaken at him. By the time he had reached the junction at Pembridge Road, his mind was made up.

After dumping the evidence in the safe at the Waldorf, Dex tubed it to St John's Wood. After all the limos and private jets, he found the normality of the post rush-hour Underground strangely enjoyable. As the Jubilee Line raced under Baker Street, he could even feel nostalgia for the drawn pallor of the pinched faces. He remembered the bad times in Kilburn when taking the tube meant a hateful start to another loathsome day in the City.

All around, Emily's face stared out from the Standard and he wondered if Kath and Mark were giving each other support. Kenny would be their tower of strength and wisdom, hampered only by the inability to explain just what he knew. The long escalator at St John's Wood brought him to the surface and for a moment, he stood under the station canopy as the traffic streamed northwards on Wellington Road, the car lights cutting swathes through the gloom of the miserable evening.

He checked his watch. He was due to phone Scotty at Otto Schneider's in ten minutes. As he entered Grove End Road, he realized that winter had set in as an icy blast straight from the Arctic slapped freezing sleet across his face. It settled in his hair and stung against his cheeks. He pulled up the collar on the donkey jacket he'd bought at the Gare du Nord. Along the darkened side street, he was alert for any sign of someone following him. Ahead, he saw the red phone box, its flicker of light barely visible in the sleet. He dialed the Vegas number and Otto Schneider handed him over to Scotty.

"It's fixed. We RV at the Barbary Coast at one am on the 23rd to deliver the evidence. No, the cops are getting nowhere. But look, my concern is a double-cross that leaves me dead but Emily free. I want people watching out for me in the Barbary Coast, Caesars, Ballys, the Flamingo and Bellagio. Discreetly."

"No problem. We'll have the area heavy with our guys. Anythin' else?"

"That's just insurance. I'm thinking of setting him up but need your help. You'll need a blow-up doll." Dex laughed even as he said it.

"S'long as its not male, she's pretty an' don' fart, you're on. What's the game? Not puttin' the kid at risk are you?"

"Here's the plan."

Scotty listened from his chair at the foot of Schneider's raised table. From this position, he could only see Otto's shiny black shoes and red socks. "Sure. I'll set that up. Anything else?"

"It'll be dangerous – that journey."

"Sure. I'll take that chance."

"Thanks, Scotty. Christ, it's cold in this phone box. My fingers can hardly hold the receiver any longer. I want Carlo watched 24 -7 in case he does a runner." He shivered as the wind whistled through the crack by the door. "Shawcross *must* be convinced I'm staying with you. Here's the idea. Using your *home* line so any Shawcross' bugs can listen in, you ring my cellphone on 21st at five pm. When I answer, I won't say anything. You'll then talk as if you're *answering my call made from your place*. Switch us round. Okay."

"You sure are cookin' with gas, tonight. Go on."

"You'll say *hi, how ya doin'*. I'll say *I'm pissed off waiting for you to come back from the casino*. You say, *shit, well, I'll be home real soon*."

"Sure. I'll do that. And then I leave home on the 23rd apparently to drop you off at the Barbary Coast by one am. Right?

"Correct." The damp chill had penetrated his bones and he was anxious to get away to restore some life into the aching limbs. "There's a real Jack the Ripper atmosphere here in London – it's a dark, filthy night and nobody but me around. Are you collecting the evidence from Otto?"

"Everything is going to my safe."

"No. I've changed my mind. Leave it with him. For now."

"Why?" Scotty knew from the silence he'd get no explanation. "As you wish. Take care then."

"Last thing. As soon we've freed the girl, we fly to London for Reverse Labby. Have the jet ready to fly at about two. Monday evening is take-on Dukes time."

"Count on me, if she's free."

Hillside Road was another two minutes walk and by the time he turned into the darkened narrow street, the raw chill had even penetrated his donkey-jacket. The sleet had soused his hair. His cheeks and ears were raw and tingling. As a motor-cycle roared along Abbey Road, he spun round, a tired over-reaction but it was only a courier heading north. Otherwise all was quiet. Not even the dog lovers were out. His well-heeled neighbors, who Dex viewed as anally retentive and boring as hell, rarely walked further than to their BMWs or Range-Rovers anyway. Dex imagined them stuffing themselves with marzipan around their Christmas trees while talking in plummy tones of pending ski trips to Whistler or St Moritz.

He looked down the street for any sign that Shawcross had the house watched. There was nothing. Nothing *seemed* different - not a car parked anywhere, no figures apparently lurking behind one of the many trees that leaned away from the wind's keen grasp. Satisfied too that the small front garden was empty, he turned between the familiar white gates to enter the garden.

Unlike the others he had passed, Porcupine House looked as austere and unwelcoming as a Scottish manse. There were no fairy lights shining from the windows and no holly displays with red bows fixed to the solid front door. As he approached the kitchen door down the side of the house, he could almost see Beth walking ahead of him, tapping her white stick against the edge of the flower–bed or sitting with him by the pond reading her books in braille. When this was all over, he would sell up.

He unlocked the door and was greeted by warm air. The central heating was running fine, the purring noise from the gas boiler beside him was reassuring. At least the house felt less unwelcoming once the kitchen light had flooded the room. The cold tap was still dripping, the biscuit tin was where it had been left before the scrambled exit. He switched on the hall light, picked the stack of mail from the mat and was about to enter the study when he changed his mind. He could resist no longer. Why die never knowing what father had written? He went to the chimney and tapped open the code for the safe. He removed the envelope and sat on a pale green upholstered regency chair to read the contents. It was a letter addressed to him dated just a month before the plane went down.

Dear Finlay,

If I live to be ninety I shall never be able to call you Dex!

As I look back on my life, by no means over, I regret that the manner of your upbringing by me wronged you grievously. You were a headstrong child with little interest in typical boyish activities. From preference, you defied authority and I could not respect your values. Your first school headmaster told me you were rather a handful in one of his politer remarks, yet he also said he saw great qualities and strength of character. The reports from public school were consistently unfavorable as you will well remember.

Wrongly, I wanted a subservient Boy! I did not want a rugger bugger like you became. I did not want a top athlete or boxer able to slug it out over ten rounds. I could take no pleasure in your trophies or your obsession with racing cars. I wanted you to be a great lawyer and to appreciate true culture with opera and ballet to the fore. I see now this was a big mistake and has I fear it cast a long shadow over your formative years. I should have given you your chance to sharpen <u>your own qualities</u> rather than subsume them beneath my selfish intentions or strangle them within a straitjacket of my design.

You must talk to the Reverend Hillyer about a young child for whom I have taken a special interest. He knows the full story. Bobby is an orphan. I will not labor you with details save to say that I most certainly am not his father! I have provided for him during his life in a manner I consider suitable. But watching young Bobby grow has made me realize the errors in my role of father to you and to a lesser extent to Beth. He too is a lively rebellious little boy, values I now cherish. To Bobby, I have been an Uncle, albeit somewhat remote as I see him only at weekends. Should I die or be incapable of visiting Bobby while he is still under 18, I should like to think that you with your wit, drive and enthusiasm for life (sometimes used in misguided directions by my fuddy-duddy standards) would help to shape his future but being careful to let him have his head.

I made a Will a few years ago in which you did not feature. I knew that you would never challenge it, despite a legal entitlement so to do. You would be far too proud to stoop to scrabble for money that you knew that I did not wish you to have. Through my love for Bobby, I have seen your childhood in a different light and have destroyed that Will by ripping it up. If I die now, you will benefit under an intestacy but I wanted you to know that in the new Will, to be drawn up by Archie Smithers, you will be a fairly treated beneficiary.

Money, you will say, cannot purge a lost childhood. I agree but I want to die knowing I have done the correct thing. Indeed, perhaps even before you get to read this, I shall have steeled myself to make the first move towards a rapprochement. I hope so. This change of heart has come solely because of young Bobby. Treat him well. He deserves better than life has given him so far. So did you from me.

Love

Father

Dex read the note twice and then returned it to the envelope and locked it back in the safe. While reading it, he had been carried back to childhood and he could almost hear his father speaking the words he had written. It was like hearing a voice from the grave. These were the words of a barrister making a speech full of heavy, worthy and soul-baring Victorian sentiments. As he walked slowly through to the study, he was still agonizing over the struggle his father must have had to write such an apology.

He went up to his bedroom. Nothing unusual there as he went to the dressing-table and removed a photo he had taken of Jude in a pose that showed more of her bare buttocks than her face. It was good enough. Jude's head was turned to the camera and she was grinning hugely as she knelt on hands and knees. He carefully cut off the body and went down to the study with the face.

Everything seemed normal. The phone message light was flashing but nothing looked disturbed. He played the messages, all routine. The telltales were unbroken. In the drawer was the new credit card which he slipped into his pocket. Occasionally, the hairs on the nape of his neck seemed to sense something but he steeled himself to carry on, doing what was essential. He ran Jude's face through the copier, enlarged as much as possible. He called the private detective agency he had traced while in the Waldorf. "Is that Ben Greenaway? Finlay Dexter here. Yes. I've got the photo. I'll drop it off on the way back to my hotel. I'll also give you the check you wanted. I want Jude tailed from tonight. She may be at Dukes. She normally leaves there by four latest. Have someone at Shawcross' address in Notting Hill too. Follow her everywhere until further notice. I want Arnie Fisher trailed too, as discussed. If you see a man of early forties around Shawcross' place who does not fit my description of him, have him followed too – that might be Fisher. I want details of all addresses they visit."

"I'll be at Joe Allen's restaurant, 13 Exeter Street until after ten."

"I'll see you there, soonest."

Dex put down his mobile still uneasy having his back to the door. He knew it was irrational with Shawcross in Vegas but he could not wait to get away. Hastily, he rummaged for his check book to pay some of the more pressing bills, especially the eight grand due to American Express. While he scribbled furiously, the feeling that he was not alone persisted but every time he flashed a quick glance over his left shoulder there was nobody there.

Heathrow Airport, London - 20th December 2002

Dex saw that it was nearly ten and he hurried to a quiet table in a café in the Departure Lounge. He found and dialed the Morden number. "Kenny Jennings, please." After a second at most, the familiar voice was on the line.

"Hi Dex. Any news?" Quickly Dex updated him on the agreed meeting. "Can I tell Mark?"

"So long as the cops aren't in earshot. But don't raise Kath's hopes too much."

"I wouldn't trust her with anything secret. Understandably, she's as taut as cheese wire."

"And as a couple?"

"United against adversity, I'd say. There's no warmth but it could be much worse. The cops are getting nowhere. It's tempting to tell them what we know, don't you think?"

"I usually agree with you, Kenny but not on this. Too risky. I'm having Jude Tuson and a man by the name of Arnie Fisher followed. Just a hunch that Shawcross might have used one of them over Emily."

Kenny sounded hesitant. "Arnie Fisher? I know that name. He's an agent, no-holds-barred. Nasty reputation. Anyway, I've just bought that pay-as-you-go. I'll call you tomorrow, same time."

"Make it earlier – say eight am. That'll be midnight in Vegas. Give Mark my best and tell him I'm not doing anything to rile Shawcross."

Dex then rang Greenaway. "News, Ben?"

"Information, not news." Greenaway cleared his throat. "Jude left Dukes alone at three and cabbed it to Shawcross' address. She let herself in. Lights went on in the penthouse and she went to bed about twenty minutes later. Nobody else appeared to be there and nobody has called there this morning. I've two men, one on foot and one with a car ready to follow her. As for Arnie Fisher, we spotted him unlocking his office in Goodge Street about two hours ago.

423

He's still there. As you suggested, I've got someone phoning on a pretext of wanting Arnie *personally* to do a job staying in Brighton for three days just to see if he's free to take it. And we're standing by to follow him."

"I'll ring when I'm next free. Thanks."

Ten minutes later, his flight was called. For the first time that morning, he was able to look forward to seeing Tiffany tonight. It was better than imagining what Emily was suffering.

Las Vegas – 22nd December 2002

The comfortable suite at the Barbary Coast was silent and the bedside lamps muted. Dex had asked Tiffany to switch off the endless babble from the TV. He had been there a long two days, happy enough but frustrated that there was nothing to do but wait for developments. Soon, he would know if Emily would be freed. Greenaway's daily reports had been unhelpful. Arnie Fisher seemed to spend his days chained to a desk before returning to a house in Loughton. To the request to be based in Brighton for few days, he had answered smoothly enough that these past three years, he liked to get home at night and had never taken jobs outside London. He offered a colleague. Watching Jude had also been wasted money. Though her days were spent more interestingly than Fisher's, she never did anything remotely suspicious – a cinema, window-shopping around Bond Street, meeting an Aussie woman friend for lunch around Piccadilly, coffees in Starbucks and evenings in the casino. "But don't stop yet," Dex had told Greenaway. It was an instruction born from desperation. With no sign that either of them were caring for the girl, Dex had been haunted by the possibility that Emily was already dead.

They were both packed for the quick dash to the airport after meeting Shawcross. Though his head was still light from the time change, the pummeling water from the recent shower had helped. He had toweled his hair dry and left it so that it looked more like the old urchin look. He reckoned Tiffany's eyes had been watching him pad round the room in his boxer shorts. Or was that wishful thinking?

A bottle of Krug in a bucket of ice lay on the low table by the two well-upholstered chairs. The Strip view, with multi-colored neon flooding the night was spectacular. The soaring metal framework of the *Eiffel Tower* rose high above them, the lights reflecting an orange-brown from the giant girders. Beyond that, unseen lay Space City. He'd ordered them Room Service – champagne, some Zinfandel from the Napa and simple lamb chops. His idea had been to keep their minds off the rendezvous which was creeping relentlessly closer.

Tiffany's face, though not drawn, nevertheless revealed her mixed emotions. "This was a beautifully romantic idea and I know it's your birthday tomorrow but I'm in no mood for seductive meals and romance. I'm too scared. Give

425

me a cuddle." Dex was deflated. His hopes for some romping had been raised when he found she had been shopping at Victoria's Secret in the Forum Shops and was now wearing a ruby-red lacy chemise with only a pair of black v-string panties. She tucked her legs beneath her as she settled on the chair. "Do you understand? I want you ... but with all this, oh, worry, I can't get excited." She flicked a smile of regret. "Just a cuddle?"

"Sounds wonderful," Dex responded with more enthusiasm than he felt as he took in the taught thigh muscles and unblemished expanse of skin. "I guess I shouldn't be drinking too much with just four hours to go." He stood behind her chair, arms around her neck, watching her gaze out at the art deco coloring of the walkway to Bally's. Gently, he caressed her shoulder and leaned over to rest his cheek next to hers.

Tiffany took in his faraway look. "You nervous?"

"I'd lie to say I wasn't. Not scared. Just on edge that so much turns on facing Shawcross and hoping he's not double-crossing me." He sat down beside her, pulling her head onto his shoulder. "You're all ready to dash to the airport?"

"I'll be ready. You're still taking on Dukes tomorrow then?"

"Yes. 23rd December. My birthday. With Shawcross over here until the opening, I expect Kyte is too. I'm gambling they'll stay here getting ready for the celebrations while we are back in London. FB will keep me posted." As Tiffany picked at the juicy pink lamb, her face grew increasingly concerned. "That last call from Scotty was odd."

"You thought so? He sounded keen enough."

"That's just it." She turned to her tomato and onion salad. "It was almost as if he hoped Shawcross would try something while he drove here. Like a death-wish."

Dex thought for a moment, one finger playing with his teeth. "Well ... I wouldn't go *that* far."

Tiffany persisted. "There *was* something fatalistic in his approach. Sort of *que sera sera.*"

"As Scotty would say, no boo-hoo. Big boys' game." He leaned across reassuringly. "If there's a chase, my money's on the F1 driver any day, injured shoulder or not." He stroked her thigh, absent-mindedly at first but then with a more meaningful longing. "I wonder where Shawcross is. He left Bellagio at lunchtime. Otto's agents haven't spotted him since they lost him in the Mirage."

"Perhaps he's in the next room." They both laughed. He pulled her closer, his body yearning for her. "God knows when we'll get another chance for some quality time." He brushed a hand across her nipples. She turned inwards to face him, her mouth slightly open, her eyes fixated.

"I'm just scared Dex. There's so much that can go horribly wrong."

He rose from his chair and eased her up so as to face him, her slender body tight against him, he with his hands softly caressing her neck. "Don't be. What we're doing is for one terrified child. It's worth the risks. The price, whatever it is, is one I'm ready to pay."

"Then make me forget the risks." She nuzzled his ear. "Take me to some distant place where this nightmare isn't happening." She tilted her head back to receive a kiss that was gentle at first but which became increasingly fervent as she responded, drowning her fears in the intensity of her own stirring emotions. Arm around her shoulder he led her gently through to the bedroom. "Make it fierce, Dex. I need to be devoured, consumed - anything to take me away from this god-awful reality."

Scotty's eleven thousand square foot mansion with garaging for nine cars, a home-cinema, gymnasium and two pools was about twelve miles west of the Strip, a journey of thirty minutes maximum for a sedate family driver. For a former world-champion driving a silver Jaguar XK8 convertible capable of nearly one-sixty mph, he knew the journey down the Summerlin Parkway and 1-15 was about twelve minutes and much less if the cops weren't looking.

On the small area behind the two seats was *the evidence* - a black bag filled with old newspapers. Beside him his blow-up *passenger* sat impassively, a cap on her head. For a moment he faltered, not starting the engine, wondering if he had made the biggest mistake of his life agreeing to go ahead when Dex had said he could back off. Outside, the temperature on the lower slopes of the Spring Mountains had dropped to freezing point, not unusual in December. A freezing drizzle was in the air, sweeping down with the cutting wind from the snowy slopes of Mount Charleston further north-west.

He thought back to the conversation. "You done your part, Dex. So hell, yes, I'll drive. I won't get no shit … but if I do, man I jus' can' wait to give them the race of their fuckin' lives. I ain't done much more'n gripe an' behave like a horse's ass so far, so I wanna justify my payback. So I drive to the Barbary Coast. Then head for the airport. The jet's ready."

"Suppose you run into trouble?"

"If I'm not there by on time, you run like fuck. Take the plane. If I'm dead, no point you grievin'. You'll know he's gonna whack you - if you give him the chance."

Despite his bravado, after the call, Scotty had fixed his own private insurance. Behind him in a tail car were four guys, all armed.

Dex had chosen the Barbary Coast deliberately. Though less celebrated and much smaller than its illustrious neighbors, he knew it was always busy far into the night. Dex wanted that as his own protection. As the appointed time approached, he left an emotional Tiffany packing her last items. He descended in the lift carrying the heavy bundle of evidence in a brown zipper bag. At the casino level, he was immediately enveloped in the clattering noise, the canned music and shouts of the packed gaming area.

The air was smoky and as usual, most of the noise, whooping, shouting and high-fives came from the craps tables. The subdued lighting gave the room a welcoming old-fashioned saloon atmosphere. Dex likened the ambience to a saloon from out of an old Western movie as he walked pensively and warily between the lines of blackjack and roulette tables towards the front of the gaming area. The main bar was to his right, not a dedicated room but very much part of the casino - a line of stools surrounding the bar counter. The location had been perfectly chosen to meet his needs. Somewhere in the endless kaleidoscope of movement were his five security guards, perhaps including the large guy sipping a beer along the counter. Shawcross too was somewhere around, perhaps also with a secret entourage - perhaps the large guy sipping a beer along the counter.

Dex jammed the heavy bag between the foot of the stool and the counter. Neither Shawcross nor any goons that *he* had hired could now appear from behind him. Perched there, he gazed for any clues of trouble ahead. Everything seemed routine, just like last night when he had come down for a dummy run. The others seated round the bar were the usual cross-section of steady drinkers - couples young and old drinking exotic cocktails or dumb-fucks staring into their beer bottles wondering why they had lost everything on their first night in town.

"Sparkling water with ice, please," he ordered as the barman nodded a greeting. Was someone even now watching and reporting by cellphone to Shawcross that he had arrived? It was now precisely one am, though typically there was no clock in the casino as a reminder. He looked to his right at the entrances leading in from the Strip. He gazed to his left into the gaming area. Nothing. Nobody interesting. No Shawcross. He sipped the water slowly and wondered what Tiffany must be thinking – probably wondering to which hotel they had gone for the handover. *So how long do I give Shawcross? Five minutes? Ten? Thirty?* This was the type of meeting where you were on time or a no-show. He gave him fifteen and went to the house phone.

"Tiffany. No Shawcross. I'm coming up. We're leaving. Book a cab to take us to the Executive Air Terminal in five minutes." He dialed Scotty's number which rang but there was no answer. He tried again when they arrived at the Terminal, just a short and quick ride away. There had been barely any time to reassess the situation but his mounting fear was that Emily was already dead. "I never doubted he would show," said Tiffany. "I mean what's the point of holding the child and not using her as planned."

"There are three possibilities. One is that Emily is dead - unlikely. Next is that Shawcross has been caught - most unlikely."

"Lastly?"

"He didn't appear because he *expected I would not be there.*"

"You mean?"

"That he had set up an ambush and expected to have retrieved the evidence and silenced me too." The implications hung heavily between them as the yellow taxi jolted to a stop.

She looked at him anxiously across the cab. "Dex – stop chewing you lip. It already looks as if I've bruised it."

In the terminal there was no sign of Scotty. Dex wiped his hands nervously down his trousers. "I'll phone him again." He waited for a moment or two listening to the ringing and again left no message. "He was insistent. We *must* not wait for him … but I can't just leave, not knowing."

"Dex, Scotty was right. We have to assume there was trouble. We must get off to London. Reckon we'll have to go to the cops. Tell them everything. The deal is not going to happen now."

Dex did not know how to respond to that wisdom. "I'll get the pilots moving. Scotty'll still have twenty minutes. The take-off slot's not until two. I've got to ring Kenny and he'll have to tell Mark." He hurried away but had only gone a few yards before he turned round. "And by the time we get to London, you'd better know Reverse Labouchère backwards. I'm not going to fail now. There's nothing to lose by poking Shawcross in the eye now."

Tiffany was unconvinced. "Me?" Her voice echoed behind him as he hurried away. A frown clouded her face as she sat on a bench seat to await his return.

Scotty switched on the ignition and blasted hot air onto the windows until the visibility improved. Cold weather didn't do favors to his shoulder or leg and he winced as he leaned across to wipe down the rear-view mirrors. He grinned at the black doll and tipped the cap to a jaunty angle. "Ready to roll, Fifi? Let's hit it." A moment later, after a word on the phone to the driver in the following car, the Jaguar purred just like the cat it was, gliding smoothly round the crescent of millionaires' homes towards the Tournament Hills security gates. Thirty yards behind was a black Mercedes Coupé. Nick, the driver had been briefed to prevent any car getting behind the Jaguar.

As he approached the gates, and on impulse, Scotty decided to change his route. The quickest way to the Barbary Coast was east down the Parkway and then south on1-15. "Okay, Fifi. I'll make a right at the gates and then turn west to the 215. That'll confuse things."

At the exit, the uniformed guard saluted him with respect as the double sized gate swung slowly open. Outside, there was the usual steady stream of traffic heading north or south on Rampart. He paused briefly for a decent gap big enough for the Mercedes to stay close. Then he pulled across to the left lane as if to turn east about half a mile away. He phoned Nick. "I'm gonna make out I'm turnin' at the *second* lights – eastbound but I'm takin' the first exit, headin' west. You be in the correct lane for that. I'll swerve in front of you."

He watched the Mercedes move across another lane and draw almost beside him. Behind him, about three cars back, a 928 Porsche appeared, the only car around that had the grunt to match him for speed. As he approached the westbound entrance to the Parkway, he swerved late and in front of the Mercedes and was rewarded with a blast of horn. In his mirror, he watched the Porsche also barge its way into the next lane in order to maintain contact. He grinned at Fifi. The ruse had smoked out the tail. "We got company, Nick. Watch out for the petrol blue Porsche. A two-seater."

Scotty knew that the Porsche could accelerate up to around one fifty-five mph, way beyond local speed limits. "Keep the line open now. We'll need to talk." He accelerated round the near one-eighty degree horseshoe turn of the slip-road to join the main traffic heading up the Parkway away from the city. He felt a slight loss of grip from the ice on the polished surface and corrected with a deft touch of his right hand. For several miles, the Mercedes kept close doing a steady sixty until they passed through the lights at the recently opened 215 Beltway where Scotty turned left again. The new road was quiet and dark except for the occasional light from an oncoming vehicle. Heading south now, Scotty checked his mirror. "Jus' the three of us now Fifi," he said quietly.

Scotty knew the traffic would build up after the Sahara junction, so any hostile move might come quickly in this more barren area of unfinished freeway. He was not surprised when he saw the Porsche's lights pull left to the overtaking lane and start to accelerate. "He's coming Nick. Don't let him pass."

Scotty pushed down his foot and the engine responded like a thoroughbred, effortlessly pushing the car up to ninety. He saw the Mercedes' lights weaving around as the car criss-crossed the lanes, weaving a zigzag path while Nick also speeded up to stick close. "You're doin' jus' great blockin' him but back off - slow the fucker down. Hold the motherfucker up! I need more time. I'm gonna really hit it now. You slow him for another thirty seconds and I'll be so far gone, they'll never get me. I'm gonna avoid Flamingo. Too obvious. I'll head east down Tropicana. Okay."

"Agreed." Nick's voice showed the strain as he swung the wheel back and forth on the treacherous surface to block the Porsche. "Jesus!"

"Problem, Nick?"

"They're shootin'. Hit the rear tire, I reckon. That ain't me swerving this sonovabitch." There was a muffled sound of someone shouting. Then Scotty heard the crack of a gun and guessed one of Nick's passengers was firing back. "Shit. Scotty, my windshield's gone. I'm losin' it." Scotty looked back and saw the big black car slew sharply right and spin out of control up the graveled embankment.

"You okay?" But the question brought no response. "Hold tight Fifi. We're goin' for the ride of your goddamned life." Scotty jammed his foot down hard and felt that glorious power force him back in the seat. Fifi's cap slipped off with the kick of power.

Scotty weighed up the options. The solitary headlights were now only three hundred yards back, far too close to confuse the driver as to which exit he'd take. He watched the speedo race through one-thirty but the Porsche had no problem keeping pace. Now he was up to one-forty. The Sahara and Town Center exits flashed past as if they did not exist. The traffic was busier now and he left a Dodge pick-up and a small Mazda for dead as he looked for the sweeping right-hander, the overpass and slip-road for Flamingo. "Fifi, we'll still take Tropicana, whatever the lights. Then I'll show them how to drive, zigzaggin' down them sleepy suburban streets roun' there."

He ignored the Flamingo slip road rising to his right, instead accelerating into the long curve under the overpass, knowing that Tropicana was still over a mile. The Porsche was matching him for pace.

"Holy shit!" His curse was aimed at a large Ford F150 truck that had been cruising at about thirty down the inside lane. Without signaling, it was now pulling across to overtake a small sedan. Suddenly, both lanes were blocked with his closing speed on them over a hundred. Slamming into the rear of the truck was not an option. Neither was hard braking on the treacherous surface. He eased off the accelerator. "Hold on Fifi! I'm gonna hit the gravel on the central reservation, get me some traction and squeeze on through." Avoiding any sharp handling, he eased left as ahead a shadowy overpass approached as quickly as Ste Devote.

At ninety yards from the Ford's rear-lights, he blasted the horn and nudged the Jaguar further left round the sweeping right-hander, desperate to get all four wheels onto the chippings The car's lights caught the wall of concrete supporting the bridge. It towered high above the road but appeared to leave a sliver of room for him to use between the wall and truck.

On the freezing surface, the back end started to slide left. That familiar waltzing feeling was something he loved. He controlled the skid without thinking but then the lights picked out a new view, a different angle. Ahead, the central verge became slim-line under the bridge but he judged it still just possible to get through, especially if the dickhead in the Ford used his mirrors and moved afoot or two to his right.

Somehow, he needed to be inch-perfect despite the loose chippings that were now flying from the left side front tire as the back end slithered on the black ice at just over seventy, the closing speed down to forty. "Move over! Move over!" He slammed his hand onto the horn again to no obvious effect. The F150's rear was now only fifty yards away as the width of the central verge dropped from three yards to just one.

" Too narrow, Fifi, that bridge is too fuckin' close!"

There was no choice, no room or time for finesse now. He decided to hit the concrete with a glancing blow at a fine angle, slowing the car and putting it into a spin. As the dark red chippings flew thicker and faster all round as both driver's side wheels ripped through them, he aimed the bonnet diagonally, hoping that with the rear left tire now biting, he would slow enough to waltz ever slower behind the Ford.

In a dazzling shower of sparks, the car slammed along the concrete, destroying the wheel and wing and spinning the Jaguar across the road behind the Ford. His speed dropped violently. Fifi was thrown across him as he fought with the wheel while the Jaguar looped 360 degrees until there was a further lurch and bang as this time the offside struck the overpass with a sickening bang. The Jaguar's right side was badly stove in as it slewed crablike across the road, coming to rest beside the slow lane. Ahead, the two other cars drove on as if nothing had happened. The lights and engine died, steam rising from the twisted bonnet. From behind, the Porsche 928 slithered through the debris and came to a standstill on the nearside verge beyond the bridge. Two men appeared and started running back to the wreckage.

Dex and Tiffany were seated alone in the grey leather chairs as the Bombardier thundered along the runway and turned north for a routing over Denver, the Hudson Bay, a thirty minute refueling stop and then across the Atlantic into Heathrow. They were silent, both thinking of Scotty, worried about his fate. The flight attendant served ham, rare beef and pickle with salads but Tiffany pushed hers to one side saying she wasn't hungry while Dex ate with relish but without speaking. Except for telling her that he had phoned Kenny, he had been silent. "I'll ring Scotty again at Gander." Occasionally, he looked across at her as he drank a fruity Sangiovese that worked well with the beef. Tiffany ordered a second vodka-martini. "No point moping, Dex. He's probably fine."

His face was expressionless, as if every muscle had frozen. "Listen to who's talking! You look more mopy than the mopiest person in a room full of mopers." He tried to sound more cheerful than he was feeling. "Let's not piss into the wind. I doubt he's okay at all. Because of me, Emily's a prisoner or dead. Because of me, Scotty's lying in a ditch with his brains blown out." He spread open his arms helplessly. "And there's me jumping onto *his* plane, drinking his booze as if I didn't care. When we refuel I'll phone again..."

"...And email Shawcross asking where the hell he was," Tiffany intervened.

"Right! He still needs the documents."

"Otto's men never spotted him at McCarran, so he was still in Vegas until we left." Greenaway's team will spot him at Heathrow or Gatwick Arrivals if they missed him here."

"And Jude?"

"Ben Greenaway is following her everywhere. Says she's lived the life of a nun these past few days. That must have had her scratching the walls in frustration." Even as he said it, he knew it was a mistake and hurried on but not before Tiffany had given him a quizzical look.

"So what next?"

"We go ahead with Reverse Labby tonight, so long as FB tells me his boss is in Vegas. If he's at Dukes, then the plan is off."

"Look Dex - the police. It was fine until tonight. By now Emily should have been freed. But surely we tell the cops that he's the man. The emails don't admit he's behind it but he's in deep shit at the very least."

"So, suppose the police nab him. They have no real evidence to hold him. What happens to Emily then? In Vegas-speak, Emily's future is a crapshoot. History shows if a kidnapping starts to go wrong, then the victim is in grave danger."

"Examples?"

"The jail sentences for kidnapping and murder are much the same, so if in doubt kill. Remember Lesley Whittle, the girl in the Midlands, kidnapped and dumped down a drain under a manhole cover and chained by a wire noose? The kidnapper tried to set up a rendezvous to get cash for her but it went wrong. She was found dead about two months later. I can't risk that."

"God! I remember now. The Black Panther wasn't it?"

"Right. Donald Neilson. Convicted of murder." He ruffled his growing hair. "Then there was Muriel McKay - another wealthy woman where the kidnappers got jumpy when ransom demands went wrong. She was never seen again. It was rumored she was fed to the pigs." He tried to find the right words when nothing he had to say was either reassuring or pleasant. "Tiffany, I've scoured the web and read every kidnap story trying to get into the psychology of all this." His voice was strained, his tone pleading with her to believe in him a while longer. He rose to his commanding height and removed his navy suede jacket. "If I go to the police about Emily, then I'd have to tell them about the murders, the fraud, the lot. That way, Shawcross would not get bail. The

434

kid will die of starvation or be murdered by an accomplice. Shawcross won't admit anything." His tone was pleading as he struggled to find the logic. "I'd still bet someone really trusted by Shawcross is involved. Must be." He spread his arms out helplessly.

"You've still got to do better than that to convince me."

"I'm going to up the stakes." He adjusted the sleeves of his black turtle-neck.

"How?"

"Reverse Labby him. Hit Dukes for ten million. Then offer to return the cash as well as the documents in exchange for Emily. He has two options. Deal with us and brazen it out, hoping for our silence. Or he can flee after grabbing the ten million. His choice."

Tiffany reached across and pinned both his arms gently to the table. "But won't winning at Dukes really anger him? Make things worse for Emily? You can't take chances with her life."

"Can they be worse? How can they *become* worse? Offering him *personally* the cash back could be a godsend. Can *you* think of anything better/"

Tiffany looked doubtful. "But aren't you getting ahead of yourself? How come you're so confident of winning ten million?"

He forced out a grin. "It's my birthday. I'm feeling lucky."

"God! So it is." She leaned across the table and kissed him. "Happy Birthday. Your present will have to wait. It's in my case. But you're not talking luck." She poked him playfully. "You're now looking ... well, rather smug if I may say so. I don't understand why. With is Reverse thingy, you said you can go for days always losing, then one day you hit it big."

"Trust me. Today's that day."

She stroked his cheek. "I'm not sure." She sighed. "Okay, if Shawcross wants to run for cover, getting ten million would help." She sighed again. "Oh come on then. Teach me how we're going to take Dukes for millions."

"We'd better knuckle down." He checked his watch. "Allowing for refueling, we should touch down around eight pm, London time. We'll check messages at the airport. If Shawcross is not around we'll go straight to Dukes."

"I don't understand. Why the rush?"

"The magic powder can only work on my birthday." She stroked his hair teasingly. "At midnight, I turn into a pumpkin." Seeing she was going to get no better explanation, Tiffany shrugged helplessly as he produced two sheets of paper. "Grab your pen, Tiffs. It's back to school time. In Dukes you'll play Scotty's role. You'll gripe, carp, and argue with me. Whatever. Beg me to stop. To cut and run. I'm serious. Understood?"

"No but I'll do it."

"Scotty was good at that. No practice needed. We must not look as if we're confident of winning. Reverse Labouchère is simple – if you don't panic. You'll play black tonight. I'll back red. That was the color I needed the night they destroyed me."

"You back red, I back black. One of us always loses. I remember that bit. Sounds as much fun as burning fifty pound notes."

He grinned again and tapped her on the nose. "Trust me."

"How much money are you risking?"

He spoke softly but with emphasis stamped on every word. "Everything. I've got Scotty's half-mill in the cage at Dukes. I'll risk it all plus what's left of the life policy cash. If he's alive, I owe him. If he's dead, then I'm only doing what he expected." His eyes watched her closely now, so determined was he to imbue her with his burning enthusiasm. "Remember I told you about visiting the graves at Bladon? Well, as Sir Winston said - that day at Bladon *was the end of the beginning. Today is the beginning of the end.*" Tiffany saw his eyes go distant. His memories were of the smell of fresh cut grass; of his mother and Beth so close, so real and yet so very dead; of the cow in distress, blaring and bellowing across the sunlit meadows in the autumnal air. Suddenly, he looked at her directly, right eyebrow raised, the smile touchingly sincere. "Of course I want Shawcross and the rest banged up. This way, we have the chance of financial retribution, the return of Emily *and* a chance to send him to jail."

"Explain what I've got to do besides being grumpy."

He looked at her earnestly. She knew there was something odd about the roulette just from the cheeky look on his face. She saw the resolute determination in every movement as he prepared to teach her and she marveled at this inner strength when so much was going wrong. Yet nothing could ease the fears that were chewing at her stomach, churning it over like a ride at a fair. "All we need is for red or black to dominate. Why? Because we increase the winning bet every time and reduce the losing bet. So if red dominates, I'm betting bigger and bigger sums – using casino winnings. Meantime little old you betting on black are staking peanuts. Right?"

"You mean red wins thirty times running? That isn't going to happen."

"No it won't. It doesn't have to win every spin – just win distinctly more often than black."

He saw understanding on her face as she wrestled with an alien concept. "But what if neither red nor black dominate. Suppose it's almost fifty-fifty as it should be. What then?"

"We lose everything."

She stared at him. "Tell me why I hoped you wouldn't say that."

Dex ignored the remark as he sipped at his wine and then steadied the glasses as the plane struck a small patch of turbulence over the Rocky Mountains. "We're each betting twenty thousand a spin - our base bet. We can afford twenty-five consecutive losing bets where the ball zigzags from red to black. That's most unlikely as well – happily. But it won't be as simple as that."

"If you say so. Bought a new rabbit's foot charm have you?"

"My middle name's Warren." The plane lurched sharply and the co-pilot came through on the intercom to say they'd be above the turbulence *real soon*. "Across the top of the paper write 10, 10, 10, 10. Each one represents ten thousand."

"You got it!" She hesitated. "Damn and blast!! I'm starting to sound like an American. Go on."

"You bet the total of the two outside numbers. 10 +10 =20 = £20,000. So do I. I win. You lose. So I add 20 to my line so it reads 10, 10, 10, 10, 20. You though strike out the two outside numbers so your line shrinks to 10,10."

"I'm with you."

"We again bet the total of our outside numbers. So I bet 10 +20 = 30 = £30,000."

"And I bet 10 +10 = 20 = £20,000 again." Tiffany showed she had picked up the idea.

"I win £30,000. So I add 30 to my line so it becomes 10, 10, 10, 10, 20, 30."

"So your next bet is 30 +10 = £40,000. But me?"

"You strike out the two remaining tens. That line is finished, down forty grand. But I'm up fifty grand, so together we're ahead ten grand. From now on, my wins will increasingly compensate for your losses. I'm starting to win much more than you're losing."

"Take it a bit further."

"You start a new line of 10, 10, 10, 10. I bet my forty grand, you stake twenty. I win again. I add 40 to my line to read 10, 10, 10, 10, 20, 30, 40. My next bet is £50,000. You strike out the two outside 10's again."

"So now we're ahead by your ninety less my sixty. Up thirty. Okay clever clogs. Suppose you lose next spin. What happens?"

"I lose £50,000 and so I strike the two outside figures from my line. They were..."

"Forty and ten."

"Right. So my next bet is ten plus thirty – my two outside numbers. My line is 10, 10, 10, 20, 30. Your line is 10, 10, 20 so you bet ..."

"Thirty grand."

"Right. It's simple. What we want is for red to outnumber black by say four to one over an hour's play. Result: a big, big win. These figures crank up hugely. Get a bit of a run at the thing and one of us could easily be betting half a million." His grin was infectious, the cocked head adding to the playful image. "Using winnings only."

"Five hundred thousand pounds on a roulette wheel?"

His eyes were flashing excitement. "Fantastic isn't it! Using our winnings to play the casino at its own game!"

"Promise me you'll stop this gambling once you've won big." He was pleased that she was now living his dream. "Will you?"

"Like you once said to me. No promises." He leaned across to kiss her and was glad she responded.

"What'll happen to Adrian Ryder? And Zara?"

"God alone knows. He'll stay over here, lying low at Scotty's if he's any sense. Waiting for developments. For him, this has been a cataclysmic disaster. Without him being corrupted by Shawcross, the Gaming Board would have discovered the frauds."

"Sounds as if he's better off without Zara though."

"He doesn't see it that way. He's lost a career at the Board *and* faces a probable prosecution and humiliation. To say nothing of the end of his dreams in Vegas."

"Fool that he was, believing that crap. And Zara?"

"Still out of sight with no sign she's ratted on us. If she's caught and arrested, she'd be jailed. Later? She'll find someone else." He stopped for a moment. "Hell. Don't let me forget. If we get through this, I owe Ryder's wife and her girlfriend two cruise tickets."

"Explain."

He looked at his watch. "Too complicated for now. Let's get some sleep. It's going to be a full day. In about twelve hours, we'll have finished at Dukes. Then I can make Shawcross an offer he can't refuse."

London – 23rd December 2002

At Heathrow, it was dark and cold, a biting easterly penetrating even the warmest clothing. After clearing Customs and Immigration, Dex went to the Business Centre eager to check emails and news. "Dex?" Kenny answered his phone at once. "It's been a difficult day here." The understatement was obvious. "Mark couldn't take it any longer. He decided to tell Kath of the failed attempt to get Emily back without the police. She went berserk. I had to go into her bedroom to calm her down. She was screaming so the street could hear. She had Mark by the throat and was strangling him. She's not big but she's tough. I had quite a struggle to pull her off. Luckily, the young woman constable in the kitchen didn't hear what was said, though she heard the commotion. I sent her packing. Said it was typical domestic stress."

Kenny sighed. "Mark is close to despair. Well, we all are, come to that! If she's not found by Christmas Day, then under the deal, no …call it an uneasy truce that I brokered, he's going to the cops about Shawcross. That's quietened her. I'm dead against the police being involved, so I exaggerated a bit. Said we were still very optimistic." His silence confirmed his embarrassment. "I had to buy you time. The girl's dead if the cops trample on this."

Dex then hooked up his laptop just as he had done six hours earlier in Newfoundland. There, he and Tiffany had disembarked during refueling. "No reply from Scotty. I'll go on line," he had told Tiffany as she peered anxiously over his shoulder hugging a cup of coffee. He checked for any email from Shawcross but there was nothing, so he fired off a blunt complaint. *"I was there at 1 a.m. Where were you? Are you serious? We must rearrange. I suggest the same venue for another night. I hope to improve on my offer."* Then, fearing bad news about Scotty, he turned to Google headlines. There was nothing.

Now in London, he surfed through to the BBC news. As usual it was still carrying a photo of Emily. There had been no developments. Surrey police were still apparently seeking clues. "At least no child's body has been found," said Tiffany but Dex was not listening, already surfing to a new page as Tiffany looked on. *"Scotty Brannigan, the racing driver and former Formula One world champion, was found shot dead in his Jaguar on the outskirts of Las Vegas last night. Witnesses spoke of Brannigan being chased by another sports car. His car hit a bridge at about 80 mph and stopped some distance away. Two masked men were seen to approach the wreck. He appears to have been executed in cold blood. The police are seeking anyone able to assist. Only in September, Brannigan was shot and injured while at a funeral in London. Police say there is no evidence linking the two shootings."*

Tiffany felt weak and clasped his shoulders for support as he let out a long groan of despair. It came from the gut, low and agonizing rising like a deep rumble through his vocal chords. "Oh no! F'Chrissake! When *will* we get a break?" For a moment there was total silence as he imagined a chase along the roads of Las Vegas and gunmen approaching the wrecked car. Tiffany pressed herself hard against the curve of his spine and wrapped her arms around his neck. "There's no going back, Dex. The hurt must come later. We have to get to Dukes. Up the stakes. Get the money. That's what Scotty wanted. Only *you* can prove he didn't die for nothing. He risked his life to prove that Shawcross wanted you dead. To give you the chance to live your dream."

Dex spoke slowly. "God!" He shouted. "Don't put it like that. It's too close to the truth."

Tiffany tried to change the moment. "Wonder if they shot the doll *and* read the newspapers." The black humor seemed odd coming from her but it worked. He grabbed her hand as they piled into a taxi. After emerging from the Heathrow tunnel, he phoned FB and a few minutes later the call was returned. "I'm playing tonight. Is either Shawcross or Kyte about?"

"Kyte is in Las Vegas working on cross-border security. He won't be back until after Space City opens. A.S. is expected back tonight. I'm told he's here for Christmas and then returns for the opening."

"ETA?"

"By eleven was what I heard."

"See you soon." He cut off the connection and his face strained, turned to Tiffany. "It's a race against time. Shawcross was in Vegas but he's flying in. We've under three hours to get there, win and disappear." Pressurized by the clock and still reeling from the reality of being murdered with Scotty, he clasped her hand so tightly that she had to break free. Along the M4 motorway, he booked a room at the Goring Hotel, close to Buckingham Palace and only a short taxi ride to Dukes. Then he called Gabe Fazziolli in Las Vegas. "Dex here in London. Where's Shawcross?"

"Try lookin' over your shoulder! We spotted him at the airport. The desk clerk said he was routed to New York and then the Concorde. But his flight was delayed and he would have missed his connection. The first subsonic flight would be at Heathrow at about ten."

"Thanks Gabe. I know about Scotty. What's new?"

"They found the Porsche the killers used. Burned out on waste ground off Russell Road. The killers also shot up my bodyguards. No serious injuries but the car was riddled with bullets. Catch up with you later."

Dex turned to Tiffany. "It's now eight-forty. We're ahead of him by under one hundred minutes."

"Is that long enough?"

"Barely. We've got to hope he goes home and Jude seduces him."

"My guess, he won't go home. After all, with your evidence, he can barely risk even going to Dukes, let alone home. Think about it. Scotty's dead with a bundle of old newspapers. You have the evidence. Shawcross will have gone apeshit, true. But he'll be as worried as hell too. My next guess? Jude will have a hotel room somewhere and he'll join her."

"It's as good as any speculation. I'll call Greenaway." He dialed again. "Is that you Ben? Dex here."

"Dex. Thank God you rang. There's nothing positive yet but I think we've cracked it. I won't know until say nine tomorrow morning."

"Thank God! I needed some good news. Tonight, put extra surveillance at Dukes and at the Shawcross home. Then follow both him and Jude to wherever they go and keep that address under watch. Where's Jude?"

"Having dinner at Pomegranates on the Thames Embankment in Pimlico. Arrived there ten minutes ago. She's with another woman."

"Don't lose her. I'll talk in the morning."

Tiffany had heard the conversation. "I hope he's got that breakthrough. Anyway, I've been thinking. Shawcross will soon land. He'll do what all top executives then do - check his phone and emails. You've fixed a meeting with him in Vegas but if Jude sees you in Dukes, hell, he'll panic. Not good."

"So you want me to come clean about being here?"

She nodded assent. He looked at the dreary properties lining Talgarth Road as the taxi made good time towards the West End. "But I can't email him. I don't have his cell number. I'll leave a message at Dukes." He rang and got

Shawcross' voicemail. "I was there at one! Where were you? As you decided to return to London rather than meet me, I suggest we do the handover somewhere like the Meridian on Piccadilly. Similar arrangements to before except I want you there this time. What about Christmas Day?"

Tiffany laughed. "He'll wonder how the hell you knew he'd returned to London."

"Let's keep him guessing." The taxi pulled up outside the Goring. Dex ran in, dumped the suitcases and zipper bag with the bellman and leaped back down the steps outside. "That two minutes might have cost us a million or so." He dialed Kenny's number. "Don't over-egg this with Kath but your crass optimism may have been prescient! There may be a breakthrough. Stand by to come to London with Mark in the morning."

Moments later they were dropped off in Mount Street and descended the elegant stairs to reception. Dex looked around the gaming area. The sights, the sounds, the smells welcomed him back with a comfortable feeling. He wondered if this would be the last time he would ever see Dukes. Everything seemed so very *mundane*. FB had been hovering between the desk and the gaming floor. "Mr Dexter! Oh, yes and Ms Richmond. So good to see you."

"Glad to be back, FB. So you're the gooseberry, stuck here, while the top brass gad about the Strip."

"The Cinderella role suits me fine. Las Vegas is so vulgar, like Southend only bigger. Will you be dining?"

"Thanks but we've just eaten. We're going to have some fun with you tonight."

FB's brow furrowed. "How so? What do you mean?" He was walking with them to the roulette tables.

"I've been reading up about breaking the bank. Norman Leigh and all that."

"Reverse Labouchère, you mean." FB nodded. "Good system – if you don't go bust while waiting for one color to dictate."

"I was telling Tiffany earlier. Four-leaf clover or no – this is my birthday *and* my lucky day."

FB raised a quizzical eyebrow before looking away at the logos on the floor. "Congratulations and good luck with your new system. We've a table open but if you're serious about having *real fun* at our expense," he coughed into

443

the back of his hand, "we'll open up a high stakes table for you. What stakes did you have in mind?"

"Twenty thousand minimum. Right up to the maximum."

"Oh! In that case, yes of course. I'll get a table opened."

"And I want Jeb Miller there - and One-Eye. I want to kill the jinx." He laughed. "Especially One-Eye. Those two put the yips on me. But today, I feel ready to take them on. This new system sound fantastic."

"As you wish. Why don't you get your funds organized. I recall you deposited, er, quite a substantial sum with us." FB went to the house phone and by the time Dex was ready to sit down, Miller's bottom was already sagging over the edge of his high stool. One-Eye was setting up the chips. Dex nodded to the Inspector. "Table Limit of two million max on outside bets, right?"

"No, Mr Dexter." Miller's brown-toothed smile was disarming. "Twenty thousand minimum to one million."

"Christ! No wonder you casinos make money. That's a bit rich. It should be up to two million maximum."

Dex saw Miller fighting to hide his smirk. He resisted his usual instinctive wish to punch the inspector's nose. "I don't make the rules. Ask FB. He's in charge."

Dex looked at Tiffany and then at his watch. It was nearly ten. Shawcross might even now be in the Arrivals Hall. "No point asking anybody here to play fair. Forget it. Let's get on." He called for two glasses of orange juice as they settled into their chairs. In front of them were their chips. Dex had yellow ones bought in for ten thousand each. Tiffany's were blue at the same value. Beside them were plaques from the cage each worth one hundred thousand pounds.

"Let's go for it!" Dex smiled at Tiffany and admired the confident way she pushed out her chips to back black. One-Eye spun the wheel with a deft flick of the wrist. "Labouchère?" he asked as the ball started to slow.

"No. Reverse Labouchère." Somehow the past didn't matter, One-Eye, Andy, and Miller. He'd lit the fuse and soon he would get them all jailed and banned from casinos for life. The feeling made his pulse race more than the excitement of at last playing the roulette game of his life.

You can put your fingers in your ears, fellas.

But it won't stop the bang.

"Eight. Black. Even."

Tiffany swooped on her winnings and added a twenty to her line of 10,10,10,10. "Start as we mean to carry on," she chuckled. "I could get to like this." Dex grimaced as if they'd lost but in fact they were even. Dex turned to Miller laughing. "I told Tiffany this was my lucky day but it looks more like business as usual." He angrily crossed off the two outside tens.

"So long as one of us keeps winning, who cares?" Tiffany sounded elated at her success. Dex knew how the gambling drug could kick in and she was looking flushed already. In a sudden movement, she grasped her juice and drank with gusto. Her eyes sparkled, her shakes of the head were exaggerated, the intoxication of a big win already racing through her. She pushed out three blue chips while Dex just repeated his first bet. "I'm on a roll," she laughed. "Swallows and summers," retorted Dex but his reference to Aesop was lost, her mind on the chance of another win.

"32. Red. Even."

"Sod that!" She crossed off the twenty and a ten from her line. "I'm losing now."

"We're *both* losing. The one thing that'll kill us is a wretched zigzag of reds and blacks. "Come on One-Eye! Red *or* black but not this zig-zagging please."

The next four numbers were all red. "Heh!" Tiffany protested. "I'm well down, just crossing off lines."

"But *we're* winning," Dex replied pointing to the extra yellow chips now in front of him.

She leaned across and stroked the chips that were multiplying in front of Dex. "Keep them coming."

Dex nodded as he turned to One-Eye. "A few repeat numbers would be good now." He saw the dealer shrug without interest. "Yeah, yeah, yeah. Don't say it One-Eye! *You can't control the ball. The wheel has no memory.* Don't give me that stuff. *You* can make that ball do anything you want."

"Dream on, Mr Dex-tah!" One-Eye's small dark eyes met Dex' stare. His moon-like face was inscrutable, his sallow features revealing nothing beneath the mop of jet black hair.

"He can, can't he Mr Miller?" The inspector did not reply and shook his head as if Dex' suggestion were mad. One-Eye spun a red number again – and again. "Don't pay me in yellows now. Cash chips, big ones please. I told you this was my lucky day."

Tiffany looked irritated with him. "Luck changes. Don't let's push it."

"I'm not stopping. Keep those reds coming my friend. I knew you could do it." Miller made a dry kissing noise used by casino staff to attract attention. A swarthy Maltese Pit Boss, his skin a deep olive, came across and Miller whispered to him, something that Dex could not hear. He left the table and spoke to a bulky, severe looking man who would have looked more comfortable in a wrestler's leopard-skin than a suit that barely contained him. Dex had never spoken to the man but knew him to be a Shift Manager. He seemed to pride himself on being a man of few words and even less charm. He was in his fifties and was answerable only to FB and Shawcross. After listening to the Pit Boss, he disappeared but returned a few moments later and stood behind Dex.

"This is what's known as *giving us heat*," he whispered to Tiffany. "Making us feel uncomfortable. Ignore it." Moments later, FB appeared with a worried frown. A few uncharacteristic brisk strides brought him to the table. He saw that red numbers 7, 3, 34, 16, 16 and 27 had all hit with only one black number between them. Dex saw FB tap the Shift Manager's arm and the two men walked to a corner of the room where they engaged in a lively debate. Dex heard One-Eye's name more than once but the context was unclear.

"Dex. It's twenty-five to eleven. I want to go dancing, remember. Haven't you won enough?"

"No. I'm enjoying myself." Dex had taken to looking at Miller after every winning spin, rubbing his hands, chortling like a child with a new toy. "You'll dance all night my sweet but not yet. Another twenty minutes or so? That was just nineteen spins. I'm ahead just over a million but I'm feeling lucky. I want more. If One-Eye keeps on like this, it'll accelerate like crazy. What are you down?"

She showed him her card with new line after new line all deleted. "Just over a quarter of a million."

"So we're ahead seven-ninety thousand. Just look at my line: 30, 40, 50, 60, 70, 80, 100, 120, 150, 180. My next bet is two hundred and ten thousand."

"You promised. No big risks and agreed to go dancing." She pouted, then down-turned her lip.

Dex reckoned Shawcross must be nearing the West End now. "Spin 'me up One-Eye." He turned to Miller who still had the Maltese Pit Boss beside him. "Great run but nothing like a *really* long run. It's not like it's been nineteen reds in a row. One-Eye, damn him, throws in an odd black. Still, I've dreamed of days like this."

"They say the world record is twenty-seven even-chances in a row. If you believe that," the Pit Boss observed in a guttural voice but still friendly enough. "What's happening is ideal for your system but nothing unusual. Nothing like any record."

"You're right. There's been no run longer than five reds."

"Take care Mr Dexter. It can change, suddenly be all black as the laws of averages take over. You could go down the tube pretty fast." The somber warning, spoken quietly came well from the swarthy features.

"He's right, Dex. Let's stop now," said Tiffany tugging at his arm and almost willing Dex to quit but there was no chance as the ball dropped into number 23, another red number.

"Whahay! This is the ride of our lives. I want to bet a million. If we were in Vegas, One-Eye, I'd be allowed to tip you. When it's over, all I can do is give you a great big kiss." He laughed at the look on One-Eye's face as his winnings were pushed across to him.

Tiffany had watched the dealer sweep her losing chips down the sorter. "Only suckers bet on black today."

He stroked her hand. "Cheer up. It's not your money you're losing. I'm thinking Dire Straits. Seems apposite. He quietly sung the words to her in a tone deaf manner.

That ain't working, that's the way you do it.

Money for nothing and your chicks for free.

She laughed. "I don't sing. Nor should you. I vowed to give up after I did karaoke in a Japanese nightclub."

"What happened?"

"Fell off the stage, singing *My Way* after too much sake, y'know their rice wine."

447

"Tap your fingers then." He pointed to One-Eye and spoke like American golf-fans. "Yo' the man, One-Eye! My *very* good friend One-Eye." He winked at the Chinese dealer who looked uncomfortable at the familiarity, knowing that the cameras were catching Dex' actions from every angle. Red came good for the next five spins but then lost twice running as One-Eye repeated on 35 black. Reluctantly, Dex crossed some tasty figures from his line. "That's knocked me back from over two million up. Only one point three odd now. Less your losses."

"Let's quit."

"No."

"Well I will. Divvy up."

He turned to Miller. "Give us a moment, will you." The inspector was nodded clearance by the Maltese. "Piss off, Tiffany." Dex spoke through tightly clenched teeth. "Don't do this to me."

"You're wasting money. You carry on alone. Bet both colors yourself. You'll find me in the bar. Drinking a large vodka. I can't take all this shit."

"Tell you what. I'll do a deal. If we drop to half a mill, we'll review. I may quit then. But no promises."

Tiffany's shoulders bristled indignation. She glared at him as if he were vermin. "Okay," she breathed the words reluctantly. You win."

Eight spins later, she was still on edge. "I've had enough of this losing. Your crazy bets, I keep thinking of starving kids, crying for a grain of rice. It pisses me off. *You* piss me off too."

"Be fair. We're up four point five million." FB appeared, rubbing his hands nervously and then stood at the head of the table beside Miller. "I'll be cashing out soon, FB. I hope you have enough cash."

"Not a check?"

"No. I'll want cash please."

"Euros? Their five hundred notes are less bulky than sterling."

"Euros? Fine. Just listen to this line." Dex was addressing nobody now in particular. "60, 70, 80, 100, 120, 150, 180, 210, 240, 270, 320, 370, 420, 470, 520 and 570. My next bet's six-thirty thousand." He turned to One-Eye. "Can you manage a few more reds?"

He could. The next seven numbers were all red, including a repeat on 27, as if some God were watching and remembering that disastrous June night when 27 red should have won him all his money back.

Surprising Tiffany, Dex suddenly asked to cash out. The phone in his pocket was vibrating, transmitting an urgent but unspoken message around his entire body like *shit, Shawcross is entering the building.*

Tiffany was surprised. "Cashing out? Thank God!"

"Time to quit. Reds can't go on like this." His watch showed eleven-seventeen.

To prevent any palming of the odd chip, Dex watched the count with meticulous care. One-Eye seemed to take an age counting out stack after stack. His hand movements were precise and fluid.

Tiffany checked the figures on the second page of her notes. "I was down six hundred and twenty thousand. I can live with that."

"Thank you, Mr Dexter," said Miller as Dex and Tiffany scooped up their winnings.

"Come on Tiffany. Let's see if they have enough money." He gave One-Eye an unsubtle wink, called him *my old friend* and then blew him a kiss across the table. As they stood at the cage, FB, Jeb Miller and the Maltese were all within earshot, locked in animated conversation with the Shift Manager who had been trying to spot any fraud or collusion.

"Dexter seemed too damned familiar with One-Eye. Even winked at him," said the Shift Manager.

"Twice, I think. *And* he'd asked for him to be the dealer," added FB. "Pity Reggie Kyte's in Vegas." FB looked at both listeners. "It may be One-Eye. We know he can land the ball damned close to any number he wants. But nobody's going to convince me he can just pick reds – or blacks. Not possible."

The Shift Manager agreed. "Impossible. But then he didn't. He hit quite a few blacks, but just not enough of them. It might be a gaffed wheel. Or good luck. We've seen these big imbalances before. An even money bet, I'd say."

"The odd thing isn't that Dexter won so much but that today was the first time he'd chosen to play a system that feeds on runs of one color."

"That's what bothers me too," said FB. He grasped his chin for a moment and looked at the cage where the cashiers were still sorting the cash payout.

"Close the table. We'll send the wheel off for testing. Huxleys' people are best. Anything less and A.S will go berserk."

The Shift Manager nodded. "Agreed. If there's anything odd about the wheel, Huxley'll be onto it in a trice."

"I'll get our security guys to take it there tonight. And I want to see One-Eye in my office in fifteen minutes. You will all sit in with me. He's a few questions to answer."

FB and the Shift Manager took a couple of steps to watch the last details of the payout. "Quite a birthday present, Mr Dexter," said FB. "I have to tell you that we're going to have the wheel checked. And question One-Eye about collusion with you. Dukes always prosecute if there's collusion with a player."

"Me and One-Eye an item? Dream on! Now listen. Being serious – do you have something I can borrow to carry this cash." He was looking at the stacks of five-hundreds that the cashier was counting.

"Lend Mr Dexter a suitcase, will you. That Italian left three here a few weeks back."

"And I want a letter from Dukes signed by you and the cashier that the cash represents gambling winnings plus the money I deposited. The taxman y'know!"

Dex watched the uncomfortable figure of the Shift Manager go across to One-Eye as the cashier typed the letter. The conversation was inaudible but Dex guessed from the arm movements and the vigorous head shakes from the Chinese dealer that he was under severe fire. Dex turned away and addressed FB. "So how's Mr Shawcross?"

"He's upstairs, in his office. Arrived here about ten minutes ago. I expect he'll come down to congratulate you."

"Splendid. Does he know I'm here?" Dex looked round. FB shook his head. "He's busy, catching up I suppose. Nobody's seen him except Reception. But if you wait in the bar, I'll get him. I expect he'd like to have a drink with you to celebrate."

"Good idea. Shall we?" Dex turned to Tiffany and saw the furious look on her face. "Silly question. I forgot. I promised Tiffany we'd go clubbing tonight. Another time."

"As you wish. Goodnight then. A limo perhaps?"

"Thanks. I don't want to lug this case round London. Get the driver to take us to the Dorchester Club."

Park Lane was thronged with Christmas party-goers escorting other people's wives to hotels and stations. Progress in the navy blue Bentley was slow as they covered the few hundred yards. "Thanks and Merry Christmas," Dex said as he tipped the driver a fiver, forgetting for the moment that he was carrying nearly ten million pounds. As the sleety wind slapped across their faces, they stood and shivered like paupers on the wide pavement until the limo had disappeared. Then Dex waved frantically for a slowly advancing cab.

"Where now?" Tiffany looked exhausted.

"I feel drained, jet-lagged, plain knackered."

"That just finished me, hearing that Shawcross was in his office."

"By my reckoning, he went straight to Dukes." The cab stopped and they piled in, their Samsonite heavy and lying on the floor between them. "The Goring Hotel please."

Tiffany looked puzzled. "Is there nothing else we can do? I mean look down there." She pointed at the tan suitcase. "I just feel that something extraordinary should be happening."

"Other than kissing you all over or counting the money, I can't think of anything. Either suits me."

She looked at him, her face showing amazement at the man beside her. "Somehow, God knows how, you've robbed Dukes of all this. There's some special kind of brain ticking away in there."

He shrugged and grinned, the naughty schoolboy look so wicked in the shadowy light. "Not robbery. Skill. Hard work. Planning." He thought back to the hours poring over books and of lunch with Walter McKay, the unknowing architect of it all. But all the time, every thought was soured by violent death and images of Emily's delicate features. "It seems a hollow victory."

"Well," she said. "It is still a victory. Now you can up the stakes. Buy her back." She twisted awkwardly to face him. "And even if you can't bring yourself to celebrate, I can." For a second she was silent and then she let out the greatest whoop of joy, pounding the suitcase with both fists. After looking shocked, Dex' eyebrows curving spectacularly at her unlikely reaction, he joined in, beating the case, punching the air and shouting mindlessly before hugging her until she could scarcely breathe.

451

"*Give me money, that's what I want,*" she sang gustily but rather out of tune. "The Beatles got it right." The cabbie looked over his shoulder at the commotion behind the glass partition, wondering what the excitement was all about. "Nine million! Nine million! Dex you're a genius."

The praise stopped him dead. He looked sheepish. "Living the dream! It's been a costly obsession. Let's hope Ben Greenaway brings good news in the morning. I don't want to give all this to Shawcross but if that's what it takes…"

"Look sweetie, Glenn wasn't your fault. If he'd not behaved like an ignorant pig when you tried to help him, he'd never have threatened Shawcross. Scotty – well… as I said, he seemed to be weary of life anyway and relished the risk. Behind that *kid-caught-scrumping-apples* look, you're a devious shit, well able to out-think Shawcross. So…with Emily? Be positive. I can't believe you won't find her. Then she'll bounce back to normal, just you see." Tiffany watched passengers stamping their feet while queuing for a bus that might still be minutes or hours away. "You know well enough, I'm not a betting person but I'm still backing you to keep the nine million. Think what good we can do for abused kids."

"I'm certainly not planning to enrich Roxy, Scotty's ex anyway. He'd never rest in peace. But there's one other thing I'd do if I keep the money. No two."

"Tell me"

"Fly in two consultants from John Hopkins, Baltimore. I read an article. They're making bigger strides with brain damage than the UK. Could help father."

"And the other?" She clutched his hand. "No. I'll guess. I'm getting to know you." She glanced at his profile, the smallish rather bent nose emphasizing why people had always underestimated the dynamo within. She saw that faraway determined look, even in the darkened cab as it waited for the lights on Buckingham Palace Road. "It's Beth, isn't it? The crash. You want the truth."

"You're right. There've been too many theories about why the plane just dropped from the sky. Someone knows why. Someone is covering up the truth. Maybe more than one person."

"Don't you say it. I will. You feel you owe it to Beth and your family."

The cab swung into Beeston Place and the Goring as he leaned across and kissed her, looking deep into her eyes. "You know me too damned well."

London – 24th December 2002

Dex put down the phone as he watched an overcast sky full of scudding rain clouds herald Christmas Eve morning. He called through to Tiffany. "Kenny's just pure gold. Fire-fighting again. Kath has been yelling and screaming—despite her tranquillizers. It must have been a crazy time in Orchard Avenue, living in a goldfish bowl, just circling each other and helpless to go anywhere or do anything. Using the door from the house to the garage, Mark's going to lie down in the back of the car and Kenny's bringing him to London. Hopefully, the media won't notice. Kath's sister and the WPC will take care of Kath."

Tiffany appeared in a wrap, her feet bare. " I hope you're not getting ahead of yourself. Ben Greenaway wasn't sure he had the big break."

"True but it's good for Mark to get out, release some tension from the pressure cooker down there. Can you imagine what it's like? Christmas Day tomorrow, presents for Emily round the tree, *Jingle Bells* and Santa on TV all day. In the living-room there's a policewoman and outside are the media waiting for the story."

"Kenny's been more than a good agent." Tiffany ran a hand across his bare chest.

"I owe him. So calm, so sensible. I owe *so many* people." He looked at his watch yet again. "I can't stand this inaction." It was only just gone eight as Dex peered gloomily into the darkness, reflecting that most Londoners had already left for Christmas in the country. The rain was now spattering on the windows. "All that money lying there and we're as deflated as a kid's burst balloon." Tiffany motioned him to stop pacing but he ignored her. "Turn off those bloody Christmassy jingles, will you?" Tiffany lowered the volume on the TV. "Thanks."

The thought that Greenaway might know where the kid was being held was too gut-wrenching for him to take a moment longer. He dialed the number and heard Ben's voice at once. "Greenaway."

"Morning Ben. So?" Dex sensed the hesitancy as if the agent was seeking to pick his words carefully. "Well, go on," he said testily, his voice sounding throaty. "Have you got the big break?"

453

"Yes. But ... hell." There was a long delay that did not improve Dex' frustration. " I've got to say it. We screwed up."

"Damn you, man. Get to the fucking point."

"We thought the man in the Goodge Street office was Arnie Fisher."

"So?"

"It was his younger brother, Ricky who runs the office. Arnie's out and about or works from his home. We traced Arnie to a right pukka home in Tyle Green, Hornchurch. He's the intelligent one. Ricky's just the front man – makeweight, answering phones and doing the VAT."

"Oh! For fuck's sake! You telling me, you've been following the wrong bloke every day?"

"We assumed the guy in the ..."

"I don't pay you to assume anything. You call yourself a detective agency. I wanted evidence not assumptions. I mean ... oh Christ! What a fucking nightmare! Four wasted days watching the wrong person. Four days and nights this kid's been terrified, sobbing her heart out. I'll sort you later. As for your bill - put it where a duck puts it. Meantime, what have you found out?"

"I'm sorry, mate."

"No time for that," Dex snapped. "Facts please. No assumptions."

"Arnie left home yesterday morning at about six. He did the same today. Yesterday he went to a flat in Dolphin Square. That's in Pimlico - by the river, the biggest block in London, between Westminster and Chelsea. He spent the day there, popping down to the off-license for some beer and to buy groceries. He left about seven last night. If the girl *is* there – and it seems possible, then she's alone overnight. I've got someone following Arnie this morning again. If he goes there today, it may be worth a visit."

"Could be a girlfriend. Probably is, based on the reliability of your assumptions so far." Dex banged the wall in frustration. "Heh! Did your guy listen at the door or peep through the letter-box and hear a girl's voice rather than the rattle of a brass bed? No don't tell me. He didn't think of that!"

Greenaway sounded sulky at the jibe. "He didn't hear anything."

"Tell him to listen this time. Give me the address." Dex scribbled down the details. "That's on the sixth floor, right? The Drake Building in Dolphin

Square. So Fisher should reach there in half an hour if he goes direct. Agreed?"

"I'll call as soon as we know where he's headed."

"Wait! Haven't you forgotten something? Like telling me where I might enjoy morning coffee with Audley Shawcross? Where I might find Jude Tuson out window-shopping?"

"Christ! Slipped my mind. Shawcross went to the Montefiore Hotel last night, just off the Edgware Road. He didn't check in - went straight to the lift with his two bags – well one bag and a briefcase. I assume you'll find Jude in the same room. She checked in there straight from Pomegranates. We followed her."

"Have two people at the hotel. Keep me posted." A knock on the door heralded breakfast. Tiffany directed the waiter to the sitting-room while Dex paced around the bedroom with angry strides, his face still twitching with fury at the cock-up.

"Calm down, Dex. You won't think clearly while prancing round like bear with hemorrhoids. There's a great English fry-up for you. Remember what Beth said. Revenge is best savored cold. So come in here. Enjoy breakfast and we'll talk it through."

Dex sat down but ate barely anything, playing with the bacon. When the phone rang, he almost spilled the tray reaching for the receiver. It was Greenaway. "Arnie Fisher has gone to Dolphin Square again. He stopped in the shop downstairs and bought a newspaper and two bags of jelly babies."

"Thanks, Ben. That's more like it." Dex turned to Tiffany. "Know what? Pomegranates is slap bang there at Dolphin Square too."

"So Arnie's been dating Jude." Tiffany saw the look on Dex' face. "Only joking."

"Kenny should be here any time now."

London – 24th December 2004

Audley Shawcross was sitting at the desk in the large suite at the Montefiore. He was wearing a toweling robe and munching the remains of an omelets. It was still early and his scar looked pink across his unshaven cheek. The frown was the product of more than one aggravation. The telephoned report received yesterday in New York that the attack on Dexter had failed had been like a kick from a stallion. The onward flight from New York had seemed endless, an irritation, but he knew he had to get to London. Leaving London without his *rainy-day kit* had been a mistake, one that had to be rectified urgently.

The news from Arnie after he had cleared Immigration that the kid wasn't too well was a lesser problem that he immediately dismissed. Then FB had told him that Dexter had walked out of Dukes with nearly ten million. Being so close and so far had been almost worse than the money. It had given him ten million reasons not to sleep as he struggled to work out a plan. He went to his home to collect the kit and had reached the Montefiore at after two. Though Jude had greeted him in a red PVC figure-hugging outfit, his mind had been in turmoil and he had been in no mood for her advances. Instead while she sat grumpily in bed watching TV, he had phoned Carlo

"You heard about Scotty Brannigan?" the American had asked.

"The guys who were after him in London got him this time? Yes, I heard. Any news on who he had upset?"

"Nah! Just speculation. Get this! The guy had a blow-up doll in his car, a black one! Sounds crazy to me. And Dexter? Is he still causing trouble?"

"All fixed."

"Not whacked?"

Shawcross had laughed. "No. I met him. We did a deal, so he's no problem. Carlo, I'm back on the 27th. Dinner at Picasso. 8 pm?" Shawcross had no intention of being there.

"That's okay."

Now, as he pushed aside the last of the omelets to check his emails, his anger had not abated. There was one from FB, just in. "John Huxley's top guy confirms the wheel is A1 perfect. I told him to check again."

"Fuck and damnation. How did the bastard do it? Pure chance?" He answered his own question. "Like hell it was."

In the next room, he could hear Jude padding about between the bathroom and bed. He felt a sudden urge to violate her, someone or anyone - her, for no better reason than that she was there. He put down his mobile and recognized that dry feeling in his throat. *Someone* was going to suffer today. He could sense the feverish sensations racing through him as he imagined slitting Dex' throat. From the next room, he heard Jude busying herself and it irritated him. He had tired of her fatty thighs and her face that looked like uncooked pastry in the morning. Everything about her had become too much – the rasping Aussie voice and the crude laugh. But she *had* done well, served her purpose. She'd get her goodbye note after Christmas. Especially after that mocking laugh when he had failed to get an erection last night.

"Damn you, Dexter. Damn you!" He wondered how he knew that he had flown to London. He read Dexter's email that had awaited him at the hotel. "Besides the documents being returned, you can have five million back for the girl's release before Christmas."

Fuck that, creep!

From his briefcase, he removed the knife. It had been the last item collected from his home. He admired the beautiful lines of the Master Bowie's stainless steel blade. He lovingly caressed the handle and fingered the point, turning the blade around so that the light bounced off the steel. Dexter would shit himself when he saw this. Then he noticed the bulging toiletry-bag, his *rainy-day kit*. He knew he would need it before the day was out. Besides three false passports, it contained everything for his short-term change of appearance. As Dexter's email again filled the screen, he returned the knife to his briefcase and thought it through again.

Maybe getting five million was a good idea.

Dukes and Space City were toast. Dexter had too much evidence, so disappearing was the best option. It was impossible to trust that devious shit Dexter to return every copy. God knows how many copies he had made but he guessed at two, probably three and all that cash would be handy once Audley Shawcross had ceased to exist. That had to be today. The botched job in Vegas had seen to that. Grabbing the girl hadn't worked too well so far but somehow he had to make her kidnap count. He paused, nose upturned, staring at the ceiling. He looked down at his briefcase. Suddenly, it all seemed so obvious. The best of all worlds was still possible. Kill the girl. Kill the bastard too. Get the money.

He fired off an email to Aruba with coded instructions following the bank's precise requirements. By two pm London time, every last dollar would have gone to another account in the name of Raymond Spencer Booth, not the name on any of these passports. Thirty minutes later, the money would be spread between seven accounts around the globe, all in names of different companies, controlled by trusts that nobody could prove were his.

He thought again of Carlo. He had no regrets at the double-cross. All the financial troubles had started from his bad management, especially the way he had handled the Unions. His thought turned to Cedric and the rest of the Board. Reggie Kyte apart, to hell with the lot of you.

Season's greetings and a happy slopping out to you all.

The shower was running and with Jude now out of earshot, he rang British Airways. Moments later, he had booked a first-class ticket for Mr Bertram Coley on the late-night flight to Singapore. He had the passport and credit card to match. Then he started typing using the Trent Harrison email address.

"I have your email. I was at the previous rendezvous. Maybe you were expecting someone different? Return the full amount you stole from Dukes plus every set of documents. I know there are three copies. Do that and I may be able to arrange with the people who are holding the girl for release. Meet me today at five pm in the lobby of the Sheraton, Knightsbridge with the documents and the money. The girl will be close by. I will have a suite booked in the name of Matthews. Like me, you will be alone. Once I am satisfied you've been straight, I will phone from the suite for the girl. I will leave and you will find her in the lobby ten minutes later. If I suspect you are trying to trick me, the girl will be dead before Christmas. Be warned."

He sent the email and poured some ice-cold orange juice. At his feet, he saw again the Master Bowie and savored the dry catchy feeling at the back of his throat. Not since Crabant's death had he felt it so strongly. He sipped at his juice and let his anger mount in preparation for 5pm.

From the bedroom, he heard Jude singing White Christmas along with the TV and he angrily pulled the door shut. He wondered how many sets of evidence there really were. Not that it mattered really now. And the full nine million? Could Dex afford not to return it all?

He went to the window and looked down on the quiet Georgian street. There seemed to be somebody slumped low in the driving-seat of a Ford Fiesta. He looked the other way and saw a woman parked in a black VW towards Marble Arch. He was not surprised. It seemed he had been under constant observation

His cellphone rang and he hurried to the desk, slopping orange juice down the robe in his haste. He snatched at the phone. "Yes? Oh. It's you Arnie. What's news?"

Shawcross at once noted the alarm in the agent's voice. "I'm no doctor but I reckon the kid's got pneumonia. I told you she was ill yesterday. Now its much worse." He seemed breathless and Shawcross guessed he did not care to bring bad news. "I just been down to the chemist. Bought a thermometer. Her temperature's 105 degrees. What little I know says that's serious. She's struggling to breathe. She needs a doctor and quickly."

"Don't be a fool," Shawcross barked down the phone. "We can't get a doctor in. Give her some cough medicine."

"She's beyond that, I'd say. Almost unconscious, eyes wild, unable to speak."

"Wait. Don't ring off." Shawcross barged into the bedroom and saw Jude sitting in black bra and pants doing her make-up. "The kid's ill. Temperature of 105. Arnie says she's probably got pneumonia. She's almost unconscious."

"That bad now is it? He's right! She needs a doctor. And quickly. Let me speak to him." She followed Shawcross to the desk and grabbed his cellphone. "I'm a nurse. Is the girl shaking?"

"Yes."

"Coughing?"

"Yes."

"Is she coughing up stuff? If so, is it brown?"

There was a pause. "I'd say it was brown."

"Tell me about her breathing."

"Hard to describe. Like short panting noises as if she's gasping for more air."

"Hold on Arnie." Jude looked at Shawcross, her face grim. "This *is* serious. She needs to be in hospital for help with her breathing for starters."

"Impossible." He seized the phone. "Get some cough stuff down her. I'm coming over." He cut the connection.

"I'll come too." Jude was already heading for the bedroom to get dressed. "This is urgent."

"You're not coming."

"What? I'm the kid's only hope, f'God's sake. You can't let her die." She looked at him and saw that he was unmoved. "If you do, I'm going straight to the police."

"Don't threaten me, bitch! She's no use to me now anyway. I'll get what I need from Dexter whether she's alive or dead."

"No Aude." She pulled at his robe but he tugged himself free. "Not that. Don't let her die. I can't let you. Kidnapping was bad enough but this is .. oh God. I mean I'm implicated in this too but not, absolutely not, in her death." She stood facing him defiantly, her body leaning forward from the waist as she challenged him, her eyes following his movements. She saw no softening in his attitude. Her Sydney accent sounded even rougher as she raised her voice. "Fuck you, Aude, you go there without me to help, I'm calling the cops. She mustn't die." She grabbed at her white jeans as he turned back towards the desk. In another rapid movement, she pulled on a pink jumper and had just crouched down to find her white boots when she saw his feet almost beside her.

She looked up and gasped as his hand clamped her mouth tight shut. The grip was ferocious. She tried to wriggle and kick. "No, no!" The words were inaudible. In his hand was the knife, the monstrosity she had seen hidden among his clothes. For a second, she saw his eyes, hard and without mercy though there was pleasure around his lips. Again, she tried to lash out, her arms and legs kicking and waving. It was hopeless. From behind her, his left hand pulled her tight against him, his palm still tight across her mouth. She saw a flash of movement coming from her right side as she unleashed a despairing backwards kick.

"Don't bother to do the room today, " Shawcross told Housekeeping over the phone. He had already hung a *Do not Disturb* sign on the bedroom door as he had cleaned the knife and packed. The blooded robe and everything identified with Audley Shawcross went into Jude's overnight bag.

Dexter's reply had then arrived as he was sipping his juice and admiring Jude's lifeless body as it lay close to his feet, blood now surrounding it. As he read the response, he had nodded in satisfaction. The trap was ready. Dexter had taken the bait. Downstairs at the front, the same two cars were still there. He took the lift to the basement and found a shabby staff exit that went out into the street behind. Moments later, he had waved down a taxi in Gloucester Place and was dropped off in Frith Street, deep in Soho. Nobody was tailing him.

Almost at once, he saw what he was looking for down a short blind alley. With nobody around, he heaved the belongings of Audley Shawcross into a seven foot garbage can outside the back of a Chinese restaurant. From a few yards away, he picked up three stinking black sacks and threw them on top. The metamorphosis had begun. After finishing with Dexter, his kit would complete the transition. In Wardour Street, he hailed a cab. "Dolphin Square."

The taxi was soon maneuvering through the usual hold-ups by Bressenden Place. The clock on the small tower at the junction with Victoria Street showed it was nearly eleven-thirty. The driver then cut down into the maze of streets behind Victoria Station until the huge but uninspiring red brick building appeared ahead. "Eleven pounds please, guv."

Shawcross handed over the money with no tip and was rewarded with a sarcastic "and a Merry Christmas to you too." Shawcross barely noticed as he entered the swing doors to the part of the building called Drake House. When Arnie had rented, he had been told that different parts of the massive block had been named after famous seafarers but now on the Chichester Street side, the former apartments were consolidated into the Dolphin Square Hotel.

He took the lift to the sixth floor and then looked in each direction, needing to get his bearings. He gazed down the seemingly endless corridors, aware that former prime ministers, royalty and Charles de Gaulle had all lived here. He walked along the green carpet past nearly a dozen doors before reaching the right one. There he paused and listened. From within, there was no sound. He used his key and swung open the door and called for Arnie. Then he saw a note on the phone-stand ahead of him. "Kid's worse! Gone down to the chemists. Trying to buy something stronger."

He closed the door and dumped his two bags on the rather dirty fawn carpet. He had not been here before and was unsure of the geography. He remembered the agents' particulars describing two bedrooms, a living-room, kitchen and bathroom, ideal if Jude had agreed to live in, which she had not. The door to the living area was open and the room empty. The two other doors were ajar as was the coat-closet in the hallway.

He drew out the knife from his belt, looked down at it and played with the point that so recently had ripped into his lover's chest, not once but six times. The familiar dryness in his throat immediately returned as he fondled the handle. Then he peered into the first room. There was a large double-bed draped with a green cover. It was empty and the room was bright, the curtains open. He pushed open the second door and saw a much smaller room with a single bed. Despite the drawn curtains, he made out a pair of child's socks and knickers lying on a chair. He stood and looked at the small huddled figure under the blankets.

For just a second, he felt a flicker of shame but then the surge of powerful forces took over. Knife clutched in his right hand, he took three steps towards where Emily was lying almost lost in the full-length bed. His lips and gums were parted wide in anticipation as he clutched the handle in both hands now. Slowly he raised the blade to head height, ready to plunge. His breathing was fast yet his hands were steady. Then he struck, almost doubling over in the violence of the movement. His senses were tingling. His nostrils were flared at the prospect of blood bursting through the linen and the sights, sounds and smells of sudden death.

With his mind intoxicated by the pleasures in hand, a slight creak made by the built-in wardrobe door behind him was lost as he drove home the knife again, deep through the cover. As he looked at the torn bedding awaiting the surge of blood, he saw a movement and felt his head being jerked backwards as a knotted rope looped around his neck and tore into his windpipe. "Arnie! Arnie." The repeat of the word came out as more of an *aaargh* than an *Arnie* as the knots dug in deep and additional torque was applied.

"Finlay Dexter to be precise." Dex jerked the garrote again as he glimpsed the Bowie flail back towards his right kidney. "Kenny! Now! Now." The yell reverberated round the cell-like room. The sound of Dexter's voice seemed to renew the killer's resolve as he tried to hurl his weight backwards to free himself. Dex slammed his knee into his captive's spine and yanked the rope again arcing Shawcross' body like a bow. "And no Emily either. You bastard!" Even as he tightened the throttle, the extra pressure was insufficient to force Shawcross to drop the knife but suddenly the right arm wilted, swinging loose.

Dex found pleasure in the pain he was inflicting yet was unsure how long it took to kill with a garrote - not long he guessed and he had no intention of risking that. When he felt Shawcross' weight increase as his knees started to buckle, he eased off the pressure, anxious not to go too far. His reward was another backward kick as his victim desperately tried to strike a telling blow. "Kenny!" he yelled. "Quickly."

Kenny barged noisily in carrying a three foot length of lead pipe and a Glock. He had squeezed himself into a walk-in cupboard off the living-room. "This'll sort him," Kenny said as he smashed the lead pipe over Shawcross' wrist. Dex saw the knife clatter heavily to the floor. Then Kenny swung the tube across the back of Shawcross' head. Dex absorbed the jolt as the body was knocked forward. The dead weight was immediate and he released the garrote so that Shawcross collapsed unconscious by the bed. Swiftly they bound his arms and legs, stuffed Emily's socks and knickers into his mouth and added handcuffs as the finishing touch.

"Don't touch the knife," commanded Kenny as Dex was about to move it far from the body. "This is a crime scene."

Dex looked down at the handsome features, the mouth jammed wide open, eyes tightly shut. He saw the strong profile and the thick black hair now matted with blood oozing from the back of his head. For a moment he wondered what drove a man to such greed and brutality. How could he have tried to murder a helpless child?

"Time to call the police, Kenny." Dex was surprised how out of breath he was. "We've done their job. Trussed him up like a turkey. Very seasonal."

"Well stuffed too," panted Kenny. "Brilliant idea of yours, tricking Shawcross to come here. Bloody marvelous."

"Born out of desperation. I didn't much fancy meeting Shawcross at the Sheraton, I can tell you."

"I thought he would bring Jude. Hell, after what Arnie said to him, the kid deserved a nurse."

Dex shook his head angrily. "Not when you saw what I saw. He had only one purpose." He pointed to where the knife had been plunged deep into the middle of the concealed pillow beside the yellow ball. "I was next in line, once I'd handed over the cash and the files."

"Come on. Let's phone the police."

Dex took a final look at the prone body. "I shall never, couldn't possibly, forget the noises I heard – first a bizarre kind of rattling sound as if he were clearing his throat. Then it was the grunts each time he plunged the knife in." He shook his head, scarcely believing what he had just achieved.

As they awaited the police response to the 999 call, Dex was able to phone Tiffany who was downstairs in the hotel and he reassured her that he was safe. "You've got a world-class scoop. A story with a happy ending. Go for it! I'll be down after speaking to the cops."

"How long will you be?"

"I've a couple of calls to make. Maybe half an hour. I want to see Emily."

"She's a smart kid. She recognized you. Said you had promised to play *Connections* with her."

"Tell her Mr Dex won't be long."

He went to the fridge and poured juice. After emptying it without stopping, he flung open the door to the coat cupboard and saw Arnie Fisher stirring slightly from the crack across the skull. Like Shawcross, he too was expertly handcuffed, bound and gagged. Dex looked at him for a moment and then could resist it no longer. With a mighty swing of his leg, he smashed his Doc Martin deep into Arnie's crotch and then repeated it. As a glob of spit slithered down Arnie's nose, he shut the door. Kenny appeared to see what the noise was.

"Nothing," said Dex. "Let's just relax until the cops arrive." He sat down on the settee looking anything but relaxed.

"Best moment" said Kenny "was when Arnie opened the door expecting Shawcross."

"He nearly crapped himself I should think! Never got time to pull out the Glock. Guess he never expected trouble." Dex leaned across to find the agent's arm as he sat on a small chair. "You did just great. No messing!"

"Not in these situations." They fell silent, Dex reliving the weasel face ducking and flinching as Kenny cracked the pipe across the man's shoulder so that he was instantly felled. Having pinned him down and secured him, they had found Emily strapped to a dining-chair, her eyes wide open, her nose streaming with cold and her mouth gagged. While Mark fell upon his daughter, Kenny and Dex frogmarched the agent to the phone, Glock at his temple.

"Your job, your only chance, is to get Shawcross to come here," Dex had ordered. "You will tell him that Emily's seriously ill – pneumonia. Got it? You are in deep shit for conspiracy to kidnap but if you lure Shawcross here, this will work as mitigation at the trial. If you bugger this up or try any tricks, Kenny here will beat you to pulp with this pipe. Understood?"

It was nearly an hour before Dex was able to head for the hotel bar overlooking the swimming-pool. A porter and a policeman blocked his way until Mark had him waved through. In Chichester Street, a media scrum had formed to cover the greatest Christmas story imaginable. Just ahead of him, he recognized Kath from the photo Mark had shown him. She was just arriving, guarded by two policemen and sobbing into a hankie. Dex followed her along the passage down the steps and towards the closed off bar area, strangely diffident now of approaching her. There, at the double doors to the bar and feeling like an intruder, he watched Kath's electric joy transform her drawn, tear-stained and weary face. Emily rushed from her father's knee as she saw her Mummy. Spilling the burger and chips with oodles of ketchup that lay in front of her, she flung herself forward, arms outstretched.

Dex watched as Kath swooped down on her daughter and then lifted her up in a convulsion of sobs, groans and sighs. Mark quickly joined them in a threesome blissfully oblivious to the rest of the world. The emotions were too much for Dex. Feeling like a gatecrasher at a very private party, he backed off into the corridor and stared down at the blue waters of the swimming-pool below. Seconds later Tiffany slipped her hand into his. "So!" She leaned across to whisper in his ear. "*Boy* did it."

Las Vegas – 30th December 2002

From their suite at the Four Seasons Hotel on the 39th floor of the Mandalay Bay tower, the view looking north over the Strip was spectacular. It was early morning, first light, and Dex and Tiffany were awake to see the sun rising to their right, the sharp golden hues emerging over the sweeping heights of the Sunrise Mountains. By the floor-to-ceiling window lay the breakfast tray just delivered. It was laden with coffee, juice, fresh raspberries, a selection of pastries, waffles and a pot of maple syrup.

Dex was still charged up with emotion. Christmas had been a whirl - rare private moments and far more public ones as a shocked world learned of the story behind Emily's kidnapping. "When we met, my life had just been destroyed. My family were in the wreckage, my money all gone. Now, everything has changed. I've got you," he pulled her close to his side. "And I've two ready-made kids."

"Two?"

"Emily of course. She'll always be special to me now. But there's someone else I've been wanting to tell you about - an orphan called Bobby. But with everything else, I wasn't ready to get my own head round it, let alone explain to you. Here goes." He ran through what he knew in economic brush-strokes. "I told father I knew about Bobby when I visited on Christmas Day. I'd like to think he understood but truly, I just don't know. Next week, please come with me to Bladon. You must meet dear old Hillyer and then maybe all three of us should go to meet Bobby. He needs some love, some permanence in his life but I'm not the answer."

"We must help if we can."

"If it's right for him."

Tiffany nodded. "I can't wait to meet Walter McKay and your father."

"McKay phoned me. Wouldn't take any credit for the collapse of the crooked empire. But I *know* differently."

"Go on. Open it," Tiffany prompted, handing Dex the envelope that had intrigued them. It had awaited them when they had checked in. He saw again his name written across the top. It had arrived in a larger brown envelope with a sad note from Brad Brannigan, Scotty's father. Dex had read that – how Brad had found the envelope at Scotty's home beside a photo of his son when aged six sitting in a pedal-car. Last night, Dex had been unable to face opening the envelope. Now, slowly and carefully, he peeled back the adhesive and pulled out two sheets of paper. Across the top of the letter-heading was a cartoon of Scotty emphasizing his generous sideburns, peaked cap at a jaunty angle. Together they read it. The letter was dated 22nd December at eight pm, just a few hours before he had set off in his Jaguar.

"Heh Dex! If you're reading this, then you'll know I ran out of luck. But no sweat. Nobody but you knows what I'm going to tell you. Please keep it that way. Life ain't been so sweet recently. My own fault. Remember Nanda Datt? You asked? Well that motherfucker suckered me into fixing races. I couldn't take his shit no more, so I told him to go fuck himself. But he fucked me – during the funeral procession. He had called again. Said I was dead meat. Man! Having a guy like Datt on your back is like being raped very, very slo-o-owly by a brown bear. You kinda hope for his orgasm, to get it over!

So taking a ride tonite for you ain't no big deal. I owe you. I sure as hell hope you win at Dukes. Keep the lot. I won't need it where I'll be. (Paper notes would burn!) There'll be life insurance too if some guys get me tonight. Plenty enough for everybody, even the leeches at the IRS and that bitch Roxy. Those insurance bastards won't wriggle free this time!

In case you hadn't noticed (!!!!), I'm a difficult kinda guy. You got too much of my wrong edge. You didn't deserve that. Matter of fact, you were maybe the only guy who ever tried to help without wanting far more back. Now I can repay you.

Look after Tiffany. She's a real big number.
Truly
Scotty.
PS: Speak to Otto. Might be worthwhile."

They sat motionless, just staring out across the Strip towards Space City. Tiffany eventually stopped mopping her eyes.

"No point spoiling his reputation." Dex meticulously destroyed the letter. "That's our secret."

"We were right about his *que sera sera* attitude." They sat holding hands, each again lost in thought, Dex wondering how someone like Nanda Datt might be brought to justice. He was sure too that Tiffany was about to fire some awkward questions. "Dex?" The watery smile was replaced by the objectiveness of the TV journalist. "Scotty set the tone. Time for some confessions from you now?"

"About?"

"Why Gerhard Hoge was not in Dukes when it was raided during their Christmas Eve party."

"You journalists! Questions, questions!" He played for time by selecting a blueberry muffin with ridiculous care. "Must have gone abroad." His gaze was even, giving nothing away. "Interpol are after over eighty people who laundered money through Dukes, courtesy of Shawcross, Jude and this Claire Weatherley woman."

"Dex, my sweet, how do you keep a straight face." She sucked her pen-top and tried again. "Hoge was laundering wasn't he?"

"Lucky to be alive."

"Why?"

"Because with Crabant and Hoge, Shawcross screwed up."

"Go on!"

"The SFO wiz told me a few things they've uncovered. This scam was a quick fix to raise enough hot money to keep the banks purring. They suspect that Shawcross was lining his own pockets too – an Aruba connection. These rich guys they brought cash from offshore accounts all over and left with a nice clean casino check."

"Call me stupid but why when these people had offshore bank accounts before."

"Not stupid at all. I only had a crash-course yesterday. These guests were mainly clients of a lawyer in Liechtenstein who introduced them to Shawcross. Even about ten years ago, hooky money flowed freely through offshore accounts and tax havens, no real questions asked. But you try shifting a million now from a bank in the Caymans to Barclays in Croydon and all hell breaks loose. The bank's compliance team could raise all types of questions and file reports."

"Give me an example."

"Take Hoge, the cheerful loser. If he brought in and then lost a million, he still received a check for £850,000 – a small price for usable money in a major onshore bank. Adrian reckons these hot-money folk never lost more than fifteen percent, the fee that Dukes took for helping them."

"And if they won?"

"Mostly they were mug players like Hoge but once when he won two hundred thousand, he would only have got a check for twenty-five percent. Shawcross had also set up several accounts where Jude or Claire was a signatory in another name. The guest became a *co-signatory* with power to withdraw on one signature."

"How's all this coming out?"

"Claire is singing like the proverbial. FB couldn't add much to what I'd already extracted."

"But the screwing up? Hoge and Crabant."

"They were the first two involved. They joined as members *in their own names*. Claire said Shawcross quickly knew it was a mistake. That's why she and Jude became involved - using the loophole of guests using false names needing no ID."

"So? I'm still not following."

"Shawcross didn't need any heat. Didn't want any *obvious* criminal laundering through Dukes. Crabant using his own name became an embarrassment when he was named as part of a massive fraud probe in the European Commission. Crabant had been taking bribes from people like Hoge to win tenders to sell surplus European wine. Both became rich. Crabant's money was red-hot and Brussels, through OLAF, was onto him. My guess is that Crabant, who was a petulant Frenchman, made the fatal mistake of crossing Shawcross over something. The SFO found a petrol receipt Shawcross had kept from Launceston, Cornwall for the day after he was last known to be alive. Tin-mine job, I'd say."

"Was Hoge named by OLAF?"

"No. That's why he was no immediate problem to Shawcross. With a wife he was harder to dump anyway."

"Hoge told you this?" Tiffany's question was answered only by an enigmatic smile.

"Apparently, Shawcross had used a shady company in Hampshire to create the paperwork. False IDs and references were set up. Players could then get bank accounts in bogus names and credit cards to match, a classic money-laundering scam. The banks wouldn't query a casino check arriving. Later, the owners could withdraw sensible amounts of cash or use the credit cards in Acapulco, Cannes or London. They could no longer as safely operate and manage an account in any tax haven. Getting most of their cash onshore like this was a great deal."

"And this American – Carlo something?"

"We'll know more today after the Feds come here to take my statement. Meantime, he's in jail charged with a shopping list of offenses. I guess he'll go down for a long stretch."

"And Zara? And Adrian Ryder?"

"He was right. She's a survivor. She's in Cyprus where she went when we ran for it. The cops may extradite her and charge them both."

"Will FB be jailed? What about the board?"

"I've put in a word for FB. He can't avoid prosecution. He was a key player but acted under pressure of his boss. Turning Queen's Evidence will help – so long as Shawcross never gets to him. He might avoid jail - unlike One-Eye, Miller, Andy and a few others – Kyte and the cashiers. My QC told me that unless the cops turn up complicity in the money-laundering, the board, like Sir Cedric, will be in the clear." He picked up an almond covered Danish, looked at his waistline and then put it back. "Haven't spent nearly enough time jogging. That's a New Year resolution." Dex was sure the two toughest questions were still to come. So far, they had been softball. Jude Tuson was one. Yet he had a feeing that Tiffany was too astute to go there. He hoped he was right.

"Our win in Dukes," Tiffany persisted. "Come on! That wasn't luck! You've got around nine million in the bank now and increasing with interest every nano-second."

Dex stood up, stretching away his fatigue. He rubbed his head, his eyes and tightened the cord on the shortie dressing-gown but said nothing. Her eyes followed him everywhere. He did a grand circuit of the suite and then another, head down, his brow furrowed. "It was just forty spins and about ninety minutes work." He produced a calculator. "Plus six months planning. Sounds better in dollars or euros – nearly fourteen million. 15% Black numbers, 85% Red."

Tiffany avoided the jugular. "Were you worried about them checking the wheel?"

"No."

"The ball?"

"No. My only worry was they'd insist on a check and that Dukes would be raided before it had cleared. But FB knew from me I'd want a load of cash if I won." He could see from the furrowed brow that she was not satisfied.

"That wheel," she began again.

"85% -15% is not a big imbalance over an hour or so. Over six months, it would be a crisis. As it was, another dozen blacks and it would have looked reasonable. If the casino has a wheel that's faulty, improperly checked or off-balance, that's their problem."

"Come on Dex! You *knew* you were going to win."

"Reverse Labouchère's a great system for a birthday-boy," he volunteered as he sipped his V8 juice and avoided her playful punch. "Walter McKay told me about it." He started another longer, slower tour of the suite, his eyes telling Tiffany that he was far away somewhere in the *Land of Truth*.

He knew that he had never needed Scotty or Tiffany to play with him. McKay had told him that but he had decided it looked less odd if he were not alone. To have played only red on his own would have attracted more heat. He wished he had been able to appreciate Max Chieseman's wheel. It had been a masterpiece of engineering with every red slot slightly larger than usual, every black slot a touch smaller. The base of every black slot had been lined with extra padding to spring the ball to the next red number. FB had done well getting it installed that morning.

Dex had never forgotten McKay's advice that what casinos feared most was collusion between player and employee. His capture and turning of FB had opened up a glorious opportunity. From behind him, Dex could feel Tiffany watching him as he enjoyed a smile at what had happened to the wheel after they had left the casino. In return for brown envelopes, the two security guys had switched the wheel on the way for testing. The gaffed wheel was dumped but its flawless twin was perfect.

Dex eventually stopped his pacing round, his face now serious. He absorbed Tiffany's quizzical look and stretched out his arms, pulling her up to stand next to him. He kissed her, softly stroking her cheek as he did so. Then he pointed down the Strip, just a few hundred yards away. Space City was like a giant white morgue - empty, shut and with security guards standing every twenty yards all around. Police cars were parked by the walkway to the hotel entrance. "Carlo Letizione is still singing to the Feds, trying to convince them he had no part in the murders." He looked her straight in the eye. "Only when you see that great white elephant does it seem real. Today the new wing should have opened. We've brought the whole rotten empire down."

"*You* have, Dex. *You alone.*" She kissed him softly. "I read it in the papers, so it must be true. The first person ever to bring down two casinos."

"Team effort. Beth would be pleased. Mission accomplished."

"Was it worth it, your obsession?"

"With so much tragedy? So much suffering? Mick, Scotty, Jude – besides little Emily's ordeal. No I can't say that. But I had to do it. Right is right."

"So, will you give me your confession now? How you won nine million?"

"Tonight I'm taking you to the greatest show in town – Siegfried and Roy. They're illusionists. They make an elephant disappear. I've seen them do it before - just feet from me. One second you see it, the next there's nothing."

"So?"

"*My* answer is the same. It would be *interesting* to know how they do it. But it would spoil everything." He winked at her, his impish look at its worst. "Some things are best left... just admired."

About the Author

Born in Glasgow, Scotland but brought up in England, Douglas qualified as a British solicitor working in London and internationally. Alongside this career in law, Douglas had his first novel published twenty-five years ago and has been writing ever since. After retiring young from his law-firm, Douglas moved to the USA where he has broadened both his legal and writing interests.

Late Bet is his seventh novel following Undercurrent, his acclaimed thriller about maritime crime. Its success led to Douglas being invited to write and publish in Germany a non-fiction title, Piraten. The English language version of that has recently been published in 2007 as The Brutal Seas and has been hailed as the benchmark on crime at sea by the Founder and first Director of the ICC-International Maritime Bureau, a non-Government agency committed to fighting crime at sea. That book delivers in vivid focus the tensions and brutality that crews of vessels, large and small, face today from piracy, hijackings, murders and fraud on the high seas.

Douglas' novels have generally involved a theme of international fraud – whether in Timeshares, Road Haulage, the Wine Trade, the Pharmaceutical Industry or at sea. Late Bet maintains that tradition and enters the murky world of international casino crime. Douglas, after years of living in London and Las Vegas and as a writer on gaming issues, knows his subject well. A strong legal background and a lifetime of global travel enable Douglas to introduce exciting locations and to weave legal themes into the rich tapestry of the thriller plots.

Douglas is married with three children. His interests include most sports and especially cricket, something much missed in America. Beyond that, his interest and experiences involving Formula 1 Grand Prix motor racing also feature large in Late Bet.

Printed in the United States
73525LV00003B/58-81